To Kayla—

the story of us

The Complete Series

CASSIA LEO

Thanks for being awesome! ♡ Cassia

The Story of Us: The Complete Series

First Edition

Editing by Red Adept Edits.

Copyediting by Marianne Tatom.

Cover art by Cassia Leo.

Interior design by Angela McLaurin, Fictional Formats.

ISBN-13: 978-1517019570
ISBN-10: 1517019575

the way we fall

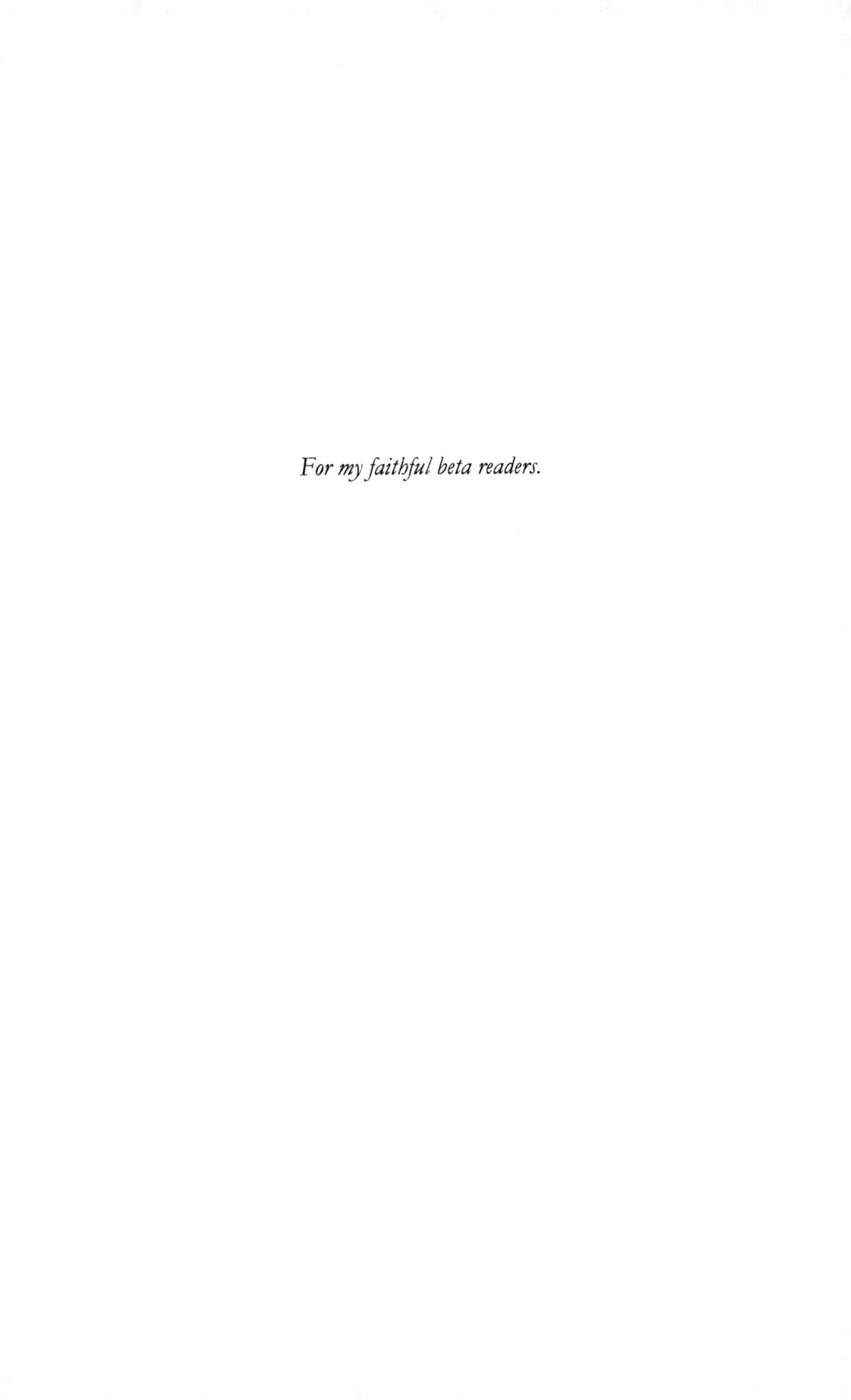

For my faithful beta readers.

Prologue

LIES ARE COMFORTING. Soft blankets we wrap around our hearts. We roll around in them like fat, happy pigs. Gorging on their decadence. We prefer lies, though we claim otherwise. Trust me. If ignorance is bliss, believing lies is orgasmic.

I should know. I'd subsisted on a steady diet of lies and orgasms while Houston and I were together. And now that he was standing before me, five and a half years after the breakup, six-foot-four inches of solid muscle and caramel-brown hair, offering me my first dose of reality, part of me wondered whether my body would reject it.

Houston sighs as he looks me in the eye. "Rory, I came here because I told you I would tell you the truth and I intend to keep my word."

"The truth about *what?*" I spit back, imbuing my words with caustic venom, hoping he'll feel just a fraction of the agony he's inflicted on me. "It's over Houston. There is no truth that needs to be spoken anymore."

He shakes his head, his blue eyes filled with regret. "I wish that were true."

He reaches into his back pocket and my stomach drops out. My limbs becomes heavy as I watch him retrieve a white envelope. I think part of me knows what's inside that envelope. Has always known. But lies are powerful. And it seems Houston's lies had the power to make me stop looking for answers when they were right in front of me, tucked away in the warmth of his back pocket.

"She left a note."

My eyes are locked on the envelope as memories swirl in my vision. The first night Houston and I slept together. The hours that came before. I begin ticking off the lies one by one, but when I move past our first night together, the lies mount up too quickly. A mountain of fiction too high for me to see over.

"Not Tessa. Hallie," he says, mistaking my horror for confusion.

The anger sets my blood on fire. I land a hard shove in the center of his chest. "I hate you!"

"I didn't want you to read it until you were strong enough."

Skippy barks as I pound on Houston's chest, half-expecting to hear a hollow thump where his heart should be. He drops the letter and grabs my wrists to stop the onslaught of violence.

"That's not for you to decide!" I shout, my voice strangled by the force of this truth. "How could you keep that from me?"

"I was just trying to protect you."

A primal roar issues from deep in my throat. "I wish you would stop protecting me! If it weren't for your stupid protection, I wouldn't be picking up the pieces of my life again."

His jaw tenses at my accusation, the muscle twitching furiously. "I need you to read it while I'm here. I… I won't leave until you've read the whole thing. Then you'll understand why."

Yanking my wrists out of his grasp, I shoo Skippy away so I can grab the letter off the floor. But he follows me as I sink down onto the sofa, hopping onto the cushion next to me, his sixty-pound black Labrador body pressed against my side. As if he can sense that I'm going to need him there.

Houston sits on the edge of the coffee table facing me, our knees inches apart, his gaze locked on the letter in my hands. I try to read his expression, try to see beyond the hardened grief and obvious regret for any indication as to what I'm about to read. What did Hallie confess in this letter that would make him think he had to lie to me for more than five years? But I see nothing.

He looks up from the envelope and our eyes meet. My heart thumps loudly, a riotous drum heightening the sense of foreboding that grips me. The anticipation crackles in the air and Houston's blue eyes narrow as he hardens himself against the intensity of the moment.

I let my gaze fall to the name scrawled on the outside of the envelope: Houston. The shaking begins suddenly, my hands trembling as if the letter I'm holding is as heavy as the Earth. But it's not heavy, it's just real. It's his name in her handwriting. In her final moments, she turned to him, not me.

I clutch the letter to my chest as tears burn hot streaks down my face, my throat a hard painful mass of anguish. Carefully, I slide the folded letter out of the envelope. The moment I see the words *Dear Houston*, the room seems to tilt on its side, throwing me off balance. But I swallow my nausea and keep reading, ripping my way through five pages, front and back, the sentences feeding into my heart like a never-ending news ticker, getting bleaker and more vile with each passing moment. Until I finally reach Hallie's parting words and magma explodes in my belly, searing my throat.

I leap off the sofa, racing for the bathroom, slamming the door behind me. The meager half-cup of oatmeal I ate this morning launches from my mouth as I grip the porcelain. More retching as milky liquid spews forth, my arms shaking as sweat sprouts over my neck, sending a chill through me.

A knock at the door, followed by more retching until I'm empty of everything. All the warm, comforting lies replaced by a single cold, empty truth.

Another knock at the door.

"Go away!" I wail, my voice a shrieking rasp.

The click of the knob turning. The tick of Skippy's nails against the tile floor as he comes to me. My diaphragm compresses angrily in my chest, attempting to rid my body of the truth. A few deep breaths and the dry heaving finally stops. I fall back, my shoulder blades pressed against the hard bathtub as I try to catch my breath.

Skippy is gone, but Houston is still there, as solid and real as the aching truth gnawing at my insides. He looks down at me, his eyes filled with regret so fiercely tangible, I could probably use it to carve out my heart. If I hadn't already given it to him thirteen years ago.

This is not the way the story of us is supposed to go.

Part 1: Denial

"Even when we want to forget,
our scars have a way of
reminding us where we've been."

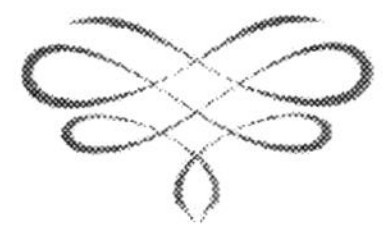

Rory

August 13th

MY NAME IS Aurora Charles, but everyone calls me Rory. Rory Charles. It's the kind of name that conjures up scuffed knees and messy ponytails pulled through the back of a dirty baseball cap, but I could not have been further from a tomboy. In fact, when I was a child, the neighbors would sometimes come check on me because they hadn't seen me playing outside in days. With a book or pencil and paper in hand, I could spend weeks indoors by myself, crafting stories or getting lost in my favorite authors' fictional worlds. I always preferred the comfort of armchair adventures over the outdoor variety. Then, five years ago, everything changed.

I've spent most of those years trying to make sense of the most beautiful and miserable time of my life. But now I have Skippy to help me put it all behind me. Skippy's always there waiting for me when I get home, ready with a sloppy kiss and all. And he never disappoints me or rejects me. He's my new best friend and soul mate.

I open the door of the dog crate and Skippy prances inside, quickly settling himself down on the plush green dog pillow. His furry black tail wags behind him, splashing in the bowl of water sitting on the floor at the back of the crate. I slip my hand into the wire enclosure and he gently licks the liver treat off my palm.

"Good boy, Skip," I coo, scratching him behind the ears as he looks up at me with those wide chocolate-brown eyes that almost seem hazel against his black fur.

Skippy is my two-year-old black Labrador retriever, adopted from a local shelter when he was five months old and still small enough to fit in my backpack. Nowadays, Skip is a hefty sixty-eight pounds and he prefers riding in my car to riding on my back. When I'm not working, Skip and I do everything together. We frequent all the dog-friendly cafés in Goose Hollow and downtown Portland. We go to the dog park where he plays with his best friend, a four-year-old boxer named Greenland, and his girlfriend Nema, a two-year-old Portuguese water dog.

"I'll be back in a few hours. Love you."

His tongue laps at my palm in what I deem a show of affection or appreciation, but in reality he's probably just trying to get the crumbs left behind by the liver treat. It's easy to anthropomorphize our pets. We love them. We tend to assign human characteristics to almost anything we love. We name our pets, our cars, even our body parts, as if they have a life of their own. So what does it mean when we have trouble naming something? That we don't love it? How about when you're trying to name a piece of art?

This is one of the few topics that was never covered in college when I studied creative writing. How do you come up with a title for a book, a poem, a play? Is it the same way you name a baby or a pet? Do you pick your favorite title and stick with it? Or do you assign it a title that has a special meaning?

My mother likes to brag that she named me Aurora because I

was conceived in Alaska under the northern lights. It's a good story, whether or not it's true. But it doesn't help me one bit. I began writing my book five years ago on an uneventful day, under a cloudless summer sky while riding the train home from the University of Oregon.

Maybe I should name my book *Uneventful Day*. Yes, I'm sure readers would clamor to bookstores for that one.

Of course, that day was only uneventful because my life had blown up a week before and there was nothing good left to salvage from the wreckage. I had no choice but to head home for the summer with my head slung low and my tail between my legs.

I grab my bike helmet off the dining table, ignoring the car keys sitting in the glazed blue dish on the kitchen counter. A hacking sound gets my attention and I sigh when I see Skippy has vomited his morning meal onto the green doggy bed. I let him out of the crate and work as fast as I can to scrub most of the vomit off in the kitchen sink. Then I grab the old dog bed I keep in my closet as a spare and lay it down inside the crate.

After I call my mom and ask her to come check on Skippy while I'm gone, I head out the front door of my one-bedroom apartment in Goose Hollow, a small community in Southwest Portland with a spirited car-free culture. I get in the elevator and press the button for the lower terrace level. When the stainless steel doors slide open, I slip the helmet over my head and buckle it tightly under my chin, wincing as I pull one of my auburn hairs out of the clasp. It's a beautiful August day in Portland, Oregon. Perfect day to ride to work.

I reach the bike storage room near the gym and laundry facilities, and enter my code on the digital padlock securing my bike to the wall rack. Pulling the bike off the wall, I double-check that the straps on my backpack are nice and tight. Then I hop on and set off toward the bridge. The vomiting incident has made me ten minutes late. I need to ride my ass off today.

I hit some gridlock on the way, so I arrive at Zucker's grocery store on Belmont twenty-three minutes late for my five-hour shift. After hastily locking up my bike in the employee rack behind the store, I enter through the back door. The refrigerated air blasts me in the face and my heated skin bristles at the change in temperature. The warehouse is always freezing and smells of stale lettuce. Edwin, the warehouse supervisor, waves at me from behind the window looking into his office where he's speaking to Minnie, the inventory-slash-payroll clerk.

I wave back and power walk to the time clock to punch in before Edwin can come outside to make small talk and realize I'm late. I tuck my green T-shirt bearing the grocery store logo—a beige *Z* in the middle of a circle—into my black skinny jeans and head straight for Jamie's office.

Jamie Zucker is the great-granddaughter of Winifred Zucker, the woman who opened the first Zucker's market in 1948 at the ripe age of forty-three. Their family suffered greatly through the Depression. Then Winifred lost her husband, Jacob Zucker, in World War II, leaving her to care for the twins, Jeffrey and John, by herself. Winifred, known to most as "Winnie," worked day and night for four years as a seamstress to save enough money to open her own shop. When the twins were old enough, they took over the market and turned it into a small chain of natural foods stores. Winnie insisted they would never sell the mass-produced junk she saw on the shelves of the big-box supermarkets. They struggled through the '80s and '90s when America experienced a cheap junk food explosion, but the organic food movement of the 21st century breathed new life into their business. And they were now opening their fifth location in East Portland, which Jamie would be running mostly by herself.

Jamie was only twenty-six, but she'd been working at Zucker's for ten years. Her grandfather, John Zucker, still came in once in a while to see how Jamie was doing. He was really there to check how she was running the store. Though it appeared on the outside that he had little faith in her, you could see by the way his eyes lit up in her presence that there was no one he adored more than Jamie. I sometimes wondered what it would feel like to have a grandfather, or even a father, who looked at me like that.

I stride purposefully past the displays of organic Braeburn apples on my left and the dairy case on my right into the rear-right corner of the store. Reaching the office, I knock three times and hear an *Oh, my God!* before Jamie yanks the door open.

"Oh, my God! I can't believe I didn't think of this," she says, her freckled cheeks flushed red and her blue eyes wide with horror. "I need you to pretend to be me."

"What?" I chuckle as she pulls me behind her desk toward the black leather office chair.

"Sit," she commands. "Just hear me out."

She takes a seat in one of the visitor chairs on the other side of the desk, where I normally sit. She pushes her hand through her thin blonde hair as she stares at me, biting her lip as she contemplates what she's going to say. I can't help staring at her one crooked tooth, the top-left pointy cuspid that hangs slightly over her bottom lip.

"Jamie, what's going on? You're sort of freaking me out."

"Rory, I need you to do something for me. As a friend."

A friend? Jamie and I are not enemies, but we're far from friends. We're only two years apart in age, but we're from two different worlds. I graduated from the University of Oregon with a degree in English—with a minor in creative writing—and she dropped out of high school to manage a grocery store. She's engaged to her high school sweetheart. I'm not dating anyone and I never had a high school sweetheart, unless you count the hopeless unrequited crush I had on my best friend's older brother.

Still, even if Jamie's tossing the word *friend* around to get me to do something for her, it does feel good to be needed.

"What do you need?"

She sighs with relief. "I have a meeting with a supplier today. He's coming in to pitch, but Grandpa John's coming. I don't want him to see the guy."

"Why? Isn't he the one who said you needed to keep the selections fresh, or something like that?"

"It's the guy from the beer company coming to discuss the joint venture for the wine bar. Grandpa is dead set against it, but the board is pushing for it."

My heart thumps painfully as I realize what she's asking me.

Management at Zucker's markets has spent the past two years discussing a project to turn some of their in-store espresso cafés into bars that sell wine, beer, and coffee. They'll do wine and beer tastings on Friday and Saturday nights. The bars are being opened only in the locations with a high walk score. A walk score is a rating given to a city based on how easy it is to get around without a car. Goose Hollow has a walk score of 90, which is higher even than New York City. All the board members agreed that the uptown shopping center in Goose Hollow is the perfect area to implement the wine bar idea. Then someone suggested they implement it across all their Portland stores and suddenly our store has been seeing a flurry of meetings over the past few weeks. Apparently, Grandpa John is not supposed to know about these meetings.

I want to get up from Jamie's chair and leave. I didn't realize how safe I felt in my cashier position until now.

"Jamie, I can't pretend to be you. I don't know anything about this wine bar deal."

She holds out her hands to stop me when I attempt to stand. "You don't have to know anything. And you don't really have to pretend to be me. Just thank him for coming and ask him to take a seat. Then you can just sit there and nod and look pretty while he pitches you his beer. I'll try to get Grandpa out of here as quickly as possible. As soon as he's gone, I'll come in and take over."

My entire body tenses with nervous energy just imagining this scenario, but I can't leave her hanging. She's my boss. And it *does* seem like a fairly simple favor to grant.

I draw in a deep breath and let it out slowly. "Sure. I think I can handle that."

"Thank you!" she shrieks as she leaps out of the chair. "You stay here. I'll go out front and wait until the guy gets here, and hope he doesn't get here at the same time as Grandpa."

I lean forward in the leather swivel chair as I watch her leave. She closes the door behind her and my heart races at the thought of what will happen the next time that door opens. Will it be Jamie? Will it be the beer guy? Will it be Grandpa? How will I explain sitting on this side of the desk if it is Grandpa John?

Too many questions for too small of a task. This is nothing. It will be over in a few minutes and I'll be able to get to work.

Leaning back in the chair, I close my eyes and take another deep breath. The knock at the door startles me. I almost trip and fall in my haste to get out of the chair and answer the door. I manage to catch myself by grabbing on to the edge of the desk, but the damage is done. My nerves are ratcheting up again.

I shake out my arms like a prizefighter getting ready to enter the ring. Reaching for the door handle, I force my lips into a smile, then I open the office door.

I'm frozen at the sight of him.

Rory

August 13th

HOUSTON CAVANAUGH.

The first boy I ever loved. And *boy*, did I love him a long time. I loved him until he was a man. I loved him until he loved me back. At least, I *thought* he loved me.

His eyes narrow and he appears confused for a moment. "Jamie?"

My heart drops to my feet.

He doesn't even remember me.

"No," I say with far too much emotion.

"Oh, my God. I'm sorry. I… I know you."

I clutch my chest, unable to breathe. Then his eyes widen with what can only be described as pure terror.

"Rory? Aurora?"

I let out a sharp puff of air. "Yeah."

His lips are still moving. I want to hear what he's saying, but my thoughts are pounding in time with my heart. Images flash in my mind: our bodies tangled in his sheets; the breakfast bar littered with sticky shot glasses and empty beer bottles; my empty dorm.

"Rory?"

I blink a few times to focus on his face and he looks at the floor, as if the weight of our history is pulling his head down.

"I'm sorry. Maybe I should come back later."

"What? No!"

He looks up, startled by my outburst.

"I mean, you came to talk about the contract, so… let's talk. I'm…" I nod toward the chair for him to sit down, then I close the office door behind him. "I'm sorry for spacing out. I was just a little surprised to see you." I take a seat in Jamie's chair and yelp as it begins to tip backward. "Shit!"

Houston laughs as I scoot forward and lean my elbows on the desk, hoping he doesn't notice how the sound of his laughter makes the hairs on my arms stand up.

"Sorry. Obviously, I don't sit on this side of the desk very often, but Jamie didn't want to reschedule this appointment. She should be here shortly."

"You don't need to apologize." The left corner of his mouth pulls up in his signature half smile and I grit my teeth against the surge of emotions welling up inside me. "I'm actually kind of glad we ran into each other."

"Really? You hardly remembered me a minute ago."

He chuckles again. "Yeah, sorry about that. I was just surprised."

I can't argue with this when I just used the same excuse. But it's no more true coming from his lips than it is from mine. We're not *surprised* to see each other. We're *terrified.*

All the times I've imagined running into Houston, I never once imagined he wouldn't recognize me. I haven't changed much. I still have the same long auburn hair he used to bury his face in and twist around his fingers. I'm still carrying the extra ten pounds I put on my freshman year at UO, my *softness*, he used to call it. I still don't wear a lot of makeup, though back then I avoided makeup because I never knew when I was going to burst into tears. Now I avoid it because I'm comfortable in my skin. This is who I am. If someone doesn't like me—or recognize me—that's *their* problem.

I swallow the lump in my throat and force a smile. "So, Houston—would you rather I call you Hugh?"

He flashes me an uncomfortable smile, but it takes him a moment to respond. "Houston is fine."

His family always called him Hugh, but he hated it. I always made it a point to call him Houston. Every time I said his name it was like a promise to be true to him. The real Houston. I wish I had known then that you can't promise to be true to a ghost. Ghosts aren't real.

"So… you're the beer guy?" I say, trying to break the awkward silence.

"The beer guy? Is that how I'm referred to around here?"

Houston's gaze is focused on the desk so he doesn't have to look me in the eye. His elbows rest on the arms of the chair and his hands are clasped in front of him. That's when I notice the wedding ring.

"You're married," I blurt out before I can stop myself.

He looks up, his eyes locking on mine, then nods just enough for me to notice.

My eyes and sinuses sting and I blink a few times. "What's her name? I mean, that's… that's great."

Shit. What is wrong with me?

He stares at the desk again, unsure how to respond to this. "Yeah, I guess. Um… Are *you* married?"

For some reason, I glance down at my hands where they rest on top of a stack of invoices on Jamie's desk, as if I'll suddenly find a wedding ring on my finger, too.

"No, I'm not married." I draw in another breath and let it out slowly as I try to think of a new topic. "You're still making beer?"

In college, Houston made his own line of homemade ale, which he called Barley Legal, since barely anyone who drank it was over twenty-one. It was very popular with the frats. I still remember the way our apartment would smell like yeast and alcohol after his weekend "tasting" parties. I'm surprised I still remember the name of the beer and the smell, considering I was pretty wasted through the last six months of my freshman year, the months we were together.

"Yep. And it's still Barley Legal."

"You kept the name?"

"Couldn't let it go."

My breath hitches at these words. They're so similar to the last words he whispered in my ear five years ago as I lay in bed pretending to sleep. *I love you, but we need to let it go.*

He doesn't seem to catch the similarity. Maybe he doesn't even remember the last words he spoke to me. How can he be so different when he looks exactly the same? The shock of caramel-brown hair on his head still has the natural ribbons of sandy blond running through it. His blue eyes still sparkle when he talks about his homemade creations, though they're probably not homemade anymore. He still looks like the guy who took my mind and body to places they'd never been. But there's something very different about him. He seems subdued. Defeated.

"Rory," he says, just loud enough to break through my thoughts. "How have you been?"

I don't know why he's asking this question ten minutes into our conversation, so I shrug. "Fine. I graduated two years ago. I changed my major after… Anyway, I got my degree in English—minor in creative writing. I've been working on a book in my spare time."

His face lights up at this news. "A book? That's *awesome.* You were always a great writer."

"Well, probably not *great*, but I graduated."

He smiles at my modesty. "You were great. I'm sure you're even better now."

My smile fades. Is it okay to accept praise from him now that he's married? Is it okay to *want* his praise when I've lived without it for five years?

My phone vibrates in my pocket and I pull it out to see who it is. My mom's cell number flashes on the screen. I usually send her calls to voicemail while I'm at work and check them on my lunch break, but I *did* ask her to check on Skippy today.

I contemplate answering her call, if only to escape the awkwardness of my conversation with Houston, but I hit the reject button. If it's an emergency, she'll send me a text. I've told her multiple times to text me in the case of an emergency, since I'm almost always with a customer when she gets the urge to call.

I look up and Houston's jaw is clenched as he stares at the food-handling certificates hanging on the wall of the office.

"It was my mom," I say, not sure why I feel the need to mention this. "Probably just wants to tell me I'm out of coffee or something."

"You still live with your mom and dad?"

"No. *God*, no. My parents divorced two weeks after… we broke up. My mom and I moved to Portland two years ago. She has her own apartment now, but she checks on my dog while I'm at work."

He smiles at my reaction and my stomach flutters. Then, I find myself wondering what shifted between us in the last minute or two, because I'm beginning to wish we could sit here talking like this forever. But any minute now Jamie is going to walk through that office door and relieve me of this meeting.

"How long have you worked here?" Houston asks as he leans back in his chair, getting a bit more comfortable.

He's dressed in jeans and a brown T-shirt bearing the logo of his company. The shirt clings to his biceps and pectoral muscles. I try not to think of the nights I fell asleep with his arms around me and my cheek pressed against his solid chest. The fact that he wore a T-shirt and jeans to a pitch meeting proves he hasn't changed. He's still the laid-back guy everyone wants to share a beer with. And if he hasn't changed, I should stop letting my mind wander to our past.

"I've worked here a little more than a year," I reply. "I interned at the *Oregonian* for a while after graduation, but I got tired of living with my mom and never having money. I applied for this job on a whim, but it ended up working out. I'm union, so I make enough to live in a one-bedroom nearby and still feed myself and Skippy."

"Skippy?"

"My dog."

"Oh."

The desk phone rings and I contemplate not answering it, but it could be Jamie calling me from somewhere else in the store. "Jamie Zucker's office. How may I help you?"

"Rory! Skip passed out and I can't wake him up." My mom is frantic and I can tell by the thickness in her throat that she's crying. My mom never cries, and the mere sound of it makes my heart race.

"What? What's going on? What happened?" I stand suddenly and Houston's smile disappears as he stands, too.

"I don't know. The apartment was pretty warm when I came inside. I don't think your air conditioner's working. He was just lying there in the crate, so I put some ice in his water bowl and put it next to his face so he could drink. He drank the whole bowl, then he passed out! Oh, my God. Did I do something wrong? I was just trying to cool him down. I swear, I didn't mean to do anything. I'm sorry, Rory. I'm so sorry."

"Oh, no. How long has he been out?"

"About twelve minutes now."

"Is he breathing?"

"I don't know. I think so."

"I'll be right there."

I hang up the desk phone and grab my cell off the stack of invoices. Then I scroll through my contacts searching for the number to Skip's vet as Houston follows me out of the office.

"*Shit!* I rode my bike today. It will take me at least twenty-five minutes to get there."

"I can take you," Houston immediately volunteers.

I gaze into his eyes, knowing that every second I hesitate could mean the difference between life and death for my best friend.

Suddenly, the memories come flooding back to me from the day my world was turned upside down five and a half years ago. The day I found Houston standing outside my dorm refusing to let me inside. The day Houston became my protector and my downfall.

My finger hovers over the call button, then I grab Houston's arm as he begins walking straight toward Grandpa John and Jamie, who are both standing at register three talking to Kenny, another cashier.

Houston glances down at his arm where my fingers are curled around his firm bicep. I quickly let it go.

"Sorry, but we can't go that way. We have to go through the back. Hurry."

He follows me into the warehouse and out through the back door.

"What about your meeting?" I mention as we skitter like mice along the back wall of the store.

"I'll work it out," he replies quickly.

We turn right at the back corner of the building into a small service alley that reeks of trash and stale beer.

"Where are you parked?" I ask.

"Right out front. Don't you need to tell your boss you're leaving?"

"I'll call her after I call the vet."

We make it to the end of the alley and Houston grabs my arm before I can walk out onto the sidewalk. "Rory, wait."

I glance down at his fingers, which are curled around my forearm the same way mine were curled around his bicep a minute ago, and I instantly grow impatient. "What?"

He's silent for a moment, then he lets go of me. "Nothing. Let's go."

I follow closely behind him as we approach his shiny, pearl-white SUV. The sight of it makes my stomach curdle. Not because it's a gas-guzzler, but because his wife probably sat next to him inside this car, holding his hand, stroking his skin. Maybe they've even had sex in there.

I know I shouldn't care. I haven't seen or heard from Houston in five years and here he is going out of his way to help me—again. As if the past five years never happened.

He opens the passenger door for me and I grit my teeth as I climb inside, holding my breath to block out the heady scent of beige leather.

Shutting the door after me, he rounds the front of the car and smoothly climbs into the driver's seat. "Where are we going?" he asks, unable to hide the hint of enthusiasm in his voice.

I stare straight ahead and think, *I wish I knew.*

Houston

August 13th

I STARE AT the dashboard so I can't see her face. She looks the same as she did five years ago, and back then that face had the power to knock the breath out of me. The curve of her cheekbones, the fullness of her lips, the softness of her skin. She was the drug that numbed the pain, but only temporarily. I just have to keep reminding myself of that so I don't do anything stupid, like telling her the truth.

We may only ever have one great, passionate love. If I had one, it would definitely be Rory. But sometimes it's best to leave that kind of love in the past. Still, there's so much unfinished business between us. As I watch her from the corner of my eye, I wonder if this chance encounter is the opportunity for absolution I've been hoping for the past five years.

"Hold on," she says as she presses the cell phone to her ear. "Hello? Yes, is Dr. Heinlein in the office today?... My dog is unconscious and I need to bring him in. It's an emergency... No, not that I know of... Blood type? Um... DEA 6, I think... Yes...

Thank you so much. I'll be there as fast as I can." She pulls the phone away from her ear and checks something on the screen. "We have to go to my apartment first. I'm in Portland Towers."

"On 21st?"

She nods and I sense a bit of tension, like she's embarrassed to live in a building mostly inhabited by college students. She probably imagines I live in a nice house with my wife and kids and maybe even a few pets. She doesn't know that Tessa and I live in a generic two-bedroom apartment downtown and we have no children.

We make it to her building in seven minutes and I find myself getting nervous. How far do I take this act of kindness? Do I go inside? Do I help take her dog to the vet? The conversation she had with her mom a few minutes ago implied she has a car of her own, but she opted to ride her bike to work today. Technically, she no longer needs my help, but I have no idea how big her dog is. He could be a teacup poodle or a huge mastiff, in which case she definitely needs my help getting the dog into the car.

I park in a fifteen-minute loading zone right in front of the thirteen-story apartment building and kill the engine. I throw open my car door to follow her inside, but she stops me before she gets out of the car.

"What are you doing?" she asks, her voice still taut with tension. "I have a car. I'm fine. You need to go back to your meeting."

"I can help you carry the dog down, then I'll take off."

She hesitates for a moment, then she nods. "Okay. Thanks."

Following her into the elevator, I hold my breath as she presses the button for the eighth floor. Just walking behind her, I've gotten small whiffs of her hair. But I know the close quarters in the elevator will only amplify that. And I don't want her to know how crazy that scent is making me.

We stand side by side in total silence as the elevator ascends.

The fingers on my right hand tingle, as if my skin can sense she's near. Then I realize it's probably because I'm holding my breath. Slowly, I breathe in, catching a strong whiff of vanilla that sends my heart racing. I clench my fist to keep from reaching out to touch her.

She glances down at my hand as she sees the slight movement from the corner of her eye. I relax my hand again so she doesn't think being this close to her is making me tense, but I don't believe for a second I can fool her.

She steps forward, closer to the elevator doors, putting more distance between us. A soft buzzing noise breaks through the silence just as the elevator doors slide open. She holds the phone to her ear as we exit onto the eighth floor.

"What's wrong?" she says, her eyebrows furrowed with worry, then her lips curl into an absolutely beautiful smile. "Oh, thank God… Yes, we just got here. I'll be right in." Holding the phone to her chest, she lets out a sigh of relief. "He's awake."

"That's great news."

She stops in front of apartment 811 and looks up at me. "I guess you can go."

"You're not still taking him to the vet?"

"Well, it's not an emergency anymore. I'll just have my mom take him in my car. She can walk him down now that he's awake."

My heart clenches as I realize I'm no longer needed. "Of course. So, you're okay?"

What a stupid loaded question.

She shrugs as she reaches for the doorknob. "As good as I can be," she replies, then suddenly she wraps her arms around my waist. "Thanks for the ride."

The smell of her hair hits me like a knife in the chest and I hold my breath to keep myself from completely inhaling her. I pat her on the back and she chuckles as she lets me go.

"Good luck with your pitch," she says, never looking back as she disappears into the apartment.

Jesus fucking Christ. I'm in deep shit here. I can't go back to the store for that meeting. There's no way I'll be able to work with Rory on a regular basis. If we open that wine bar, I'll have to check in at least once a week, probably more like two to three times a week.

I won't survive seeing her that often. I've barely survived the past five years.

But I can't throw away a multimillion-dollar joint venture contract. There's too much competition in the craft beer market these days. I need to take whatever bones are thrown my way.

I just wish I knew if Rory were *truly* okay. I can put myself through the agony of seeing her on a regular basis if I know it won't affect her. The last thing I want to do is make her work situation unbearable. She doesn't deserve that after what I did to her.

I MANAGED TO avoid bumping into Rory on the way out of the meeting at Zuckers by leaving the shop while she was busy with a customer. The pitch meeting with Jamie went well. When she heard why I stepped out earlier, she was quite impressed with my kindness toward the staff. I considered telling her that Rory is far from just a staff member to me, but I opted against it. If Rory wants her boss to know about our past, she should be the one to tell her.

As I drive away from Zucker's market, I think of going back to the brewery to see how Dean, our production manager, is coming along with the new winter lager. We've been brewing it in small batches in the pilot brewing system since January, and it won a gold medal at the Portland International Beer Festival last week. But today we're brewing the first large-scale production batch. Scaling up can be a bit tricky, but I'm confident Dean can handle everything on his own.

This batch of winter lager won't be ready for another twenty-three days. And if this deal with Zucker's goes through, it will be on tap at the new wine bar just in time for the holidays. I can relax tonight knowing I've done all I can today. Right now, I need to get home and see Tessa. I know that once I see her face, I'll know what I have to do.

I park the truck in the underground lot, then I head for the elevator. I pass the dog grooming station on the way, which Tessa always complains about. She thinks it's nice that the complex was built with the needs of pet owners in mind, but she thinks the wet-dog smell seeps into the underground parking structure and "infringes" on the other residents. Yet, as I breathe in the barnyard scent of freshly washed canine, all I can think of is what it would be like to help Rory give her dog a bath in there, suds flying everywhere, laughter echoing off the concrete walls.

I shake my head, trying to clear these dangerous thoughts as I enter the elevator. The doors are almost closed when someone sticks their arm through the gap. The doors slide open again and in walks Kendra Gris, our neighbor from across the hall and Tessa's new best friend. Kendra's a stay-at-home mom with an eight-month-old baby boy, Trucker. I'm not one to speak ill of a child, but I will say that Kendra and her husband, Aaron, really screwed their kid with a name like Trucker Gris.

"Hey, Kendra," I mutter, trying not to sound too annoyed.

She flashes me a tight-lipped smile as she pushes the stroller into the elevator then glances at the panel to make sure I've pressed the button for the third floor. She sighs as she flips her dark hair over her shoulder.

"Hey, Hugh."

I think back to the moment in Jamie's office earlier when Rory asked if she should call me Hugh or Houston. After five years, she still remembered that I prefer Houston, but this woman who sees me almost every day still insists on calling me Hugh.

"You're awfully quiet," Kendra remarks as the elevator doors open. "Bad day at the brewery?"

I exit right behind her as she pushes the stroller down the hall. "It's been a long day."

"It's two o'clock," she sneers when she reaches her door. "Maybe you just need a few cold ones."

She pushes open the door with her back and pulls the stroller in backward, all the while flashing me a condescending smile. Kendra has told Tessa on more than one occasion that I drink too much. I don't.

I drink two, maybe three, beers a night to unwind after work. Sometimes when we're testing a new recipe, I'll drink too much, but I never get so drunk I black out or lose time. Beer is my life. I'm supposed to be a connoisseur. It's my job.

I enter the apartment and Tessa is sitting at the kitchen table with her computer. Her eyes widen when she looks up and sees me in the doorway. She deftly closes the laptop as she rises from the chair.

"Hey, I didn't expect you back so soon. Is something wrong?"

I shake my head as I drop my keys into the glass bowl on top of the table constructed out of salvaged Brazilian pine. "Everything's fine. I think the pitch went well. I'm… optimistic."

"That's great!" she replies, pulling her straight blonde hair into a ponytail at her nape as she walks toward me. "Why don't you look happy?"

"I am happy." I force a smile as I head for the refrigerator to grab a beer.

"Houston, it's two o'clock."

I glance at the beer in my hand then back at her. "Does it matter what time of day it is?"

"I'm not talking about the beer. I was just wondering why you're home so early on a Wednesday."

I can't tell her that I ran into my ex-girlfriend today and how the wall I'd built around my memories of Rory was knocked down in an instant. I can't tell her that I'm home early today because I didn't trust myself to be anywhere but here right now. I can't tell her that I hoped the sight of her would remind me of all the reasons I can't be with Rory.

Being married means having someone, just one person, who knows everything about you. Someone you can share everything with, even the ugly bits of your soul you'd rather sweep under the carpet and completely forget about. But Tessa doesn't know anything about Rory. That time of my life is a discussion I hoped I would never need to have with her.

"I told you. The meeting went well, so I just decided to take the rest of the day off. I wanted to see you."

I set the cold beer on the marble countertop, then I grab her waist and pull her body flush against mine. Gazing into her blue eyes for a moment, I will myself not to compare her to Rory, but it's difficult. Her sharp hip bones are pressed against me and I can't help but remember how much I loved the softness of Rory's body.

Leaning forward, I take her earlobe into my mouth. Her breathing quickens as I trace the tip of my tongue inside the shell of her ear. Her hair smells like the lavender-mint shampoo we share and I inhale deeply to rid myself of the memory of Rory's hair, the way it smelled like vanilla frosting.

"Houston," she breathes, her fingers curling tightly around my biceps. "I… I have an appointment."

She pushes me back and her face is flushed as she opens a drawer and takes out a bottle opener. "I didn't know you were coming home early. I booked a hair appointment for this afternoon."

She pops the top off the bottle of beer I set down on the counter a few seconds ago, then she hands it to me.

I wish I could say that this is the first time Tessa has rejected my sexual advances, but that would be a lie. Any married couple will tell you that these kinds of things just don't always line up. Sometimes she has an appointment. Sometimes I have to get to work for an important meeting. Sometimes one of us is just not in the mood. But it's not the response I was hoping for. I wanted to lose myself in her today. Maybe even go for an all-nighter.

"You have a good time, baby."

She laughs nervously. "A good time at the hair salon?"

Before she can say anything else, I kiss her. Hard. Tangling my fingers in her hair, I thrust my tongue inside her mouth. She whimpers as she clutches the front of my T-shirt. We move in unison and I'm reminded of the first time I met Tessa, at a beer festival three years ago.

She was wearing a floral crown on her head and totally blasted on free beer when she showed up at our booth. I probably could have taken her home with me and fucked her once then never called her again. It was what I had done for two years and it had worked just fine. But something she said changed my mind about using her.

She sampled our pale ale, then she looked me in the eye and said, *You look like my brother… He's dead.*

She cackled loudly at this proclamation and spilled the rest of the beer sample on her chest. Then she looked up at me again and her eyes swelled with tears. She apologized as her friend pulled her away from our booth, but I knew then that I wanted to know her.

I pull away, placing a soft kiss on her cheekbone before I whisper in her ear. "Hurry home. I don't think this beer is gonna quench my thirst tonight."

She nods as she reaches for her purse in a daze. "I'll be back soon."

As the door closes behind her, my eyes are drawn to the laptop on the table. Tessa never brings the laptop out here while I'm home. She says she doesn't like having electronic devices between us. So one of our unofficial wedding vows is to leave all electronic devices, other than cell phones, in the office. That way when we're home together we give each other our undivided attention.

I guess it's not a big deal if she brings the laptop out here while I'm at work. I take a seat on the sofa, but my gaze is still drawn to the table. Was it my imagination or was she nervous when I walked in at two o'clock?

No, that's just my own guilty conscience making me paranoid.

I stare at the laptop and for a brief moment consider opening it up to see what she was doing, but that would be a gross invasion of her privacy. Tessa is allowed to have her own personal space where I don't intrude.

And so am I.

Rory

Five years ago, May 28th

I SLIDE THE dollar bill into the vending machine on the first floor of the sociology building and, once again, it spits it back out.

"Piece of shit."

I smack the front of the machine as if this will make me feel better. I'm still thirsty as hell. Stuffing the dollar into my jeans pocket, my fingers bump into the new cell phone Houston gave me yesterday. The least romantic gift I expected to get, especially since I wasn't even expecting a gift. He's the one graduating next week and I still haven't decided what I want to get him.

I'm sure he would gladly accept a blow job as a graduation gift, but I had hoped we could do something a normal couple would do. Maybe a private dinner or even just a weekend alone without a dozen frat guys spilling beer all over our carpet. Actually, I'd settle for just a decent truthful conversation.

For more than a month, Houston has dodged my questions about his plans for the summer. He's graduating with a degree in business. He got accepted to the UO School of Law, but I have a feeling he's not going to stay here. I'm not sure I understand throwing away that kind of opportunity. I'm also not sure I wouldn't do the same. Not a day goes by that I don't wish I could quit school, move somewhere no one knows me, and start over.

Houston pretty much told me he wanted the same, though he was rip-roaring drunk when he confided in me two weeks ago. I'm still not sure I believe that he was too drunk to know what he was saying.

Silver brushstrokes of moonlight painted across his muscular shoulders as he brushed the backs of his fingers across my cheekbone and looked me square in the eye. "Let's go. Let's get out of here."

His lips swept softly over mine as he leaned closer. I could smell the sweet ethanol fragrance of too much beer on his breath, but he could probably smell it on mine too. He slipped his knee between my legs as he slid closer to me, until his body was flush against my right side and his growing erection was prodding my hip.

"Go where?" Six months together and I still got breathless whenever he was this close.

He kissed my jaw and nuzzled his face into the curve of my neck. "I don't know. South America. Indonesia. Anywhere. As long as it's just you and me and no one knows where we went. Let's do it."

"We can *do it* here," I replied with a soft chuckle.

He didn't laugh at my joke as he laid a tender kiss on the corner of my mouth. "Rory, we can fuck each other into submission anywhere." His hand slid behind my neck, lifting it so my head tilted back, so he could suck on the hollow of my throat. "But we can never be together here."

My heart stopped. "What are you talking about? We *are* together here."

He chuckled and the sound made my skin prickle with goose

bumps. "I'm kidding. I'm just drunk." He climbed on top of me, lifting my leg so I could feel the tip of his solid erection pressed against my panties. "I love you, baby."

Then he kissed me and I forgot about that conversation and haven't thought about it since. Until this morning when I visited the university health center.

How am I going to tell him I'm pregnant? I'm pretty sure Houston wants a child as much as I do, which is *not at all.* This is not the kind of graduation gift I wanted to give him.

Maybe I should just get it taken care of without him. If I tell him, he might think I'm trying to imply that we should keep it. Or worse, he might think I'm trying to ask him to commit.

I know he likes to talk about the future and how we're going to get married after I graduate in three years, but I don't like to think that far ahead. Hallie had her whole life planned out and it didn't work out very well for her.

I love Houston. And I know he loves me and he would support me if I told him I wanted to terminate the pregnancy, but part of me is terrified of changing anything between us right now. We already have too much change to deal with this summer with him graduating and possibly moving two hours away to Portland, if he decides not to go to law school. I'm not sure our relationship could survive this.

Sometimes I wonder if our relationship is even real.

Hallie and I became best friends on the first day of sixth grade when the teacher sat us next to each other and we both discovered we were obsessed with Blink 182. She invited me over to her house after school that day so we could burn some songs onto a USB drive, and that's when I fell in love with Houston. I was eleven and he was fourteen, but in my warped prepubescent mind I was already concocting fantasies of us married with three children.

It's weird how our fantasies change as we mature. Now, I'd

be happy just to *know* Houston after I graduate. Our connection is tenuous at best, no matter how many times he tells me he loves me and that we're going to spend the rest of our lives together. We're connected by a million fragile filaments, memories we've tried our hardest to pretend aren't there.

I once made the mistake of asking Houston if he remembered Hallie's favorite song.

His response: *I'm sure I'll completely forget after this fifth beer.*

We're not allowed to talk about the past in Houston's apartment. I sometimes wonder if it's this mutual desire to forget that brought us together or if he genuinely wanted to protect me when he asked me to move in with him six months ago. I could have moved in with Houston and kept to myself. I could have moved into another dorm. Or I could have opted not to move out of my old dorm at all. But I wanted to escape the memories as much as he did. I would have accepted a sleeping bag under a bridge at that point, anything not to have to enter that dorm ever again.

Instead, I moved in with Houston the same day he offered, and we slept together that first night. After seven years of pining for him, I convinced myself it was natural. We were meant to be together. It was okay to give myself to him so willingly.

I think I would have believed that even if we weren't brought together by tragedy. I was always ready to belong to Houston. But I was not ready for what came after.

I make it back to our off-campus apartment a few minutes after three and I'm not surprised to find I'm alone. Houston doesn't get home until a quarter after four on Wednesdays. I bought a couple of at-home pregnancy tests on the way home, just to make sure there wasn't a mix-up with my specimen at the health center. Five minutes later, I'm confused. The test is negative.

I take another brand of test and the results are positive. Now

I'm even more confused. I lift the package off the bathroom counter to read the instructions again. I'm so lost in the small type, I don't notice when Houston walks in.

"What's that?"

I drop the box in the sink and let out a sharp yelp. "Jesus Christ, Houston. You scared the shit out of me. You're home early." I reach for the box, but he beats me to it. "Give me that."

His eyes widen as he holds the box up so I can't reach it. "A pregnancy test? Are you pregnant?"

"No! I mean, I don't know."

"I thought you were on the pill," he counters, but I don't appreciate the accusatory tone.

"I am! But it's not 100% effective, especially when consumed with alcohol."

He laughs. "Oh, so it's *my* fault you drink so much?"

"What? I don't drink that much!" I shout. "You drink more than I do."

"Did you do this on purpose?"

I stare into his blue eyes, unable to hide the anger boiling inside me. "Fuck you."

I push past him, but he grabs my wrist before I can leave the bathroom. "I'm sorry. That was a stupid thing to say."

I shake my arm free and head for the kitchen.

"Rory, I said I'm sorry. I didn't mean it. I know you wouldn't do something like that."

He follows me into the kitchen and pins me against the counter as I search for my car keys in my purse.

"Stop it, Houston."

"Are you pregnant or not?"

"Why do you care? I'm not keeping it."

He grabs my waist and turns me around roughly. "Are you saying I don't have a fucking choice?"

I lay my hands flat against his solid chest and try to push him back, but he doesn't move. "Get off me."

"Answer the question, Rory. Are you pregnant?"

"I don't know." I twist my body and duck under his arm to get away from him, then I head for the bedroom, where I left my backpack.

He follows so close behind me I can feel the heat of his body radiating on my shoulders. "What did the test say?"

"It was negative."

"So you're *not* pregnant?"

I grab the backpack on the bed and pull it upright so I can unzip the top. "I took three tests today. Two in the bathroom and one at the health center this morning… Two out of three were positive."

I pull my laptop out of the backpack and he takes it from me, flinging it onto the bed. "You're pregnant."

This time it's not a question. And it makes me sick to my stomach because I know it's true.

"I'm sorry," I whisper, staring at his chest as I wipe away the tears. "I don't know how this happened."

He grabs my face and tilts my head back so I can see the tears in his eyes. He doesn't speak for maybe a minute or two, but it feels like an eternity.

"We can do this."

"Do what?"

His arms envelop me, crushing me against him so tightly I feel as if my shoulders may dislocate. "We'll have the baby. We can't get rid of it… It's… This can't be a mistake."

My face is pressed against the solid warmth of his chest, so close I can hear his heartbeat, slow and steady. He's serious.

Houston

Five years ago, May 28th

I CAN'T TELL Rory the truth, that I'm no more ready to have a baby than she is. But this realization that she's pregnant has flipped a switch in me. It's as if everything I've fucked up over the past six months has faded away and I can finally see clearly. This is the opportunity I've been waiting for. This is going to make all the lies and the guilt worth it.

I kiss the top of her head and she sobs into my T-shirt. "Hey," I whisper in her ear. "I know you're scared, but I think I know how to fix that."

She swipes the back of her hand across her nose and I can't help but smile. I grab the back of her neck with one hand and with the other hand I pull up the bottom of my T-shirt to wipe her nose.

She laughs as she pushes me away. "What are you *doing*?"

I chuckle as I grab her face so she can't get away. "Come here, Scar. Let me wipe your snot."

"Ew! Stop it!" she protests, giggling hysterically as I try to wrangle her in.

She loves it when I call her Scar. It's short for Scarlet, for her red hair, but also because sometimes she's as mean as Scar from *The Lion King.*

"See, I'll make an excellent father. I've watched *The Lion King* and I know how to wipe snot. You don't have to be afraid."

"Shut up." This takes some of the fight out of her, but she's still smiling uncontrollably as I pull her close. "Stop trying to make me laugh. This is serious."

I kiss the tip of her nose and wrap my arms around her shoulders. One of the things I love the most about her is that, at five-foot-four, she's twelve inches shorter than I am. I just want to tuck her in my pocket and keep her with me everywhere I go.

Plus, it makes for great wall sex.

"I know this is serious, which is exactly why I'm trying to make you laugh. That's the only way we'll get through this."

Her arms loosen around my waist and she looks up at me with those round hazel eyes that have never seen the real me. "What do you mean by 'That's the only way we'll get through this'? How are we going to get through this?"

I know there's only one correct response to this question, but I don't know if I can bring myself to say it. Once I say the words, there's no taking them back. I'll have to back up those words with actions, because there's no other alternative. Not for me.

I consider leaving the room to get the ring I have hidden underneath our bed, but I'm afraid I'll talk myself out of it in the short time it will take to do that. I've already spent the past couple of weeks since I got her the ring trying to talk myself out of it, convincing myself that nothing good will come of it.

That's it. I'm doing it.

I take both her hands in mine, then I step back and look her in the eye as I get down on one knee. Her eyes widen and her whole body begins to tremble. She knows what I'm about to do.

"Rory—Aurora—well, I—I don't know the proper way to do this."

"Houston, please, you don't have—"

"No, just listen."

Rory knows there's no use trying to talk me out of doing something once my mind is set. But is my mind really set on this?

She smiles as she kneels before me. "Then I'm coming down here with you."

"Get up, baby. It's *my* turn to get on my knees."

She smacks my arm and I smile as I try to help her back to her feet, but she refuses to stand. "I'm not getting up. If we're doing this, we're doing it together… from beginning to end."

Her words make my stomach vault into my throat. I can't do this. If I marry Rory, then I'll have no choice but to tell her the truth. And I love her too much to do that.

"Get up, Rory. We can't do this."

"What?"

I stand up and hold my hand out to help her up, trying not to look her in the eye so I can't see the hurt. She stands up and I don't see her hand coming at me until it's too late. Her palm lands hard on my jaw, making a popping sound so loud I think she may have broken something.

"What the fuck?" I roar at her, rubbing my face to soothe the burn.

"I knew you were an asshole, but I never thought you'd do something like this. You just made a fool out of me. What kind of person stops proposing in the middle of the proposal? An asshole."

"Getting married isn't the answer."

She storms off toward the bedroom and stuffs her laptop back into her backpack. "I'm leaving."

"Rory, please, just stay. We need to talk about this."

"I don't want to talk to you." She pulls the backpack on and rounds on me. "I don't want to see you. I don't want to know you."

My chest aches as I finally grasp that this is it. This is the solution I've been waiting for since the day I realized inviting Rory to live with me was a huge mistake. Though I know this is what I've been waiting for, there is no sense of relief and it doesn't hurt any less. On the contrary, it fucking kills.

"You don't have to leave. The rent is paid up until the end of June. That's thirty-four days. You can keep the apartment and I'll stay with Troy until I find another place."

She laughs as she wipes tears from her cheeks. "I knew this would be your reaction. I knew the minute they told me the test was positive that this would happen. You're so fucking predictable it's disgusting."

I know I deserve this, but I wish I could grab her and shake her and force her to see the truth. The truth that has been right under her nose for six months. The truth that I have so foolishly hidden from her when I should have told her everything from the beginning. Then I wouldn't feel like the past six months of my life were a lie.

I want to take her in my arms and apologize for not being a better man, but she needs a clean break. She doesn't need me begging for forgiveness and further confusing the situation. This is the end. It has to end now or it will only get worse before it ends later.

"What do you need?" I ask, breaking the heavy silence.

She looks up at me, confused by this question.

"I mean, do you need money for the… procedure?" I clarify.

Her lips tremble as she presses them together and turns her head so she doesn't have to look at me. "I need you to get out."

"I don't want you to do this alone."

"Just get out," she whispers.

"Baby—I mean, *fuck*, Rory. Come on. You can't do this

alone."

She steps around me. "Fine. I'll leave."

I grab her forearm to stop her. "No, I'll leave. You stay."

I can't allow her to leave this apartment. I don't know where she'll end up. She doesn't have any close friends anymore.

Striding past her, I turn around when I reach the doorway, marveling at the mess I've made. "You're staying. I'm leaving." I grab the doorframe for support as it hits me that I've just made the worst mistake of my life. "And I promise I won't bother you, but I need you to promise me something, too."

She stares at the carpet, unwilling to meet my gaze.

"Rory, please promise me you'll call if you need anything. Ever."

She steps backward and sits down on the edge of the bed, still refusing to look up at me. "Just get out."

Rory

August 15th

MY DOG HAS diabetes. I thought the vet was joking when he told me this. *My perfect Skippy can't have diabetes.* But he does. And he will need insulin injections for the rest of his life. My poor Skip.

After spending two nights in the animal hospital, and after waiting patiently for me to receive a thirty-minute lesson on how to test his blood glucose and give him an insulin shot, Skippy was ready to come home. The moment he climbs into my twelve-year-old Toyota, his tail wags relentlessly and he whines for me to open the window.

"Settle down, Skip. We'll be home soon."

I roll the passenger window all the way down and he grins as he juts his head out. He closes his eyes, panting heavily as the sun warms his face. I love him so much. I don't know what I would have done if I'd lost him.

My phone vibrates in my pocket and I slip it out to check the number. I don't recognize it so I hit the red button to decline the call, then I drive home.

The streets of Portland are lively with the trappings of summer. Outdoor patios at cafés are bustling. Bicyclists swish by when I'm stopped in traffic. Protestors are picketing in their shorts and tank tops outside the Justice Center. The air blasting through my car window smells like hot concrete and there are few clouds in the sky, but the threat of rain is always present.

I moved to Portland after I graduated from UO. It seemed like the logical next step. I was born and raised in McMinnville, about an hour's drive from Portland. Even after the population doubled, McMinnville is still the kind of small town that is too spread out to have a true small-town feel. Don't get me wrong, everyone knows everyone's business in McMinnville, but there's still a disjointed quality to the town that never sat right with me. As if the town had been planned by someone with attachment issues.

Hallie and Houston moved to McMinnville the summer before we began middle school and Houston began high school. Looking back, it seemed like a logical time for them to move, I suppose. Their parents had just divorced and their mom, Ava, wanted to start fresh. Their father had been having an affair for years and Ava couldn't seem to escape all the people who had kept it a secret from her.

This must have affected Houston, knowing that his father was the one who had betrayed his mother for so long and still *she* was the one who'd had to move away to escape the memories. I often wonder if Houston was cheating on me while we were together, which is why he insisted I keep the apartment out of some misplaced sense of guilt. So he wouldn't feel like a total bastard like his father. But I think the truth about why Houston left is much worse.

The truth is, Houston probably never loved me.

It took a near-miss with a wedding proposal to jolt the truth out of him. As painful as it is to know I spent so many years of my life loving someone who was incapable of loving me back, I'm still grateful for the months I spent curled up next to him, wrapped in his arms. Even if it was all a lie, those were still the best moments of my life.

Skippy and I are settled on the sofa, ready to spend Friday night catching up on the past few episodes of *The Good Wife*. I flinch a little when my phone buzzes. I snatch it off the coffee table and Skip and I both look at the screen. It's the same unknown number that called me earlier.

"Should I answer?" I ask the dog and he looks up at me, his brow furrowed, wondering when I'm going to make the stupid thing stop buzzing.

I sigh as I hit the green button. "Hello?"

"Rory, it's Houston. Do you have a minute?"

My first instinct is to hang up. I can't talk to Houston on the phone. He's married.

"Houston, what are you doing?" I whisper, as if his wife is sitting next to me. "You can't call me. How did you even get my number? Forget it. I don't care how you got it. Just don't call me."

The last thing I hear as I hang up is Houston calling my name. I stare at the phone for a second, expecting him to call back. Foolishly *wishing* he'd call back. Then I hug my knees to my chest as I wonder what he could have possibly been calling about.

Skip breaks me out of my trance by stuffing his snout under my armpit. I laugh as I push his head back. "Is that a hint? Are you saying I need a shower?"

I stretch my legs out and rest my feet on the coffee table so he can lay his head on my lap, then I turn on the TV and try not to think about Houston. But, at this point, trying not to think about him is like trying not to breathe.

After he drove me to my apartment two days ago, I was on high alert at the store. As I bagged groceries and punched in product codes, I'd glance over my shoulder at the sliding doors, watching the customers as they came and went. I don't know if I was more afraid or excited at the prospect of seeing him. All I know is that I didn't want to be caught unaware again. But he never came back to the store after his meeting with Jamie on Wednesday. And I've been too afraid to ask Jamie whether or not their meeting went well. I don't want to show too much interest in this wine bar project as I have no intention of telling Jamie that Houston and I have a past.

An hour later, I have no idea what happened in that episode of *The Good Wife*. I may as well just take a shower and go to bed. I clip on Skip's leash so I can take him outside to do his business before I give him his insulin. When I exit the front entrance of the apartment building, my stomach flips at the sight of a white SUV parked next to the curb.

An Asian woman climbs down from the passenger side and waves at the driver. I squint through the darkness and, through the glare on the windshield, I can barely make out another woman in the driver's seat. Letting out a soft sigh, I lead Skip around to the back of the building where there's a small greenway for him to do his duty.

I clean up after him with a biodegradable waste bag and toss the bag into the receptacle at the end of the greenway marked "Doggy Bags." I round the corner to the front of the building and the SUV is back. I never noticed how many people in this complex have white SUVs, though I suppose I'll probably start noticing them everywhere now. That's the way these things work. After Houston and I broke up, my heart would stop every time I saw a gray Chevy truck.

Of course, I wasn't really afraid of running into him then. Houston had moved to Portland right after graduation, less than one week after we broke up. It was my memories of him I was afraid of.

"Rory."

I jump at the sound of his voice. Whipping my head around, I catch Houston entering the lobby behind me.

"You scared the hell out of me."

"Sorry," he says with a smile that's sexy enough to stop my heart.

My cheeks get hot and this makes me irrationally angry. "Go home, Houston."

"Nice to see you, too," he replies, following me to the elevator. "I need to talk to you. We need to talk."

I punch the elevator call button and look up at him. "We didn't speak for five years and we did just fine."

The elevator doors open and I roll my eyes as he steps in after me. I coil Skippy's leash around my hand to pull him closer. Houston smiles as the dog licks the back of his hand.

"Hey, buddy. You feeling better?" he says as he scratches Skip behind the ear.

Skip pulls on the leash as he tries to get closer to Houston, but I maintain a tight grip.

"You can't get to me through my dog."

"I'm not trying to get to you. I just need to talk."

He kneels down and laughs as Skippy laps at his jaw, and for a moment all I can remember is the raw feeling I used to get from hours of kissing Houston. He used to refer to his scruff as a "free exfoliating treatment." I turn away so I don't have to see Houston kneeling down before me, scratching Skippy's throat. So I don't have to wonder if that's what he looked like when he proposed to his wife, supplicating and still so damn happy.

I never understood the tradition of a man kneeling before a woman and begging her to marry him. Which is why I also got down on my knees when I thought Houston was going to propose to me. I wanted him to know he didn't need to beg me to be with him. I was already his.

Houston stands as the elevator doors slide open. "I need to

talk to you about the work situation," he says as he follows me out. "I got the contract, but I want to make sure you're okay with this before I sign it."

"You want to know if I'll be okay working with you?"

I slide the key into the doorknob and Houston places his hand over mine to stop me from turning the knob. "I can't go in there with you. Please stay out here until we're done talking."

I shake his hand off and turn around to face him. "There's nothing to talk about. You have to sign the contract. The way I feel about working with you shouldn't matter."

"But it *does* matter. I don't want to upset you. You were there first."

I can't help but laugh. "So this is a territorial thing? You think because I was there first that I have some sort of right to keep you out?"

His left eyebrow shoots up the way it always does when he's confused, and it nearly renders me mute.

I shake my head to clear the momentary distraction. "Houston, if I didn't work there you wouldn't think twice about signing that contract. So that's what you should do. Just… please stop making this into something it isn't. We hardly know each other anymore, and that's the way it's going to stay."

He swallows hard as he lets this sink in. "I guess you're right. I'm sorry I bothered you. I only wanted to… Never mind. I'll get going. I have to get up early to go sign that contract. Not that you care."

He shakes his head in disappointment as he walks away and I'm glad I don't have anything solid in my hand other than Skippy's leash or I might throw it at the back of his head. So *I'm* the one who doesn't care? *Ugh.* Typical Houston and his endless psychological games.

Maybe I should have told him to walk away from the contract, but that would have meant admitting that he still has this much power over me. It also would have been the truth, and the truth has never gotten me into trouble. In fact, the truth is something my previous relationship with Houston was sorely lacking.

Nevertheless, I don't need to right the wrongs we made while we were together. I don't need to tell Houston that the sight of him makes my throat dry and my stomach flutter. He doesn't need to know that I still go to sleep with scenes from our life together playing on repeat in my mind. Or that sometimes I wake with his name tumbling from my lips, the remnants of dreams where he never left and nightmares where he hovers just out of reach.

Before Wednesday, the last time I had seen Houston was the day after he met me at the Planned Parenthood clinic. I didn't ask him to come, and I don't know how he found out the date and time of my appointment, but he was there when we pulled into the parking lot. Lisa, a girl from my Social Inequality class whom I'd had coffee with a couple of times, had graciously agreed to take me to the clinic. The moment we pulled into the lot and I saw Houston leaning against his truck, I knew I had to send Lisa home. He would insist on driving me back to the apartment after the procedure, to watch over me.

It was the last thing I wanted, to have Houston doting over me after terminating the pregnancy. But it was also the only thing I wanted. It was as if he was performing the last rites on our dead relationship.

It took me a while to wake up after the D&C. I didn't want to be conscious while they did it, so I opted for a sedative in addition to the local anesthesia. The nurse pushed me out the back door of the clinic in a wheelchair all the way to Houston's truck. He scooped me up out of the chair and gently placed me in the passenger seat as if I weighed nothing. I closed my eyes and pretended not to feel it when he kissed my forehead before turning the key in the ignition.

I head into my apartment and hang up Skippy's leash inside the coat closet. As I'm getting undressed to get into the shower, my phone lets out a short buzz. I'm almost afraid to look at it, but it could be my mom. She loves texting me. She thinks it makes her a "hipster."

Houston: *I promise this is the last message you'll get from me. I just want to thank you for not making this more difficult when you have every right to.*

I sit on the edge of my bed and stare at the words on the screen in a daze. Is this how mature adults behave when they're confronted with the painful memories of a past relationship? Should I be trying to sabotage his contract? Is that what he expected me to do?

I take a deep breath and let it out as I begin typing my response.

Me: *I'm not trying to make this less difficult. I'm trying not to fall. I'd appreciate it if you could respect that.*

My index finger hovers over the send button. As much as I want to be honest with Houston, I know I can't send this message. The window of opportunity for honesty closed the minute he got married, whenever that was.

I delete the words I typed without sending the message, then I delete Houston's text message to me and his phone number from my call history. *Hey, Houston, how does it feel to be erased? Again.*

Houston

August 15th

MY ATTEMPT TO clarify my position with Rory failed spectacularly. And I can't say I'm surprised. Rory always had a way of calling me out on my bullshit, even if she was completely oblivious to the biggest lie I ever told her. Actually, it was the biggest lie I've ever told anyone.

The truth: Hallie left a suicide note. The bigger truth: That note is the reason Rory and I got together. And the biggest, most despicable truth of all is the one conveyed to me, and only me, in that suicide note. Hallie's last words.

I know most people wouldn't understand it. And most people would be absolutely disgusted with me for what I did to Rory. But the truth is that I allowed my loyalty to my sister to eclipse my loyalty to the only girl I've ever loved. The only girl I may *ever* love.

So when I come out of the bathroom with sweat beaded on my chest and a towel wrapped around my waist, I'm a little disgusted—not just with myself—to see Tessa checking me out.

She's lying on the bed with her phone hovering above her. When we first started living together, I loved watching her in this position because inevitably she would drop the phone on her forehead. It's one of her cuter quirks.

Today, I find myself wishing she'd drop the phone on her face just so she'll stop staring at my body. I'm a bad person. I know that. But I can't help wishing it were Rory lying in my bed.

"Hey, handsome," Tessa purrs as I open the top drawer of our dresser and pull out a pair of gray boxer briefs.

"Hey, baby."

I shed the towel and toss it onto the chair by the window, then I pull on the boxers.

"I don't think you're gonna need those tonight."

I turn around and she's casting her best come-hither expression in my direction. I try to see Tessa the way I saw her three days ago, as my hot, blonde twenty-six-year-old wife. The woman who gave me a distraction from the painful memories when I thought they would consume me. But all I see when I look at her is two words flashing in bold letters: NOT RORY.

I smile at Tessa and squint my eyes a bit to return her sexy glare. "Is that an invitation?"

The words feel wrong and misshapen in my mouth. Like I'm rehearsing lines from a movie script.

"Do you *need* an invitation?"

She lays her phone down on the nightstand and I know there's no getting out of this. A man can't refuse sex the way a woman can. And, of course, I am only a man. I also have needs. I can't save myself for Rory when there's probably zero chance she'll ever take me back.

I push down my boxers and kick them off as I climb onto the bed. She giggles as I slide between her legs, placing my hands on each side of her head as I lean down to kiss her. She tastes like toothpaste and betrayal.

I reach down and hastily pull off her panties and she yelps. "Hey! Take it easy, tiger."

Sliding my hand behind her nape, I pull her head to the side, exposing her neck, then I suck hard on her pale flesh. She pushes me back.

"What are you doing? You're gonna leave a mark."

"Sorry." I push up on my hands and look down at her, trying to convey the hunger in my eyes. "Turn around."

She gazes into my eyes, trying to figure out what's going on with me, but she decides not to question it. She flips over onto her belly and I wrap my arm around her middle to lift her up onto all fours.

Doggy-style is a primal sex position. It's the position we perfected as apes and we carried it with us when we became human. I think this is probably why so many women are opposed to it. When sex became less about procreation and more about emotional connection, women lost their love for doggy-style.

Now women want to look into your eyes when you come. They want to imprint the image of their face in your memory at that climactic moment so you associate their visage with your ultimate desire. It's all a psychological game.

Tessa doesn't like doggy-style, but she tolerates it because I like it. The worst part is that she'd be right in assuming I'm imagining someone else when I fuck her from behind.

I slide the tip of my cock over her clit a few times to get her extra wet, then I glide into her. "Fuck," I hiss through gritted teeth.

I close my eyes and try not to picture Rory as I slide in and out of Tessa, but all I can think is how Rory's cheeks were softer and creamier and how much I'd rather be buried inside her right now. I have to stop this. I'm coveting that which I cannot have.

I open my eyes and focus on Tessa's body. I lean forward, sliding my hand under her tank top to grab her breast. She looks back at me over her shoulder and I feel myself getting strangely annoyed by the look on her face. Letting go of her breast, I stand up straight again and grab her hips to drive her harder. But she keeps looking at me.

I close my eyes and force myself to think of anything other than Rory. First, I think about work, and visions of brew tanks and bags of barley and hops flash in my mind. Then I think of my office and suddenly I remember that box I have hidden in the closet of my office.

I open my eyes to clear away this memory. My thrusts are slow and deliberate as I try to focus on anything but Rory and her soft, pliant body laid out beneath me. I try not to think of the perfect fit of my mouth on hers. Or the time we became parents for two seconds. Then it was over.

When I took Rory home, after she had the abortion, I waited until she had slept off the sedative. Then I waited until she had washed up, pretending not to hear the aching song of her cries in the shower. Then I waited some more, until she had eaten solid food and fallen asleep. Then I left.

I've been waiting five years to tell her the truth. The truth about Hallie. The truth about why we were together. And, most of all, the truth about how I've never stopped loving her. I'm tired of waiting.

I pound Tessa from behind, completely oblivious as to whether or not she's actually enjoying herself. All I can see and hear over my blinding memories of Rory is the vague curve of Tessa's hips and the faint sound of her moans. Whether those are cries of pain or ecstasy I don't know.

Because even if those are cries of ecstasy, Tessa will still find a way to complain. No matter how many times I fuck her senseless. No matter how many times I make her come so hard she cries real tears. No matter what, it will never be enough unless I fuck her with the intention of making a baby.

I told Tessa from the beginning of our relationship that I don't want children. But she was undeterred. She probably convinced herself that she could change my mind.

I will never change my mind about wanting children with Tessa. And the reason is simple: I don't want to have to choose.

If Rory ever wanted to give me a second chance, I wouldn't want to choose between her and my children. And I know it's crazy to risk losing my wife over something that may never happen—will almost *certainly* never happen—but I can't bring children into my life when I'm still living a lie.

My cock twitches and I pull out of Tessa. She waits as I come on her ass, then I grab a tissue off the nightstand and quickly wipe it off. She turns over and narrows her eyes at me. I know what she's thinking.

I always come inside her. She has an IUD implanted in her uterus, which means she has less than half of one percent chance of getting pregnant. Not a single pregnancy has been reported with the use of this particular IUD, so I've always been quite happy to release my load inside her. But I can't bring myself to do it tonight.

Rory was on birth control when she got pregnant. And I know a .05 percent failure rate on this IUD means it's basically impossible for the same thing to happen with Tessa, but I can't take the chance anymore. I *won't* take the chance anymore.

"Why did you do that?" she asks as I climb off the bed and head for the door.

"Do what?"

"You know what."

I keep walking into the corridor. "I don't know what you're talking about."

I make it to the kitchen and manage to pour myself a glass of cold water before she catches up with me. Her panties are back on and her face is contorted in disbelief.

"Are you fucking someone else?"

This wouldn't be the first time Tessa has accused me of having an affair with absolutely no evidence. I'm pretty certain she does it just to remind me how much I don't want to end up like my father. But this tactic isn't going to work with me tonight.

"What?" I reply calmly, placing the empty glass in the sink.

"You heard me. Are you fucking someone else?"

I let out a soft chuckle as I shake my head. "I didn't come inside you, so now I'm having a fucking affair? What if I happened to read an article on the ineffectiveness of IUDs today? Nope. Right away you jump to the worst fucking conclusion."

She gets in my face. "*Did* you read an article on IUDs today?"

I roll my eyes as I try to step around her, but she blocks my path. "No. No, I didn't. Are you happy now?"

Her gaze falls to my chest and she swallows hard. "I think I'm gonna be sick."

I sigh as I grab her face. "Tessa, I'm not cheating on you. I'm just… I'm sorry."

She looks into my eyes. "Sorry for what?"

What am I supposed to say? *I'm sorry for not coming inside you… I'm sorry for fantasizing about someone else while I was fucking you.*

I'm sorry I never loved you.

"I'm sorry for being in a shitty mood. It's not your fault. I'm just stressed about this new contract." I pull her face to mine and kiss her softly on the lips. "I love you. Come to bed and we'll do it right this time."

She lets out a soft sigh as her shoulders slump with defeat. She nods and I take her hand as I lead her back to the bedroom for round two. I'll let her win this one.

Rory

August 16th

DURING MY SENIOR year at UO, I worked as a fiction editor for *Unbound*, the university's literary arts magazine. It was my job to work with submitting writers to get their pieces ready for publication. Though, since I was the new kid on the editing team, most of my time was spent reading through submissions, some of them terrible enough to make my eyes bleed. But every once in a while a submission would come through with the kind of prose that made my insides ache with envy. Sometimes, it wasn't just words arranged on a page. Sometimes, I would open up a submission and smell the fumes of gasoline and smoke after a furious car crash; hear the echoing cries of a sick child in my mind long after their passing; feel the searing tendrils of lust curling inside me from a passionate affair. Sometimes, I would get a sensory experience.

It was my semester working for *Unbound* that inspired me to write my *own* sensory experience. At first, I tried writing something completely fictional, a story about a detective who's investigating a murder where her longtime lover is implicated. But I couldn't seem to rein in the story. There were too many plot lines and plot holes, and none of it really made sense. Then I decided I would write a children's book. It was safe. But I quickly realized it was *too* safe. I needed something a bit more challenging.

Then it dawned on me that the one project I was avoiding would probably be the most challenging project of them all: the story of us.

Over the past two years, I've written 227 pages in the as-yet-untitled story of Houston and me. But six weeks ago I reached the climax where everything falls apart and I can't bring myself to write anymore. My mind knows how the story ends, but my heart is demanding a rewrite.

My mom brings me a steaming mug of black coffee, setting it down on the table in front of me. "Shouldn't you be at work?" she asks, taking a seat at the other end of the sofa.

Skippy lies peacefully between us, having just ingested his morning ration of dog food and insulin.

"I switched with Kenny so I could stay home with Skip today on his first day back from the vet. Right, Skippers?" I scratch his shoulder and he stretches his arms and legs out lazily.

My mom rolls her eyes as she brings her cup of tea to her lips, takes a slow sip, then sets the mug down on the coffee table. She flips back her shoulder-length prematurely gray hair and leans back. She's going to tell me what I *should* be doing today.

"You should be working on your book, not watching TV. Where's your ambition?"

I grab my cup of coffee off the table and take a sip, mentally cursing my mom for knowing how to make coffee better than I do. "My ambition, or lack thereof, has nothing to do with why I'm not writing."

"Are you stuck? Because you know I'd be glad to help you. Just give me a few pages and I'll tell you why you're stuck."

My mother taught high school English for twenty-five years, until she retired a little more than three years ago. My parents' divorce came about six months after Hallie died; just two weeks after Houston and I broke up. That was definitely the worst summer of my life. Then one year later, my mother retired. She declared her classroom days were over and she would be starting fresh, without my father.

I assumed this meant that she would finally write that novel she'd had kicking around inside her head for the past twenty-some years, but I was wrong. She's spent the past three years trying to live vicariously through me. She desperately wants *me* to write my novel, though she has no idea if it's actually any good, since I refuse to let her get anywhere near it with her English-teacher-eyes.

"I don't need you to look at it. It's not even edited. It's a first draft. I just need to put it in a drawer for a while. Come back to it with fresh eyes in a month or two."

My mother crosses one slender ankle over the other and purses her lips at me. "You're so afraid I'll hurt your feelings by insulting your writing. That actually hurts me, you know. I would never purposely tear apart your work."

Yeah, she would never *purposely* tear it apart. *Oops! What's this dangling participle here and that cardboard character there? And how about this misguided attempt at theme? Really, Rory, you call this fiction?* My mother is probably the perfect person to provide feedback on my novel, but she will never get her hands on it because it's too personal. I don't want her to know how deeply I fell.

"Fine. If you're not going to write, then you need to get up and get out of those lady boxer shorts. Go find yourself a man so you can wear *his* boxer shorts."

"Ew!" I shriek. "Don't talk to me about that kind of stuff."

"Oh, please, Rory. You're twenty-four years old. You can have an adult conversation. You can't keep denying yourself. We all have needs."

"Double-ew. Please don't talk to me about *needs.*"

She glances around the living room as she slides my mug aside and sits on the coffee table in front of me. "Maybe you should make one of those online dating profiles. You're a beautiful girl, Rory." She smiles as she reaches forward and pets my hair. "You're smart. You're self-sufficient. You're healthy."

"And I'm purebred."

"Oh, Rory, stop making everything into a joke. Men will see it as a defense mechanism and they'll wonder what you're hiding."

"I'm hiding from men. Isn't that obvious?"

She sighs heavily as she lays her clasped hands in her lap.

"Okay, that's enough, Mom. If you want to make an online dating profile, make one for yourself. Leave me and my defense mechanisms out of it."

I stand from the sofa and scoop the coffee mug off the table to take it to the kitchen. I don't know why I'm taking it to the kitchen, other than I need an excuse to get away from my mother.

She calls out after me. "You know, you have more than one soul mate in this world, Rory." She pauses to let this sink in. "There really *are* plenty of fish in the sea."

"Yeah, and most of them are slimy eels or boring sand dollars," I shout back at her as I dump my coffee into the steel sink. "I want a smart, spunky dolphin. Is that too much to ask?"

A smart, spunky dolphin named Houston.

Just thinking these words makes me sick to my stomach.

My mom arrives in the kitchen with her tea mug. "A smart, spunky dolphin? Is that how you remember Houston? Because I remember him being an arrogant frat boy."

After five years of hearing these kinds of insults directed at Houston, it still makes me as angry as it did the first time. "This conversation is over."

She follows me out of the kitchen and I brace myself for

more criticism as she trails behind me. "Rory, you don't need to be ashamed for loving Houston as he was, but it's been five years. You need to stop remembering him through the telescopic view of young love. You need to look at the big picture. At reality. And the reality is that he left you. He. Left. You."

"That's enough, Mom." I stop in the hallway and round on her. "That's. Enough."

Her eyebrows knit together as she nods. "I'm sorry. I just want you to be happy. You deserve to be happy again."

Why is everyone always trying to tell me what I deserve? My mom insists I deserve to be happy. Houston insists I deserve to decide whether or not he should sign a contract. It's as if everyone knows something about me that I don't know about myself.

I'm no more deserving of happiness than anyone else. I'm just a screwed-up girl with a billion stories racing through my mind on any given day. And only one story I really want to tell.

Rory

August 17th

MY NERVES ARE buzzing as I make my way through Zucker's icy warehouse. Taking a deep breath, I push through the swinging door and enter the store. Right away, I busy myself with tidying up a display of dried apple chips in the produce section. Then I keep my head down as I make my way to the cash register. I don't know if Houston is coming in today, but I know he came in yesterday to sign the contract, which is the real reason I switched shifts with Kenny.

Kenny and I are both working today and I breathe a sigh of relief when I see him standing behind register four. He's the only person in this store that I could *maybe* call my friend, though I've only hung out with him outside of work on one occasion. He's also the only person in this store I would trust to balance my cash drawer if I were to suddenly drop dead while ringing up a bottle of organic shampoo.

Kenny is ridiculously attractive and completely gay, so he's as safe as a children's book. But that doesn't stop him from flirting with me. I'm sure in his twisted twenty-two-year-old mind, I'm as safe as a children's book to him, because I'm hopelessly incapable of forming new attachments. He knows I won't misinterpret his flirtations.

"Hey, beautiful," Kenny says as I slide in behind register three.

Unlocking the drawer, I pull it out completely. Then I walk past Kenny's register toward the service register at the front of the store, where Jamie is on the phone. We exchange my empty drawer for the drawer she has waiting for me under the counter. Checking the amount on the register slip, I sign it and hand it back to her. She time-stamps the slip and tucks it beneath the money tray inside the service register.

Carrying my cash back to my station, I easily lose myself in the monotony of setting up my drawer. I don't notice there's someone at my register until I hear the unmistakable sound of a woman clearing her throat. Looking up, I want to say something, but I find myself stunned into silence. The girl at my register has the same straight, light-brown hair as Hallie. She's wearing a crooked smile as she tucks her hair behind her ear while holding out a pack of gum to me.

"Are you open?" she asks so softly I can barely hear her over the sound of Kenny's scanner beeping.

I nod hastily and turn back to my register to punch in my password. "Yeah, just a minute." The system takes a few seconds to log me in and I smile as I take the pack of gum from her to ring it up. "Do you want a bag?"

"No, thanks," she replies, taking the gum back and walking away, completely oblivious of her resemblance to my dead friend.

"Hey, sexy, can I trade you a ten for a roll of quarters?"

I look up and Kenny winks at me as he holds out a ten-dollar bill. I grab a roll of quarters out of the drawer and exchange it for the ten, then I turn back to the keypad in front of me, trying not to think about Hallie.

The one thought I couldn't escape after she committed suicide was the idea that I may never have truly known her. Hallie and I had both known of kids who had taken their lives and, at the time, we could see how it was inevitable. *Joe was always wearing black… Stacy never had any boyfriends… Paul was always playing those violent video games.* But in the end, it was my own best friend's death that stumped me. I didn't see it coming.

It didn't help that she didn't leave a note.

Closure is a weird word. It implies that something is closed. Finished. But how can you find closure when someone you love dies? They're already gone. The case is closed. There's nowhere to go from there.

There's no one to give you answers that make any sense. Which is why, after the shock of Hallie's death wore off, I became very angry with her. How could she leave me behind without any explanation? Did I not deserve to know her story?

There goes that word again: deserve.

I make it through the rest of the workday without any appearances from Houston. Kenny walks me out to the back of the store where my bike is parked.

"Want to go to Ración with us tonight? We have a reservation at eight, but someone in our party canceled. You know you want to come."

It's been about five months since I've taken Kenny up on one of his offers to get out of the house. I've been using the excuse of writing my book, but I can't really use that anymore since I haven't written a single word in six weeks.

I kneel down next to my bike to punch in the code on the padlock. "Who's going? I'm not going if Lina's there."

Lina is Kenny's bisexual friend who hit on me the last time I went to dinner with him and his crowd. She made some pretty crude remarks after I rejected her, too. I would have left the restaurant right then if it weren't for Heather, Kenny's straight friend who explained to me that Lina was going through a bad breakup. That was something I could relate to.

"Lina moved to Seattle with her new boyfriend months ago."

I climb onto my bike and nod. "Sure. I'll meet you there."

"Yay!" Kenny shouts as he throws his arms around me so suddenly I almost lose my balance. "I've missed hanging out with you."

I hug him back and refrain from reminding him that we've only hung out once before. "I've missed you, too."

He kisses my cheek as he lets me go. "What are you going to wear?"

I open my mouth to reply, but no words come out. My gaze is locked on a white SUV parked at the end of the service alley behind the market. I know it's just my mind playing tricks on me again, my subconscious fear of running into Houston.

Kenny follows the direction of my stare to the SUV. "Who's that?"

"No one."

The driver's side door opens and my breath hitches as Houston steps out. What is he doing here? Is he following me?

"Sure doesn't look like no one," Kenny says. "Looks like a very delicious someone."

I swallow hard and turn back to Kenny and throw my arms around him again. "I'll see you later."

He chuckles as he seizes the opportunity to squeeze me firmly. "Oh, yeah, baby. You know how I like it. Hug me tighter."

I squeeze a little harder. "Is this tight enough?"

"No, harder!"

I laugh as I push him away. "Go home."

He kisses my forehead before he turns to walk away. "Don't stand me up, gorgeous."

I slide my helmet off the handlebars and try to pretend I

don't notice Houston walking toward me.

"Hey," he says, his voice a bit breathy, as if he's nervous.

I look up and try to think of a response other than *Go home to your wife*. "Hey," I reply tersely.

Houston looks back over his shoulder at the corner of the building Kenny just disappeared behind. "Who was that?"

I should slip this helmet onto my head, ignoring his question as I ride off into the sunset. But I can't.

"Why does it matter?"

He smiles at my impertinence. "I guess it doesn't. Do you need a ride?"

I narrow my eyes at him in disbelief. "Are you seriously offering me a ride?"

The muscle in his jaw twitches. "Rory, I don't know what's going to happen when I come in here to oversee the setup of the bar, but I know that this"—he wags his finger to indicate the space between us—"can't continue. We can't work together with all this animosity."

"Why?"

His eyebrows furrow in confusion. "Because it's not healthy."

"Suddenly you're worried about maintaining a healthy relationship with me?"

He sighs as he looks down at the asphalt. "I deserve that."

"Look, Houston, if you want to maintain a healthy working relationship with me, I think the first part of that would entail not questioning my friendships with other guys. The second part would probably entail not showing up at my apartment. How about we start with those two things?"

That muscle in his jaw is working again and I wonder if he's going to explode from all that pent-up emotion. Finally, he looks me in the eye and his face relaxes, the corner of his mouth pulling up into a soft crooked smile.

"You haven't changed at all."

"Is that an insult?"

He shakes his head. "Quite the contrary."

I draw in a deep breath and let it out slowly as I stare at my helmet in my hands, unable to respond. When I look up again, I catch a glimpse of the inside of his forearm as he runs his fingers through his hair. He got the old tattoo partially covered. He quickly tucks his hand into his pocket so I can't make out the new tattoo.

"Let me give you a ride, Rory."

My stomach cramps at the idea of being alone with him in the car again. "Does your wife know you're here?"

"Yes. I told her I had to give a friend a ride home."

"You lied to her?"

"About you being my friend?"

"About having to give me a ride home."

He smiles, his eyes lighting up with hope. "Does that mean we can be friends?"

"Houston… That hopeful look in your eyes is making me very uncomfortable."

He laughs and takes a step back. "Sorry. I guess I suck at this friendship thing. Maybe I can get some pointers from your friend… what was his name again?"

"I didn't tell you his name."

He bites his lip in a sheepish expression and my heart flutters with longing. I should *not* be alone with him. Ever.

He nods toward his car and smiles. "Come on."

I stare at his SUV for a moment and I suddenly remember the last time I gave him a blow job in his old Chevy truck. We were leaving a UO football game. The traffic around the stadium was horrendous and both our phones were dead, so I jokingly offered to strip for Houston to keep him entertained. He offered to do all the dinner dishes for a week if I followed through. Dishes being one of my least favorite chores, I quickly yanked up my green

Oregon T-shirt and flashed my breasts at him.

"Houston, we have liftoff," he replied with a sexy grin.

I groaned as I tried not to laugh at his awful pun. Then I glanced around the crowded streets. When I was certain no one was looking in our direction, I ducked down to undo his jeans.

I chuckle to myself as I recall how crazy we were. "Thanks, but I have a ride," I say, tapping my handlebars. "See you later, Houston."

I pedal away, trying to pay attention to motorists while contemplating what just happened. Does Houston really want to be my friend? Does he only want to do what's best for his business? Or was he feeling me out to see if I'd be open to having an affair?

RACIÓN IS A Spanish tapas restaurant that's quite popular for its mastery of molecular gastronomy. I've never been to Ración, but I've read some of their reviews online and heard people talking about the place. The moment I walk in and see the tasting menu on the blackboard, I know this is going to be the kind of eatery that serves tiny portions that will break my budget.

I'm starving, since I normally have a late lunch when I get off work at four p.m., but I skipped lunch today to save my appetite for this special dinner. I love food, which is why I ride my bike to work most days, even when it's raining. So I can burn enough calories to justify my need to stuff my face.

I rode my bike to the restaurant tonight. I figure if I get a little tipsy, the worst-case scenario is I have to push my bike to the bus stop or the rail station. It will take me forty minutes to get home instead of fifteen. No big deal.

Kenny stands up and waves at me from the far left end of the bar. I make my way over, taking in the laid-back attire most people are wearing. A lot of vintage dresses paired with cardigans, plaid shirts and thrift-store jeans, and Gor-Tex jackets. I sigh with relief as I dressed pretty casually in my only pair of designer skinny jeans, an airy coral blouse, and some nude flats.

Kenny bumps his cheek to mine and wraps his arm around my shoulder. "Everyone, this is my gorgeous friend, Rory, short for Aurora." He stretches the syllables on my given name and I try not to blush. "Some of you may remember her from that one wonderful night in March when she graced us with her presence. Well, it only took five months for me to convince her to give us another shot."

I wave as everyone says hi, some of them offering me a handshake. Kenny asks Judy, the girl sitting next to him, to scoot over so I can sit next to him, then he orders me a Looking Glass cocktail.

"What's a Looking Glass?"

He shakes his head. "All you need to know is it contains absinthe. You'll like it."

Two drinks later, Judy and two of her dining companions have to leave and a group of three guys is seated at the bar on my right. The guy seated next to me has a full beard, which I've come to appreciate after two years living in Portland. Around here, growing a beard is a pissing contest; the fuller and longer the beard, the more virile and manly you are. It's cute to see men publicly fluffing their feathers in an attempt to attract mates.

The guy glances sideways and catches me staring at him. I quickly look away, but not before I catch a glimpse of his smile and the perfect teeth underneath that beard. I press my lips to keep from smiling and I hook my arm around Kenny, my social lifeline.

Kenny turns to me and smiles. "Are you having fun?" His

eyes widen when I reply with a clumsy nod. "Oh, my goodness, Rory. Are you drunk off two cocktails?"

"Cocktails? Why do they call them *cock*-tails?"

"Oh, you're too adorable." He waves at a waiter, who quickly comes over. "Can you please hurry with the food?" He nods toward me and the waiter nods back, as if he can divine how tipsy I am with a single glance. "Thanks, man," Kenny calls out as the waiter walks away.

"Thanks," I mutter. "I'm starving."

"Then you came to the wrong place."

I whip my head to the right and Beard-guy is sporting a twinkle in his eye, looking very pleased with his comment as he takes a sip from his beer. I slip my left arm out of Kenny's and sit up straight so I can respond.

"Excuse me?"

He smiles, showing off those perfect teeth again. "I said you came to the wrong place if you're hungry. This place is for tasting, not eating."

"Are you saying I have to spit my food out after I taste it?"

He chuckles as he sets down his beer and turns his shoulders a bit so he can get a better look at me. His eyebrows scrunch up. "Rory?"

I squint at him through the dim lighting and I can just barely make out the crystal blueness of his eyes. "Do I know you?"

"You probably don't recognize me because of the beard." He holds his hands up to cover the lower half of his face.

My eyes widen with surprise. "Liam?"

He drops his hands and smiles. "In the flesh."

I lick my partially numb lips and reach for my glass of water, taking a few gulps before I set the glass down. "How long have you lived here?"

Liam was in my Art of the Sentence class junior year. We partnered up during an exercise where the professor asked us to construct a five-sentence-minimum short story. The catch was that it had to be done one word at a time, going back and forth for each word. The experience was memorable. Liam and I met at the local Starbucks and spent four hours sipping lattes and laughing at our ridiculous short story.

It was the first time I'd felt comfortable in the company of a man since Houston had left almost two years earlier. I was having such a good time, I didn't even notice he kept hitting the ignore button on his phone. Until we left Starbucks and he apologized before making a quick phone call—to his girlfriend.

"I actually just moved here a few months ago," he replies. "Got a job at Intel."

"Intel? What do you do there?"

He smiles as he reaches for his beer. "Corporate affairs. Totally boring. What are you doing these days? Still writing?"

Nothing like a question about what I'm doing with my career to sober me up. "I work at Zucker's for now. Yeah, I'm still writing."

"Zucker's? The grocery store on Burnside?"

"Actually, the one across the river on Belmont. But, yeah. It's temporary, you know, just until… I don't know. Until I decide it's not temporary, I guess."

He flashes me a reassuring smile. "Nothing wrong with that. I actually wish I had done something a bit more temporary. It's easy to feel trapped once you're in a so-called dream job. Competition is fierce. The pressure is on not to screw up."

I raise my eyebrows in agreement. "Yeah, I know that pressure."

"Are you…?" He looks down at my hands and smiles. "You're not married?"

I glance down and his left ring finger is bare, but his right hand is concealed behind the glass of beer he's holding. "No, are you?"

"Nope. I dodged that bullet shortly after graduation."

"Dodged that bullet?"

He laughs and takes another sip of beer as he tries to think of a response. "It ran its course."

I nod as if I understand what this means. The waiter arrives with our first course and I'm a little perplexed by what looks like a shallow bowl of purple goop.

Kenny gives my forearm a light squeeze. "Purple potato. Dig in, sweetheart. I can't have you passing out on me."

I turn to Liam and he looks confused as to why I was chatting him up if I'm here with someone. "This is my friend Kenny. We work together."

Kenny turns his head at the mention of his name, and his eyes twinkle as the sight of Liam. "Pleased to meet you," he says, reaching his hand out to Liam.

I lean back so they can shake hands and I get a weird feeling, like Kenny is sizing Liam up to see if he's good enough for me. And my suspicions are cleared up as soon as Kenny opens his mouth again.

"If you hurt her, I'll cut you."

"Kenny!" I squeal, but Liam just laughs as he goes back to nursing his beer. "He's kidding. He wouldn't hurt a fly."

"I've got your back, gorgeous," Kenny whispers in my ear, then he goes back to chatting with his friend George.

After a delicious, but slightly unsatisfying, five-course meal, Kenny insists on paying my $134 bill. He gives me a warm hug and I thank him profusely before I stand up to leave.

Liam grabs my hand as I begin to walk away. "Wait up. I'll give you a ride."

I glance at Kenny and his eyebrows are raised skeptically, then I turn back to Liam. "I rode my bike."

"I have a truck. We can put your bike in the back."

Liam quickly settles his bill and Kenny blows me a kiss as we head out.

"I'm really not that far," I insist as we head south on Washington.

"Yeah, but it's late. You shouldn't be riding alone at this time of night."

A desperate chill has fallen over the streets of Southwest Portland, fluttering the sleeves of my coral blouse. I rub my arms to warm up and Liam quickly removes his gray twill jacket.

"Put this on."

"I'm fine."

"Are you always this stubborn?"

"Yes."

He stops in the middle of the sidewalk and holds up the jacket for me. I roll my eyes as I slip my arms inside. But my reluctance quickly melts away as I'm comforted by the residual warmth and crisp scent left from his skin.

"See, that wasn't so bad, was it?"

"It's awful. I'll need therapy after this."

I unlock my bike and he pushes it for me toward his truck. Once he's satisfied that the bike is secure in the truck bed, we hop inside and head toward my apartment.

"Can I ask you a question?" he asks as we come to a stop at the first intersection.

I sigh as I anticipate a question about why I'm single or something else equally awkward. "Shoot."

"I never asked you this when we were partners in class, but I remember what happened to your friend freshman year. It was one of those things that people talk about for a week or so, then it gets forgotten. But I imagine it was quite different for you."

I clench my fist, digging my fingernails into my hand. "Is that a question?"

"Sorry. Actually, what I wanted to ask is… how are you doing?"

I'm silent for a moment as I contemplate his question. It's not an inappropriate thing to ask. It's actually a very intimate question, which I'm not obligated to answer. But he does seem genuinely concerned. And somehow, I find myself wanting to tell him the truth, that sometimes I still lie awake replaying the last few days I spent with Hallie over and over in my mind.

"Like you said, it's just one of those things," I reply, hoping he doesn't hear the painful thickness in my voice. "You learn to live with it."

Liam makes small talk the rest of the eight-minute ride to my apartment. Once we're in front of my building, he scoops the bike out of the truck bed and sets it down gently in front of me.

"Thanks for the ride." I begin to peel off his jacket and he holds up his hand to stop me.

"Keep it. I'll get it back next weekend, when you let me take you out."

I sigh audibly because I hate having to reject guys. "Liam, I'm not the kind of girl that can be saved. I'm beyond damaged… I'm destroyed."

"Damaged goods, huh?" he replies with a smile. "Does that mean I get a discount? Can I take you to McDonald's instead of Ración?"

I try not to smile. "I'm serious. I… I pretty much swore off relationships five years ago. I'm a lost cause."

He laughs at this. "Rory, you're twenty-four years old. We're all lost at this age." He reaches forward and my skin prickles as he brushes a lock of hair away from my temple and tucks it behind my ear. "Let me take you out and I'll decide whether you're defective."

As I gaze into his crystal-blue eyes, my mind drifts to thoughts of Houston. Earlier today, I refused to let him give me a ride home. But I allowed Liam to give me a ride. Does that mean I feel safer with Liam? And by safe, do I mean children's book safe?

I guess it doesn't matter what I mean. It just matters that he's the kind of guy my mom would want me to date. Maybe this will get her off my back.

"Okay."

His eyes light up. "Awesome. I'll pick you up here at eight next Saturday. Is that good?"

"Maybe… Maybe you should just come over and hang out. I haven't been on a date in a long time. I think I need to ease my way back into this."

He chuckles. "Well, you're definitely out of practice. Because, while I have no problem hanging out with you in your apartment, that's usually what happens *after* the date."

I shake my head in dismay at my own ignorance, but I don't offer to change the plans. I still think I'd feel more comfortable with him in my domain than surrounded by a bunch of strangers.

We quickly exchange phone numbers before I head inside. As I enter the elevator, a thought occurs to me that I hadn't considered before. If I'm dating other guys, that will make it much easier to resist Houston once we start working together.

Houston

Five years ago, April 5th

RORY WAS BORN with an affliction I like to call spontaneous hugging syndrome. Whenever someone does something really nice for her, she can't help but throw her arms around them in a wild embrace. This affliction is one of my favorite things about her. Often I find myself conspiring to do something nice just so I can trigger her hug reflex.

Today I'm using the excuse of our four-month anniversary. I ordered her a custom nightgown bearing an image of her head on Britney Spears's body and Justin Timberlake kissing her cheek. Rory is mildly obsessed with Justin Timberlake. I like to pretend it makes me jealous, but I actually find it pretty fucking adorable. I guess I'm also hoping this surprise will detract from the fact that it's the four-month-and-one-day anniversary of the day Hallie died.

I open the front door of the apartment and call out, "Honey, I'm home!" But there's no answer.

I head past the kitchen toward the bedroom, my mind

immediately concocting the worst-case scenario. Reaching the bedroom door, I open it slowly and find Rory curled up on the bed with her laptop open next to her. The blanket clutched in her fist, her auburn hair tumbling over her face. I would let her continue sleeping, but I know she'll feel even more awful if she doesn't finish whatever homework she was working on before she fell asleep.

I set the package containing the nightgown on the foot of the bed, then I take a seat on the edge of the mattress next to Rory. "Baby, wake up." I give her shoulder a light squeeze and she lets out a soft groan. "Rory, are you okay?"

I reach forward to push the hair out of her face and she shoves my hand away. "Don't touch me."

"What's wrong?" I should probably be asking her, *What did I do this time?*

She sits up and her eyes find the package wrapped in silver paper, but she doesn't look pleased. "Celebrating something?"

I don't bother responding. I know this is a jab at my attempt to distract her from yesterday's anniversary. Most of the time, Rory is too smart for her own good. She can spot my hidden motives before I act on them. Most of the time, but not always.

"I just wanted to give you something that might cheer you up. It's a cheesy gift. You can toss it out if you don't want it."

"Cheer me up?" She glares at me and I know today is going to be a bad day. "You want me to cheer up, Houston, then how about you let me have a night out with my friends! Oh, no, you can't do that because the only friend I ever had is dead." She slams her laptop shut and kicks the gift onto the floor as she slides off the bed. "With no *fucking* explanation."

My heart clenches with guilt, but I follow closely behind her as she heads for the bathroom. "It's okay to be angry."

"I'm not angry. I'm furious."

She opens the medicine cabinet and immediately reaches for a bottle of allergy medicine, the one she uses when she can't sleep.

"It's okay to be furious, too. Everyone deals with death differently."

She dumps eight pills out of the bottle into the palm of her hand, then she turns to me with a wicked smile. "Everyone deals with death differently? Like the way some people choose to not deal with it at all?"

I resist the urge to lash out at her. "You can't take that many, Rory."

She glances at the tiny pink pills in her hand. "Well, the six I took earlier didn't keep you from waking me up."

"Rory, this is not the way to handle this."

"Fuck you! Who are you to tell me how to handle it when all you do is ignore it? She killed herself, Houston. She killed herself and she didn't have the decency to tell anyone why." Her hands begin to tremble as the tears stream down her cheeks and the pills fall into the sink. "Sometimes I hate her."

"Don't say that."

She grips the edge of the sink tightly, her shoulders leaping with each chest-racking sob. "I do. I hate her."

"Don't you fucking say that."

"Why?" she mewls. "I just want to know why."

The words in Hallie's suicide note scroll through my mind like closing credits in a movie. I could end Rory's misery right now if I wanted to, and I do. I hate seeing her suffer like this. But my baby sister confided her darkest secret to me in that suicide note and I will never betray her.

"You don't hate her," I say, stepping forward to place my hand on the small of her back.

She smacks my arm. "Why can't you just let me feel the way I want to feel?"

"How would she feel if she heard you say that?"

She turns her head to face me, her mouth gaping wide with

shock. "Are you serious? Hallie *can't* hear, because she's dead, Houston. She's fucking dead."

"Stop that."

"What are you gonna do? Are you gonna hit me?"

I clench my jaw to keep myself from calling her all the foul names racing through my mind. "Stop it, Rory."

She places her hands on my chest, probably to push me, but I grab her wrists to stop her.

"I said stop it. Stop acting like a fucking child."

She laughs as she tries to free her wrists from my grip. "Is that what I am to you? A fucking child? Is that why you love getting my underage ass drunk so you can fuck me?"

I glare at her for a moment, a million insults about her sexual inexperience teasing the tip of my tongue. Instead, I let go of her wrists and leave the bathroom.

"Where are you going?" she shouts as she follows me. "Going to get drunk and fuck another underage piece of ass?"

"Fuck you." I'm almost at the front door when she lands a hard shove in the center of my back. I round on her, grabbing both her elbows. "I told you to fucking stop it! That's enough!"

Her hazel eyes are wide with fright, but she's not ready to back down. "What are you gonna do?"

Our chests are heaving as we stare into each other's eyes and that's when I know there's no one in this world who will ever understand me like Rory. She knows I'd never hurt her. She knows she can rail against my sister and I'll still want nothing and no one but her. Because no one but me knows how brightly the pain burns inside her.

I let go of her elbows and tangle my fingers in her hair as I crush my lips against hers. I grab a fistful of hair at the crown of her head and tug. She whimpers as she reaches for the button of my jeans. Our mouths nip at each other clumsily as we frantically undress each other.

"I'm sorry," she whispers.

I shush her as I lift her naked body onto the kitchen table. Her legs coil around my hips and I hook my arm tightly around her waist as I slide into her. She moans and the sound sends a chill through me.

"God, I fuckin' love you."

She whimpers as I thrust my cock deeper inside her.

"I'm so sorry," she whispers a few more times, until I kiss her to silence her apologies.

She moans into my mouth and the sound is so damn beautiful it sends a shiver through me. I pull my head back and grasp her jaw in one hand so I can look her in the eye as I slide my other hand between her legs.

She gasps. "Oh, God, Houston."

I stroke her firmly as I move in and out of her until I feel her muscles spasming around my cock. I pull out of her and get down on one knee so my head is between her legs. Then I slide two fingers inside her as my mouth devours her swollen clit.

Her legs squirm and she screams my name with ecstasy. When I slide into her again, I feel as if I might collapse from the pure euphoria of being inside her. She grabs my face and kisses me hard, but I can hear her cries have changed. I tilt my head back to look at her face and she's on the verge of sobbing. I sweep her hair away from her eyes and I move slowly in and out of her as I kiss each of her eyelids.

"It's okay," I assure her and her legs coil tighter around me, her arms squeezing me closer. "It's okay, baby."

"I love you," she whispers in my ear as I come inside her. "So much it scares me."

I kiss the tip of her nose, then lean my forehead against hers. "You don't have to be afraid… I'll never leave you."

Rory

Five years ago, April 6th

MY HEAD TWITCHES to the left, but it takes me a moment to realize what's happening. There's something on my face. I let out a piercing shriek as I try to bat away whatever spider or fly is perched on my eyebrow, then I freeze when I hear soft laughter.

I open my eyes and Houston breaks into a full cackle. "Was that you?"

"Sorry," he says, trying to keep a straight face. "I was just brushing your eyebrow with my finger to wake you up."

"You jerk. What time is it?"

"It's 6:30." He holds his arms out and beckons me to come closer. "Come here. You don't have to get ready for class for another hour."

I scoot in next to him and drape my arm across his solid chest. "Is it really 6:30?"

"Yep. Are you still tired?"

"I haven't slept that well in… months."

I trace my finger down the center of his chest, smiling as

goose bumps sprout over his skin.

"I'm glad you slept," he says, kissing the top of my head.

"I'm sorry about the things I said yesterday," I whisper, my voice choked with regret. "I didn't mean it."

"No need to apologize," he murmurs. "Sometimes… Sometimes I get angry with her, too."

"She doesn't deserve that."

"No, she doesn't."

I trace a heart shape over his firm abs and smile when I see his erection rising beneath the sheet. I lightly rake my fingers over his ribs and back up to his chest. Then I trace the letters of the tattoo that stretches from one side of his chest to the other: LOYALTY. His other tattoo is on the inside of his left forearm: REMEMBER. Followed by the date Hallie died. He got both tattoos within the past six months.

Though he almost always avoids talking about Hallie, I know he hasn't forgotten her. And I know he's dealing with this in his own way. I shouldn't have accused him of avoiding the issue. But I do hope he'll open up to me at some point. I don't know if it's realistic to hope for something like that.

I take a deep breath and decide to give it a shot. "Remember that time Hallie got an iPod for Christmas?"

He lets out a soft puff of laughter. "Yeah, and she gave it to your grandma."

"I didn't even notice until the day after Christmas. My grandma was wearing headphones when I went to hug her goodbye."

"She was always way too mature for her age."

"My grandma?"

He laughs again, squeezing my shoulder as he plants a kiss on my forehead. "Remember when we used to go to the public pool and I had to discipline that fucking eight-year-old kid for staring at her?"

"She was thirteen and too pretty for her own good, but she loved the attention." I smile as I recall those summers I spent in Hallie's shadow. "I, on the other hand, hated the pool. All I wanted to do while I was there was watch you, but you never paid me any attention. No matter what bikini I wore."

"Maybe that was the problem. I would have noticed you if you weren't wearing a bikini."

I shake my head as I slide my hand under the sheet and wrap my fingers around his erection. A grin spreads across my face as I realize I finally got all I ever wished for during those summers at the pool. But the smile quickly disappears when I realize it was at the expense of my best friend's life.

I slide my fist down the length of his erection and his breathing quickens, but he reaches down and pulls my hand up.

He lifts my chin so I'm looking up at him. "I'm sorry."

"For what?"

"For never noticing you. If I had known… maybe everything would have turned out differently."

I snuggle up closer to him so I can whisper in his ear. "Different isn't always better."

BY THE TIME Houston pulls his truck into the lot of the sports bar, I'm ready to tell him to turn around and take me home, but I hold my tongue. It's been four nights since our blowout fight over Hallie and I've been trying to keep the peace. I kept my cool when he got drunk last night and asked me, in front of all his friends, if I wanted to fuck him in the bathroom. And I kept quiet when we slid into bed a couple of hours later and he accused me of flirting with his best friend, Troy. I'll just promise to give him a really long blow job if he agrees to be the designated driver tonight.

God, sometimes I hate the person I've become.

"What's tonight's forecast?" Houston asks as he kills the engine.

"Rainy with a ninety percent chance of beer," Troy replies from the backseat.

"Just another night of grueling research," Houston replies and all I can do is roll my eyes.

As soon as we're seated at a table in the bar, I lay my hand on top of Houston's thigh and lean in to whisper my proposition in his ear. He grins broadly and Troy just shakes his head.

"Is that a yes?" I say, taking a sip from my glass of water.

He turns to me and his smile is gone. "If you don't want to watch me drink, you can take the truck home. I'll call a taxi."

He slides his car key across the table and bile rises in my throat as I stare at it. He's lost all perspective.

I know Houston took the brunt of the impact from Hallie's death. He was her older brother. He was supposed to protect her. He wasn't supposed to find her dead body in our dorm. He's probably suffering from post-traumatic stress disorder, but he refuses to see a therapist. He thinks this obsession with creating and consuming craft beer is a healthy alternative to therapy.

I don't know how much longer I can pretend everything's okay.

I take the key from the table and smile as I tuck it into my pocket. "I'll drive us both home… later."

"How about me?" Troy asks, leaning back in his chair so he can check out the waitress serving beers at the table next to us.

Troy is Houston's oldest and best friend. They met in ninth grade around the same time Hallie and I met in sixth grade. Hallie had a crush on Troy for about two minutes when she was fourteen, before she decided he was too young for her. Hallie always had a thing for older men.

"Maybe you can get *her* to drive you home," I remark, and the waitress turns around.

Her glossy lips curl into a seductive smile as she catches Troy staring at her ass. Troy nods at her and she shakes her head as she walks off with her empty tray. His eyes are locked on her as she leans over the bar, flirting with the bartender while stealing the occasional glance in Troy's direction.

He stands up and pushes up the sleeves of his hoodie to expose his muscular arms. "I'll be back."

"You'd better come back with a pint," Houston calls out as Troy walks away.

He turns to me and the corner of his mouth turns up in that signature crooked smile. He leans forward and kisses my cheekbone. His lips hover over mine and suddenly I'm grinning like an idiot.

"You look beautiful tonight." He plants a tender kiss on my lips and I wish we were home so I could make out with him for hours. "I'll drive us home. You can be my beer taster and I'll be your designated driver."

He kisses me again and there's no way I can resist him when he's laying on the charm like this.

Another waitress arrives with the two pints we ordered earlier and Houston pushes the one she placed in front of him over to me. The waitress smiles and apologizes for mixing up the order.

"No worries," he says, waving off the apology. "My wife is planning on pounding about a dozen of these tonight, so keep 'em comin'."

I shove Houston and the waitress just smiles as she walks away. "Way to make me look like a lush."

"You're not even going to mention the fact that I called you my wife?"

I don't know how to respond to this. I didn't mention it because I assumed it was just part of the joke; it's funnier if you say *wife* than *girlfriend.* But now that he's calling attention to it, I don't know what to think.

I shrug as I lean in to take a sip of the farmhouse ale. "It was part of the joke."

He waits for me to swallow my ale, then he grabs my hand. "One day, we're going to get married. You know that, right?"

I chuckle and roll my eyes. "Yeah, of course."

"Did you just roll your eyes?"

"I just think it's a bit early to be making those kinds of proclamations. It's probably best not to make any promises we can't keep."

His gaze falls to the table and he nods. "You're right." For a moment, I think this is it. The topic has been closed to further discussion. Then he sits up a little straighter and looks me in the eye. "No, you and I are going to be together forever. Even if we break up, we'll always make it back to each other; mark my words."

I nod as I reach for the beer again. "Do you want to know what I think of this beer?"

He smiles at my attempt to change the subject. "Shoot."

"It's too citrusy. You can taste a hint of honey, maybe even caramel, but the top notes are definitely orange and bitter lemon. The hops deliver a bite and they're lingering."

"IBU?" he asks.

IBU is an acronym for International Bittering Units, a measurement of the amount of bitterness or "hoppy-ness" in a beer.

"Probably thirty to forty."

He shakes his head. "I'm in love with a beer snob."

"Does that turn you on?"

"Put your hand under the table and you'll feel my beer-ection."

I almost spit out my ale, but I manage to swallow it down.

Houston laughs as I grab the cocktail napkin to wipe the dribble from my chin. Then he rubs my back as I cough out the small bit of farmhouse ale I inhaled.

"That's what you get for killing Mufasa," he says.

I shake my head as I take another long sip of ale to cool my throat, then an idea comes to me. "Did you decide what you're doing next week?"

"For Spring Break?"

"No, for Christmas," I reply sarcastically. "Of course for Spring Break."

He looks uncomfortable with this question. "Troy and I made plans."

"What kind of plans?" I regret the question as soon as it comes out. I don't want to be the nosy, clingy girlfriend. That's not me.

"Troy and I are gonna try out some new formulas."

"But… you guys do that every weekend."

The muscle in his jaw twitches and that's my signal to let it go. I want to say, *So that whole thing about us being together forever is only true if we never get too close?* but I hold my tongue… again. Then I down four more beers and give my detailed analysis of each one. Houston drives us home and fucks me over the bathroom sink. And when we wake the next morning, with the rain tapping on our bedroom window, Houston's head is lying on my abdomen, facing the foot of the bed.

I can't see his face so I reach down and run my fingers through his hair to wake him gently. At first, I think he's still sleeping. Then I hear a small sniff and I feel the wetness on my skin. This is the second time I've seen Houston cry and, somehow, this time is worse than the day Hallie died. Because today I don't know why, and I don't know if I ever will.

Houston

August 17th

LOVE IS A strange concept. That the very sight of someone, the very mention of their name, can cause an intense chemical reaction inside you is crazy. The fact that many people settle for less than that explosive chemical reaction is even crazier. Yet here I am, sitting next to Tessa in church on Sunday, praying to a god I stopped believing in five years ago.

Why am I sitting here watching people line up to eat a piece of bread impersonating the body of Christ? Because I'm afraid of what would happen if I weren't here. In other words, I'm afraid of becoming a cheating bastard like my father.

When I met Tessa at that beer festival three years ago, I recognized something in her. Something we both shared: the need to forget. And I knew that, having honed that skill over the previous two years since Rory and I broke up, I had to be the one to teach Tessa how to do it.

I'll admit that the lessons were mutually beneficial in the beginning. But once Tessa began to put her brother's death behind her, I recognized something even more important in her: We had nothing in common other than our mutual grief, which we had so cleverly locked away.

I glance sideways at her and even the way she sits in the pew with her ankles crossed and her blonde hair hanging over her shoulders in perfect loose curls makes me bristle. I want to grab her slender shoulders and shake her and ask her why we're still pretending to love each other.

After we consume our piece of the Lord, we make it out to the parking lot before He's even dissolved on our tongues. We walk in silence as the warm summer breeze rustles the trees along the edge of the lot. I open the car door for Tessa and she raises one eyebrow.

"What's with the chivalry?"

I want to make a joke, maybe call her m'lady, but I can't muster up the energy to force the words out. "We need to talk."

She climbs into the car and stares straight ahead through the windshield. "Okay. Let's talk."

I shut the passenger door and hurry around to climb into the driver's side. Once my door is closed, the sound of the breeze disappears and the silence takes a seat between us. I swallow hard as I try to think of how to start this conversation, but I'm dumbstruck.

Tessa knows nothing about Rory other than the few photos she's seen in Hallie's room of Rory and Hallie together. I asked my parents to destroy the few pictures they had of Rory and me. And I put all my own pictures of us on a flash drive I keep hidden in my office at the brewery. How do I even begin to explain to Tessa the kind of love I shared with Rory?

"Fine. If you're just going to sit there silent, then, yes. Yes, I contacted a fertility clinic. Are you really so mad you can't even speak?"

My vision blurs as my heart thumps inside my skull. "You…

contacted a fertility clinic?" I turn toward her and she looks confused. "What the fuck were you thinking?"

"You… didn't know?"

"What were you thinking, Tessa? You went to a fucking fertility clinic without my consent?"

Her eyes widen with sheer terror. "I thought you knew. I thought that's what you wanted to talk about."

"You thought I knew? How the fuck was I supposed to know if you were *hiding* it from me?"

"But, I thought… I thought that's why you… you didn't come inside me. I… I thought you had looked at my laptop when I went to the appointment."

"You thought that's why I didn't come inside you? I didn't come inside you because I don't *want* to have a child. What is so fucking difficult to understand?"

"I thought you would change your mind! All young guys think they don't want children, but I've seen you with my nieces. You'd make a great father, Houston." She reaches for my hand and I yank it back before she can touch me. "Houston, please. Let's do this… together."

"Or what? Or you'll do it alone? When were you planning on telling me about going to the clinic? *After* you get pregnant?"

She turns away to look out the passenger window and a sick knot of fear grips my insides. "I'm four weeks along."

I'm tempted to tell her to get the fuck out of the car. Instead, I turn the key in the ignition and pull out of the lot without another word. By the time we get home, I know there's no way I can go inside with her. I leave her in front of the building, then I head for the brewery.

Twenty minutes later, I pull into a parking space in back of Barley Legal headquarters in Northwest Portland. On the outside, it looks like an old three-story shoebox brick building, which takes up half a city block in the industrial district. But on the inside, that's where all the magic happens.

I began brewing my own beer my sophomore year at UO. I majored in business with the idea of going to law school after graduation and subsequently selling my soul to the legal interests of corporations. But a girl I was dating that year gave me a dinky little home-brew starter kit. She knew my friends and I were beer snobs, so it was actually a pretty thoughtful gift. That relationship didn't survive past the new year, but I still have that starter kit in my office here at the brewery.

I enter through the back door and quickly punch in the code to shut off the alarm. No one comes in through the back on Sundays. Only the front and side entrances are open to let in the servers, management, and customers at the Barley Legal Brewhouse pub and restaurant. They won't even know I'm here.

I take the stairs up to the offices on the third floor. I pass the glass receptionist's desk, where Tessa worked for two weeks last year before she decided she preferred being a stay-at-home wife. I never had a problem with Tessa's choice to stay home. I make more than enough to support us. But I've always wondered how she can stand not having anything to do.

Tessa does have hobbies. She works out at the gym on the first floor of our building one to two hours a day with Kendra. Kendra's husband is a network security consultant who works from home, but they have a nanny who watches the baby while she's at the gym. Tessa also likes to make handmade event invitations. She takes orders on Etsy.com, where she gets an order once or twice a month. As I enter my corner office, I can't help but wonder if she'll be making her own baby shower invitations soon.

Just the thought of it makes my palms sweat. I can't have a baby with Tessa, but I also can't ask her to terminate the pregnancy. If Tessa's Catholic parents find out I "made" her get an abortion, I'll never hear the end of it.

I head for the corner of the office and open the closet door where I hang my coats and spare clothes and shoes. You never know when someone's going to spill some beer on you. And the Portland weather often leaves me craving a dry set of clothes. I reach into the back of the top shelf and feel around the dusty surface until I find the small tin box.

I take the box to my desk and set it down on the glass surface. Taking a seat, I lean back in my chair and stare at the box for a moment, as if gazing at it will tell me whether or not I should open it. I should call Troy and ask him to come have a beer with me. But I can't talk to him about Tessa tricking me into getting her pregnant. He'll say, *I told you so. Contessa Dracula sank her teeth in and now she's gonna suck you dry.*

Troy likes to call Tessa by her full name, Contessa. When she's not around he tacks on Dracula because he has insisted, from the day Tessa and I met, that she's after my money. She's not. Her parents do pretty well. Her dad's a pediatrician and her mom was a stay-at-home mom to their four children. Tessa is the youngest and therefore the most spoiled of them all. The oldest of the four, Jasen, is the one who died in a car accident four years ago.

But Troy and Tessa share a mutual dislike for each other. Troy has been my best friend since ninth grade, and he's always been a man-whore. He even gave me a run for my money after Rory and I broke up and I was fucking anything that moved. But he's actually been in a steady relationship for more than a year now, so you'd think Tessa would no longer feel the need to tense up every time I tell her I'm going out for beers with Troy. The problem is that he claims he's never going to get married. And he actually managed to find a smart girl who is willing to stay with him despite this.

Now, with Tessa pulling this baby crap on me, I'm wondering if women view these sorts of proclamations as temporary obstacles. Maybe Troy's girlfriend is only waiting until the right moment, until their lives are completely commingled, then she's going to spring the ultimatum: Marry me or get out of my life.

I grab the metal box off the desk and hold it up at eye level. Every picture I ever took of Rory is stored on a tiny flash drive inside this box. But I can't figure out if I should pop it into my laptop and let my mind wander back to the happiest and most miserable time of my life, or if I should toss it in the waste bin.

I'll never have the balls to leave Tessa if we have a child. I know this about me and she definitely knows this about me. So maybe I should just get it over with now. Completely erase Rory from my life and move on.

The lid on the box is embossed with a forest scene. In the center is a painted logo for Sierra Nevada Brewery. A chill passes through me as I slowly pry the lid off. I lift it away and set it down on the desk as I stare at the two objects in the box: a simple white USB flash drive and a three-carat princess-cut diamond engagement ring.

I had every reason to take this ring back to the jeweler after Rory and I broke up. I'd saved up almost every single penny of the money Troy and I made at our "beer tastings." We had a cover charge to get in, but once you were in, it was all-you-can-drink. We financed production of the home brew with our meager savings, so the money we made on cover charges seemed like pure profit.

After graduation, Troy used half his money to get a new car. Three weeks before graduation, I used about three-quarters of my earnings to buy this ring for Rory. I kept worrying about what would happen to us once I graduated and moved two hours away to start the brewery. I foolishly thought that an engagement ring would keep her committed to me while we were apart. But I didn't know how us staying together would work, logistically. I knew I could never go back to McMinnville with her. And I couldn't expect her to always visit her parents alone. So I kept the ring tucked away until I could figure it out.

Then a week later, she told me she was pregnant and I almost went through with it. I almost proposed. But I couldn't do it. Not to myself. Not to Hallie. And especially not to Rory.

"Hey, man. What are you doing?"

The sound of Troy's voice startles me and I drop the box into my lap. The ring and the flash drive tumble out and onto the wood floor. Troy's eyes immediately lock on the ring and I quickly get on my knees to retrieve it from beneath the desk.

"What's that? Renewing your vows with Contessa already?"

I bump my head on the glass as I get up. "*Fuck*. No, this is nothing. It's old." I drop the ring into the box and hastily put the lid back on. "What are you doing here?"

He has one eyebrow raised as he fixes me with a *stop-bullshitting-me* stare.

I sigh as I set the box on my lap to semi-hide it from Troy. "It's a ring I got for Rory… a long time ago."

"And you still have it?" he says, taking a seat in a chair on the other side of the desk.

I think of lying to him and saying the jeweler wouldn't let me return it, but that's such a load of crap. I don't think a kindergartner would believe that.

"I ran into her," I say as casually as I can.

"Who, Rory?"

I nod and he lets out a soft chuckle.

"Wow. Is she living in Portland?" he asks, his eyebrows perking up with curiosity.

I nod again as I place the metal box back on the desk. "I'm gonna be working with her."

"What the fuck? Did you *hire* her?"

"No! No, it's nothing like that. It's that wine bar."

"The contract we signed on Friday?"

"Yeah, she works at the market."

"Well, I'll be." Troy lets out a cackle of laughter as he smacks his knee. "There you fuckin' go, man. That's your ticket out. Now you can kick Contessa to the curb and get back with Rory."

"What the fuck are you talking about? I'm not going to divorce my wife because I ran into my ex-girlfriend."

"Then why the fuck are you sitting alone in your office staring at a ring you bought five years ago? Because if you're not planning on doing something with that ring, then that just seems pathetic."

I shake my head. "One of these days I'm gonna build a balcony just so I can throw you off."

"Yeah, yeah. Don't get mad at me. You're the one sitting here pining for a girl you could probably still have in a heartbeat. Unless she's with someone else. Is that what it is?"

"I don't know."

"Then find out." He stands from the chair and heads for the door. "I don't know much about relationships, but I know I've never seen you as miserable as you were when you two broke up. And I know I've never seen you as happy with Tessa as you were with Rory."

"Now you're calling her Tessa?"

"I'm trying to be serious. But whatever, dude. Do what you gotta do. I just came in to get my racket. Meeting Joey at the gym. Wanna come?"

"Nah, I'm good. I'm just gonna sit here and stare pathetically at this ring a bit longer."

He shrugs. "The lube is in my top drawer. Don't use it all."

"You take it. You'll need it when Joey makes you his bitch."

Troy walks away cackling and I lean forward to stare into the shallow depths of the tin box. He's right. Staring at this ring is pathetic.

But I can't keep it. It doesn't belong to me.

It's time to give it to its rightful owner.

Tessa

August 18th

KENDRA'S APARTMENT IS exactly the same as ours. The same two bedrooms with windows; her windows face the courtyard while ours face Savier Street. The same concrete counters and black kitchen cabinets. The same layout and, oddly enough, it even smells the same since she gifted me the same scented oil diffuser she uses. The one major difference is that her apartment is overrun with baby gear.

You walk in the door and, if you're not paying attention, you'll bump into the black stroller with the lime-green polka-dots. Her kitchen sink is always piled high with baby-food containers that she sterilized and set out to dry. I've never understood how they're supposed to remain sterile while drying in that dish rack. Her living room is cramped by a playpen and, half the time, her coffee table is pushed against the wall under the window so eight-month-old Trucker can crawl around without knocking his head on the furniture.

I take a seat on Kendra's overstuffed sofa and try not to stare at Trucker in his high chair. He has Kendra's dark hair and gray eyes, but his face is round and bright, just like Kendra's husband, Aaron. Aaron is a great guy, but he can be a bit abrasive sometimes, like Kendra. The few times Kendra has tried to get him to hang out with Houston and me, he accused her of trying to set him up on an adult playdate. Kendra gave up trying to force us into a four-way friendship months ago.

"So, I had to go to Aaron's cousin's house in Salem for a birthday party this weekend. So trashy. I swear, it's like I married the only sane person in that whole family. How was your weekend?" Kendra asks as she shovels a spoonful of organic pureed peas into Trucker's pursed baby lips.

I tear my eyes away from Trucker and sigh. "I told Houston I'm pregnant."

"You're pregnant? *Already*?"

"No, I lied to him."

"You what? Why?"

I get an itch on my forearm, but I know it's just the guilt irritating my scars, so I resist the urge to scratch. "Because I'm stupid. I thought he had found out about the appointment with the fertility clinic."

"Because he came home early?"

"Yeah. I was convinced he had opened up my laptop and saw the website in my history. Especially because, just a few days later, we were having sex and he pulled out for the first time since I had this IUD implanted fourteen months ago."

Kendra uses Trucker's bib to wipe away some green goop from the corner of his mouth, then she turns to me with a very suspicious look in her eyes. "He pulled out?"

"Yeah, I know. It freaked me out. But he was acting like it was no big deal, so I accused him of cheating on me."

"Oh, because that's always smart."

I lean forward and grab a travel magazine off the coffee table, which is right where it's supposed to be today. "I know. I've been doing a lot of stupid things ever since I had that consultation. Dr. Menlo told me that even if I take the IUD out now, I probably won't get pregnant for four to six months. And that's only if we track my ovulation patterns and have sex during peak times. I can't even get Houston to come inside me with an IUD. How am I ever supposed to have a baby?" I sigh heavily. "Why doesn't he want to have a baby with me?"

"He doesn't want to have a baby with anyone. You know that."

Kendra is referring to the conversation I had with Ava Cavanaugh, Houston's mother, shortly before Houston and I got married two years and three months ago. Houston doesn't know his mother told me about the ex-girlfriend he got pregnant. According to Ava, they broke up right after the girl got an abortion. She wouldn't tell me the girl's name, but I got the feeling Ava loved her very much, which makes me even more insecure. The reason she divulged this information to me was as a cautionary tale. In other words, she was silently warning me, *If Houston didn't want children with her, then he will definitely never want children with you.*

I flip the travel magazine open to a random page and land on an advertisement for vacation rentals in Bali. "I know, but that's what all guys think."

"No, it's not, Tessa. Aaron and Houston are not all guys. Besides, once Aaron found out I was pregnant, he completely flipped sides and couldn't get enough of my juicy birth canal."

"Ew."

"Whatever. The point is that you have to accept that Houston doesn't want kids. And you have to emotionally prepare for the possibility that he may leave you if you do get pregnant without his consent or if he finds out you're bluffing about this pregnancy."

I turn another page and roll my eyes at the happy couple pictured next to an article about chic honeymoon locations. "You're the one who told me to get pregnant. Now you're telling me to consider the consequences?"

"I didn't tell you to get pregnant. All I said is that it worked for me. Results may vary. But I guess it doesn't matter what I think 'cause Houston is the type of guy who needs to be trapped or someone else is gonna sneak in there. He's totally Vanessa's type: hot, rich, and married. Like, you should totally keep him away from Vanessa or she'd be all like, 'Lawd! I'd let him ram me so hard my lunch would fall out.'"

My stomach curdles at the thought of Vanessa and Houston together. "Ugh. I hate that girl."

Vanessa is Aaron's sister, who likes to come over and visit Kendra every once in a while. She has a disgusting habit of dating married men. She claims it's because she likes excitement and expensive gifts, especially when they come without commitment. I think it's because she's a dirty home-wrecker.

Kendra pulls Trucker out of the high chair and he flashes her a gracious smile as she balances him on her hip. His gray eyes find me across the room and I smile, though I know his eyes aren't developed enough to see me clearly. His chubby hand smacks his mom's chest as she clears the bowl of food from the chair.

"Settle down, Trucker."

I set the magazine on the coffee table as I rise from the sofa. "I'll take him so you can clean up."

Kendra's brow furrows with pity as I hold my hands out to her and I know what she's thinking. And she's right.

She hands him over and I get a weird sensation in my chest the moment his soft body is snuggled against my hip and inside the crook of my arm. Trucker reaches for my hair and I gently grab his hand to redirect his attention. He smells so soft and clean with just a hint of sweet earthiness on his breath from the baby food. He nods at me and I nod back. Kendra has been teaching him to nod and shake his head as well as a few simple phrases in sign language. I don't know why Trucker's nodding at me, but I'd like to think it's because he approves of my prospects as a baby handler.

I just wish I could get Houston to feel the same.

Rory

August 23rd

MY JAW DROPS when Jamie finishes making her offer. She waits patiently for me to respond, but after a couple of minutes of stunned silence, she finally has to speak.

"Is that a yes?"

"I… I can't run a wine bar."

"Yes, you can. If Theo can run the coffee bar, you can take over at the wine bar."

When Jamie pulled me into her office ten minutes ago, I never imagined she'd be offering me a management position. But that's exactly what she's done. Assistant manager of the wine bar at the Goose Hollow location. A seven-minute walk from my apartment. And more than twice what I'm currently making.

The current assistant manager of the coffee bar, Theo, is only nineteen years old and won't be allowed to keep the same position when it's converted into a wine bar. He's being promoted to Assistant Manager II of customer service. They need someone to take his place and, somehow, Jamie got it in her head that I would be perfect for this position.

"Why me? Isn't there anyone else at the Goose Hollow store you can promote?"

"So you don't want the promotion?"

My throat goes dry as I realize I'm botching this up. "No, I didn't say that. I was just wondering why… I… Oh, forget it. Yes, of course I want it. Thank you so much, Jamie. This is… amazing. Thank you."

She smiles and her crooked tooth shines under the fluorescent lighting in her office. "You're welcome. I'm sure you'll do great."

She winks at me as I get up to leave and I hold in my laughter as I exit her office. Then it hits me. What if that wink was meant in a wink-wink nudge-nudge sort of way? What if she was trying to tell me something? *Oh, God.* What if Houston is the one who told her to give me the management position?

No, that's crazy. As far as Jamie is concerned, Houston is just a supplier. He has no power over hiring decisions. And I'm flattering myself to think he would care enough to do something like recommending me for a management position. Besides, if he did recommend me for that promotion it was probably because he's planning on spending less time at the Goose Hollow location. Not the other way around.

I finish out my last day as a cashier at 4:37 p.m. when Kenny arrives to start his shift. I run into him in the warehouse as he's clocking in.

"Hey, sexy. You look happy. Did you finally get some?"

My happiness is quickly deflated when it dawns on me that I'm no longer going to see Kenny four to five times a week. "I got a promotion."

"To what?"

"Assistant manager of the wine bar…"

Kenny's gorgeous green eyes widen.

I continue, "In Goose Hollow. Today's my last day here."

"*WHAT?*"

"I know. I'm so sad I'm not going to see you anymore."

"What are you talking about? You're not getting rid of me that easily. But what in the fuckity-fuck is up with that promotion? I mean, don't get me wrong, it's not that you're not qualified. You're obviously *over*qualified for every position here." He winks at me, then continues. "But isn't a promotion like that a bit out of left field? Did you apply for the position or something?"

I shake my head. "No, I didn't know about any of this until Jamie called me into her office this morning."

Kenny shrugs and gives me a quick hug. "Doesn't matter. You deserve it. And now I have an excuse to stalk you—I mean *visit* you at your apartment."

"I'd love for you to visit me." A sudden urge overcomes me and I throw my arms around him again. He chuckles and I let go quickly.

"You're so weird, Rory."

"In a good way?"

"In a beautiful way. I'll call you later. You still have to tell me all about the lumberjack you went home with Sunday night."

A chill passes through me at the mention of Liam. He called me last night as I was getting into the shower, but I didn't call him back when I got out. I listened to his voicemail once before I deleted it, then I stared at my phone for about two hours while thinking of Houston.

My mind constantly draws back to the memory of him telling me that we would be together forever, even if we broke up. I held on to that memory like a totem of our relationship. An intangible relic. A wispy promise, easily forgotten and even more easily broken.

But we did make it back to each other, just like he said we would. Only now it's impossible for us to be together. Yet, he seems intent on having a presence in my life as some sort of heroic chauffeur. I laugh out loud at this thought and only then do I realize I'm still standing next to Kenny in the warehouse.

He shakes his head at me. "You need to get laid, sweetheart."

I let out a deep sigh. "Working on it."

EVERY TIME THE phone rings I become more nervous. Until I'm so nervous I feel physically sick to my stomach. Finally, on the fourth ring, Liam answers.

"Rory?"

I suck in a sharp breath and my reply comes out far too high-pitched. "Liam! Hi!"

He chuckles. "Hi. How are you doing?"

Skippy yelps to tell me I'm scratching his head a bit too hard. "I'm fine. Just lying in bed with my dog. Wait. That sounded weird. I'm just relaxing. Yeah, that sounds better."

"Actually, I liked the visual of you lying in bed."

I swallow hard as I try to think of a response, but Liam laughs it off.

"Well, I could try to make some more small talk," he says, and I sense another proposition coming, "or you can invite me over."

"This whole dating thing is still kind of weird for me, so I'll need you to be patient."

"I don't do patient," he replies, and an awkward silence settles in between us, then he laughs. "I'm kidding. I've actually been sitting by my phone waiting for you to call me since I dropped you off last Sunday."

"Who sits by their phone anymore? Doesn't your phone sit

by *you*?"

"I guess you're right. I'll have to work on the accuracy of my guilt-trip material. So how was your day?"

I sigh audibly. "Ugh. This sucks. I hate small talk."

"When I come over, I promise I'll only talk big."

"Talk big? What does that mean? Are you going to make bold claims about yourself all night?"

"If that's what you're into. I might even back up those claims with some action."

My face flushes with heat. "Don't get any funny ideas, okay? I barely know you and, like I said, I'm not looking for anything serious right now."

"That's fine with me. We can keep our relationship strictly based on shallow sexual encounters."

"Hanging up now."

I stare at the phone for a second wondering if this is a good idea. I haven't had sex with anyone since Houston. I know it's totally lame, but he was my first. And he was so patient with me that I quickly opened up to him. Less than a month into our relationship, we were trying things some couples would consider kinky. But I always felt safe and adored when I was with Houston. The idea of having sex with someone and not feeling that way doesn't appeal to me. I want to feel that intense emotional bond as well as the primal sexual attraction.

It's way too early to expect to feel that with Liam, so I'll have to ask him to take it slow. As I told him before, I'm damaged goods. I sigh heavily at this thought. Five years later and the pain is still as intense as it was the day Houston hand-fed me a bowl of soup then snuck out of our apartment in the middle of the night, when he thought I was sleeping.

I consider getting dolled up to hang out with Liam, but if he's going to like the real me, then a messy ponytail is the least disturbing part of me he's going to have to accept. As a small courtesy, I apply some powder and blush to my cheeks and some tinted lip balm. Skippy and I get settled down on the sofa with Animal Planet on the TV, but we're quickly interrupted by a knock at the door.

Skippy lets out a soft bark as he jumps down from the sofa.

I point at the cushion he just vacated. "Sit, Skippy."

He casts a forlorn glance in my direction before he hops back onto the sofa.

"Stay," I say, for good measure.

My heart is beating so fast and hard, I can feel my pulse in my fingertips. I reach for the knob and take a slow breath as I open the door.

My jaw drops. "Houston. What the hell are you doing here?"

I peek my head into the corridor and I'm only slightly relieved to see Liam hasn't arrived yet. But he'll be here any moment. I have to get Houston out of here.

"Were you expecting someone else?" He looks me up and down for a second, taking in my messy ponytail, gray leggings, and UO hoodie. "You look—"

He stops himself before he can finish this sentence and I find myself wondering if he was going to tell me I look pretty or that I look like shit. I want to ask him, but I don't have time.

"Houston, you need to leave."

"Are you expecting someone?" he replies, glancing toward the elevator.

"That's none of your business."

His jaw clenches. "I came to bring you something."

"Bring me something? Bring me *what*?"

His whole body seems to tense and that's when I notice his hands are clasped behind his back. Is he hiding something back there?

"What is it?" I whisper.

He gazes into my eyes for a moment and I'm flooded with a

gust of raw emotion. I desperately want whatever he's going to give me.

"Houston, what is it?"

He opens his mouth to speak, but he's interrupted by the ding of the elevator. I whip my head to the right and I watch anxiously as Liam glances at the sign on the wall pointing him in our direction. He turns left and his eyes lock on Houston and me, then he proceeds toward us cautiously.

I don't know what to do. How do I introduce them to each other? *Liam, this is the ex-boyfriend who destroyed me. Houston, this is my new friend Liam, who I hope will help me get over you.*

Houston's hand closes around my elbow, but surprisingly I don't flinch. "Rory, you're trembling. Are you okay?"

Liam arrives and seems a bit confused, so I quickly push Houston's hand away. And now I'm shaking again, even more than I was before.

"I'm fine. Houston, this is my friend Liam." I turn to Liam and hope he can see the plea in my eyes to cut me some slack for this very awkward, unplanned encounter. "Liam, this is… my old friend Houston."

Houston narrows his eyes at my description of him, but after an awkward few seconds, he turns to Liam and offers him his hand. "Good to meet you."

Liam nods at him as they continue to shake hands. "You too."

Houston doesn't seem to be ready to let go of Liam's hand, so I finally grab Liam by the arm and pull him inside. His body is almost flush against mine, so close I can feel his warmth and smell his crisp scent. I whisper for him to go ahead and take a seat on the sofa and he smiles as he heads inside.

I shut the door behind me so I'm alone in the corridor with Houston. "I told you not to come here."

"Is that your boyfriend?"

"No, it's not my boyfriend. Actually, it's none of your business. You need to leave."

I reach for the doorknob and he grabs my hand to stop me. "Tell him to leave."

"Are you kidding me? No way."

"Do you see that?" He nods toward where his hand is covering mine. "You're not trembling anymore."

I slide my hand out from under his and shake my head. "No, Houston. You're married. You're not allowed to come here and fuck with my life. Go home."

He pulls his other hand out from behind his back and brandishes a small metal box with a Sierra Nevada logo on the top. He stares at the box for a moment before he holds it out to me.

I take the box from his hand and my heart sputters. There's something small and hard sliding around inside the box.

"What is it?"

"It's my promise to make this right." He takes a step toward me and I'm frozen as his hand lands on my cheek. He brushes his thumb softly over my cheekbone, then he leans in and plants a soft kiss on my forehead. "You look beautiful tonight."

I want to hurry inside the apartment so I don't have to watch him walking away, but I can't tear my gaze away from him. As I watch him getting into the elevator, I get the urge to run after him and kiss him. Instead, I close my eyes and listen to the soft swoosh of the elevator doors closing.

I heave a deep sigh as I turn around and head back inside the apartment. The sight of Liam sitting on my sofa with Skippy's head in his lap instantly puts me at ease.

"Is everything all right?" he asks, and I sense another question in there. *Do you want me to leave?*

I smile as I set the small metal box on top of the breakfast bar, then make my way to the sofa. "Never better."

I consider not asking Skippy to move, but that would mean I'd have to sit on the opposite end of the sofa from Liam. And right now I think I need to be close to someone. I gently order Skippy to get down and he begrudgingly obliges, then I take a seat on the middle cushion next to Liam.

"Do you like Animal Planet?" I ask, trying to keep my voice casual.

"I thought you asked me over here because you hate small talk." He smiles at me and I'm treated to the sight of his gorgeous teeth framed by his perfectly groomed beard.

"You want to know who that was?"

He shrugs and I take that as a yes.

I let out a soft sigh and continue. "He's the one… the one who changed everything."

"Oh." He nods as if he totally understands, but I can tell this information has made him uncomfortable. "So… he wants to get back together?"

I glance at the metal box on the breakfast bar. "He wants to make things right, whatever that means."

"Is that possible—to make things right?"

I stare at Liam for a moment as I contemplate this question. "I don't know."

He smiles and I take the opportunity to scoot a bit closer to him. He quickly takes the hint and wraps his arm around me so I can lay my head on his shoulder. It's only ten p.m., but I can already feel myself getting very relaxed and sleepy in his arms. He must feel it too, because a few minutes later he kisses my forehead and uncoils his arm from around my shoulders.

"I should let you get to sleep."

"But you didn't get to talk big."

He chuckles as he stands from the sofa. I move to get up, but he holds his hand out to stop me. "Thanks for being honest with me, Rory."

"Why would I not be honest with you?"

He shakes his head. "You know, the thing about honest people is that they can't imagine why someone else would be dishonest."

"Are you calling me naive?"

He laughs again. "No. No way. I'm just saying that you're an honest person and… I find that very sexy."

"Sexy?"

He smiles, then heads for the door, leaving me feeling a bit unsatisfied with his twenty-minute visit. Though, I get the feeling he's leaving out of a need for self-preservation. What did I expect? I invited him over and he found me talking to my ex-boyfriend in the doorway. Then I went and told him the truth, that I don't know if things can ever be made right between Houston and me. I should have lied and told him that Houston and I are irreparable.

Maybe Houston was right. Maybe we *will* always make it back together.

Then we'll never stop hurting each other.

Houston

August 23rd

I SIT IN my car for about five minutes, contemplating my next move. I consider waiting for Liam to leave. Maybe—hopefully—my presence scared him and he'll leave early. Then I consider going up there and dragging him outside where he can't touch her. But I lost my right to be territorial with Rory five years ago. Ultimately, I decide to take Rory's stern advice and go home to face my wife.

I pull out of the curved driveway in front of Rory's building and set off in the opposite direction of my apartment. I need to figure out how to approach Tessa before I get there. If there's one thing I've learned in two years of marriage, it's that you must have a plan when arguing with a woman. If you go in blind, you'll be knocked over the head and slaughtered before you know what hit you.

My mind draws back to the day I asked Tessa to marry me. We had been together a whopping four months before I decided that she was exactly the type of woman I needed to spend the rest of my life with. Someone who would stay with me no matter how often she suspected she should leave. Someone who wouldn't question why I was never fully hers.

It was December 4th, the third anniversary of Hallie's death. As always, my plans were to get so drunk that I blacked out. Tessa knew my sister had committed suicide, but she didn't know all the grisly details of how I found her. Or how the next six months I spent with Rory were the best and worst months of my existence. And she certainly didn't know about my tradition of getting blackout drunk on the anniversary of Hallie's death. So when Tessa tried calling and texting me a dozen times with no reply, she didn't know why I wasn't calling her back. And when she showed up at my apartment and found me shit-faced drunk, fucking a girl I'd met at a bar and took home because she reminded me of Rory, what she did next changed everything.

I expected Tessa to hit me, or the girl whose pussy was wrapped around my dick. I expected her to cry or storm out of my apartment. I expected her to do pretty much anything other than what she actually did.

She threatened to kill herself.

She told me, rather calmly, that if I didn't make the girl leave she would take her own life. She insisted that after losing her brother she wouldn't have anything to live for if she lost me, too. That was when I knew I couldn't leave her, and that I didn't really want to, because she didn't care if I loved her. She didn't care that I was still in love with Rory. All Tessa wanted was for me to stay with her. To me, this made her perfect.

It was quite a dramatic scene, getting the Rory lookalike out of the apartment and convincing Tessa that I was going to stay with her and she didn't need to kill herself. Dare I say I even relished the moment? It was a second chance to save her the way I couldn't save Hallie. Once Tessa was wrapped safely and calmly in my arms, I asked her to marry me right there. And she accepted, with no ring.

I had never felt more disgusted with myself and more relieved at the same time. The burden of trying to find someone to measure up to Rory was lifted. I could settle for someone who accepted me at my worst, as long as my worst was merely that I loved someone else from afar.

But showing up at Rory's apartment and presenting her with an engagement ring that's far more expensive than the ring I ultimately gave my wife is not quite "loving her from afar." And normally I would deal with this type of problem by drinking myself into unconsciousness, but all I can think of right now is *What would Rory want me to do?* She tolerated my drinking binges when we first got together, often trying to outdrink me. But by the end of our six-month relationship, just the sight of beer annoyed her.

Half of me wants to get blasted so I can deal with Tessa. Because I know she won't care. She'll probably use my drunken state to her advantage to try to have sex with me. The other half of me wants to stay sober so she knows I mean it when I tell her I'm leaving.

I'm leaving? This thought surprises me even though it originated in my mind. Am I really going to leave Tessa for getting pregnant behind my back? That would make me the worst husband in the history of Tessa's Catholic family. Maybe the more important question is: Am I going to leave Tessa because she deceived me into getting her pregnant or am I leaving her for Rory, and if I leave her… what will she do?

I get my answer as I'm pulling the SUV into the underground parking garage. A text message from Rory.

Rory: *This box won't stop staring at me.*

I smile for a split second as I imagine going back to Rory's and slipping the ring on her finger. Then I remember what happened the last time Tessa caught me cheating on her and my smile evaporates. I stare at the message for at least a minute before I respond.

Me: What's in the box?!

I hit send, hoping she'll understand the reference to Brad Pitt's famous line from the movie *Seven.* I always used that line whenever Rory ordered something online and the package arrived on our doorstep.

Rory: *If this box contains Gwyneth Paltrow's severed head I'm going to be very disappointed.*

I shake my head and grin like an idiot. She's still the same Rory I knew five years ago. I have to stop myself from responding with a dirty text about giving good head, the way I would have responded when we were together. Then I try to come up with a clever response, but after a couple of minutes I decide to call her instead. I'm surprised when she answers.

"Houston." The way she says my name, preceded by a small, reluctant sigh, makes me smile.

"Rory."

"What's in the box?"

This is the moment of truth. Whatever I say right now will change my marriage forever.

I draw in a long breath and she waits patiently as I let it out slowly. "I'd rather open it for you and show it to you myself."

She's silent for a moment. An excruciatingly long moment. "Fine. I won't open it until tomorrow."

"Tomorrow?"

"That's when I start my new job. Are you saying you had

nothing to do with me getting a promotion?"

I can't sneak anything past her.

"I may have had a little something to do with that. Are you upset?"

"Upset? Why would I be upset? Because I'm making double what I used to make and I can walk to work now? Yeah, I'm totally upset. I'm writing my manifesto right now before I go blow up the grocery store."

I smile though there's an ache inside me when I think of how much I've missed her quick comebacks.

"I knew I should have told Jamie to fire you instead. Is there anything I can do to make it right? Maybe I can help with that manifesto."

She's silent for a moment and I wonder if I've said something wrong. Then it dawns on me that she mentioned she was working on a book in her spare time.

"Rory?"

"Yeah?"

"What's your book about?"

She's silent again, but this time there's no fidgeting or background noise. As if my question has created a vacuum of space between us, sucking out all the sound and energy.

I glance at my phone to make sure the call didn't drop, then I bring it back to my ear. "Rory?"

"Yeah, I'm still here."

"You don't have to tell me. I was just being nosy."

"No, it's fine. I'll tell you what my book is about when you show me what's inside the box."

And just like that, all my trepidation over whether I should give Rory that ring disappears. Because I want to know what she's writing. I desperately want to know what's important enough for her to spend months or even years thinking about.

Who the fuck am I kidding? I want to know if she's writing

about me. And, yes, I'd give up my marriage to find that out.

Rory

Five years ago, February 13th

THIS IS MY fifth trip to Barnes & Noble this week and I've come away empty-handed each time. I'm in a rut. I haven't read anything for two weeks straight. If I don't find something to keep my mind occupied outside of studying, I'll go crazy.

I trace my finger along the edge of the wooden table as I enter the Barnes & Noble off campus. The table is stacked with all the latest new releases from authors like Danielle Steel and J. D. Robb. Some nonfiction bestsellers are mixed in, but nothing that catches my eye.

Normally, I'd just pick up the latest book from one of my favorite authors, but I've read all the most current releases. And I'm not in the mood for the same type of romance or family drama I normally read. I'm trying to avoid that kind of story right now, seeing as I'm unable to escape those things in real life.

Tomorrow is my first Valentine's Day with Houston and he hasn't mentioned it at all. I've been silently obsessing over it for a few weeks now. Which is probably why I haven't been able to read for pleasure lately.

A hardcover near the back of the table grabs my attention and I pick it up to get a better look. The jacket cover depicts a quaint arched bridge set in front of a rich midnight-blue sky. A gray satin ribbon appears to be gently falling from the sky toward the glistening water under the bridge. I brush my thumb across the embossed title: *The Fall* by Amanda Cabot. I've never heard of this author, but I make an impulsive decision to buy the book without reading the description on the inside flap.

I pull up in front of our apartment building twenty minutes later and I'm surprised to see that Houston is parked next to the curb. We switch between parking at the curb and using the carport that came with the apartment. There's only space for one car in the carport, so he parks his truck in the space Friday through Sunday and I park my seven-year-old Toyota there Monday through Thursday. It's Friday evening, so he should be parked in the space tonight. I assume he's invited a friend over and they took the carport, so I park my car next to the curb behind Houston's truck and head inside.

I open the front door and I'm surprised to find Houston lying shirtless on the sofa with no one else around. "Are you alone?" I ask, throwing my keys and my backpack onto the kitchen table. I take my Barnes & Noble bag to the sofa and he sits up to make room for me.

"No, my imaginary girlfriend is in the shower."

"Why are you parked at the curb?"

He watches intently as I pull my new book out of the bag. "I forgot to park in the space and by the time I remembered I was already lying here in my boxers. I'll move it in the morning. What'd you get?"

"I don't know. I just picked a random book off the display table and bought it."

He laughs as he takes the book from my hand. "You're such a

dork." He holds up the book and reads the title aloud. "*The Fall*? Sounds literary."

"I guess I'll find out soon. I'm gonna go take a bath."

I reach for the book and he holds it above his head so it's out of my reach. "What are you talking about? You can't read it without me. That's not fair."

I can't stop the stupid grin spreading across my cheeks. "Fine. But I have to take a shower. I smell like the smoker dude who sat in front of me in the lecture hall today."

He narrows his eyes at me. "What were you *doing* with the smoker dude?"

"Oh, you know, the usual bj followed by lots of cuddling."

I stand up to go to the bathroom and Houston grabs my hand. "I'll cuddle with you, Scar."

"But will you give me a bj?"

He lets go of my hand and smacks my ass. "Go take a shower, dirty girl. I'll get the bed ready for your bj."

Houston

Five years ago, February 13th

WHENEVER RORY STARTS reading a new book, she always wants to read the story aloud to me. I think it's cute, but I've never cared for women's fiction or romance, which is what she mostly reads. A month ago, after shooting down her fourth request to read to me, I told her I'd only listen if she took off all her clothes while she read. I thought she'd get a little pissed, then resume her book without me. I didn't expect her to say yes.

I've acquired a new appreciation for women's fiction and romance ever since then. Especially the love scenes. No matter what the circumstances are in the novel, I always imagine the characters are us. The difficult part is trying to keep my hands off Rory's creamy skin.

She comes into the bedroom with a towel wrapped around her body and another wrapped around her head. She heads for the dresser to get some clothes, but pajamas go against everything I have planned for her tonight. I leap out of bed and slide between her and the dresser.

"I'll go turn up the heater. No clothes is part of the deal."

She shakes her head as I set off into the hallway to turn up the heat. When I come back, she's gone. I peek into the bathroom and she's standing naked in front of the sink, brushing her hair. I enter behind her and take the brush from her hand. Her reflection smiles at mine and I continue brushing. I grab her towel off the rack to squeeze more water out of her hair, then I finish by blow-drying it.

Rory loves when I do girl stuff with her. I try not to imagine that this is because my sister isn't around to do this kind of stuff with her anymore, but it's hard not to. What's worse is that I actually enjoying blow-drying her hair and painting her nails because I know how happy it makes her. As long as she keeps her promise never to tell anyone I do these things, I'll probably be doing it for the rest of our lives.

I hang the blow-dryer on the rack she asked me to install in the bathroom last week for her hair tools. She turns around to face me and I just want to lift her up and slide my cock inside her right there, but I have to be patient tonight. Tonight is about the long game.

I grab her neck gently, placing my thumb over her pulse, then I kiss her tenderly until I can feel her heartbeat racing. Pulling away slowly, I place a soft kiss on her cheekbone before I take her hand and lead her into the bedroom. The book she bought today is lying on her side of the bed. I hold the covers up for her to get in, then I take off my boxers before sliding in next to her.

"Is this historical fiction?" I ask, as she settles in under the covers.

"I think it's—"

"Wait. Don't tell me. I want to try to figure it out."

"Of course. You like to be surprised." She drags out the "i" in "surprised" to mock me.

I reach over and gently grab her breast and she gasps because my hands are a little cold. "See? You like being surprised too."

She lightly smacks my hand. "All right. You've made your point. Can I have my breast back?"

"But it's so warm. Can I hold on a little longer? I promise I'll still listen."

She rolls her eyes as she begins reading the first page. "In the light of my grandmother's torchère, the one with the fringed lampshade, I wrote my first letter to my dead husband." She stops and slowly closes the book. "Maybe I should read something else."

"Why?"

She turns to me with tears glistening in the corners of her eyes. "I don't want to read this."

I let go of her breast and take the book from her hands. I lay it on my nightstand and by the time I turn back to her, she's composed herself. My hand slides under the sheet, quickly finding her soft abdomen. I brush the backs of my fingers over her skin as I slide my hand to her waist.

Burying my face in her neck, I whisper against her skin. "You want to tell me another story?"

She arches her back a little, pressing her chest to mine. "What kind of story?"

I slide my knee between her thighs as she coils her arms around my shoulders. "Your story."

She moans softly as I lightly dig my teeth into her neck. "My story is boring."

I suck on her neck and she wraps her legs around my hips. "Then tell me our story. Tell me how long you've wanted me." I slide my hand behind her knee and lift her leg so my erection is pressed against her throbbing pussy, but I don't enter her. "Then tell me how our story ends."

She squeezes her thighs together to tighten them around my hips and I gasp as my cock slides about an inch inside her. She grabs my face so she can look at me as I sink in slowly. Her eyelids flutter with ecstasy until I hit her cervix and she lets out a tiny gasp.

"Talk to me," I whisper as I move slowly in and out of her.

She smiles as she gently rakes her fingernails down my back, then back up to my shoulders, sending shivers through me and making my cock twitch. "The first time I saw you… you were on your skateboard."

I let out a soft chuckle, but she continues undaunted, as do I.

"You had your hat on backwards and… I think you were fourteen and you were already almost six feet tall. It was August and you were all sweaty."

I lift her left leg a bit higher so I can dig deeper. "You like it when I'm all sweaty?"

"Yes," she moans. "Yes… but I didn't realize I was in love with you until I was fifteen."

"Four… years… later?" I time my words with my thrusts and this makes her smile. "Why… so… long?"

She lets out a long sigh as I reach between her legs and massage her clit. "Because that's when I started touching myself."

"And you'd think of me?"

Her pussy clenches around my erection as I move my finger in slow circles around her swollen bud. She closes her eyes and tosses her head backward, exposing the graceful arch of her neck. The sensation of her muscles spasming around my dick is getting me too excited, so I pull out of her and her eyes flash open.

"Keep talking, baby," I urge her as I lay a hot trail of kisses down her neck all the way to her breasts.

She whimpers as I take her nipple into my mouth and suck gently. "That was when you went away to college… I thought of you all the time and… I think I was touching myself at least once a day."

I tease her nipple with my tongue, smiling when she writhes a bit. "Is it wrong I find it hot you were fantasizing about me at that age?"

"Well, technically, you were eighteen and I was fifteen… so you would have been taking advantage of me if we actually did all the things I imagined we were doing."

My cock becomes painfully engorged at this comment. "Well, you're eighteen now, so tell me… what did you imagine us doing?"

I slide down and lay a soft kiss on her abdomen, then my head is between her legs. One of my favorite things about Rory is that she lets me shave her in the shower. Probably because she knows I'll make her come when I'm done. But nonetheless, it's one of my favorite parts of showering with her.

She draws in a sharp breath as I use my fingers to part her swollen lips, then I take her perfect clit into my mouth. "Oh, God, Houston."

"Keep talking or I'm gonna stop."

She laughs, but she quickly resumes her story. "This. This is what I used to imagine. And… I was a virgin, but I used to imagine you being my first."

"I *was* your first," I mutter, then I go back to licking her.

She threads her fingers through my hair, holding on for dear life as her legs begin to quiver. "I know… and it was *way* better than I imagined it would be."

I softly lick her up and down right at the one o'clock position on her clit and, as usual, she comes within seconds. I continue stimulating her, relishing the sound of her moans, until she grabs chunks of my hair and pulls me up.

I mash my lips to hers as I slide into her. I try to move slowly, but she grinds her hips into me, urging me on.

I pull back so I can look her in the eye. "Slow down, baby. The story's not over yet."

She smiles and pulls my mouth to hers again. Her kiss is hot and hungry, making it difficult for me to slow my pace, but I'm determined to make this last. I lift her leg again so she can watch my cock dipping in and out of her as I pierce her slowly and methodically.

Finally, she continues. "You know what comes after our first time together… What else do you want me to say?"

I pull out of her as my arms begin to shake. "Holy fuck. I'm getting so close to blowing my load. Give me a second."

"Holy fuck. I'm getting so close to blowing my load. Give me a second," she says, repeating my words back to me as if this is what I wanted her to say.

I laugh at her attempt to inject humor into the situation, but it's not helping as my dick keeps twitching with an impending orgasm. "Don't move," I whisper, then I take a deep breath as I wait for the sensation to pass.

"Okay, I'll just keep talking. You wanted to know how our story ends?"

I look up at her and she smiles as I very slowly ease my cock back inside her. "How does it end?"

She gazes into my eyes for a moment before she responds. "It doesn't have to end, does it?"

Unable to hold back any longer, I press my lips together to keep from grunting as I come inside her. Then I think of how our relationship began and how I've always known that it's going to end.

I lay a soft kiss on the corner of her lips. "I hope it never ends."

Rory

Five years ago, February 14th

HOUSTON IS GONE by the time I wake up Saturday morning. Our first Valentine's Day together. Or *not* together, I guess. I forgot about Valentine's Day while I was with Houston last night. I don't know if that's a testament to how much I love him or how good he is at making me forget that anything and anyone else exists.

I consider lying in bed and wallowing for the rest of the day, but I know I'll start thinking about Hallie and I'll be a crying mess before long. I should go back to Barnes & Noble and find a more uplifting book, but uplifting is not exactly better. I finally decide to just get up and go for a run.

By the time I have my running shoes and yellow fleece jacket on, Houston bursts through the front door soaked from head to toe and shivering.

"What happened to you?" I ask as I rush over to help him out of his UO hoodie. The rainwater soaking his clothes is so frigid, the cold penetrates through my fleece jacket. "You have to get out of those clothes. You're freezing. What were you doing out there?"

He pushes my hands away to stop me from removing his hoodie. "Stop, stop. You need to come outside."

"Are you crazy? You need to change your clothes."

He smiles. "We can do that later. Right now, you need to come outside with me. But grab an umbrella."

I shake my head as I grab an umbrella out of the stand next to the door. "You're acting weird."

He leads me through the courtyard and out to the parking lot. The freezing rain batters the top of my umbrella, but Houston doesn't bother trying to take shelter with me. He doesn't even flinch as the rain batters his hulking shoulders, as if he's a god impervious to the elements.

Where Houston's truck should be parked under the carport, I spot another car, a brand-new silver Prius tied with a soggy red bow. That's why he was parked on the street last night?

"What the fuck is that?"

He laughs as he pulls me toward the car. "It's yours. The ribbon got a little wet while I was tying it. Do you know how hard it is to tie a ribbon on a car in the middle of a rainstorm?"

"The *ribbon* got wet?" I reply, looking him up and down. "You're insane."

"I'm in love. It kinda goes with the territory. Happy Valentine's Day."

In love? Houston has never told me he loves me. This is the first time he's hinted at it. Well, I guess buying me a car is also a pretty huge hint. I want to scream *I love you!* loud enough for it to echo in a neighboring galaxy, but I'm speechless.

The hand holding my umbrella falls to my side and raindrops fall steadily on my cheeks. I drop the umbrella and stand on my tiptoes so I can throw my arms around his neck. He squats down and wraps his arms around the tops of my thighs, then he lifts me up so I'm about six inches taller than him.

I cradle his beautiful face in my hands and kiss him with such ferocity our teeth clack against each other. We both chuckle, then I slow down a little so I can savor the sensation of his warm tongue brushing against mine. The rain taps the back of my head, slithering through my hair, then down our faces. I turn my head to catch my breath and Houston sets me down gently.

"You're shaking. I'm taking you inside." He grabs my hand and sets off toward the courtyard, but I dig my heels into the asphalt.

"Wait! I didn't get you anything."

He turns back to me, confused. "Yes, you did. You told me a story."

"But… I'm sorry. I can't accept the car. I don't deserve it." My protests are slightly garbled by the staticky sound of rain pouring all around us.

"What are you talking about? Of course you do. And, no offense, but your car is a piece of shit. You need this car."

A green SUV pulls into the lot and Houston pulls me aside so we're under the carport.

I wipe the rain from my face and eyelashes. "But what happens if we break up? I can't afford to make a car payment with a part-time minimum-wage job. That's why you took me in. I'm poor."

"That's not why I took you in."

I flash him my best *don't-even-try-to-bullshit-me-right-now* expression.

He laughs. "Okay, fine. That *is* partially why I took you in, but the important thing is that we're not going to break up. The story never ends, remember?"

"Houston, that was a story. It's not real life. In real life, shit happens."

He lets out an impatient sigh. "Fine. If it makes you feel better, you can keep your old car in case we break up."

"But where are we gonna keep it? *Oh!* I can keep it in the garage at home. Can you follow me home in your truck—or better yet, follow me in the new car so I can show my parents?"

He's silent for a moment as he contemplates my request, then he smiles. "I can't. I promised Troy we'd go to the game tomorrow. But I'll buy you a train ticket for the ride back. Go visit your parents, on me."

I consider whining to get my way, because I really want my parents to see my new car. And I really, really want them to see me with Houston, to see how happy we are together. So they can see there is still one bright spark of hope in my life. But he did just buy me a car. I can't be too demanding right now.

I reach for him and he leans down so I can wrap my arms around his solid neck. "Thank you, from the bottom of my heart, for taking me in. And for giving me a fucking car."

He laughs as he tilts his head back so he can kiss the tip of my nose.

"But most of all," I continue, "thanks for being my friend. I… I…"

He squeezes me harder, and for the first time since we left the apartment I feel warm. "I love you more," he whispers in my ear. "But all I ask in return for this car is that you let me tie you up tonight."

"I knew there was a catch." I grin stupidly as the words *I love you more* repeat inside my mind like a beautifully broken record.

He slides his hand underneath my jacket and I flinch a little when his icy fingers whisper over the small of my back. "There's always a catch."

Part 2: Anger

"We're all searching for
someone whose demons
play well with ours."
-Anonymous

Houston

Six years ago, December 24th

CHRISTMAS EVE IS usually the day I'm reminded of how my father's affair tore our family to shreds. Hallie and I normally spend the day commiserating over our mutual dislike of our stepmother, Ilsa, while also expressing how glad we are that we'll never have to spend another Christmas with her family again—not after the scene Hallie and I caused during our first post-divorce holiday dinner.

I grab a bottle of Hallie's favorite sparkling cranberry juice out of the fridge and head toward the dining room. As I make my way around the corner, I can already hear her voice, bubbly and sweet as the contents of the bottle in my hand, chatting with Rory and my mom. Rory must have just arrived. I consider going back to the kitchen to grab something for her to drink, but I don't really know what beverage she prefers with her Christmas dinner. This is the first time Rory will be spending Christmas Eve with us.

I'm not supposed to know that Rory has a crush on me, but it's kind of hard not to notice the way she quickly turns away whenever I look at her. Or the way it takes her a few seconds to compose herself whenever I answer the phone or the front door.

Also, last year, Hallie confessed that Rory has had a crush on me for a long time, though she won't tell me how long. I don't think Hallie meant to betray Rory's trust by telling me this. It's just really hard for Hallie and me to keep anything from each other. Considering Hallie told me about Rory's crush more than a year ago, it's possible she's over it by now, especially since it's been about sixteen months since I left McMinnville for UO.

I enter the dining room and stop in the middle of the archway when I see Rory bent over the table arranging the silverware. She's wearing a short-sleeved, curve-hugging sweater dress the color of fresh milk. The dress is cut just above her knees, exposing her fair skin, which looks just as soft and creamy. A fiery longing ignites my insides as I'm unable to tear my gaze from her perfect ass.

How have I never noticed that body?

"Uh… Houston, we have a problem?"

I turn sideways and find Hallie standing right at my left, her eyebrows raised. "What?" I shake my head to clear the image of Rory, then I hold up the bottle of cranberry juice. "What do you mean? This isn't what you wanted?"

My eyes flit back to Rory, but she's on the other side of the table helping my mom open a bottle of wine. Now I have a view of her from the front and it's even better, if that's possible. The dress clings to the swell of her breasts and the curve of her hips, accentuating her hourglass figure.

When did Rory grow up?

Suddenly, Hallie yanks me by the arm until we're outside of the dining room, out of Rory and Mom's line of sight. Her blue eyes bore into me, seeking answers. But I stare back at her, pretending not to know what she wants.

"What was that?" she demands.

"What?"

She tilts her head. "Don't play dumb with me, Huey."

I scrunch my nose at the sound of my mom's old nickname for me. Hallie only uses it when she wants to get something out of me. She knows I'll cave just so I don't have to hear it anymore.

"I was just looking. Don't worry. I know she's off limits."

She looks confused by this statement. "What do you mean, she's off limits? I don't care if you get with Rory. You know that."

"It's not that. She's off limits because she's seventeen."

I don't say it aloud, but it's pretty much the duty of every man over eighteen to know the age of consent in their state. In Oregon, the age of consent is eighteen. I'm twenty. Rory is seventeen. She's off limits.

"That's so lame," Hallie replies, rolling her eyes. "Rory would do backflips if you stuck your wiener in her. She wouldn't go to the cops."

I shake my head. "Yeah, I'm not having this conversation with you. Besides, if she did backflips when I stuck my dick in her, I'm pretty sure *I'd* be the one calling the cops."

She curls her lip at this reply. "Yeah, I don't need that kind of visual right before we eat."

"You started it."

She takes the bottle of sparkling juice from my hand and we both head into the dining room together. My mom is pulling her dark hair up into a ponytail as Rory pours her a glass of wine.

"Geez, what temperature is the thermostat set at. It's hotter than Satan's waiting room in here."

Hallie sets her juice on the table and takes a seat. "How do you know Satan's a doctor?"

My mom fans her face with one hand as she grabs her glass of red wine with the other. "Someone turn down the heater."

"It's just a hot flash, Mom," I say, trying not to look at Rory as I take the seat between her and Hallie at the round dining table.

"*Just* a hot flash? Well, now it'll be *just* a little cold. You can put on your Christmas sweater."

I try not to laugh as I get up from the table to adjust the thermostat.

Hallie holds her hand out to stop me. "I'll turn it down. I have to show Rory something in my room really quick, anyway." She looks at Rory and nods toward the corridor, but Rory looks confused. "Come on."

Rory shrugs and flashes my mom an adorable smile as she gets up from the table. I don't bother trying not to look at her as she walks away. It's just my mom in here now, and she's too busy holding the cold bottle of juice against her cheek to notice.

When Hallie and Rory return a few minutes later, I search their faces for any sign that Hallie may have told Rory about how she caught me ogling her. But Rory appears as uncomfortable around me as she always does, looking everywhere but at me as she smooths her dress and takes a seat in her chair. I find myself wondering what kind of bra and panties she has on underneath that dress. Or if she's wearing any at all. Just the thought of that makes my cock twitch.

I need to get this under control. Too bad I'm not twenty-one, or I'd be pouring myself a glass of red wine to dull these unexpected urges. Though I'm pretty sure my mom knows I drink, I know she won't condone it in her house. Besides, getting a drink or two in me might actually backfire.

We each take turns passing around the mashed potatoes, string beans, maple-glazed carrots, and the tray piled high with sliced turkey smothered in gravy, until our plates are overflowing with food. Every time Rory passes me a dish, I look her in the eye to keep from staring at the way her dark red hair falls softly over her cleavage. As we eat, I find myself stealing glances at her, watching the fork as it disappears inside her mouth, her lips wrapped tightly around the steel before it comes out clean again.

Hallie clears her throat. "Ahem. So Houston, how's that new business coming along?"

I narrow my eyes at Hallie. She knows Mom doesn't know about my little side business. I don't know what she's getting at by bringing this up now.

My mom looks up from her plate. "What is she talking about, Hugh? I haven't heard anything about this."

Hallie smiles. "Oh, it's nothing. Troy and Houston are brewing non-alcoholic beer."

I look at her like she's crazy, but she just smiles and continues.

"Yeah, they named their company Barley Legal. Isn't that cute? *Barley* Legal." She looks very pleased with herself as Rory covers her mouth to keep from laughing. "Get it? Because it's non-alcoholic beer, so it's legal for him to make it and to drink it. Pretty cool, huh? I think Houston's going places with that one."

I shake my head at her. "You're insane, but I still love you."

"Ew, Mom. He loves me. Tell him to stop."

My mom rolls her eyes. "Oh, you two, that's enough. Finish your food so we can open presents. I'm sure Rory's dying to get back to her normal family."

"That's not true," Hallie replies as she stabs her fork into a string bean. "Rory loves our crazy family. Don't you, Rory?"

Rory glances at me then goes back to staring at her plate of food. "Yes, I do. Almost as much as I love… Um…"

"Don't hurt yourself," Hallie says with a wink of her eye. "The word you're looking for is turkey. You love us almost as much as you love turkey. Right?"

Rory nods as she presses her full lips together, trying not to smile. She's wearing red lipstick today, which accentuates her fiery auburn hair. Everything about her looks different. I don't think she normally wears enough makeup for anyone to notice. I normally prefer the girls I date to look naturally beautiful, but if

Rory hadn't worn that red lipstick and that white dress today, I may never have noticed her.

What the fuck am I am thinking? I can't date Rory.

I shake my head as I mentally cross her name off my to-do list.

When we're done eating, Rory offers to do the dishes, the way she always does when she has dinner at our house. But this time, I offer to help her instead of sitting back and letting Hallie do it. My sister cocks an eyebrow at me as she and Mom walk out of the kitchen to start sorting the presents in the living room.

When I turn around, Rory is already washing the large roasting pan my mom used for the turkey. I place my hand gently on her arm and she flinches. Her gaze is fixed on the sudsy water in the pan as she waits for me to say something.

"I'm sorry. I didn't mean to startle you," I say, gently taking the pan out of her hands. "I'll wash, you dry. I don't want—I mean—you don't want to get your dress dirty."

She smiles as she rinses the soap off her hands, then she steps aside and grabs a clean dish towel out of a drawer. We spend the next five minutes in relative silence. I pretend to care whether every bit of grease comes off every dish, drawing out the moment until I can work up the nerve to say something to her. She alternates between crossing her arms, biting her lip, and staring at the floor. Finally, I get an idea.

I finish rinsing my mom's wine glass, but when I reach out to give it to her, I pretend to accidentally drop it. "Shit!"

"Oh, no!" Rory says, immediately squatting down to clean it up, giving me a spectacular view of her ass.

It takes me a moment to tear my gaze away from her body, then I kneel next to her, reaching for her towel. "I'll clean it up. It was my mistake."

She stares at my hand on hers and seems unable to speak. I gently ease the towel out of her grip and she finally looks up at me. I flash her a warm smile and she looks confused. It takes a moment, but she seems to get her bearings and quickly stands up, leaving a soft cloud of vanilla-scented air in her wake. I sigh as I breathe in the fragrance while cleaning up the glass.

"You can go ahead," I say, as I carry the jagged shards to the trash bin. "I'll finish up in here."

I'm drying the last few pieces of silverware when Hallie comes into the kitchen. She crosses her arms and tilts her head, waiting for me to say something.

"What?"

"That's how it starts," she says. "First, you try looking for ways to be around them. Even doing shitty stuff like washing the dishes seems fun if it means you get to spend one moment with them."

I place the forks in the utensil drawer and cock an eyebrow. "Are you speaking from experience? I don't seem to remember you bringing any guys around here."

"What makes you think I'd bring a guy I like around you?"

I slide the drawer shut and lean back against the counter. "It's not what you think it is. She just… She looks different today."

"Yep, that's how it started for me, too. You have to tell her, Houston. Don't be a pussy."

I laugh as I shake my head. "No fuckin' way. She's not old enough. If I still feel the same when she's eighteen, I'll think about it."

A dull sadness washes over her features. "Fine."

She turns around and heads back to the living room. I wait a moment before I follow after her. When I enter the room, I find Rory sitting on the sofa with a pile of presents at her feet. Hallie hands her the gifts one at a time and Rory shakes each box to try to guess what's inside before she places it on the cushion next to her.

Hallie holds up a long, thin box and reads the gift tag. "From

Hallie to Rory," she says, handing Rory the box. "You don't have to bother shaking that one. It's your new battery-operated boyfriend."

My mom's jaw drops. "Hallie, you didn't."

"Oh, yes I did, Mom. And I got you one, too."

Rory and I burst into hysterics. She whips her head around at the sound of my laughter and quickly tries to hide the long box behind the other presents on the sofa.

"Oh, my God," she mutters, covering her face with her hands.

I try to keep from laughing even more at her embarrassment as I make my way toward the sofa. Sitting down on the opposite end so Rory's presents form a barrier between us, I hold out my hand for Hallie to give me my first gift.

"To Houston from Hallie," she says proudly.

I take the shirt-sized box wrapped in green paper from her hand, and sure enough I can feel the soft weight of some type of clothing sliding around inside. "Is this the butt-plug I asked for?"

She shakes her head. "Can't sneak anything past you."

I wink at Rory as I set the box down next to her vibrator. "She knows me so well."

My mom sighs as she yanks the hair-tie out of her hair and plops down onto the recliner on the other side of the Christmas tree. "How did I raise such twisted children? Where did I go wrong?"

Hallie pats my mom's knee. "Don't worry, Mom. It's the kids that are too afraid to have the butt-plug conversation with their parents who end up in trouble."

"That's very reassuring," my mom replies.

Once Hallie has sorted the presents by recipient, we all open our gifts at the same time. This is the tradition in our home ever since Mom and Dad divorced. My mom felt the need to change all the traditions that reminded her too much of my father, which is also why we celebrate Christmas on Christmas Eve now instead of Christmas Day.

Hallie helps Rory stuff her five gifts into a couple of grocery tote bags so she can carry them back to the house. But she leaves the unopened vibrator box behind. Hallie joins me in the living room to clean up the boxes and wrapping paper while my mom puts a couple of logs in the fireplace.

I grab a couple of Rory's discarded boxes and stuff them into the large trash bag Hallie's carrying. "That wasn't so bad."

"Speak for yourself. You really confused Rory."

"What's wrong with Rory?" my mom asks as she grabs the lighter off the mantle.

My stomach clenches at the thought that I may have made Rory uncomfortable or confused. "I guess I should just back off."

"Or you could, you know, follow through and ask her if she has any plans for New Year's Eve."

I take the trash bag from Hallie. "No, I'll just wait it out. These things pass."

She sighs as she stares at my mom with a far-off look in her eyes. "Like I said, speak for yourself."

"What does that mean?"

She shakes her head and grabs another piece of torn wrapping paper off the carpet. "It's not that easy. True love doesn't disappear with time."

"Are you saying Rory is in love with me?" My heart races at this thought, but I can't decide if I'm more excited or scared.

"I don't know. Just forget it. It's probably best if you two don't hook up. I don't want you getting between me and Rory."

"Are you trying to set your brother up with Rory?" my mom calls over her shoulder as she pokes the small fire in the grate. "That's a dangerous situation, Hallie. You have to be prepared to accept the consequences if it doesn't work out."

Hallie sinks down onto the sofa cushion. "I just want

everyone to be happy. Love makes people happy."

My mom shakes her head. "Love can also make you crazy and miserable. Don't forget that."

Hallie sighs as I take a seat next to her, then she rests her head on my shoulder. "And I'll bet it's totally worth it."

Houston

August 24th

I GET UP an hour earlier so I can get out of the apartment before Tessa wakes. I grab a light rain jacket. It's one of those rare August days in Portland where the rain clouds roll in and attempt to dampen everyone's summer plans. Not that anyone in Portland can be deterred by a smattering of rain. I'm almost out the front door when Tessa stumbles out of the bedroom, squinting at me through the gray morning light.

"Why are you leaving so early?"

I'm tempted to tell her that it's none of her business. That she lost the privilege to question me when she betrayed me by getting pregnant behind my back. That she never really earned the privilege to question me because our whole relationship has been teetering on a knife-edge waiting for something exactly like this to happen.

Picturing the two of us careening off the edge reminds me of a quote I read in college: *This is the way we fall. First we lose our balance, teetering precariously on the edge of uncertainty, until, mercilessly, gravity takes over. You can't outshine gravity.* Tessa and I are about to topple over and she's either too stubborn to admit it or too delusional to see it.

"I'm heading to work early."

"But, we didn't get to talk about…"

"About what? If you're truly pregnant, you need to get an abortion."

"Abortion?" she shrieks, her face contorted with disbelief. "I'm not getting an *abortion.* How can you even *suggest* that?"

I step back inside the apartment and push the door closed. "How can I suggest that? What else do you propose we do? Raise a child in a home built on lies? Is that what you want for your child?"

"*Our* child. And it's not a lie if I told you the truth. I didn't hide the pregnancy from you."

"No, you just lied about being on birth control. So where are the test results? How do I know you're really pregnant? Am I supposed to take your word for it? Because right now your word holds zero value with me."

"Why do you hate me? Is it because I'm not *her*?"

"I don't even know what you're talking about," I reply, in no mood to listen to more accusations of adultery.

I cheated on her one time before we were engaged and I'll never live it down. I wish Tessa knew how fucking badly I want to cheat on her with Rory right now and how her accusations only serve to chip away at my loyalty even further.

Loyalty. You'd think I'd know the meaning of the word since I have it tattooed across my chest. But it seems the older I get, the line between loyalty and treachery becomes thinner and blurrier.

Marriage is not simple. I knew that going into it. But there are all types of betrayal in a marriage, and most of them don't involve adultery.

I turn to leave and she rushes to my side.

Latching on to my arm, her face is wrought with fear. "Wait. I'm sorry. I didn't mean that. Don't go. Please. We can talk about this."

My stomach vaults at her desperation. "I have to go to work." I try to wrench my arm out of her grasp, but she tightens her grip. "Let go, Tessa."

She shakes her head. "No. Come to bed." She reaches for my face and I flinch.

"Stop it."

Her hand slides down and I look her straight in the eye as she curls her fingers around the bulge in my jeans.

"Don't do this, Tessa. Let it go."

She moves her hand up and down, stroking me through my pants. "Fuck me, Houston."

I grit my teeth and will myself not to get an erection. How is it that my wife's touch makes me feel as if I'm cheating on Rory?

I look her in the eye as I push her away. "I'd rather fuck my hand."

Her eyes widen in utter disbelief. "I'm leaving." She storms away toward the bedroom. "I'm going to my mother's. At least she'll miss me when I'm gone."

I want to roll my eyes and call her bluff, but I can't. I knew a guy named Greg in high school, a friend of a friend, who used to threaten to commit suicide whenever his girlfriend, Alisha, was on the brink of dumping him. It worked for about three years, until Alisha finally called Greg's bluff. He ended up in the hospital that night after taking thirty Tylenol. Any asshole with half a brain knows thirty Tylenol won't do anything to a healthy person, except maybe make you vomit or possibly pass out. Alisha didn't visit Greg in the hospital and he got himself a new girlfriend a few months later. If Greg was the only example of attempted suicide following a breakup I've ever come across in all my twenty-seven years, I would totally call Tessa's bluff.

I follow her into the bedroom and find she has two magenta suitcases open on the bed. Her clothes fly haphazardly out of her dresser drawers and somehow most of them find their way inside her luggage.

"Tessa." I call her name from where I stand in the safety of the doorway. "Tessa, look at me."

"Why?" she wails, her voice thick with tears. "You've been trying to get rid of me since before we even got married. This is what you wanted, isn't it?"

"What are you talking about? I never tried to get rid of you."

She rounds on me, clutching a bundle of panties to her chest. "You never loved me, did you? All that stuff about *my pain is your pain* and all that other crap was just bullshit. Wasn't it? You don't give a damn about me or what I've gone through." She lifts her left arm to show me the scars on the inside of her forearm. "You don't care how I got these. You've never even asked. You probably even think I'm bluffing when I say I'll kill myself."

"Don't say that. Just… don't even say it."

"Why? You don't want to be responsible for another suicide?"

Her words spark a jolt of violent rage within me. "Shut up! Shut your *fucking* mouth! You don't know what the fuck you're talking about."

She's stunned for a moment, then her lips begin to tremble. "I'm sorry." She whispers this a few more times as she sinks down to the floor. "Please don't make me go."

I take a few steps closer and find her sitting on the carpet near the foot of the bed. "Make you go where? You're the one who said you were leaving."

"I don't want to leave." She looks up, her blonde hair sticking out in all directions as her eyes plead with me. "I'll get an abortion. I'll see a therapist. I'll do anything. Just please don't leave me." She sobs as she grasps chunks of her hair. "I don't… I don't… I don't know who I am without you."

I stare at her for a moment, trying to hold on to the anger and disgust I felt a moment ago, but I can't. I sink down next to her and take her into my arms, where she sobs heavily for a while. And as I stroke her hair and wait for her to finish, I wonder how long Rory will wait to find out what's inside that box.

Rory

August 24th

I TAKE MY time walking to my new workplace on Burnside, turning a seven-minute walk into a ten-minute leisurely stroll. The contents of the Sierra Nevada tin box are clinking around inside my backpack. It sounds like a ring, but I refuse to peek inside. If Houston would rather present it to me himself, he must have a good reason. And I'm pretty certain he knows I have no desire to be his mistress. Maybe whatever's in the box is a sign that he's leaving his wife.

Is that what I want? Do I want to be responsible for breaking up a marriage? Would it be fair to call me a home-wrecker if I haven't actually had an affair with Houston and *he* was the one who pursued me?

I don't know the answers to any of these questions. All I know is that I do miss Houston. He was my first love, my default best friend after Hallie died, my protector and provider, and, for a split second, the father of my unborn child. Of course I miss him and everything we had. That doesn't mean that we belong together.

I enter the Zucker's on Burnside through the front and my gaze lands on the plastic sheeting on my right. Behind the semi-transparent veil, people are moving inside the coffee bar. A signpost standing in front of the plastic shroud reads: Excuse our dust. New Zucker's Café & Wine Bar coming soon!

I look left and spot a door behind the customer service counter, which must lead to an office. Jamie told me to ask for the store's general manager, Benji. A blonde cashier spots my green Zucker's T-shirt as she's bagging some produce for a customer. She flashes me a warm smile and I return it.

"Is that Benji's office?" I ask her, pointing at the door behind the customer service counter.

She nods. "Yep. He's in there right now."

"Thanks."

I slip behind the counter and knock on the door. A few seconds pass before a guy's face appears behind the small window set into the door at eye level. I can't see him very well through the wire mesh between the window panes, but he looks pretty young to be a general manager.

The door opens inward and Benji smiles at me. "Are you Aurora?"

"Yeah, but everyone calls me Rory."

He motions to a chair. "Well, have a seat, Rory, and I'll get you up to speed. I'm Benji Zucker, by the way."

I try to focus as Benji explains the job to me, but all I can think is that Grandpa Zucker must really trust his young grandkids to give them such powerful positions in the company. Benji is very friendly, which makes me think he was born, or bred, to do this kind of job. He doesn't patronize me when he explains the magnitude of my new responsibilities. He turns his computer screen toward me so he can give me a tutorial on the new inventory system they implemented a few weeks ago. When he explains the tasks associated with vendor management, my eyes glaze over as I imagine trying to "manage" a relationship with Houston's company.

"Rory?"

I blink a few times and smile. "Yes. Sorry, I got a little distracted. I was just thinking about the vendor management stuff. Does that entail meeting with vendors *in person* or would it just be phone meetings?"

He looks confused by my question. "Do you have an issue meeting with vendors?"

"No, no. I'm just, as you can tell, a bit awkward in person. I'm much better on the phone. But I have no problem meeting with vendors in person. I was just curious." The skeptical look on his face tells me he's not buying it. "I swear, I'm fine. I promise I'll do a good job. You have nothing to worry about."

He nods as he dials a number on his desk phone. I have a weird fantasy that he's calling security to have me hauled out of here. This makes me grin and he smiles back at me.

"Bella, can you come get Rory from my office? She's ready for you." He sets the phone down on the cradle and smiles as he turns his computer monitor around so I can't see the screen anymore. "Bella is the manager of the wine bar, but she's four months pregnant. You're going to have to pay close attention to what she does so you can take over when she goes on leave in five months. Do you think you can handle that?"

"Absolutely."

He nods as he types something, then he pushes his keyboard aside and looks me in the eye. "I heard you're a writer."

This catches me off-guard. I've only mentioned my writing to Jamie once. I don't know what that has to do with anything.

"Uh… I write sometimes. Not sure I'd call that being a *writer.*"

"But you know how to write? Like, you know the basic rules

of grammar and stuff, right?"

I chuckle. "Yeah, I hope so. I have a bachelor's in English."

"Cool. I might have a project for you that involves writing."

"A work project?"

He flashes me a sheepish grin. "It's a personal project. I... need help writing my wedding vows and Jamie recommended you. Is that okay? Obviously, you don't need to do it if you're not comfortable with it."

"Yeah, totally. Anything I can do to help."

"Cool. I'm getting married in three weeks and I'm shitting bricks over these vows."

I open my mouth to reply, but I'm interrupted by a knock at the door. I stand quickly and begin smoothing down my T-shirt as if we've been caught doing something naughty. Bella is a tall, doe-eyed brunette with ample breasts and a small baby bump. Her perfectly understated makeup makes me feel a bit self-conscious about my lack of makeup. If a pregnant woman can take the time to look that good, I have no excuse not to.

Bella holds out her hand for me to shake. "I'm Bella." She pats her belly, then glances at Benji. "And this little guy in here is Benjamin Jr."

I turn to Benji and he's grinning from ear to ear. "Bella and I are getting married in three weeks."

I swallow hard as I realize I just agreed to write wedding vows for *both* of my bosses' weddings. *Great!*

BELLA AND I spend a couple of hours in the stockroom updating inventory for use with the new software. All the while dodging construction workers who scurry back and forth from the warehouse to the stockroom then to the bar area, installing supply cabinets, patching drywall, connecting the plumbing for three different sinks. I make it through the first couple of hours of inventory management with ease. Then Bella informs me we have a city building inspector coming in at two p.m. to inspect the coolers in the basement where the draft beer will be stored. And a beer vendor is coming in to oversee the inspection. We work in silence a bit longer, scanning boxes of coffee syrup, tea, and coffee stirrers into the computer system, but my curiosity soon gets the best of me.

"So, this guy who's coming to oversee the inspection… what company is he with?"

Bella chuckles, but she doesn't look away from the box she's scanning. "It's called Barley Legal. I think it's a cute name. And the guy's über hot, too. Maybe you could, you know?" She sticks out her chest and jiggles her boobs a little. "Unless you're not single, then disregard my advice."

Heat rises into my cheeks, but I can't tell if I'm blushing because she's complimenting my ex-boyfriend or if I'm flushing with jealousy because she called him über hot. Either way, I need to figure out how I'm going to approach the situation when Houston gets here. Do I let him go about his business and pretend I don't know him? Do I opt for honesty and tell Bella he's my ex? Maybe the honest approach will help me get closer to Bella and get to know her better. Then I'll be better equipped to help Benji write his vows.

Of course, getting in good with the boss is positive for my working environment, but how long do I actually plan to work here? The plan is to eventually make my living as a writer, isn't it? That was the point of changing my major after Houston and I broke up, wasn't it?

I shake my head as I scan a case of cinnamon syrup. Maybe I just want to stick my flag in Houston, claim him as mine again, if only in the past tense. That's so pathetic.

On cue, my phone buzzes in my pocket and I quickly retrieve it, heart pounding as I imagine it's Houston with his promise to show me the contents of the box when he comes in. But it's not Houston. It's Liam, with a text that makes me laugh so loud Bella drops her scanner gun.

> **Liam:** *In the most boring meeting of my life and thinking, this would be less boring if* Rory *and her ex-boyfriend were here.*

Bella picks up the scanner gun and stares at me. "Well? What's the joke?"

I shake my head. "It's totally lame. Sort of an inside joke."

"I wouldn't get it?"

"Ugh. I hate when people say that, but it's actually true. Here, you can read it."

I hold my phone out with the screen pointed at her.

"So this guy, Liam," she begins, not looking particularly impressed, "I take it the last time you two hooked up, your ex-boyfriend showed up and decked him, or you had a threesome. Which is it?"

I laugh as I stare at the text. "No violence or sex involved, but everything else is correct."

She moves toward the door leading out to the warehouse. "No violence or sex? That must be a *really* boring meeting he's in."

I follow her into the warehouse and she takes me down to the basement, where the walk-in cooler was installed yesterday. She introduces me to a few stock boys along the way, waggling her eyebrows when one of the better-looking ones glances repeatedly at my boobs. Finally, we make it down to the cooler, which is installed below the wine bar. A notice on the steel door has the name of the company and the man who installed the cooler, the company phone number, and the date of the installation.

"Wait right here so you can greet the inspector when he comes down. That way I can stay up there in case any of those guys need anything."

"But I don't know anything about inspections or coolers."

"You don't have to. That's why the Barley Legal dude and the installer are coming at the same time. They'll talk to the inspector. You're here in case they need a manager to sign off on something."

I open my mouth to remind her that I'm not a manager, but I stop before I can make a fool of myself. "Got it. I'll just wait here."

Once Bella is gone, I pull my phone out of my pocket again to respond to Liam. It takes me seven excruciating minutes to come up with something remotely clever.

Me: *I hope your next visit is less traumatic.*

Liam: *Next visit? Are you hitting on me? Don't answer that. I accept. I'll be there at 8.*

I laugh as I tuck the phone back into my pocket. When I look up, I nearly jump out of my skin at the sight of Troy Bingham, Houston's best friend through high school and college. They must run Barley Legal together. Is this the über hot guy Bella was referring to?

His blue eyes are bright with excitement. "Rory? Are you shitting me? Holy fuck. Look at you, girl."

He holds his arms out for me to give him a hug. I give him a quick pat-on-the-back type of hug, but he holds on a few seconds longer than expected. He lets go and looks me up and down a couple of times, shaking his head.

"Houston told me he ran into you, but I didn't really believe it. I mean, what are the fuckin' odds, you working here while we're setting this up?"

"Houston told you he ran into me?"

"Yeah, of course. He couldn't keep that to himself. You know how crazy he was about you."

My hands begin to shake, so I tuck them behind my back. "So… you're here for the inspection?"

"Oh, yeah. You probably thought Houston was coming. He was supposed to, but he had some kind of emergency at home. I think there's trouble in paradise, if you know what I mean."

Is Troy trying to convince me to have an affair with Houston?

"I don't really know," I reply, unable to disguise the tremor in my voice. "I don't know Houston anymore."

"What are you talking about? Houston's the same guy he always was, just richer."

"And married-er."

He shrugs as he chuckles. "If you can call it a marriage. Whatever. None of my business."

"Or mine."

"That's debatable."

"Excuse me?"

He waves off the comment. "Nothing. I was only kidding. So where's the inspector?"

I draw in a deep breath to calm my nerves. "I was told he would be here at the same time as you and the installer. I don't really know. This is my first day at this store."

"I guess we'll just wait, then." He smiles as he tucks his hands into his jeans pockets and leans back against the steel door. "Rory, can you do me a favor?"

"What kind of favor?"

"Can you not tell Houston what I said about his marriage? The thing is… He spoke to me about you in confidence and, to be totally fucking honest, I've never liked his wife. I guess I let my personal feelings about her get away from me. I shouldn't have said that stuff about his marriage being on the rocks. I don't know if that's true."

I'm silent for a moment as I try to remember what it was like not to want Houston. I wish I could call him right now and ask him if there's any truth to Troy's assertions. What kind of emergency at home kept him from coming here today? Did something happen to his wife? Did she find out about his visit to my apartment last night?

Or maybe Houston just didn't want to see me today.

"No worries," I say, leaning against the door. "Anyway, Houston's marriage is none of my business."

After a stiff, awkward silence, Troy turns to me and smiles. "But I wasn't lying when I said he was crazy about you… And if you ask me, he still is."

Rory

August 24th

AFTER MY FIRST day as the assistant manager of the former coffee bar slash soon-to-be wine-slash-coffee bar, Benji sends me off with a worn, folded sheet of paper containing his best intentions. I'm tempted to read his attempt at wedding vows on the walk home, but I'm afraid the light rain will ruin the thin, worn paper. The moment I walk inside my apartment, my mom greets me at the door with Skippy. The salacious grin on her face is a bit frightening.

I set my backpack containing Benji's vows and the Sierra Nevada box on the breakfast bar and crouch down to smooch Skippy. His tongue makes a loud clopping noise as he laps my face, his tail wagging so hard his whole butt shimmies from side to side. Holding my arms out for a hug, I smile when he lays his paws on my shoulders like a good pup. Then I squeeze him hard, burying my nose in his black fur as he whines and continues to lick my cheek and ear.

"I know, buddy. I missed you, too." I let him go and get to

my feet, trying to ignore the backpack as I make my way into the kitchen. "Did you check his blood glucose? And why are you so happy?"

My mom follows closely behind me. "Yes, I did, twenty minutes ago. He's fine for now. And I heard you had a man here last night. Actually, *two* men."

I roll my eyes as I imagine Mrs. Vernor from across the hall standing inside her door last night, listening to what was going on in the corridor. Then she took it upon herself to pass the juicy gossip onto my mom today.

"It was nothing. Just a couple of friends."

"Since when do you have boyfriends?"

"Not boyfriends. Just friends who happen to be guys."

I pour myself a glass of water from the tap and gulp it down, leaving the glass in the sink to use it later. As expected, my mom pushes me aside so she can wash it now. She hates the sight of dirty dishes in the sink.

"Don't play coy with me, Rory. And don't be so secretive. It's good to talk about your love life. It helps you work out problems you might not be able to work out on your own."

"Who says I'm having problems? And who says I have a love life?"

"Well, you're going to have to work pretty hard to maintain a love life if you bottle everything up."

For a moment, I consider telling my mom everything that happened last night with Houston and Liam. Then I remember how much she hated Houston after he broke my heart. She may have been a strict grammarian during her days as a schoolteacher, but she threw all the rules of language out the window when she spoke of him during that time. Of course, it probably had to do with the fact that she was so stressed over the divorce at the time. She was on a man-hating kick for a while there.

"Why are you so concerned with me getting a boyfriend? It's

been five years since you and dad divorced and you're still single."

"That's different. I'm old. I've done the whole marriage, career, family thing. I can take my time finding my next partner."

I shake my head as I head for the bedroom with Skippy and my mom trailing right behind. "That's such a load of crap, Mom. If anything, being old means you have *less* time to find your next partner. I'm the one who can take my time. I'm twenty-four. I have at least fifty or sixty good years left in me. You're fifty-one, Mom. You're the one who needs to get laid."

"Rory!" She grabs a pillow off my bed and throws it at me. "Watch your mouth."

I laugh as I grab a pair of clean skinny jeans and a T-shirt out of the closet then head for the bathroom. My mom watches me curiously, probably waiting for me to tell her why I'm taking a shower right after work instead of right before bed, the way I've done it all my life. Finally, I move to close the bathroom door and she stops it with her hand.

"Do you have a date tonight, young lady?"

I smile at her, knowing she's expecting me to deflect the question. "I may even get laid."

I close the door and shake my head when I hear my mom shout, "Yes!"

TWO HOURS LATER, my mom has left the building and Skippy is sitting at my feet under the dining table, watching me eat a bowl of homemade udon. The folded sheet of paper and Sierra Nevada box are sitting on top of the table in front of me. I clamp my chopsticks around some noodles and bring them to my mouth, slurping the rich broth as I try to decide which one to open first. I know I promised Houston I'd wait for him to open the box for me, but my curiosity is reaching epic levels the longer the box remains unopened. I sigh as I reach for the paper and unfold it, laying it on the table next to my bowl so I can read as I eat.

My dearest Bella,

The love of my life, and I know you didn't want me to mention this but the mother of my child.

I shake my head in dismay. He's going to infuriate his future wife with these vows. If she doesn't want him to mention the pregnancy or the baby, that means she wants to try to hide her baby bump, which is totally her prerogative. At least Benji recognizes he needs help.

I read the rest of the vows to myself, then I read them again aloud, just to see how they sound when spoken. It's even worse. Though Skippy does respond to my recitation by putting his paw on my thigh, so maybe Benji's on to something.

"You want to marry me, Skip?" I say, shaking his paw as he stares at me dumbly.

I finish my udon and clean up, then I plop down on the sofa with Benji's vows. My new best friend, the Sierra Nevada box, keeps watch from the coffee table. I'll attempt to rewrite Benji's vows while I wait for Liam to come over in an hour. The first thing I do is type up what Benji has already written into a notes app on my phone, then I begin thinking about what I would want my future husband to say to me when I get married.

Houston's face materializes in my mind and I suddenly have trouble breathing. I hold the phone to my chest as I think of him saying the words I've needed to hear for five years. *I was wrong to let you go, and I'd rather die than let it happen again.*

The vibration startles me. I pull the phone away from my chest and I can't believe what I'm seeing. I answer the call and slowly press it to my ear.

"Houston?"

"I'm sorry I couldn't make it to the store today."

The sound of his voice, smooth and sweet with a slight crackly finish, reminds me of toffee. And it makes my chest ache with longing.

"Is everything okay?" I ask, remembering my promise to Troy not to say anything about the things he shared with me today.

Houston is silent for a moment and I count each breath until he responds. "No, actually, everything's pretty messed up right now."

His honesty catches me off my guard. "What are you saying? Are you… Are you getting divorced?"

"I want to, but it's not that simple. I need to see you. Can I come over?"

I let out a deep sigh. "Houston, I can't be on this side of a list of excuses. If you want to be married, you should stay married and stop jerking me around."

"Rory, don't hang up. Listen to me. Just… please listen." He expels a large puff of air, and I brace myself for whatever he's about to say. "My wife is sick. Mentally, not physically. She's… threatening to kill herself if I leave her. And I know this has nothing to do with you, but you know me. You know… how much I loved Hallie."

Tears well up in my eyes the moment he says her name. "I know," I whisper. "But you can't save everyone, Houston."

I think of how he saved me from having to live in a dorm haunted by my best friend's memory. How he gave me a car to save me from having to drive my shitty Toyota, though I was very lucky I held onto that Toyota or I wouldn't have a car right now. Then, of course, I think of how he saved me from making the mistake of marrying him when he obviously wasn't ready. And how he tried to save Hallie when he found her.

"That's why I want to see you," he replies. "I think… I need you to save me this time."

I bite my lip to keep from turning into a complete sobbing mess. *This* is what I've needed to hear. Not that he was wrong, just that he needs me.

"Rory?"

"Yes?"

"Open your door." His words are followed by a knocking that sends my heart racing.

"Wait. I'll be right there."

I end the call and immediately open my text messaging app. My fingers tremble as I tap out a vaguely honest message to Liam, telling him something came up and I'll have to call him tomorrow. He doesn't respond right away, so I head for the front door. I take a deep breath and let it out as I pull it open.

Houston leans with one hand on my doorframe, a simmering cocktail of quiet desperation and raw sex appeal. His eyes are fixed on mine, communicating silently, but the message is loud and clear as his gaze falls on my lips.

I take a step back. He steps forward. I begin to stumble. His right arm catches me around the waist. His left hand pushes the door closed. The excitement pulsates between us as we stare into each other's eyes.

My gaze wanders over the sharp angles of his cheekbones and jaw. The perfect slope of his nose and the dark desire in his blue eyes. And, *oh*, that mouth. The mouth that spoke the words I couldn't forget. The tongue that taught me how to surrender every part of myself to him.

His fingers brush my cheek. "God, I've missed this," he whispers as he runs his fingers through my hair and tucks it behind my ear.

My arms slacken at my sides as I feel myself dissolving into him with each stroke of his fingers. "What are we doing,

Houston?"

He traces his thumb over the shell of my ear, then he gently squeezes my earlobe. My chest heaves as the throbbing between my legs intensifies. His other hand moves up to cup the other side of my face. Cradling my head in his massive hands, he holds my gaze as I grab his wrists to steady myself.

"Whatever you want to do."

He leans forward and I hold my breath. His lips hover over mine. My heart pounds a roaring beat in my ears. I tighten my grip on his wrists. I may collapse at any moment. Then, his mouth is on mine.

His lips are as soft as I remember. His breath hot on my mouth, so hot my insides are burning up. I want to part my lips and kiss him like we haven't seen each other in five years, but I'm afraid. I'm afraid I've never been more afraid.

"I can't," I whisper desperately.

"You can't what?"

"I can't… I can't believe what I'm about to do."

Houston

August 24th

I THREAD MY fingers through the soft hair at her nape. As I firmly clasp the back of her neck, her head tilts to the side and her lips part for me. The heat of her shallow breaths stir a primal longing inside me. Leaning in closer, I brush my lips over hers and lay a soft kiss on the corner of her mouth. Her lips are still slightly parted as she lets out a soft whimper, waiting for me. Just that small sound is all it takes. My erection grows until it pushes painfully against the zipper of my jeans.

Her willingness to give herself to me is hotter than she could possibly imagine. I kiss her luscious top lip and she exhales as I take it into my mouth and suck gently. Then I tilt my head slightly as my lips cover hers. Our mouths fit together like puzzle pieces, and we let out a collective sigh followed by a soft chuckle.

"I still love you," I murmur into her mouth. "You believe me, don't you?"

She tightens her grip on my forearms. "How could you forget me?"

I tilt my head back to look into her hazel eyes and my stomach twists when I see the tears collecting at the corners. "Forget you? I never forgot you."

"When you first saw me at the store, you didn't recognize me."

I hoped she would have forgotten that embarrassing moment. I consider lying to her and telling her I was only kidding. That I totally recognized her. But if I want any chance of keeping her, I know I have to be honest.

"I started going to a therapist after we broke up, and she treated me for PTSD."

"PTSD? Are you saying I gave you PTSD?"

I chuckle. "No."

"Then what does that have to do with forgetting me?"

She loosens her grip on my arms so I let go of her face and grab her hands.

"I asked her to help me forget what happened with Hallie and she started me on an experimental PTSD treatment that uses anesthesia and CBT to modify painful memories."

"CBT?"

"Cognitive behavioral therapy. They gave me low doses of xenon gas for a few months and I also had to change my behavior whenever something happened that reminded me of the day Hallie died."

"But…"

"Yeah, almost everything associated with you reminded me of Hallie."

She lets go of my arms. "You really forgot me?"

I feel physically sick at this question. Not because I resent the accusation. I resent myself for ever making her feel like I'd forgotten her. As much as I wanted to erase the mistakes I made with Rory and Hallie from my memory, it's impossible to erase the bad stuff without also erasing the good.

"No, you don't understand," I reply, taking both her hands in mine and looking her in the eye. "I went through the program, and it seemed to work for a while, but every day that passed, every visit to my mom's house, and every conversation about Hallie chipped away at what little progress I'd made. The effect wore off. And three years ago, I was pretty much at square one."

She looks up at me and the hurt in her eyes makes me sick with myself. "But you still forgot me because you didn't have any more reminders of me?"

"I could never forget you," I whisper, letting go of one of her hands so I can brush a piece of hair out of her face. "But I tried really hard to because I was in a world of pain after we broke up. And what happened the day we ran into each other two weeks ago was a split-second error. Bad programming. I can prove it to you. Where's the box I gave you?"

Rory

August 24th

THE MOMENT HE lets go of my hands, I'm struck by how cold I feel without his hands on me. Then I remember his question and I turn around to face the coffee table where the Sierra Nevada box sits. I move toward it and Houston follows me, reaching for the box before I can grab it.

"Sit down."

I take a seat on the sofa, but he doesn't follow suit. He stands next to the coffee table, staring at the box in his hands. I wish I knew what he was thinking, because all I can think of right now is the promise I made to him last night. If he shows me what's inside the box, I'm supposed to tell him what my book is about.

Finally, he tears his gaze from the box and tilts his head as he notices the sheet of paper sitting on the coffee table. He's six-foot-four. Can he really read the words scribbled on that worn piece of paper from all the way up there?

"What is that?"

I reach forward and swipe the paper off the table. "It's

nothing. It's just something I'm working on for my boss."

"Your boss asked you to help him write his wedding vows?"

Suddenly I feel guilty, as if I've somehow betrayed Houston. "Yes. He found out I have a degree in English and he was kind of desperate for some help. It's not a big deal."

He smiles as he looks down at me. "Can I see what you've written?"

"No!"

He laughs. "Why not?"

"Because I haven't had a chance to write much of anything yet, and it's embarrassing."

"Why is it embarrassing? It's just me." He sits next to me on the sofa and I get a strong whiff of his clean, masculine scent. "Let me see, then I'll open the box."

"I thought you wanted to know what my book is about."

"I want to see both."

His words echo in my mind and the guilt hits me hard. Houston wants both me and his wife. And I was about to let him have his way.

"You have to leave," I say, tucking the vows into my back pocket as I rise from the sofa.

He stands up with me. "Why? What did I do?"

"It's not what you did. It's—" I'm interrupted by the vibration in my front pocket. I slip my phone out and shake my head when I read the text message.

Liam: *Rory, if you're not ready to go out yet, just let me know. I'd rather keep you as a friend than risk one of us getting hurt.*

"Who's that?" Houston asks, glancing at the back of my phone.

"It's a really nice guy who's not married."

His chest is heaving and his jaw is clenched tightly as the anger percolates inside him. "Don't shut me out, Rory. Give me a chance."

"A chance to do what?"

He doesn't answer right away, so I begin typing a response to Liam. Houston grabs my phone and gently slips it out of my hands. He lays the phone facedown on the coffee table and smiles as he opens the Sierra Nevada box.

I gasp when I see the ring lying on its side. "What is that?"

He lifts my chin up so he can look me in the eye. "I bought this engagement ring for you two weeks before we broke up."

I clutch my chest as I try to keep breathing. "What? I don't understand. You… you said we couldn't get married. You… you broke my heart."

"It was the biggest mistake of my life. I could see it then and I can see it even more now. Letting you go was the single stupidest thing I've ever done." He plucks the ring out of the box and sets the box on the table next to my phone, then he holds the ring between his thumb and forefinger. "Rory, you're the only one who knows me, which is kind of sick because I spent so much of our time together lying to you."

I shake my head in disbelief. "What do you mean?"

He blinks back tears. "There's so many things you don't know about me that I need to tell you, so you'll understand everything that happened back then and afterward." He takes my hand and my entire body trembles, the way it did when I thought he was going to propose to me five years ago. But this time, he lays the ring in the palm of my hand and closes my fingers around it. "This is yours. It's my promise to you. I swear I'm going to do everything I can to get that ring on your finger."

I squeeze my fist around the ring, savoring the sharp prick of the diamond as it digs into my skin. "Houston, I'd rather have the truth than this ring."

"That ring is my promise to tell you the truth, but only when the time is right. I need to get out of my marriage first. I need you to know how serious I am first." He takes my face in his hands again and I draw in a sharp breath. "Promise me you'll wait for me and I promise I'll tell you everything."

I would be stupid to make that kind of deal with a married man, but Houston isn't just any man. He's the only man I've ever loved. He may be the only man I'll ever love. I can't risk throwing it all away again.

"It's about us," I whisper.

He looks confused. "What are you talking about?"

"The book. It's the story of us."

He sighs as if he's been waiting to hear these words all his life. "I hope it never ends." He brushes a tear from my cheek and kisses my forehead. "Wait for me."

I nod and wrap my arms around his waist to bury my face in his chest. He holds me tightly for a long while, occasionally kissing the top of my head and rubbing my back. I breathe in the scent of his warm skin through his T-shirt and I find myself not wanting to let go. Like we could stand here for the rest of our lives and I'd be perfectly content.

A while later, it could be ten minutes or ten days, Houston tilts my face up and the smile on his face makes my heart happy. He leans in to kiss me and I have no desire to stop him anymore. He may not be mine on paper, but I know his heart is mine. I can feel it in the way he kisses me, exactly the way he used to kiss me. Like we've picked up right where we left off, never skipping a beat.

His fingers are tangled in my hair, tugging lightly so my mouth falls open in a silent gasp. Seizing the opportunity, he pushes his tongue farther inside. I close my lips around his tongue and suck gently. His moans drive me crazy. I bob my head a little to give him a preview of what's to come. Then, I release his tongue and smile as I tuck the ring into my pocket.

Reaching up, I coil my arms around his solid neck. His arms

lock around my hips as he lifts me up, like I weigh about as much as a sparrow. My legs curl around his waist and I tilt my head back as he kisses my neck.

"I missed you," I whisper.

"I missed the fuck out of you, Scar."

I laugh so hard I almost choke on my saliva. "You killed it."

He carries me over to the sofa and lays me down with the utmost of ease. "What are you talking about? I'm just getting started. Can you feel the love tonight?"

I sigh as he slides his hand under my T-shirt and settles himself between my legs. "I can feel *something.*"

His fingers squeeze my breast. "So can I."

He kisses me hard and I lose myself in him until we're a tangled mess of hot, unrestricted desire. Suddenly, his T-shirt and my shirt and bra are off and I don't remember removing them. He's still so good at operating in stealth mode while I'm lost in the throes of lust.

His lips are hot and firm as he kisses his way down to my breast. My back arches the moment he takes my nipple into his mouth. The throbbing between my legs intensifies as he firmly squeezes my other nipple. Tangling my fingers in his hair, I slide my hands down to his shoulders, digging my fingernails into his skin as he devours my sensitive flesh.

"Oh, God, Houston."

"What do you want me to do to you?" he whispers as he kisses his way to my other breast.

Just hearing him ask the question makes me writhe with anticipation, but it's been so long since we've been together, I don't know if I remember how to do this.

He kisses his way down to my navel, his fingers poised on the button of my jeans as he looks up at me with a cunning smile. "I'm going to make you come so hard tonight."

I swallow hard as he undoes my button. "Oh, God."

He slowly eases me out of my jeans, smiling when he sees my pink G-string. Tracing his finger downward along the lacy edge, he stops when his hand is between my legs. He looks up at me, watching my reaction as he slips his finger beneath the fabric and easily finds my clit. My abdominal muscles tighten and I try to focus on breathing as he gently teases me with the soft pad of his finger.

"Look me in the eye."

I gaze back at him, my mouth gaping as he strokes my clit. He varies the pressure, first soft and then firm, then soft again. I pant steadily, my mewls subdued by my insecurity.

"Let go, baby," he reassures me.

I bite my lip as I look him in the eye and swallow my reserve. My hips buck in time with the rhythm of his hand. And almost instantly, the orgasm hits me in waves. My body curls inward feeding the fiery hunger in his eyes. He holds me tighter, his gaze fixed on mine as my legs twitch with the force of the pleasure. My body spasms uncontrollably as he continues to stroke me, and I get a strong urge to push his hand away. The pleasure is so intense it's almost painful.

"This is mine," he murmurs as he caresses me. "Say it."

I exhale a sharp breath coupled with a moan as the orgasm reaches epic levels. "It's yours."

My thighs tremble and I let out a few sharp whimpers, but he continues until the orgasm passes. He's going for orgasm number two.

"You're going to come so many times tonight, you'll be begging me to stop just so you can catch your breath."

I haven't been touched in so long, the second orgasm comes easily. He smiles as he slides his hand back and slowly pulls my panties off. The moment his mouth is on me, I throw my head back and let out a loud sigh.

"Holy shit."

His tongue swirls around my clit, torturing me, until orgasm number three begins. He senses it, so he pulls his head back and slides two fingers inside me. I look down and he's watching me so he can see when he's found my G-spot. He curls his fingers inside me, massaging in a firm back-and-forth motion until he locates it. My body jumps a little and he smiles as he focuses his stroking on that one sensitive area.

Then his mouth is on me again and the pleasure is almost too much to handle. I grab fistfuls of his hair and try not to kick him as he brings me to orgasm again. He reaches up to tweak my nipple, keeping his mouth closed around my clit. My body quakes violently as he stimulates me beyond the point of comprehension. Until I feel as if I'm panting so hard I'm going to black out.

When he's done, he plants a soft kiss on the inside of my thigh and moves to get up. I watch in wonderment as he stands from the sofa and strips before me. He's more beautiful than I remembered. His perfect pecs and abs flow effortlessly into his oblique muscles, which draw a glorious arrow pointing down toward his velvety smooth erection.

He settles down on top of me and I coil my arms around his muscular shoulders as he kisses me deeply. His erection rubs against my sensitive clit as his hips thrust slowly back and forth, using my moisture to massage me and work me into a frenzy.

I push his shoulders back so I can look him in the eye. "Put it in… please."

The left corner of his mouth curves upward, then we both look down to watch as he slowly slides his cock inside me.

"Fuck," he hisses, as he pushes in a bit farther. "You're so tight." He plunges into me a little at a time, watching my face to see my reaction. "Have you been with anyone else?" He freezes with half his erection inside me when I shake my head. "Really?"

I would expect myself to feel embarrassed about this, but I'm not. I shouldn't be ashamed of the fact that I don't want to have casual sex.

"Is that weird?" I reply.

He smiles and kisses my forehead. "It's not weird. It's sexy as fuck."

He lifts my leg a little so he can slide farther into me. It takes a few minutes, but he finally gets his entire erection inside me and I gasp when he hits my cervix.

His brow furrows as he looks me in the eye. "Am I hurting you?"

I shake my head. "I don't think I've ever been this happy to feel a bit of pain."

He leans down to whisper in my ear. "I love you, Scar."

I tighten my arms and legs around him and close my eyes as I attempt to burn this moment into my memory. "I love you, too."

He pulls his head back a little and grabs my face, forcing me to look him in the eye. "I love you, baby, but tonight I'm going to fuck you until you question that." He smiles and plants a kiss on the tip of my nose as he thrusts his hips back and forth. "I've been waiting five long years for this."

I whimper as he moves in and out of me. His considerable girth gently stretches the walls of my pussy, tenderizing me, preparing me for whatever he has in mind.

I gaze back at him as I whisper, "I'm ready. And I'll never question that."

Houston

Five years ago, January 3rd

"WHAT ARE YOU here for today, young man?"

I swallow hard as I try to work up the courage to say what's on my mind. "My sister died last month and I… I've been having trouble sleeping, and I've… been feeling sort of… sad. Is there something you can give me to make it go away?"

Dr. Greene flashes me a tight smile. "Being sad is not a disease that I can prescribe medication for. Depression is a disease for which I can prescribe an antidepressant, but it is not the same as being sad. Being sad is a single symptom of depression. And depression is not the same thing as grief."

I sigh audibly. "Can't you just give me something to make it go away?"

"Make *what* go away?"

I want to shout, *The fucking grief!* But my subconscious beats me to it. "The memories."

Dr. Greene casts a pitiful look in my direction and that's when I realize I've diagnosed my own disorder. And I know exactly how to treat it.

I don't need drugs for depression. I need alcohol for forgetting.

I slide off the exam table and grab my coat off the plastic chair. "Sorry I wasted your time. I made a mistake."

By the time I hop into the driver's seat of my truck, I'm shaking like a leaf as the memory of Hallie's death replays in my mind. I told myself I would get over that by getting revenge on the person responsible for her death, but nothing I've done over the past month has brought the justice Hallie deserves. I've only made things even more complicated. I've fallen in love with the person I intended to destroy.

Rory

August 25th

ALL DAY LONG, no matter what I do or where I go, I can't seem to get rid of the giddy, nerves-zinging sensation. I discussed my thoughts on the wedding vows with Benji and couldn't stop thinking of the engagement ring tucked inside the pocket of my jeans. As Bella taught me how to make a billion different espresso drinks, I grinned stupidly while imagining Houston standing naked in my kitchen, gulping a postcoital glass of water. While passing the produce department on my way out of work, I smiled coyly at the sight of the bananas. So when I step onto the sidewalk outside the store, where Kenny waits to walk me home, he instantly spots me grinning from ear to ear. There will be no hiding from him what happened last night.

Kenny looks me up and down and cocks an eyebrow. "You got your kitten smashed."

I shrug as I fall into step beside him. "Maybe."

"By the lumberjack?"

I chuckle at this. "That's quite a violent image you've

conjured, but no. Not the lumberjack."

He grabs my arm and stops me in the middle of the sidewalk on Burnside. "You have *another* suitor I don't know yet? That's not allowed, Aurora."

"Suitor? I didn't realize I needed permission from Sir Kenneth to get my kitten smashed."

"Who is he? Whoever he is better not cut into our quality time."

I smile as I lock arms with him and continue down Burnside. "I can't really say too much about it. He's…" I glance around as if any of the random strangers walking around us are interested in our conversation. "He's married," I whisper just loud enough for Kenny to hear.

"Oh, my goodness," he gasps, covering his mouth. "I didn't know you were such a slut."

I nudge his shoulder. "I'm not a slut. It's complicated. He's my first love. And the only guy I've ever been with."

He shakes his head as if he's trying to physically clear away his confusion. "Whoa, whoa. Wait. So, have you been with this guy the whole time he's been married? I'm so confused… and intrigued."

"No, we broke up five years ago while we were in college. Then he got married and… We ran into each other at the Belmont store."

"While you were working there with me?"

I nod and he gasps.

"Oh, my God, Rory. Was it that guy in the back of the store?"

I nod again and his eyes widen.

"He's gorgeous," he replies, continuing down Burnside. "I am truly jealous."

"You don't think I'm a disgusting human being for having sex with a married man? It was only one night, but I do feel slightly, or maybe totally, ashamed."

He slows down to a stroll and flashes me a warm smile. "Of course not. I know a thing or two about complicated relationships. No one's perfect. And anyone who expects you to be perfect is just hiding something."

I chuckle at this statement. "No one has ever explained that to me so simply. How did you get to be so wise at the age of thirty?"

He gasps and lightly smacks my shoulder. "Don't ever insult me like that again. And my wisdom is just plain common sense earned over a very messed-up childhood. I mean, my mother named me Kenny, for God's sake. You'd be surprised how much crap one person can endure in twenty-two years."

I sigh as I think of how much I had endured by the age of eighteen. "Not surprised at all, actually." I hug his arm. "That was a hug for your messy childhood."

"Thank you. That made it all better."

After Kenny and I gorge ourselves on Korean barbecue tacos at the food truck on Burnside, we head to my place to let our food digest while watching a chick flick. When we arrive at my apartment, I take Skippy out of his crate and walk him outside to do his business. Then I check his blood glucose before I feed him. And he is more than happy to snuggle up with me on the sofa.

Kenny beckons me to cuddle with him while we watch *How to Lose A Guy In 10 Days*. I cock my eyebrow at his invitation, but he waves off my skepticism.

"Oh, come on. You're safe with me. You and I both know cuddling is totally gay."

I scoot closer to him and lay my head on his shoulder. He lies back so he can put his leg on the sofa and I wind up with my head lying on his chest.

He sniffs the top of my head. "Your hair smells delicious. What is that?"

"It's vanilla birthday cake shampoo and espresso. I was

making coffee all day."

"It perfect, just like you."

We settle into a comfortable position and soon we're lost in the adorable antics of Kate Hudson and Matthew McConaughey. An hour later, I'm woken by a vibration in my pocket. I glance up and Kenny is still awake and watching the movie. I slide my phone out of my pocket and find a text from Houston.

Houston: *Do you work tomorrow?*

I carefully sit up so I don't poke Kenny with my elbow, then I begin typing my response.

"Is that him?" Kenny asks as he sits up.

"Yes."

"Houston is a cowboy's name. Hmm… A cowboy and a lumbersexual? I'd pay to see that."

I shake my head as I hit send.

Me: *No. I'm taking Skippy to Wallace Park to mingle with his own kind.*

Houston: *How about Wednesday?*

Me: *Yeah, I'll be there.*

Houston: *Good. Bring the ring with you.*

I tuck the phone into my pocket and lean back as I wonder why he wants me to bring the ring to work. When I glance to my left, Kenny's wearing an awkward smile. I'm almost afraid to ask what he's thinking, but I have to know.

"What?"

He shakes his head. "What are you going to do if he doesn't

leave his wife?"

"I don't expect you to understand why I feel this way, but I honestly think that's not something I have to worry about."

"You guys bumped into each other just two weeks ago and you had sex once and now he's just going to leave his wife?"

"We had sex *four* times," I reply with a grin, but Kenny doesn't look impressed. "I told you, it's not that simple. We have a history."

"Enlighten me. What is this *history* that makes the situation so complicated?"

I heave a deep sigh and stare at the ceiling as I begin. "I've loved him since I was eleven years old."

"Holy pedobear. You two were together when you were eleven?"

"No. That's how long I've loved him. We didn't get together until I was eighteen. Houston's sister was my best friend." I close my eyes and take a deep breath as I try to keep my emotions in check. "Hallie committed suicide our freshman year in college and I ended up living with Houston the rest of the year. We broke up a week before summer break."

"So you were there for each other at the most painful time of your lives, but the pain wasn't enough to keep you two together?"

I open my eyes to look at Kenny. "I wish it were that simple." I reach into my pocket and pull out the engagement ring. "He was really messed up by what happened to Hallie. He was the one who found her."

"Holy jeebus. Look at the size of that rock. He gave you this engagement ring and you *still* broke up with him?"

"No. He gave me that ring last night. He never gave it to me when we were together. He broke up with me when he found out I was pregnant."

Kenny shakes his head adamantly as he rises from the sofa. "Uh-uh, Rory. This isn't *complicated*. This is Kardashian-level *fucked up*. You're gonna need to get me a stiff drink if you expect me to listen to this."

I laugh as I get up and head for the kitchen to get some tequila and lime wedges. I rarely ever drink, hence the easy buzz I got when Kenny and I went out last weekend. I think drinking is one of the things that reminded me too much of Houston. The tasting parties and the research trips to the pubs. Getting tipsy and having frenzied drunken sex was so common for us that just walking down the beer aisle at work can be a haunting experience.

Two hours and four tequila shots later, Kenny has heard the story of Houston and me. I've arrived at the climax where, apparently, Houston comes back into my life, gives me a very expensive diamond engagement ring, and tells me he's going to leave his wife. And it all happens at the same time I run into a totally nice, unattached lumberjack I once knew in a past life.

"Oh, I almost forgot!" I pull my phone out of my pocket and Kenny lunges for it, but I hold it out of his reach. "I told lumberjack—I mean, Liam—I'd call him today. I have to call him."

"Nuh-uh. You are not drunk-dialing him at eleven o'clock at night on a Monday. Give me that phone."

I laugh as he struggles to take the phone from me, then I jump up from the sofa and race to the bedroom, laughing maniacally as I lock the door behind me.

"Nothing good can come of this!" he shouts at me through the door.

I dial Liam's number, then I press my fingertips to my cheekbones to see how numb my face is. He answers on the second ring.

"Hey."

"Hey," I reply, trying not to laugh.

"I thought you'd forgotten about me."

"Nope. Just got a little sidetracked. I'm drunk."

He laughs. "You drunk-dialed me?"

"Yeah, sorry. I was drinking with my friend and I just remembered that I promised to call you today. I didn't want you to think I'm flaky. I'm really not flaky, but I am forgetful. And both of those words begin with the letter *F*."

He chuckles. "An astute observation. Other than getting drunk, what are you and your friend doing?"

"Exchanging sob stories." I hear a soft barking noise in the background and I get really excited. "Do you have a dog?"

"Yeah, a shepherd mix named Sparky, short for Sparkle Motion."

I chuckle at this reference to the movie *Donnie Darko*. "He must be a great dancer."

"He is. You should see him go from a pirouette straight into a perfect *Dirty Dancing* lift."

"I'd love to see that. Maybe he could teach Skippy a thing or two. I'm taking Skip to Wallace Park tomorrow. You should bring Sparky."

Liam is silent for a moment, and when he finally responds his voice sounds a bit weary. "Rory, tomorrow's Tuesday. I work tomorrow."

"Oh, crap. Sorry. Sometimes I forget that not everyone works retail. Just forget I asked. I'll let you go. You probably need to get to sleep so you can wake up early. Sorry."

"Wait. Don't hang up. I'm just… Ah, fuck it. I'll meet you at the park tomorrow at ten a.m. But you're really drunk right now, so I'm calling you at nine a.m. to remind you, 'kay?"

Suddenly I feel a little sick to my stomach as I realize Liam is going to skip work tomorrow to hang out with me. I want to tell him to just forget it. I don't want to lead him on. But Liam was the one who said he'd rather be friends with me than risk getting hurt. I guess that means I'll have to come clean with him tomorrow about Houston.

"Okay. See you tomorrow."

I open the door and Kenny is wearing a look of disappointment. "You just asked him on a date."

"No, I didn't," I reply, making my way to the kitchen to rehydrate with a glass of water. "I asked him if he wanted to meet me at the dog park. That's not a date."

"Don't play coy with me, young lady. You can't pass this off as a doggy playdate. That lumberjack thinks you're interested in more than his dog."

My buzz is wearing off quickly as I reach for a glass in the cupboard. "Even if that's true, the point of this date is to clarify that. I can do it over the phone, but he's the one who said he wanted to be friends with me."

Kenny sighs as he leans against the counter. "Fine. But if you break his heart, make sure you do enough damage that he turns gay."

I laugh as I fill my glass with water from the tap. "Now you're into lumbersexuals?"

"Honey, a luxurious beard works wonders for oral sex."

"Ew!"

"Don't knock it till you try it!"

Houston

August 26th

THE SMILE ON Troy's face tells me he's very pleased with my plans. "You're finally gonna do it?"

I take a long pull on my bottle of Barley Legal Double IPA. "I know. It's been a long time coming, but I'm still nervous as fuck."

Steve, the bartender in the Barley Legal pub, exchanges my empty bottle for a fresh, cold one. I nod at him and he goes back to pouring some pints for a group of girls who came in on one of those Portland brewery bike tours. Not that I don't appreciate the extra business, but riding around on a bike while drinking beer all day sounds like a good way to get hit by a bus.

"So when are you gonna do it? Can I get it on video?"

I shake my head. "Tessa's gonna flip. It might be a good idea for someone to be outside in case she pulls out a gun or something. I don't know what the fuck she's been doing behind my back, but I could totally see her at the gun range aiming at a poster of me."

"Dude, she's crazier than a coked-up raccoon. You'd better

watch yourself."

"I can handle Tessa. And she's not crazy, she's sick."

"Whatever." He takes a few gulps from his glass of double bock. "You didn't ask me what happened when I ran into Rory the other day."

"I assumed you were probably scheming to sway her in my direction. I didn't send you there by mistake."

"You fucking bastard."

I shrug as I bring the bottle to my lips. "I need all the help I can get."

"That's what friends are for," he replies.

"Interesting. When I was with your mom last night, she said friends are for cock-gobbling."

Troy strokes his chin as if he's considering this. "That *is* interesting because *your* mom said friends are for enemas. Followed by sweet backdoor action, of course."

"Of course." I leave half my beer in the bottle and slide off the bar stool. "I'll see you tomorrow, brother."

"Good luck, man."

It's eleven a.m. when I leave the pub. As I open the door to get into the SUV, I spot a silver Lexus that looks like Tessa's parked at the end of the block. I can't be sure, but it doesn't look like there's anyone sitting in the driver's seat. I shake my head as I hop into my car. There must be dozens of silver Lexuses in this area at any given time. I'm being paranoid.

I've only had one and a half beers, so I decide to drive by Wallace Park to see if Rory is still there with her dog. Seeing her will give me the motivation I need to break away from Tessa.

Being with Rory two nights ago was like being myself again after five years of pretending to be someone else. I finally felt like I was living more than half a life. The worst part is that I didn't even realize I was living in black and white until I bumped into Rory two weeks ago. Now I can't get the color of her hair and the taste of her skin out of my head.

I want to carve out a place for her in my life, sow the seeds of trust, and watch our story grow. I want to stir up the ideas in her mind and drink in the tales she'll tell me into the early hours of the morning.

I want to bore into her, physically and mentally, unearthing every glistening jewel of pleasure and pain. I want to take her to bed every night and worship at the altar of her hushed beauty. I want to lose myself in the luscious curves of her hips and the delicate scent of her skin.

I want to slide that ring on her finger and kiss her madly in front of hundreds of people. I want to have a family with her. I want to make her deliriously happy.

I turn left on Raleigh Street and quickly find a space for my car across from the park on the corner of Raleigh and 25th. I cross the street, trying to peek through the trees and the wire mesh fence surrounding the dog park, but I don't see anyone. I head through the waist-high gate and I finally glimpse some people and dogs in the grassy open field. I spot the black Labrador first, which has to be Rory's dog, Skippy. He's playing with a tan dog that appears to be some kind of shepherd mix. My gaze follows the dogs as they run, tongues wagging, toward an area shaded by some trees.

I'm about twenty yards from the trees when the black Lab collides with Rory. She orders the dog to sit, but I quickly lose sight of what she's doing when I notice the guy standing next to her. It's the guy who went to her apartment the other night.

A roaring wave of jealousy swells inside me, flooding my veins with pure adrenaline. My fists are urging me to destroy him, the one thing standing between Rory and me and everything we've ever wanted. But my brain is yelling at me, *Down, boy. Sit. Stay.*

I approach slowly, consciously trying not to clench my fists so

I don't look *too* intimidating. Rory spots me when I'm a few yards away. Her eyes widen and she drops the dog treat in her hand, which the tan dog quickly snatches up.

"Houston?" she says, her voice breathy with shock.

She glances at the guy next to her and he refuses to look at me, but the sight of the muscle in his jaw twitching drives me over the edge. This asshole thinks *I'm* inconveniencing *him*? He's the one infringing on *my* territory.

"Is there a problem?" I ask, my voice taut with tension.

Rory opens her mouth to respond when she realizes I'm not talking to her. "No!" she shouts, as if we're two dogs who can be called off each other with a simple command. "No, this is not happening here, or anywhere, so just come off it."

I tear my gaze away from the hipster lumberjack and look Rory in the eye. "We need to talk."

I nod for her to follow me and she calls Skippy to join us as we walk a few yards away. "Houston, this is not what you think it is. Liam is just a friend."

"It doesn't matter what you think it is. What matters is what *he* thinks it is. And he doesn't think you two are just friends."

"You're misreading this. Really."

I gaze into her hazel eyes, searching for a trace of deceit, but Rory has always been the most honest person I know. She really thinks they're just friends.

"I'm leaving Tessa tonight."

She draws in a sharp breath. "Tonight?"

"Yeah. I need to know if you're ready to do this. Just you and me. See where the story takes us."

She smiles and nods as her eyes well up with tears. "I'm ready."

I cradle her face in my hands and kiss her forehead. "I'll tell you everything tomorrow." I kiss her cheekbone and she grabs the front of my shirt. "Then I hope you'll let me put that ring on your finger."

She exhales a soft sigh into my mouth as I kiss her slowly. I let go of her face and smile when I see the far-off look in her eyes.

"How do you do that?" she murmurs.

I crouch down and scratch Skippy behind the ears as he licks my face. "Do what?"

"Make me forget where I am."

I smile as I look up at her. "That's because everywhere we're together is the only place and the only moment that exists."

Rory

August 26th

HOUSTON LAUGHS AS Skippy shoves his head into his lap, begging for even more attention. I shake my head as I watch my boy hamming it up, then I glance over my shoulder at Liam. He has Sparky by the collar as the dog jumps up and down excitedly, eager to join his new buddy Skippy. I want to invite Liam and Sparky to come over, but I feel like it would be too awkward. And I don't want to give Houston the wrong impression about Liam and me.

"Houston, I know you've already met Liam, but can I please reintroduce you?"

He takes a deep breath before he stands up, glances in Liam's direction, then flashes me a reluctant smile. "Anything you want."

"Thank you."

I tear my gaze away from his gorgeous face and turn back to Liam. I wave at him, but he doesn't notice me. I take a step toward him and suddenly I'm knocked onto the grass face-first.

"Tessa! What the fuck?" Houston roars.

It takes me a moment to realize I've been hit in the head with something. I reach up to feel the back of my head, but I'm yanked backward by my hair. The whiplash cracks the joint in my neck, then it's over as quickly as it began and I'm lying facedown on the grass again.

"What the fuck are you doing?" Houston's voice sounds panicked, but I can barely hear it over the sound of Skippy and Sparky's barking.

"Is that her?" a shrill female voice echoes inside my skull. "I knew you were cheating on me!"

"Rory, are you okay?"

I turn my head toward Liam's voice and Skippy's tongue sloshes across my nose several times. "I think so."

"It's over, Tessa. Let it go."

Houston's words make my chest ache as Liam helps me sit up. I can't help but be reminded of the time Houston whispered those same words in my ear. If anyone knows how this woman feels right now, it's me. If she didn't knock me over the head, I might actually empathize with her.

When I'm sitting up, I finally see her. Her blonde shoulder-length hair is as wild as the look in her eyes. She's breathing heavily, seething with anger as she brandishes a steel thermos in her right hand. I rub the back of my head, wincing at the sharp pain.

Houston is standing like a six-foot-four wall of muscle between me and his wife. He looks back at me over his shoulder, a worried expression in his blue eyes. I gasp loudly when his wife takes a swipe at him with the thermos.

"Watch out!" I scream.

She hits Houston square in the side of his head and he curses as he covers his ear.

"Call 911," I urge Liam, but he's already on it.

"Let it go, Tessa," Houston repeats the phrase, and I finally understand he's referring to the thermos, not the marriage.

I'm sure he could easily take it away from her, but he probably doesn't want to be seen in public struggling with a woman. That could easily be misconstrued if a stranger were to stumble upon the scene.

She throws the thermos at Houston's face and he catches it in his right hand. "It's all your fault. Everything is your fault!" she shrieks. "I hope you're happy knowing you killed your baby."

She takes off running toward the street and Houston drops the thermos onto the grass as he takes off after her. My heart is pounding so hard, my fingers are going numb. I grab Skippy and pull him into my lap so he doesn't chase after them. And so I can hug him.

"Should I go after them?" Liam asks, holding his phone to his ear in one hand, his other hand clenched around Sparky's collar so he doesn't bolt after Houston and Tessa.

I nod as I stand up so I can grab on to both Sparky and Skippy. Liam takes off in the same direction as Houston and Tessa, his phone still pressed to his ear. But seconds later, everything seems to stop. Sound. Time. My heart. Everything.

The sound of tires squealing is followed by a loud crash.

"*NO!*" Houston roars so loudly, his cry ruptures the silence.

Liam picks up his pace toward Raleigh Street and I let the dogs pull me after him, though I almost don't want to know what we'll find. I think I'm going to be sick. But I keep putting one foot in front of the other until we're at the fence surrounding the dog park. I take the dogs through the gate and they whimper as they try to pull away from me. Their instincts kick in as they sense someone needs their help.

A leaf falls off a large elm tree and flutters across my line of sight. Only then do I realize I'm crying. I move forward slowly toward the space between my Toyota and Liam's truck. The first thing I see is an Asian woman standing on the sidewalk across the street. She's covering her mouth and staring wide-eyed at something on the other side of the truck. Skippy, Sparky, and I squeeze through the gap between the vehicles and the scene is laid out before me.

Tessa is lying facedown on the asphalt and Houston is on his knees next to her. Liam is standing over them, his phone still pressed against his ear as he looks up and down the street. Probably looking for any sign of an emergency vehicle. My heart stutters when I see Tessa's arm move. She attempts to roll onto her back, but Houston stops her.

"Don't move, baby. The ambulance is on the way."

The word *baby* coming out of Houston's mouth in reference to another woman makes me sick to my stomach. And when I think about the fact that the other woman is his wife, this only makes me sicker. I have no right to be sickened. *I'm* the other woman.

Liam spots me standing between his truck and my car and shakes his head. I don't know what he means by this, but I take it to mean that I don't need to watch. They have it covered.

I turn around and lead the dogs back onto the sidewalk. I unlock my car and let them into the backseat. Then I sink down onto the curb, rest my head in my hands, and cry as I replay the events of the past twenty-four hours over and over in my mind.

Oh, God. What have we done?

It seems that without knowing it, we fell into the same pattern we fell into five years ago. We were so busy looking in the rearview mirror, we didn't realize we were about to crash. Only this time, it wasn't just Houston and me who got hurt.

Houston

Five years ago, December 4th

HALLIE RARELY CALLS me during the week. She almost always saves her calls to me for the weekend. Then she'll blabber on and on about her classes or all her suggestions for the many ways I should ask Rory on a date. I should never have expressed interest in Rory last Christmas Eve. It was a huge mistake. Rory was still seventeen and I was twenty. I knew she was off limits. But that tight white sweater dress she wore to Christmas Eve dinner at our house completely changed the way I saw her. Then, when I saw her laughing as she and Hallie shook the presents to try to guess what was inside, laughing about vibrators as Christmas gifts, it was like a switch was flipped inside me. And I wasn't able to stop thinking about her for months.

Then I started going out with Kim a couple of months ago, a few months after Rory turned eighteen, and Kim's been doing an okay job of keeping my mind off my sister's friend. But that hasn't stopped Hallie from trying to set us up. She insists Rory and I belong together, whatever the fuck that means. I think it's possible to believe you belong with *anyone* if you spend enough time with them. It's like Stockholm syndrome.

Nevertheless, I'm surprised to see Hallie's name flashing on my phone screen on a Thursday morning. If it were anyone else, I'd hit the red ignore button. But part of being a big brother to a pretty girl like Hallie is that I always worry about her when she's not around. Especially now that she's in college.

I hit the green button to answer the call and whisper into the phone so my Financial Markets professor can't hear. "Hey."

"Houston, I need you to come over here at one o'clock."

"Why?"

"I need to talk to you… about Rory… before she gets back from class. Please." Hallie's voice sounds strangled as if she's been crying or she's about to start.

"Are you okay?"

She lets out a frustrated sigh. "Yes. Will you come?"

"Yeah, I'll be there."

"At one o'clock. Don't forget. And don't be late. Rory gets here at two so you need to come before that. Okay?"

Professor Hardwick casts a sharp glare in my direction.

"Yeah, yeah. I'll be there."

I end the call and flash the professor a tight smile as I tuck my phone back into my pocket. I don't know what Hallie needs to talk about, but it better be more urgent than another attempt to set me up with Rory. If it's not, I'll need to have a stern discussion with her about calling me during class.

An hour and forty minutes later, I pull my hood over my head and trudge through the light snow across campus to Hamilton Complex. The snow showed up as soon as we got back from Thanksgiving break three days ago. Most everyone grumbles about it, but we hardly ever got snow in McMinnville so I've enjoyed it since coming to UO three years ago.

The snow crunches under my boots and the fresh white

powder reminds me of Rory in that dress. I wonder what Hallie wants to talk to me about. Maybe she's going to tell me that Rory's really a man and I can stop lusting after her. Or maybe she's not even going to be in the dorm when I get there. Maybe she's tricked me and Rory into meeting up without her. The same way she used to force her Barbie and Ken dolls to go on dates. *Now kiss!*

I enter Watson Hall at Hamilton Complex and make my way up to the third floor corridor. I reach room 301, Hallie and Rory's dorm room, and knock three times. Hallie doesn't answer so I knock a little harder this time, in case she's wearing her headphones. That's when I notice the door isn't closed all the way. I knock again, in case she's changing or something, then I push the door in slowly.

"I'm coming in," I say, announcing myself as an extra precaution.

Once the door is all the way open, my vision blurs. My heart gets a massive jolt, like a horse kick in the chest. Hallie is lying in her twin bed, a clear plastic bag over her head. I rush in and quickly undo the Velcro around her neck. I yank off the bag, but she doesn't open her eyes.

"Hallie, this isn't funny. Wake up!" I shake her shoulders. I yell her name. But she doesn't respond. "What the fuck?"

I glance at the bag on the floor and notice a couple of plastic tubes that must have fallen out when I tore the bag off. The tubes lead to a helium tank. *What the fuck was she doing?*

"Wake up, Hal!" I shout, crouched at her bedside as I press two fingers to her neck to check for a pulse. "Come on. This can't be happening. This can't be fucking happening. No, no, no. What were you thinking?"

I can't find a pulse. I stand up and pull my phone out of my pocket to dial 911, but I'm interrupted when I notice a white envelope clutched in Hallie's right hand. My heart hurts so much,

I'm afraid I might be having a heart attack. I reach for the envelope and let out a wretched groan when her stiff fingers don't immediately let go.

I cover my mouth to stifle the sobs when I see my name written on the envelope. She planned this. From the moment she called me two hours ago, and probably well before that, she knew.

"Hey, what's going on here?"

I whip my head around at the sound of the female voice and for a moment I'm terrified it's Rory. But when I turn around it's a brunette I don't recognize.

"Call 911!" I shout at her. "Now!"

"Holy shit," she whispers as she fumbles in her pocket for her phone.

I learned CPR when I was sixteen and I got a summer job as a lifeguard, but I never expected I would need to use what I learned to try to bring my baby sister back from the dead. I scoop her up off the bed and lay her gently on the floor. Then I proceed with the chest compressions and mouth-to-mouth.

My mind knows it's too late, but my heart tells me to keep going. So I keep plunging her fragile breastbone and pumping breath after breath into her deflated lungs. When the paramedics arrive, it takes them a moment to pry my arms from around her limp body. Then, I begin to lose time.

I see flashes of what's happening around me, but I can't make sense of any of it. It's as if my body is here, tucked in the corner of Hallie's dorm, watching as the medics work on her, but my mind is somewhere else. This must not be happening. Or it's happening to someone else. That's not my sister. That is *not* my sister.

I collapse onto the wooden desk chair in the corner of the dorm and it's as if the hardness of the chair has woken me to the harsh reality I've found myself trapped in. Hallie is placed on a stretcher and the medic continues to apply chest compressions as they roll her out of the dorm.

What time is it? If Rory gets here now, she'll be beyond shattered. I reach into my pocket to check the time on my phone as I follow the stretcher down the corridor. It's 1:36 p.m. Hallie said Rory would be here at two. She obviously didn't want Rory to find her, either. But why did she want me to find her? Did she think I could handle this better than Rory?

They wheel the stretcher into the elevator and I squeeze inside with them, trying not to look at her gray skin.

The medic who's pumping the oxygen bag sees my discomfort and offers me his condolences. "I'm sorry, man."

"Why do you guys keep doing that? She's obviously dead."

"Do you have a DNR for her?" the guy applying the chest compressions asks. "If not, we have to keep doing this until she gets to the hospital."

It's a cold response. No apology or attempt at consolation. Just a big *Shut the fuck up and let us do our job.* I want to shove him into the wall of the elevator, maybe break his head open, so he'll stop repeatedly crushing my dead sister's chest. This day couldn't possibly get any worse, could it?

It can. I need to honor Hallie's final words to me and make sure Rory doesn't make it back to the dorm before I explain everything to her. I can't let her come back from class and find out on her own from some stranger.

When the elevator reaches the first floor, I let the medics out first. I follow behind them a few more paces, ignoring the onlookers, then I poke the oxygen bag operator on his shoulder.

"Do you need me to ride with you or can I meet you all at the hospital? I have to call my family."

"No, go ahead and do what you need to do. She's going to Sacred Heart on Hilyard."

I call my mom as I head back to the dorm, but I can't understand a word she says after I break the news to her. Her incoherent wailing fills my chest with an excruciating ache. Somehow, I maintain enough composure to convince her to call a friend so she can get a ride to the hospital.

When I get to the third floor, the campus police have blocked off the entrance to Hallie's dorm to conduct their investigation. I keep glancing at the time on my phone as I answer their questions. Finally, one of the officers asks me why I keep looking at my phone.

I squint at him in disbelief. "You have some fucking nerve to ask me that. My sister just committed suicide. I promised my mom I'd call her back after I talked to you all. And I have to notify the people that care about her before they find out from someone else. Are we done here?"

He looks like he's ready to chew me out, but his partner beats him to it. "We're good. If we need anything else, we'll give you a call," he says, patting my arm. "Sorry about your sister."

"Yeah, thanks."

I turn to head back toward the elevator when I see Rory stepping out into the corridor. Her eyes are wide with fright and her fair skin is flushed pink. Someone must have already told her what happened.

"No!" she wails as she sees the officers and the crime scene tape over the door. "Hallie!" She races toward us and I catch her around the waist to stop her. "Where is she?"

"She's gone." My voice is gruff and shaky as the tears return. "Hallie's gone."

"No! Stop lying! Let me go!"

She fights me every step of the way as I carry her back to the elevator. Once we're in the cabin, she stops fighting and collapses into a heap on the floor. When the elevator reaches the first floor, I help her up and we both walk out of Hamilton Complex in a daze.

I have to call my mom to make sure she found a ride, but I

can't bring myself to do it with Rory here. I know it will only cause her to break down. Ten minutes later, Rory and I arrive at the Jordan Schnitzer Museum of Art. Instinctively, I grab her hand and lead her up the icy steps toward the entrance. We need to get out of the cold, though I'm not sure it matters. I don't think either of us can feel anything right now.

I fumble in my wallet when they ask for my student ID so they can let us in for free. We walk the halls like zombies, searching for something to bring us back to life, some piece of art that proves beauty transcends pain, but nothing stands out. We reach the Reflection Garden and head outside again, undaunted by the dusting of snow covering the path around the reflection pool.

The garden is small and empty, so we instantly gravitate toward the stone statues. Two genderless stone figures kneel in front of a large stone shell. One figure plays a flute while the other strums a small instrument held against its chest. We stare at the statues for a moment before Rory finally speaks.

"I can't go back there."

Fat tears roll down her cheeks and I glance over my shoulder, hoping no one comes out here to interrupt us. Then I take her in my arms and she sobs into my chest, thick, pitiful cries that sound about as pleasing as nails on a chalkboard. But only because I can't make them stop.

"You don't have to go back. You can stay with me."

She sniffs loudly and draws in a stuttered breath. "No, I can't."

She lets go of me and covers her face. I reach up and gently pry her hands away, but she still won't look at me. Her eyelids are puffy and the whites of her eyes are bloodshot, but she looks even more beautiful than she did when I first noticed her in that white dress.

"Yes, you can. You're coming to my apartment now."

"I can't. I need my stuff."

"We'll get it later. Besides, I have to go somewhere private so I can call my mom." I brush the moisture away from her cheek. "Come with me. I don't think I can do it alone."

She finally looks up at me, but she only meets my gaze for a second before she turns away. "Okay." She tucks her hands into her coat pockets and stares at the statues for a moment. "She told me not to come back until two. Why were you already there?"

"She told me to come at one. She said you were coming back at two."

She shakes her head and wipes more tears. "My class ended at 12:30. She texted me and told me not to come back till two. I just don't understand why."

I think of the white envelope tucked in my back pocket, and consider opening it up right here, but it was addressed to me, not Rory. I have to open it alone.

I place my hand on the small of her back and lead her back into the museum. "We may never know why."

Houston

August 27th

THE WALK UP to Rory's apartment feels like a death march. I couldn't call her to let her know I was coming. I didn't know if she'd actually see me. And I'm sick at the thought that Liam may be in there with her. After what happened yesterday, I have no right to question who Rory spends time with. And after what I'm about to do today, I have no doubt that I'll probably never be with Rory again.

I knock on the door and try not to look at the peephole. I can hear the jingling from the tags on Skippy's collar. I stare at the doorknob, waiting for it to move, but nothing happens.

I step forward and lean my face closer to the doorframe. "Rory, please open the door."

Skippy lets out a soft bark followed by a desperate whine. I hear her shushing him, but he responds with another baleful howl. The doorknob begins to turn and I step back so I don't startle her. Skippy wags his tail and whimpers as I greet him with a good scratching around his scruff.

"Skippy, get inside."

Rory issues this order a few times before he listens to her. She turns to me and fixes me with a dark glare replete with five years of resentment. After a moment, she steps aside and waves me in.

"I know I'm probably the last person you want to see right now."

"I had to call the hospital myself to try to find out if she was alive and, of course, they wouldn't tell me anything. Yeah, you could have at least texted me."

"She's fine. It's just a broken arm. How's your head?"

"*Now* you care?" She scowls at me for a moment, letting her disdain sink in before she snatches the Sierra Nevada box off the coffee table and holds it out to me. "I don't want this."

I clench my jaw against the wave of nausea that sweeps through me as I take the box from her. "She wasn't pregnant. She was *never* pregnant. She was lying."

"Thanks for clearing that up."

I heave a deep sigh and let it out slowly as I look her in the eye. "Rory, I came here because I told you I would tell you the truth and I intend to keep my word."

"The truth about *what*?" she demands. "It's over Houston. There is no truth that needs to be spoken anymore."

I shake my head. "I wish that were true." She watches intently as I reach into my back pocket and retrieve the white envelope containing Hallie's suicide letter. "She left a note."

She stares at me for a moment, her face contorted in a mixture of horror and confusion.

"Not Tessa. Hallie."

The confusion quickly morphs to a fury I've never seen, then she pushes me square in the chest. "I hate you!"

"I didn't want you to read it until you were strong enough."

Skippy barks as Rory tries to pummel my chest. I tilt my head back, out of her reach, then I drop the letter so I can grab her wrists.

"That's not for you to decide!" she says, the anguish choking her words. "How could you keep that from me?"

"I was just trying to protect you."

She groans so loudly it sounds like a thunderous roar. "I wish you would stop protecting me! If it weren't for your stupid protection, I wouldn't be picking up the pieces of my life again."

I grit my teeth at the truth in her words. "I need you to read it while I'm here. I… I won't leave until you've read the whole thing. Then you'll understand why."

She yanks her wrists out of my grasp and gently pushes Skippy out of the way so she can snatch the letter off the floor. She heads to the sofa and the dog hops onto the cushion next to her. I sit on the coffee table, facing her so I can see her reaction when she reads the letter. I know the moment she opens that envelope, everything is going to hell. And even if she claims to hate me and resents my attempts to protect her, she's going to need someone to hold, or someone to punch, when she's done reading Hallie's words.

Her hands tremble violently as she stares at my name scrawled on the outside of the envelope. Judging by the tears rolling down her cheeks, she recognizes the handwriting. I hold my breath as I watch her slip the folded five-page letter out of the envelope. She unfolds it slowly and covers her mouth the moment she sees it's genuine. Clutching the letter to her chest, she closes her eyes as she takes a few deep breaths. Finally, she holds it up and begins reading the words that changed my life forever. The words that gave me a purpose and a love like no other while also destroying everything I knew to be true.

Dear Houston,

First of all, please don't show this letter to anyone else. Not Mom. Not Dad. And especially not Rory. And please forgive me for what I've done, and what I'm about to do.

You're probably wondering why I did this. You think there weren't any signs and that none of it makes sense. You think I had everything going for me and so much to live for. But you need to know the truth. And the short version of the truth is that I was destroyed by love. Now let me give you the long version.

It all began about twenty-eight months ago. I was sixteen and it was the end of the summer before my junior year. Rory and I had made plans to go to the movies on a Friday night, but when I got to her house an hour early, she wasn't there yet. No one answered the door. So I went down the driveway toward the backyard to see if she was laying out trying to catch a suntan, but she wasn't there. But her dad was back there, standing on a tall ladder and cutting branches off the big elm tree in their backyard.

He didn't have a shirt on. His T-shirt was draped over one of the lower branches. The tanned skin of his back was glistening with sweat. He'd been working on getting the yard ready for the fall for a couple of weekends. But it wasn't until that day, when I was able to look at him without wondering if Rory was watching me, that I finally realized what a beautiful body he had.

I'd always thought James was handsome. Even as a young girl, I thought he was the coolest dad ever. When I first met Rory and she told me her dad used to be an activist and now he was a lawyer, I thought there probably wasn't anyone in our town as cool as him. But I didn't really develop a crush on him until I found him sawing the branches off that tree.

It wasn't just the sight of the muscles working under his skin, it was the thought of what they were working for. He was working to make the yard better for his family. Rory's mom hated it when the elm tree dumped all its leaves in the fall and winter. And Rory hated it when she had to spend the weekend raking leaves, so he was trying to make their life easier by trimming the tree before autumn.

I think I was feeling more vulnerable that day because I hadn't seen Dad in almost five months, since I visited him in Salem during Spring Break. But he kept making excuses for why we shouldn't visit him that summer, so we gave up trying by the end of June. If I had not been feeling so vulnerable, maybe none of this would have happened. I don't know.

All I know is that it took a few minutes for James to realize I was watching him. He was friendly as he explained that Rory and her mom had to go to the store to pick up a few things for a teachers' potluck at school. He said I could wait inside the house, but I told him it was a nice day so I'd just wait on the back deck. The truth was that I just wanted to watch him.

He didn't seem to catch on the first three or four times I showed up when I knew Rory and her mom would be gone. I told him a couple of times that I had accidentally changed the time on my phone when I reset my alarm clock, which was why I kept showing up at the wrong times, and he seemed to believe me. But when I showed up at their house a couple of days before the first day of school, he finally caught on.

It was about seven o'clock at night and Rory and her mom had left to go shopping for school clothes. When James answered the door, he didn't bother telling me that Rory was gone or that she'd be back in a couple of hours. He didn't even invite me in, he just flashed me a reserved smile and opened the door.

I was so nervous. I had been up late the night before trying to figure out how I was going to approach him. School would be starting soon and I thought my opportunities to be alone with him would dry up. I knew I was crazy, but I didn't care. I couldn't stop thinking about him and, in my mind, something had to be done or things would get very awkward very quickly.

I wore a short, flouncy skirt and the UO T-shirt you'd bought for me. I thought this would lull him into a sense of false security, like I wasn't actually sixteen.

He sat down on one end of the sofa and kept on watching Monday night football while I sat on the other end and pretended to wait for Rory. *It took a few minutes for me to work up the courage to slip out of my flip-flops and put my feet up on the coffee table the way* Rory *and I normally did when we were hanging out in her living room. I watched him from the corner of my eye as I crossed and uncrossed my legs. He seemed to be stealing glances every few minutes, so I upped my game by scratching a pretend itch on the inside of my knee, then I left my hand resting between my legs. This got his attention.*

He stared at my hand for a moment before he looked up at me and said, "That's a nice skirt."

I was so desperate for more praise, I could hardly speak or breathe. But no matter what position I sat in or how many times I scratched an itch, he never said another word to me that night. Over the next twenty-two months, things went on the same way. Occasionally, I'd find myself alone with him and, occasionally, he would compliment me, but he never touched me or made any verbal propositions. Still, I knew he was interested. And I had convinced myself that everything would change when I turned eighteen. And it did.

Rory *and I drove to Salem for my eighteenth birthday. We actually went on May 17th, three days after my birthday, because we had to wait until the weekend. We snuck a bottle of Mom's whiskey out there and got drunk before we went to the Enchanted Forest theme park. It was the best birthday ever. Once we were sober, we drove back to* Rory's *and got ready for bed.*

About one in the morning, I got out of bed to go to the restroom when I saw a faint glow coming from the staircase. I decided to creep downstairs and see if it was James, and it was. He was in the downstairs office with his computer on. I tiptoed in, but he looked up from his laptop immediately. His eyes scanned my body for a few seconds before he told me to close the door.

I closed the door and locked it just to be safe, then I slowly walked around the desk. I was a little disappointed when I saw him working on a legal brief instead of watching porn. But the disappointment melted away when he beckoned me to sit on his lap.

He spoke to me softly, asking how my birthday went and how I felt about going away to UO after the summer. With my head resting on his shoulder, he stroked my leg with the tips of his fingers as he spoke. He told me about the case he was working on and it made me feel smart. But I knew if I didn't make a move, he would probably send me upstairs unsatisfied.

The scent of his skin was crisp and cool like he had just showered, so I took a chance and kissed his neck. He froze and I began to wonder if I had misread his kindness. Maybe he was just comforting me, indulging my schoolgirl crush on my birthday. But then I felt something going on beneath me and I knew he was getting excited.

He told me multiple times that this would only happen once. That he was only doing this because he knew how much I wanted him. And that it could never happen again. But I didn't care.

Part of me believed it would be the last time, but a larger part of me knew I could make it happen again. And I did.

Why do you think I got a summer job thirty-five minutes away from home? James and I would meet at a hotel where he would pay cash, but I put my debit card on file and used my name to register. I was crazy with jealousy when I wasn't with him and I was miserable with guilt every time we parted. I knew I couldn't ask him to leave his wife, so we just never spoke of those kinds of things. When we weren't screwing, we talked about work.

But the worst part was knowing what would happen if Rory *ever found out. I reasoned with myself that I would end the affair before it got too serious and way before* Rory *or her mom found out. When in reality I knew that I was already in way over my head. I had loved James from afar for two years. Now that I had him, I knew I wouldn't be able to give him up. And in a sick way, this also made me feel closer to* Rory.

She's loved you since she was eleven years old. And I know that if you two ever got together, it would be a dream come true for her. That was the way it was for me, only I was acting out a disgusting schoolgirl fantasy. I was on the verge of destroying a family. And not just anyone's family, my best friend's family.

I hated myself throughout the whole thing, but I couldn't stop. Then Rory and I went off to UO and I tried to pretend to be happy. I even tried going out on a few dates, but I hated all those guys almost as much as I hated myself. Still, I kept pretending.

Then Rory asked me if I wanted to spend Thanksgiving with her family. I knew I could split my day between our house and Rory's house if I played my cards right with Mom. So I began to get excited at the prospect of possibly being alone with James again. But when Rory and I arrived the Saturday before Thanksgiving, he was very cold with me.

I thought he was just doing it so as not to arouse suspicion, but when I managed to catch him alone in the garage later that night, he told me very clearly that it was over between us. I insisted that it didn't have to be. That I could keep it a secret as long as he wanted me to, but he was adamant that the affair couldn't continue.

Still, I didn't believe him. I went inside the house and cried in the bathroom for a little while. Then I decided I'd just try to show him what he would be missing. I did pathetic things like sitting across from him at the dinner table and squeezing my breasts together just enough for them to appear larger. I would wait in the bathroom until I heard him coming out of his bedroom, then I'd walk out of the bathroom in nothing but a towel. I'm not certain, but I think Rory's mom began to notice what I was doing, and if that wasn't embarrassing enough, I began texting nude pictures of myself to the pay-as-you-go cell phone he bought over the summer. I think the number was disconnected, but I kept sending them in the hope that it wasn't.

When Thanksgiving finally came, I tried to sit next to him, but he decided to change seats so he could "carve the turkey at the head of the table." That was when it finally started to sink in that I had been used.

He never told me he loved me, but he always made it a point to tell me how beautiful I looked and how much he missed me when we were apart. I mistook this for love. But I was finally starting to realize that I had spent more than two years of my life loving someone who would never love me back. Even worse, I'd spent two years of my life dreaming of a life that would ruin my best friend if it were to come to fruition.

I've spent the past week absolutely sick with myself. I hate knowing that I grew up to be as sick as Dad. Absolutely no respect for the sanctity of marriage. I don't want to live with what I've done. And I don't want Rory to live with it either. That's why you can never show her this letter. And you need to promise me that you won't punish her for what James and I did.

I knew what I was doing, which only makes me even more guilty. Please don't take it out on Rory. She's the victim in this whole fucked-up scenario. All she's ever done is love me and trust me, and I couldn't bear losing her over something like this.

I'm sorry that you had to find out this way. And I'm sorry that you're the one who had to find me. Please know that I didn't want to hurt you. I just didn't want to hurt Rory any more than I already have. Please help Mom and Rory get through this.

I love you always.

Hallie

Rory

Eight years ago, September 23rd

I HAVEN'T BEEN to the Gallery Theater since I was eight, so it's been eight years since the last time I came with my parents. Hallie has never been there in the five years since she moved to McMinnville with her mom and Houston, so I'm sure this visit will be more interesting than my last. Hallie and I get tickets for *Oklahoma* at 7:30 p.m., then we get in line behind a family of four to get inside the theater.

Hallie's quiet as she stares at the family, then she turns to me and leans in conspiratorially. "What is it like to love someone for as long as you've loved Houston?"

I'm a bit taken aback by this question. It's not the type of light banter that usually happens while standing in line at the theater. We reach the door and an usher takes our tickets, then leads us through the lobby and to our seats. The whole time, I sense Hallie anxiously awaiting my reply to her question. I don't know what's prompted her to ask me this, unless she has a crush that she hasn't told me about. But Hallie and I share everything.

The usher leads us to a pair of seats three rows back from the main stage. Once he's gone, Hallie turns to me with a smile on her face, awaiting my reply.

I shrug. "I don't know. I guess it's… crippling."

Her smile disappears. "Really?"

I think about Houston and how much I've missed him since he left for college last year. And how every time I see him at Hallie's house during holidays, my stomach cramps up and my thoughts get all jumbled. How I fall asleep most nights with thoughts of what it would be like to have those feelings reciprocated. And wake up with my heart broken when I realize the happiness I felt moments ago was just a dream.

"Really. It's awful."

Her shoulders slump as she lets out a soft sigh. "I want to be in love."

"With someone in particular?"

"No, I just want to feel like there's more than this, you know?"

I chuckle, feeling slightly confused. "No, I don't. More than what?"

She raises her hands, palms up, to indicate the stage cloaked in a velvety red curtain in front of us. "This! This place where we have to pretend to be someone we're not." She turns to me with a glint of electricity in her blue eyes. "It's not fair that you have to pretend you don't love my brother because he's nineteen and you're sixteen."

"Well, that's not the only reason. I asked you to never tell him because I don't want to get hurt. Then things would get awkward between you and me. Losing my best friend would be worse than never having Houston at all."

She stares at me for a moment, then her mouth curls into that signature half smile she shares with Houston. "That's completely corny."

I roll my eyes and stare at the stage. "Whatever. I guess I'm corny, but I stand by what I said. Your friendship is more important to me than taking a chance with Houston."

Her smile disappears and she sits back in her seat. "Friendship is more important." She repeats these words and I get a weird feeling she's not telling me something. "It's the *most* important thing."

"Without friendship, there's no love," I reply, though the phrase surprises even me.

Hallie nods in agreement. "No friendship, no love." She sighs as she ponders this, then she turns to me. "I think you and Houston are gonna end up together."

I try not to let her see how hearing these words come from her mouth makes me absurdly happy. "I doubt it. I'll never have the courage to make that happen."

"Maybe you won't, but maybe someone else will."

My eyes widen. "You wouldn't!"

"No, not me. But you never know. Maybe one of these days Houston will finally get a clue and make it happen on his own."

I let out an exasperated sigh. "It would be kind of hard for him to get a clue when he's ninety miles away."

"Yeah, but you'll be going to UO in a couple of years. Maybe you can show up at a party he's at and pretend to be drunk. Then he'll carry you back to your dorm and—*Ew*. I don't want to imagine that."

I give her a playful shove. "Stop it."

She laughs. "Yeah, you might not love him so much if you knew he used to sleep with my mom every time he got sick."

"That's adorable," I say, feigning a dreamy smile.

She cocks one eyebrow. "The last time he did it he was thirteen."

I imagine six-foot-four Houston lying in bed next to his petite momma. "Still adorable."

"You're sick."

I laugh and we continue chatting until the seats fill up around us. When the curtains part, I hold my breath, as if I'm one of the actors on the stage waiting for my cue. Well, according to Hallie, I *am* an actor. I guess she's right. I've gotten very good at pretending.

I pretend I don't love Houston. I pretend I'm going to UO so I can study, when the only reason I'm going is to be near him. And worst of all, I pretend not to be afraid that I'll never love anyone else.

After the show, Hallie and I walk home together arm-in-arm. It's a bit chilly, but the sky is clear, so we don't bother rushing home. We take our time, just breathing in the crisp autumn air and chatting about the play. We're a block away from my house when I remember that Hallie never answered my question earlier.

"Hey, you never told me if you have a crush on someone. Is that why you were asking me about Houston?"

A small part of me is hoping she asked me about him because he mentioned me to her. But I know that's next to impossible, so I make sure not to look too eager for her response. Still, the demure smile she's wearing as she thinks about this question is making me nervous. I wish she would just hurry up and answer me.

"No. I don't have a crush on anyone other than Justin Timberlake."

"Justin Timberlake doesn't count," I reply, shaking my head both at Hallie and at myself for thinking that Hallie would keep the identity of her crush from me. "He's an alien. It's not possible for a human to be born *that* hot, with *that* much talent."

We arrive in front of my two-story house on Evans Street and Hallie tucks her light-brown hair behind her ear as she stares at the upstairs windows. "Then I guess the answer is no. But that might change. We *are* juniors now."

"Is that supposed to be some sort of achievement? I thought turning sixteen was only a big deal in Texas."

"Everything's a big deal in Texas. Especially Justin Timberlake." She winks as she begins to walk away. "Call me later."

She heads off in the direction of her house around the corner and I can't help but wonder if Hallie is lying to me. She's stretched the truth before, but only to spare my feelings. Maybe Houston *did* say something about me, something about how I'll never have a chance with him.

My chest hurts just considering this. I stroll up the walkway toward the front steps and my dad opens the front door before I even reach the porch. "Hey, sweetheart. How was the show?"

I think about the amazing costumes and the energy of being that close to the performers. "It was great," I reply, taking off my jacket as I adjust to the warmth of the living room.

My dad takes my coat and I sit on the sofa to reflect on how much I liked the play. Then I think of the conversation Hallie and I had before the show about the importance of friendship. And I find solace in knowing that it doesn't matter if Houston asked Hallie about me, because what I said to her today is all that matters. I'd rather keep pretending not to love Houston than risk getting my heart broken and possibly losing her as a friend.

Because Hallie and I are more than friends. She's the sister I never had and the only person I don't have to pretend with.

No friendship, no love.

Houston

August 27th

RORY CLOSES HER eyes when she finishes reading the letter. I hold my breath waiting for her response. The tears fall silently down her cheeks and I want to pull her in my arms and hold her until I've soaked up all her pain.

She opens her eyes and throws the letter at me as she leaps from the sofa and runs to the bathroom. Skippy and I race after her, but she slams the door to keep us out. The sound of her vomiting makes my stomach ache. But the sobs that come between each chorus of retching make me absolutely sick with myself.

I knock on the door when I hear a few seconds of silence, but her response echoes in the toilet bowl. "Go away!"

She's dry heaving now, but she manages to tell me to get out a couple more times. If it were anyone but Rory I would listen. I push the bathroom door open slowly and she's sobbing with her cheek resting on her arm, which is resting on the toilet seat. Skippy peeks inside the bathroom, sees her near the toilet, then turns around to go back to the living room.

I kneel next to her and she looks up at me, her eyes full of absolute despair. "I'm sorry I didn't show you the letter sooner," I begin, "but you can't tell me you don't understand why."

She covers her mouth as she sits up and leans back against the tub. "I don't understand any of this." Her shoulders fold inward as she tries to hold back the sobbing and retching. "And I don't know if I even *want* to understand it. I'm so disgusted with myself. I'm so stupid."

"You're not stupid. You're the only smart person in this whole fucked-up situation."

"No, I'm an idiot. I've spent thirteen years loving someone who was incapable of loving me. How, Houston? How could you pretend to love me for so long?"

I clench my jaw as I look into her eyes. "I wasn't pretending," I reply. "I couldn't ask you to choose between me and your father. Just because our relationship was built on a lie, it doesn't mean I didn't love the fuck out of you… I still do and I always will."

She rests her elbows on her knees and closes her eyes as she covers her face. "I knew you were hiding something from me, but I never expected this." She draws in a long, stuttered breath, then she looks up at me with a question in her eyes. "You said our relationship was built on a lie. What does that mean?"

I let out a deep sigh as I prepare to tell her the most damaging secret of them all. "When I asked you to move in with me, I hadn't read Hallie's letter yet. But after we went back to my apartment, I sat in the bathroom with the letter and tried not to punch the mirror as I read Hallie's words. I've never been so mad in my life. I wanted to burst into the bedroom where you were sleeping and take my anger out on you even though Hallie had just begged me not to in that letter."

Rory shakes her head as she covers her face again. I wish her father were here to see what a frightening mess all of us have made of this beautiful girl. This innocent girl whose only sin was to love and trust with all her heart.

"But I decided that instead of hurting you right there and then, I would bide my time. And I'd hurt you when you least expected it. I wanted you to hurt as much as Hallie did, then maybe your dad would feel the gravity of what he'd done to my sister. Maybe then he'd feel just a *drop* of the pain I was feeling."

She looks up at me, her eyes wide with shock. "That's why you broke up with me when I told you about the pregnancy? To *destroy* me?"

I shake my head adamantly. "No, you don't understand. Initially, I wanted to hurt you. But it only took a couple of days for the anger to subside. And in less than a month, I had fallen so utterly and completely in love with you, Rory.

"When you told me about the baby, I broke up with you because I was afraid if we got married, and I had to see your father walking you down the aisle or holding our child, I wouldn't be able to keep on lying to you. But I knew the truth would knock the stilts out from underneath us and we'd fall so hard we might never get up. I didn't want to ruin you. All I ever wanted was for you to move on."

"Move on?" Her hands tremble as she wipes the tears from her chin. "How was I supposed to do that when you were holding on to the one thing that would give me closure?"

"I'm so sorry I didn't show you the letter. It's the biggest regret of my life."

"Your biggest regret?" She shakes her head as if she can't believe what's she's hearing. "Fuck you and your regrets. Your regrets ruined me. Get out."

I reach for her face and she smacks my hand away. "I know you hate me right now, but this isn't over."

"Yes, it is." She rises from the floor and I follow her out of the bathroom. "This is where it ends." She stops just inside the front door, her lips trembling as she presses them together and looks me in the eye. "Good-bye, Houston."

"We'll always make it back to each other."

"Back to *what*? There's nothing left."

Stepping forward, I take her face in my hands. "Back to *us*. This isn't the end of us, Rory. You know it as well as I do." My lips brush softly over the tracks of tears glistening on her supple skin and she lets out a muffled sob. "The world can fall to pieces around us, but in the end, we'll always make it back to us."

She grabs my wrists as I kiss the corner of her mouth. "No, Houston, don't."

"We're the only thing that makes sense in all of this." I kiss her again and she whimpers. "Just give me some time to make this right."

Tangling my fingers in her silky hair, I kiss her tenderly. Her lips are salty and moist with tears, but she kisses me back. I want to lift her up and carry her to the bedroom, but I don't want to make this even more difficult. After today, Rory and I will have to go back to being strangers until I can figure a safe way out of my marriage.

She groans as she pushes me away and whispers, "Stop." Her gaze is fixed on Hallie's letter and the Sierra Nevada box where I left them on the coffee table. "Get out, Houston. And don't ever knock on my door again. Ever."

I stare at the box on the table and consider taking it with me—she did try to give it back to me earlier—but I decide to leave it. Telling Rory the truth doesn't change the fact that the ring is hers. If she doesn't want it, neither do I.

I also want to grab the letter. It's been such an important part of my life for the past five and a half years. It's my last connection to my baby sister. It's proof of her suffering. But I think that's exactly why I have to leave it with Rory.

I may have loved Hallie, but Rory knew and loved her like no one else. Rory deserves to hold on to that letter so she can seek the answers she needs to finally find some peace. I only hope I'll be there when that happens.

I sigh as I reach for the doorknob. "You'll always be the deepest scar on my heart."

Rory

Seven weeks later

THE LINE FOR the wine tasting is so long it extends from the bar, out along the glass walls enclosing this area from the rest of the market, and snakes around the glass until it reaches the sidewalk outside. The grand opening of Zucker's Café & Wine Bar looks like it's going to be a huge success. After the stress of the past seven weeks, I should be excited for all the preparation to finally be over. But I can't think of anything else right now except the guy staring at me from where he stands at the front of the line of customers.

He looks a little nervous, with his hands tucked in his pockets and a bashful smile lighting up his boyish good looks. I smile at him as Bella and I walk in and take our place behind the bar. He beams and I shake my head as I wonder how someone can be born with such a perfect smile.

"I'll take the first person in line," I say, looking straight at him. He steps forward as Bella takes the customer behind him. "What can I help you with, sir?"

He scratches his beard as he reads the options on the menu board on the wall behind me. "I'll take a bottle of Lagunitas IPA and"—he cocks an eyebrow and I wait for him to finish—"a date to my brother's annual Hipster Halloween party next Saturday."

I raise my eyebrows. "That's a tall order. Let me get your beer first." I grab his beer out of the cooler behind me, then I pop the top off and set it down in front of him on top of a cocktail napkin. "That will be $7.50."

He hands me a ten-dollar bill and tells me to keep the change. "And the party?"

"Who's going to be there?"

"Just a bunch of people wearing irony as if it didn't go out of style last year."

"Irony is so over!"

He laughs at my reference to *Portlandia*. "Looks like you'll fit right in."

I sigh as I look at the impatient line of thirsty patrons waiting behind him. "Okay, but you have to promise not to leave my side. I'm terrible at parties. I'm… way out of practice."

"Don't worry. I'll stick to you like a beard on a hipster."

He winks at me as he sets off to sit at a small table in the corner. I steal glances at him every few customers and every once in a while I catch him looking in my direction. His presence is making me a little nervous. I keep wondering if either Houston or Troy are going to show up for the grand opening.

I haven't seen Houston since he brought Hallie's letter to me seven weeks ago. Troy has been handling the setup of the beer taps. I don't know if this is because Houston is trying to respect my desire to not see him or because he's the one who doesn't want to see me. But seeing Troy six times in the past seven weeks has been more than enough reminders.

Every time Troy walked into the bar, I practically held my breath the entire time he was here. I was just waiting for him to say something about Houston. Sometimes, I'd try to guess what he might say, but that became too painful a game to play. What if Troy broke his silence only to tell me that Houston and his wife were now living happily ever after?

Just imagining this scenario makes me sick with emotional agony. And the nausea only worsens when I realize how deeply I'm still in love with Houston. And how, no matter how toxic things got between us, the good still outweighs the bad in my lovesick recollection.

After three hours and forty minutes without a break in the line of customers, Bella and I are relieved by Benji and Hernando, the only person at the grand opening with actual bartending experience. Bella makes herself a skinny latte and I grab an iced green tea before heading over to join Liam at his table.

"Those are some impressive beer pouring skills," he remarks.

"It's all in the wrist." I sigh as my aching feet tingle with relief when I sit down. "I'm sorry I haven't been answering your calls."

"Or texts, but who's keeping track?" He smiles as he stares at the empty beer bottle on the table. "I figured you had a lot on your mind, and you did respond that one time to tell me you were okay, so I probably should have taken the hint. I guess I'm just a glutton for punishment."

"It's been a weird seven weeks."

"Want to talk about it?"

I look up from my iced tea, and the inquisitive expression on his face makes me want to tell him everything, but I don't want to scare him away. Plus, my coffee break is nowhere near long enough to explain how I fell in love with a boy thirteen years ago and he, along with my best friend, proceeded to smash my heart into a billion pieces. Or how I looked up to my father as a role model most of my life and how, until seven weeks ago, I was unable to comprehend why he's hardly spoken to me in the past five years. Or how my mother could possibly think I didn't want to know her suspicions about Hallie. Basically, I don't have enough time to tell Liam how everyone I've ever given my heart to managed to stomp all over it.

"I think that conversation should be saved for a moment when you have about ninety-two hours to spare."

He chuckles. "I'll have to check my calendar, but I think I can fit you in next month."

"Lucky you." I take another sip from my tea, then I sit back in my wooden chair. "Why do you like me?"

He laughs and I realize how weird that must sound to him.

"I'm serious," I insist. "I'm a hot mess."

"That's probably why I like you," he replies. "I like my girls like I like my… girls: hot and messy."

"That's an amazing analogy."

"What can I say? When I was in college, I was partnered up with this really smart girl who taught me how to construct the perfect sentence."

"Really? So what's the perfect sentence?"

He smiles and leans forward as if he's about to divulge a secret. "Then, she let it go."

I don't know if it was his intention, but these five simple words stir a newfound energy inside me. A sudden awareness that I don't have to tell Liam anything about Houston. Liam can be my fresh start. All I have to do is let it go.

I smile as I rise from the table. "Sounds like a triumphant last line in a book."

"Feel free to use it."

I nod as I turn to leave. "I just might."

As I walk back to the bar, I glance at Liam over my shoulder, but he's already out of his chair and heading toward the recycling bins near the coffee prep station. I turn back toward the bar, but something I see out of the corner of my eye makes my heart stop. I whip my head around to get a better look, but no one's there.

I shake my head in disbelief. A half a second ago Houston was standing right there near the entrance. I can still see the green Barley Legal hoodie and the soft light bouncing off his golden-brown hair. But now he's gone.

Am I going crazy?

I rush back to the bar before anyone realizes how disturbed I am. Liam leaves the store and I spend the rest of the night trying not to sweat as I slide glass after glass of beer and wine across the bar. Bella and Benji offer to give me a ride when we leave the store at eleven p.m., but I decline their offer and set off on my own.

I don't mind walking the streets of Goose Hollow late at night. Besides, it gives me a chance to walk off some of the leftover anxiety from seeing Houston's ghost.

I stroll casually through the misty rain, inhaling deep breaths of cleansing Oregon air as I contemplate how much of the truth I should share with Liam and where this new adventure may take me. Maybe Liam will be the equivalent of Houston's PTSD therapy. Perhaps he'll help me forget everything I've lost and found.

I was eighteen when I got lost in Houston, and in him I found myself. They say love is just two souls recognizing each other. With Houston and me it was more like two souls staring into a mirror, my left hand aligned with his right, our hearts skipping a beat at the same moment, our lungs choking on the same noxious air, our scars as perfectly aligned as mountains and fault lines. If ever two souls were perfectly right and perfectly wrong for each other, it would be us.

Us.

I guess the story of *us* ends here.

But Hallie's story continues. And I won't rest until I know her truth inside and out.

Right now, all I know is that Hallie was drowning, but she

was too afraid to reach for a lifeline. As heartbroken as I am that she didn't give me the opportunity to understand her, I'm even more grateful to her for loving me enough to try to protect me in her last moments. And for teaching me the most important lesson I've ever learned.

You can't erase love without erasing yourself.

the way we break

For my father.

Part 3: Bargaining

"Before you bargain for more,
decide how much you're
willing to give up."

Rory

December 4, 2014

THE FRENCH HAVE A PHRASE I've become quite familiar with: *la douleur exquise.* Translated to English, it literally means exquisite pain. But the French use this phrase to refer to the excruciating pain of wanting something—*or someone*—you cannot have.

For me, *la douleur exquise* refers to the friendship I lost when my best friend Hallie Cavanaugh took her own life exactly six years ago today. The friendship I so desperately want back.

La douleur exquise also alludes to Hallie's older brother, Houston Cavanaugh. Everything about him. From the magical moment I first laid eyes on him when I was eleven years old, to the disenchanting moment when his wife attacked me just over three months ago. Houston is the one wish I've held on to for more than half my life. You can't hold onto a wish for that long without incurring the agony of deprivation. And the pain of wanting Houston has been the most excruciating anguish I've ever endured, until he showed up on my doorstep three months ago and completely obliterated my heart.

The tattoo artist holds my wrist steady as he focuses on the design he's carving into the delicate skin on the inside of my left forearm. Each stroke of his tattoo gun delivers microdroplets of ink deep beneath the surface of my skin. I try to focus on the shades of blue and green hair sticking out the sides of his baseball cap as he leans over my arm, to block out the sharp burning sensation, but it doesn't help.

"I'm almost done," he says, lifting his head to flash me a sparkling smile. "Just relax your hand."

I glance at my left hand, where I have a white-knuckled grip on his pinky. I quickly relax my fingers and he shakes out his hand. Then he grabs my wrist again.

"Sorry. It's my first time," I reply. "It…"

"Hurts? No worries. I'll try and make it quick." He winks at me then bows his head to get back to work.

I can't help but blush at the innuendo in our conversation. Biting my lip, I close my eyes and try not to flinch as he retraces the lines of my tattoo. Yes, it hurts, but not as bad as the pain of losing my best friend, my parents, and the only man I've ever loved.

My mind draws back to August 27th, the day Houston handed me Hallie's suicide note. The words Hallie never intended for me to see. In that note, my best friend confessed to having had an affair with my father the summer before our freshman year at the University of Oregon. She took her own life just one week after my father made it clear the affair was over. Hallie couldn't live knowing she had betrayed me. And Houston held on to that note for more than five years, trying desperately not to betray Hallie.

After Houston left my apartment, I called my mother, crying hysterically. My world as I knew it was falling apart. I needed someone to hold me and tell me everything would be okay. That this was as bad as it would get. I wanted her to stroke my hair, tell me I had hit bottom and there was nowhere to go but up.

I was so wrong.

My mother arrived at my apartment and immediately took me in her arms the moment I opened the front door. I buried my face in her silver shoulder-length hair and wept even harder when I recalled how her hair, once naturally auburn like mine, had turned almost completely gray during the seven-month period after she divorced my father five years earlier. She had also suffered. But… did that mean she knew about the affair?

She stroked my hair, just like I wanted her to, and squeezed me tightly. "Oh, honey. I knew Houston would hurt you again. I hate that you had to find out this way."

A flash of anger sparks inside me and I push her away. "This way? What do you mean by that? How long have you known about the affair?"

Her eyes are wide as her mouth drops open slightly, her mind grasping for the right words, which seem to be just out of her reach.

"*How long?*" I shout at her and she flinches.

"I didn't know. I… I had my suspicions, but your father denied it. Kept on denying it, even after she…"

"Is that why you divorced him?"

She swallows hard, but she doesn't answer me.

"You've suspected it all this time and you never told me?"

Her eyebrows furrow beneath her silver fringe. "I'm sorry, Rory, but I didn't want to hurt you. Not if there were even the slightest chance that I could be wrong."

I shake my head in dismay. "Everyone is so busy trying not to hurt me. No one stops to think about how much it hurt for me to be in the dark all those years."

"I'm so sorry, honey." She reaches for my hair and I push her hand away. Her mouth tightens into a hard line as she clasps her hands in front of her. Her disappointed-teacher stance. "Rory, please try and understand this from my point of view."

"Your point of view is that you didn't want to hurt me. I get that, Mom. What I don't get is why you felt you had the right to decide what pain was too great for me to face. Because I lost my best friend and, somehow, I got through that. I even managed to build a small semblance of a life for myself. When did I ever give you the impression that I couldn't handle pain?"

She presses her lips together as her eyes well up with tears. "You're right," she whispers. "I should have told you. You're stronger than I gave you credit for." She lets out a soft sigh as she looks me in the eye. "I'm sorry for underestimating you."

It's been three months and eight days since that conversation with my mother and I don't know what hurts more: not knowing if I can ever trust my parents again or not knowing if they were right. What if I'm *not* strong enough to handle this level of pain? What if I've fallen too far, without Houston to catch me this time?

Zack, the tattoo artist, begins wiping away the excess ink and blood from my left arm, then he sits up and smiles. "Want to take a look and tell me if there's anything you want me to go over again before you leave? Anything you want changed or detailed?"

I hold up my arm, but the tattoo is upside down from my vantage point. I smile at the beautifully scripted words. Looking up at him, I shake my head. "No, it's perfect the way it is. Thank you."

"Pleasure's all mine."

My stomach flutters a bit at the warm expression in his green eyes, but I flinch when I hear Liam's voice.

"You're all set?" Liam asks from the doorway of the private tattoo suite.

Zack's face gets serious. "Hey, you gotta stay outside until we're done. Shop policy, to avoid contamination."

I smile at Liam over my shoulder. "All set."

Liam glares at Zack. "Can I come in now?"

Zack responds with a wave of his hand, as if to say, *Be my guest.* As he rolls away on his stool to grab a bandage kit off the supply counter behind him, Liam makes his approach.

He leans over my chair to get a better look at the tattoo, letting out a soft puff of laughter. "What does it mean?"

I didn't tell Liam what I was getting tattooed on my arm. I was afraid he would know what *la douleur exquise* means, both in French and to me. I stare at the tattoo as I try to think of how to answer Liam. It's a heart with a banner underneath bearing the phrase *la douleur exquise.* Above the heart is the date December 4, 2008. Inside the heart is the phrase "No friendship, no love."

"It means I miss my friend."

Liam flashes me a tight-lipped smile then heads back outside while Zack cleans and bandages my new tattoo. Zack sends me off with a plastic bag filled with a packet of gauze, antiseptic cream, and saline wash.

Once we're outside, Liam and I keep our heads down, and I keep my arm tucked into my coat, braced against the sudden onslaught of rain. We walk quickly to the truck, where Liam opens the passenger door for me to climb inside, but he doesn't say anything. I can sense some tension, though I'm not sure if it's because of the tattoo or because he's as nervous as I am right now.

I wipe away the cool droplets of rain on my forehead as he climbs into the driver's seat. "Are you okay?" I ask.

He chuckles as he slides the key into the ignition. "I'm fine. Are *you* okay?"

I should probably explain the tattoo in more detail, but I'm afraid it might disturb the delicate balance Liam and I have established between friendship and… I don't even know how I would characterize our relationship. Some days, I feel as if Liam came into my life at just the right moment. Almost as if it were fate. Other days, I feel as if we were thrust together by extenuating circumstances, and now we're just riding comfortably on the inertia of that initial push.

"I'm good," I reply with a smile I hope hides the way my nerves are buzzing beneath my skin, making my skin itch.

"You don't look so good. Are you sure you want to do this?"

There could be two meanings to this question, since there are two terrifying things Liam and I are doing today. The first is something I've been putting off for years and the second is something I should probably put off for a few years. I decide to answer his question as if he's referring to the first thing.

"One hundred percent sure. It's not that I want to do it. I *need* to."

"Right," he replies, pulling out of the parking space outside the tattoo studio. "Needing something and wanting something are two very different things."

I'm not sure if this is a jab at the meaning of my tattoo, so I decide to ignore that possibility. Instead, I carefully slide the sleeve of my jacket up to my elbow and pull off three of the four pieces of tape holding the bandage in place over my tattoo. Then I slip my phone out of my pocket to text Kenny a picture of it. I replace the tape and wait anxiously for his response, which comes less than a minute later.

Kenny: Ooh, la la. French. What does it mean?

Me: The exquisite pain of wanting something you cannot have.

Kenny: You should just start wearing turtlenecks and move to France already. You've got that tortured artist thing down.

Me: I don't think I've graduated to that level of artiste yet, but I'm working on it.

Kenny: What does Liam the lumbersexual think of your new badge?

I glance at Liam to make sure he can't see my phone screen, then I type my response.

Me: Not sure he knows what it means. Not even sure I do.

Kenny: Sweetheart, you can pretend with him and you can pretend with yourself, but you cannot pretend with me.

Me: I have to go. I'll call you later.

Kenny: Oh, yes you will. And don't forget who you're spending New Year's Eve with. Hint: He doesn't have a luxurious beard.

I look at Liam and he's wearing that soft smile that always makes me feel as if he knows something I don't know. "What?"

"Nothing. What did Kenny think of your new tat?"

"How do you know it was Kenny?"

He shakes his head as he turns onto the highway toward Salem. "Who else would it be?"

"He thinks it makes me a tortured artist."

He chuckles as he looks over his shoulder to change lanes. "No comment."

"What does that mean? Do you agree with him?"

"Are we really going to argue over whether or not you're a tortured artist?"

I turn my attention back to the rain pounding on the windshield. "Sorry. Automatic response."

"We've gone over this, Rory. I respect you. You don't have anything to prove to me."

I let out a deep sigh. "I know. I'm sorry."

I've been picking fights with Liam a lot lately and I think it's just a way for me to prove I'm not weak. I can stand up for myself. But it's a stupid way to prove myself to him, especially when he's made it clear I have nothing to prove. It's my parents and Houston who didn't think I was strong enough, not Liam.

My stomach clenches as I think of the last time I saw my parents, five weeks ago, October 24th. It had been eight and a half weeks since Houston handed me Hallie's suicide note. My mom had come to my apartment to try to talk to me again. After two years of almost-daily visits from my mom, not talking to her for eight weeks was taking a toll on both of us. But when I saw her, the anger over her betrayal came flooding back to me and I demanded she leave.

"You can't keep shutting me out, Rory. It's not healthy."

"You want to know what's not healthy? That my father hasn't returned a single one of my calls in eight weeks. Eight weeks! You want to see me, then next time you come, bring him with you."

She pursed her lips the way only a former schoolteacher could. "That's not fair. I have no control over what your father does. I never have. You have to stop punishing me for his mistakes."

I looked her in the eye and gritted my teeth. "You're right. You have no control over him… But maybe I do."

I slid my phone out of my pocket and dialed my father's office number, anxiously tapping my foot as I waited for an answer.

"Talbert, Charles, and Associates, may I help you?" the receptionist said, her voice husky with boredom.

"James Charles, please."

"May I ask who's calling?"

"Mrs. Leiderbach," I replied coolly.

"Just a moment, Mrs. Leiderbach."

My mom's eyes widened at my fake name. She knew I was serious. There would be no more hiding. This was all going to come to a head now.

"James speaking."

My dad's voice knocked the breath out of me, and suddenly I couldn't speak. We hadn't spoken in months. Though I knew his voice hadn't changed, he sounded different. Just hearing him speak brought up memories of the times he'd carry me to bed after I'd fall asleep on the sofa. I remembered the crisp scent of his aftershave and wondered if Hallie had loved that smell.

This thought brought my voice back. "You inconceivable asshole."

"Excuse me?"

"You heard me, Dad."

"Rory? What—what's going on here?"

"Oh, don't play dumb with me. You've been avoiding me for eight weeks. You know exactly what's going on. But I'm through being ignored."

"Rory, I don't know what you're talking about. I've been working a death row appeal for months. I don't have any messages from you."

"Stop lying! I'm tired of being lied to." I took a moment to unclench my fist, rubbing my hand over my jeans to soothe the nail marks. "You're coming to my apartment right now and you're going to tell me everything or, I swear to God, I will come down there and tell everyone in that office what you did to Hallie."

"Jesus Christ, Rory. You can't call my office and do this. I'm in the middle of a very important case."

"Yeah, well, I think the story of you seducing an underage girl is going to make a very important case with the Disciplinary Board. Don't you?"

Every seething breath he took rustled loud and clear through my phone speaker. "I'll be there in thirty minutes."

My mother busied herself making coffee while I checked my phone obsessively, waiting for him to arrive. I expected to get a text message from him saying he couldn't make it. He'd been called away to a meeting, or some other excuse. But no text messages came through and thirty-two minutes later, the knock at the door made me jump.

I leaped off the sofa and raced to the front door, glancing over my shoulder at my mother's worried face as I reached for the doorknob. Turning the knob, I braced myself for the inevitable fury that would hit me the moment I saw my father's face. But when I pulled the door open, I wasn't prepared for the avalanche of grief that cascaded through me.

Each breath I took came in short deliberate gasps as the tears flowed freely from my eyes. Overwhelmed with heartache and the images painted in Hallie's letter. I had not been allowed to grieve properly when Hallie died. I'd been denied the answers I needed for closure. Now, I had the answers, and the sickening mental images, and the one person who could have prevented it all was standing right in front of me. The grief slammed into me like a freight train, violent and unstoppable.

My father stood in my doorway in his gray suit and black overcoat, his brow furrowed below his closely cropped dark hair. "Rory."

"How could you?" I whispered, my voice strangled by the knot in my throat.

He reached for me as I clutched my chest, as if I could physically hold the splintered pieces of my heart together.

I held out my hand to stop him. "Don't touch me."

He took a step back, his face flushed with frustration. "It's not what you're thinking," he insisted.

"*How could you?*" I bellowed from somewhere deep inside me, a place where my memories of Hallie weren't distorted by the knowledge of their affair. A place I longed to get back to.

The door across the hall opened immediately, as if Mrs. Vernor had been waiting for this confrontation with as much anticipation as I had. Her silver hair curled and poofed, her dark-brown eyes widened when she saw my father.

"Are you all right, honey?" she asked me.

I didn't want her to know that this man who had never once visited me at my apartment was my father. He was always too busy. For the past two years, he'd insisted we meet for lunch downtown instead of at my place or his. Lord knew how many young minxes he kept at his downtown condo.

"I'm fine, Mrs. Vernor," I replied, then I opened the door for my father to step inside. "Sorry if we disturbed you."

Mrs. Vernor didn't look convinced, but she retreated inside her apartment as I closed my door behind me.

I needed to get a grip on my emotions. But as I turned around to face my parents, all I could see was the words I'd read in Hallie's letter. No matter how many times I read it, I couldn't figure out if Hallie was trying to cover up for my father. What if their affair *didn't* begin three days after Hallie's eighteenth birthday? What if it started when she was underage? And even if it *did* begin when she was eighteen, did that make it any less wrong?

My mother and father glanced at each other and exchanged a curt nod as he stood awkwardly next to the coffee table. They had spent more than twenty years together as each other's most intimate confidantes, and now they were reduced to brusque gestures. This affair had torn my family apart and yet I couldn't bring myself to be angry with Hallie. She had gone through a very similar situation when her father was caught cheating on her mother. Only, Hallie had to go through it at a much younger age. It was no wonder she pursued my father. Just like it was no wonder I got caught up in an affair with Houston.

I am my father's daughter.

I swallowed hard at this thought. As I opened my mouth to voice my disgust with what my father had done, a knock at the door interrupted me. Sighing with frustration, I yanked it open, prepared to tell Mrs. Vernor to mind her own business. But it wasn't Mrs. Vernor. It was Houston.

Liam's truck hits a bump and I'm yanked out of my thoughts. The scene before me materializes, then reality punches me in the gut. We're now bumping along a narrow road at Pioneer Cemetery. The rain is coming down so hard, I can barely see the grave markers. But I remember quite clearly we have to take the first right and go all the way down until the road begins to curve left.

Liam parks the truck and reaches for the umbrella in the cab.

I place my hand on his arm to stop him. "I need to go alone."

He nods. "Okay, but you need to take the umbrella."

I take the green umbrella from him and gaze into his crystal-blue eyes. "Thank you for bringing me here. It means a lot to me."

He smiles faintly. "I know."

I push the passenger door open and stick the umbrella out of the truck so I can open it before I step into the downpour. The rain batters the nylon and a few fat drops hit the back of my head as I hop out of the truck. Landing in a shallow puddle, I mentally curse myself for wearing sneakers instead of rain boots.

I slam the truck door shut behind me then slog across the soggy grass toward the second-to-last gravestone in this row of markers. The ground sloshes under my feet as the rain batters my umbrella, making it almost impossible to hear my own thoughts. The smell of wet stone and decaying earth is overwhelming.

A deep chill settles into my bones the nearer I get to the end of the row. I walk between the banks of stone crosses and Gothic tablets memorializing people who were once as alive and vibrant and loved as Hallie. Finally, I reach the plain stone marker with Hallie's name on it and my fingers tighten painfully around the umbrella handle.

The stone reads "Hallie R. Cavanaugh. May 14, 1990—December 4, 2008. A much loved daughter, sister, and friend. Forever in our hearts."

Six years later and I still can't believe it. Like it's just an elaborate hoax and Hallie is going to walk up behind me right now and say, *Gotcha!* The rest of my life seems hazy and incomplete when I try to imagine it without her. She won't be my maid of honor. I won't be her firstborn's godmother. We won't be playing bingo together in a nursing home. She's just gone.

The cold seeps inside my twill jacket and I instantly begin to shiver. Wiping the tears from my face, I kneel before the gravestone, paying no mind to the muddy rainwater soaking through the knees of my jeans. I reach out and trace the *H* of Hallie's name.

"Hallie." I whisper her name aloud. "I miss you so much." The patter of the rain on my umbrella fills the spaces between my words, a solemn drumbeat. "I'm sorry… I'm sorry I never saw this coming." Once the first apology tumbles out of my mouth, the rest come in a relentless torrent. "I'm sorry I didn't see how badly you were suffering. I should have pushed you to talk to me, or someone. I should have known something was wrong with you that morning instead of thinking everything was about me. I'm sorry I wasn't a better friend."

I rub my fingertips over the pain in my chest as I take a long draw of cold December air, letting out each caustic breath slowly in an attempt to calm myself. After a few deep breaths, the pain in my chest lessens to a dull ache.

"Most of all," I whisper, "I'm sorry for all the times I've been angry with you the past six years. You were my sister, Hal. I've never hated you. And I never will." I kiss the tips of my fingers and touch them to the rough wet stone as I stand. "I'll never stop wanting you back."

My tattoo starts burning as I walk back to the car. Glancing at my arm, I see my left sleeve is soaked with rain from touching the gravestone. The bandage is probably wet, too. Liam hops out of the car and rushes around to the passenger side to open the door for me. I hand him the umbrella and he closes the door behind me before making his way back to the driver's side. He shakes out the umbrella a little before he sticks it in the backseat, and Skippy and Sparky finally wake from their doggy nap.

Liam's face is impassive as he scratches Skippy's head. "How do you feel?"

"Better."

"Good. So you're ready for an eleven-hour road trip?" He flashes me that perfect smile that always warms my insides and I have no choice but to say yes.

Even if I'm actually terrified I'm making a huge mistake. The truth is, I've been living my life too carefully for the past six years. My world has been hermetically sealed off from any possibility of pain or mistakes for far too long. It's time to tear off the wrapper and take some risks. Maybe stumble a bit. That's the stuff that makes every story more interesting.

I'm certain that's why I had trouble finishing my book before Houston came back into my life. And why, ever since he returned, I've been writing more pages than my fingers can keep up with.

"I'm ready," I reply with a genuine smile. "Let's move to California."

Houston

September 5, 2014

I DIDN'T KNOW there was such a thing as pre-divorce counseling until I handed Tessa divorce papers last week and she responded by handing me a business card with the name of a therapist who specializes in it. Now I'm sitting in this therapist's office, gritting my teeth and trying to convince myself the next four to six weeks of my life won't be a complete waste of time when I can go back to Rory a free man. Four to six weeks is how long it will take for the divorce to go through, which isn't very long compared to some other states, where it can take as long as six to twelve months. But it still feels like an eternity.

"How are you feeling today, Houston?"

Dr. Mansfield crosses his ankle over his knee as he asks the question, making himself comfortable as he's in the process of making me uncomfortable. I want to ask him if he has any compassion for me. *Can't he see I'm suffering?* Isn't there an unspoken bro-code that says he's not allowed to indulge Tessa's need to draw this out?

"I'd be better if I didn't have to be in this bogus counseling session," I reply, trying to sound as bored as possible.

Tessa crosses her arms over her chest and shakes her head. "See? This is what I have to deal with every time I try to talk to him. He doesn't take me seriously."

"I take you very seriously. Otherwise, I wouldn't be here."

"You don't take me seriously. You just want this divorce to be finalized."

"You're right about that. If it were up to me, the divorce would be finalized today."

She turns to Dr. Mansfield. "*See?*" she shrieks, her blonde hair flying as she points her skinny finger at me, like I'm not sitting three feet away from her. "That's what I'm talking about. He doesn't even want to *try* to talk about it. He just wants it *over*!"

"What do you expect when you emotionally blackmail me into staying with you for three years and then you *lie* about being pregnant?"

She leans over the arm of her chair as if it's the only thing stopping her from charging me. "I didn't lie! I thought I was pregnant!"

I lean back in my chair, shaking my head. "Stop lying, Tessa. It's over. This is over. There's no reason to lie anymore."

Tessa opens her mouth to shout something, but Dr. Mansfield holds up his arm to stop the madness. He begins speaking again, but my thoughts drift to the day I found out Tessa was lying about the baby.

After Tessa got clipped by that car on Raleigh Street, I wanted to ride with her in the ambulance, but the EMT wouldn't allow it. It wasn't until I pulled my SUV away from Wallace Park to follow the ambulance that I realized I couldn't see Rory anywhere. I thought of getting out to look for her, but I didn't have time. I had to get to the hospital. I had to make sure the doctors and nurses knew Tessa was pregnant. Besides, after what Tessa did, I doubted Rory would want to see me. She'd probably already left the park.

I didn't think it was possible to hate myself more than I did when I left Rory five years earlier. But the moment I drove off toward the hospital to try to save the child Tessa was carrying was a defining moment for me. It wasn't that I loved Tessa or our child more than I loved Rory, or the child I had conceived with Rory. It was that *I* had changed. I was ready to come clean with Rory about the letter. I was ready to live the truth instead of the lie. And if the truth was that I was going to become a father, I had to accept my new role and all the consequences that came with it.

When I arrived at the hospital, the ER nurse informed me that Tessa was conscious and had already been wheeled away to Radiology for X-rays.

"Didn't the EMT tell you she's pregnant? I told him to tell you." I tried to keep my voice even, but the nurse could see by the way I gripped the counter I was about two seconds from jumping onto her side of the desk.

She didn't look very impressed. "Sir, please head down the hall and to the right to complete the registration forms for your wife."

"Did you hear a single word I just said?"

"Sir, please step back and take a breath. Your wife is in good hands. We will update you as soon as we have more information."

My mouth fell open in disbelief. "Did you just tell me to step back and take a breath?"

"Sir, I'm not going to ask you again. Please go down the hall to complete registration, then have a seat in the waiting room. When we know more, we'll call you."

My nostrils flared as I drew in a deep breath and let it out slowly. Then I marched my ass to Registration to sign all the paperwork. Two and a half hours later, another nurse called me out of the waiting room to take me to Tessa's room. But first, she had to tell me they were ordering a psychiatric evaluation. In her words, Tessa seemed "a bit confused."

"What the fuck does that mean? Does she have amnesia or something?"

The nurse's brown curls bounced as she shook her head adamantly. "No, she doesn't have any head injuries. Her only injuries are a few scrapes and bruises and a broken arm. Her arm is in a temporary cast, but you'll need to make an appointment with an orthopedic surgeon to get a permanent cast."

I followed as we turned the corner into another hospital corridor. "I don't get it. Then why is she confused?"

The nurse cleared her throat and I had a sense she was trying to find a delicate way to break the news to me. "She seems to think she was pregnant, but the ultrasound and blood tests don't show any evidence of that. She told us to contact her fertility doctor to ask him and he said she was never pregnant. But she insists this doctor helped you two conceive a child. Was your wife pregnant?"

I stopped in the middle of the corridor, my vision blurring as fiction and reality seemed to be blending together. "She's not pregnant?"

"Have you been to a fertility doctor, Mr. Cavanaugh?"

I shook my head in utter disbelief. "She was never pregnant."

The nurse glanced at my clenched fists and shook her head. "I'm sorry."

Dr. Mansfield's voice cut through the fog of this memory. "Okay, okay. Let's move on to something else. How do you both feel about this divorce? And by that I mean, do you feel you will be stigmatized by this divorce? Do you fear this may affect your chances of finding a romantic partner in the future?"

Tessa laughs at this. "It won't affect him. He already has a *romantic* partner just waiting in the wings for him. Don't you? Why don't you tell the doctor how I caught you cheating on me with that slut?"

I grip the arms of the chair I'm sitting in and clench my jaw so I don't say anything I'll regret in front of the therapist. "Watch your mouth, Tessa."

"*See?*" she cries again. "He defends *her* and he hates *me*. He treats me like I'm *nothing*."

I want to storm out of this office and never come back, but I promised myself I would do the mature thing and make it through at least four counseling sessions. This therapist better up his game and start reining in Tessa's hysterics. I can't take much more of this.

"Okay, let's try something different," Mansfield says, sitting up straighter in his chair. "How about we do an exercise? Why don't the both of you each give me three positive things that will come out of this divorce?"

My mind instantly conjures Rory's face. The one positive thing that will come out of this divorce: I'll be free to make room for her in my life. Then I try to think of three things I love the most about her, but it's hard to narrow it down. Her vanilla-scented hair is pretty high on the list. Her constant movie references. Her creamy skin and the way it feels when her legs are wrapped around me. Her many facial expressions: adorably confused, scary angry, her *come-fuck-me* expression, and, my personal favorite, her smile. But it seems all she's done lately is cry.

Which is why I'm stumbling my way through these counseling sessions. It's why I'm giving Rory the space she needs to work things out with her parents. I just hope her father took my threat seriously.

I've wanted to throttle that son of a bitch for nearly six years, but I've put it off because of Rory. After she tossed me out of her life last week, I had nothing left to lose. I showed up at his law offices in downtown Portland and managed to finesse my way past the receptionist. I found the glass-walled conference room where James stood at the head of a long mahogany table. He was in the middle of a meeting, but not for long.

I stepped into the conference room and pointed at him. "You and I need to talk. Now."

"We're in the middle of a meeting," said a blonde woman sitting in a chair a few feet away from me.

"No, it's fine, Christina," James said, making his way toward me. "Carry on without me. I won't be long."

I clenched my fists as I followed him to his corner office. The first thing I saw when I stepped inside was the row of framed pictures on the console table behind his desk. There were two pictures of James and Rory together, one of him kissing her forehead as they stood next to a backyard grill. The other picture was obviously from the family vacation they took to Hawaii when Rory was in high school. I couldn't remember how old she was during that vacation, but I found myself wondering if Hallie had already developed a crush on James by then.

This thought made me more sad than angry. How would Hallie feel if she knew why I was here? What would she think of the way I've handled her secret?

James's office smelled of leather and hardwood. It reeked of money, with the tufted leather armchair behind the mahogany desk and the walls lined in bookshelves and certificates. Light poured in through the window painting a silver glow over every gleaming surface. But that was only the first impression. Upon further inspection, an uneasy feeling rippled through me.

The stain on the mahogany desk didn't match the stain on the mahogany shelves. And the leather chairs appeared worn, as if all these pieces were scrabbled together from purchases made at a used office furnishings warehouse. I tried to determine what this said about James, but I didn't know if it meant he was pragmatically frugal, or maybe he took on a lot of pro bono cases.

Did that mean I should admire him? The man who was once an activist, fighting for the rights of the wrongfully accused, until he settled down and had a family.

Before I went off to college, I barely noticed Rory, and I sure as hell didn't notice her father. But I'd had six years to consider how I felt about what happened between Hallie and James, and I still couldn't figure out why I was so angry. By all accounts, Hallie's letter made it clear she had pursued James for two years before *he* gave into her advances after her eighteenth birthday. I guess what made me most angry was knowing that, in the end, *he* rejected *her*. Not the other way around.

"Have a seat." He spoke cordially, his face somber as he motioned to the guest chair and took a seat behind the desk. As if I were there to discuss litigation instead of his illicit affair with a teenager. "Let's talk."

I glanced at the chair James motioned to, but I didn't move. "No, I'm going to talk. You're going to listen." Glaring at him across the desk, I waited for him to challenge me, but he simply nodded. I found this a bit disappointing. "You took advantage of my sister."

"It's not—"

"*I'm* talking!"

He clenched his jaw, his gaze falling to the desk as he leaned back in his chair. "Do your worst."

"This is far from my worst. I'd much rather be throwing you out that fucking window."

His nostrils flared as he bit back a reply.

I took a deep breath to slow the frantic pounding of my heart, then grabbed the back of the chair in front of me. "What happened with Hallie is over. I can't get her back and your sneaky lawyer brain made damn sure you couldn't be prosecuted. But there's still one person who deserves a massive fucking apology from you." I gritted my teeth against the twist of emotion in my gut. "Rory lost her best friend. And she's lived almost six years not knowing why because my sister was too ashamed to tell her."

I swallowed the lump in my throat as he finally met my gaze. "I hope that's remorse I see in your eyes, because Rory's in a world of pain right now. And, God help her, you're the only one who can make it right. So you'd better come out of your dark closet and get down on your knees for her. Or the next time I come here I won't be so fucking polite." My entire body was trembling with rage. I knew my only option was to leave before I did anything stupid. "You have six weeks."

That meeting in his office took place last week. I've spent every day since then hoping Rory will call me and tell me her father went to see her. That he's apologized and she's ready to let me back into her life. But I haven't heard anything from her.

I've avoided showing up at her apartment or cornering her at work. The last thing I need is to give Tessa another reason to go after Rory. But once this divorce is finalized in the next four to six weeks, I'm going back to her. And her father better have made amends with her, or at least attempted to, by then. Though I'm not exactly sure how he's supposed to make amends with Rory when I'm still trying to figure out how to do that with my mom.

Rory and my mom are the collateral damage of this affair. As much as I want to show my mom Hallie's suicide note, I don't know if I have it in me to break her heart when it's just beginning to heal again. Just last week, she showed me a vase she made in her new pottery studio in the garage. She'd painted it pink and orange, Hallie's favorite colors, and used a new shimmering glaze to make it glitter in the sunlight. A year or two ago, she would have shown me that vase with tears in her eyes, but last week she held it up to the light shining through her kitchen window and smiled broadly, as if the vase were the very embodiment of my sister's lustrous soul.

I don't think anyone has judged my actions, and inaction,

these past years more harshly than I have. No one understands the burden I've carried. The power to destroy someone emotionally is not the kind of power I wanted bestowed upon me. But that is the gift my baby sister left me. And it's all I have left of her.

Rory

December 4, 2014

THE FIRST TWO HOURS of our road trip to Silicon Valley pass fairly quickly. We stop once to let Skippy and Sparky have some water and stretch their legs. And Liam can't stop talking about how much I'm going to love Mountain View, California. He's been there for business trips at least half a dozen times and he claims it's a Mecca for tech-savvy grown-ups. One of my favorite things about Liam is that he refers to adults as grown-ups.

I wish I could say I feel like a grown-up, but I feel quite the opposite today. The truth is that I agreed to come to California with Liam on a crazy whim. And if Houston hadn't shown up while my mom and dad were at my apartment five weeks ago, I may not have said yes.

When I opened my front door and found Houston standing there, with my father standing just a few feet behind me, it was the first time I had seen Houston since he'd handed me Hallie's suicide note. He wore a black Barley Legal T-shirt that hugged his broad shoulders, and a smile as warm as a speck of dust caught in a sunbeam. I hadn't seen that smile since the day at Wallace Park, when he told me that everywhere we're together is the only place and moment that exists. And that was exactly how I felt as I stood frozen on my threshold.

He held up the stack of papers in his hand and proclaimed, "It's over."

His voice was softer and clearer, as if his soul had been brushed clean of everything that had been weighing him down. I tried to imagine what he meant by this phrase, but in his presence, my brain wasn't operating on all cylinders.

"What's over?" I asked.

"My marriage," he replied, tempering his smile as he seemed to realize the need for less hubris. "We need to talk, Rory."

"Is that Houston?" my mom called to me from the kitchen.

Houston's smile vanished. "Is your mom here?"

My pulse raced as I tried to figure a way out of this. "Yes," I replied, stepping over the threshold toward Houston as I tried to sneakily shut the door behind me.

"Who else is in there?" His blue eyes narrowed as I tried to close the door. "Rory, who's in there? Is it Liam? I saw him talking to you yesterday at the opening."

"You were there?" As soon as the words came out of my mouth, I wanted to smack my own forehead. Of course he was there. He owns a fifty percent stake in the wine bar. So I wasn't imagining things when I thought I saw him.

"Don't change the subject, Rory. Is Liam in there?"

I chuckled nervously as I pulled the doorknob. "What? No. Liam's not here." The door clicked shut behind me, and I leaned back against it to keep from collapsing. "No, it's just my mom. She came over to talk."

His gaze fell to the floor, disappointed. "It's your dad, isn't it?"

My fingers gripped the doorknob so tightly my knuckles

cracked. "Yes."

The muscle in his jaw twitched as he drew in a sharp breath through his nose. "Did he apologize to you?"

"He… He just got here."

He looked me in the eye, his brow furrowed with confusion. "You haven't spoken to him until now? But… it's been eight weeks since I gave you that letter. I told him eight weeks ago that he needed to apologize to you."

"You *what?*" I shrieked, unable to believe what I'd just heard.

"I told him to apologize to you." He looked even more confused by my anger. "Yes, I went to his fucking office and I told him to make things right with you or he'd have to answer to me."

"He's my father, Houston. My relationship with my father is none of your business."

"Your relationship? What fucking relationship? It took him eight weeks to talk to you about this. He hasn't even *tried* to see how you've been doing?"

"Neither have *you*!"

The doorknob turned and I fell backward a little as the door opened. Then the sound of my father's voice filled me with dread.

"What's going on out here?" he asked. "Are you okay, Rory?"

Houston's face contorted with rage when he saw my father. Before I could stop him, he shoved my father back, but with me in the way he was only able to make contact with one hand.

"Eight fucking weeks!" Houston roared. "Do you have no fucking conscience?"

I pushed Houston back into the corridor, but it was like trying to push a bull back into a pen. "Stop it!" I shouted at him, gripping his T-shirt like reins, trying to steer him away from the door.

"Get off me," he growled as he attempted to pry my hands off his shirt.

"Don't you touch my daughter," my dad warned Houston, and I wished I could turn around and slap him for even thinking he had a right to try to defend me.

"You shouldn't have touched my sister!" Houston shouted back at him.

The tears stung my eyes and I didn't realize I'd let go of Houston's shirt until my hands fell to my side. "Stop it," I whispered. "This is *my* family, Houston. Not yours."

"Keep your fucking family."

After he walked away, I assumed that would be the last time I ever saw Houston. But he began texting me apologies that same night. And he's showed up at my apartment three times in the past five weeks. All three times I pretended I wasn't home. Though I almost opened the door on the third instance when I heard Mrs. Vernor from across the hall threatening to call the police on him if he didn't leave me alone. I would have told her the police aren't necessary. But he left pretty quickly after she threatened him and he hasn't been back since. Not even today, on the anniversary of Hallie's death. I thought for sure he'd come today.

I guess I didn't really give him the chance to since I left my apartment this morning at nine a.m. to get my tattoo. But I'm probably the last person he wants to see today. I'm sure he's probably spending the day with his mom. I wonder if she knows about the letter yet.

"Can you change the playlist?" Liam's voice pulls me back to the present.

"Which playlist do you want me to put on?" I ask, opening up the Spotify app on my phone.

"My Halloween playlist."

"What? I don't want to listen to Halloween music."

"It's not Halloween music," he says, rolling his eyes. "It's music they played at the Halloween party."

"Oh" is the only response I can muster as I turn on the 80s playlist.

Liam's brother's Hipster Halloween party in October was our first official date and our first kiss. Liam tends to make too big of a deal about it. It's not like we're teenagers anymore. On November 30th, four days ago, Liam took me out to Ración for the one-month anniversary of our first kiss. But the restaurant was so busy that we got pretty terrible service. So when Kenny texted me midway through our meal to ask if I wanted to meet up for drinks, we jumped at his offer.

We arrived at Kells Brew Pub around 9:30 p.m. with three drinks in our bloodstream. We found Kenny and two of his hottest pals sitting at a table near the back of the dark pub. Kenny leaped out of his chair at the sight of me. His ash-brown hair was freshly cut and I swear he looked even taller and stronger than the last time I'd seen him. He was working with a new personal trainer to gain muscle, though he freely admitted to fantasizing about blowjobs while he was bench-pressing.

I gladly accepted Kenny's bone-crushing hug. "This is not your typical hangout," I said, squeezing his waist tighter, just the way he likes it.

He planted a loud kiss on my cheek before he let go. "Nope. We're trying something new tonight. We just left Timber Stadium, where we were watching Gastón Fernández get fondled—I mean *fouled* by David Beckham. So hot. Anyway, we thought we'd try to hook us some soccer fans, but it's kind of Deadsville in here. Then I thought, *Hey! My fabulous friend Aurora lives in this neighborhood.*"

"I love being your last resort," I teased him as I took a seat on his right and Liam sat next to me.

"Honey, if you had a penis, you would be my *first*… woman with a penis?"

I laughed as I reached for the pint of beer in front of Kenny.

"Is this yours?"

"It's yours now, gorgeous. John, get us all a round of shots," Kenny said to his blond friend with the obscenely long eyelashes.

"So, if I had a penis, I'd be your first woman *with* a penis. Does that mean I wouldn't be your first woman *without* a penis?"

Kenny bit his lip as his gaze fell to the table. "Guilty."

"Oh, my goodness! When was this? You have to tell me so I can fantasize about it."

He smacked my arm. "Shame on you! You have a handsome someone to fantasize about right here," he said, waving his hand in a flourish, as if Liam were a brand-new car on *The Price Is Right*. "Besides, that was a very dark and confusing time in my life. I'd rather not go there."

One beer and three shots later, I was seeing double. I excused myself to the restroom, and when I returned, Kenny and Liam were singing "My Way" by Frank Sinatra. The notes blended together in my sloshy drunk mind, or maybe Kenny and Liam were slurring. Either way, by the time they were done, I was smitten.

I plopped down in the chair next to Liam and curled my arm around his, locking elbows with him. The alcohol swimming through my veins washed away all thoughts of Houston. It even numbed the lingering discomfort in my belly, which seemed to reside there whenever I spent time with Liam.

"That was incredibly sexy," I murmured.

"You should see me sing Christmas carols," he replied, then took another sip of his beer.

"We should totally sing Christmas carols!" Kenny replied with way too much excitement.

I shook my head as I reached for Liam's beer. "Oh, my God. That reminds me. Zucker's is having a Christmas party this year."

"What!" Kenny shrieked. "Oh, girl, you and I are going to crash that thing into the ground like a couple of terrorists."

"Nuh-uh. I'm taking Liam," I slurred as I nudged Liam's shoulder. "That will be, like, the one-month-twenty-five-day anniversary of our first kiss. Maybe we can go to second base, eh?" I wriggled my eyebrows at him and he shook his head. "What? You don't want to hang out with me and my awesome coworkers? Come oooooonnn."

"I would like nothing better than to score a home run with you, but I won't be here for Christmas."

"What?" I replied, my face slackening with confusion.

Kenny laughed as he pointed at me. "Oh, my goodness. The look on your face when he said that."

I shushed him as I turned to Liam. "Why aren't you going to be here?"

Something about the sober look on his face combined with his lumberjack beard made him look even more serious than I thought possible.

"I need to talk to you about something." He scratched his beard as he pondered how to answer my question. *Digging for wisdom in his fur* was what I called this gesture. "Actually, I need to *ask* you something."

Kenny and his friends' voices melted away into the clamor of drunken chatter that filled the bar. The amber glow of the bar lighting seemed to dim on all sides of us, spotlighting our table. My nerves sparked with curiosity and I shivered as I waited for Liam to continue.

"Rory, do you want to move to California with me?"

A needle screeched across the record in my mind as Kenny and his friends turned to me wide-eyed. I could hear the noise in the bar again, now that our table was eerily quiet. I didn't know what was worse, the pressure of having Liam ask me something like this in front of so many people or the fact that my immediate answer wasn't no.

I barely knew Liam. We had been dating for a month and we

hadn't slept together yet. Our first kiss was questionable, but after a few make-out sessions, I had trained him to kiss more like—like the way I wanted to be kissed. But the best thing about Liam was that he didn't just listen to me when I talked. He asked questions.

He wanted to know what happened with Houston and me. I didn't tell him everything, but he knew enough to know what he was getting into. The fact that he was asking me to move in with him, in another state, told me he didn't think I was as screwed up as I thought I was. Maybe there was hope for me after all. With Liam.

Still, this was not the kind of question I was expecting Liam to ask.

"But…" I swallowed hard, trying to ignore Kenny's penetrating glare. "I live here. I *work* here."

Liam grabbed my hand and leaned toward me, his face inches from mine. "You can take some time off to write while you look for another job."

Glancing sideways, I saw Kenny's lips pressed together, anticipating my response. He knew as well as I did that Liam had just said the magic words. I didn't want to work at Zucker's grocery store for the rest of my life. I've wanted to be a writer since I was six years old, lying in my bed with a big book of fairy tales, twisting my hair around my chubby finger as I imagined one day creating a story as magical as the one I was lost in. And now, just like in those fairy tales, Liam was offering to be my knight in shining armor. He was offering to make my dreams come true.

"Yes."

Liam looked confused by my response. "Really?"

"What?" Kenny shrieked.

"Yes, I'll go to California with you."

My phone vibrates in my hand, and the sensation pulls me out of my memories, but the soft buzzing sound is drowned out by the '80s music blasting through Liam's car speakers. I turn the phone over and my breath hitches at the sight of the name on my screen: Houston.

He hasn't called me in more than a week. I assumed he'd packed up his suitcase of lies and headed back to the level of hell from which he came.

I hit the red button to decline the call and glance at Liam to make sure he didn't notice the name. I should really change Houston's name in my phone to something that will remind me not to answer. Heart Obliterator is one option. Lying Cheating Demon from Hell is another. Or maybe, God of Orgasms. I bite my lip at the thought of that one. That would definitely *not* keep me from answering his calls.

I went more than five years without having sex with anyone. Now, it's been three months since my sex marathon with Houston and I can't stop thinking about it: his smooth skin sliding over mine, his strong hands gripping my ass, his hot mouth between my legs, his cock stretching me, sending me soaring into a blissful sex haze.

A couple of minutes later, my phone vibrates again and a voicemail from Houston appears in my inbox. I stare at the message for a while, wondering why the voicemail is so long. One minute and thirty-six seconds. His messages are usually ten to fifteen seconds of him begging me to call him back. Of course, today is December 4th. Maybe he just wants to talk to me about Hallie.

Or maybe he went by my apartment and realized I'm gone.

My heart pounds with anticipation. I want to check his message so badly, my finger itches to hit play. But I can't. And not just because I'm sitting here with Liam.

I can't check that message because Houston and I are over. All we ever brought each other was one layer of pain mortared atop another. I need to tear down the monument of memories I've worshipped for the past five and a half years. Shed the pain like a bear sheds its winter coat. It's time for me to come out of hibernation and move on. Okay, maybe that's too many metaphors, but they're all accurate.

I delete Houston's message without listening to it and instantly I'm filled with a deep heaviness in my gut, not unlike the way I felt after Hallie died. Like the world was spinning around me, but I was completely still, weighed down by the force of my grief. Certain that at any moment, I would be knocked off my axis, set adrift in the universe, flailing in the ether for all eternity.

My phone begins to vibrate again, but this time it's Kenny. He's probably going to try to convince me to stay in Portland again, but I really don't need another lecture right now. Not when my stomach is still aching from deleting Houston's message. I'll call Kenny back in four hours, when we get to our place in California. Until then, it's just me, Liam, and Def Leppard.

Houston

December 4, 2014

THE WORDS ON THE SCREEN blur into a soft network of incoherent lines. I can hear the faint ringing of a telephone in the distance, but can't break myself out of the haze. I try to blink, but my vision only sharpens for a split second before everything goes into soft focus again. All I see is her.

Her features slackened. Golden-brown hair fanned out across her pillow. Blue eyes vacant. Skin so cold.

All the PTSD therapy and the blackout drunk episodes had no effect on my recollection of Hallie. The day she died is seared into my memory like a scar from a cigarette burn. For so long, I tried to ignore that scar, but I've finally accepted that it's a part of who I am. I have to wear it proudly, like a war wound.

Now, if I could only get Rory to do the same.

Five weeks since I ran into James at her apartment and she still refuses to take my calls. And her nosy neighbor has made it pretty clear I'm not welcome to knock on Rory's door anymore. But Rory has to see me today, or at least speak to me.

I close the email I received from my divorce lawyer and lean back in my chair. Suddenly, the simple decor in my Barley Legal corner office seems too simple. I took down the one picture I had of Tessa, which used to sit on my glass desktop. It would be weird to put up a picture of Rory, but I need to put something up in here. It feels sterile.

I pick up the phone and call my assistant into my office. Adaline arrives promptly with her iPad Mini in hand, ready to take notes. I hesitate for a moment, realizing how odd my request is going to sound.

"I'm going to send you some pictures of my sister. I need you to get them printed and framed. They're for my office." I rise from the desk and head for the closet in the corner to retrieve my coat. "I'm going out for a few hours. I'd appreciate it if you could have that done by the time I get back."

She nods and flashes me a cutesy grin. "I'm on it."

Pulling on my coat, I return the smile and head out of the office quickly. A few of the girls in the office have taken to flirting with me ever since the divorce was finalized. Though Rory is rejecting my every advance, I have no intention of getting involved with anyone right now. Even a no-frills fuck with a random girl would probably just overcomplicate things if Rory ever found out.

That said, I am a man and I have thirsts that need to be quenched. I sometimes find myself wondering if I should just go back to Tessa. Her therapy must be going well. She hasn't tried to contact me in about three days.

Maybe I don't deserve Rory after what I did to her. Maybe she's better off with that guy she's been hanging out with for the past few weeks. Liam.

Just thinking his name makes me sick. I don't want to imagine what he might be doing with Rory. The thought of his hands or his mouth on her lights a fire inside me. Every atom of my being still feels possessive toward Rory. Or maybe it's the other way around. Maybe I'm possessed *by* her. Either way, I can't entertain thoughts that I don't deserve her or that she should be with someone else.

Rory and I are better together. We're like beer and pizza. Or beer and a Blazers game. Or beer and anything.

I slide into the driver's seat of my SUV and shake my head at this thought. I haven't had more than a single beer in one sitting in more than two weeks, which is a huge accomplishment for me since I usually toss back at least three or four beers anytime Troy and I have lunch together. And we usually do lunch about two or three times a week.

I haven't felt like drinking much lately. My mind is too busy trying to figure a way out of this mess I'm in with Rory and her family, and *my* family. I've had so much on my mind, getting drunk seems like the last thing I need right now.

As I'm turning the key in the ignition, a knocking on the window startles me. It's Troy. He's gesturing with his palms turned up as if he can't believe I've forgotten something important.

I cock an eyebrow as I lower the window. "What's up?"

"Hey, man. Where are you going? You know the rules. It's beer o'clock all day today."

"Nah, I gotta stay sober today. I'm going to run a few errands, then I'm going to see Rory."

"Again?"

"She can't keep ignoring me. At least, not today."

He nods in agreement, though I detect a hint of pity in his eyes. "Hey, I don't know if today is the right day to bring this up, but…"

"But what?" I ask after a long pause.

"Well… Um… Will you be my best man?"

"Your *what*?" I reply with a chuckle. "Is this a joke?"

He looks me dead in the eye. "No bullshit. We're making it official on May 30th."

The ridiculous grin that spreads across his face tells me he's very sincere, and happy. I knew Troy and his new girlfriend, Georgia, were getting serious, but I never expected to get this kind of news just five weeks after my divorce was finalized, and especially not *today*. But it's exactly the kind of news I need right now. It gives me hope. If Georgia can get this bastard to settle down, then I still have a shot with Rory. I just have to remind her why she's loved me for more than half her life.

"I guess I'll be throwing *you* the bachelor party this time," I reply with a wink.

"Like yours? Fuck no," Troy insists, shaking his head. "Georgia will call off the wedding if I pull some shit like that. Let's do something local and a bit more low key. Pub crawl or something."

I grin as I remember the debauchery of the bachelor party Troy threw for me in Vegas before I married Tessa. I got married on zero sleep, yet I still had a few beers to "calm my nerves" before I got up on the altar to say *I do*. Now I realize the only reason I had a "last meal" bachelor party was because I felt like a prisoner shuffling toward my execution. I allowed myself to be emotionally blackmailed into marriage because I thought marriage would help fade the scars of my previous heartbreak.

Now all I want is my Scar back.

"I'll figure something out," I assure him. "I gotta get going. I'll be back later."

Troy nods and begins to turn around.

"Hey… thanks," I call to him.

He looks over his shoulder at me. "For what?"

"For asking me today."

His face gets serious, but he forces a smile. "We all loved her, man. Sometimes a little good news goes a long way."

We nod at each other to acknowledge the depth of this gesture, then I watch for a second as he heads off into the boxy brick building known as Barley Legal headquarters. I pull out of the parking lot behind the building and set off toward Morrison Bridge.

My favorite tattoo studio in East Portland is owned and operated by the coolest tattoo artist I've ever met. It helps that Miss Mayhem is also the hottest woman over forty I know. She's never actually told me how old she is, but she's been tattooing since 1986, and that's all I need to know. She only hires female artists, though she occasionally hires male "guest" artists. I'm sure it's no coincidence that all three of her female employees are smoking hot and insanely talented. But I don't go to Mayhem Tattoo for the eye candy. I go for the quality ink. And I guess the scenery isn't so bad.

When I enter the tattoo studio on Burnside, I'm surprised to see a guy with bluish hair sitting behind the counter. Must be one of those "guest" artists. Miss Mayhem works by appointment only and she's usually booked out two to three months in advance. But I can usually get a walk-in appointment with one of the other female artists.

"Is Missy here?" I ask, so he knows I'm on a first-name basis with his boss.

He looks up from his phone screen and shakes his head. "Nope. She'll be back in a few minutes, but she's all booked up."

"How about Vega or Nancy? Or Katy?"

"Katy should be here in about an hour, but she has two appointments before she starts taking walk-ins."

We stare at each other for a moment, knowing I have no other choice but to ask if he's available. He cocks an eyebrow, waiting for the question.

I let out a sigh. "Are you taking walk-ins?"

He smiles and nods. "I've got about ninety minutes before my next appointment. What do you need?"

I pull off my coat and hold out my left forearm so he can see where I covered up the date of Hallie's death with some leaves. Above the leaves, the word REMEMBER is now covered up with a rose. My arm itches with guilt just looking at it.

"Missy helped me cover up some words a few years ago. I want to bring 'em back."

The guy chuckles as he holds his hand out for me to shake. "I'm Zack."

"Houston," I say, shaking his hand.

He nods over his shoulder. "Come on back."

He leads me into a private suite and I lie in the chair as I begin discussing the tattoo I want to get to replace the one I covered up. I explain in detail the shape of the hand that will be reaching for the rose and where I want him to put the date of Hallie's death. When I'm finished, Zack's tattooed arms are crossed over his chest and his eyebrow is cocked skeptically.

"December 4, 2008?"

"Yeah, you think you can do that in ninety minutes?"

"December 4, 2008?" He repeats this as if I haven't said it at least three times in the last five minutes.

"Yeah," I reply, trying not to sound too annoyed.

He shakes his head. "That's crazy, bro. Some girl just came in here today and got that same date inked on her left arm."

"What?"

"Same exact fucking date? That's some crazy shit, right there."

I sit bolt upright in the chair. "What was her name? What did she look like?"

He tilts his head as he tries to remember her name, then he shrugs. "I can't remember her name, but she had red hair. Pretty face, sweet body. She just left like an hour ago."

I resist the urge to give him a thwack on the head for having impure thoughts about Rory. "Where did she go?"

His eyebrows knit together in disapproval. "Are you some kind of stalker or something?"

"What? No. That's my—she's my ex. That date is… significant to both of us."

He narrows his eyes at me, then he smiles and nods. "Now I get it."

"Get what?"

"Her tattoo."

"What was it?"

He purses his lips and shakes his head. "Nah, I won't even try to pronounce that shit. You gotta see it."

Pronounce? Did Rory get a tattoo in a different language? What could it possibly be if she also included the date Hallie died?

Then I remember a phrase Rory and Hallie used all the time: *No friendship, no love.* Maybe she got that tattooed on her arm in another language. That sounds like something Rory would do. Maybe she even did it to piss off her English-teacher mother. That's definitely something Rory would do.

"No friendship, no love," I say the words aloud and Zack nods in agreement.

"Yeah, and something else in French." He stares at me for a moment then sighs. "You're gonna make me say it."

I give him my best pleading face.

"Okay." He clears his throat. "La dollar exquisite. I mean, exercise. I mean, holy fuck, I'm butchering this."

"*La douleur exquise?*"

Zack points at me excitedly. "That's it! Whatever the fuck you just said. Yeah, that's it."

I leap out of the chair. "Where did she go?"

He shrugs. "Beats me. She left with some other dude."

A wave of jealousy surges through me and I clench my fists to stanch the emotion. "Thanks, man. I'll have to come back and get this tat another time."

"No worries, man. Good luck."

I shake my head as I head out of Mayhem Tattoo, thinking about how this total stranger knows way more about my personal life than I intended when I walked in here today. I jump in my car and fly back across the river toward Rory's apartment building. I don't care if Liam is at her place, and I really don't give a fuck if her neighbor calls the cops on me today. Rory still loves me and that tattoo she got on her arm is solid fucking proof.

La douleur exquise is a French saying Rory used when we were together. She said it was the perfect phrase to describe how she felt for so many years while Hallie was still alive. The pain of wanting me and not being able to have me for fear of ruining her friendship with Hallie. She once confided in me that our relationship made her feel guilty, like she was doing something wrong. She compared herself to a kid who throws a house party the moment their parents go out of town.

"It's like, Hallie's gone now, so it's time to party."

"It's nothing like that. You know she would have wanted this as much as we do," I reassured her. "She was always trying to push us together."

Getting that phrase tattooed on her arm tells me Rory is still in pain. She knows she can have me, but she still feels this insane obligation to Hallie. And she probably thinks she can't trust me anymore. I'm going to show her she's wrong.

I park in front of the building and head up to the eighth floor, my heart pounding with the anticipation of seeing Rory's face. I don't even know what I'm going to say to her. All I know is it's time for Rory to stop trying to write me out of the story. It's *our* fucking story. Not Rory and Liam's.

I knock on the door loud enough for someone inside to hear, but I hope it's soft enough that it doesn't attract the neighbor across the hall. More than a minute passes with no answer. I knock again, just a bit harder, and sure enough the door across the hall creaks open.

"I thought I told you to leave that sweet girl alone."

I grit my teeth and force a smile as I spin around. "I'm sorry to bother you, but do you know if Rory is home?"

"You know damn well she does *not* want to see you. Am I gonna have to call the police?"

I nod as I set off toward the elevator. "Right. Thanks for your help."

"You're wasting your time," she calls out. "She don't even live here no more."

I stop in the middle of the corridor and spin around. "What?"

"You heard me. She don't live here no more. So don't come back, ya hear?"

The tension in my shoulders eases a bit as I head back toward the elevator. I'm on a fucking wild goose chase. *Where the fuck is Rory? Did she move to get away from me?*

Fuck. I really fucked up this time.

I sit in my car for a few minutes, trying to think of my next move. Finally, I decide to go to Zucker's and see if I can catch her working.

I haven't tried to talk to Rory at work. I don't want to be responsible for jeopardizing her job. I couldn't live with myself if I got her fired or even reprimanded. Not after everything I've already done to her.

But today is different. Today she's hurting without me just as much as I'm hurting without her.

It takes me another twenty minutes to get to Zucker's and figure out that Rory no longer works there. She's moved out of state, and her coworker Bella is hesitant to give me her forwarding address.

Technically, I'm Bella's boss since I own half the stake in the wine bar where she's working at this very moment. But technically, Rory no longer works for Zucker's, so she no longer works for me. Therefore, Bella is not allowed to give me her forwarding address.

I flash Bella my best puppy-dog eyes. "I know she's talked to you about me."

She purses her lips. "Yes, she has definitely spoken of you. Where were you when she needed a date to my wedding?"

"Bella, please. You know as well as I do that Rory's making a mistake. Help me out here."

She sighs heavily. "That girl is hopelessly in love with you. You know that, don't you?" She shakes her head. "I'm her boss. I can't give you her address. But you can talk to Kenny. Tall handsome guy who works the register at the Belmont store."

I grin like an idiot. "Thank you, Bella. I won't forget this."

"Don't thank me yet," she mutters as she wipes the top of the bar clean with a wet rag. "But don't forget my annual review is coming up."

I shake my head as I head back outside and hop in my car to go back across the river to the Zucker's on Belmont. The whole time I'm crossing my fingers and toes that Kenny will be working when I get there. My wishes come true when I find him at register four. The moment he sees me, he freezes with his hand stuck halfway in a paper grocery bag, as if time has stopped.

"Oh, my God," he squeaks.

"You're Kenny?"

"Oh, my God. You know my name?"

The elderly woman whose groceries Kenny is bagging looks confused. She tilts her head, examining me, probably trying to determine if I'm a celebrity she should recognize.

"Where's Rory?" I ask, getting to the point.

Kenny drops the item into the grocery bag as he comes out of his trance. "Oh, crap. I knew this was going to happen. I *told* her this was going to happen." He continues scanning and bagging the woman's groceries, all the while shaking his head in dismay. "But *noooooo*, she didn't listen to me."

"Kenny, can you please just tell me where she went?"

"Nuh-uh," he replies without looking up from the grocery bag. "She made me promise I wouldn't tell you and I am not breaking a promise. Even if she did just up and abandon me."

My stomach clenches as I see my last opportunity to get Rory back slipping through my fingers. I went almost six fucking years without her and now I'm losing her all over again. And I don't know how to stop it.

I lean back against the check stand at register three and heave a deep sigh.

Kenny looks up as he waits for the woman's receipt to print, rolling his eyes as he hands it to her. She walks away with her two bags of groceries, glancing at me over her shoulder, like she's still trying to figure out who I am.

Kenny flicks the light off on his register and stares at me for a few seconds. "Look at you. You look like a kid whose parents became Jehovah's Witnesses on Christmas Eve."

I chuckle at the comparison. "Yeah, only I should have seen this coming."

"Oh, God. I am going to get in so much trouble." He slips his phone out of his pocket. "She went to California."

"California? Why?"

He flashes me a sideways glare. "The lumberjack."

"Liam?" I reply, and just saying his name makes me sick to my stomach. "She moved to California with *him*?"

He raises his eyebrows and purses his lips at the same time. "Yup. Poor girl is more confused than I was the time I saw Scarlett Johansson naked."

"I need her address."

"No, that's all I'm giving you. And only because I think Rory's gone a little crazy and she needs a good talking-to. Then maybe she'll get her gorgeous little ass back here where it belongs."

I smile because I finally think I've finally found someone who's on my side. I dial Rory's number on my phone and Kenny smiles when he realizes what I'm doing. The phone rings a few times before her voicemail greeting comes on.

"This is Rory. I'm on a road trip, so I can't pick up right now. But leave your name and number and I'll get back to you as soon as I can."

Just hearing her voice speak the words *road trip* makes me want to throw the phone at the fucking window, watch it shatter the way my world has in the past hour. When the beep sounds, I take a deep breath to compose myself before I begin.

"Rory, I went to your apartment today because... Well, because there's no one in this world who understands what I'm feeling today better than you do... But when I knocked on your door, your neighbor came out and told me you were gone. Then, I went to the bar and imagine my surprise when they told me you quit yesterday... At first, I was ready to blame myself for pushing you away. Then I tracked down your friend Kenny and...

"Rory, please don't do this. Running away is not the answer. Trust me, I tried it for more than five years. But I'll never be the same person I was before I ran into you in Jamie's office, or before I took you in six years ago. I'm forever altered by you… We don't need more distance between us, Rory. We need truth. And that's all I'm offering. Just give me a chance to show you that nothing else matters to me anymore except you and the truth… You don't love him, Rory. You still love me… Let me convince you this is not how our story ends."

Rory

FOUR HOURS INTO OUR ROAD TRIP to California, Liam stops off to gas up the truck because, according to him, the gas I'm holding in is not enough to get us there. He insists I've been holding in my farts since we started dating after the Halloween party, and this long road trip is the test of just how far I'll take this charade.

The argument is ridiculous, but it makes me think of the first time I passed gas in front of Houston. It was just a week after we'd moved in together. If that wasn't bad enough, it happened while we were having sex. After hiding my head under the pillow for a few minutes, Houston managed to convince me that it was completely natural… considering I'd been holding that one in for a week.

Liam pulls the truck into the gas station in Medford and he waits as the attendant fills up the tank while I take Skippy and Sparky for a short walk to do their business. Afterward, we head down the block to the Real Deal Café.

I slide out of the passenger seat and plop down onto the

asphalt with a crunch. The sky is a dark marbled gray, covered with clouds amassed in brilliant silver swirls. The rain must be taking a midafternoon break, but it will surely start up again by the time we're done stuffing our faces with greasy diner food. Despite the lack of rain, the air is cold enough to siphon the hot breath out of my lungs within seconds. Reaching into the cab of the truck, I grab my coat and pull it on for the short walk to the restaurant.

"You stay in here, Skip," I say, patting Skippy on the head when he whines to be let out. "We won't be long."

Sparky tilts his head as his shepherd ears perk up, but he makes no attempt to sit up or get out of the truck. He just lies there waiting for my command. Skippy, on the other hand, continues whining and pawing the back of the passenger seat. His black fur and playful Labrador temperament shine through even on the gloomiest of days.

"Sit tight, buddy. We'll take you to the park after we eat."

I shut the door and Liam flashes me a gorgeous smile as I cross my arms across my chest and hunch my shoulders against the cold.

"You're such a sucker," he says, wrapping his arm around me and rubbing my shoulder to generate some heat. "They'll be fine in the truck for another couple of hours. That's all it's gonna take to get to Redding. Then we'll make another stop."

With his arm locked around me, we walk awkwardly, our bodies bumping against each other, until we reach the front door of the Real Deal Café. He opens the door for me and I rush toward the warmth that blasts me in the face. The door closes softly behind us as a skinny waitress with dark hair pulled into a low bun walks by with plates of food balanced on her forearm.

She nods at us. "Sit anywhere you want."

Three of the six booths are open in this tiny restaurant that, according to the maximum capacity sign on the wall, only seats forty people. But the air smells of coffee and bacon and my stomach growls at the sight of the large stack of pancakes being consumed at the table nearest us. I take a seat in a booth and raise my eyebrows when Liam sits next to me on the same side of the table instead of across from me.

"Just in case you need help staying warm," he says with a wink.

I reach up and tug his beard and his eyes widen with surprise. This has naturally evolved into my signal to him that I want to be kissed. It all started with the first time he kissed me on Halloween and it's continued from there.

Liam dressed up as an old-timey-outlaw-slash-hipster for Halloween, complete with a handlebar mustache, suspenders, bowler hat, and antique pistol. I dressed up as a librarian-feminist-hipster in a dowdy ankle-length skirt, Birkenstocks, faux hipster eyeglasses, and a dreadlocks wig. He had offered to pick me up at my apartment and take me to the party, but I insisted on driving to his brother Jared's house in Tualatin. It was my way of making sure I didn't drink too much and make a fool of myself on our first official date.

New social settings and I went together like sandpaper and condoms, so I was very pleased when Liam went out of his way to make sure I felt comfortable in my new environment. He waited outside until I arrived, so I wouldn't have to search the house for him. Then he introduced me to everyone he knew, which was almost all of the thirty-some guests. Though I felt a bit like a first grader being introduced to my classmates, it was cute.

Anytime I began to feel awkward, he could sense it. He would excuse us both, then he'd pull me aside to chat, just the two of us. When one of Liam's female college buddies recognized me from our days at the University of Oregon and asked if I was doing okay, he rescued me by answering, "She's definitely not okay. Look at her! She hasn't cut her hair in five years. Why do you think she's wearing such a long skirt?"

I laughed so hard I almost peed my pants. And, as seductive as a joke about ankle-length pubic hair can be, I managed to keep myself from ripping his clothes off and blowing him right there. Though I was quite content when he later pulled me aside into a dark hallway to ask if I was *truly* okay.

I reached up and tugged the two-inch-long beard at the base of his chin. "Pretty soon you'll need a long skirt to cover this."

His eyes locked on mine and a beautiful smile curled the edges of his mouth. "Two steps ahead of you. Already put one on layaway at Walmart."

The kindness in his eyes turned into a dark hunger, and I gulped down my nerves in anticipation of his next move. His head tilted slightly as he moved in. The curve of his smile disappeared as I let go of his beard. Then I closed my eyes, waiting for the first contact.

I could feel his breath on my mouth, soft and warm. Then he pressed his lips to mine and my body froze.

I hadn't kissed anyone other than Houston in a long time. I'd seen other guys after Houston and I broke up my freshman year, but I hadn't dated anyone in a long time until we ran into each other in Jamie's office. Still, when Houston kissed me for the first time in five and a half years, it was as if no time had passed between us. As if the universe had imploded and exploded in a single instant, scattering us across the sky like the shimmering stardust where we were created. Houston knew how to use his mouth to tease me unlike anyone I'd ever known. Part of me was terrified of kissing Liam. I didn't want to compare him to Houston.

As soon as Liam opened his mouth, his beard brushing over my chin, I grasped the front of his shirt to hold myself steady, so neither of us could escape. His tongue parted my lips and glided into my mouth slowly. He tasted like the candy corn punch we were both sampling a few minutes earlier. I tried to kiss him the way he kissed me, tilting my head and moving my tongue and lips in sync with his, but something felt off. *Was he using his tongue to explore the roof of my mouth?* This thought made me burst into a fit of giddy laughter.

I pushed him away and took a step back. "Oh, my God. I'm so sorry," I said, covering my mouth to stifle the lingering giggles. "I'm sorry. I'm just nervous."

He scratched his beard and cast a handsome smile in my direction as he reached into his pocket and withdrew his pistol. "That's okay, little lady. I reckon we should rustle up some grub and head on out to rob us a Starbucks before you turn into a pumpkin patch at the stroke of midnight."

I laughed again. "I reckon you oughta put away that pistol and pick up a book, mister. You're mixing up your children's stories."

"Figures a librarian feminist like you would say somethin' like that."

I stepped forward and tugged his beard again. "Say librarian feminist one more goddamned time."

"W-w-w-what?" he stuttered.

I smiled, knowing he'd understood my movie reference to Samuel L. Jackson's famous scene in *Pulp Fiction*. Then I kissed him. It was much better the second time. And after that, a soft tug of his beard was all Liam needed to shut up and kiss me.

We stuff our bellies with omelets and fruit at the Real Deal Café, then we head back to the truck to continue our journey to California. Tonight will be the first time Liam and I sleep in the same bed. We'd fallen asleep on my couch last week while watching a documentary on honey badgers, but we didn't have sex. When I woke up at six a.m., Liam had turned the ringer off on my phone and sent me a text thanking me for an awesome movie night. I assumed he turned the ringer off because I didn't have to work that day and he wanted me to sleep in, but I hadn't asked him to do this so it only served to annoy me.

I glance repeatedly at Liam as the truck carves its way through the winding mountain roads, wondering if he can see how nervous I am about sleeping in the same bed with him tonight. Maybe I'm hiding it well. Or maybe he's just as anxious as I am.

Maybe I'll just sleep with Skippy.

Houston

December 4, 2008

RORY AND I cut a dark path through the fresh dusting of snow as we head across campus toward Lot 42, where I parked my truck. Hallie's letter calls to me from my pocket, begging me to read her final message to the world, but I don't know if I'm ready to see her last words. Maybe I can just burn the letter and pretend this day never happened.

When we reach the truck, I open the door for Rory to get in, but she just stands there looking like a zombie. Her fair skin is taut with dried tears and her nose is pink from the cold, evidence that she's alive and hurting, but her vacant stare appears lifeless, like Hallie's eyes when I was trying to revive her today.

I place my hand on Rory's elbow to help her inside and she looks down at my hand for a moment, confused. I don't know what to do, so I do the first thing that comes to mind. I scoop her up in my arms then place her down gently in the passenger seat. As I step back, her eyes are locked on mine. She presses her lips together, probably trying not to cry. Then she reaches for the door handle and I move out of the way so she can close the door.

The whole drive to my apartment, she rests her head on the inside of the window. Her eyes are closed, but I can still see an occasional tear slide down her face. My apartment is less than ten minutes from campus, but when we get there she doesn't sit up or make any attempt to get out of the truck. I reach over and my hand hovers an inch above the top of her thigh, contemplating whether I should tap her leg to wake her. If she's really asleep, I don't want to disturb her rest. God knows how difficult it will be to try to get to sleep later, when the reality of what happened today really starts to sink in.

I pull my hand back and quietly slide out of the truck. Shutting my door softly behind me, I open the passenger door slowly so Rory doesn't fall out. When the door is open a couple of inches, she sits up straight and looks around, appearing dazed. I scoop her up in my arms again. She wraps her arms around my shoulders and buries her head in my neck as I carry her to my apartment. She almost looks drunk when I set her down to unlock the door. Then I scoop her right up again, and by the time I lay her down on my bed and step back to look at her, her eyelids have fallen shut and she's asleep within seconds.

I've never seen anything like it. The emotional exhaustion must be too much for her mind to deal with right now. I pull a folded blanket out of the linen closet in the hallway and lay it over her, tucking it snugly around her body, then I head to the bathroom.

Pulling the envelope out of my pocket, I push the shower curtain aside and sit on the edge of the tub. Seeing my name on the envelope again hits me almost as hard as it did when I first saw the letter clutched in Hallie's stiff, lifeless fingers.

Why me?

The paper feels warm from being in my pocket, especially against my cold skin. I lay my hand flat over the envelope, covering up my name and hoping the warmth will seep into my hand. Taking a long, deep breath, I turn it over and rip it open with one swift swipe of my finger. I yank the folded sheets of paper out and toss the envelope onto the floor like a discarded piece of Christmas wrapping. Then I read.

Just seeing the words *Dear Houston* in Hallie's precise handwriting has me trembling. But the first paragraph confuses me.

Dear Houston,

First of all, please don't show this letter to anyone else. Not Mom. Not Dad. And especially not Rory. And please forgive me for what I've done, and what I'm about to do.

There was a reason she wrote my name on that envelope. She doesn't—*didn't* want anyone to read this except me. My gaze scans to the bottom of the page, then I turn it over and count the number of pages: five. I lay the letter facedown on the edge of the sink without reading another word and try to imagine what kind of secret my sister is about to tell me. What kind of confession takes five pages, front and back?

My mind wanders to horrible things. Maybe my father sexually abused her and that's why he hardly speaks to us anymore. Maybe she was sexually assaulted at that Halloween party she went to in October where she got completely wasted. Or what if…? What if she was in love with Rory?

Holy shit. Maybe that's why she doesn't want me to show the letter to Rory. And what if that's why she was always so excited to spend the night at Rory's house? *What the fuck?* Are Rory and Hallie more than friends?

No way. Hallie's been trying to set me up with Rory for ages. She wouldn't have done that if she were carrying on a secret relationship. But then, what else could it be?

I stare at the letter almost too afraid to pick it up again, but I can't *not* read it. Just twenty feet away from here, Rory is lying in my bed too tired and heartbroken to function. Even if Hallie told me to keep the contents of this letter a secret, if her confession will help Rory feel better about my sister's death, then I'll *have* to tell her. I have to read this letter for Rory and my mom and dad. And for myself.

I grab the letter off the sink and turn it over to start reading again.

Dear Houston,

First of all, please don't show this letter to anyone else. Not Mom. Not Dad. And especially not Rory. And please forgive me for what I've done, and what I'm about to do…

It all began about twenty-eight months ago. I was sixteen…

The moment I realize what kind of confession Hallie is making, my eyes begin to skim over the details, searching for the words I know I'll find. And with every paragraph I read, my world turns blacker and my rage grows stronger.

He didn't have a shirt on… I'd always thought James was handsome… I think I was feeling more vulnerable that day… He said I could wait inside the house… The truth was that I just wanted to watch him.

He didn't seem to catch on the first three or four times I showed up… But when I showed up at their house a couple of days before the first day of school, he finally caught on… Rory and her mom had left to go shopping… I was so nervous… trying to figure out how I was going to approach him. I knew I was crazy, but I didn't care. I couldn't stop thinking about him… I wore a short, flouncy skirt… I watched him from the corner of my eye as I crossed and uncrossed my legs... This got his attention... I was so desperate for more praise, I could hardly speak or breathe. But no matter what position I sat in or how many times I scratched an itch, he never said another word to me that night. Over the next twenty-two months, things went on the same way. Occasionally, I'd find myself alone with him and, occasionally, he would compliment me, but he never touched me... Still... I had convinced myself that everything would change when I turned eighteen. And it did.

My stomach coils tightly inside me. I don't know if I can continue. Do I *want* to know what happened between Hallie and Rory's dad? I know if I keep reading, my life will never be the same. But Hallie wanted me to read this, or she wouldn't have spent God knows how long putting it all down on paper for me. And only me.

I heave a deep sigh and steel myself for whatever comes next as I continue reading.

Rory and I drove to Salem for my eighteenth birthday. We actually went on May 17th, three days after my birthday, because we had to wait until the weekend. We snuck a bottle of Mom's whiskey out there and got drunk before we went to the Enchanted Forest theme park. It was the best birthday ever. Once we were sober, we drove back to Rory's and got ready for bed.

About one in the morning, I got out of bed to go to the restroom when I saw a faint glow coming from the staircase... He was in the downstairs office with his computer on. I tiptoed in, but he looked up from his laptop immediately. His eyes scanned my body... I closed the door and locked it just to be safe... he beckoned me to sit on his lap.

He spoke to me softly, asking how my birthday went and how I felt about going away to UO after the summer. With my head resting on his shoulder, he stroked my leg with the tips of his fingers as he spoke. He told me about the case he was working on and it made me feel smart. But

I knew if I didn't make a move, he would probably send me upstairs unsatisfied.

The scent of his skin was crisp and cool like he had just showered, so I took a chance and kissed his neck. He froze and I began to wonder if I had misread his kindness. Maybe he was just comforting me, indulging my schoolgirl crush on my birthday. But then I felt something going on beneath me and I knew he was getting excited.

He told me multiple times that this would only happen once. That he was only doing this because he knew how much I wanted him. And that it could never happen again. But I didn't care…

Why do you think I got a summer job thirty-five minutes away from home? James and I would meet at a hotel… the worst part was knowing what would happen if Rory *ever found out. I reasoned with myself that I would end the affair before it got too serious and way before* Rory *or her mom found out. When in reality I knew that I was already in way over my head. I had loved James from afar for two years. Now that I had him, I knew I wouldn't be able to give him up. And in a sick way, this also made me feel closer to* Rory.

She's loved you since she was eleven years old. And I know that if you two ever got together, it would be a dream come true for her. That was the way it was for me, only I was acting out a disgusting schoolgirl fantasy. I was on the verge of destroying a family. And not just anyone's family, my best friend's family.

I hated myself throughout the whole thing, but I couldn't stop. Then Rory *and I went off to* UO *and I tried to pretend to be happy. I even tried going out on a few dates, but I hated all those guys almost as much as I hated myself. Still, I kept pretending.*

Then Rory *asked me if I wanted to spend Thanksgiving with her family… I began to get excited at the prospect of possibly being alone with James again. But when* Rory *and I arrived the Saturday before Thanksgiving, he was very cold with me.*

I thought he was just doing it so as not to arouse suspicion, but when I managed to catch him alone in the garage later that night, he told me very clearly that it was over between us… When Thanksgiving finally came, I tried to sit next to him, but he decided to change seats so he could "carve the turkey at the head of the table." That was when it finally started to sink in that I had been used…

I mistook this for love. But I was finally starting to realize that I had spent more than two years of my life loving someone who would never love me back. Even worse, I'd spent two years of my life dreaming of a life that would ruin my best friend if it were to come to fruition.

I've spent the past week absolutely sick with myself. I hate knowing that I grew up to be as sick as Dad. Absolutely no respect for the sanctity of marriage. I don't want to live with what I've done. And I don't want Rory to live with it either. That's why you can never show her this letter. And you need to promise me that you won't punish her for what James and I did.

I knew what I was doing, which only makes me even more guilty. Please don't take it out on Rory. She's the victim in this whole fucked-up scenario. All she's ever done is love me and trust me, and I couldn't bear losing her over something like this.

I'm sorry that you had to find out this way. And I'm sorry that you're the one who had to find me. Please know that I didn't want to hurt you. I just didn't want to hurt Rory any more than I already have. Please help Mom and Rory get through this.

I love you always.

Hallie

My blood is pumping with so much fury, I can't see the words on the page anymore. I want to burst out of the bathroom and into the bedroom to show Rory what a sick, depraved father she has. I want to shove this letter in her face and tell her that she and I will *never* be together after what he did to my sister. Rory had to have known.

I wrench open the bathroom door and enter the bedroom

without trying to be quiet, but Rory is unperturbed by the sound of the latch clicking or the hinges squeaking. She remains dead asleep, as still as Hallie when I entered her dorm today.

In a sudden flash of clarity, I realize there's no way Rory could have known. That's why Hallie didn't want me to show her the letter. And that's why Rory has literally been knocked out from the news of Hallie's death. If I show her this letter right now, God knows what it would do to her.

I back out of the room slowly, but the back of my head bumps into the door. "Shit!" I whisper, reaching up to rub my head.

In the bed, Rory begins to stir. I quickly hide the letter behind my back before she opens her eyes. Carefully, I fold it up and tuck it into my back pocket as she comes to.

"What? Where am I?" she whispers, as she looks around and pushes herself up onto her elbow.

I try to think of a clever reply, a thinly veiled jab at the fact that she's in my home being taken care of by me instead of her disgusting father. But I can't bring myself to direct my anger at her. Rory's not the one I want to hurt right now. Her father is the one I want to run over with my truck a few times.

No. Physically assaulting James wouldn't be enough. He needs to feel the kind of pain I'm feeling right now. He needs to know what it's like to see someone you love with all your heart lose themselves to the pain and desperation of love. As this thought crosses my mind, I'm hit by an even more sobering realization.

I know what I have to do to hurt James. I have to break Rory's heart.

Holy fuck. I don't think I have it in me to do something like that. Especially when all I see when I look at her is a tired, fragile girl who just lost the most important person in her life. But I can't let James get away with what he did to Hallie. And what he did with Hallie was technically not illegal. Hurting Rory is the only way to hurt him.

I push Hallie's letter farther down into my back pocket and flash Rory a warm smile as she sits up in bed. "You're home. Go back to sleep."

She stares at me for a moment, then she lies back down and turns away from me. I hear a few sniffles as she curls up into a ball, but I don't stick around to see if she's okay. I head out of the apartment and back outside into the freezing cold to call my mom. Her friend Lorna answers the phone and tells me my mom is in no condition to speak, but they should be arriving at the hospital in about an hour. They'll meet me there.

I hang up, trying not to dwell on the fact that my mom is too heartbroken to speak right now. Just like Rory is too heartbroken to do anything. I don't know if I should wake Rory to go with me to the hospital. I wonder if Rory's mom has heard the news. If so, is she already on her way? Maybe I should check Rory's phone for messages, but it's tucked in the pocket of the coat she's still wearing.

My biggest fear is that my mom will get to the hospital and they'll ask her to identify Hallie. My second biggest fear is that Rory's mom will go to the hospital with *him*.

I'll let Rory rest. There's nothing for her to see at the hospital anyway.

I ENTER THE APARTMENT six hours later to the sound of silence, and it fills me with dread. I don't know if I'll ever feel the same way about silence after today. Dropping my keys on the table, I head straight for the bedroom. Rory didn't try to call me while I was at the hospital, but I don't know if she has my phone number. Up until today, she was just my little sister's best friend. The quiet girl with a deep, infectious laugh and a body that could make a grown man weep.

As I push open the bedroom door, I shake my head to clear away the image of Rory's body pressed beneath mine. I find Rory in bed, lying on her side and facing the door. The blanket I laid over her earlier is bunched up in her arms as she hugs it tightly to her chest. Her eyes find me, but her face quickly contorts with grief and she buries her face in the blanket.

My chest aches watching her from this distance. I want to take her in my arms and tell her that everything's going to be okay. That I'm going to take care of her. But part of me knows that the closer I allow myself to get to Rory, the more difficult it will be to let her go if I decide I can't be with her, knowing what her father did. And it will definitely make it more difficult to go through with my plan to hurt her, if I can even bring myself to do that.

I should tell her to look for someplace else to live, but I can't bring myself to do it. There's no one else who knows what she's feeling right now more than I do. And I can't deny how much I *want* to take care of her. How much I want to hold her and kiss her and…

I approach the other side of the bed and take a seat on the edge of the mattress. The movement of the bed gets her attention and she looks up at me, eyelids swollen, her nose red and sniffly, cheeks flushed pink, and still as gorgeous as she looked when I first noticed her beauty last Christmas.

"I meant what I said before. This is your home for as long as you need it. You don't have to rush to find another dorm or off-campus housing."

Wiping at her face, she sits up and stares at the blanket in her lap as she bunches it up in her fist. "Thank you, but… Why are you doing this?"

Her hand is balled up tightly around the fabric of the blanket, as if she's holding on for dear life, waiting for me to answer the question. I could tell her I have ulterior motives, but I don't know if I do. Or I can tell her the truth.

I reach forward and gently lay my hand over hers. "Because you were my sister's best friend. And she loved you like a sister. And…" She seems to stop breathing when I pause, so I place my other hand under her chin to tilt her face up. "Because I've wanted you for almost a year. And if there's one thing I've learned today, it's that you can't put off telling someone the things you feel deep down inside. Because the day may come when you don't have another day."

Her eyes are wide with shock. "You… want me?"

I scoot closer to her and cup her face in my hands, brushing my thumbs over her moist cheeks, marveling at her delicate bone structure. "I've wanted you for a very long time, Rory."

Rory

December 4, 2008

HEARING THESE WORDS coming from Houston's mouth is surreal. I feel weightless. As if I'm floating on a dream, looking down on myself. Maybe I *am* still asleep. This can't be happening. Because if this is really happening, then that means Houston wants to be with me, and Hallie is *really* dead.

He leans in until his mouth hovers over mine, so close I can smell the faint musk of melted snow in his hair. I can feel the cloud of warmth each time he exhales and my whole body aches to touch him, to wrap myself around him and become part of him. But Hallie's name keeps sounding in my mind, a broken-record reminder of why we're even here.

I would *never* say yes to Houston unless Hallie was gone.

Hallie is *gone.*

He whispers softly, his breath stroking my lips. "Do you want me?"

"Yes," I respond, my voice as thin and wispy as the air between us. "Yes, I want you."

He presses his lips gently to the corner of my mouth. "How long have you wanted me?"

My eyelids flutter as he drags his supple lips across mine to the other side of my mouth and lays another kiss there.

"For a very… long time."

He reaches up, firmly clasping either side of my face. The skin of his hands is rough, pressed against my cheeks like leather on satin. My mouth falls open, readying myself for his lips, but he tilts my head to the side and lays a soft trail of kisses from the corner of my mouth to my jaw, then up to my earlobe. The resonance of his breathing reverberates in my skull, each lustful breath a deep rumbling wave crashing inside me as he teases the shell of my ear with the tip of his tongue.

"What do you want me to do to you?" he whispers, sending a crackle of electricity racing down my spine.

The throbbing between my thighs intensifies. I swallow hard as he kisses his way down my neck and his hands move down to unzip the coat I never removed.

"I… I want you… to kiss me."

A loud gong goes off in my mind as I realize how stupid that probably sounded to someone as experienced as Houston. He probably expected me to say I want him to fuck me. I might as well just carve the word VIRGIN into my forehead.

Houston tilts his head back, his eyebrows screwed up in an adorable expression of confusion. A slight smile tugs at the corner of his pillowy lips. His gaze travels over my face, as if he's just seeing me for the first time.

"Rory, are you a *virgin*?"

"Shit," I mutter, and he responds with a soft chuckle. "Go ahead, laugh. I know it's stupid."

"I'm not laughing at that. I'm laughing at your reaction." He holds on tighter when I try to push his hands off my face. "There's nothing wrong with being a virgin. That's a good thing.

It means you value yourself and…"

"And what?"

He smiles softly and my stomach explodes in a chorus of butterfly wings. "And you also value the person you've been waiting for."

I close my eyes so he can't see the black fear gripping me. I'm not just afraid of having sex for the first time. I'm afraid of having sex with Houston. I'm terrified it won't be good… for *him*. Then he'll never speak to me again and every time he sees me on campus he'll remember that awkward moment when he had the worst sex of his life with his sister's best friend.

He presses his soft lips to my forehead and I open my eyes. "You've been waiting for me?"

He's so close I can see the layer of gritty stubble on his jaw. I want to rub my lips over it until I'm raw and scrubbed clean of every fantasy I've ever had involving Houston.

I draw in a deep breath and let it out in a soft whoosh as my gaze falls to his chest. "Yes."

He tilts my face up again so he can look me in the eye. "Don't look away from me." His blue eyes shine with silver ferocity. "Don't you see what's happening here?"

"What's happening?"

His gaze falls to my lips and, I can't help myself, I wet them so I can see his reaction. The glint in his eye flashes white hot. He wants me. *Holy crap.* Houston wants to fuck me.

"This is our chance, Rory." He brushes his lips over my cheekbone then lays a soft kiss on my temple. "You and I… we were both waiting for this."

The words lodge in my throat, then sputter out like puffs of smoke. "But Hallie."

His lips skate across my cheek and back to my ear, where he whispers, "Hallie wanted us together." He nips my earlobe, dragging his teeth over the tender flesh. "You know it and so do

I." He pulls away and his eyes take me in again, his gaze wandering over my hair, my face, my neck, my chest. "You're so goddamned beautiful."

"No, I'm not."

He looks genuinely confused by my response. "Are you fucking kidding me?" He gently brushes his thumb over my cheekbone. "Look at this skin… so creamy and perfectly soft." He reaches up and sparks of energy tingle over my scalp and down my neck when he runs his fingers through my hair, pulling his hand all the way through until he reaches the tips, where he rubs a lock between his fingertips. "Your hair is like silk and the most gorgeous color I've ever seen. Like… scarlet ribbons."

All the breath has left my body. I'm drifting on a sea of Houston's mesmerizing words.

He grabs my chin between his thumb and forefinger. "And this face." He pauses as he looks me over. "Beyond beautiful. There are no words to describe your beauty."

"Stop," I whisper, making a halfhearted attempt to push his hand off my chin.

"No. I will never stop telling you this until you believe it. You *have* to believe it." He cups my face in his hands again to force me to look him in the eye. "You're not just physically beautiful, Rory. You're radiant. Inside and out. You're vulnerable and smart and sexy as fuck and…"

His chest is heaving as his eyes lock on mine. Then he crushes his lips to mine and reality quickly dissolves. All I can feel is his rough hands on my face, his soft lips covering my mouth, his hot tongue brushing against mine. *Holy shit.* This is what it's like to kiss Houston? Everything fades out of existence except us, and the electric friction of our bodies touching, our mouths hungrily seeking each other. His hand tangles in my hair as he grabs the back of my neck, commanding me to stay put. But he must know there's nowhere I'd rather be.

He pulls away slightly, his teeth tugging my lip, and a deep, ravenous moan sounds in my throat. Then his tongue is back in my mouth, teasing me with a sensual dance of slow and fast, soft and hard, deep and long. The kind of kiss that says I'm going to fuck you slow and fast, soft and hard, deep and long.

My clit aches just thinking about it. Houston is the only guy I've ever thought about while touching myself. Now he's here in my arms, solid as hot steel. And he wants me. Houston wants *me.*

I coil my arms tightly around his shoulders. "I want to do it," I breathe, my fear unraveling inside my body as a new me rises from the depths of my desire. "I want to fuck you, Houston."

He pulls back immediately and looks me in the eye. I bite my lip and hold his gaze, emboldened by his need for me, a newfound resolve burning inside me like wildfire.

"Say it again," he says, his voice a low growl that raises goose bumps over my skin.

"I want to fuck you, Houston."

The words are like hard candy on my tongue, solid and sweet, but he can hear the determination in my voice. A feverish yearning sparks in his eyes as he slides my coat off my shoulders. Then he commands me to say it again.

"I want to fuck you." I slip my arms out of my coat sleeves and he tosses it onto the floor. "Fuck me, Houston."

He removes his jacket and throws it behind him. Then we both sit up so we're kneeling in front of each other.

He gazes longingly at my chest. "Take off your shirt."

I'm glad he didn't say please. There's something primal about seeing him take control. I yank off my long-sleeved shirt and draw in a sharp breath as a cool breeze sweeps over me, my nipples hardening under the flimsy fabric of my lavender bra.

He stares at my breasts for a moment, the fire in his eyes searing holes straight through my flesh and into my heart. Reaching forward, he grabs both sides of my waist and pulls me toward him. He presses his lips to the satin curve of my breast. A small hiss sizzles through my clenched teeth. His hand reaches up and cups the underside as he massages my softness. Without my noticing, he's managed to unclasp my bra, and suddenly my straps are falling.

He tosses the bra aside as he takes my stiff pink nipple into his mouth. The warmth of his tongue and the firmness of his lips send sparks of electricity coursing through me. He kisses and sucks on my flesh, looking up at me occasionally to see my reaction to the sweet pleasure. I curl my fingers in his caramel-brown hair as he traces his tongue around my areola, a circle of heat that cools under his breath, my panties getting wetter with each torturous lick.

His hand slides down my lower back and inside my jeans until he's palming my ass. His fingernails bite into my cheek firmly as he pulls my hips against his so I can feel the rigid bulge in his pants. His mouth covers mine again as his other hand begins to undo the button of my jeans, his every movement a note in a symphony of sex.

Brrrr. My zipper goes down.

Shhhh. There go my pants.

Ahhhh. His hand sliding into my panties.

His finger lights on my clit and I gasp. "Is that it, baby?"

"Yes," I whisper.

My fingernails dig into his shoulders as I tighten my arms around his neck. His finger twitches methodically, a purposeful beckoning. Every muscle in my body is taut, quivering, balanced on the edge of his careful command.

He leans his head back to look me in the eye. "I want to watch your face while I touch you."

He drags his finger slowly back and forth, and I whimper as each scratch of his calloused skin on my clit lights me up with a sharp lustful spark of pain. My gaze falls to his chest as my body begins to curl inward. He kisses my mouth to pull my face back up.

"Look at me." His finger glides around in light circles over my clit and I dig my nails into his neck. "That's it, baby. Hold on tight."

"Oh, God," I whisper, my body twitching with every movement of his hand, a finger puppet in a sinful spectacle.

Ladies and gentlemen! Watch as this man turns this woman into a jellified, quivering mass of obedience!

"Let yourself feel it, Rory," he murmurs, his hot lips against my jaw. "Savor it… but don't pass out on me. This is just a preview."

I swallow hard as I lean back and gaze into his eyes. His fingers are magic, turning my body into pure liquid lust. Every stroke coaxes a wave of pleasure out of me, a waterfall of desire cascading through me, until my muscles are too weak to support my own weight. I crumble in his arms.

He holds me tighter, propping me up as he slides his hand farther into my panties until his middle finger is buried inside me.

"Holy shit," I wince and he freezes.

"Does that hurt?"

"No," I insist, gathering up the small threads of energy scattered inside me, bundling them into just enough vigor to reassert my hold on his shoulders, so he can't pull away. "It feels good. Don't stop."

He grunts softly as he tightens his arm around my waist again and slides his finger back inside me.

"You're soaking wet," he says, a devilish smile curving his mouth. "And I'm just getting started."

"Oh, my God," I whisper under my breath as he rakes his teeth down my neck.

It's the most decadent pain I could have imagined. Sharp, like an oddly pleasurable knife twisting inside me as he moves his finger up and down, in and out. The flat of his palm rubs against my still-throbbing clit, my thighs trembling with ecstasy as an orgasm approaches. But he stops just before I reach my peak. The teasing is pure torture, and the godly smile that tugs at the left corner of his mouth tells me he's enjoying his role as tormentor.

He slips his hand out of my panties and fixes me with a glare so seductive it should be criminal. Slowly, and without taking his eyes off mine, he lifts his hand and slides the finger into his mouth. I swallow hard as he pulls it out slowly, his eyes darkening with a craving as volatile as gasoline. One flicker of flame and we're going to ignite, burning up until there's nothing left of us but ash and bone. I can feel the explosive charge coming, like a tremor in my marrow, but it doesn't scare me. I want it. I want to walk into the flames, let them engulf me.

He licks his lips as he reaches down and tugs on the waistband of my panties. "Take these off so I can taste all of you."

I swallow hard and focus on my breathing, trying not to let him see how pleased I am to hear those words. He slides off the bed so he can undress as I lie back to remove my underwear.

First, he tears off his T-shirt and I'm mesmerized by the sight of his perfectly sculpted physique. He looks like a goddamned fitness model. I've seen Houston shirtless plenty of times. He's always been lean, with well-defined musculature. He swam competitively and played rugby in high school. Still, I haven't seen him with his shirt off in three years. So I've *never* seen him like this.

His shoulders are broad and strong, a slight sheen shimmering on his taut skin. His neck is solid, and as thick as his biceps. But his chest and abs are a testament to whatever he's been doing to stay in shape for the past three years. Sculpted to perfection, every groove and valley points my gaze downward toward the enormous bulge in his jeans.

He flashes me a sexy half grin as he begins undoing his pants. His confidence radiates off him and fills the room with the headiness of his masculinity. He knows how fucking hot he is. No, he's not just hot, he's gorgeous, exquisite, beautiful, yet exceedingly male.

In a flash, his pants are off, quickly followed by his navy-blue boxer briefs. And there it is. I clap my hand over my mouth to keep from blurting out something stupid about his huge cock.

Is it too late to back out?

My blood stands still in my veins. I've never seen an erect penis anywhere other than the few porn videos I've watched out of curiosity, but this is definitely the largest one I've ever seen. Thick and long, the skin stretched tight over the hard shaft. And it's pointed straight at me.

No! There's no way I'm backing out of this. This is the moment I've been waiting for since I first laid eyes on Houston seven years ago. Okay, maybe I wasn't thinking about it at the age of eleven. But still, there's no fucking way I'm backing out now.

He reaches into the top drawer of his dresser and pulls out a long strip of condoms.

Holy shit. Is that how many times we're gonna do it?

He tears one foil wrapper off the strip, then he rips it open and unrolls it over his cock. He approaches as I lie down on my side, propped up on my elbow, watching him move across the bed toward me. He reaches up and pinches my nipple, tugging a little until, like magic, I can feel the tugging sensation between my legs. Letting go of my nipple, he leans in and kisses me tenderly, his hand landing on my hip and sliding back to softly caress my butt.

I lie back and wrap my arms around his neck and we make out like this for a while. Our bodies stealing each other's warmth, his hands exploring every inch of my skin, banking my wetness like currency as he readies me for the main event. After a while, he begins to move down on me and I have to keep reminding myself not to tense up.

I've never had oral sex. I'm not one of those virgins who thinks oral doesn't count. I don't know what to expect. What if I scream or kick him or something else even more mortifying?

He plants a soft kiss on each of my hip bones before he looks up at me with a smile in his eyes. "You're so fucking gorgeous." He kisses the spot just below my navel. "I'm going to put my mouth on you, then I'm going to lick you until you're begging me to stop." He places a soft kiss right above my clit and my stomach clenches. "But I need you to promise me one thing."

"Anything," I reply, breathless with anticipation.

He looks up at me, a cunning smile curving his lips. "Don't hold back. I want to hear you scream."

I nod and draw in a deep breath as he lowers his head between my legs. Then his mouth is on me and my whole body convulses. He looks up at me, his eyes full of excitement, watching my reaction as he slides his tongue between my folds and drags it upward ever so slowly. The ecstasy is overwhelming. My eyelids flutter as his tongue moves slowly up and down, teasing me, dragging out the pleasure, until finally it's on my clit.

"Holy shit," I whisper, grabbing chunks of his hair to hold my body steady as his tongue swirls around my swollen bud.

He wraps his soft lips around my clit and gently sucks, the tip of his tongue applying pressure as his lips work the outer regions. Together, it creates a sensation that reverberates through every inch of me, sending my mind and body floating into the outer reaches of space where time doesn't exist.

The orgasm builds quickly, bringing me back into the moment, and I'm aware of everything again. My muscles are warm and twitchy. Sweat beads on my chest, slides down my neck, tickling my skin as my body floods with magma. My legs begin to quake as the first sound comes out. It's a sharp whimper, a desperate cry for release.

His tongue flicks my clit rapidly as he senses the orgasm rumbling through me. My back arches and my feet push against the mattress, my body desperately trying to escape the intensity of the orgasm. Then comes the scream.

It starts off as a moan and quickly evolves into a burning howl. I push him away as the sensation becomes painful. He chuckles as I let out one more exhausted groan.

My body melts into the mattress as pinpricks of colorful light burst in my vision, tiny fireworks celebrating that earth-shattering orgasm. I'm *actually* seeing stars.

"Holy fuck," I breathe, blinking furiously to clear my vision. "Holy fucking shit."

He moves up, his bare chest sliding over my heated skin. Despite the snow falling outside the bedroom window, we're both slick with sweat. He kisses me hard, not giving me a chance to recover from that unbelievably intense orgasm. And I go with it, wrapping my legs around his hips and kissing him back with the same ferocity, reveling in the taste of me on his lips. More proof that this is not a dream.

The tip of his erection presses against my entrance and I resist the urge to grab it and shove it inside me. I know that's not possible. He's going to have to ease that enormous thing inside a little bit at a time.

He plants his hands on either side of my head and pushes himself up so he can look down at me. "Are you ready for me?"

I nod. "I'm ready."

He leans his weight on one elbow so he can look down at his beautiful cock, probably admiring it just as much as I am. Taking it in his hand, he glides the tip through my wetness, and my body twitches when he hits my clit. Then he slides it in about an inch and I let out a soft gasp.

The thickness stretches me painfully. This is going to hurt. I harbor no illusions about that. But I try not to let the pain register on my face.

He looks up at me, a slightly guilty grimace on his face as he guides his erection in just a bit farther. I bite my lip to hide the agony, then I lock my arms and legs tighter around him to pull him back on top of me. The change in position pushes him even farther inside and I let out a high-pitched whimper.

"Are you okay?" he asks, his brow etched with worry.

I gaze at the perfect slope of his nose, the peaks of his soft lips, and the messiness of his lush caramel-brown hair, nodding as I smile through the pain. Because Houston is right. This is the moment we've been waiting for. This is our destiny. From now on, this is us.

Rory

December 4, 2014

LIAM'S TRUCK pulls up to 13 Harbor Court, our new suburban address, just before eleven p.m. and my heart races at the sight of it. It's an actual house. Not an apartment. I haven't lived in a house since the few months I lived with my mom after graduating from UO.

The porch light is on, illuminating the lawn and the front of the house. The light-gray stucco looks as if someone slathered cement on the walls and forgot to come back and paint it. The clay tile roof reminds me of the sprawling Spanish-style estates you see in the movies, but this house is far from sprawling. It's tiny. And the lush green lawn makes me question whether we're at the wrong house.

"Is this the right address?" I ask as Liam pulls into the driveway in front of the one-car garage. "That grass is so green. It looks like someone lives here."

Liam laughs. "This is a planned unit development. I'm sure keeping the grass green is one of the stipulations in the association bylaws."

Planned unit development? Association bylaws?

If my heart could speak it would say, "I don't belong here. Take me home. To Portland… and Houston."

Hearts are stupid, which is why the phrase "listen to your heart" is an idiom, not an axiom. Idioms are figurative. They're not meant to be taken literally. Axioms are accepted truths. And the truth is something Houston is unfamiliar with.

I can forgive him for keeping Hallie's suicide note from me out of some misguided attempt to protect me. But I can't forgive him for deceiving me into a relationship. For making me believe he wanted me just as much as I wanted him that first night we were together. I don't care how many voicemails he leaves me claiming he had wanted me since the Christmas before Hallie died. I don't believe a word of it. I have no reason to believe it. He's proven to me that the truth means nothing to him.

If he had really confessed his feelings about me to Hallie that Christmas, why didn't she mention anything about it in her suicide note? I know the note wasn't addressed to me, but she could have said something like *"I know you don't want to hurt Rory any more than I do."* Something as simple as that would have made me believe Houston, because I so desperately *want* to believe him. I don't want to accept that the most amazing moments of my life weren't real.

But that's the truth. Not that bullshit Houston is spouting at me in all his messages. I'm glad I deleted the last one without listening to it. That is how I will deal with all his attempts to contact me from now on.

We take Skippy and Sparky into our new gated backyard, then we yank our suitcases out of the truck bed, dragging them up the driveway and along the short concrete path leading to the front door. Liam slides the key into the deadbolt and the sound is so loud it grates on me. My skin is itching with anxiety just wondering what we'll find inside.

Liam's relocation contract with this new start-up in Mountain View included ten thousand dollars and first and last months' rent on the property of his choice. This is what he chose. A two-bedroom Spanish bungalow in a planned development. The question is, is there a bed in each bedroom?

Liam pushes the front door open and the smell of fresh paint wafts out on a cloud of hot air. "Wow. The painters must have just left," he says, heaving his suitcase over the threshold.

I let him grab mine as I step inside. "It's furnished," I remark as I wander into the living area.

"Of course it is. All we brought are these enormous suitcases."

The living room is appointed in modern, understated furniture in shades of gray and cream. The coffee table is a gnarled slab of wood, sanded down and shellacked into submission, held up by thin metal legs that crisscross like the legs of a TV tray. The drapes and accessories are all various shades of aqua and orange with a few hammered metal lamps and bowls. It feels very yuppie-ish. I can't decide if I genuinely don't like the decor or if I'm just looking for something to pick on because I miss my plain apartment.

I wonder if Kenny has moved in yet. He agreed to take over my lease since he was on a month-to-month contract on his apartment in Killingsworth. He was more than happy to make the move to Goose Hollow, but he wasn't certain when he would be moving in since he was still looking for someone to help him move his stuff into a storage unit. I smile as I imagine Kenny sleeping in my bed and watching Netflix on my sofa.

Liam's hand lands on the small of my back and I flinch. "You want to see the bedroom?"

"I thought there were two." I try to say this casually, as if this is a normal reaction when the guy you've been seeing for a month asks you if you want to see the bedroom, but he looks a bit put off by this question.

"Only one of the bedrooms is furnished," he says, sounding a bit annoyed. "But if you're not comfortable sharing the bedroom, I can sleep out here."

"What? Don't be ridiculous. You didn't move all the way to California to sleep on the sofa. I'll sleep out here."

He cocks an eyebrow. "Are you serious?"

"No, but that look on your face? Priceless." I lean in to kiss his cheek. "I have to shower. I won't be long."

"I'll get you back for that one," he calls out as I drag my suitcase into the hallway. "Hold on. Let me get that."

He grabs the handle of my suitcase from me and rolls it into a short hallway that branches out in two directions. Looking both ways, he decides to go left and I follow close behind him. We stop just outside the door at the end of the hallway. Liam sticks his hand inside and flips the light switch. Then we step into our new bedroom.

It's decorated in the same colors and materials as the living room. Nothing to see here. I grab the handle of the suitcase from Liam and lay it down on the floor so I can open it up and get my bag of toiletries. Liam sits on the edge of the bed watching me, and I wish I knew what he was thinking. Because I'm thinking that this is going to be a very long shower.

Forty minutes later, I emerge from the tiny, but modern, master bathroom with my auburn hair mostly dry and my heart racing with anticipation. When I catch sight of Liam sitting up in bed with a book in his hands and both our suitcases lying on the floor totally empty, I feel like the scene has been staged.

"You unpacked everything?" I ask, my voice a bit shrill as my heart goes a million miles a minute. He must have seen the Sierra Nevada box containing Hallie's suicide note and the three-carat diamond engagement ring Houston gave me.

"You look upset. Did I do something wrong?"

"No, I'm just… No, you didn't do anything wrong, it's just that…"

He puts the book down on the bedside table. "I put the box in the top drawer of the dresser with your other unmentionables."

I wish he would flash me that perfect smile, just so I know that he didn't look inside the box, or if he did look inside, the contents didn't upset him. But he doesn't smile. He just waits for me to respond and I don't know what to say, other than "Thank you… for putting everything away."

This pulls a smile out of him. "You don't have to thank me. That's part of living with someone. You help each other out. I've got your back." He winks at me and continues flashing me that gorgeous smile, but all I can think is *Does he think this is the first time I've lived with a man?*

I know the ups and downs of cohabitation. I know what it's like to trade off the duties of cooking and doing dishes. I know what it's like to wash a man's dirty laundry, and what it's like to bury your insecurities when it's his turn to wash yours. I know what it's like to spend all day feeling as if the weight of adulthood is pressing down on you, crushing you, only to come home and find your boyfriend has purchased a special edition of your favorite childhood book, just to remind you that love can bring stuffed bunnies to life. Or what it's like to comfort your boyfriend with silence when you wake to find his tears shimmering on your belly as he cries over the loss of his baby sister.

It's only just dawned on me that the few times I saw Houston cry over Hallie, he wasn't just mourning her loss. He was flooded, overflowing with conflicting emotions, anger, frustration, sadness, over not being able to share her suicide note with me. *God, how did I not see that before?*

I don't notice Liam is standing next to me until he clears his throat and I jump at the sound. "Shit. Sorry."

He chuckles. "I'm gonna take a shower. I won't be long."

Eight minutes later, Liam comes out of the bathroom wearing nothing but a pair of snug black boxer briefs. It's the first time I've seen him with his shirt off and he's gorgeous. The light smattering of hair on his chest and the happy trail leading down beneath the waistband of his boxers make me giddy. I've grown a bit obsessed with running my fingers through Liam's beard over the past five weeks. I should probably just skip the denial phase and get an "I love furries" bumper sticker already.

Oh, yeah, I can't get a bumper sticker since I left my car in Oregon. Liam assured me I won't need my car here until I start working, then I'll have enough money to lease one.

The left corner of Liam's mouth pulls up in a ridiculously sexy smile. "Are you checking me out, young lady?"

I close the e-reader app on my phone and set it down on the nightstand. "Maybe."

He stops when he reaches the other side of the bed, then he spins around to show me his backside. "What do you like better: my tits or my ass?"

"Why not both?"

He turns back to me wearing a sly grin. "I like the way you think."

He slides under the covers and the clean scent of his skin makes my nerves tingle. I've never slept with anyone other than Houston. It feels so strange knowing that Liam and I moved in without having slept together. But considering that's exactly how things progressed with Houston and me, I guess that's just my modus operandi.

I can only hope that tonight is as beautiful as my first night with Houston.

Liam turns off the lamp on his bedside table and I take a deep breath as I turn mine off, too. I lie back as we're plunged into cool darkness. Clasping my hands over my belly, I wait for Liam to say something, or *do* something.

"The road to hell is paved with awkward moments like this," he whispers into the darkness.

I smile as we both turn onto our sides to face each other. "Are you saying we're going to hell?"

"After we do all the dirty things you've been thinking about since I walked out of the bathroom, we're definitely going to hell." He reaches forward and lightly brushes a lock of hair out of my face, tucking it behind my ear. "But I wouldn't want to go there with anyone else."

He leans forward and I close my eyes as his lips fall softly over mine. His hand slides down from my face, skimming over my shoulder and landing on my hip. Houston's face flashes in my mind and I let out an involuntary gasp. Liam takes this to mean I'm urging him on and he responds with a soft moan as he gently eases me onto my back.

His knee slides between my legs and I tangle my fingers in his hair to keep reminding myself where I am and who I'm with. Liam's dark hair is cut in an undercut, about three inches long on top and about a half inch everywhere else. It's very different from Houston's caramel-brown hair, which is thicker and about half as long on top. I used to love that I could manipulate his hair to stick out in just about any direction. Liam's hair is very soft and requires manly hair products in order to stay put.

But he's fresh out of the shower now, so all I feel is the softness of his hair. I tug lightly and his erection twitches against my thigh. He uses his knee to push my legs open as his hand glides down my waist, stopping briefly as he finds the waistband and slides his hand underneath. He's not going to waste any time tonight.

We've made out for hours at my apartment. There's no reason to spend hours on foreplay tonight, especially when it's almost one a.m. But I must admit that I'm a bit disappointed in this approach.

His finger slides into me and I tighten my arms around his neck as I brace myself. He fucks me with his finger for a few minutes, feeling me out, exploring me, then he gathers my wetness and drags his finger up to my clit. I whimper into his mouth and lean my head back, waiting for him to keep going, but he moves his finger slightly to the right and the pleasure is gone.

He rubs the area just to the right of my clit for a couple of minutes before I give up. Through the darkness, I look him in the eye as I reach down and move his hand into the right position. The moonlight glints in his eyes when he smiles. He continues to stimulate me in the right spot, only I'm no longer wet and his finger is actually hurting me.

"Do you have a condom?" I ask, my subtle hint that we should move on.

He nods. "Did you come?"

"Not yet, but I will. I just need you inside me." *Need* is a strong word for what I'm feeling right now.

He rolls off me and reaches into the drawer of his nightstand to get a condom. He pulls out a single foil pack and I watch as he rolls it over his erection. I feel as if I'm floating. As if this is happening to someone else. The irrational center of my brain is attempting to disconnect from this experience while also sending out warning signals tingling throughout my entire body: *Red alert! Intruder!*

My body belongs to Houston. I've held this belief bone-deep inside me for as long as I can remember. It's my gospel. The doctrine I've followed for a billion years. I belong to Houston.

It's not too late to stop this.

Liam climbs back on top of me, settling himself between my legs. Placing his elbows on either side of my head, he leans down and kisses my forehead. I wrap my arms around his middle, ignoring the slight sting on my tattoo arm, then I coil my legs around his hips as the tip of his erection presses against my entrance.

"Thank you for coming with me," he whispers, laying a soft kiss on the corner of my mouth.

I know he's referring to my decision to come with him to California, but I can't help but notice the irony in the fact that I haven't actually *come* with him yet.

"And thank you for being so goddamned sexy," he continues, running his hand down the length of my thigh until it's clasped behind my knee. "You make me feel lucky."

I sigh as he kisses my neck. I want to say something like *I'm the lucky one*, but I can't bring myself to do it. So I say the one thing I know will move this evening forward.

"Fuck me," I whisper in his ear.

The words cause his erection to twitch against me. He reaches down and guides himself into me, then he lifts my leg so he can slide farther inside. My nails dig into his back and I close my eyes as I try to push aside memories of the first time I had sex with Houston.

I can't keep comparing Liam to Houston. They're different. I have to expect them to do everything differently. I can't expect homogeny or I'll always be bored and disappointed.

I reach up and grab Liam's face to force him to look me in the eye. He grunts softly as he moves in and out of me. The smell of sweat and stale bedsheets is at the forefront of my thoughts. I push it aside, trying to focus on the sensation of his hard length piercing me slowly and deeply. He kisses me and I shove my tongue into his mouth, as if I can force him to swallow my traitorous thoughts to rid myself of them.

He pulls his head back and looks me in the eye, a quizzical expression painted across his boyish features. "Are you okay?"

I nod and tighten my legs around his hips. "Much better than okay."

He flashes me a tight smile, though I'm certain it's only because he can't control his mouth anymore. He's about to blow.

He thrusts a few more times, then I grab his face and turn his eyes back to me. His arms shake with the effort of holding his own weight and his eyebrows scrunch together as if he's in pain. I hold his head still, forcing him to look at me as he comes.

We need to imprint on each other, and there's no easier way to do that than gazing into someone's eyes while they're coming inside you. Houston taught me that. There's no reason it shouldn't work with Liam.

Houston

December 5, 2014

THE MOMENT I step inside my office at seven a.m. my heart stops. Adaline did exactly as I asked and got the photos I gave her printed, and some of them framed. Three new sleek silver frames are propped up on my desk, their backs facing me as I approach. I round the glass desktop slowly, drawing in a deep breath as I prepare to see her face.

I haven't seen my sister's face since the last time I visited my mom in McMinnville, more than a year ago. The moment I see the first picture, I breathe a sigh of relief. It's a picture of Hallie and me when she was just a baby. I'm about three or four years old and baby Hallie is sitting in my lap as I awkwardly try to hold her while one of my parents takes a picture.

I shake my head as I look at the next picture. Hallie is about eleven years old and she and Rory are dressed up as CatDog. Rory's face is painted with whiskers and her hand is making a clawing motion, but I can definitely see her blushing under the white face paint. Hallie's tongue hangs out the side of her mouth and her "paws" are raised like she's begging. My mom stands off to the side positively beaming at how adorable they look. I remember taking this picture and thinking how lame their costume was. I might have actually said the words, "Who likes CatDog anymore? That's so lame."

Now I see how perfect that costume was for Hallie and Rory. From the very beginning, they were inseparable. We had just moved to McMinnville two months before this picture was taken. I get a deep ache in my belly thinking of how much pain Rory must be in right now.

The third picture frame holds a picture that instantly relieves the gnawing sensation inside me, replacing it with a dull, warm ache as I recall the day this picture was taken. Troy, Hallie, and I were watching the Olympics on the TV in the living room. At my mother's insistence, I'd come home for a few weeks that summer to help Hallie get ready for college and take her back with me to UO in August.

Hallie had been happier than I'd ever seen her before that summer. Though her summer job in Salem was keeping her busy, away from the usual summer festivities, she didn't seem to mind. And watching the Olympics was usually one of her favorite things to do. But on this day, she was sullen and moody, sitting in the corner of the couch with her arms crossed over her chest and her Blazers hoodie pulled over her head.

"Put your game face on, Hal," I said, setting a bowl of potato chips on the coffee table in front of her. "Phelps is going for his eighth medal today."

"Fuck Michael Phelps."

Troy laughed as he reached for the bowl of chips. "What crawled up *your* vagoo?"

"Can you please not use that word? It's disgusting," she said, recoiling when Troy offered her the bowl.

I snatched the TV remote off the table and plopped down

into my mom's favorite armchair. "Why don't you ask Rory to come over? Maybe she can help you pull that stick out of your ass."

"Hey! Rory's eighteen now," Troy said, as if this should mean something to us.

It definitely meant something to me. And the glare Hallie was shooting in my direction told me exactly what it meant to her. She was probably pissed that Rory had turned eighteen more than a month ago in June and I still hadn't asked about her, despite my griping about her being underage last Christmas Eve.

Hallie turned to Troy. "Who told you Rory's eighteen now?"

He cocked an eyebrow. "Facebook."

"Fucking Mark Zuckerberg," she huffed.

Troy looked at me questioningly, and I shot him a look to let him know I'm just as confused by Hallie's shitty mood.

"Like I said before. Why don't you just invite Rory over so you're not stuck here with us?"

"Invite Rory over?" she responded, and I knew if I didn't drop it she was going to say something about how I needed to man-up and ask Rory out already. So I dropped it.

"Whatever. Then go over there."

She rolled her eyes. "I can't go over there. She's gone. She went to dinner with her parents, some corny anniversary crap."

"Anniversary of what?" I asked, scrolling through the guide on the TV to see when the swimming finals were coming on.

"Anniversary of when her parents met."

I glanced at Hallie and she was pulling the strings on her hoodie tighter, as if she were trying to disappear into her sweater. "That's real fucking sweet," I replied as I stopped scrolling when I find the right channel. "That's too bad. Rory's gonna miss out on today's festivities." I jump out of the chair and toss the remote to Troy. "I'll be right back."

I disappeared into my room and locked the door, otherwise

Troy might walk in, and I wanted this to be a surprise. I changed out of my clothes into my new "festive" outfit, digging through the top drawer of my nightstand for the final piece. When I reentered the living room, Hallie and Troy fell over laughing. Troy actually rolled off the sofa onto the floor.

I strode confidently into the living room in my old Speedos from when I worked as a lifeguard four years ago. To say they were snug would have been the fucking understatement of the century. I was shitting bricks with every step I took, hoping my junk wouldn't sneak out. I couldn't find my old swim cap, so I opted for an extra-large Magnum condom pulled securely over my head. The wrong head.

"I'm the Baltimore Bullet, Michael Phelps, baby. You ladies ready to see me get medal number eight?"

Troy seemed to understand the photo opportunity and quickly leaped up from the carpet, digging into his pocket for his phone.

I held up my hand to stop him. "Hold on. Let me get in position."

Hallie and Troy couldn't stop laughing as I laid on my belly and pretended to swim on the carpet while Troy took pictures of me in various swimming positions, freestyle, butterfly, breaststroke, which is a bit tricky. Finally, Hallie came over and joined me in the pictures. She pretended to swim in the "lane" next to me. I pretended to drown her when she got ahead. Then I pretended to be a surfboard while she stood on my back.

And that's the picture Adaline decided to use for this frame. I'm laid out on the carpet of our old house, my arms and legs stretched out, pretending to be a surfboard while Hallie pretends to hang ten on my back. Her eyes are squinted, mouth wide open as she cackles with laughter. From bitch-face to this beauty in zero seconds, or the speed of Magnum.

Man, I think Adaline's gunning for a raise.

I HAD PLANNED to tell my mom about Hallie's suicide note after Tessa and I were divorced and Rory and I were officially back together. But after everything blew up with Tessa and Rory at Wallace Park, that plan was also blown to bits. I don't know if I've felt more guilt for keeping the letter from my mom or Rory. They would both be devastated by the news of Hallie's affair with James, but there was nothing my mom could do with that knowledge other than use it as fuel for her anguish in the moments when she missed Hallie most. Rory, on the other hand, might lose her father forever.

I struggled for so many years with the burden of Hallie's secret. And now I'm passing the weight of it on to the two people I love most in this world. It doesn't seem like a very loving or fair thing to do. Though the uncomfortable truth can sometimes seem like the less humane option, in the long run comforting lies are far more destructive.

I stare into the mirror in my new bathroom in my new apartment. My gaze falls on the word tattooed across my chest: LOYALTY. For a long time, this tattoo was my reminder to hold tightly to the lies.

The truth is that lying is not humane, it's just easy. Lying is an easy way of postponing consequences. It's especially easy to lie in the name of a noble cause, like loyalty. I hid behind my loyalty to Hallie. My loyalty was the perfect shield, protecting me, Rory, and my mom from the truth. I regret using Hallie's note this way. But most of all, I regret that it took losing Rory a second time for me to understand this.

I raise my gaze to look my reflection in the eye, then I make myself a few promises.

I promise I will never lie to the people I love.

I promise I will be loyal to people, not ghosts.

I promise I will find Rory *and I'll never lose her again.*

I pull on a blue hoodie and head out into the rain to visit my mom. The one-hour drive to McMinnville gives me time to refine my approach. Rory still has Hallie's suicide note in her possession, but I have pictures of it on my phone. I don't know what I'll do if my mom doesn't believe the note is real, but I have to prepare for that possibility.

I climb the steps to the porch of the house where I spent most of my teen years. The house I've visited a handful of times since Hallie's death. I reach for the doorknob, then I stop myself from turning it. Instead, I press the doorbell and wait. This isn't my home anymore, and after today who knows when or if I'll ever be welcomed back.

An excruciatingly long minute of silence passes before the sound of footsteps comes to me from inside the house. The door swings open and my mom's eyes widen with surprise. Her dark-brown hair is cropped into a short pixie cut and the way her taupe cardigan hangs a bit loose tells me she's lost about five or ten pounds since the last time I saw her, three months ago.

She came to visit me in my hotel room after I found out Tessa lied about being pregnant. I begged her not to come. I didn't think I could face her knowing that I wasn't ready to tell her about Hallie's letter. But she's a mother above all else and she refused to stay put.

"Hugh, what are you doing here?" she says, pulling her sweater tightly closed to shield against the stiff winter air.

"Is that how you greet your only son?"

She purses her lips as she opens the door for me to come inside. "Get in here. It's freezing out there."

I plant a kiss on her forehead as I step over the threshold. "I missed you."

She shuts the door and leads me through the living room toward the kitchen at the rear of the house. "Oh, bologna. You don't miss me. Something's wrong. What is it this time? Did Tessa drive her car over a cliff?"

"Mom, that's not nice."

She rolls her eyes as she reaches into the refrigerator and pulls out two bottles of Barley Legal oatmeal stout. Her favorite. She hands me the bottles and I open up the drawer to the left of the dishwasher to get the opener. Then I hand one of the beers back to her.

"Well, it's also not very nice to lie about being pregnant. Or threaten to kill yourself if your husband leaves you."

We clink bottles. "Touché. I can't argue with that."

"I should hope not," she replies then takes a long pull from her stout. "So why are you really here?"

I take a long draw on my beer then set it down on the granite counter. "I think you should sit down for this."

She eyes me skeptically as I beckon her to the living room to sit on the sofa. As she takes a seat, I glance around the living room, hyperaware that Hallie is watching me from at least six different framed photos in this room. Once we're both settled on the sofa, I take a deep breath and slip my phone out of my pocket. Then I look into my mother's kind blue eyes, the same eyes Hallie and I inherited from her, as I prepare to annihilate her heart.

"Mom, there's something I've been keeping from you."

She looks confused and leery of the serious tone of this confession. "Houston, what did you do?"

Shit. She only calls me Houston when she's upset with me. This is not setting a good tone for this conversation.

I let out a deep sigh. "I did something very bad. Awful. Maybe even unforgivable. But I need you to understand that I did it because I thought it was the only way to protect you and… and Rory."

Her eyes widen at the mention of Rory's name. "What happened to Rory?"

"Nothing," I reply quickly. "I mean, physically she's fine. Not sure I can say the same for her emotional state."

"Houston, I am *not* going to ask you again. What did you do?"

I feel like fifteen-year-old Houston, sitting on the sofa as I confessed to shoplifting a video game when my mom insisted I tell her how I got the money to buy it. But keeping a secret isn't illegal. Maybe it *should* be illegal to hurt someone the way I've hurt Rory, and the way I'm about to hurt my mom.

I swallow my fear as I reach forward and take her hand in mine. "Mom, I've been keeping a secret from you… about Hallie."

She narrows her eyes at me and I squeeze her hand to reassure her as I continue.

I draw in a deep breath and spit out the next sentence in one exhalation. "Hallie was having an affair with Rory's dad before she killed herself. She left a suicide note explaining the whole thing."

In an instant, the flame in my mom's eyes burns out and the muscles in her face slacken. "She left a note?"

Of all the things I just confessed, I expected her to comment on the affair first. But I suppose it's her motherly instinct that makes her want to know if there's a piece of her daughter left.

"Yes. She left it to me and she asked me not to show it to anyone. Not even you."

She covers her mouth and her eyebrows knit together with grief as tears well up in her eyes. "Where is it?"

I let go of her hand so I can grab my phone and open up the photos app. "It's in here. I took pictures of the letter, but I gave the actual letter to Rory because… because of what it said about her dad. I'm sorry, Mom. I didn't want to keep it from you for this long, but I thought I was honoring Hallie's last wishes. I know now that I should have shown you the note right away. I'm so, so sorry."

She stares at my phone as I hand it to her, but she doesn't take it. "I can't." She shakes her head as she rises from the sofa and heads for the kitchen.

I follow closely behind her. "What do you mean? You don't want to read it?"

"Not right now. I just… I've finally learned to accept it. If I read that, it will just set me back."

This is not the reaction I expected from my mother. "Mom, did you know about any of this?" I ask, holding up the phone to indicate the contents of the letter.

Her lips tremble as she presses them together and nods her head. "He came to confess to me right after you and Rory broke up."

"He came here? When? In August or… Not the first time we broke up?" My eyes widen as she nods. "Five and a half years ago?"

She nods again, crossing her arms over her chest as she leans back against the kitchen counter. "I wanted to kill him, but I couldn't. He was beside himself with remorse and basically *begging* me to do with him as I pleased." She wipes the tears from her face and stands up a little straighter. "I didn't know what to do. I didn't know if he was telling me the truth, that the affair began after she turned eighteen, but I knew there was no way to prove it now that she was gone. All I knew was that the man who stood before me was broken. He wasn't like your dad. He was truly sickened by what he had done." She glances at the phone in my hand then looks me in the eye. "Does the letter say when the affair began?"

I nod. "After her eighteenth birthday." I run my fingers

through my hair, unable to comprehend how she's so calm about this. "Why aren't you more angry about this? If not with me for keeping the letter from you, then with *him*. She's *gone* because of him."

She sighs with exasperation. "You're right, she's gone. But it's not because of him."

"What do you mean? It says so right here. She was disgusted with herself. She couldn't live with what she'd done to Rory."

She closes her eyes, pressing her fingertips to her temples. "No, Hugh. She's gone because she didn't know how to cope with her feelings. Your father and I weren't the best examples of a loving relationship. She didn't know how to deal with what she was feeling. That's the *only* reason she's gone. No one made her do what she did. She made that choice on her own."

I clench my jaw as her words penetrate me, grow inside me, until I'm so full I can't stop the tears from coming.

"We have to let her go," she continues, her voice serene yet firm. "We have to let her go peacefully and with love. And we have to forgive him, and *ourselves*, for not knowing. It's the only way to move on."

"You can't tell me you forgave him."

She sniffs, wiping away more moisture from her cheeks. "It took a couple of years, but yes. Hallie would have wanted me to. She loved him."

"She was a kid," I reply, narrowing my eyes in disbelief. "She didn't know what love was."

"Are you trying to tell me it's impossible for an eighteen-year-old to be in love? Isn't that how old Rory was when you two were together?" She sighs with frustration. "Love makes people crazy. If it wasn't love that drove her to the brink, then it was something else. But I'd rather believe it was love."

"I refuse to believe she loved that—"

My mom's expression is sober as she looks me in the eye.

"Hugh, I found the old phone she used to contact him. There were tons of emails and messages, many of them unsent."

A flame of anger flickers inside me. "She wasn't in love. She was obsessed."

"Is there really a difference?"

"Yes. He didn't love her back."

"How do you know that?"

This question coming from my mother's lips stops me cold. I've never once considered that James may have loved Hallie. It never even crossed my mind. Yet, he *did* get divorced soon after Hallie's death. Is it possible his grief tore his marriage apart?

I shook my head, unable to process this idea. "I messed everything up with Rory."

"What happened?"

"After what happened with Tessa, I went to Rory's apartment and gave her the letter, and she was… well, devastated doesn't begin to describe it. Now she never wants to see me again."

"Oh, that poor girl. Losing her best friend and you and now finding out about the affair like this. I'll go talk to her. Just give me her new address."

"I don't have it. She moved to California yesterday."

"California? Why?"

I tuck my phone into my pocket and pick up the beer I set down on the counter earlier. "She moved there with another guy. She's not returning any of my calls."

"Well, what are you doing here? Go to California and get her back."

"I don't know her new address. And I can't just go there and drag her back to Oregon, caveman-style. I need a plan."

She grabs her beer off the counter and takes a swig as she thinks of a response. "Well, I'm terrible at planning, but I'll help in any way I can."

"Thanks." I take the beer from her hand and set both our

drinks on the counter so I can give her a proper hug. "I'm sorry I didn't show you the letter earlier."

"If that's the way Hallie wanted it, then I can't fault you for it. In fact, I'm not sure I'd have wanted to hear it from you anyway. I might never have forgiven him if I knew you'd been dragged into this."

I kiss the top of her head before I let her go. "I guess all that's left to do now is to try and get Rory back." I smile as I realize there's only one person other than me who knows Rory well enough to help me formulate a plan. "I'll come back soon, Mom. I have someone else I have to see today."

I'M A BIT CONFUSED and annoyed when I arrive at Kenny's apartment in Killingsworth and find him and one of his friends struggling to load a refrigerator onto a U-Haul truck. Kenny is standing on the steel ramp holding the dolly with the fridge tipping backward toward him while his skinny blond friend is attempting to push it up the ramp.

"Push harder!" Kenny shouts at his friend, who proceeds to laugh so hard they drop the fridge back into its upright position.

"I'm sorry!" the blond guy shrieks with laughter. "You said push harder. It's just… too funny. I'm sorry."

Kenny grunts with frustration before he spots me crossing the street toward him. "Oh-my-God-oh-my-God-oh-my-God."

"You guys need some help?" I ask.

The blond guy spins around and gasps. "Who is *that*?"

Kenny smacks the guy's arm. "He's taken."

"God, you never share."

I clear my throat. "You need a hand?"

"Yes, please," Kenny replies.

I grab the handle of the dolly. "Just push the top back a little so we can tilt it."

They help me tilt the fridge toward me, and I haul the appliance into the truck myself. Once I've moved it safely into place, I undo the straps and slide the dolly out. Then I push the fridge against the inner wall of the truck and head down the ramp.

"That was hot," the blond guy remarks.

I wipe the dust off my hands onto my jeans and reach my hand out to him. "I'm Houston."

The guy looks at my hand as if I've offered him a snake.

Kenny rolls his eyes as he nudges his friend out of the way. "To what do we owe the pleasure of your company, Houston?"

"Actually, I have a favor to ask of you."

"Go on."

I flash him a modest smile, hoping to raise my chances of getting a *yes* out of him. "I need you to help me get Rory back."

Kenny turns to his friend. "John, go inside and take a break. I'll be in in a minute." When John is gone, Kenny purses his lips at me. "You wrecked Rory. How do I know you're not going to hurt her again?"

"Because I'm done being a lying dirtbag."

Kenny narrows his eyes at me. "Sounds like you've been rehearsing. Okay, what do you plan to do if you get her back?"

I'm stumped by this question, but I know he won't accept *I don't know* as an answer. "I'm… going to ask her to marry me."

"That's it?" He doesn't look impressed.

I take a deep breath to calm my nerves. I suddenly feel as if my entire future rides on the next words out of my mouth. This is the most important pitch of my life.

"I'm going to spend the rest of my life loving her and proving to her that my love is real by making her every wish come true."

Kenny covers his mouth and lets out a soft *oh*. "Curse you for being straight."

"So does that mean you'll help me? Because I'm fucking dying here. I need your help."

He's silent for a moment as he considers my request, then he stands up straight and salutes me like a soldier. "Private Kenny Rhodes reporting for duty on Operation Gay Agenda."

I laugh. "So what's the agenda, Private?"

He looks at me like I'm stupid. "You just said it. You're going to make her every wish come true."

"Well, that's over the span of our lifetimes. I can't make her every wish come true in the next few weeks or months or however long Operation Gay Agenda takes. There has to be an end in sight. And I need a clear objective."

"Okay, you're going a little too far with the military metaphors."

I try not to laugh. "This is serious. I need help."

"All right, all right. There's only one way she's going to take you back."

"How's that?"

He flashes me a smug grin. "You have to give her the one thing she wants most in this world, other than you."

I'm seized by fresh panic. "I don't know what she wants. I mean, wait! I know what she wants. She wants to finish her book, but I can't finish her book for her."

Kenny scratches his chin as he ponders this. "Hmm… You can't write her book, but maybe you can do something even *better*."

Rory

December 5, 2014

"SORRY I DIDN'T CALL you back yesterday." I begin my conversation with Kenny with an apology. "We were on the road until late, so we just crashed as soon as we got here. Are you moved in yet?"

Kenny sighs. "Yes. I got all my stuff into the storage unit this afternoon, with some help."

"Great," I say, taking a sip of my slightly over-sweetened coffee as I stare out the kitchen window onto our plain backyard, where Skippy and Sparky are chasing each other around like a couple of kids playing tag. "I'm so glad you found someone to help you. I know I sprang this on you kind of quickly."

"Yes, you did. And yes, I did find someone to help me. Someone you might know. Someone who may have left you a heartfelt voicemail yesterday, which you seem to have completely ignored."

I sit back in the spindly metal dining chair with the white plastic seat. "What are you talking about?"

"Oh, I think you know what I'm talking about. Houston helped me move my stuff into storage today after you completely ignored him yesterday."

I choke on this news, literally, as if the air in my lungs has become toxic. "He what?"

"Have you gone mad?" Kenny responds, not waiting for me to recover from my hacking fit. "Did you hear the voicemail he left you?"

I let out a few stray coughs and gulp down some coffee to soothe my throat. "No, I deleted it. But wait a minute, he helped you move?"

The thought of Kenny and Houston together, without me, fills me with a deep physical ache in my chest. I don't know if it's jealousy or just that I miss them both terribly, but I suddenly feel my soul folding in on itself with regret.

"Yes. Houston came to my apartment asking about you," Kenny says, sounding both exasperated and consoling. "And I was there when he left that voicemail for you yesterday. Rory, just talk to him. For the love of David Beckham's boxer briefs, hear him out."

"You were with him?"

I clamp the lid on my curiosity, throwing away the key to my mouth to stop myself from asking Kenny what Houston said in the voicemail I deleted. Or why the hell the two of them were hanging out in the first place. Part of me wants to know the answer to both of those questions, but a larger part of me knows that, in the grand scheme of things, it doesn't matter. Kenny and Houston both want me to go back to my old life, where I'll be surrounded by lies and painful memories.

There's nothing wrong with wanting to start over.

Kenny sighs. "Yes, I was with him. He poured his heart out. It was beautiful. Oh, so beautiful… God, that man is gorgeous. Get your ass back here, young lady."

Why is everyone trying to protect me? Why can't anyone just support me?

"Okay, I'm hanging up now. I don't need another lecture. I'm a grown woman, Kenny. I'm allowed to make life-changing decisions."

I close my eyes and the gray winter sunlight pouring through the kitchen window becomes dark crimson on the backs of my eyelids. I visualize my life as a book. And all the pages in this chapter have been glued together. I'm trying to turn the page, but it's stuck. And the harder I try, the more torn and messed up the pages become. But I'm going to keep trying. So help me, I will get to that next chapter.

"Okay, okay, I'm sorry," Kenny replies. "Don't hang up."

I take another sip of coffee and clench my teeth against the crabby remarks resting idly on the tip of my tongue. I swallow them down and let out an audible sigh so he knows I'm holding back.

"Aurora?" Kenny says after a minute of silence, though his voice sounds a bit far away.

"What?"

"I'm sorry, gorgeous. I just put you on speaker so I can kneel before my phone whilst begging your forgiveness, m'lady."

"Shut up and take me off speaker."

He chuckles as he comes back on the line crisp and clear. "Change of subject. How do you like Techlandia?"

My mind flashes to my lackluster evening with Liam. "I haven't really seen much of it," I reply. "I took the dogs for a walk around the housing tract this morning. Liam unpacked everything last night while I was in the shower, so I haven't had much to do. I've just been lazing around in my yoga pants all afternoon, contemplating doing some writing or looking for a job if I should get a burst of motivation."

"You should write. Or hop on your bike and go get yourself a barista job."

"I need a new bike. I feel like my vintage ten-speed isn't techie enough for Silicon Valley. I need a bike with a jetpack."

"Your green bike is totally hipster. Roll up to Starbucks on that green machine, whip that gorgeous hair over your shoulder, and just bat your eyelashes as all the men flock to you."

I roll my eyes. "I don't need men to flock to me. Anyway, I want to get a nice bike, but I don't want to dip too far into my savings. I'll have to wait until I assess the job market around here, to see if my cash will be better served sitting in my bank account rather than under my ass."

"Honey, that money would be privileged to sit under your ghetto booty."

"You always know what to say to make me feel special."

"That's my job. But I do have another job I need to get to. I have the six-to-eleven shift tonight. We'll talk later, snookums."

"Goodnight, handsome."

I wash my coffee mug and leave it upside down in the sink to dry, then I take my laptop to the sofa and open up my book file. I've written another hundred-some pages in the book since Houston came back in and out of my life. I finally got caught up with the most recent events two nights ago. Now I need to write about the road trip and my first night with Liam.

After staring blankly at page 349 for a few minutes, I type my first sentence: Saying good-bye to the things that cause you pain sometimes means saying good-bye to the things and the people—the addictions—who once brought you pleasure.

"Hey, babe."

I jump at the sound of Liam's voice as he appears before me in front of the sofa. "Holy shit. I didn't even hear you come through the front door."

He laughs as he sits down next to me. "What are you writing?"

I slam the lid of the laptop shut. "It's my book!" I shriek, as if we're both ten years old and he just tried to take a peek at my diary. Though, I guess this book sort of is my diary. "It's not ready yet."

He rolls his eyes then leans in to plant a kiss on my cheek before he rises from the sofa. "Are you telling me you're never gonna let me read it?" he asks as he walks toward the kitchen.

I tuck the laptop under my arm as I follow him. "Not until it's finished," I reply, though I'm not sure if that's true.

Do I really want Liam to read the story of me and Houston? And, if this is the story of Houston and me, why am I still writing it if we're over?

No, I can't show the book to Liam. I don't want him to know how dysfunctional Houston and I were together. But that means I just lied to Liam by telling him he could read it when it's finished. It seems Houston has rubbed off on me in many ways.

I turn away from Liam and look out the kitchen window, trying not to smile as I imagine Houston rubbing himself on me.

"What are you smiling at?" Liam says as he grabs a jug of organic orange juice out of the fridge.

I was shocked to find that Liam's new assistant at SaltMedia had stocked our fridge and pantry with the essentials, from skim milk and orange juice to peanut butter and my favorite ice cream, Häagen-Dazs Swiss Almond. I mentioned my favorite ice cream flavor to Liam only once, when I was complaining how they were out of it at Zucker's. But I think it was even weirder to know that his assistant had been in our house, opening our cupboards, before we even arrived. Maybe I'm just being silly, or maybe just a touch jealous.

"I'm just smiling because I had a good day off," I reply. "How was your day? How's your new assistant?"

Is she pretty?

"Sonia is cool. She got me up to speed. As far as how my day went, I had a bunch of boring meetings about a press release that's going out next week to our investors. What did you do?"

I think back on my day of leisure and my conversation with Kenny. "Not much. I was a little truck-lagged from the road trip, so I took the day off. I think I'll ride my bike downtown tomorrow. Maybe hook myself a barista job."

"You don't have to rush to get a job," he says, setting the orange juice down on the counter so he can grab my waist. He wiggles his eyebrows as he pulls me close. "You can work from home."

"Like a sex slave?"

He throws his head back with laughter. "I meant like a writer. Writers work from home, don't they?"

I narrow my eyes at him as he leans in to kiss my neck. "Sure, that's what you meant."

His lips skate softly over my neck, sending a shiver down my spine. He grabs the laptop from me and I tighten my hold on it instinctively.

"I'm just going to put it on the counter," he assures me.

I relax my grip and he slides it out from under my arm, then sets it down on the counter next to the orange juice. His lips quickly return to my neck. I raise my hands tentatively to lay them on his chest.

"You know, I get a two-hour lunch break every day," he whispers in my ear as I coil my arms around his neck and breathe in the woodsy scent of his skin. "Maybe you should stay home tomorrow and I'll bring you some lunch. We can have a picnic outside with the children, then… who knows?"

I swallow hard as I realize he's suggesting I not leave the house so he can come home and have a picnic with me and the dogs, followed by a quickie. Like he's trying to entice me not to leave the house.

I push him away and grab my laptop. "I think I should look for a job," I say, heading back toward the living room.

"Do you want to borrow my truck?" he calls out behind me.

I turn around and the sweet lumberjack smile he's wearing makes me realize I'm just being defensive. He's not trying to trap me here. He's just horny.

"You can drop me off at work then go job hunting," he continues.

I smile at him. "No, I'm fine. I need to get out for a bike ride. Thanks."

He nods. "Let me know if you ever need the truck. What's mine is yours."

My stomach twists into a mass of heavy guilt as I remember how I lied to Liam about my book earlier. Apparently, what's mine is *not* his.

Houston

December 6, 2014

"HI, MRS. CHARLES," I say when Rory's mom opens the front door.

She flashes me a tight-lipped smile. "I go by my maiden name now, Hensley, but you can call me Patricia. No need to be formal. I haven't stepped foot in a classroom in four and a half years."

I pull off my slightly damp raincoat as I step inside her apartment in the Pearl District, which is just around the corner from the apartment I shared with Tessa until four months ago. It doesn't surprise me that Patricia's place is impeccably clean and more modern than Rory's apartment in Goose Hollow. I never spent time with Patricia while Rory and I were together, but her perfectionism was one of Rory's favorite topics of conversation. Rory never squandered an opportunity to express how happy she was to be at UO, away from the scrutiny of Mrs. Charles, the grammar Nazi.

"What brings you here on this dreary Saturday?" she says, taking my coat from me so she can hang it on a hook near the front door.

"I can't stay long. I have to go visit my mom. But I wanted to talk to you about Rory… and James."

She presses her lips together at the mention of his name. "I don't know what I can say that will make this easier for you."

"I don't need you to say anything. I need you to do something."

Her face puckers a bit as her gaze falls to the floor. She's not comfortable with the direction of this conversation. Finally, she turns on her heel and heads for the kitchen.

"Did you want a cup of tea or cocoa or something to warm up?" she asks. "You must be freezing."

I follow her into the kitchen. "I'm fine, thank you. Can we talk about this?"

She reaches for the cupboard above the coffee machine, but she doesn't open it. Standing silently with her hand clasped around the silver door pull, she lets out a soft sigh and turns to face me.

"Houston, I know you want me to help you bring Rory back. And believe me, I want her back just as much as you do. But we have to let her figure out what she wants on her own." She stands up straight, putting on her dignified teacher expression. "And she deserves that after everything she's been through."

"You mean, after everything we put her through?"

This takes the air out of her sails and her shoulders slump a bit. "Yes. I guess we deserve to be left behind." She clasps her hand over her mouth as she begins to cry.

I take a step toward her and she shakes her head.

"I'm fine," she insists, her fingers swiping clumsily at her tears.

"No, you're not." I take another step forward and beckon her to come to me.

She stares at me, dumbfounded, then she lets out a gut-wrenching sob as she buries her face in my chest. "How could we be so careless with her heart, Houston?" she pleads.

I wrap my arms tightly around her slight shoulders. "We thought we were protecting her."

"What if she never comes back?"

"She'll come back," I reply fiercely. "She has to come back, or I'm going to have to move to California."

She chuckles as she pulls away, still wiping a few stray tears. Looking up at me, I'm struck by how she has the same round hazel eyes as Rory and the same cute button nose. This is probably what Rory will look like at Patricia's age.

"I apologize for always working against you," she says, though she doesn't appear very apologetic. "It's just… you made it so easy to hate you."

I let out a soft puff of laughter. "Thanks. I'll make sure to add that to my dating profile."

Her smile disappears. "Houston."

"I'm kidding. I'm not dating anyone. Rory is the only woman I want, but I need your help getting her back."

She crosses her arms over her chest. "I don't know how I can help you. She's not very keen on speaking to me either. She called me yesterday from her new place, but she seemed to remember halfway through the conversation that she's still angry with me, so she ended the call quite abruptly. She's still *so angry*. I've apologized a million times. I don't know what to do anymore."

"There is something you can do. Something *big*."

She narrows her eyes at me and I laugh.

"Sorry. That came out wrong. Just please hear me out." I clear my throat and take a deep breath as I prepare to put phase two of Operation Gay Agenda into action.

Rory

December 23, 2014

AFTER ALMOST THREE weeks of testing out all the cafés and quiet zones in Mountain View, I've finally settled on my perfect writing spot: the Good Bean Café. I've yet to submit any job applications, since I wanted to make sure my first application was submitted to whichever café turned out to be my favorite. But my plan is to hang out at the Good Bean for at least a week, get to know the staff a little, let them get to know me, before I spring my desperation for employment on them.

I lock up my bike outside the café and head inside to order my usual skinny latte. The scrawny guy working the register doesn't smile as he swipes my card, but I don't mind. I don't need constant kindness. I'm from Portland, not Mayberry. But when I turn around to look for an empty table, the woman behind me flashes me a warm smile. I return the gesture and set off toward a small table in the corner.

I set up my laptop, plugging the charger into the outlet on the wall behind my chair, then I head back to the front of the café to grab my latte off the bar. Sitting back down at the corner table, I take my first sip and cringe. This is not a skinny latte with no syrup. This is a full-fat mocha. I'm about to stand when the woman who smiled at me earlier turns around in her chair and holds up the cup of coffee in her hand.

"I think I may have grabbed yours," she says, her eyebrows screwed up under her black fringe in what appears to be a sincere expression of apology. "Sorry. I can buy you another… whatever this is. I can't really tell. There's no sugar."

I try not to roll my eyes. "It's fine," I say, holding out her mocha. "We can just swap if you're okay with that."

She smiles as we exchange cups. "What's in there, if you don't mind my asking?"

"Skinny latte. No syrup. I'm trying to cut back on sugar."

She nods as if she totally understands. "I tried the whole black-coffee movement in the '90s and could never stick with it. More power to you."

"Thanks," I say, setting my coffee down next to my laptop and opening the lid to start writing.

But the woman doesn't seem to be turning back around, so I look up again.

She smiles as she takes a sip of her mocha then reaches her hand out to me. "I'm Hannah."

I shut the lid of my laptop so I can reach forward and shake her hand. "Rory. Nice to meet you."

"I'm sorry. I must be bothering you. You're probably trying to get some work done or write the next great American novel. I'll let you get back to it."

"Oh, you're not bothering me. I'm sorry if I gave you that impression. I'm just new here. Haven't really gotten used to the local customs yet."

Her eyebrows shoot up with interest. "Oh, really? Where are you from?"

"Portland. I moved here a few weeks ago with a friend."

"That's wonderful. I moved here from Salem about thirteen years ago. My ex-husband was a software engineer. We divorced three years ago, but I decided to stay here. I just love the California weather. How are you liking it so far?"

I smile as my mind digs through the past three weeks of experiences to find the positive things, like the fact that Skippy has a new playmate who has quickly become his new best friend. Or how I love being able to ride my bike in the winter knowing that nine times out of ten I won't need a raincoat. Or how grateful I am to Liam for giving me the opportunity to move on from my painful past.

"I love it," I reply. "I do have some friends I miss, but I'm certain that will fade a bit with time."

She flashes me a knowing smile. "Ah, I know that feeling. I was homesick for Salem for about four years. Looking back, I think I should have known then that—Excuse me. I'm sure you don't want to hear my boring ex-husband stories." She glances at my laptop then looks me in the eye. "Are you a writer?"

One of her eyebrows is cocked as she awaits my answer and suddenly I feel extremely nervous. It's a simple question, which I have absolutely no idea how to answer. Can I call myself a writer if I've never actually published anything?

I shrug as I stare at the laptop. "Uh… I don't know if I'd say that. I mean, yes, I'm writing something, but it's still in the beginning stages. It's very rough. I've never actually published anything."

Her lips curl into a smile, but I can't tell if she's feeling smug or if she's genuinely impressed. "Sweetheart, if you write, you're a writer. Doesn't matter if anyone but you ever lays eyes on it."

I bite my lip, trying to hold back a cheesy grin. "I guess so. Are you a writer?"

She shrugs. "I guess you could say that, though my agent

prefers to call me a word trafficker, whatever that means."

Her words fill me with panic. This is a *real* writer. No, not just a writer, an *author*. She has an agent. And I almost dismissed her when she started talking to me. She probably thinks I'm such an amateur.

"That's so cool. I've never met a real writer. Um… do you mind if I ask what you write?"

She takes a long sip from her mocha, then she rises from her chair and grabs the back of the empty seat at my table. "Do you mind?" She sits down as I'm still shaking my head. "I write thrillers." She says this very seriously. "In my opinion, if it doesn't send a chill running down the reader's spine, it's not worth writing. What are you working on?"

I glance at my laptop and wonder if anything I've written in my book would send a chill down Hannah's spine. Maybe the lies Houston has told. Or the spine-tingling sex scenes.

"It's a memoir, of sorts."

"A memoir? How old are you? You look young enough to be my legitimate offspring."

I chuckle. "I'm twenty-four. I guess it's pretty presumptuous of me to assume anyone would want to read my story."

She shakes her head in dismay and her black hair sparkles in the morning sunlight shining through the café storefront. "Sweetheart, lesson number one: Never let anyone question the legitimacy of your work. It's art. It's subjective. Whether or not it's salable has no bearing on whether or not it's necessary."

"Well, I suppose it's more of a romance, though I'm not sure I can call it that if the events are true and it doesn't have a happy ending." The words are out of my mouth before I can stop myself. "I didn't mean that. I mean, it's not like I'm unhappy. It's just that—"

She holds up her hand to stop my jabbering. "You don't have to explain to me." She flashes me a warm smile and I exhale slowly. "So I take it you majored in creative writing or something similar?"

I nod. "Yeah, though college feels like a lifetime ago."

She chuckles at this. "Well, how would you like to brush up on the boring stuff you learned in all those godawful writing workshops?"

"How?" I ask, resting an elbow on my laptop as I lean forward.

"Well, I know you mentioned college feels like a lifetime ago, but I'm actually looking for a college-aged beta reader right now. It's a thriller and the stalking victim is a college student. It'd be nice to get a younger beta reader on board for this one. All my current betas are pretty crotchety, like me. Our memories of college life are probably a bit different than yours."

My eyes widen. "I'm sorry. Was that a question?"

She chuckles. "I suppose I should know how to phrase a question at this stage in the game." She clears her throat. "Would you like to beta read for me? It may help you with that memoir."

My phone rings and I jump slightly. "Sorry," I mutter as I slip the phone out of my pocket and glance at the screen.

It's Liam calling me from his cell phone, which means he's not at work. He always calls me from his desk phone when he's in his office.

"Excuse me. I'll just be a minute." I press the green button to answer. "Liam?"

"Hey, babe. I'm on my way home for lunch. Do you want me to pick you up a sandwich or something?"

A chill passes through me as I'm filled with an emotion I don't recognize. I can't decide if it's guilt or fear for not being home.

"I'm not home," I reply. "I'm at the café. I won't be home for a while. Go ahead and get whatever you want for yourself."

He's silent for a moment. "You're at the café *again*?"

My first instinct is to explain to him how I'm so close to finishing the book, but I don't want to bring up the subject of the book knowing that I won't be able to show him the finished product. And I'm not sure what he meant by adding the inflection on *again*. I don't want to read into it, but I almost feel as if he's trying to make me feel guilty for not being home and at his beck and call.

"Yeah, I'm just having a coffee then I'm going for a bike ride." It's not a lie if I go for a ride after I leave the café.

Every second of silence makes the nervous feeling in my belly intensify. I glance at Hannah to see if she can sense the tension, but she's not even looking at me. She's waving and smiling at an older gentleman outside the café window as he walks by with his Yorkie on a leash. The man waves back at her and continues on his way.

"So you'll be home when I get there after work?" Liam asks.

I nod, though he can't see me. "Yes, definitely. I'll be home in an hour or two, tops."

"If you can get home in an hour, I'll still be there."

My stomach drops as I realize he's not going to let it go. "I actually just started chatting with a very cool author here at the café. I might be a bit longer."

"An author? What's his name?"

"*Her* name is Hannah."

"Ah, I see," he replies, and I hear the smile in his voice. "All right, pretty lady. You have your writers' meeting and I'll see you later."

"See you later." I tuck my phone back into my pocket and Hannah flashes me a tight-lipped smile. "Sorry, you were going to ask me something."

"Actually, I already asked you. Would you like to beta read for me? Assuming your boyfriend would be okay with it."

The sour contents of my stomach bubble up into my throat

as I realize she definitely sensed the tension in my phone call with Liam. She probably thinks I'm a weak girl who followed a boy to California because she has no aspirations of her own. She doesn't know that Liam basically rescued me from a life spent fending off Houston's lies.

"I'd love to beta read for you, but I've never actually done that before."

"If you've done a peer review in any of your creative writing classes then you're all set. And if you do a good job, maybe I can give you some feedback on your memoir. Have you ever edited a piece of fiction?"

"Yes! I was a junior fiction editor for the university's literary magazine. Does that count?"

She smiles broadly. "That's more qualifications than I could have hoped for." She extends her hand to me again. "You're hired."

I WAKE TO FIND Liam's side of the bed empty. Stretching my limbs, I reach across and the sheets are still warm. He hasn't been up very long. I consider getting up and going to greet him right away, but my limbs don't seem to agree with this plan. I feel listless and weighed down, as if I could sink into the mattress and all the way through the floor, disappearing somewhere deep inside the earth.

It's difficult not to think of Hallie on a day like today. She spent her last Christmas Eve with me, Houston, and her mom, doing what she did best, making us laugh. I've gone over and over the events of that day in my head, racking my brain for signs that Houston was developing feelings for me or that Hallie was suffering the woes of unrequited love. But that Christmas Eve came almost a year before Hallie's death. She hadn't even begun her relationship with my father yet. And I think I would have been too flustered around Houston to notice if he were interested in me.

Resisting the urge to pull the covers over my head, I slide out of bed, enter the bathroom, and lock the door behind me. Then I turn the water on in the shower and lower the lid on the toilet so I can sit down and think. As I stare at the phone in my hand, my mind drifts to Houston and our first Christmas as a couple, six years ago.

Houston's aunt had bought his mother, Ava, a plane ticket to visit their family in Pittsburgh. She didn't want Ava spending the holiday alone so soon after Hallie's death. When I asked him why he didn't go to Pittsburgh with his mom, Houston replied simply, "Because she said I didn't have to."

At first, I thought this was him being a typical insensitive male. But when I woke up on Christmas Eve to the smell of Kung Pao chicken, I began to suspect he had other motives.

"What's this?" I asked, rubbing away the cobwebs of sleep from my eyes.

Houston slid the breakfast tray laden with Chinese food containers to the side so he could sit on the bed. "Christmas dinner."

"Dinner? What time is it?" I glanced at the bedside table, but my phone was gone.

"Almost noon. I let you sleep in. You looked pretty zombie-esque last night." He sat on the bed and slid the tray between us. "Sit up so we can eat. I slaved away all morning on this meal."

I rolled my eyes as I sat up and crossed my legs. "It was that hard to drive to the restaurant?"

"It was raining. I had to turn on my wipers."

"Oh, you poor thing."

He smiled as he used his chopsticks to pick up a piece of chicken and pop it in my mouth. "I did it for *you*."

His words gave me pause. I chewed my food slowly and swallowed.

"You stayed here for me."

The charming smile he wore while feeding me disappeared in an instant. I'd never seen him look more uncomfortable.

"It's no big deal. I didn't really feel like traveling," he explained. "Have you seen the weather they're having over there in the Northeast? All kinds of flights getting delayed. People getting stranded. It's…" He seemed anxious, his chest heaving as his lungs attempted to keep up with his racing heart. "It's stupid, I know… But I wanted to be with you."

I bit my lip to stanch the tears. "It's not stupid. I've never heard anything more not-stupid in my life."

He chuckled. "Me try to be not-stupid."

"You are *much* not-stupid."

He shook his head as he dropped his chopsticks onto the tray and looked me in the eye. "I really like living with you, Rory. A lot."

I swallowed hard as I held his gaze. "I like living with you, too."

"I'm serious. I've… never felt like this about anyone. You're not just a fuck buddy or a roommate or my sister's friend. You're *my* friend." He pushed the tray to the foot of the bed so there was nothing between us, then he reached forward, gently brushing the backs of his fingers over my jawline. "You're all mine. Say it."

His fingertips drifted lightly over my neckline as his lips inched closer to mine.

"I'm all yours," I murmured.

He brushed his lips over my mouth. "Then I guess I got everything I wanted for Christmas." He laid a soft kiss on the corner of my lips. "Now we have to give you what you want."

The memory dissolves when Liam knocks on the bathroom door. "You okay in there?" he calls to me.

My phone screen is completely fogged up. *How long have I been sitting in here?*

"I'm fine!" I shout back at Liam. "Just taking a shower. I'll be right out."

I take a five-minute shower and hastily brush the tangles out of my hair before I head out into the kitchen to see what Liam's doing. I find him standing by the stove with his hand clutched around a wooden spoon as he stirs something in a large pot.

"What are you doing?" I say as I approach.

He holds up his hand to stop me. "Don't come any closer. This is a surprise."

I chuckle. "What are you cooking? Surprise Cream of Wheat?"

"Oh, I'm cooking up a creamy surprise, all right."

"Ew."

He laughs and shoos me out of the kitchen. "Go wait out there. Actually, wait. I need some bananas. Can you take my truck and go to the store and get bananas? They close early today so you'll need to go right now."

"Do we really need bananas?"

"Yes! Everyone knows you can't have a creamy surprise without bananas."

I grab his keys and my purse off the hooks on the wall next to the door that leads into the garage. "Okay, I'll be back soon. I'll grab some moist towelettes while I'm there."

"Good idea."

The grocery store is packed with people picking up rolls of tape and wrapping paper and last-minute items for their Christmas dinners. I grab a bunch of bananas and a box of condoms, just to mess with the woman working the cash register. But she pretends not to notice, or she's just too cranky about working on a holiday to care about my joke.

By the time I pull Liam's truck into the garage, I'm a little annoyed. I managed not to run anyone over, but only just barely. My idea of a relaxing holiday does not entail battling hordes of Northern California drivers who seem to panic at the first sign of a light drizzle. I can't even imagine how bad this phenomenon must get in Southern California.

The sound of my phone ringing as I reach for the door handle startles me. Retrieving the phone from my purse, I'm not surprised to see it's my mom calling.

I sigh heavily, then I answer. "Hey, Mom. Merry Christmas."

"It's not Christmas yet," she replies, never missing an opportunity to correct me. "Rory, how are you doing?"

This question catches me off guard. She's been so busy trying to explain away her misdeeds for the past few months, I can't remember the last time she asked me how I was feeling. And suddenly, I'm not feeling so well.

I swallow the lump in my throat and reply, "I'm fine. How are you?"

"You don't sound fine. You sound upset."

"Mom, if you called to berate me, then you picked the wrong time. I'm not in the mood."

"Rory, I called for no such thing. I just wanted to know how you're doing over there." Her voice softens and I think I hear a stitch of sadness woven through it. "You're so far away. I just wish I was there so I could see you and give you a big hug. Make sure you're truly okay."

I think of yesterday's conversation with Hannah and how Liam kind of embarrassed me by questioning why I was at the café instead of home. Hannah's comment about my boyfriend possibly not being okay with my beta reading her novel was a clear indication that she could sense the power struggle going on between Liam and me.

I've always thought of myself as a strong person. Without siblings to guide me, I learned to be independent at a young age. By all accounts, following Liam to California so I could focus on finishing my book was very out of character for me. But I guess the romantic in me hoped that the start of my relationship with Liam would be just as abrupt and passionate as the way it was when Houston and I moved in together. Now I see I've been just as stupid as my mother told me I was to cling to the idea that every love has to be as passionate and volatile as the love I shared with Houston.

"Mom, I'm more than okay. I'm happy. I promise. I… I have to go. I have to help Liam in the kitchen. I'll call you tomorrow."

"Oh, okay. Say hi to Liam for me. I love you, sweetheart. Merry Christmas."

"Love you too," I say with a smile as I realize she's ending our conversation with the same faux pas she just corrected earlier. Her way of sending me the hug she can't give me from six hundred miles away.

I enter the kitchen through the door adjoining the garage and Liam is nowhere in sight. Hanging up his keys and my purse, I head into the living room and drop the grocery bag I'm holding.

Liam is dressed up as Santa Claus and Sparky and Skippy are dressed up as reindeer. And he's holding a selfie stick, taking pictures of the three of them while they stand in front of a tiny Christmas tree that's been propped up on the coffee table. The dogs sit obediently at his feet while Liam snaps the shot, until I begin to cackle. Skippy whines as he gallops toward me and I practically fall over with laughter as I crouch down to greet him.

"What's going on here?" The words barely make it out of my mouth.

Sparky comes over to assist Skippy in smothering me with kisses. Liam joins them with his selfie stick, offering his free hand to help me up.

"Ho, ho, ho. Are you ready for Santa's surprise?"

I smack his arm. "Santa! Keep talking like that and you'll be on the naughty list."

"Ho! I've been on the naughty list a looooooong time. Why do you think Rudolph's nose is permanently red? Right, Rudolph?" Sparky looks up at Liam on cue and I have to take a few deep breaths to calm a second bout of uncontrollable laughter.

My belly is getting sore, but I can't seem to compose myself, so Liam holds up the selfie stick to take a picture of us while I'm indisposed with my fit of the giggles. I usually try to cover my face when he takes pictures of us. He snaps a few shots and I finally calm myself.

"Oh, my God," I gasp. "This is the best Christmas present ever. Thank you."

"We're not done yet," Liam says, grabbing my hand and leading me toward the armchair near the living room window. "It's time for you to sit on my lap and tell me what you want Santa to bring you for Christmas tomorrow."

He takes a seat on the gray chair and whistles to get the dogs' attention, then he tells them to go to the garage and they obey him instantly. They disappear around the corner into the kitchen and the last thing I hear is the flap of the doggy door.

"Wow. How did you get Skippy to do that?"

"You've gotta learn to be the pack leader," Liam says, patting the top of his thigh. "Sit down, young lady."

I try not to laugh as I take a seat on his lap, but the moment I sit down I can feel he already has a slight erection. I press my lips together to hide my grin as I adjust my position and his erection grows.

"What's so funny?" he whispers in my ear.

"Your banana."

"You find my banana funny, do you?" He sets the selfie stick down on the carpet and grabs my legs to turn me sideways. "What if I told you that bananas are radioactive? Would you still think that was funny?"

"No, now I'm just scared."

"Okay, I was just kidding."

I laugh again, but not for long. He turns my face to kiss me and it takes my breath away. Once I have my bearings, I twist my body around so I can wrap my arms around his shoulders and kiss him hard. Placing my knees on either side of his hips, I lower myself down on his erection and grind against him as he kisses my neck.

"You've been a very naughty girl this year," he says, reaching under my shirt to undo my bra. "Do you know what happens to naughty girls?"

"They get coal in their stockings?" I reply, snatching the Santa hat off his head and tossing it onto the floor so I can tangle my fingers in his silky hair.

"No, they get bananas in their creamy surprise." He wraps his arm tightly around my waist, surprising me with his strength by carrying my full weight as he stands from the chair. "I'm sorry I freaked out yesterday when you were at the café."

His words surprise me more than his strength.

"It's okay," I say as he gently sets me down on the carpet. "You wanted to see me on your lunch break. You were frustrated that I wasn't there. It's forgivable."

"No, it's not. I shouldn't have questioned you. I was just… a little stressed about this new job and I was taking it out on you. It was wrong. I'm sorry."

I brush my fingers over his cheekbone. "Is everything okay at work?"

"Yeah, yeah," he nods. "Just takes a little getting used to a new work culture. It's… not the same as Intel, but I'll get used to it. Anyway, enough about me. I just wanted to apologize, and now that I have, I want to make it up to you."

He begins slowly undoing the button of my jeans. I smile as I help him out of his ridiculous Santa suit, until we're both completely undressed. Once again, he surprises me by taking the lead and forcing me into the chair he just vacated. Then he kneels before me.

Liam has only performed oral sex on me once, and it wasn't that great. Though I chalked that one up to the fact that it was almost pitch black in our bedroom. He probably couldn't see very well. But it is definitely not dark in this room right now. He can see everything, which makes me more than a little nervous. No one other than Houston has ever seen me in the light of day in such a compromised position.

He spreads my knees apart and looks up at me with that perfect smile. "I hope you like tonight's surprise. Tomorrow, I'll give you your real Christmas present." Then he lowers his mouth onto my throbbing center and my eyes roll back into my head.

I let out a soft whimper and reply, "I love it."

Houston

December 31, 2014

I PULL UP to the curb next to the United Airlines check-in terminal and turn to Kenny. "Do you have everything you need? I mean, do you need money for cab fare or anything? My assistant took care of the flight. It's first class, so feel free to get drunk on the plane."

Kenny purses his lips as he stares at the revolving door leading into the terminal at Portland International Airport. "Houston, you're making me feel like a whore or a slave. A slave-whore to Operation Gay Agenda. This is *not* the way it's supposed to feel."

"Sorry, I just… I don't want anything to go wrong."

He turns in his seat and stares at me for a moment before he sighs. "Oh, the things I do for you and Rory. I could be home, sipping hot toddies with a hot Toddie, and Rory would be coming to *me*."

"Kenny, we went over this. I need you to go to her. I need you to make sure she's okay."

He purses his lips again. "She's fine. As we speak, she's probably huddled safely *in the arms of the lumberjack*." He sings the last six words to the tune of "Angel" by Sarah McLachlan.

I clench my jaw and take a deep breath so I don't fly off the handle. "Don't say stuff like that. You make me want to get on that plane with you and that would not turn out well."

He rolls his eyes. "I was just trying to draw a comparison between Rory and an abused shelter dog."

I fix him with a searing glare to let him know I'm getting dangerously close to calling off the whole operation.

"I'm kidding," he insists. "Rory's more like an adorably helpless lost puppy who was taken into a stranger's home, but *not* abused."

"Okay, I think we get the point. Let's just drop the comparison."

"Okay." He slings the strap of his carry-on bag over his shoulder and reaches for the door handle. "I'll report back to you tomorrow."

"Tonight."

He rolls his eyes again and grumbles his agreement. "Tonight."

I watch as he heads into the terminal, my stomach fluttering with anxiety, my mind drifting to sickening thoughts of Rory curled up in Liam's arms. Is she really safe with Liam? If she is, is it time I let her go?

A car horn blasts me back into the present moment and I quickly set off out of the airport, toward Barley Legal headquarters in Northwest Portland. When I arrive at the pub on the first floor, I find Troy holding a meeting with the servers in the kitchen. He's going over the agenda for tonight's Barley Legal New Year's Eve party. It's only our second year doing it, so the servers have to be prepared for the madness that's going to descend upon this building in about six hours.

"There are four holiday cocktails that Wilma created just for tonight: the Holiday Ménage, Absolutly Legal, the Portland Legspreader, and Just the Tip for the Bartender. They're not the same drinks as last year, so make sure you learn the specials before the doors open," Troy says, scrolling through the notes on his iPad. "And we're running low on bottles of Red Light District, but we still have it on tap."

"Denny from Cascade sent us a few cases of blackberry ale. We can offer that if we run out of Red Light," I say, grabbing the plate of pizza the cook just handed to me.

Chef Ramos knows I don't have Tessa to cook for me anymore, so I've been eating in the restaurant a lot. I've had to ramp up my workout routine and substitute some meals with protein shakes so I don't gain weight from this new diet of pizza and burgers. I fucking hate being a bachelor.

Troy watches me scarf down a slice of pepperoni pizza, almost in awe. "Blackberry ale and cranberry cider are not exactly the same thing, but I guess there's no harm in offering." He turns back to the servers and waves them off. "Go see Wilma and get to work. And don't forget, it ain't fun unless it's Barley Legal."

Everyone rolls their eyes at Troy's cheesy tagline, then they head out into the dining area to see Wilma, the head bartender.

Troy watches as I wolf down my second slice. "Are you training for a fucking eating competition? Slow the fuck down."

"I'm starving. I haven't eaten all day," I reply through a mouthful of food.

He shakes his head. "You need a girlfriend. Or you need to get laid."

I set down the plate of pizza on the stainless steel prep station and wipe the grease from my lips with a napkin. "You don't know what the fuck I need. Besides, I have a girl. She's just temporarily indisposed."

"Have you invited Rory to my wedding?"

"No, I haven't spoken to her."

He shakes his head in dismay, as if I'm a total fucking amateur. "Then give me her fucking address and I'll send her the invitation myself."

"Don't tell me Tessa's making your invitations."

He glares at me with utter incredulity. "Are you fucking kidding me? I wouldn't let her within a hundred miles of my wife."

I shrug. "A hundred miles is hardly an obstacle for Tessa. You'd need at least a thousand miles and a unit of Navy SEALs to stop her."

"Bullshit. All I'd need is one clone of you to distract her."

I shake my head. "Damn. How I wish that were a joke."

"She hasn't contacted you?"

I lean back against the steel prep table. "She's trying to get me to go to her niece's birthday party. Don't get me wrong, Morgan's cute as shit. Great kid. But she's not mine. I've got enough girls in my life to drive me crazy without feeling responsible for some kid I've hung out with three times in the last year."

"Don't let her get to you, man. First it's the guilt, then she starts asking for small favors, then she's calling you just to chat and showing up at your work… Just cut her off."

"I did. But she keeps calling me from different phone numbers. One time she called me from her mom's phone. Then her cousin's phone. Then she changed her number and called me from her new phone. I can't fucking keep up."

"Just get a fucking restraining order."

"I can't do that. She could lose her job and then she'll really come after me. At least now she's got a steady job to keep her busy forty hours a week. That's forty hours I don't have to worry about her."

"What about when Rory comes back? What do you think Tessa's going to do if she catches you two together?"

"I hope she knows better than to go near Rory again, because I won't hesitate to take her down if she threatens Rory."

Troy shakes his head as he makes his way toward the dining room. "You're so fucked."

Ten hours, five double IPAs, and one glass of champagne later, I'm blasted out of my gourd. I've hardly been drinking lately, so the IPAs hit me hard. But it's the one glass of champagne innocently handed to me by one of the new servers that tips me over the edge.

Troy pulls me toward the front corner of the brewhouse where we've set the 66-inch TV screen jutting out of the wall above us to a countdown clock. Troy's fiancée, Georgia, clumsily climbs the steps onto the small stage we sometimes use for live entertainment. Troy wraps his arm around her shoulders and plants a hard kiss on her cheek. She pretends to wipe it away as if she's grossed out. I can't hear what she's saying over the music and the roar of voices in the pub, but as I watch them, I find myself wondering what Rory's doing right now and why Kenny hasn't called me yet.

The countdown begins at sixty seconds to midnight, and my pickled brain is having a hard time keeping up. I glance around the room, blinking furiously to keep the spinning to a minimum. Then I see her.

The count is at twenty seconds and she's shoving her way through the drunken crowd as if it were a sea of puppies and she were Cruella de Vil. Actually, come to think of it, Cruella would be a great nickname for Contessa.

Ten, nine, eight, seven…

She climbs up the steps onto the stage and smiles as she saunters toward me. A glowing million-watt smile that reminds me of the way she looked on our wedding day.

Four, three, two…

Rory

December 31, 2014

KENNY SETS his bag down on the bed in the newly furnished spare bedroom and looks around. "It's perfect," he says, though his smile looks a bit forced.

I wait for him to say the room is perfect just like me, the way he normally finishes that statement, but he just smiles and waits for me to respond. I didn't realize how much I've come to rely on Kenny's positive affirmations until now.

"Great!" I reply, ignoring the burning emptiness in the pit of my belly. "I guess I should offer you a drink or something. That would be the hostess-y thing to do, right?"

He glances at Liam, who's standing right behind me in the doorway, then he looks back at me. "Aurora, can we please chat first? In private?"

The burning emptiness swirls into a sinking feeling. "Sure."

I look to Liam and he flashes me a tight smile before heading down the hallway toward the kitchen. When I turn back to Kenny, his smile is gone. Why do I have a feeling he didn't offer to come here to save me the plane fare?

"What do you want to talk about?" I ask, using the heel of my boot to push the bedroom door closed behind me.

He pulls off his gray scarf and sits on the edge of the double bed, patting the mattress for me to join him. Taking a seat next to Kenny, I begin to feel like a teenager about to be chastised for coming home too late on a school night. Kenny reaches out and threads his fingers through mine, squeezing my hand gently. A small gesture to assure me that, despite what he's about to say, he has the best intentions.

"How have you been, gorgeous?"

I glance sideways and he's wearing a soft smile that instantly breaks down my defenses. "I'm fine," I assure him, my voice taut with emotion. I try to swallow the knot in my throat, to make a second attempt at this lie, but the lump only grows painfully. "I'm just a little homesick."

He wraps his arm around my shoulders and pulls me close so he can kiss my temple. "Honey, it's okay to miss your home." He wraps his other arm around me and squeezes. "It's also okay to admit you made a mistake."

And just like that, my defenses are rock solid again. I gently push him off me and stand from the bed.

"Can we please not go there?" I say, already heading for the door.

"I'm sorry, honey," he says, jumping off the bed and beating me to the door. "I'm a jerk. I shouldn't have said that." He turns his face sideways and taps his jaw with his index finger. "Go ahead. Slap me like a soap opera star so we can both feel better."

I try not to smile, but it's impossible. "Get out of my way. We're supposed to be getting drunk. Not crying and slapping each other."

"You are one million percent correct, as usual. Let's go get Liam drunk so we can spank him instead."

"I think he might go for that."

He smacks my arm. "Don't corrupt me. Besides, I'd much rather spank you. You naughty little minx."

I sigh as I smile up at him. "I've missed you."

"I've missed you like crazy. Zucker's is so dreary without the glow of my precious Aurora." He reaches up and tucks my hair behind my ear. "Jamie hired a new cashier to replace the guy who replaced you then quit a month later. The new girl has red hair almost exactly like yours, and she's totally boring. I think Jamie misses you, too."

"Are you saying I'm boring?"

He flashes me a radiant smile then takes me into a bone-crushing hug. "You're the least boring, most screwed-up girl I know."

"Thank you."

"You're welcome," he says, letting me go. "Now let's get you drunk so I can take advantage of you."

Opening the door for us, I head into the kitchen with Kenny following close behind. Liam is rearranging the food in the fridge to make room for the beer and champagne we bought on the way home from the airport. He sees us enter behind him and offers us a couple of bottles of Pliny the Elder. I don't say it aloud, but in my head I'm thinking how this is one of Houston's favorite beers.

Kenny, Liam, and I decide to stay safe and low key tonight and we celebrate the New Year at home with Pliny, Ryan Seacrest (on mute), Kenny's Sinatra playlist, and Cards Against Humanity. Liam and I sit on the sofa while Kenny sits cross-legged on the floor, collecting the cards from each round. When Liam dazzles me with the winning combination of [Oedipus complex] + [kid-tested, mother-approved], I lean over and tug his beard to show my appreciation for his literary acumen.

He smiles as he leans in to kiss me. "I should break out my knowledge in traumatizing ancient literature more often." He stands from the sofa. "But right now, it's time for me to drain the lizard."

Kenny watches Liam as he heads for the hallway, turning to me the moment he's gone. "What time is it?"

I dig my phone out from between the sofa cushions. "It's 11:23. Why?"

He reaches for the bottle of Jim Beam on the coffee table and pours me a double shot. "Here. You're not drunk enough."

I cock an eyebrow as I take the shot glass from him. "I'm just buzzed enough to not question your motives right now."

"Drink," he urges me on.

I down the double shot of Jim and instantly reach for my bottle of room-temperature Pliny to chase away the biting alcohol flavor. "There. Are you going to seduce me now?"

"Oh, you wish," Kenny replies, then he purrs at me. "I'm just trying to get you drunk so you can drunk-dial your ex."

"What?" I ask, my drunk brain having trouble deducing whether this is a joke.

Liam walks out of the hallway and Kenny busies himself with dealing another round of cards. "What did I miss?"

Kenny casts a furtive glance in my direction and the double shot I just drank spirals inside me. I down the rest of the bottle of Pliny I'm holding and set it down on the coffee table without answering Liam's question. Liam grabs the three empties off the table and retreats to the kitchen for refills.

I want to ask Kenny what the hell he meant by that. Is he trying to get me to call Houston? But that's absurd. Kenny wouldn't suggest something so ridiculous, not while hanging out with Liam in the house we share together. Would he?

Liam is gone longer than expected, so I take the opportunity to try to get my answers.

I tap Kenny with my foot. "What did you mean by that?" I whisper.

He glances at the kitchen area to make sure Liam is nowhere in sight, then he sits up on his knees and leans in close to whisper to me. "I think you should call Houston and wish him a Happy New Year. He must be having a really hard time tonight. He divorced his wife, then he lost you again. He's all alone."

I can't tell if the burning in my stomach is the alcohol or the guilt. Or something else. But I quickly realize that Kenny's right. I should call Houston, if not to wish him a Happy New Year, then I should at least call to make sure he's okay.

A loud pop from the kitchen startles me out of my Jim-Beam-slash-Houston haze. I look up just as Liam walks in with three wine glasses and a bottle of champagne.

"Almost midnight," he proclaims, passing around the glasses.

As Liam fills them to the brim with bubbly, I imagine Houston sitting in his apartment, watching Ryan Seacrest (not on mute), drinking Pliny or probably Barley Legal all alone. We toast to a Happy New Year and I guzzle down my entire glass of champagne. The effervescence flows through me, bubbling inside me. It's not like liquid courage. It's like liquid happiness. I feel light and airy, bursting with all the things I want to say to Houston.

I turn to Kenny and nod at him to let him know I'll do it. I'll call Houston. I just have to figure out a way to excuse myself.

A few minutes later, I settle on the bathroom excuse. "I have to go potty," I mumble. Or was that a slur? Am I slurring?

I close the bathroom door behind me, my fingers fumbling over the wall as I search for the light switch in the darkness. Finally, I locate it and the bathroom is flooded with intense fluorescent light. I blink to clear the spots in my vision, then I splash some water into my mouth to clear the yeasty aftertaste of the champagne.

Lowering the lid on the toilet seat, I sit down and stare at Houston's number in my address book. Goose bumps sprout all over my body just thinking about calling him. Will he sound different? I know it's only been about a month since I last heard his voice, but people change. Maybe Houston has changed for the better.

It's not until after I press the number and the line begins to ring that I realize it's 11:59 p.m. It's almost midnight and I'm sitting in the bathroom calling my ex-boyfriend instead of kissing my current boyfriend.

What is wrong with me?

I should end this call and stumble out of this bathroom to go tug Liam's beard. Give him a sloppy drunk kiss. Just as I begin to pull the phone away from my ear, Houston picks up.

"Rory!" he shouts into the phone.

I can hardly hear him over the roar of celebratory cheering in the background. He must be at a party. How stupid of me to think he would be spending the holiday alone.

I open my mouth to wish him a Happy New Year, but the sound I hear on the other end of the phone stops me cold.

"Is that that bitch on the phone? Give me the phone, Houston!"

Then the line goes dead. And so does a piece of my soul.

Part 4: Depression

"And then it all fell apart."

Rory

January 3, 2015

MY FIRST POST-HOLIDAY meeting with Hannah Lee falls on a cloudy day when the dark sky looms heavy over Mountain View. As I ride my bike across town, I imagine reaching up and poking a hole in the fat clouds, the sky bursting open into a gushing torrent, washing me away into the Pacific Ocean. Of course, Liam might not appreciate my phone getting wet. Then he might be unable to reach me.

Liam seems to teeter between perfect boyfriend and jealous boyfriend most days. I can't decide if it's because I made a mistake in telling him everything he wanted to know about Houston, or if it's just that he's really insecure. It's probably a little of both. Either way, I think I need to just keep asserting my own independence while reassuring Liam that Houston and I are over.

We are *so* over.

I stop behind the white painted line of the crosswalk at a red light, thinking of what it felt like to call Houston and hear his ex-wife calling me a bitch in the background. It felt like my guts had been ripped clean out of me and tied around my throat, rendering me mute. I couldn't speak. I couldn't breathe. I couldn't move, until Kenny knocked on the door, snapping me out of my despondent haze.

The line had gone dead, but I held the phone in front of me, almost perplexed by the sight of it. As if someone else had dialed Houston's number, not me. The alcohol in my belly bubbled like lava, scorching my throat. Finally, I powered off the phone and tucked it into the back pocket of my jeans before I opened the bathroom door.

"Are you okay?" Kenny asked. "You missed the countdown."

Our eyes met and in that brief moment I imagined handing the burden of Houston's lies over to Kenny, like a heavy shoe box full of old pictures and letters. And he would take the box and do whatever needed to be done. Burn it, bury it, hand it back to Houston. Anything to make sure I didn't have to ever see it again. Then I realized I didn't have to imagine this. I could give Kenny the Sierra Nevada box.

Without uttering a word, I grabbed his hand and pulled him into my bedroom. As I retrieved the tin box from my nightstand, a sharp longing twisted inside me, urging me to look inside it one last time, but I resisted.

"You can take this to Houston or you can get rid of it. I don't care." I placed the box in his slender hands, trying not to read the expression on his face as pity. "And never speak to me about Houston again."

He nodded and placed a soft kiss on my forehead before heading back to the guest room to hide the box. I slept fitfully for two nights. I dreamed of living in a house with transparent walls, which afforded me no refuge from a shadowy figure that stalked me relentlessly. I tried hiding under the bed and found myself yanked out from beneath it by the hair.

I woke with a start two nights in a row, Liam reaching over to console me. I couldn't tell Liam what had happened with Houston. He was blissfully unaware of the murky waters I'd been drowning in since that New Year's phone call, but he threw me a life vest nonetheless. Didn't ask me to tell him how I'd gotten myself into this mess. Just tossed out the lifeline and pulled me in, cradling me in his arms until I fell back to sleep.

A car honks behind me and I set off toward Hannah's house. *Hannah Lee.* Her name reminded me of a Peter, Paul, and Mary song my parents used to listen to when I was a kid, "Puff the Magic Dragon." My parents weren't even old enough to be hippies, but you wouldn't know it looking at old photos of them together in the '80s. My mom with her feathered auburn hair and bell-bottom jeans. My dad, a year younger than her, trying desperately to grow a mustache to make up the difference. Even though he was taller than my mom, you could see he was the younger of the two. He was always looking at her with the kind of adoration you only see in cartoons. Draw hearts in his eyes and the picture would be complete.

I don't know what happened to my parents. Why my dad felt the need to fuck my best friend. She was my age, for fuck's sake. Maybe that's the most sickening part of it all. Because it doesn't seem consent was an issue. It's that Hallie was just one month older than I was when their affair began. If he found her irresistible enough to throw away his entire marriage, what did that say about his taste in women? Or did my dad see more in her than just a young, ripe easy fuck? Was he in *love* with her?

I can't rule that out. It's not as if I'm not familiar with how easy it was to love Hallie. She had guys falling all over her in high school. She had the most contagious laugh and she could drone on and on about sports and music for hours. When she loved something, a song, a sports team, a new hair product, she felt the need to shout about it. It must have killed her to have to keep her feelings about my father to herself.

And she was such a planner. She had her whole life mapped out. She was going to move to Seattle and be a sports commentator for ESPN. Then she was going to coin a phrase even catchier than "cooler than the other side of the pillow."

She must have tried to come up with a plan for what would happen if I ever found out about the affair. But I guess, in the end, it seemed like too big a risk. She chose death over gambling with our friendship.

The world is a worse place without her. Of that I'm certain. But I do have moments of doubt where icy fingers of anger creep up inside me, trying to flip the deck, until I'm silently blaming her for breaking up my family, just the way she feared I would.

I wish I had the slightest fucking clue what I should believe.

I arrive at Hannah's vanilla and peach townhome on the east side of the city. The streets in this tract are lined with a mixture of young maple and eucalyptus trees. It's obvious that the association maintains the neighborhood well, but I'm not sure how I feel about all these planned unit developments in California. It's just neighborhoods of pretty houses, all indistinguishable from one another, where people seem to spend most of their lives indoors. You hardly ever see kids playing in the street. They're all tucked away in their air-conditioned bedrooms playing video games or pretending to feel safe while chatting with strangers on the internet.

News flash: The predator will find the prey wherever it may roam, whether it be in the privacy of an online chat space or outside under the butter-yellow sun. Might as well drink in the fresh air while it's still somewhat breathable.

God, I miss the clean Oregon air.

I prop my bike up behind the railing on the small porch, then I ring the doorbell. Clasping my hands together, I rub my thumb in circles over the inside of my palm. I've never been more nervous in my life. Not even when Houston and I first slept together. I've spent the past week and a half since I met Hannah feverishly reading as many of her books as I could. I don't normally read thrillers, so it was a nice change of pace for me. And, thankfully, they were quite addictive and fast-paced, so I was able to make it through eight of her seventeen books.

She answers the door with her red lips pulled into a broad smile. "Rory! So glad you made it. Come on in."

I step inside and immediately I'm overcome by the scent of green tea and lemon. Glancing at a small console table under the stairs, I spot a scented oil warmer. The living space is cozy, with sumptuous oatmeal linen sofas and rustic ash-colored tables that look heavy and expensive.

"I just put on a pot of coffee," Hannah proclaims, clapping her hands together.

She moves like a wraith across the dark wood floor toward the kitchen and dining area, her lithe arms and legs gliding gracefully as her beige cardigan billows slightly behind her. I follow her into the kitchen, where the smell of green tea and lemon melts into the aroma of freshly brewed coffee. The machine sputters its last few drops into the glass pot as she approaches the counter.

"I read your email," she says, her voice reverberating off the white kitchen cabinets as she reaches for a couple of coffee mugs. "Your feedback was spot on. I *was* skimming over the details of the murder scene a bit, but I don't think the readers will notice. Want to know why?"

I place one hand on the cool marble countertop. "Why?"

She flashes me a devious smile as she pours the coffee. "Because they won't yet know what to look for." She slides the carafe back into the machine and spins around to retrieve the cream from the giant stainless steel refrigerator. "You can't give the reader all the details right up front. Writing is twenty percent telling, thirty percent showing, and fifty percent holding back. So, for instance, with this story you're working on—your memoir—you can't call it a memoir."

"Why?" I feel like a toddler, spouting off the only word I know in the presence of an adult who obviously knows way more than I do.

"It has to be a love story based on true events," she replies, handing me a cup of coffee with cream and no sugar. "If you call it a memoir, readers will examine your life to see how true it actually is and how the real story ends. And you're not dead yet, honey." She takes a sip of her coffee then continues. "If it's a love story, the readers will go wherever you take them and, when the story ends, they'll move on to the next one. You want to eventually write fiction, don't you?"

"Yes."

"Then you don't want readers examining your life. You need to keep an air of mystery about you. Readers *want* to imagine you sitting at a laptop in your bathrobe, coffee rings staining your desk, hair sticking out in all directions, a cigarette leaning perilously over the edge of your lip. Let them hold on to that image whether or not it's true."

I pause with the coffee mug pressed against my bottom lip, but I don't take a sip. "Why?" I ask again and she smiles before she takes a drink from her steaming mug.

"Lesson number one about being an author: You can't allow another person's opinion of you define who you are. You can't allow readers or critics or interviewers to attempt to define you based on the bad decisions you made in college or the extra ten pounds you gained while writing your last book. Your work should be judged on its own merit, not on how hideous your skin looked in your last Instagram selfie. You'll understand soon enough."

I suddenly feel my jeans getting tighter around my belly and my skin getting itchy.

"Everyone will try to define you based on their own perception of you, but the only thing that matters is what's between those pages. That's who you are. Whether you're writing fairy tales or spy novels. All that matters is the truth in the words."

I take a sip of my coffee to give myself time to think of a response, anything other than *why*. I can't help but smile when I realize Hannah makes coffee as good as my mom's. She would be totally creeped out if I shared this with her, but this small fact, coupled with this conversation about truth, has endeared me to her.

"So, you mean, even if I'm writing fiction, I have to tell the truth."

She winks at me. "It ain't rocket surgery."

I open my mouth to say, "That's one of my dad's favorite phrases," but I stop myself. I don't want to bring my dad into the conversation at our first meeting. She's not my therapist.

Hannah nods toward the dining table in the breakfast nook and we take a seat. "This may be a bit early, but I'd like to see what you're working on. I think you'll find a second opinion to be most helpful with stories that are close to your heart."

My skin tingles at the idea of her reading my story. "It's not finished."

"I don't mind," she replies with a warm smile. "I probably won't read the whole thing anyway. Just a few chapters to get a sense of the voice and flow of the story. If it's any good, we can submit it to my agent with a proposal. She's been looking for something fresh in the romance genre."

My hands tremble at the thought of Hannah and her agent reading the story of Houston and me. My mind races with thoughts of all the horrible things she can say about my writing. Or the terrible things she'll think of me when she learns what happened with Houston and Hallie.

No, she said she'd only read a few chapters. I'll just remove the prologue, which shows the moment Houston brought me Hallie's suicide note. If I delete that, she'll start from the beginning of my obsession with Houston and she'll probably stop somewhere around where we move in together. Yes, that's what I'll do. I'll send her a link to a duplicate Google doc that *doesn't* contain the prologue.

Then a sobering irony slams into me: My first attempt at telling the truth involves me hiding the most honest and raw part of the story.

I have to let her read the prologue.

If someone offered to help fix your stalled car on the side of the road, you wouldn't hide the wrench before handing them the toolbox. You'd give them every fucking tool they could possibly need to help you.

That's what I have to do. I'll send her the link to access the unedited document in my Google Drive. She'll pluck the truth from the digital cloud and watch it blossom on her computer screen, live and uncensored. And I'll wring my hands and try not to throw up as I wait for her to reply.

Houston

January 5, 2015

Toss me the bag.

I hear the words, but they mean absolutely nothing.

Seth repeats the sentence louder. "Hey, toss me the bag!"

The scene before me materializes like a camera gradually shifting into focus. The cold concrete floor of the warehouse. The bags of grain stacked on the dead forklift next to me. The herbaceous fragrance of hops and the sweet nutty scent of chocolate malt settling around us in a cloud of dust. Seth, my warehouse manager, standing in front of me looking mystified.

"Sorry, man. Must have drifted off for a second."

I grab a fifty-pound sack of malt and pass it to him. He tosses it to Hector, who then tosses it to Quinn, then the assembly line disappears into the grain room. The forklift that's used to transport the pallets of grain from the warehouse into the grain room has broken down. Troy is already upstairs in his office calling our heavy-equipment mechanic to see how soon he can come out. In the meantime, we need to get two hundred fifty-pound sacks of Cascade hops and malt out of the warehouse to clear space for the next delivery of malt extract coming in less than three hours.

My mind must have taken a vacation. It's been doing that a lot since I received a text from Kenny this morning asking me to meet him at the Zucker's store on Belmont. I didn't bother calling to ask him how his New Year's visit with Rory went. It's been almost five days since then and I know I'm pretty well fucked.

When I saw Rory's name on my phone, I completely forgot Tessa had been making her way toward me on the stage in the corner of the Barley Legal brewhouse. In a split second, I went from horrified at the sudden appearance of my ex-wife to elated at the prospect of hearing my Scar's voice. I wasn't fucking bullshitting when I told Rory that when we're together it's as if nothing and nobody else exists. Even with her being six hundred miles away, there's nothing that can pull me out of time and reality like her name. Her voice. Her scent.

But I never got to hear Rory's voice because Tessa knocked the phone out of my hand and it was shattered under the crush of bodies celebrating the promise of a new year. I used Troy's phone to try to call Rory back. I wasn't certain she had heard Tessa's insults. But the call went straight to voicemail, which told me she *had* heard Tessa. If there was any hope of Rory taking me back before, it vanished in a single sickening instant.

I don't know what Kenny wants to talk about or why he wants me to meet him at the store instead of at Rory's apartment, where he's now living. Maybe Rory asked him not to let me in her apartment. *Fuck*. The thought of her making that kind of request burns, but I can't say I'd blame her.

Once all the bags are stacked neatly in the grain room, I head out to meet Kenny at Zucker's. With just ten minutes to get across town, I rush into the store in time to meet Kenny at the time we agreed on. I ignore the stunned looks from the employees who are used to seeing me in clean clothes. The dust from the chocolate malt is all over me, smeared over my cheeks and crusted under my fingernails.

I spot Kenny sitting at a table in the wine bar, sipping a frothy white drink. "What's up?" I say, pulling out a chair to take a seat across from him.

He looks me over for a moment, taking in my grunginess. "What happened to you?"

"I was working in the warehouse today. I didn't have time to go home and clean up. What's going on?"

He bites his lip and I don't want to imagine the dirty things he's imagining right now. Finally, he shakes his head, throwing up his hands in defeat. "I can't even…"

He twists around and reaches into the backpack hanging on the back of his chair. When he turns back to me, my heart drops at the sight of the Sierra Nevada tin box. He slides it across the table toward me and my first instinct is to lean back, to distance myself from the grating sound it makes as it scrapes over the wooden surface.

"What are you doing?" The words issue from my mouth, low and threatening.

"She asked me to give it back to you." He waits a moment for me to respond, then sighs. "She asked me not to talk about you anymore."

My nostrils flare as I suck in large breaths. A fiery storm rages inside me. Before I can stop it, the box goes flying across the small floor space reserved for the café. It lands with a clatter underneath the seat of the chair next to me. The ring clinks across the floor, coming to a stop next to the feet of a man who's standing next to the bar waiting for the bartender to pour his beer. The letter lands softly at my feet. I scoop it up and storm out of the store, adrenaline surging through my veins. My resolve stiffens like steel tension cables corded through my muscles.

I get in my car and drive south toward Tessa's parents' house in Healy Heights. My fingers grip the steering wheel as if it's the only thing anchoring me to my sanity. I could probably rip it clean off the dash right now.

I can't let Tessa fuck with my life anymore. But what the fuck am I supposed to do to get her to stop? I can't show up at her parents' house and threaten her, get myself thrown in a jail cell. And I sure as hell can't reason with her. But Troy was right, I need to take care of Tessa before I can even think about bringing Rory back to Portland.

The firestorm inside me rages out of control when I think of Rory in California with another guy. I know I brought this on myself, but I need someone else to blame. I've been taking on the full burden of my mistakes and Hallie's mistakes for a very fucking long time. It's time I start holding other people responsible for their mistakes. And Tessa's first on my list.

She fucked this up for me by showing up at our New Year's Eve party. I'm not going to let her continue to ruin my chances with Rory.

I take a few deep breaths to douse the fire raging inside me. Then I slide my phone out of my pocket and dial Tessa's parents' house phone. After the fourth ring, I'm about to hang up, when Tessa's voice comes on the line, desperate and breathless.

"Houston?"

I recoil at the yearning in her voice. "Tessa, we need to talk."

She lets out a sharp breath. "Yes. Of course. I'll be at your place in twenty minutes."

"No. I'm coming to you. We're going to discuss this with your family."

"But… I don't mind going to your place."

"I'm coming to you."

I end the call before she can protest, and five minutes later I pull up outside their rambling ranch-style home overlooking downtown Portland and Mt. Saint Helens. This five-bedroom home with the million-dollar view in this stellar neighborhood with the best schools wasn't enough to fix the things wrong with Tessa. Maybe I'm kidding myself by thinking a stern talking-to is all she needs to back off. But my only other option is to sit back and let her repeatedly knock my train off the tracks.

I was so close with Rory. So *fucking* close. *She* called *me*. At midnight. On New Year's Eve. When she could have been kissing that fucking lumberjack, she was calling me instead. And now I'm not even back at square one. It feels like I'm at zero fuck-all.

I won't let it happen again.

Pressing the doorbell, I try and wipe some of the malt dust off my face using the inside of my T-shirt. When I pull my shirt back down, Tessa is standing in the doorway wide-eyed.

A lascivious smile curls her lips. "What happened to you?"

"Forklift broke down. Can I come in?" I ask, ignoring the gleam in her eyes.

She steps back, opening the door wider as her gaze rakes over me. I nod at her as I step inside. The first thing that hits me is the smell of oatmeal. Tessa loves to eat oatmeal for breakfast, lunch, and dinner. Times when I worked late, she wouldn't bother cooking dinner for herself. She'd always make a bowl of oatmeal. I didn't realize how the smell of oats and cinnamon has become so deeply associated with Tessa in my psyche.

I get a weird sensation in my belly. I wouldn't call it a longing. It's more of a sadness, because neither of us wanted to face reality while we were together. And yet, there were still good times. Times we laughed so hard our bellies ached. Times we fucked so hard our minds numbed. But nothing we ever did could fully mask the fact that we were dangerous for each other.

I used to think that Rory and I had a toxic relationship, but the three years I spent with Tessa were far worse. Lying to Rory was a disgusting thing to do, but at least it allowed me to love her honestly for a brief moment in time. Lying to myself while I was with Tessa almost made me forget who I was.

We enter the living room and Tessa's mom, Marie, is sitting on the brown leather sofa with Tessa's one-year-old nephew, Jasen, bouncing on her lap. Jasen was named after Tessa's eldest brother, who died in a car accident four and a half years ago. Pictures of the older Jasen are plastered all over the living room, atop the mantle, on the walls, and in the hallway. A pang of guilt overcomes me as I remember why I'm here and how I'd feel if Rory came to my office and told me the things I'm about to say to Tessa.

No, I can't equate the love Rory and I share to the obsession Tessa has with me.

"Marie," I say, nodding at her as Tessa sits down on the love seat, patting the cushion next to her. I ignore Tessa's invitation and address Marie directly. "I came to talk about Tessa."

"Hello? I'm right here," Tessa says, her mouth hanging open in an expression of incredulity. "You can talk to me, Houston."

I draw in a long breath to stop myself from saying anything stupid. "I came to talk to your mom." I turn back to Marie. "Is that all right?"

Marie purses her lips as she stands from the sofa, balancing Jasen on her hip. "Houston, I think it's very inappropriate for you to be here. You two are divorced. Can't you just let her be? You've done enough damage."

"Excuse me? I know I haven't been a saint, but I think I've been more than fair with Tessa since the divorce was filed."

Tessa stands up. "Fair?" she says, with a laugh. "You think it's fair to cheat on me and kick me out onto the *streets*?"

"I didn't kick you out on the streets. I divorced you and that means we no longer live together. It's not my fault you didn't have a job."

"It's not your fault? It's not your *fault*? It's *all* your fault! You told me I never had to get a job if I didn't want to."

Jasen starts crying and Marie tries to console him. "It's okay, sweetheart. Don't cry, honey." Her eyes shoot daggers at me. "See what you did?"

I clench my jaw to keep from blowing up at this woman who hardly tried to know me in the three years I was married to her daughter. Tessa once admitted to me that her mom didn't care who she married, as long as he had money to take care of her. I imagine Tessa's parents probably didn't want to have to deal with her shit anymore. It's true that I never asked about the scars on Tessa's arms, and I didn't ask a whole lot of questions about her family while we were together. I sensed she wanted to leave the painful memories behind her and I used that to my advantage. It meant I was able to keep Tessa at arm's length. Close, but not *too* close.

But I can't fucking believe Marie, blaming me for upsetting the baby when clearly Tessa is the one yelling. It was a mistake coming here.

"Marie, I'm here to ask you *nicely* that you keep Tessa away from me."

Tessa's shrill laughter echoes off the stone fireplace and Jasen actually reaches up to cover his ears with his chubby hands.

"I'm serious," I continue. "I don't want to have to get a restraining order, but if she comes near me again, I will. Do you both understand? It's over. It ends today. No more showing up at my work or calling me on the phone, from *anyone's* phone." I point at Marie. "She's your daughter. Take care of her for a fucking change."

As I walk away, Marie calls out, "Don't you turn and walk away from me! I take care of my daughter!"

I continue out the front door, ignoring Tessa as she screams at my back, "I hope you die! I hope you *both* die!"

I'm shaking with fury as I pull the car away from the curb and drive off. I don't know if they'll listen to a single word I just said, but at least I said it. And they'd better know how fucking serious I am.

Instead of going home, I head to the gym to burn off the tension. Despite the fact that I spent three hours doing intense manual labor today, I spend another hour on the treadmill and two hours lifting weights. I finish my workout and shower away all the grime of the day. When I pull my phone out of the locker, I find three voicemails from Marie. I'm instantly filled with dread. Marie has never once called my cell phone, which means this is probably another deranged call from Tessa.

I let out a deep sigh and hit the play button to listen to the message.

"It's all your fault!" Marie's voice is frantic. "She took the whole bottle! Are you happy now? I hope you rot in hell!"

Rory

January 5, 2015

SOME CATHOLICS BELIEVE you can exorcise demons with a determined priest and a little holy water. I'm going to exorcise mine with a little determination and a lot of hair dye.

Toasted Marshmallow is the color. It's a stupid name. Everyone toasts their marshmallows to varying degrees, which basically means I could end up with hair in the spectrum of a soft pillowy white all the way up to charcoal black. But the model on the front of the box has hair that's more of a golden chestnut color. Yes, golden chestnut is more accurate. Maybe I should get a job naming hair dye colors.

I walk out of the bathroom forty minutes later, my hair still slightly damp, clutching my phone and wearing nothing but a green Timbers T-shirt and pink panties. Liam cocks an eyebrow as he watches me approach my side of the bed. Slowly, he sets his tablet on the nightstand and sits up straighter as I plop down next to him.

"What do you think?" I ask, rubbing a lock of my new dark,

slightly damp hair between my fingers.

His eyebrows can't seem to decide if they want to shoot up or scrunch together in confusion. "It's… not red anymore."

"No shit, Sherlock. But what do you think about the color? Do you hate it? Love it?" I trace the tip of my finger over his knee. "Want to pull it?"

He smiles at this proposition, but he seems unable to respond.

"You hate it."

"No, I don't," he insists, grabbing my hand before I get out of bed. "It's just going to take some getting used to. That's all."

"Which is code for *I hate it.*"

He laughs as he pulls me toward him. "I don't hate it."

"But you don't love it."

"Would you shut up already?" he says, sliding his hand behind my neck as our eyes meet. "Just shut up and listen."

I swallow hard as his gaze is locked on my mouth for a moment, then it shifts to his hand as he slides it through my hair.

"I like brunettes," he murmurs, reaching up to cradle my face in his hands. "But I'll like you whatever color your hair is."

A pinprick of guilt punctures my heart.

"I like you, too," I reply, to which he responds with that perfect smile and those perfect teeth. "How often do you floss?" I ask, my voice shaky as I try to distract myself from the intensity of his gaze.

He laughs at my ridiculous question. "Twice a day. But I can make it three," he says, his hand sliding down until it's between my legs. He kisses my neck as he slips his hand inside my panties. "Everyone should floss more often," he murmurs, his finger finding my clit. "It's healthy."

He strokes me softly and suddenly I'm reminded of the first time Houston made me come with his magic fingers. "Oh, my fucking God."

For the first time since Liam and I moved to California, this feels wrong.

I'm lying on my bed getting a hand job from Liam while somewhere, just a few blocks away, Hannah is possibly sitting in her comfy armchair reading about my many sexual adventures with Houston. The ink hasn't even dried on my breakup with Houston and I'm already getting fondled by another guy.

"Fuck," I whisper, pulling his hand out of my panties. "Sorry. I just remembered I have to check my email. Hannah's supposed to send me some feedback."

I slide off the bed, stumbling a little as I head for the bathroom, all the while trying to ignore the unfulfilled ache between my legs.

"You're gonna check your email in the bathroom?" Liam says, a note of bitterness in his voice.

I glance at him and immediately look away when I see him adjusting his boxers over his erection. "Do I have to tell you every time I'm going to piss?"

He narrows his eyes at me and I check my tone.

"I didn't mean it like that," I clarify, though I absolutely did mean it just the way it sounded. "I'm just nervous about the email. Sorry."

Before he can reply, I disappear into the bathroom and lock the door behind me. I sit on the toilet and stare at my phone screen, breathing deeply as I try to calm the throbbing between my thighs. But I can't help myself. I keep imagining Houston's hands on me.

Suddenly, the photo app on my phone is open and I'm scrolling, images flying by in a soft blur of silver asphalt and blue ocean, road trip pictures. Then I reach the images of Houston and me in my Goose Hollow apartment. His face buried in my neck, my face radiant with that post-sex glow, as I snap a selfie of us in my bed. His hand splayed over my ribs, slightly cupping the underside of my breast.

Spreading my knees open, I slowly pull up my T-shirt and slide my hand inside my panties. I'm still tender and warm from Liam's touch. Another pang of guilt at the thought that Liam just warmed me up to fantasize about Houston, but I quickly push the thought aside.

I don't want to feel guilty right now. I just want to feel good.

I drag my finger through my wetness, bringing it up to my aching clit as I imagine Houston's tongue licking me, up and down and in slow torturous circles. Drawing out the pleasure one luscious flick at a time. His mouth kissing my clit tenderly, as if it were my mouth, savoring my taste. His tongue firm and purposeful as he slides it inside me, fucks me with it.

"Houston," I cry out and my eyelids snap open, mechanical and doll-like.

My hand is frozen inside my panties, my heart punching my ribs, as I listen for movement outside the bathroom.

Did Liam hear me?

What the fuck am I doing?

I wash up quickly and take a few minutes to blow-dry my hair, to give Liam a couple of minutes to process what just happened, if he did hear me. Then I draw in a deep breath, straightening my spine and pulling my shoulders back as I walk out of the bathroom. He watches me silently as I leave the bedroom, but as soon as I cross the threshold, I hear the soft rustling of him sliding off the bed to come after me.

The living room is as dark and cold as my blood. I quickly turn on the lamp by the sofa and jump when I turn around and Liam is standing right behind me.

"Holy shit. You scared the fuck out of me." I slither past him to scoop my laptop off the coffee table and plop down on the sofa with it.

"Were you on the phone in the bathroom?"

Without raising my face, I roll my eyes. "It was Kenny. He won't stop calling me and updating me on everything that's happening with Houston. I finally told him to never mention Houston to me again." *At least that last part is true.*

Liam takes a seat next to me as I begin typing in the password to log into my computer, then I stop before I finish entering it. "Why does he keep talking to you about Houston? I thought you two were finished."

"We are, but Kenny just needs a little extra convincing." I scoot a few inches away from Liam, angling my laptop a little so he can't see my fingers as I type in my password. "He means well. He just misses me and he's looking for an excuse not to let go. He'll drop it, eventually."

Liam lets out a soft chuckle, his gaze laser-focused on my computer. "You don't seem very worried about the fact that it's been a month since you left and he's still trying to get you to go back."

I look up from the screen and meet his suspicious glare. "Exactly. It's only been a month. He's my *best* friend. You can't expect him to stop wanting me back after just one month."

He stares at me for a moment as we both probably wonder who I was just referring to. "Do you want to go back?"

"No," I reply flatly, turning back to my computer screen.

He doesn't respond. He just sits there, stealing glances at me as I pretend to check my email with the screen slightly turned away from him. My eyes glaze over the text in front of me. I know I don't have an email from Hannah. She said she'd call me after she's read the chapters. I only gave her access to my Google doc a few days ago. I don't expect her to get in touch with me anytime soon, unless she needs feedback on her own novel.

Something simmers inside me as I sit there pretending to check my email. I don't know if it's resentment over Liam making me feel as if I need an excuse to leave the bedroom at night. Or if it's a sudden steely courage that has eluded me for the past month, buried under my desire to believe that my sensitivity is the problem, not Liam's insecurity. If I weren't so thin-skinned, I could handle the occasional bout of jealousy. I could even understand it considering Liam is very much aware that he has big shoes to fill. But it's not that I'm being touchy. It's that Liam doesn't trust me.

And how could he? Our relationship got off to a rocky start in August, with him *convincing* me to give him a shot despite the fact that I was deeply messed up over running into Houston. Then I went and had an affair with Houston while he was still married. And Liam had to watch as Houston's wife attacked me in broad daylight. And despite all this, he knows, he can *sense* that, though my mind and body reside in California, the roots of my heart are still firmly planted in Oregon.

I haven't given Liam a reason to trust me. I made the mistake of presuming the default status of any new relationship is 100 percent trust. That the trust doesn't begin to erode until there is *actual* wrongdoing. But it seems I was wrong. I feel as if Liam and I started at about 50 percent trust. And each mistake I've made with him over the past five months has only served to chip away at that number.

"Why did you and Savannah break up?" I ask, hoping I sound as casual as I'm trying to sound.

He stares at the side of my laptop screen for a moment before he answers. "I told you, it just ran its course. It never would have worked out between us. We were too different."

"Different how?" My fingers click over the keys as I begin typing a fake email to no one.

I can feel his gaze lift from my screen to my face, but I keep my eyes pointed downward. My heart ripples inside my chest, a ghostly flutter of anxiety.

"She cheated on me with her boss."

The irony of this statement is not lost on me. I am fully aware that Houston was technically my boss before I left Oregon.

My face tilts up and our eyes meet. "She cheated on you?"

So that's why you're so insecure?

"Yeah, that's why I don't offer up the story unless someone asks. I don't like talking about it." He turns his torso toward me and puts on a smile, though I'm sure he's not feeling very smiley right now. "Enough about that. How about we forget about our shitty exes and go out for drinks tomorrow? Me and a guy from work are going to a local place for Taco Tuesday. We can go down a few shots of Patrón then come home and I'll show you how much I like brunettes."

He wiggles his eyebrows and I smile as I realize Liam is just a different version of me. He's me in two or three years, after all this stuff with Houston has blown over. I'll probably still have trust issues too, but if I don't screw things up with Liam, I might have someone who understands why.

I slam my laptop shut and place it on the coffee table. Then I climb into Liam's lap, my knees on either side of his hips, as I reach up and softly tug his beard. He smiles as I lean in, the crotch of my panties rubbing against his erection as I kiss him slowly. When I pull away, his eyes are glazed over and hooded with lust.

I lean in and whisper against his lips. "Let's chase down our demons together."

Houston

January 6, 2015

I ENTER THE HOSPITAL a few minutes past midnight, rubbing my itchy palms against my jeans. I wish I didn't feel the need to check on Tessa. I wish I could fall asleep in my bed and not give a fuck. Because this is exactly why she downed that bottle of pills. She knew it would bring me to her and she didn't care if I came on a white horse or carrying a pitchfork.

I'll just check in with the hospital staff. Make sure she's okay. Maybe look in on her really quick while she sleeps, then I'll leave. If Marie is still here, I won't even drop into her room. I'll just speak to the staff to ease my mind, then I'll turn around and never look back.

I head for the nurses' station, but from the corner of my eye, I glimpse a doctor coming out of a hospital room. I walk casually past the nurses' station as they chat, pretending I know my way around, then I speed up to catch the doctor.

"Excuse me, sir?"

He turns around and cocks a bushy silver eyebrow. "May I

help you?"

"Yes, I'm looking for Tessa—um, I mean, Contessa Cavanaugh." She hasn't changed her last name back to her maiden name yet, but this could work to my advantage. "Is that her room?" I ask, nodding toward the door from which he just emerged.

Confusion settles over his wrinkled face. "I'm sorry. Are you family?"

"Houston Cavanaugh," I reply, swallowing the nausea blistering up my throat. "Her husband. I was away and my flight just came in. I just want to make sure she's okay."

My skin feels itchy as the lies stream out of my mouth. I wonder if he's even buying this. I'm certain I look more repulsed than grief stricken.

"I'm very sorry, Mr. Cavanaugh," he begins, and my heart falls with a thunk. "Your wife is stable, but she's being admitted to Cedar Hills in about eight hours on an inpatient basis."

"Cedar Hills?"

"I didn't see any notes in her chart about them trying to notify you, but I guess if you were out of town that would have been difficult." His expression becomes pained. "Her mother agreed it would be best if she were put under a physician's hold… She's considered a danger to herself, so she's being admitted for psychiatric treatment."

I blink a few times, trying to process this information. "Is she going to… to get help at this Cedar Hills place? Or is it like some looney bin where they just pump them full of meds and roll them into a corner?"

"They have specialists there who have a lot of experience with BPD, and she'll only be in the Crisis Stabilization Unit for one to five days. But after that, they'll talk to you about further inpatient and outpatient options. I'm sure you're aware that medication isn't very effective on BPD, so they'll discuss the various therapeutic options available."

"BPD?"

The doctor waits for me to come up with the definition of this acronym, but quickly realizes I'm completely lost. "Borderline Personality Disorder. Your wife has suffered with this disorder for, well, according to her chart, about thirteen years. Were you not aware of this?"

I want to say, *Do I fucking look like I was aware of this?*

I don't know if having this knowledge in my possession from the beginning would have changed my decision to marry Tessa, but it sure as hell would have changed my approach to the divorce. And the past four months I've spent trying to get Rory back. I probably would have listened to Troy when he told me to get the fucking restraining order from the beginning.

I always knew Tessa was sick, but I thought it was just her obsession with me that drove her to do crazy things. I thought it was her fear of being alone that compelled her to continually throw out her hook in my direction, trying to get our lines helplessly tangled together for all eternity.

"Thank you," I whisper, dazed and somewhat relieved to have answers.

Turning around, I walk past the partially open door of Tessa's room, not bothering to peek inside. No need to keep up the charade of concerned husband anymore.

I came here feeling as if it were my duty to make sure Tessa's family gets her some help, but they've known she has BPD all along. And they never said a goddamned thing to me about it. Tessa spent three years with me not taking meds, not seeing a therapist, until our fucking pre-divorce counseling sessions, which were basically *shit on Houston* sessions. And all that fucking time she could have been working on getting better.

Instead, her family basically pawned her off on me. *Like a fucking mushroom, fed shit and kept in the dark.* One of my mom's favorite sayings. She used it a lot to describe her years with my dad, when he was living a double life with two families. That was me. *Fed shit and kept in the dark.* I was a fucked-up twenty-four-year-old in the midst of my own PTSD crisis, trying like hell to forget the worst fucking day of my life. And Tessa's family thought *I* was the answer to her problems?

Jesus Christ. I thought Rory's family was fucked up.

I step out of the swishing hospital doors, under the fat starless sky, hoping it will rain. I want to feel the cold prick of raindrops on my skin. Inhale the freshly cleansed air, smelling of wet concrete and ozone. And run all the way to California on a single breath.

But I have to be patient.

My problems with Tessa may be reaching some semblance of resolution, but my problems with Rory are far from finished. I have to stick to the plan Kenny and I hashed out. Even if I have zero chance of getting Rory back, I have to follow through with the plan for her sake.

I slide into the driver's seat of my car feeling buoyant with hope. Tessa's going to be taken care of. Her family knows what's wrong with her. The doctors will make sure they have the tools to help her. Whether they use those tools is no longer my responsibility.

As I slide my phone into my pocket and drive out of the hospital parking lot, my mind conjures the sharp snip of ropes being cut. I get a strange feeling that if I look in my rearview mirror, I'll see the frayed ends trailing behind my car. But I keep my eyes focused on the road ahead of me. I'm not looking back anymore.

When I pull into my parking space in my new apartment building, I slide my phone out of my pocket and begin typing an email.

Hi Hannah.

I hope this message finds you well. I'm emailing you instead of calling you because I didn't think you'd appreciate a rambling phone call at one a.m. Plus, Patricia said I shouldn't call you because it will ruin something with the book. I can't remember exactly what she said, but anyway, I'm thinking we may need to speed things up a bit. I know you're busy with your own deadline, but I'd love to hear your thoughts on the book as soon as possible. I don't doubt it's good enough to submit to your agent, but I need to know for sure, so I can start making other plans, if necessary.

By the way, thanks so much for all your help. When Patricia told me she was going to approach you, I thought this whole thing was a long shot, but you've made me believe in the goodness of people again. That's something I'll never be able to repay you for.

Please respond at your earliest convenience.

Houston

I send the message and pray there aren't any typos. Then I recall how I would sometimes purposely put typos in my emails and text messages to Rory, just to drive her nuts. If the lines of communication between us hadn't gone dead, I'd text her right now: I can't loose you again. Your my scar.

Rory

January 6, 2015

I SIT DOWN at the table in Hannah's breakfast nook, my insides squealing with a mixture of fear and delight at the sight of what's laid out on the wooden surface. A maelstrom of paper with words I recognize: Houston, Hallie, Scar… An explosion of black emotions on white canvas with red blood scrawled in the margins.

Every. Single. Page. Redlined.

"Don't let that scare you," Hannah says, handing me a steaming mug of coffee, which I'm certain is made just the way I like it. "First drafts are always a steaming pile. And your pile is teeny tiny compared to most beginning writers. And very fresh. Not a single fly."

I glance at the steamy brown liquid in my cup and set it down on the table instead of taking a sip, pushing aside a stack of paper to make room for it. "Did you… Did you read the whole book?"

Hannah takes a seat in the chair across from me and brushes aside some papers to make room for her mug. "Yeah, I'm going to be totally honest with you. You hooked me with the prologue.

I'm not sure the notes I added in the first 75 percent will make any sense because I was pretty much just cramming the words down at that point." She takes a sip of her coffee and I hope my face doesn't look as red hot as it feels. "And once I got to the scene with the letter, well, I had to keep flipping pages just to see when these two would get back together." She raises her eyebrows at me. "So when do they get back together?"

I stare blankly at the chaotic layer of paper in front of me, unsure how to answer this. "I… don't think they get back together. I mean, if I'm going to sell this story as a romance, I guess I'll have to change the characters' names and give them a happy ending."

She waves away my suggestion. "Pfft! No, this is not a romance. This is a love story based on true events. You've acknowledged that. A love story doesn't need a happy ending the way a romance does, but it *does* need a conclusion. And there is no resolution in this story. How does it *end*?"

"How does it end?" I repeat the question, and my nerves crackle, lifting the hairs on my arms. "I don't know."

Hannah tucks her dark hair behind her ear as she reaches for the red pen that rests innocently between two stacks of paper in front of her. "Well, then I guess we'd better figure it out."

THE VIVE SOL restaurant on the west side of Mountain View is just beginning to fill up with the dinner crowd. Liam grabs my hand, lacing his fingers through mine as we traverse the cracked black asphalt in the parking lot. We pass a faux stone water fountain on our way inside. It trickles water that smells like rain and I smile at the warm rush in my veins.

Matt, Liam's friend from work, opens the door for us to enter the restaurant and I flash him an appreciative smile. Liam tightens his grip on my hand as he leads me toward the host station. The aromas in the restaurant make my mouth water: fresh-cut lime, roasted peppers, warm tortillas. I skipped lunch today, opting for a skinny latte and a bike ride instead, gearing up for tonight's gluttony.

The hostess informs us that the wait is currently forty minutes, but we can sit outside in the outdoor bar-slash-patio right away. Liam looks to me as if sitting outside is even an option.

"It's, like, fifty degrees out there," I remind him. "We'll freeze."

"There are heat lamps," the hostess says.

Liam tilts his head. "Come on. I promise I'll keep you warm."

I glance at the hostess, wondering how many times she's heard that line uttered. I gaze longingly at the cozy amber glow from the Moravian star pendants hanging in the warm dining room. Letting out a soft sigh, I follow the hostess and my two male companions to the outdoor bar area.

Ten minutes after we place our order, the sound of my teeth chattering gets Liam's attention.

"Should I order some shots?" he asks, wrapping his arm around me and rubbing my arm to try to create some heat.

I nod hastily. "Yes. Order me two."

Liam and Matt exchange a look. "Not fucking around tonight, are you?"

I roll my eyes and steer the conversation toward Matt.

What do you do at SaltMedia? Programmer.

How did you get into it? My dad's a programmer.

How long have you lived here? Uh… I was *born* here.

Matt is kind of quiet. His answers are short and monotone, only infusing some inflection when he feels the answer is a bit obvious. The typical nerd cliché wrapped up in a slightly overweight, yet boyishly handsome package.

"So, do you have a girlfriend?" I mutter, my lips starting to feel numb from the two Patrón shots we just downed.

Liam flashes me an exasperated look, but I don't know what it means. Does he think it's time to change the subject to something other than Matt or does he think I'm flirting with him?

"Nope. No girlfriend. Just a really big collection of—"

"Socks?" I say and Matt laughs.

"I was going to say *Star Wars* figurines, but I guess my sock collection is just as impressive."

Liam is definitely looking perplexed by this conversation, which is exactly what I expected. Actually, I'm getting a kick out of it.

"Okay, can we change the subject from cum rags to something a bit more palatable?" Liam suggests.

"Oh, my God!" I say, pulling my phone out of my pocket. "Have you seen that Whitest Kids You Know sketch about The Jizzle? It's disgusting."

Matt smiles as I scoot my barstool closer to him so we can both watch the video on my phone. I can feel the heat of Liam's annoyance scorching my back as he waits for us to watch the one-minute and twenty-three-second fake commercial for a cum rag called The Jizzle, an obvious parody of the Sham Wow infomercial.

"That's disgustingly awesome," Matt says, his fair skin flushed with laughter and tequila.

I smile as I mentally pat myself on the back for getting Matt to loosen up, but when I turn to Liam he does not look very impressed with my technique. I sit up straight and flag down the bartender to order myself another shot, and a house margarita chaser.

By the time our food arrives, I'm pretty sloshed, but I don't give a single solitary fuck about whether I'm upsetting Liam with my behavior. And I don't know if it's because I'm drunk, but it seems Liam gives up on trying to make me feel guilty halfway through dinner. Or maybe I'm just too numb to correctly interpret the malicious intent in his sideways glances.

Either way, I leave the restaurant feeling positively jubilant, the flame of tequila in my bloodstream lighting me up like a Moravian star. The kind of euphoria that only comes when you're just the right amount of drunk. The kind of drunk that makes you do stupid things like professing your love in a drunk text and falling into bed with the first person you see.

Liam and I fall into bed just before midnight, while Matt falls face-first onto our couch. As usual, Liam is careful not to wake me when he gets ready for work in the morning. And I wake to find two aspirin and a large glass of water on my nightstand.

As I guzzle it down, I consider sending Liam a text message apology for the way I behaved last night, but ultimately I decide I need some coffee to clear my brain fog first. After a long hot shower, I fix myself a pot of coffee and sit down cross-legged on the sofa with my laptop.

Something is off.

I stare at my laptop and try to breathe normally. A shaft of hazy morning sunlight pierces through the space between the curtains, illuminating the dust suspended in the air above my lap, shining a spotlight on the greasy fingerprints glistening on the edge of the screen.

Somebody was snooping in my computer.

Houston

January 8, 2015

THE BROADWAY DINER is closing in ten minutes, but Jenny, the manager, won't mind us staying late to avoid the crowd. I just hope Patricia and Kenny aren't too miffed that I'm running late. With Troy getting called away by Georgia to do wedding stuff more and more often, I've latched on to the opportunity to put more hours into work, even throwing in my time and muscle to help out in the warehouse. Anything to keep my mind and body busy, to stave off the sense of doom that comes with being idle.

I enter the diner and find Kenny and Patricia sitting on a couple of stools at a tall table in the back of a small dining nook at the rear of the restaurant. The instant she sees me, Patricia's mouth curls into a warm smile that reminds me so much of Rory it makes my chest ache.

Kenny slips his arm through hers, hugging her bicep possessively. "Don't get any crazy ideas. She's mine. Right, Patty?"

She rolls her eyes and pats his hand. "Of course, dear."

I take a seat on the stool across from them and swallow hard, feeling like a child being called to the principal's office. "So what have I done? I mean, what have you got?"

Patricia purses her lips. "Oh, Houston, don't look so grave. You have to keep a positive outlook or the wait will only get more difficult as the weeks go by."

"Weeks? Is that how long it's going to take to finish?"

She exchanges a knowing glance with Kenny, and I have a feeling they're keeping something from me. "It could take weeks. Maybe even months."

My heart cracks under the weight of this news. "That's too long."

Kenny cocks an eyebrow. "Excuse me? But the girl didn't stop loving you after five years apart. I hardly think a few months with a lumberjack is going to change her sexual appetites."

"Kenny!" Patricia chides him.

He shrugs. "Sorry, Patty, but Rory's trying to pray away the gay. Trust me, it doesn't work."

"Well, she can't pray away the gay agenda," I say, and he flashes me a proud smile. "Fine. So it's going to take a while. Tell me where we're at."

Patricia slides her arm out of Kenny's, her face suddenly serious. "I got the first six chapters last night." Her hazel eyes are locked on mine. "Let me just start off by saying that I do *not* condone this type of writing. It's... gritty and... filthy."

I swallow the lump of trepidation forming in my throat. I don't know what Rory has written in this book, but I can only imagine she's poured her blood and tears onto those pages, the way she's always done with everything. Her friendship with Hallie. Her love for me. She's always been a violently raging ocean disguised as a tranquil sea.

Patricia sighs. "But it's heartbreakingly real," she continues, fixing me with an unnerving glare. "You two really did a number on each other." She stares at the table for a moment. "I'm only up to your first month living together, but the years before… when she loved you from a distance… As a mother, it chills my bones. I didn't know the intensity of her feelings for you. I assumed it was a childhood crush that she'd grow out of when she got to university and saw you with other girls."

My muscles are taut with tension, hanging on her every word. I want to ask her to send me the chapters. I want to bury myself in Rory's words the way I used to bury myself inside her. But I can't violate her privacy.

I've justified bringing Patricia and Hannah in on my plan, knowing that they will help make her book better. But I'm not a writer or an English teacher. I have nothing to contribute to Rory's story other than acting as the hero who's desperately trying *not* to get written out.

"I want to know." The words come out of my mouth in a tense rasp. "I wish I could read it, but I know I can't. So… thank you for doing this, Patricia. You can't imagine how happy I am knowing that Rory's story is in your hands. I know you'll take good care of it."

Kenny wraps his arm around Patricia's shoulders and squeezes. "We're all lucky to have Patty on our side, especially Rory."

"Well, don't start with the flattery yet. I'm only six chapters in," she replies, then takes a sip from her iced tea. "Hannah is working on extensive rewrites with Rory. They made it through the first six chapters fairly quickly, but I have a feeling the next fifty-some will take longer."

"Fifty-some *chapters*?" I blurt out, unable to contain my disappointment.

Kenny nods his head knowingly. "Figures it's fifty-some chapters, as filthy as you say it is. It's like *Fifty Shades of Houston*." His eyes widen. "Hey, you should suggest that title to her."

Patricia smacks his hand and shrugs out from underneath his arm. "Stop it. She's not writing erotic literature."

"But there are sex scenes, right?" Kenny asks, grabbing his glass of ice water.

"Enough about my daughter's sex life," she replies, her gaze focused on her glass of tea.

That's when I realize Rory must have gone into a lot of detail in those love scenes, because Patricia can't even look at me right now. My mind draws back to our first month together, poring through the thousands of images of us in bed, in the shower, in the kitchen. I come to a screeching halt on the image of Rory pressed up against the brick wall in the back of a German restaurant.

It was New Year's Eve. Troy had wanted us to join him at a frat party, but I knew Rory would feel more comfortable ringing in the New Year just the two of us. The restaurant was packed with people who either had the same idea as us, or who just wanted to take advantage of the free New Year's Eve beer sampler. I parked my truck in the back of the restaurant, which stood like a giant two-story box in the center of a dark corner lot.

The front of the restaurant was lit up by a gaudy neon sign and the sodium-yellow glow of a solitary streetlamp. But the back of the restaurant was flush in dark-blue shadow, and the occasional glint of moonlight on chrome. There was one other car parked back there, but it was a brand-new Lincoln SUV. Probably belonged to the manager or the owner of the restaurant. They wouldn't come out until the place closed down at two or three in the morning.

"Do you think they'll have champagne?" Rory asked, grabbing her phone out of her purse and tossing the handbag into the truck cab.

"Doesn't matter. You won't be able to drink it," I said, reaching into the cab to grab an old blanket I kept back there out of habit, laying it on top of her purse to further conceal it.

"You don't know that. I don't always get carded."

I can barely see the arc of her cheekbones through the hazy moonlight. "I don't know. It's New Year's Eve. They might let you slide." I reach forward, my fingertips skimming over her knee-high tights, landing softly on the top of her thigh. "Or they might take one look at you in that skirt and those schoolgirl socks and decide you're just too much of a risk."

Rory and I had never role-played, but ever since I saw her slink into this outfit, I'd thought of nothing else but bending her over a desk and fucking her as if our grades depended on it. Being three years apart, Rory and I didn't share any classes. But that didn't change the fact that I thought of nothing but her while sitting through hours of boring lectures. Fucking her in that schoolgirl outfit would make up for all the times I'd sat in class trying my damnedest not to get hard while fantasizing about her mouth around my cock.

I began sliding my fingers beneath her wool tartan skirt, but she grabbed my hand. "Stop trying to distract me."

She threw open the passenger door and twisted around to get out. My eyes locked on the curve of her hips, the bounce of her ass as she plopped down onto the asphalt. It hadn't quite been twenty-four hours since we'd last fucked, but I was already hungry for her again. I stepped out of the truck and headed her off near the tailgate.

"What are you doing?" she said, making a move to sidestep me.

I moved with her, my hands reaching forward to grab her waist. "Don't move."

"Houston."

My gaze fell on her chest, the rise and fall of those soft mounds. The way they curved down into her waist made me dizzy. The snug cream sweater she wore left just enough to the imagination. My eyes raked over her entire body, landing on her lips, my mind lingering on the memory of the sweet taste of her. Finally, I looked up, and the moment our eyes met she knew.

Her arms stretched up, latching onto my neck as I bent down, my arms locking around her thighs to lift her up. Her legs clenched around my waist as our mouths collided in a hot fervor of passion. I carried her past my truck, toward the back wall of the restaurant, my muscles saturated in my need for her.

"What if we get caught?" she whispered.

I pressed her against the brick wall, leaning my weight into her as I kissed her deep and hard. Without saying a single word, I was answering her question: *Who gives a fuck?*

"Fuck me," she breathed as I ground my hips into the wet cotton of her panties.

"Not yet. I want to watch you come undone."

I set her down on the asphalt and knelt before her. Her chest heaved with anticipation as she watched me lift the edge of her skirt. Sliding my hand behind her thigh, I lifted her leg to rest it on top of my shoulder, opening her up to me.

"Oh, God," she whimpered, as I slid her panties to the side and spread her swollen lips.

My tongue found her clit easily and she tasted just as sweet as she did the night before. The leg she was standing on buckled at the knee as I sucked on her flesh.

"Is it time to learn your ABCs?" I muttered against her hot skin.

"*Holy shit*" was her only reply as I moved my tongue over her clit in the shape of an A.

When I made a B, her body folded inward, her fingers digging into my shoulders to keep herself from collapsing. The tip of my tongue curved around her clit to make a C and she whimpered softly.

"What letter comes next?"

"D," she replied with haste.

"Nuh-uh. The D comes *after* the O."

She chuckled as I buried my face between her legs again, making her say each letter aloud as I traced the shape of it over her throbbing clit. We never made it to O before she begged me to stop.

I undid my pants before I lifted her up again. She couldn't stand on those jelly legs if she tried. Then I slid into her and I almost fucking collapsed myself.

"Jesus fucking Christ," I hissed into her neck.

She tightened her leg-lock around my waist, beckoning me deeper inside her. Each thrust of my hips sent me into a frenzy. I pounded her harder and deeper as she clutched my hair, pulled so fucking hard I swore she'd tear it out.

"Houston!" she screamed as I came inside her.

"Uh, Earth to Houston. We have a problem." Kenny's voice cuts through the hazy sultriness of this memory.

The heat in my cheeks rises the moment I see Patricia staring at me. *What the fuck?* I'm actually blushing.

Is that scene behind the restaurant the kind of stuff Patricia has been reading about in Rory's book?

I clear my throat. "What's the problem?" I say, shifting my gaze to Kenny.

"I don't know what it is. I talked to Rory last night and she sounded off."

"Off? How?"

"Yes, how?" Patricia echoes my concern.

Kenny raises an eyebrow as he thinks of a response. "I don't know. She was asking me weird questions. Like, she asked me how I was liking the new neighborhood. I mean, I've been living in her apartment for a month. She hasn't asked me how I like it there in, like, two or three weeks. Now all of a sudden she wants to know. So I told her I *love* Goose Hollow. I love being close to

23rd Street and the MAX Line and, I could be misinterpreting this, but she seemed kind of bummed to hear me say that. Like she wanted me to tell her I hate it."

"Maybe she was just hoping you'd say it's not the same without her," Patricia says.

"No, I don't think so," Kenny continues, glancing at me for just a split second. "I don't know what it is, but I'll work on trying to figure it out."

"Kenny?" I say, trying to keep my voice even. "If you think Rory's in some kind of trouble, you'd better tell me. If that fucker hurts her, I swear to God I'll never forgive you for keeping this to yourself."

"Houston, calm down," Patricia says, waving a finger at me as if I'm a dog that can be chastised into compliance. Turning back to Kenny, she adds, "He's right, Kenny. If you think Rory's in any kind of trouble, physically or emotionally, you need to tell us."

Kenny leans back a little, trying to distance himself from this inquisition. "I don't know. She didn't sound scared or hurt. She sounded kind of… agitated. Like she was annoyed with my answer. Then Liam walked in and she—"

"She what?" I demand.

Kenny's eyes widen and he finally looks as if he's going to crack under the pressure. "She got off the phone really fast, like she didn't want him to see her on the phone."

"That motherfucker. He's got her on fucking lockdown. I know it."

Patricia holds up her hand. "Hold on. We don't know that. We don't know anything about what's going on with them."

"Because she's probably too fucking ashamed to talk about it. Why else would she rush to get off the phone with Kenny?" I insist, the tension I worked out at the gym this morning coiling its way back into my muscles. "I'm going to California."

"No!" Patricia points her coral fingernail at me again. "You are going to wait until she's finished with that book. Do you hear me, young man?"

Holy fuck. I'm bringing out the angry teacher in her.

I slide off the barstool and stare at the surface of the table, my chest heaving with fury. "Two weeks." I look up and they're both waiting for me to finish this statement. "I'll give you two weeks to finish as much as you can, then I'm going. I'm done waiting."

Rory

January 16, 2015

WHEN I ARRIVE at the SaltMedia corporate office, I'm not at all surprised to find it's just around the corner from the Googleplex in a shiny new business park where the parking lines are a bright reflective white and the building gleams like diamonds in the late morning sunshine. I've had about six days of rain in the past six weeks since I moved to California. It's winter, for God's sake.

I guess you really don't know what you have until it's gone.

I lock up my bike outside and enter the reception area wearing a smile as phony as the receptionist's boobs. Her dark hair is pulled into a messy braid that hangs over her shoulder, drawing even more attention to her cleavage. She beams at me, her silver earpiece glinting with her smile.

"May I help you?" she asks in a husky porn-star voice.

"I'm here to see Liam Murray."

She reaches for the touchscreen tablet propped up on her sleek glass desk. "May I tell him who's here to see him?"

"No, you may not."

The girl stares at me blankly. "Excuse me?"

"Only kidding. You can tell him Rory is here for him."

She flashes me a tight smile, not at all impressed with the joke as she touches the tablet, waits a few seconds, then Liam's face appears on the screen.

"Yeah, what's up?"

"There's a *Rory* here to see you. She didn't give a last name."

"What? No way. I'll be right there," he replies excitedly, quickly disappearing from view.

I do feel a twinge of guilt as I flash the girl a shit-eating grin, especially knowing what I've come here to do. But it does feel a bit nice when she clears her throat and pretends to busy herself with something on the tablet screen.

I wait a few minutes for Liam to come down from whatever floor it is he works on. During those minutes, moments from our relationship flash in my mind, all the way back to when we took that Art of the Sentence class together our junior year at UO. Moments I've been suddenly seeing through a very different lens. Hindsight is a microscope.

I remembered recently a bit of the conversation Liam had with his girlfriend after we spent four hours at Starbucks working on our class assignment. I distinctly remember him saying the word *ugly*. Like he was trying to convince his girlfriend he'd been hanging out with an ugly classmate for the past four hours. I'm not sure why it took so long to remember that, but it came to me when I realized Liam had enlisted Matt to help him spy on me.

It was then that I began looking through all my old correspondence, searching my Gmail inbox (on my phone) for four-year-old emails from Liam during that time. What I found was I *wasn't* misinterpreting his flirtations in Starbucks that day. He'd been flirting with me for days following up to that meeting. Asking if I had a boyfriend and if I wanted "to study at Starbucks or in my dorm. It's warmer in my dorm. ;-)" He never tried to make a move on me during our study session, but he definitely established a pattern of dishonesty, which I didn't realize until he decided to spy on me.

The elevator twenty feet behind the receptionist's desk dings and the brushed metal doors slide open. "Hey, babe," Liam says as he strolls confidently in my direction, completely oblivious as to how much I now know about him and why I'm here.

"Hey!" I reply enthusiastically, trying not to cringe as he leans in to plant a kiss on my cheek. "TGI Friday! I'm here to take you to lunch, but I was hoping to say hi to Matt while I'm here."

Liam looks confused. "You want to see Matt?"

"Yeah. I haven't seen him since we went to Taco Tuesday. Just wanted to say hi and see how he's doing."

Liam glances at the receptionist, knowing he can't say Matt's not here because she'll know he's lying. "Sure. Let's go see Matt."

His hand lands heavily, possessively, on the small of my back as we head into the elevator. He presses the elevator for the third floor, then places his hand right back where it was, just an inch above my ass, which he still thinks is his. It takes considerable effort to maintain my composure, but I grit my teeth and hold on, knowing this will all be over soon.

I smile at a few people as we walk down an aisle of cubicles. Liam doesn't bother trying to introduce me to any of his coworkers. Halfway down the aisle, Liam stops at Matt's cube.

Matt looks over his shoulder at us and I'm certain there's a flare of panic in his eyes before he remembers to put on his friendly façade. "Hey, Rory!"

"Hi, Matt," I say, leaning in to give him a one-armed hug while he remains seated in his generic black desk chair. "I just wanted to drop by and say hi and ask you a technical question, if you don't mind."

I know how much techies hate being asked for tech support by friends and family, so I hope to God I'm bothering the shit out of him right now. Or at least igniting a flame of terror under his ass.

He swallows hard, glancing at Liam. "Uh… sure. What kind of question?"

"Well, I think I might have a virus or something. I'm getting this weird process listed in my Activity Monitor. I don't recognize it. And I'm totally not tech-savvy, so I was wondering if you recognize it. I wrote the name in a note on my phone. Hold on." I dig my phone out of my pocket as slowly as possible to see just how sweaty his armpits can get in the interim. "See? This is the name."

He blinks a few times in rapid succession as he stares at the name on my phone screen and tries to formulate a response. "I… I've never seen that on a Mac, but it's probably in your best interest to run a spyware and antivirus scan just to be safe. You know… when you work on your laptop at cafés, all you have to do is walk away to use the restroom for a couple of minutes and someone can install something on your computer." He taps his fingers on the desk. "You have to be really careful."

I grit my teeth, wanting so badly to smack the shit out of him for allowing himself to be Liam's lapdog. Instead, I force a smile and nod as I tuck the phone into my pocket.

"Thanks, Matt. I really appreciate your help."

He nods, his eyes darting around the office. "Any time."

Liam and I get back in the elevator to head downstairs, and as soon as the doors slide shut he chuckles. "What was that about?"

"What?"

He glances at me sideways, wearing a poker face. "Nothing. Let's go eat."

As the elevator doors open, an Asian guy in a sharp gray suit beams when he sees Liam and me. "Liam! Is this the famous Rory?"

Famous Rory?

Liam's poker face withers away as we step out of the elevator. "Yeah, this is Rory." He turns to me, his hand landing on the small of my back again. "Rory, this is my boss, Mr. Xiu."

The man cocks an eyebrow at Liam's introduction, then he reaches out his hand to me. "Please call me Jian." He shakes my hand gently and I can't help but marvel at how soft his hands are. "It's such a pleasure to finally meet you. And we're so glad you convinced Liam to take the position. We understand moving to a new state, new city, from a place like Portland can be a wild experience. Culture shock! Where's the rain?"

He laughs like a madman, but I'm too stunned to join in. *Liam told his boss that I convinced him to take the position in California?* Is there a man on this fucking planet who doesn't feel the need to lie to me?

Liam excuses us, his hand never leaving my back as we walk out of the SaltMedia building. As we walk to Liam's truck, I remember the first time I rode with him. He had basically refused to let me ride my bike home from Ración. Then he insisted I let him take me out despite the fact that I clearly told him I was still fucked up over Houston. He was so persistent. At first I thought it was cute, maybe even a little sexy. But now I see it was just the first brick laid in the wall between me and my entire former life in Portland.

How long had he known about the position in Mountain View?

Ugh. I don't even want to know the answer to that question. All I want to do right now is get him to a public place so I can confront him with all the pieces of the puzzle I've collected over the past eleven days. A puzzle that paints a very disturbing picture. A picture that shows he's been spying on me and trying to separate me from my friends and family since we first met.

Liam opens the passenger door for me to get inside. I don't bother flashing him a phony smile as I climb in. The time for lies is over. Now is the time for truth.

He slides into the driver's seat and sticks the key in the ignition, but he doesn't start the engine. "You think I'm stupid? You think I don't know what you were doing back there with Matt?"

"Oh, I know you're not stupid," I reply, glaring at him across the bench seat, each breath burning my lungs with seething anger. "You were smart enough to fool me and Matt, and apparently Mr. Xiu!"

He throws his head back with laughter. "So *I'm* the one deceiving people? How about you?" He waves his arm at me. "You lie to me. You lie to yourself. You lie to everyone. And you expect *me* to trust *you*?"

"I have done no such thing!"

"Oh, yeah! What's in your book, Rory? Huh? How about we start with that?"

I suddenly feel as if the truck walls are closing in on me. Heat rises into my neck, into my face, stinging the corners of my eyes.

"You read my book?"

He glares at me, nostrils flaring and completely silent. Liam has been poring through my deepest, most private thoughts and memories of Houston, not to mention my thoughts about him. I can see it in the way he looks at me, his eyes mirroring the fury in mine. He knows everything.

He knows how I lost my virginity the day Hallie died. He knows every gruesome detail of the abortion and the breakup. He knows every word Hallie wrote in her suicide note. He knows about her affair with my father. He knows I called Houston on New Year's Eve. He knows about the Sierra Nevada box and the engagement ring.

He knows I've been trying to force myself to love him.

"*You read my book?*" I howl at him.

He doesn't even flinch, he just nods ever so slightly, his gaze locked on mine as his top lip curls into a snarl. "Yeah, I read your fucking book. I read that pile of steaming dog shit that no publisher in their right mind would touch with a fucking ten-foot pole."

There should be a word to describe the kind of insult that's delivered with surgical precision. The kind that cuts through bone and sinew straight into the heart and implants itself in there, then multiplies. A flesh-eating virus that will consume you unless it's carved out and disposed of immediately.

I suppose Liam might refer to this insult as a flawless takedown. I'd prefer to call it the striking of the match that set my blood on fire.

My vision blurs momentarily as his words search the dark recesses of my heart for the best place to take root. The places where I'm most vulnerable. My weaknesses.

My mind flashes to the smooth pretty-boy face of my fellow junior editor at *Unbound* magazine. He had to stifle a laugh when he read one of my short stories. He also thought my work was a steaming pile of dog shit.

My throat thickens painfully, tears stinging the corners of my eyes. Liam's words carried the weight of an anvil dropped straight on my head. Yet, I feel weightless. Intangible. As trifling and insignificant as a discarded piece of trash floating across the highway. My first instinct is to curl into myself and skulk away into obscurity. But if Liam has taught me anything, it's that first instincts are not always trustworthy.

I sit up straighter in the passenger seat, my eyes burning into him. "Never call me again."

I reach for the door handle to let myself out and he throws himself across my lap to grab my hand.

"Wait! I didn't mean that."

"Get off me!" I shriek, pounding on his back.

He twists around slightly, lying on his side across my thighs as he struggles with me. He wrests both my wrists into his grasp.

Then he sits up again, one foot on the floor of the truck, his other knee planted firmly on the middle of the bench seat. The painful hold on my wrists never loosens as he looks down at me with a boiling madness in his eyes.

"Listen to me, Rory." His voice is a dark, seething snarl that makes my bones quiver. "I'm trying to apologize!"

My mind shuffles through the various ways this can end. Is he going to hit me? Does he really just want me to listen to him? If I listen to him, will he let me go without further injury?

His fingers dig painfully into the tendons of my wrist as the back of my head is pressed against the cold passenger side window. As hard as I try, I can't stop the tears from sliding down my cheeks.

How could I move in with someone I hardly knew? Why didn't I see that Liam and Houston were two different people? Two different circumstances. Liam wasn't my second chance to get it right. He was my second chance to get it wrong, because moving in with someone you hardly know is *stupid.*

Shit. I'm already blaming myself, like any typical victim of violence.

Fuck that.

"Liam, please let me go so we can talk," I say, hoping he'll excuse the tremor in my voice instead of seizing on it and using my fear against me. "Please. I know you didn't mean what you said. You're just hurt because of what you read in my book. I know that. Please let go so we can talk."

"You just don't fucking get it," he says, and the anguish contorting his face scares me more than the thunder-grip on my wrists. "I love you, Rory. I fucking love you! And you love that fucking piece-of-shit cheater! That's fucked up! I did everything for you."

His weight is leaning into me now and I begin to fantasize about making a quick yank on my wrist, just hard enough to reach the door handle. I'll probably tumble out of the truck and land headfirst on the asphalt, but I don't fucking care at this point. Why can't somebody just walk by and see us in the truck?

"Liam, you don't understand. All that stuff with Houston is in the past." My stomach somersaults as I force out the next lie. "What I have with you is… it's real."

His grip on my wrists loosens a little. "Don't fucking lie to me, Rory. I'm sick of the fucking lies."

"I'm not lying to you!" I shriek, my voice tinged with panic. "I'm… I'm trying to tell you that it's different. What Houston and I had was based on lies. What you and I have is true… It's… it's better. Maybe it's not love *yet*, but…"

His eyes gleam with understanding as he lets go of my left wrist. "Maybe it's not love," he says, reaching up to brush my hair out of my face. He swallows hard as he looks down at me in wonderment. "Maybe it's something less traumatic."

"Yes," I whisper, then I press my lips together, praying he interprets these as happy tears.

Bile rises in my throat as I realize how stupid I've been to think I could run away from my love for Houston. That I could force myself to love someone else. Maybe I did lead Liam on, but I never once implied that I loved him.

His hold on my right wrist loosens even more, and I seize the opportunity. In one swift motion, my hand and knee come up at the same time, my hand reaching for the door handle while my knee lands squarely on his crotch. He curls inward, covering his crotch as I pull the handle and the door flies open, assisted by the weight of my body. I manage to catch the lip of the doorframe just enough to slow my descent, but I still land on my back with a hard thud that knocks the breath out of me.

I roll over, my hands scraping over the rough asphalt as I scramble to my feet. Racing toward the front door of the SaltMedia building, I'm certain if I look back Liam will be right behind me. I'm a couple dozen feet from the entrance when I hear the familiar chug and scrape of the ignition. When I glance over my shoulder, all I see is Liam's truck screeching out of the parking space, almost hitting a black sports car behind him.

"*Coward!*" I scream as his truck peels out of the parking lot.

He knows if he leaves now it will just be my word against his. And why would any of these people believe me over the gentle lumberjack they've worked with for the past month and a half?

I'm shaking uncontrollably as I watch him set off down Shoreline Blvd. Then the sobbing begins, chest-wracking, soul-shifting sobs. I don't know if I'm more happy I got out of that situation almost completely unscathed, or if I'm more ashamed that my life is in shambles. Again.

I shuffle toward my bike, taking deep breaths to calm myself, hoping no one walks out of the building right now and sees me looking like such a mess. I kneel before my bike, the adrenaline coursing through my veins giving me a serious case of the jitters. It takes a moment for me to remember the code for the padlock on my bike. Finally, I pull my bike free, but I don't get on.

I walk my bike to the Starbucks next door, savoring the sensation of the cold steel of the handlebars against the burning scrapes on the heels of my hands. I lock up the bike and use the Starbucks restroom to wash my hands and wash the dried tears from my cheeks. As I stare in the mirror in the Starbucks bathroom, it dawns on me that the story of Liam and me started in a Starbucks. I guess it's fitting that this is how it should end.

I slap on a bit of fresh makeup and buy myself a small hot tea, so I don't feel bad about using the café as my headquarters for however many hours it takes for me to figure out what I'm going to do with my life.

I set the tea down on a small table and slip my phone out of my pocket. Then I take a seat in an uncomfortable velvet armchair sandwiched between a window and a display of Sumatran coffee beans. I cast a furtive glance at the girl behind the cash register, then pull my feet up onto the chair so I can hug my knees to my chest. My mom would die if she saw me put my sneakers on someone else's furniture.

I stand the phone on my knee and scroll through my contacts until I get to the name I'm looking for. There's only one person I want to talk to right now.

My splintered heart is telling me to call Houston. My fractured mind is worried he'll judge me for being so wrong about Liam. But it was my warped logic that got me into this mess. My clinical approach to love, thinking Liam and I could magically grow to love each other if we were kept in the same environment for long enough, like rats in a cage.

I press the number and my heart races as I wait for the ringing to begin.

One ring.

Two rings.

"Rory? What's wrong?"

My sinuses sting painfully and I turn away from the guy sitting across from me so he can't see my face, as if it's possible to hide that I'm coming apart at the seams. "Houston," I whisper, my voice strangled by the force of my regrets. "I need you."

Houston

The Barley Legal restaurant is always busy during the lunch rush, so Troy and I opt to eat in the second-floor dining area, which we only open up if the first floor gets too crowded. Right now, we have it all to ourselves, enjoying our burgers and beers amidst the far-off sounds of chattering voices, clinking silverware, and whatever Pandora station Wilma decided to put on today. But it doesn't take long for Troy to break the silence.

A sober expression comes over him as he sets down his sandwich and looks me in the eye. "You think Jennifer Lawrence is a loud fuck or a quiet fuck?"

I shake my head. "I don't fucking know. I'd guess pretty loud."

"You think every time she fucks it's like a fight to the death?"

I stare at him, unable to believe this shitty pun. "Is there a point to this conversation?"

He sighs as he stares at his burger for a moment then sets it down on his plate. "I don't know if I can do this."

"Are you fucking kidding me? I know you're trying to watch

your weight, but it's a fucking burger. Chef made it for you with love. Don't be a bitch. Eat that shit."

"I'm not talking about the burger," he says, pushing his plate aside. "I'm talking about the fucking wedding. I don't know if I can get married. This shit's getting to me. Yesterday, she sent me a dozen emails with houses for us to look at. We're shopping for houses! That's a serious fucking commitment."

I stop mid-chew, unable to believe what I'm hearing. "Where the fuck is this coming from?"

He leans back in his chair and crosses his arms over the Barley Legal logo on his hoodie. "I don't know. I've just been doing a lot of thinking."

I get a sneaking suspicion Troy's been secretly overanalyzing the drama I've been going through with Tessa since the divorce.

"Look, I can't lecture you on honoring your commitments. I'm the last fucking asshole you want to hear that from. But Georgia is *not* Tessa. She's not hiding a mental illness from you."

"You don't know that."

I try not to laugh as I take a long draw on my pint, savoring the sharp bitterness and the sting in my throat. "You're right. I don't—"

My phone vibrates in my pocket and I wipe my hands on my napkin before I dig it out. Seeing the words "Rory calling" on my screen sends my body and mind into an instant panic. My muscles tense and my heart starts pumping wildly.

"Rory? What's wrong?"

"Oh, shit," Troy whispers, but I hold up my hand to quiet him so I can hear Rory.

There's a pause on the line and a soft rustling. After a few seconds, I begin to wonder if she butt-dialed me. Then her voice comes through, and the sound puts me even more on edge. She's crying.

"Houston," she whispers, sniffling softly. "I need you."

Three words. Three words I've wanted to hear for what feels like a lifetime.

When you dream of something happening for so long, and it *finally* happens, it's never the same as you imagined. I thought I wanted to hear Rory say those words. But I never realized what it would take to make it happen. And now, I'd give anything not to hear those words over the phone when she's six hundred fucking miles away, and God knows what has happened to her.

"Rory, what happened? Are you hurt?"

Troy's eyes widen as I rise from my chair. I plug my ear with one finger as I hold my phone to the other ear, trying to block out the noise from the patrons downstairs. Rory lets out a soft whimper that might as well be a dagger in my chest.

"Rory, talk to me, baby. What happened?"

"I'm fine," she whispers, a bit louder this time. "I'm… I'm sorry."

"Sorry for what? You didn't do anything. Rory, where are you? Are you safe?"

Fuck. Fuck. Fuck! I should have gone to get her last week instead of giving Patricia another two weeks to finish working on the book.

"I'm at Starbucks. But… I want to come home. I would have called my mom, but I don't want to hear her say *I told you so.* I don't think I could take that right now."

"Why? Did that fucker hurt you? I'll fucking destroy him."

"No!" she replies forcefully, then her voice goes back to a whisper. "No, Houston. I just need your help. Can you help me? I need… help with a plane ticket. I'm low on funds."

"Don't worry about the ticket," I say, racing down the steps to the first-floor dining area. "I'm coming to get you. I'll be there in three or four hours, tops. Listen to me, Rory. I want you to tell me the truth. Are you safe at Starbucks?"

She sniffs softly, then she's silent for a moment. I dash

through the dining room, dodging customers and wait staff as I head outside to go to my car.

"I don't know. Should I go somewhere else? I don't think he'll come here, but… I don't know."

The dark clouds loom ominously over the parking lot behind Barley Legal. I don't know if it's going to rain, but I do know this: Liam is going to regret whatever he did to Rory today. He's going to regret it for a very fucking long time.

"Listen to me, Rory. I don't have time to explain. I'm getting in my car right now to go to the airport. But I need you to do something for me. Can you please promise me you'll do something? Just one thing?"

I deactivate my car alarm and hop inside the SUV, not moving or blinking as I wait anxiously for her reply.

"Yeah, okay."

Slamming the car door shut, I breathe a sigh of relief when the world goes quiet. "Rory, I need you to call Hannah and ask her to pick you up and take you to her house for the next few hours. I'll be there to pick you up soon. Okay?"

She's silent again as I turn the key in the ignition. *Tick. Tick. Tick.* The seconds pass by painfully slowly as I wait for her response. Right now, she's wondering how the fuck I know Hannah. She's probably wondering if I somehow planned for Liam to do whatever he did to her.

I pull my car away from the curb and head toward the freeway, knowing that no matter what Rory is thinking right now, nothing is going to stop me from going to California today.

"Rory? Are you still there?"

"How do you know Hannah?"

"I'll explain everything when I get there. Just know that Hannah's been looking out for you, on my behalf—and your mom's. We've been worried. I promise I'll tell you everything when I get there."

She sniffs again, but her voice sounds stronger when she replies. "Okay. I'll call Hannah."

"Rory?"

"Yeah."

I turn onto the freeway and clench my teeth against the anger raging inside me, forcing it aside momentarily so I can speak to her from my heart. "Rory, I've been dying to hear your voice again, but not like this."

"Oh, God, Houston, I'm such an idiot," she says, crying even harder this time.

"Don't say that. And don't worry about anything. I'll take care of the plane ticket and anything else you need, okay?" I swallow hard, unable to believe I'm about to say the words I've been dying to say for the past six weeks. "Rory, I'm coming for you."

Rory

AS SOON AS I end the call, a chill runs through me, lifting the hairs on the back of my neck. I'm not one to spook easily, but part of me wonders if I'm sensing Liam is near.

No, that's ridiculous. That only happens in horror films. This is no movie. This is as real as it gets. I'm really, truly fucked.

It takes a few minutes for me to work up the courage to call Hannah. I don't want her to know what a mess my life is. But I promised Houston I'd call her. How the fuck do Houston and my mom know Hannah Lee? I guess it's not a total stretch that my mom would know her. If Hannah is truly from Salem, maybe they both attended the same writers' workshop a million years ago when my mom used to actually do stuff like that. Before she gave up on her book.

I use the cuff of my sleeve to wipe away the stale remnants of tears on my cheeks, then I turn around to face the other patrons in Starbucks. The guy sitting in the armchair across from me glances up briefly from his laptop, quickly returning to whatever he's working on. Why should I care what these people think about me? The people who truly matter to me don't give a shit if I cry in the middle of Starbucks. Because the people who truly matter to me know what a drama-filled joke my life has become.

I shake my head at this thought and take a few breaths to calm my racing heart. Then I dial Hannah's number and wait. She picks up on the third ring.

"Rory! I'm so glad to hear from you. I just got a text from Houston, so I'm getting in my car right now. Which Starbucks are you at?"

My stomach clenches at her cheerful tone. She wants me to know I'm not bothering her, and maybe even that she doesn't judge me for needing to be rescued. Tears of shame well up in my eyes again, but I manage to blink a few times to hold them back.

"I'm at the Starbucks on Shoreline and Pear Avenue."

A soft chugging noise followed by a repetitive dinging sound. Then she sighs. "Oh, dear. Whatever you do, don't talk to the customers or you'll be stuck there for hours listening to someone's start-up idea."

I almost feel guilty for chuckling at this.

"Okay, honey. I'll be there in about five minutes," she says before the line goes dead.

It takes us twenty minutes and the help of a very kind Starbucks customer to get my bike positioned in a way that it will fit in the trunk of Hannah's SUV. Though I promised Houston I'd go to Hannah's house, there's only one place I want to go right now.

"Hannah, wait," I say before she can pull out of the Starbucks parking lot. "I need to make one stop… at my—I mean, Liam's house. I need to get my dog."

Hannah presses her lips together as she contemplates this request. "Are you sure that's a good idea?"

"Skippy's my best friend. I can't leave him there. I don't think Liam would hurt him, but I don't think I can be sure of anything anymore." I sigh heavily. "I'll just sneak into the backyard through the side gate. If Liam's there, he won't see me."

She flashes a warm smile. "Of course."

Liam's truck isn't sitting in the driveway when we arrive at 13 Harbor Court. Hannah parks her SUV next to the curb and a low humming anxiety settles into my bones. My fingers tremble as I reach for the door handle.

"I won't be long," I say to Hannah, though I think it's more of a reminder to myself. *This won't take long. Just get in, get Skippy, and get out.*

Pushing open the car door, I slide out onto the curb and shut the door as softly as I can, just in case Liam *is* home. He always parks in the garage when he's home. Even though he's technically still supposed to be at work, I can't take any chances. I wouldn't put it past him to be here waiting for me to come get Skippy and my laptop.

I creep across the lush green grass toward the right side of the house, where the slate-gray wooden fence opens onto the backyard. My heart sinks when I see the gate is wide open. I don't think Liam would open the gate to set Skippy free. He knows Skippy wouldn't go farther than the front yard before he turned back. The open gate is a message to me. *If you want your dog, you'll have to come inside and get him.*

My blood goes from a slow simmer to a hot rolling boil in two seconds flat. I storm across the grass and dash up the steps, not one bit surprised to find the door unlocked. I throw open the front door and it crashes into the wall, bouncing back toward me. Skippy and Sparky bark as I step inside, holding my hand out in front of me to stop the door from hitting me in the face.

Liam is sitting on the sofa with both dogs standing at his feet. His eyes narrow at me, unimpressed with my dramatic entrance.

"You!" I roar. "You can manhandle me all you want, but you leave my dog out of this. You hear me? If you touch my dog I will kill you!"

He flashes me a confused look, as if I'm speaking a different language. "Rory, I brought them in because I was… feeling kind of lonely. I would never hurt your dog. That's insulting."

"Oh, save the Saint Liam act for someone who buys it. Just give me my dog and my laptop so I can leave."

"You're just going to leave? Just like that? We can't even talk about this?" He stands from the sofa, grabbing Skippy's insulin kit off the coffee table.

I take a step back, closer to the open front door. "Stay right fucking there and toss me the kit," I warn him. "I have no desire to talk about this with you. I don't want to talk to *anyone* about this. You've made me feel sick with myself. I *hate* myself with you."

He tosses me the insulin kit and my stomach clenches as tears form in his eyes. "Rory, I'll get your laptop, just please sit down and listen to what I have to say. I know I was wrong. I fucked up."

"Don't do this, Liam."

"Just hear me out," he pleads, rounding the coffee table toward me.

"Stop!"

"Is everything all right in here?"

I whip my head around at the sound of Hannah's voice, then I turn back to Liam. "Skippy, come here, boy," I call out sweetly and Skippy gallops to me. I grab his collar and lead him toward the threshold where Hannah's standing. "Can you take him to the car, please? I'll be fine."

She glances at Liam as she grips Skippy's collar. "I'd… rather stay here."

Turning back to Liam, I straighten my back and harden my glare. "Where's my laptop? It was right there on the coffee table when I left. Where did you put it?"

He tilts his head as if he can't believe I'm worried about my laptop at a time like this. "Come on, Rory. Just give me a minute to explain. I know I fucked everything up, but I swear to God I'll fix this. I'll… I'll change."

A chill rolls through me as I realize he's begging. "You don't get it, Liam. I don't *want* you to change. I just want my fucking laptop!"

"Why are you being such a bitch?" he says, his voice going up an octave as his face contorts with anger. "All I'm asking for is a fucking minute of your time. What? Are you too fucking good for me now?"

"Fuck you! Where's my laptop?"

He takes a step toward me and his face changes again, ripe with penitence now as if he has two dueling personalities fighting for control inside his puppet body. "I'm sorry. That was a fucked-up thing to say."

"I said stop!" I hold out my hand to keep him from getting closer, but I lower it when I catch a glimpse of my trembling hand.

"Rory, I think we should leave," Hannah suggests gently as Skippy struggles to try to lick the hand holding his collar.

"Who's that?" Liam finally asks, glancing at Hannah. "Have you been planning this?"

"Planning what? Planning for you to attack me? Are you fucking crazy?"

His mouth drops open like he can't believe what he's hearing. "Attack you? I think that's a bit of an exaggeration."

"All right. That's it. Keep my fucking laptop. You probably need it for jerk-off material."

I turn to leave and he grabs my wrist. My instincts kick in and twist around, landing a hard smack on his cheek with my free hand. His blue eyes narrow, ablaze with a fury I recognize from when he throttled me in his car earlier. Against my better judgment, I thrust my leg upward to kick him. My knee barely clips his crotch area, but it's enough for him to release his grip on my wrist.

"You fucking bitch!" he roars as I race out the front door, trailing closely behind Hannah and Skippy.

"He can sit on my lap," I say, grabbing hold of Skippy's collar and giving Hannah the insulin kit so I can get in the passenger seat.

I wrench open the car door, glancing over my shoulder to see Liam standing on the front porch, his chest heaving, his eyes narrowed with seething anger, that perfect lumberjack smile nowhere in sight.

Sliding into the passenger seat, I pat my lap for Skippy to hop up. He's a bit hesitant at first, so I reach down and grab his collar with my right hand and slide my left hand under his belly, pulling him up as Liam lumbers down the steps.

"Go!" I urge Hannah as I reach for the handle to pull the door closed.

The inertia helps me slam the door shut as she drives away from 13 Harbor Court. Away from Liam and every hope I had for a fresh start. Away from my laptop and every password to every account I've ever created. He can log into my Google Drive right now and delete every version of my novel I've ever saved.

I hug Skippy at this thought, burying my nose in his black fur, partially for comfort and partially to hide my tears from Hannah. Skippy whines as he tries desperately to turn around so he can lick my face, but I hold tight to him, using him as a shield for my shame.

Other than my occasional sniff, the drive to Hannah's townhouse is awkwardly quiet. I don't know if she's waiting for me to offer an explanation, or if she's waiting for me to demand she explain her connection to Houston. Either way, I don't have the courage to ask, and the silence only amplifies my mortification over today's events.

No matter how many times I remind myself that I'm not at fault for Liam spying on me and attacking me today, I still feel like none of this would have happened if I hadn't been stupid enough to move six hundred miles away from home with a guy I hardly knew.

Hannah pulls her SUV into her garage and I insist on getting the bike out myself. I lean it up against the wall and follow her through a door leading onto a small patio, which connects us to the back of the townhouse. We enter through the back door leading into the kitchen, leaving Skippy outside with a bowl of water since Hannah's home is pet-free.

As we enter the kitchen, the last bit of resolve I had crumbles as the guilt takes its place. Hannah and I have spent every other day at this kitchen table for the past ten days feverishly processing rewrites on my book. She said her agent is looking for a fresh romance right now and she wanted me to get at least half of the book edited before she sent her the sample. What if Liam deleted all our hard work?

Even after spending so much time here over the past ten days, I still feel like an annoying imposition. Especially under the current circumstances. I know this is stupid. It's not as if I'm asking Hannah to give me a place to spend the night. I'm just waiting for Houston to get here in a couple of hours. But coming here without my laptop, I feel like a guest coming to a dinner party empty-handed. I have nothing to offer her.

I sit down at the round white table in the breakfast nook while she heads for the refrigerator. "Thank you for doing this," I say, my voice small and lifeless. I don't even sound like myself anymore.

She waves off my gratitude then grabs a pitcher of iced tea out of the fridge. "Please. This will be the highlight of my week. I think that guy who helped us put your bike in the back of my car was checking me out."

I wait until she's poured us a couple of tumblers of tea and sat across from me before I address the elephant in the room. "Hannah, how do you know my mom?"

She smiles as she stares at the glass of tea in her hand, as if she's remembering something fondly. "Your mother and I met at a writers' conference in Salem about fourteen years ago. I don't know how old you were then, but I was twenty-six. And your mother, if I remember correctly, she told me back then that she was thirty-seven."

She looks to me for confirmation and I nod.

"Ah, I guess my memory's not so bad after all," she continues. "Well, anyway, we ended up seated next to each other at the luncheon and we chatted up a storm. We griped about our mutual disdain for pitch sessions and the difference between extroverted and introverted writers. Then, we decided we'd go to the next workshop together. Barry Winters was giving a workshop on applying cinematic plot structure to a novel."

She pauses for a moment, staring off into the distance as if she's trying to remember something. Then she turns back to me and sighs. "Anyway, the point is she helped me change some really shitty elements in my plot. She also corrected some of my grammar gaffes. I thought she was being kind of petty at the time, but when that manuscript got me my agent, I silently thanked her. Then I thanked her again by sending her a copy of that book two years later, with a letter about how I was happily married and living in Mountain View, California." She takes a long drink of tea then looks me in the eye. "She sent me a letter congratulating me and thanking me for the book and, I regret, I never tried to get in touch with her again."

"What happened after that? Did she just call you and ask you to help me edit my book?"

She nods. "Pretty much."

"And after all these years you just said yes?"

"I think I was more surprised that she actually remembered me than the fact that she was asking me for such a strange favor."

"You obviously don't know my mom. She probably couldn't stand the idea of my finishing this book without her having some sort of input."

"Heh. I can see that."

I laugh louder than both of us expected. She really does know my mom.

"But how do you know Houston?" I ask, taking a sip of tea to fill the quiet space between my question and her answer.

"Well, I suppose he's the one whose enormous erection I've become quite familiar with over the past few weeks."

I spit my tea all over the table and she laughs as she shoots up to get a towel. "Oh, my God. I'm so sorry," I say, searing heat rising in my cheeks as I hold out my hands for her to toss me the towel.

I catch it and swiftly sop up the liquid I just spewed onto her white shabby-chic table.

"I'm so sorry. I hope it doesn't stain."

"Please stop apologizing. I should be apologizing for the crude remark," she says, taking a seat across from me again. "The truth is I've never spoken to Houston. Your mother contacted me first, and when she told me what she wanted me to do—to help you with the story of you and Houston—I knew I couldn't speak to him. I didn't want my impression of him tainting your picture of him. So we communicate solely through your mother and text messages."

I can't help but smile at this answer. "I can't believe you've gone through all this trouble just to help me."

She shrugs and her smile disappears. "Yeah, well, you might not be so grateful when you hear that your mom has been helping me edit your manuscript."

"What?" I say, my voice cracking slightly as I'm gripped with shock.

She laughs, actually, it's more of a soft girlish giggle that gives me the impression she's nervous. "Yeah, I told her I could only help with the developmental editing, but she would have to do the copyediting. She's the English teacher, after all, and I'm on a pretty tight deadline myself. So, yeah, she's read at least half your book. But—"she holds up her hand"—before you say anything, let me just tell you that she loves it. It breaks her heart and she's cried to me a few times, but she loves it. And you know that's big praise coming from Patty."

I cover my face with both hands, shame rising inside me like hot steam. "Oh, my God. My *mom* read it? Oh, my God. She must think I'm so screwed up and…" My hands drop as a sobering reality hits me. "She read the sex scenes?"

At first she shrugs, then she nods, her face screwed up with pained regret. "Yeah, but I really don't think it's anything to be worried about. I'm not kidding when I said she loves it. And so does my agent."

"What?"

Hannah's red-lipped smile returns. "Bernadette loves it. I sent her the first fifty pages a week ago and she wants more. She asked me to send her the full manuscript when you have it, but I told her she needed to decide now."

"You told her that? But it's not finished."

"Not to worry. Bernadette and I have a strong relationship. She knows I wouldn't back a project I didn't fully believe in. Anyway, after a little back and forth, and a couple of days of radio silence, she responded to my email yesterday asking me to call her about the manuscript. I figured I'd give her a call next week when we have more of the manuscript edited, but then you called me from Starbucks and plans changed. First thing I did when we got off the phone with you was call her. She wants to meet with you."

My mouth goes dry as I try to think of how to respond to this, but words escape me. "I… I don't know what that means."

She lets out a hearty chuckle. "It means she wants to meet with you to discuss brokering a deal. You'd work with a cowriter—a screenwriter—to turn the manuscript into a screenplay."

"Holy shit," I whisper, then I clap my hand over my mouth. "Sorry."

"Honey, I witnessed the beast come out of you a few minutes ago when we went to get your dog. And I've read your book. I don't think anything you say can faze me anymore." She smiles and takes another sip of tea. "Does that smile mean you're not upset about your mom correcting the typos in your sex life?"

"Ha. My sex life could probably stand to be shredded and completely rewritten." I let out a deep sigh. "I guess there are far worse things than your mom knowing your approach to blow jobs."

"Yes, there are. So, shall I agree to the meeting? Bernadette is in Manhattan. If you want to meet her, you'd have to fly out sometime between Sunday and Thursday. That's when Rick Bender will be there discussing his contract on a Nicholas Sparks film that's in the works."

"Why does she want me to discuss turning it into a screenplay? She doesn't like it as a book?"

"Oh, yes, she still wants to submit the book to the usual suspects, but she and Rick have been tossing around the idea of trying to develop a manuscript and a screenplay at the same time to sell the rights simultaneously. It's not the way things are usually done. But she liked your book enough that she'd like to at least discuss it with you and Rick."

My skin tingles as I imagine myself sitting in the office of a literary agency in Manhattan, probably nodding and pretending to know what the fuck I'm talking about. As scared shitless as this thought makes me, I'd be an idiot to pass up that kind of opportunity. But how am I supposed to get to New York? I've been unemployed so long, I can't even afford a plane ticket from California to Oregon.

These people are so rich, they can just hop on planes, probably first class, and jet off to meetings on the other side of the country. Maybe I should just give up now. I'm obviously not cut out for this career or lifestyle. Unless…

"This was Houston's idea?" I ask.

She nods. "The man is determined to make your dreams come true."

My lip trembles from the effort of trying to hold back a flood of tears.

"Honey, you can cry here," Hannah assures me. "I mean, I saw what happened with your boyfriend today. Holding back those tears won't do you any good. You need to let it out so you can go to New York fresh-faced and all business."

I smile as I swipe the back of my hand over my damp cheeks. "I'm just… overwhelmed, I guess. I never in a million years would have expected Houston to do something like this."

She raises her eyebrows at me. "Really? The guy who bought you a car for your first Valentine's Day together? I would say grand gestures are kind of his M.O."

I laugh as I realize how right she is. This woman I didn't know a month ago knows Houston almost as well as I do now.

"Hannah? Can I ask you a question? And I'd really prefer an honest answer."

She chuckles as she leans back in her chair. "I don't do bullshit. You should know that by now."

I nod and take a deep breath. "You've read the truth about Houston and me. You've probably formed your own opinions, which you may or may not want to share with me. But… Do you think Houston and I belong together?"

She smiles at this question, as if she was expecting it. "Honey, I don't know much about love. I've been divorced for three years and still can't figure out the dating game. But I do know this. Many times in your life, you'll be expected to choose between two roads. Not like the Robert Frost bastardized 'Road Less Traveled' metaphorical road. I'm talking actual roads." She begins ticking off the different "roads" on her fingers. "Go to California or not? You chose to go. Go to New York or not? I think that's a no-brainer. Go back to Houston or go back to your old apartment and your old life? That's up to you.

"It's always tempting to choose the safer road. The one you think will get you to your destination in one piece. But as you learned today, sometimes the safe roads are nothing but dead ends. And I'll tell you one thing I know for sure. No matter what your destination is, there's no safer road than the one you take with someone you love."

Houston

THE EARLIEST FLIGHT out of Portland to San Jose isn't until 5:30 p.m. After four and a half excruciatingly long hours, they finally start boarding Alaska Airlines flight 7116. Once I'm seated on the plane, I shoot off a text to Rory.

Me: Just boarded the plane. Should be there in about three hours. How are you doing?

Rory: I feel like my insides have been scraped raw, but other than that I'm just happy to have Skippy here with me.

Me: Can't wait to see him. And you too, of course.

Rory: I knew you only liked me for my dog.

Me: Busted. Guess I'll just have to learn to love you since the two of you are a package deal.

She's silent for a moment and I wonder if maybe she misinterpreted the joke. The plane begins to taxi away from the gate toward the runway. Pretty soon I'll lose the signal. The pilot comes on to relay the flight information and weather conditions, then my body is pressed into the seat by the force of inertia as the plane sets off down the runway. As the jet lifts away from the tarmac, I get a notification of another text message.

Rory: I miss you.

Me: I've missed the fuck out of you. I'll be with you soon.

As soon as the plane lands in San Jose, I race through the terminal, past the throng of travelers gathered around the baggage claim, toward the ground transportation area. I hop into a cab waiting at the front of the taxi line and blurt out Hannah's address.

The cab pulls up to Hannah's townhouse fifteen minutes later and I tip the driver handsomely. He drives away as I stand on the curb staring at the front of the peach and beige house sandwiched between two other similar houses. My heart hammers in my chest as I realize this is it. I'm finally getting another chance to be the man Rory needs. Not the scared-shitless boy I was six years ago. I can't fuck this up.

Before I even reach the front steps, the door opens and Hannah's standing there with a sober look on her face. This is the first time I've seen Hannah, other than the pictures I found on the internet when I googled her. She looks exactly the same in person.

"I'm sorry I got here so late. It was the earliest flight they had." I offer my apology, but she just shakes her head.

"No need to apologize," she says, opening the door wider. "I'm just glad you're here. She's… she's not doing well."

"Why? What happened?"

I step inside and my gaze lands on Rory curled up in a large armchair with Skippy.

Hannah closes the door then leans closer to me so she can whisper. "She wasn't able to get her laptop back. And Liam deleted her manuscript from her Google Drive before she could download it."

"It's all gone?"

"I was able to recover the first fifty pages from my agent, and I have a few chapters I printed a couple of weeks ago, the ones she hadn't taken home with her to edit yet, but that's it. She's lost at least 150 pages and… a lot of emails from you and Hallie that she had saved."

"But how about Patricia? Doesn't she have a copy?" I whisper, unwilling to believe that someone could do something so supremely evil.

Hannah shakes her head. "I gave her my log-in to access the document so she could edit the manuscript without Rory knowing. I feel so terrible."

"It's not your fault."

"I know. I just wish I had downloaded the whole manuscript instead of just pasting the first 50 pages into that email I sent to Bernadette. If I'm this frustrated, I can't begin to imagine what she's feeling."

I try to process this information, but all I can think is that I've never wanted to murder someone more than I do right now. I make my way toward Rory, and Skippy opens his eyes at the sound of my footsteps. As soon as he sees me, he leaps off the chair and rushes toward me, his butt wagging along with his tail.

Rory sits up, hugging her knees to her chest. Her eyes are pink and puffy, her hair damp with tears and plastered to the side of her face, but she's still the most beautiful thing I've ever seen. She stares off into the distance as I kneel before her.

"Just tell me what you want me to do and I'll do it."

She lets out a soft sigh then looks me in the eye. "Take me home."

Rory

HOUSTON STANDS UP and holds his hand out to me, an offering of support that feels more like a lasso thrown around my heart to keep it from falling apart. I take his hand and he pulls me up, crushing me in the rigid warmth of his arms as he kisses the top of my head.

I coil my arms around his waist, clenching the soft fabric of his shirt in my fists as I sob into his solid chest. "I'm so sorry."

"Shh. You don't have anything to be sorry for."

Every breath I take, my senses are overwhelmed by the crisp masculine scent embedded in his shirt, the feeling of his skin on mine as he grasps the back of my neck firmly. I try to focus on his solid presence and how happy I am to see him instead of the years of work I lost today, but it's not working.

"I feel so defeated," I whisper, placing my hands on Houston's chest as I look up.

He looks down at me and shakes his head. "You're not defeated." He plants a firm kiss on my forehead. "You'll see. You're gonna rewrite that book and it will be even better. Like a phoenix rising from the ashes. You know, like Dumbledore's bird in *Harry Potter.* That will be your book."

I can't help but smile at this as I'm reminded of the weekend we spent watching all the Harry Potter movies while lying on the sofa in our PJs. I was appalled when Houston admitted he'd never read the series, but we both agreed it would be too weird for me to read those aloud while naked. So we settled for a movie marathon that culminated in a different kind of marathon. Needless to say, I found popcorn kernels in odd places after that weekend.

"You're just trying to make me laugh to distract me from the truth," I grumble.

"I'm serious, Rory. I'll help you rewrite the book. We'll *all* help you."

His gaze wanders over my face as he strokes my hair, and I feel more relaxed than I've felt in weeks. I want to say something, but my limbs feel leaden and my mind woolly, as if I'm in a trance. I close my eyes and he kisses my forehead again.

"You colored your hair?" he whispers.

My eyelids pop open in a panic. "You probably hate it."

"Are you kidding me? It's beautiful."

"You're just saying that."

He smiles as he rubs a piece of my hair between his fingers. "I'd love you if your hair were burnt sienna. Oh, wait. It *is* burnt sienna. Gross."

I smack his chest and he laughs. "That's not nice."

"I'm kidding. Get your stuff so we can leave." He kisses my cheekbone before he lets me go.

"Are we flying home tonight?"

He shakes his head as he steps back so I can get around him. "There aren't any more flights to Portland tonight. But there are a bunch tomorrow. We'll be home by tomorrow afternoon at the latest."

I pat my leg and Skippy stands from where he was lying on the rug and comes to me. Hannah was gracious enough to let him hang out with me indoors after we discovered what Liam had done and I became pretty much inconsolable. I grab Skippy's insulin kit off Hannah's coffee table and head toward the front door, where she stands wearing a careful smile.

"I know you told me to stop apologizing, but I'm so sorry all your work was lost," I begin. "You'd probably have your own book done by now. Instead, you've been helping me, and now—"

"That's enough," Hannah says, cutting my apology short. "None of this is your fault, and I have absolutely *no* regrets. I'm actually very glad I took on this project." She looks back and forth between Houston and me. "I feel like I'm watching your story being rewritten as we speak."

I reach my arms out tentatively and she smiles as she envelops me in a warm hug that makes me miss my mom. *God, I can't wait to go home.* When I let her go, she sniffs as she wipes a tear from the corner of her eye.

"Oh, don't mind me. I'm just being a silly woman." She waves off my concern. "Go on. I'm sure you two have lots of catching up to do."

I watch Houston as he uses an app on his phone to call a cab, then I turn back to Hannah. "I'll find a way to repay you for what you've done. I swear I will."

"I told you, you don't owe me anything."

I fight the urge to cry as Houston grabs Skippy's collar and opens the front door. "Thank you, Hannah, from the bottom of my heart, for helping me believe in myself."

She nods as we step outside into the sparkling January night. The cab arrives a few minutes later, our chariot here to whisk us away to a hotel in Palo Alto. I spend the twenty-minute drive huddled safely in Houston's arms with Skippy's warm body snuggled against my hip. The whole time, I have to keep reminding myself that everything happens for a reason. Maybe Houston's right. Maybe the next version of my book will be even better. Or maybe I'll give up on the book. Maybe I'll decide to *live* the story instead of writing it.

My eyes widen when we arrive at the Four Seasons hotel. "Why are we staying here? Isn't this a bit much?"

Houston pays the cab driver and slides out of the cab, holding his hand out to me as he replies, "There aren't many pet-friendly hotels in this area."

As if he understands what Houston just said, Skippy hops over me and leaps out of the cab. Houston reaches down and scoops him up easily, scratching him behind the ear as Skippy licks his face.

"That's right, buddy. Only the Four Seasons will do for you."

I shake my head as I slide out of the cab. "I knew you liked him better than me."

The hotel is well prepared with a complimentary leash and dog biscuit for Skippy.

"A bellman will come up to your room shortly with a doggy bed and bowls for water and food," says the handsome guy in a suit behind the check-in counter.

I gasp. "I don't have any of his food."

The guy winks at me. "We'll take care of that. Does he have any food allergies?"

Houston and I exchange a look, silently asking each other if this is real.

I turn back to the guy. "No. No allergies. Regular dog food is fine, thanks."

Once we're checked in, we walk Skippy outside to mark his territory, then we head back into the lobby. As we enter the hotel elevator, I'm reminded of the first time Houston and I rode in the elevator at my apartment building in Goose Hollow. I accused him of trying to get on my good side by being nice to Skippy.

Here we are, five months later, and Houston is the one holding Skippy's leash and insulin kit.

I look at the reflection of Houston's face in the shiny metal elevator door and he stares right back at me, but he doesn't smile. I don't know if he's having the same thoughts I'm having, but something has shifted between us. A bone-shaking realization grips me and it's unlike anything I've ever experienced.

What if the whole purpose of writing and losing my book was to bring Houston and me back together?

The elevator dings and the doors slide open. Houston and Skippy exit right away, but it takes me a moment to get my bearings and follow.

"What's wrong?" he asks as we head down the corridor toward room 1822. "Something's wrong. I can see it in your face."

I take a deep breath that rattles inside my chest. "Nothing, I just… I can't shake the guilt from wasting so much of your time and Hannah's time by coming out here."

"Come on, Rory. You have to give yourself a break. You couldn't have known what was going to happen." He slides the card-key into the slot and looks over his shoulder at me as he pushes the door open. "You just need to get some sleep and you'll feel a lot better when you're home tomorrow."

"I don't have a home," I reply, making no attempt to enter the room.

He looks a little confused by this, then he sighs as he unclips the leash from Skippy's collar so he can go sniff out the room. He sets the insulin kit down on a table in the entryway, using his foot to hold the door open.

"I have an extra bedroom," he says. "Kenny can stay there. When he finds a place, I'll help him move his stuff out of storage again. Okay?"

I shake my head in amazement. This man is willing to do anything for me.

"No," I whisper.

"Rory, please just come inside and we'll talk about it."

"No, you don't understand. I don't want Kenny to live with you. *I* want to live with you."

His eyes lock on mine and the muscle in his jaw twitches. "Are you fucking with me?"

I chuckle at this response. "Did you read my book? I've been in love with you for thirteen years."

"I didn't read your book."

For a moment I'm stunned, considering everyone seems to think it was their right to read my book lately. "You didn't?"

He looks confused. "I wasn't going to read it without your permission."

I shake my head again. "You make me feel like the goddamned luckiest girl in the world."

I step inside, reaching up to grab his face so I can kiss him. His hands land on my waist and he pushes me inside so he can let the door fall shut. His tongue slides into my mouth and I let out a soft moan as he presses me up against the wall. He tastes a little like beer and a lot like mint, like he had a beer on the plane then popped a breath mint. I tangle my fingers in his hair, hungrily pulling him into me. Willing him to lift me up so I can wrap my legs around him.

But he does the exact opposite. He pulls away, breathing heavily as his gaze falls to my chest.

"Not that I don't want to fuck you, but maybe we should feed Skippy and give him his insulin first."

"Oh, shit. How can you remember that and I don't?" I ask as I head into the one-bedroom suite to search for Skippy.

He chuckles sheepishly. "I was repeating it in my head the whole ride over here. I knew the first thing I'd want to do when we got to the room was rip your clothes off."

I find Skippy in the ensuite, drinking toilet water. "Skippy, no." He looks up at me, scrunching his brow together in an apology. "Come on, boy. I'll get you some clean water and food."

Once the bellman has brought up Skippy's doggy bed and food, we get him fed and medicated and settled down for a nap. The tension in the air grows thicker as Houston watches me from where he stands near the door leading onto the balcony, his eyes glued to me as I make my way to the bedroom. I enter the master suite and, without looking over my shoulder, I can sense him behind me, following me into the ensuite.

By the time he enters behind me, I have the shower turned on and the water set to the perfect temperature. I turn around and he stares at me for a moment, drinking me in, a love-drunk look in his eyes. Then he reaches up and softly brushes his thumb over my cheekbone, sending a chill through me.

"I wanted to believe this would happen. I knew I had to be strong, but I'd be lying if I said there weren't nights where I wanted to give up." His fingers graze the side of my face as they move down until he has my chin softly grasped in his thumb and forefinger. "You're the only thing in this fucked-up world that makes sense to me. I don't ever want to lose you again."

I lay my hand gently on his chest. "I don't want to lose you either."

He reaches up to cradle my face in his strong hands. "You'll never lose me. You're stuck with me." He smiles and plants a soft kiss on my forehead. "You're the only one I want to be with." He kisses the tip of my nose. "You're the only one I want to kiss."

I hold my breath as his lips fall gently over mine. This is the kiss I've been waiting for, slow and sensual and breathtaking. His hand clasps my face firmly, his velvet tongue brushing gently over mine, stoking the fire in my blood. He groans softly and the sound sends a bolt of electricity straight to the apex of my thighs. Taking my bottom lip between his teeth, he tugs gently then lets go when I open my eyes.

He smiles as he reaches down to grab the bottom of my shirt and lift it over my head. "You're the only one I want to touch," he says, tracing a line down my chest with the tip of his finger from my collarbone down to my navel.

He kisses me one more time before grabbing my hips to spin me around slowly until my back is to him. His fingers work deftly to undo the clasp on my bra, then he tosses it aside. His large hands lie flat against my belly as he pulls me into him, his lips landing on my shoulder as his fingers slide down to undo the button and zipper on my jeans.

I have to keep reminding myself to breathe as he kisses my neck while pushing down my pants and underwear. Then he kneels down behind me and helps me step out of my jeans, tossing them aside with my bra and panties. But he doesn't stand up. He remains knelt behind me, his fingers softly skimming over the inside of my ankle. My skin tingles as he works his way up until his hand is resting on the inside of my thigh.

He lays a soft kiss on the small of my back as his fingers trail their way upward, finding the wetness between my legs. "You're the only one I want to fuck."

I gasp as his finger slides into me. But he pulls it out right away and glides it forward through my swollen lips until it lands on my clit.

My body shivers as his finger caresses me. "Oh, Houston," I breathe.

He lays his free hand over my abdomen, pulling me closer to him as he presses his hot mouth to my hip. His other hand continues to stimulate me, sending rivers of pleasure flowing through me. I grasp the shower door handle for support. My knees tremble as the heat between my legs intensifies.

He presses his lips to my ass, kissing my cheek as his finger works my clit. He lets out a sexy chuckle as my body convulses. He's relishing his control over my body, enjoying this every bit as much as I am.

"Are you going to come?" he murmurs, his lips right against my cheek so I can feel his hot breath.

"Yes."

He slows the roll of his finger over my clit, drawing out the pleasure as he kisses his way down to the sensitive area where my ass melts into my thigh. "Bend over, baby."

I fold my body forward, my forehead almost pressed against the glass shower door as his mouth kisses a hot trail from the inside of my thigh up to my clit.

"Oh, God!" I cry out, my body spasming as he sucks on my flesh. "Don't stop. I'm gonna come."

My muscles flood with warmth, my body trembling as the orgasm rockets through me, lighting me up with white-hot painful pleasure. I let out a high-pitched scream, but he doesn't stop. He flattens his tongue over my clit, curling it intermittently to coax the full orgasm out of me.

"I can't," I breathe, my knees weakening. "I can't stand up."

He wraps his arm around my thighs to hold me steady as he drags his tongue up to my entrance and drives it inside me, lapping up my juices as if it were his first drink of water in ages.

"God, I fucking love the way you taste," he growls as he kisses his way up over my ass and the small of my back.

He stands up behind me, hooking his arm around my waist to steady me as he pulls me flush against him so I can feel the massive bulge in his jeans. His lips brush softly over the curve of my neck until his mouth is next to my ear.

"I'm going to fuck the shit out of you."

His voice is so primal it sends a shiver through me. I need him inside me.

"Fuck me, Houston," I plead, my hand reaching back to clasp his neck.

He bites my earlobe, his breath heavy in my ear, severing the last shreds of control in me. "Get in the shower."

I turn around and reach for his pants. "Let me do that."

He flashes me that criminally sexy half smile as I sink to my knees and begin undoing the button of his jeans. I slide the zipper down slowly, glancing up to savor the hungry look in his eyes. Then I help him out of his pants and boxers the way he helped me out of my clothing. His erection flings up as soon as I push his boxers down and, even though it's only been five months since I last saw it, the enormity of it still takes me by surprise.

I shove his clothes aside as he yanks off his shirt. Looking up at him, I see a glint of impatience in his eyes, which only makes me hotter. I curl my fingers around his shaft and slide my hand down to the base, stretching the skin taut. Then, I wet my lips and smile up at him as I take him into my mouth. I taste a hint of saltiness on the tip, so I pull him out and lick it off so I can use it.

"Holy fuck," he hisses, as I trace the tip of my tongue around the head, massaging the sensitive ridge.

My tongue stops on the underside of his cock, teasing the delicate frenulum until his body begins to quiver. I take him in my mouth again, making sure to keep my lips wrapped over my teeth as I bob back and forth. My right hand pumps his cock as my left hand grips his firm ass.

"That's it, baby. Keep going."

I slow the bobbing a little so I can focus on taking him in deeper. The tip of his cock hits the back of my throat and my eyes water as my gag reflex kicks in. He grabs a chunk of my hair to hold me steady as he pulls out then back in slowly, each time hitting just a fraction deeper in my throat.

"Fuck!" he growls. "I'm coming."

He slides out of me, and I pump my fist over his cock as he releases himself on my chest. As he softens, I take the tip of his cock into my mouth to lick him clean.

"Get up," he commands, offering me his hand to help me up.

I finish licking the last few drops, then I rise from the floor as he opens the shower door. Stepping inside, I chuckle when he smacks my ass.

"That ass is mine," he says, stepping in behind me.

I smile as I turn around and reach up to coil my arms around his neck. Within moments, I'm pleasantly surprised to find his cock reawakening. His rising erection presses against my abdomen as he kisses me deeply. I reach down to curl my fingers around him, but he grabs my hand and places it back on his neck.

"Slow down," he murmurs against my lips. "We've got all night."

His lips skim over my jaw, landing on my neck. His teeth scrape gently over my skin as he sucks on my flesh.

"No," I protest.

"What?"

"No," I insist, grabbing his shoulders to push him back. "We can go slow later. Right now, I want you to break me."

He narrows his eyes, as if he's unsure how to respond. After a moment of silence, he kisses my forehead then leans down to whisper in my ear. "Your wish is my command."

Houston

RORY GASPS as I press her against the shower wall, my cock sliding between her supple cheeks. Her hands splayed across the travertine tiles, her perfect mouth hanging slightly open with anticipation, she looks positively fuckable. I grab both her hips and pull her ass toward me, then I take my cock in my hand and glide it through her wetness.

"Oh, God. Put it in," she begs, and the sound gets me rock hard.

I slide in just an inch and instantly meet some resistance. I try not to dwell on thoughts of her and Liam together, but in a way it pleases me to know the lumberjack never broke her in. She's still mine.

I grasp her hips hard, digging my fingers in as I thrust into her. She lets out a high-pitched whine and I groan as my cock meets more resistance.

"You're so fucking tight," I growl, working my hips back and forth, slowly penetrating her a bit farther until finally I'm all the way in. "Oh, fuck, that's it."

"Oh, God," she whimpers, her fingers curling into fists as she tries to grip the slippery tile. "Fuck me, Houston."

Her face is pressed against the shower wall as I crush into her from behind. Each thrust of my hips drives her cheekbone harder into the tile. I curl my fist around a large chunk of her hair and pull her head back so she doesn't end up with a bruise on her face. She moans as I thrust my cock deep inside her, holding tightly to her wet hair.

"Harder!" she urges me.

I slam into her, my cock driving into her pussy until I can't fucking stand it anymore. The motion of my hips slows as I unload inside her, not at all concerned with whether or not she's on birth control this time. I'd be on cloud nine if I got a second chance to see our child growing inside her perfect body.

I lose my grip on her hair as I finish coming, my body folding forward as my cock twitches inside her. "I love you, Rory. I love you so fucking much," I murmur, my hands sliding over her abdomen as I help her stand up.

She twists her head around so I can kiss her and she tastes so fucking good. I want to devour her again. I slide my hand between her legs and swallow her gasp as if it were my lifeblood.

Three more orgasms later, we manage to get cleaned up before we drag our spent bodies out of the shower. Once we're dried off, she smiles at me as she holds up the hotel hair dryer and I know exactly what she wants. I carefully comb my fingers through her hair as I run the blow-dryer over it, smiling when I see goose bumps sprout over her creamy skin. When her hair is dry, we put on some bathrobes and head out into the bedroom to relax.

"We should order room service. I'm starving," she says, grabbing the TV remote off the nightstand as she plops down on the king-size bed.

I lift the Guest Services binder off the other nightstand and sit down next to her on the bed so we can look at the menu together. An hour later, we're stuffed to the gills with pizza and chocolate-covered strawberries. Not to mention the beer, which has us both a bit loopy.

She lies back on the bed, rubbing her full belly. I lie next to her, propping myself up on my elbow so I can slide my hand inside her robe.

"I can't believe you're buzzed off two beers," she teases me.

"I haven't been drinking much lately," I say, my hand inching upward toward her breast.

She grabs my hand to stop me. "Houston?"

"Yeah?"

She takes a long pause. The kind of pause that gives other people time to contemplate all the horrible things that may follow. Like maybe she's going to tell me we should just be friends. Or worse. What if she tells me she's pregnant with a tiny lumberjack?

She turns her head to look me in the eye, and the words that come out of her mouth hit me like a punch in the gut. "What if I can never forgive my father? What will that say about me?"

My jaw clenches at the mention of him. The fact that she's worried about what people will think of her only fuels my anger. She shouldn't be the one worried about keeping up appearances. He's the one who shattered their perfect family, and my *not-so-perfect* family.

I draw in a deep breath and let it out slowly before I respond. "Rory, I talked to my mom about Hallie a while ago and… I don't know if I'll ever get there either, but I want to try."

Her hand reaches up and lands on my cheek as she looks me in the eye. "I'll try with you."

I nod, turning my face to kiss the inside of her delicate wrist. "I'll try *anything* with you."

She chuckles as I kiss my way up her arm. "Anything?"

I grab her hip as I slide my knee between her legs and lean

down to kiss her neck. "Anything."

She curls her arms around my neck, pulling me on top of her so she can whisper something dirty in my ear. I let out a hoarse chuckle at the vulgarity of her suggestion.

"Holy shit, Rory. I didn't realize you were so filthy."

She tries to push me off. "Don't be mean."

I laugh as I resist her attempts to push me away. "I'm kidding, baby," I say, looking her in the eye. "I'll do that with you any day."

She narrows her eyes at me like she's angry, but the way she bites her lip tells me otherwise. She's thinking dirty, dirty thoughts.

I kiss the corner of her mouth. "You're my dirty bird," I whisper, sliding my hand between her legs. "Are you ready to sing again?"

She whimpers when my finger finds her clit. "Yes," she gasps.

No more than ten seconds pass before Rory's phone begins to chime with a weird robotic buzzing noise. "Let it ring," I insist, but she grabs my hand and this time I let her push me away.

She slides off the bed to grab the phone off the nightstand. "Hello?" Her nostrils flare as her eyes widen with shock. "Where is it? What did you do with it?"

In a flash, I'm out of bed and standing right beside her. I want to grab the phone out of her hand. I know it's that fucking piece of shit. But I have to trust her to handle this.

"Is it him?" I whisper, but she doesn't nod or respond.

"I can't believe you would do something like this," she says, shaking her head. "This is lower than low, Liam. If you have a shred of decency you will leave it at the front desk and go home."

"What the fuck? Give me the phone," I say, reaching for the phone.

Rory pushes my hand away and shakes her head. "I already told you, I don't want to talk to you." In an instant, her face goes from pure anger to sheer terror. "Wait! Okay! Okay, I'll talk to you. Just… Just give me a minute to get Skippy ready."

"No, Rory! No *fucking* way!"

But she's already ended the call.

She shakes her head. "He has my book on a flash drive. He's in the lobby right now."

"How the fuck did he find us?" My heart thumps crazy fast when her eyes widen. "You don't even know, do you? He could have a tracking app on your phone for all you know. He's fucking psycho! I'm not letting you go down there. Not even with me and Skippy. *Fuck* that."

The tears begin streaming down her face as she sinks down onto the edge of the bed. "I don't know what to do. I just want it back. I worked so hard on it. And it's not just the book. It's the emails." She looks up at me and the pleading look in her eyes is like a knife in my chest. "Please. Just let me try. I don't think he'll hurt me. He just wants to talk."

I kneel before her, resting my hands on her knees. "That's what he says, baby, but that's not what he means. Please trust me, just this once."

She covers her face with her hands, and I know there'll be no talking her out of this. That fucker knows the one thing she cares about more than anything is that book. She's going down there no matter what I say to try to convince her otherwise.

Fucking coward.

"Okay," I continue. "I'll go down with you. If he won't give it to you with me there, then we're coming back up, okay?"

She pulls her hands away from her face and the glint of hope in her eyes makes my stomach twist. She really thinks this asshole is going to give her the book just like that. At least I'll be there if he tries anything. If he so much as breathes on her, I'll annihilate him.

Rory

MY SKIN IS BUZZING, my blood pressure rising to the point that I'm seeing spots as Houston and I get dressed in the clothes we came in. Houston clips Skippy's leash to his collar and I try to focus on my breathing as we walk down the hotel corridor. Once Houston hits the call button, each second ticks by excruciatingly slowly. The ding of the elevator makes me jump.

Houston grabs my hand to stop me from going in. "Are you sure you want to do this? I can go down there and try to get it without you."

"No, he won't give it to you. I don't even know if he'll give it to me, but I have to try." I sigh as Houston uses his foot to stop the elevator doors from closing again. "If he doesn't give it to me within two minutes, we'll come back up."

Houston doesn't look appeased by this promise, but we head into the elevator without further discussion. I'm so anxious I could cry. I feel as if my heart is going to explode out of my eyeballs. But I manage to keep from unraveling as the elevator descends to the lobby.

As soon as the elevator doors slide open, I tighten my hold on Houston's hand. "Don't let go of me, please."

He kisses the top of my head and gives my hand a gentle squeeze. "Never."

Suddenly, everything gets fuzzy. Time and space seem to blend until reality feels hollow, dreamlike. I can't remember how many steps it takes to reach Liam, or how many seconds it takes for him to throw the first punch, or when Houston lets go of my hand, or how long it takes him to wrestle Liam onto the marble floor, or which direction the security guards come from, or why Liam refuses to stop fighting.

Four times.

The security guards Tase him with the stun gun four times.

Time passes in clips. The security guard performing CPR. Red lights flashing everywhere, bouncing off every reflective surface in the glitzy lobby. People shouting numbers that make no sense. The paramedics lifting his limp body onto the gurney.

Then, it's as if time stops and in one solitary instance, my mind is cleared of all the chaos. All I feel is stillness. And as the paramedics wheel him away, it finally hits me: If Liam dies, it will be my fault.

All because I wanted my stupid book back.

I *hate* that book.

Houston takes me in his arms, crushing me to him as I sob into his chest. But the small respite of comfort lasts only a few seconds before he lets me go. The first thought that hits me is that Houston is just as disgusted by me as I am. But when I look up at him, he nods at something behind me.

I look over my shoulder and find an attractive blonde woman in a black leather jacket and close-fitting jeans, her hair pulled into a low messy ponytail like she just yanked off a motorcycle helmet.

"Good evening. I'm Detective Dana Locke. I just need to ask you two a few questions about what went down here tonight."

She nods toward the cluster of armchairs in the middle of the lobby. "Want to have a seat?"

When we explain to her the reason for Liam's visit, she excuses herself for a moment so she can step aside to get the lead detective in the Cybercrimes Division on the phone. As she steps away to make the call, my stomach goes sour.

"I don't want to press charges against him," I whisper urgently to Houston. "I can't be responsible for almost killing him *and* putting him in jail."

"You didn't do any of this," he replies in a hoarse whisper. "This is not on your head. He did this to himself. You didn't make him spy on you and steal your files and you sure as fuck didn't make him fight those guards."

"But if I hadn't come down, he would have just left."

"You don't know that. He probably would have tried to climb up the eighteen stories to our floor and the security guards would have headed him off in the stairwell. This is *not* your fault. Do you understand me?" I stare back at him, unable to respond. "Say it, Rory. Say the words: It's not my fault." His blue eyes shine with a fiery determination to make me understand, but I can't bring myself to say the words aloud, so I just nod. "Rory, say the words."

I turn away from his intense glare and mutter, "It's not my fault."

RIDING IN THE BACK of a cop car feels ominous, even if they're just giving us a ride to the hospital. Even with Skippy sitting next to me, slobbering on the window, and Houston's fingers laced through mine, I still feel as if we're being driven to our doom. I don't know what we'll find when we get to the hospital. All I know is that I can't go to sleep tonight wondering if Liam is okay.

Maybe I've come down with a case of Stockholm syndrome, where the person held captive begins to sympathize with her captor. I can't just suddenly stop caring about Liam. My heart doesn't have an on-off switch. It's just a mess of tangled wires, and I haven't figured out which one needs to be snipped to get Liam out of my system.

Houston squeezes my hand and it takes me a moment to realize the car has stopped. We're parked in a space just a few dozen feet from the curb in front of the emergency room. The cold Northern California air seeps into my skin as we step out into the black night. Houston coils Skippy's leash around his hand to keep him close as we set off toward the hospital entrance.

The emergency room is relatively quiet for a Friday night. I haven't been to the emergency room since the time I took my mom when she accidentally stabbed her hand while opening a package of bacon with a chef's knife. It was a horrific experience. There were so many people coming into the ER that night, they mixed up my mom's chart and tried to make her put on a gown just to get stitches in her palm. But this emergency room is eerily quiet. Except for an elderly couple slumped over and snoring in the corner of the waiting room, the place is empty.

We turn into the corridor on the right, just inside the sliding doors, and quickly find a chest-high desk labeled "Emergency Room Check-In."

"Sir, you're not allowed to bring pets in here. Service animals only," says a woman with frizzy auburn curls behind the desk.

"We're just trying to find out the status of a patient," Houston replies gently, but not gently enough for the woman's taste.

"Sir, take the dog outside or I'll have you both physically removed."

Houston turns to me and I nod. "I'll be right outside," he says, kissing my forehead before he heads back out through the sliding doors.

I get a weird feeling as he disappears into the blackness, as if that's the last time I'm going to see him; not ever, just *that way*. Like the next time I see him, he won't look the same. Not because he'll have changed, but because I will have changed.

I turn back to the lady behind the desk, taking a moment to gather my fortitude. "I'm here for Liam Murray. He was brought in tonight. Um… He was in cardiac arrest."

The woman's harsh features soften a bit. "Let me check."

She types on her keyboard for a couple of minutes before she picks up her phone to make a call. "You have Murray, Liam?" she asks the person on the other end. "Yeah, I have someone here to see him… All right, thanks."

"He's in ICU. Immediate family, spouses, and domestic partners only."

"We live together," I blurt out the lie easily. Technically, it only became a lie a few hours ago. It hasn't had time to ripen yet.

"Honey, unless both of you are over 62 or the same sex, you're not even eligible for domestic partnership. So… are you married?"

Her gaze is locked on mine and I don't know if she's willing me to lie or if that's just my way of justifying it, but the words tumble from my lips faster than I can catch them and stuff them back inside.

"Yes. We're married. In Oregon. We just moved here."

She raises her eyebrows, probably noting how I'm not crying. "All the way down the hall, hang a left. Turn right into the second corridor, then right again. You'll see the ICU at the end of the hall. He's in room 153."

"Thank you."

I'm only a few yards down the first corridor when I hear

hurried footsteps tapping the floor behind me. I turn around to find Houston slowing down as he catches up.

"Where's Skippy?"

"One of the officers offered to let him sleep in the backseat of his car for at least twenty minutes. I wanted to be with you."

My heart melts at these words, but the feeling doesn't last. Houston reaches for my hand and I feel sick to my stomach when I yank my hand away, holding it protectively against my belly.

I glance over my shoulder to make sure no one noticed, then I look up at him. "We can't do that. I have to pretend I'm married to Liam so they'll let us see him."

As we turn the corner at the end of the corridor, his face screws up like he just smelled something bad. "You can't pretend to be married to him. That's sick."

I continue walking fast, right past the first corridor. "You have no right to judge me for this lie when you lied to me for five years."

From the corner of my eye, I can see him shaking his head. But it's not a ridiculous argument.

"I'm not trying to imply that I deserve to lie," I continue. "I just can't believe that you wouldn't understand why I feel responsible here."

"Hallie's death was *nothing* like this," he says in a deadly whisper as we turn right into the second corridor. "Don't even attempt to compare her to him."

The tears I needed earlier appear, lush and plentiful, an unstoppable torrent. I stop at the first corridor, where the lady told me I'd find the ICU at the end of the hall. When I look up at Houston, there's a small hint of regret in his eyes, but his mouth is set in a hard line, unwilling to back down.

"I just want to know he's going to live. I just…" I take a moment to catch my breath and wipe the tears from my face. "I just want to be able to sleep tonight."

Houston's face softens as he shakes his head. "Rory, it doesn't work that way. You can't justify lying. 'Cause if you can justify a lie, you can justify anything. Trust me on this."

My mind flashes to the words Houston said to me while we were in the hotel room earlier, when he was trying to convince me not to go downstairs to meet Liam: *Please trust me, just this once.*

I should have listened to him then. I should probably listen to him now. I look up and our eyes meet and we both know it's time to go. There's nothing more we can do here. Houston is right. I can't tell such a hideous lie, even if it's with the intent of easing my mind. That's exactly how Houston and I got here in the first place. The cycle of lies has to end somewhere. It might as well end here, in the middle of an ICU corridor, with the man I love asking me to trust him.

I step forward, wrapping my arms around his waist, pressing my face to his solid chest. He kisses the top of my head and we stand there for a while, lost in the warmth of our bodies, the comfort of knowing we can get through anything as long as we have each other. It takes a moment for me to snap out of this trance when a woman's voice comes over the hospital paging system.

"Code Blue. Code Blue. First Floor. Room I-1-5-3. Repeat. Code Blue. First Floor. Room I-1-5-3."

the way we rise

For all the "Hannahs"
who encouraged my writing.

Patricia

January 17, 2015

When you become a mother, it's easy to believe your life no longer belongs to you. In an instant, your most pressing objective shifts. No longer does it matter whether your hair and makeup are perfect, not when you have to worry about whether the human being you brought into this world is hungry or sick or unhappy. It's easy to lose yourself in the day-to-day needs of others when you become a mother.

It's seven in the morning and I'm standing outside the six-story building where James has worked for the past five years, rain gushing over my umbrella, the smell of ozone and wet leaves saturating my senses. I can't help but realize how I'm still putting Rory's needs before my own. There's beauty in selflessness. There's honor in putting aside your fears to make sure the ones you love are taken care of. But I can't help but wonder if that's the only reason I'm here.

It's true, I had my suspicions about James and Hallie. When you get to know someone as well as I knew James, it's difficult not to notice the slight changes in mood and schedule. Showering more often. Working longer hours. Volunteering to do laundry. I knew what it all meant, but I didn't know *who* he was having an affair with. Not until Rory's RA called me on December 4, 2008, to tell me Hallie was dead and Rory was gone.

I enter the lobby of the high-rise building, which is conveniently near the courthouse downtown. The hefty gentleman manning the front desk looks more like a bodyguard than a concierge. He's quite polite when he asks me to sign in before heading up to the sixth floor.

The moment I step inside the elevator, my heart pounds wildly. The way it did when James first smiled at me during our first class together at the University of Oregon. He was taking the Classics course to fulfill a general education requirement. I was there to soak in every word my professor spoke about Proust and Dostoyevsky. But he was such a distraction, the clean-cut boy with the dark hair and a smile that could light up the universe. And, oh, could he carry on a conversation.

He'd graduated from high school a year early, which meant I was a year older than him when we met. He was at UO on a full scholarship, though he refused to tell me his major, until I figured it out on our third date. As we sipped Coca-Colas and ate greasy cheeseburgers at a seedy diner in Eugene, James refused to back away from his position on the deindustrialization of the American workforce. He insisted it was good for America to move toward a more service-based economy, while I argued passionately for keeping manufacturing jobs in America. It was then that I guessed correctly he was going to be a lawyer. And a damn good one.

After twenty-eight years and countless disappointments, you'd think I wouldn't give the slightest damn what my hair or makeup looks like on a day like today. Quite the contrary, I find myself utilizing the shiny steel elevator doors as a mirror to adjust a stray piece of silver hair on the left side of my head.

God help me. I'm a worse cliché than my philandering ex-husband.

The elevator dings as the doors slide open and I'm immediately hit with the strong scent of leather and kefir lime. The scent is like a knife twist in my gut. It's exactly what James's home office smelled like. Now that I know what happened in that office, it makes me sick to my stomach. The scent also reminds me of why I'm here, renewing my anger and determination. I almost feel like taking that piece of silver hair and pulling it out of place as an act of defiance.

Almost.

The receptionist is young, as expected. Her blonde hair is pulled into a neat updo and her blazer fits well, though she seems to have missed a spot with her lint brush this morning. Maybe she has a young child who was screaming to be fed while she was trying to get dressed.

"May I help you?" she says, her voice smooth and congenial.

"I'm here to see James Charles," I reply.

"Do you have an appointment?"

I smile, though I try not to look too smug. "I don't think that's necessary. I'm the *ex*-Mrs. Charles. I'm here about our daughter." I place my hand on the chest-high desk and lean forward as she reaches for her phone. "And, dear, I'd appreciate it if you'd not tell him I'm here."

She flashes me a tight smile. "Of course." She points behind her with her thumb. "Just behind this wall, you'll see a couple of paralegals and two hallways. Take the one on the left all the way down to the end. If he's not in his office, you can just come back here and I'll try to find him."

"Thank you… I'm sorry, I didn't get your name."

She smiles as she reaches her hand toward me. "Hailey."

I swallow hard as I take her hand and give it a light shake. "Nice to meet you, Hailey."

I take a few slow, deliberate breaths as I make my way around the wall bearing the firm's name, Talbert, Charles, and Associates, in large silver letters. I find two paralegals, just as Hailey said I would. A young man in a dark-gray suit nods at me and I attempt a smile. My skin must look as translucent as my resolve because he instantly stands from his desk.

"Ma'am, are you all right?"

I nod adamantly. "Yes, yes. I'm fine. Take a seat, young man."

He cocks an eyebrow as I head toward the corridor on the left. He probably hasn't been called a young man or told to take a seat since high school, and he's clearly in his late twenties or early thirties. Still a young man to me. He could be one of my old students from my days teaching high school English. Age seems inconsequential in this situation, but I suppose the number of years a person has lived—or not lived—is the reason I'm here.

If Hallie were thirty-five when she'd had an affair with James, she probably would have shouldered more of the blame. As it was, she was a child. A child pretending to be a woman to seduce a man.

I don't blame Hallie for the affair. Quite the contrary, I actually thank her for exposing a gaping crack in the foundation of my marriage. I'm also a realist.

I don't think James would have pursued her had Hallie not pursued him first. I'm not saying he wouldn't have strayed. All signs pointed to James's discontent, not just with the marriage, but also with himself. If Hallie had never pursued James, he almost certainly would have betrayed our marriage vows in some other fashion. And if he had not given in to the feminine wiles of a confused eighteen-year-old girl, Hallie might still be alive today. It takes two.

Yet, only one person survived this affair, and it's time for him to repent.

When I reach the end of the corridor, James's office door is open. I can hear him before I see him. I try not to recall my past with James often, but it's hard not to when it comes to his voice.

James has the kind of voice that sets a person at ease and commands attention all at once, the clear, resonant timbre carefully layered over a soft grittiness. It used to be one of my favorite things about him, watching him argue a case in that voice.

I approach the doorway slowly and find him leaning back in his chair, his phone pressed to his ear as he talks to someone about filing a habeas corpus petition.

"If they didn't Mirandize him or allow him to see his lawyer, then he wasn't officially under arrest. File the habeas and I'll accompany you to the hearing tomorrow..." He finally looks up to see who's standing in his doorway and his mouth drops. "Uh... I'll have to call you back."

He sets the handset down on the receiver and blinks a few times as if he can't believe his eyes. "Patricia."

"James." We stare at each other for a moment before I continue. "Can I come in?"

He stands up quickly. "Yes, of course. Come in," he says, waving me in as he rounds the desk to close the door behind me. "It's good to see you."

I roll my eyes as I watch him head back to his chair. "No, it's not. I'm probably the last person you want to see here."

"That's not true. I've been hoping to speak to you about Rory, but I've been swamped with death-row cases and—"

I hold up my hand to stop him. "Please don't patronize me with lackluster excuses, James. I'm not here to chastise you for being a substandard father for the past six years. I'm here to make you an offer."

His eyebrows shoot up. "I guess there's no need for niceties." He shakes his head as he takes a seat and waves at one of the visitor chairs for me to follow suit. "What are you offering me today, Patricia? A one-way ticket to hell? A free grammar critique of my latest brief?"

I smile as I take a seat across from him. "That's the James I used to know and love."

He shrugs. "Well, you created him, didn't you?"

I sigh as I attempt to take this insult in stride, but he still has the power to eviscerate me with such precision. "Yes, we molded each other into the people we are today. The difference between you and me is that I can acknowledge you made me a better person than I was before you."

His eyes widen at this response. "I'm… I'm sorry. I can't help but feel a bit defensive. But you're right. You're a better person today. A much better person than I am, that's for sure."

"No. I will not allow you to hide behind self-pity or self-deprecation. That is not an excuse to continue being a bad father."

His gaze is fierce and unwavering as he considers my words.

"You're a good father, James, under all those layers of guilt and self-righteousness and misdirected anger. And that's why I'm here, to give you a chance to shed the nonsense and do the right thing for your daughter. She needs you now more than ever."

His gaze falls to the top of the desk where his left hand rests, the hand that used to bear his wedding ring. I can't help but notice the tan line and ridges we once thought would be permanent have faded.

"I know you probably don't want to hear this, but I haven't forgiven myself." He looks up, his eyes glistening with unspent tears. "How can I expect absolution from Rory if I don't think I deserve it?"

"Simple," I reply. "You give mercy in order to get it. Take mercy on Rory and stop withholding your love, and she will have mercy on you."

Rory

January 17, 2015

Skippy's body twitches and the sound of his tags jangling on his collar wakes me. I glance at the alarm clock on the hotel nightstand and sigh. It's just past eight in the morning. I've slept a whole ninety minutes.

I tighten my hold on Skippy's stout Labrador body and he whines. Then he turns to me and begins loudly licking my face. He needs to go potty. He's spent the past five hours locked in my arms as I soaked his black fur with tears and snot. And he still loves me enough to kiss me when his bladder is ready to burst.

More tears come as I realize how I came so close to losing Skippy just five months ago, before he was diagnosed as diabetic. It would have been the second time I'd lost a best friend. And by some odd twist of fate, Houston was there with me when Skippy almost died. I hadn't seen Houston in five years, and yet there he was, suddenly and unexpectedly.

He was there when Hallie died and he was there when Skippy almost died. And now, he was there when Liam died. If I didn't know better, I'd wonder if maybe Houston is my unlucky charm.

An omen.

"I'll take them out." Houston's voice is clear, not an ounce of grogginess, as if he's been awake for a while.

I look down at Skippy and his chin is resting on my pillow next to my shoulder, waiting patiently for me to let him out. Then I look at Sparky, Liam's shepherd mix, lying on the chaise in the corner of the bedroom in our master suite at the Four Seasons hotel.

"I can take them out," I reply, without turning around to look at Houston.

Houston slides out of bed before I can even pry my arms out from underneath Skippy's seventy-pound body. The sound of Houston's feet on the hotel carpet prompts Skippy to leap down. Sparky jumps off the chaise and begins stretching his hind legs. I watch silently from the bed as Houston pulls on the same shirt and jeans he was wearing last night. He hooks the dogs' leashes on their collars and casts one indecipherable glance in my direction before he leaves.

I consider pulling the covers over my head and going back to sleep, but I know better than that. Sleep will not come easy today.

When Hallie died, I slept for hours. After Houston and I had sex for the first time later that night, I slept another twelve hours. The day of her funeral, I fell asleep at seven p.m. My mind seemed unable to cope with reality then. Now, I feel as if I can't escape reality.

My mind refuses to shut down. As if Liam's ghost is somewhere near me, haunting me, whispering in a voice I can't hear, but nonetheless refuses to let me rest.

This is your fault.

I drag myself out of bed and the same force that weighed me down after Hallie died propels me toward the bathroom. I turn on the hot water and undress, then I sit down on the marble floor of the shower and wait.

I don't know what I'm waiting for. A plane to crash into our hotel. A moment of clarity where all of this suddenly makes sense. Houston to find me and save me, again.

A moment after this thought crosses my mind, Houston enters the bathroom. I want to look up at him and see that beautiful face. Look into his fierce blue eyes and see the strength I know I need. But I don't want him to see me like this, grieving over the man I left him for.

He stands there a moment longer, but when I don't look up he leaves without saying anything. He probably doesn't know what to say. He can't say, *I know how you feel.* And he probably doesn't even care that Liam is dead. Why should he? Almost all he's ever seen of Liam were his worst traits: the jealousy and anger and duplicity.

He didn't know that Liam was a good person with a good heart, and the worst taste in music. He never saw Liam fall asleep on the sofa with Sparky in the middle of the day. He never heard Liam talk about his older sister as if she were his idol. He never caught Liam taking selfies in a Santa suit.

I wash up quickly in the shower and put on the clean outfit I brought with me when we went to pick up Sparky at three in the morning from the house Liam and I shared for the past month and a half, until yesterday. I open the bathroom door and Houston is sitting on the edge of the bed, leaning forward with his elbows on his thighs as both dogs lie at his feet.

He looks up as I come out of the bathroom and manages a weak smile. "How are you feeling?"

I sniff loudly and let out a deep sigh. "Never better."

"Don't do that, Rory," he says, beating me to the doorway before I can leave the bedroom. "Don't shut me out."

I stare at his chest and wonder what's going on inside there. Does his heart ache even a tiny fraction as much as mine does right now? Does he feel even the slightest bit of remorse for what happened last night?

I swipe my hands down my face then wipe the moisture on the front of my jeans. "I can't. I can't talk to you about him. It's just… It's not right. I'm sorry."

He reaches out slowly and gently takes me into his arms. "It's okay."

His shirt smells like yesterday.

I reach up and close my fist tightly around the fabric, bringing it to my nose. I inhale the scent slowly and deeply, aching to be transported back to last night. To the moment when I could have chosen to stay in my damn hotel room.

Then a pitiful, involuntary whimper leaks out of my mouth. Houston tightens his grip on me as he feels my body becoming heavy. In one swift motion, he swoops me up in his arms and carries me to the bed. Then he sits on the edge and waits for me to speak.

I pull the sheet up, use it to wipe my eyes, hoping to conceal my grief and my shame, but Houston won't allow it. He pries the sheet out of my hands and pulls it down, away from my face, so he can see me.

"Look at me, Rory."

I angle my face upward to look at him and the change in position sends two fat tears sliding down my cheeks.

He reaches for me, wiping one of them away. "I realized something when I woke up this morning and found you lying next to me for the first time in five and a half years."

I want to ask him what he realized, but I can't bring myself to speak.

He tucks my damp hair behind my ear. "The world looks and feels different when I'm with you. Better and easier." His gaze wanders over my face and hair for a moment before he continues. "That's how I know we're going to get through this, because we're better together."

I look away from him, almost feeling disgusted. Is he trying to tell me we're better off now that Liam is gone?

"Rory, talk to me."

I rub my left cheek on the pillow to wipe away some of the moisture. "I don't know what to say."

"Tell me how you're feeling."

I shrug. "I feel like a different person than I was when I arrived in this hotel room last night."

He lets out a frustrated sigh. This is not what he wanted to hear.

"Are you saying you're having second thoughts… about us?" His voice cracks a little on the word *us*, and this sends me into a bit of a panic.

"No." I force the word out through the sobbing. "I'm sorry."

"Sorry for what? Baby, come here." He slides his arm underneath my back and pulls me into him firmly. "You don't have anything to be sorry for."

"I'm sorry for making you think I was having second thoughts." I'm filled with a desperate need to make sure he knows I still need him. "I'm not having second thoughts, Houston. I swear."

"Okay, okay. Shh. It's okay," he whispers as he kisses the top of my head and strokes my hair.

We sit like this for a while, him comforting me while I try to figure out what's going to happen when we go back to Portland. How am I supposed to live with Houston while I'm mourning another man? Finally, the tears stop and Houston heads into the bathroom to take a shower, after asking me ten times if I'm going to be okay alone.

While he's cleaning up, I set up Skippy and Sparky's food bowls with the morning portion of dog food, but when I open up Skippy's insulin kit to get his shot ready, I realize there are no more vials in the kit. I forgot to bring the box of insulin vials from the house when we went to pick up Sparky. I guess it's not a big deal. We have to take Sparky back there today to hand him off to Liam's parents, whose flight should be arriving soon. I'm not looking forward to facing them.

I've never met his parents. They live in Salem and we didn't bother visiting them on the road trip from Portland to California because they were supposed to visit us within a few months. The first time I'll meet them is to offer them condolences.

I'm sure they'll want to know what happened. The police will only give so much information in an ongoing investigation. I wish I hadn't told that detective about Liam stealing my book file and my emails. Now that he's dead, I don't have to press charges, but my statement is part of the investigation into his death. It's bad enough that I was at a hotel with another man. Now Liam's parents will know he was there because I accused him of stealing from me.

When Houston walks out of the bedroom, I'm tempted to bury my face in his chest just to get a whiff of the past, to lose myself in the memory of the happiness I felt before Liam arrived at the hotel last night.

"We need to go to the house," I say, reaching for the dog leashes on the coffee table in the sitting area. "I left Skippy's insulin."

He nods and reaches for the hotel phone on the breakfast bar. "I'll just call the concierge to make sure they have the rental car I requested."

The car rental is ready and waiting for us when we head down to the lobby, a shiny black Infiniti that smells like leather conditioner. Sparky and Skippy hop into the backseat and each take their place on either end of the bench seat, waiting for Houston to roll down the windows.

The morning sky is dark and swollen with an impending rainstorm, the air crackling with friction. As Houston drives toward Mountain View, I find myself wishing the sun would come out. I imagine dazzling rays of sunlight beaming down and setting the streets ablaze until everything is on fire, my heart reduced to ashes, swept up into the wind, becoming part of the atmosphere we all breathe, and everywhere, everyone will understand, I never wanted Liam to get hurt.

Houston pulls up to the curb in front of the house. I don't bother asking why he doesn't want to park in the driveway. I figure he's leaving the space open for when Liam's parents arrive. The dogs begin whining and wagging their tails when they see their home, probably thinking they're going to see Liam. I don't bother leashing them before I let them out of the car. Sparky races across the lawn and up the steps toward the front door. Skippy makes a quick pit stop to relieve himself on a fern in the garden before he follows his best bud.

My heart races as I unlock the front door and let everyone inside. The house still smells a little like fresh paint and carpet, but there's also a faint hint of Liam's cologne laced through everything. When he was alive, I never found myself purposely inhaling the scent just to feel close to him. But now, it smells perfect. Crisp and woodsy, like freshly chopped pine.

"Are you okay?" Houston asks, and I realize I don't know how long I've been standing in the middle of the living room, inhaling the wood-scented air.

I nod vigorously. "I'm okay."

I quickly set about administering Skippy's insulin, then I head outside to leave the box of insulin vials in the car, so I don't forget them. When I enter the house again, Houston is standing on the threshold of the back door leading to the yard. I come up behind him and wrap my arms around his waist, resting my cheek on his shoulder blade.

He grabs one of my hands and pulls it up to kiss my fingers. "I'm sorry I haven't offered much sympathy. I'm just afraid of saying the wrong thing." He turns around and takes my face in his hands. "But you know I love you and I'm here for you no matter what, right?"

I nod and wrap my arms around him again, then I bury my face in his chest. He squeezes me tightly and we stand in silence for a while, until the silence is broken by my growling stomach.

He chuckles. "I'll go get us something to eat."

"Okay, I don't have much to pack. I'll do that while you're gone."

I let go of him reluctantly and he kisses my forehead before heading out. I watch Skippy and Sparky frolicking a moment longer, then I head to the bedroom to pack my things. The woodsy scent is more intense in here, especially the nearer I get to the bed.

My stomach burns with nausea as I breathe through my mouth while stuffing my suitcase with my clothing. Every time I see Liam's favorite jeans or his favorite T-shirt, I just want to fall to my knees and give up. And I do give up, halfway through. I don't need all these clothes anyway. I yank the zipper shut on the suitcase and push it off the bed until it falls to the floor with a deep thud.

The creak of the front door opening startles me. Hurriedly, I drag the suitcase out of the bedroom. I don't want Houston to come looking for me in the bedroom where Liam and I used to have sex. But when I come out of the hallway into the living room, my heart clenches in my chest at the sight of Liam's parents and sister.

His mother is a small woman, shorter than I am, and so thin she almost looks sick. His sister looks like a female version of Liam, minus the facial hair. His father, on the other hand, doesn't seem to share Liam's taste in facial hair. His square jaw is clean shaven, his dark hair cut and styled neatly. He's about six-one, Liam's height, and quite burly. His blue Oxford is pressed perfectly and I suddenly realize where Liam inherited his need for control.

"Rory?" his mother murmurs this soft plea to which I nod. "What happened?" she bellows, clutching her chest. "What did they do to him? Tell me how it happened."

The tears come instantly and I open my mouth to speak, but Liam's father cuts me off.

"Why are you crying? My son died because of you and *you're* crying?"

My jaw drops. "What? I don't—"

He turns to Liam's sister. "Leah, give me your phone."

I don't know if Leah looks more embarrassed or frightened by his request.

Liam's father turns back to me. "She has the texts from Liam on her phone."

"I don't know what you think happened," I begin, "but—"

"Don't play dumb with me, girl. I talked to the cops and they said you were there with another guy. Liam caught you at a hotel with someone else and now he's dead."

"That's not how it happened," I insist, my heart pounding with fear. "I was there with someone else because Liam and I broke up. He erased my computer files and attacked me!"

"You're telling me my son died over some fucking computer files? *Bull-fucking-shit!*" his father shouts, and my entire body begins to shake uncontrollably.

"I'm not lying," I whisper. "I would never cheat on Liam. I would never hurt him. Please, you have to believe I never wanted to hurt Liam."

His father looks disgusted with me. The look on his face reminds me of the look that flashed across Liam's face last night, when he saw me approaching him in the hotel lobby with Houston at my side.

"You never meant to hurt him when you cheated on him?"

"I didn't cheat on him!" I shout so loud my throat burns, as if screaming it will make this man believe me. I'm just a stupid whore to him.

I turn to his sister, but she refuses to look at me. Either she doesn't believe my story or she's too afraid to say anything.

"You have to believe me," I plead. "I had no money for a hotel room or a ticket home after Liam hurt me. I had to call someone to come and get me."

"After Liam hurt you?" his father jeers. "He's dead! He can't defend himself and you expect me to just take your word for it?" He steps forward and I can hardly breathe as he gets in my face, the vein in his forehead throbbing with fury. "He should have hurt you. Convincing him to move to California so you could go behind his back the first chance you got."

"Step away from her! Now!"

We all turn toward the front door and I've never been so relieved to see my father in my life.

"Dad?"

My father's face is contorted with rage, his gaze locked on Liam's father. "You touch her and it'll be the last thing you do."

Liam's mother shakes her head. "It just doesn't make any sense. Liam never got in any trouble with the police. He never hurt anyone."

His sister sighs as she wipes tears from her puffy eyes. "Yes, he did, Mom. He just never got caught. He's the one who torched Savannah's car. He told me all about it."

"What?" his mom says with genuine confusion.

"Don't you talk about your brother like that," his father warns her.

She shakes her head. "It's true," she whispers as she finally looks at me. "I believe you."

I can't speak or move, until my father's hand lands on my arm. I look up at him and the pain in his eyes at seeing me like this hits me hard.

"Yeah, get her out of here before we call the cops," Liam's father says, delivering another kick to my already-broken spirit.

A fiery aura of anger pulses around my father, but he grits his teeth and keeps his eyes locked on me, careful not to take the bait.

He kisses my forehead then reaches for my suitcase. "Come on, sweetheart. You don't have to stay and listen to this."

"I have to get Skippy. He's in the backyard."

He nods then carries my suitcase as he follows me through the back door. The rain has started coming down in a light sprinkle, creating a crystal web across the back lawn. I kneel down on the damp grass to hug Sparky good-bye.

"I probably won't see you again," I sob into his tan fur as I squeeze him tightly. "I'm sorry, buddy. I'm so sorry."

Liam's father watches from the back door as we leave through the side gate. I try to ignore Sparky's cries as I leave without him, but each high-pitched whine pierces straight through my heart. My dad throws my suitcase in the trunk of his gray rental car and Skippy jumps into the backseat, tail wagging and tongue lolling, completely oblivious to the fact that the world is a darker place today.

I plunk myself down in the passenger seat, but I don't close the car door. "Houston will be here soon. He went to get us something to eat."

"Just call him and tell him to meet you somewhere else." His eyes plead with me, but for what I don't know. "I'm not letting you stay here. I don't want you anywhere near those people."

I sigh as my mind immediately begins to conjure reasons for why my dad is here. Is it because of the investigation into Liam's death? Or is he really here just to be a father?

He sighs as he waits for me to shut the door. "Rory, I just can't stand the thought of you thinking any of this is your fault." He reaches across the space between us and brushes a tear away from my cheek. "Let me do this. Let me help you."

I don't know what's going to happen when I call Houston and tell him I'm with my father. All I know is that right now, I desperately want to let someone else carry the burden of my sorrows. And if that person is my father, someone who won't judge me for mourning a man who attacked me and spied on me in our last days together, then maybe he's exactly what I need right now.

I take a deep breath and close the car door. "Okay."

Houston

January 17, 2015

As I turn the corner onto Harbor Court, my phone vibrates in the cup holder. I snatch it up and answer right away when I see Rory's name.

"Hey, baby. I'm almost there."

"Don't go to the house. I'm not there anymore," she says, her words rushed. "Liam's parents are there and his dad is… very upset. Please don't go there."

My heart races at the thought of running into Liam's parents. Do they think I had something to do with his death? Then I think of how anxious Rory sounds and I'm suddenly angry with them for upsetting her. She was fine when I left a few minutes ago.

"But what about your stuff? And—wait a minute," I say as I pass the house and try to get a glimpse through the window, but the curtains are drawn tightly shut. "If you're not there, where are you?"

She pauses for a moment. "I'm at Cuesta Park, on Grant and Cuesta."

I pull the car over next to the curb to enter the cross-streets into the rental car's GPS. "How did you get there? It's almost two miles from the house."

She lets out a soft sigh. "My dad. He showed up when Liam's dad was yelling at me, basically calling me a cheating whore. He didn't want me to stay there. *I* didn't want to stay there."

She continues talking, but I can't hear what she's saying. All I can hear is Hallie's last words to me. *Don't forget. And don't be late. Rory gets here at two so you need to come before that.*

I should have known something was wrong. Hallie had never called me during class and, even with all the distractions of the lecture hall around me, I could hear in her voice that she wasn't okay. I should have left class and gone straight to her dorm right after she called, then none of this would have happened.

"Houston?" Rory's voice is small and hesitant, the way she sounded when she called me yesterday to tell me she needed me.

"Yeah, I should probably let you two talk," I reply, my voice a bit taut. "I'm sure you both have a lot to say to each other."

My chest muscles tense as I force myself to breathe through the anger. With every second of silence and every breath I take, the tension increases, until I feel as if my chest might explode.

She sniffs. "Okay. We'll talk later."

"Do you have your room key?"

"Yes."

"Good. I'll meet you at the hotel later." I say the words quickly, hoping she'll get the hint that I want to get off the phone.

"Okay… Houston?"

"Yeah."

She sniffs a bit louder this time. "I love you."

"I love you more," I reply without hesitation, then I end the call.

I drop the phone into the cup holder and clear the address out of the GPS. Then I sit back and close my eyes as I try to think of how I'm going to make it work with Rory if I can't stand the thought of being anywhere near her father.

I wish I could take Rory somewhere far away, where our past is just a distant memory. A place where we could wake up next to each other every day. And I'd look into her hazel eyes, brush her hair off her face, and she'd smile at me. We'd live for each day, not worrying about the pain we left behind, not hoping for a future that may never come. We'd be totally present. We'd never check the weather or save up for a summer vacation. Or look at old photos or read the same book twice. We'd always be looking for a new surprise. A new adventure.

But that's a fairy tale. Real life is messy. People hurt each other, even when they love each other. All you can do is deal with it.

Pain is stronger and faster than you. It will outlast you. Running from pain is like running from a hungry lion in a maze with no exit. You can't outrun the lion. You might be able to hide from it for a while, but eventually it will find you. Better to take your chances and face it. It might be the end of you, but at least you'll die with dignity.

What if that's why Hallie took her own life? And why she didn't want me to show her suicide note to anyone. She wanted to die with dignity.

I head back to the hotel, but once I'm in the lobby, I turn in the opposite direction of the elevator, heading for the bar instead. The moment I sit down on the stool at the glossy mahogany bar, the thought of Hallie losing the battle against that lion comes back to me. Hallie's suicide note was my lion. I hid from it for years. I drank those years away in complete denial, until I finally got the courage to stare down my lion. And the battle isn't over yet. If I get shit-faced drunk right now, the way I want to, it will all have been for nothing.

The bartender nods at me, waiting for my order.

"Your best bourbon, neat."

He nods again and sets off toward the other end of the bar to grab a bottle of Wild Turkey Tradition, but my conscience won't allow it.

"Wait!" I call out and he turns around, his hand poised on the bottle. "Make it a club soda."

The guy doesn't miss a beat as he removes his hand from the bottle of Wild Turkey and sets about fixing me a glass of plain old club soda on ice. He probably gets recovering drunks in here all the time pulling the same stunt on him. He's seen it all. He doesn't bother patronizing me with a slice of lime in my soda. He sets it down in front of me, and I give him my room number to charge it.

But as I watch each bubble rise to the surface of the soda and burst, I can't help but wonder if staying sober even matters anymore. How am I supposed to face the man who destroyed my sister when he brings Rory back to the hotel today? How am I supposed to keep myself from slamming his fucking face into a wall?

How am I supposed to marry Rory if the thought of her father walking her down the aisle makes me sick?

I down the glass of club soda and head up to the room to call my mom. She's the only person in this world who has any clue what I'm feeling right now. Somehow, she was able to forgive James. I need to know how she did it.

I sit down on a stool at the wet bar in our suite and dial my mom's number. She picks up on the third ring, sounding somewhat out of breath.

"Hugh, what's wrong?" she asks, and I can tell she's engaged in some kind of physical activity.

"Nothing. Why do you sound out of breath?"

The rustling stops and she takes a few breaths before she answers. "Sorry, honey, I'm on my morning wog."

"Your *what*?"

"Wogging. It's a cross between walking and jogging. Lisa and I go wogging every Saturday and Sunday morning and weekday evenings. How do you think I stay fit? Sitting on my butt, drinking Barley Legal?"

I shake my head. "Call me back when you're done *wogging*."

"I can talk. I'm wearing my Bluetooth." I can practically hear her smiling at the mention of her Bluetooth, as if it makes her hip.

"I'd rather wait until you're alone. It's… it's about Hallie."

"Honey, Lisa and I hide nothing from each other. We can talk now."

I let out a sigh. "Do you remember when Hallie and Rory dressed up like CatDog for Halloween?"

She hoots with laughter. "Yes, I remember that. I remember Hallie said, 'I never realized how weird it is that CatDog has no butt. How does he fart?'"

"Then she ripped one and she couldn't stop laughing," I reply, leaning back on my barstool. "And Rory's face when she smelled it inside the costume… She was redder than a traffic light."

"Well, you're the one who used to say Hallie's stink bombs were lethal. Rory was probably red because the poor thing couldn't breathe."

I laugh out loud and silently thank myself for calling my mom. She's exactly the person I needed to talk to. As she chats with Lisa, I take a moment to compose myself, drawing in a deep breath as I prepare to steer the conversation in a different direction.

"Mom, there's something I need to ask you… about James."

The chatter on the other end stops. "What do you want to know?"

"I want to know what he said when he came to you all those years ago to confess. Like, his exact words."

"Oh, honey, I don't remember his exact words."

I think of how she just recited Hallie's words a moment ago from a Halloween that came years before, and I know she's not being honest.

"Mom, I need this. I'm…" I sit up straight on the stool. "I'm going to ask Rory to marry me, but I want to do it the right way. I want to ask her dad for his blessing."

"Hugh, you don't have to do that. No one does that anymore. It's a stupid tradition."

"No, it's not. It's a good tradition. Especially in this… this type of circumstance."

She sighs heavily. "Honey, you don't need anyone's blessing to be with the person you love. But if this is about more than getting her father's blessing… If this is about giving him your forgiveness, then I can tell you what he said."

"Tell me," I say, my voice coarse with emotion. "Tell me how you forgave him."

She's silent for a moment, though I can hear the faint sounds of cars passing. "He came to me and confessed what he and Hallie had done. And I didn't know if I wanted to kill him or if I myself wanted to die. Until he said something that made me realize… that there was no doubt in my mind that Hallie loved him."

"Mom, you told me about the messages and the stuff you found on the burner phone."

"No, I told you that when you came to me last month, but that was just more proof. There's… There's something I need to tell you."

"What is it?"

"Hold on, Hugh." She takes a moment to say good-bye to Lisa as they part ways, then I hear her padding up the steps and opening the front door. As the outdoor sounds fade away, she speaks again. "Hallie made me promise I'd never say anything to you. But ever since you came to me and confessed you'd been holding on to that note for her, I've been trying to figure out how to tell you this."

Rory

The park is bustling with picture-perfect families and their dogs. They're everywhere, except the tennis courts. Only one of the twelve courts is occupied by a couple of teenage girls engaged in a leisurely match. My dad and I take a seat on the bleachers farthest from the girls. Skippy sits at my feet, his chin resting on my knee.

I scratch his head as I gaze into his chocolate-brown eyes. "How did you know to come here?" I ask my dad.

"You're the one who told me to come here. We can go somewhere else if you want. Are you hungry?"

"No, Dad. How did you know to come here, to *California*? Did Mom talk to you?"

He leans forward on the metal bench, resting his elbows on his knees. "Yes, your mother came to speak to me this morning. She told me you were in trouble."

"I'm not in trouble. Houston is here."

He nods. "I know, sweetheart. I was just hoping you'd let me take the reins on this one."

I let out a sharp puff of laughter. "Did you come here just to piss him off?"

"What?" he says, turning his head to look at me. "Is that what you think this is about?"

Skippy's eyes begin to close as I continue petting him.

I shake my head. "I don't know what this is about. I feel like I don't know anything anymore. No one is who they seem."

My dad lets out a long sigh. "Rory, I had a professor in law school, Professor Houseman. He taught First Amendment Constitutional Law and he was a big proponent of a journalist's right to protect their sources. He would begin every lecture by asking us to write down a secret we knew about someone we loved, without disclosing the person's name, and dropping it into a box. At the end of the semester, he was going to read aloud some of those secrets and the names of the persons the secrets referred to."

I scrunched my eyebrows together in confusion. "I don't get it. If there were no names, how would he know?"

"He said that he had a fifty percent success rate in guessing who the secret was about and he would only read a few of them aloud. Participation in the exercise was mandatory."

"But… that's a terrible exercise."

He smiles. "Exactly, but it sure kept everyone on their toes. We were all certain we were going to hear some juicy secrets come the end of the semester. But when the day came, Professor Houseman admitted that only a few students had actually written down secrets, and he was not going to read them aloud."

"I don't get it."

My dad raises his eyebrows. "Neither did we, until Houseman explained it was an experiment to see who would sell out their friends' and family's secrets, while knowing there was a remote possibility those secrets could be revealed before the class. And in the end, less than a handful wanted to risk betraying their loved ones. He did it to make a point about freedom of the press. How laws that protect a journalist's sources allow journalists to tell the secrets the American people need to hear."

I heave a deep sigh. "I'm having a hard time seeing how this relates to my current situation."

"It has everything to do with you and Houston… and Hallie."

Hearing her name come out of his mouth makes my stomach burn. I cross my arms over my belly and lean forward.

"Rory, if Hallie had left you that suicide note instead of Houston, would you have told him what Hallie had confessed to you, and only you?" He pauses to let these words sink in. "You don't know, because just like Houston loved his sister, you loved your best friend, and you wouldn't want to betray her. Even after she was gone. It's human nature to protect your loved ones' secrets."

"Why are you telling me this? I've already forgiven Houston for keeping the note from me."

He sits up straight and turns to face me. "Because I want you to forgive me… and Hallie."

Anger crashes inside me. "I've already forgiven Hallie."

I expect my exclusion of him in this statement to get some sort of reaction out of him, but he continues, undaunted by my remark.

"Rory, there's a reason Hallie did what she did."

"I don't want to know her reasons. I don't want to know anything about it." I begin to get up, but he grabs my hand.

"Rory, you need to hear this. Then you'll understand why Hallie did what she did and why Houston did what *he* did, and why… why I never told you about any of this before today."

My empty stomach gurgles in protest. I should stop this conversation now. Whatever "secret" my father feels he needs to tell me now will most likely destroy any goodwill he accrued when he came to my rescue today.

I draw in an extended breath of air that smells like fresh-cut grass and morning dew. This park reminds me a little of Wortman Park, where Hallie and I often went after class let out when we were in middle school. Hallie and I would head straight past the picnic tables to the park restroom, so Hallie could freshen up her makeup, which had inevitably worn off during the rainy school day. Then we'd do our homework under the picnic shelters and wait. Once in a while, guys from McMinnville High would come by and I'd be stuck talking to the awkward one who couldn't stop stealing glances at my chest, while Hallie sneaked off to make out with one of his more experienced friends.

It was hardly ever the same group of guys. Eventually, word spread around the high school about Hallie, and Houston decided to show up at the park. He found Hallie and Greg Lerner making out under the eaves of the restroom building. Houston got in one good punch before Greg and his friends took off running out of the park. Hallie was more pissed with Houston than I had ever seen her, but I fell even more in love with him that day. Not just because he had protected Hallie from her growing bad reputation, but because he had saved me from all those awkward conversations with creepy high school boys.

I gaze out across the green and red rubberized tennis courts and let out a defeated sigh. "Hallie told us why she killed herself. In that note, she told us everything. Why should I believe whatever you're about to tell me?"

My father glances at me, then back to the empty tennis court, his lips pressed tightly together as if he's trying not to cry. "Because," he begins, his voice thick, "Hallie kept this a secret from everyone, even you and Houston. She wouldn't have put it in that note. The only people who know are me and Ava." He raises his head and turns to me. "Hallie was molested by a stranger when she was eleven years old."

My body begins to tremble and it takes me a moment to realize I'm not breathing. I let out a stale breath as tears roll down my cheeks.

"How do you know this?"

"She told me."

I shake my head. "Why would she tell you? Why didn't she tell me?"

"Rory, it has nothing to do with trust. It has everything to do with shame."

I close my eyes and cover my face as the tears come harder and faster. Because now *I'm* ashamed. I'm ashamed that Hallie didn't feel she could talk to me about this. I'm ashamed that my father knew my best friend's darkest secrets before I did. I ashamed that I never knew Hallie the way I thought I did.

"It happened shortly before they moved to McMinnville, when they were still living in Salem," he continues. "Ava and Darren had just divorced and Hallie went to a birthday party at one of the neighbors' houses. When she was there, a man she didn't recognize followed her into the bathroom. She told her mom a couple of days later, but since she didn't know who the man was, the neighbors didn't believe her and refused to cooperate. That's when Ava decided to move to McMinnville."

My stomach is clenched so tight, I have to keep reminding myself to breathe. I can't stop thinking about all the signs that were there, right in front of me, and I never saw them. Actually, I did see them, I just didn't know what they meant.

Hallie's promiscuity and occasional bouts of self-loathing… Her affinity for older men… Her drinking when we started college… Her shame over the affair… I thought it all stemmed from daddy issues, due to her father's virtual disappearance from her life. But it was so much more.

"But… why didn't she tell Houston?" I plead. "She told him about the affair. Why didn't she tell him about that?"

When I turn to my father, the sight of him brushing a tear off his cheek fills me with unfathomable sadness.

"Because in her mind, the affair made her a bad friend. But the molestation, and her father's abandonment, made her unworthy of love." He turns his face away from me to wipe away more tears. "That's why she never told you or Houston. She lived with an insurmountable fear of you two seeing her the way she saw herself."

I pull Skippy close to me and hug him, burying my face in the scruff of his neck. He smells a little like the dog food the hotel gave us, and suddenly I'm reminded of Houston, back at the hotel, completely oblivious to the bombshell my father just dropped on my heart. How is he going to take this? Does he already know?

"You didn't answer my question," I say, sniffing loudly as I turn to face my father again. "Why did she tell you?"

His face is dry now, but the regret etched into his face is unmistakable. "She loved me… And… in the short time I spent with her, I came to care for her very deeply."

"Did you love her?"

He clenches his jaw and takes a breath before he looks me in the eye. "I did. Not the way I loved your mother, but yes, I loved her. I wanted her to be okay, which is why I ended the affair after she told me about the abuse. I knew our relationship would do more harm than good to her." He lets out a sharp puff of air, as if a huge weight has been lifted from his chest. "I've spent the past six years ashamed of the things I've done. The many ways I've hurt you, your mother, Hallie's family… It wasn't until your mother stepped into my office this morning and told me I deserve to be forgiven that I even fathomed that might be a possibility." He reaches out and rests his hand on mine, and I stare at it. "Please look at me, Rory."

I swipe my other hand across my nose and look up.

"Rory, I'm sorry I haven't been there for you." He uses his other hand to wipe a tear from my cheek. "My greatest regret is that I allowed my guilt to get in the way of my responsibilities as a father. You deserved more from me… You deserved the truth, from the very beginning."

He pulls me into him as he wraps his arms around me, rubbing my back as I cry on his shoulder.

"All I ask is that you *try* to forgive me. I know it will take more than a trip to California to prove myself to you, but I'm willing to do whatever it takes."

I nod because I couldn't speak right now if I tried. He lets out a deep sigh of relief. But within seconds, Skippy begins to whine from being left out.

I let out a congested chuckle as I pull away from my father and pull Skippy into a tight hug. "Is that better, Skip?"

He responds by licking the salty tears off the bottom of my chin. I hold him tighter as I realize it's time to go back to the hotel and tell Houston what I've learned. I don't know what will hurt him more, knowing that Hallie was molested and she never told him, or that I'm ready to forgive my father.

Houston

The moment I end the call with my mom, I stand from the barstool and hurl my phone across the hotel suite. The phone shatters against the creamy wallpaper, falling to the carpet in a dozen useless pieces. I instantly feel a pang of guilt when I think of my mom begging me not to do anything stupid. But the feeling only lasts an instant, immediately replaced by a rumbling anger so loud it drowns out every other emotion.

A dark voice in the back of my mind begs to be heard over the roaring rage, whispering the same sentence over and over. *Hallie deserved better.*

She deserved the kind of brother she could trust with her darkest secrets. She obviously didn't feel she could trust me. Instead, she trusted *him.*

I walk toward the door leading out to the balcony. I pull the door open and the 101 freeway is barely visible through the thick luminescent clouds hanging low over Palo Alto. Somewhere out there Rory is with her father. Is he telling her Hallie's secret? If I know Rory the way I think I know her, it will destroy her. She was as much Hallie's sister as I was her brother.

How well do I really know Rory?

She waited most of her life for me, then the moment I made myself available to her, she left me for a guy she barely knew. Last night she didn't know if she'd ever be able to forgive her father, now she's sitting at a park with him. After I dropped everything to come save her yesterday, it's a fucking slap in the face.

Maybe it's not intentional, but it shows me that Rory has needs I can't fulfill. Demons she must slay without me. Pieces of her I've never truly known. May never know, unless we press pause to sort through the tangled mess we've made.

I glance at the clock on the wall behind the wet bar: 11:04 a.m. *Fuck.* It's not even noon and that's the third time today I've gotten bad news. I quickly clean up the shards of my smartphone and toss them in the trash. Then I use the hotel phone to call Rory, but the call goes straight to voicemail. Either her phone is turned off or it died. Come to think of it, I don't remember her charging it in the hotel.

As I place the hotel phone back on the cradle, I hear the soft buzz of an electronic lock followed by a soft click, then the door opens. Skippy gallops inside, tongue lolling as he jumps up on me. I crouch down to give him some love, but I keep my eye on Rory as she enters. Her back is to me. Even after she pulls her suitcase inside and closes the door, she stays facing the mahogany slab, her hand gripping the brushed metal handle.

I stand up and make my way to her. "Rory, what's wrong?"

She turns around and I'm not surprised to see her eyes are even puffier than they were this morning. "Detective Locke called. She said they found a flash drive in Liam's personal effects." She looks up at me and she doesn't have to finish that sentence for me to know what the detective told her. "There was nothing on it. The book is gone."

I pull her into my arms, wrapping my arms around her shoulders. "I'm so sorry," I mutter into her hair.

"It's not your fault."

"I know. I just wish there was something I could do to make it right."

She nuzzles her face into my chest as she holds me tightly. I squeeze her shoulders and rub her back. She feels so small. Smaller than usual.

"Baby, have you eaten?"

"I'm not hungry," she replies automatically, gently easing herself out of my arms. "Actually, I feel kind of sick." She reaches for the handle of her suitcase, but I take it from her.

"Maybe you feel sick because you haven't eaten."

"No, I feel sick because Liam is dead. My book is gone. And…" She turns away from me. "And because of what my dad just told me about Hallie."

I watch as she walks into the sitting area, unable to move as I realize we both got the same bad news at the same time. She has every right to be sickened by everything she's had to endure in the past twenty-four hours. There's no way I can lay my anger with her father on her right now.

She sinks down onto the sofa, absentmindedly scratching Skippy's head as he rests his chin on top of her thigh. He probably misses Sparky. This whole situation is ten levels of fucked up for everyone, especially for Rory.

Just like Hallie, I couldn't protect Rory from all the shit that's gone down in the past few weeks. I can't help but acknowledge that if I had protected Hallie from what happened to her when she was eleven, we probably never would have moved to McMinnville and met Rory. And if I had protected her and prevented her from taking her life, Rory and I probably never would have ended up together.

Maybe Rory doesn't need me to protect her. Maybe she just

needs me to be there. To be her friend.

I take a seat next to her on the sofa, but I don't wrap my arm around her. I just sit there for a few minutes in complete silence, waiting for her to say something. Finally, she turns her head to look up at me.

"Did your mom tell you about Hallie?"

I nod. "Just a few minutes ago." I reach for her hand, lacing my fingers through hers, relishing the softness of her skin. "There's no way we could have known. We can't blame ourselves."

She sniffs loudly then nods in agreement. "I guess so. I just… I wish I had known. I think things would have turned out differently."

"Maybe. But maybe everything would have happened the same way. There's no way to know. Besides, it's not so bad that after everything that's happened, we still ended up sitting right here, next to each other."

She looks up at me and flashes me a tiny smile.

"That's your first smile of the day," I remark. "I guess there's hope for you yet."

She heaves a deep sigh as her grip on my hand loosens. "But my book is still gone."

I squeeze her hand, then I use my other hand to lift her chin and look her in the eye. "Sometimes, when the story gets too complicated, it's best to toss it out and start again, from the very beginning."

She draws in a stuttered breath as she gazes up at me. "How did you get so wise about storytelling?"

"I had a very good teacher," I reply, pulling a stray piece of newly dyed brown hair away off her sticky cheek. "She used to hold class in the nude."

She chuckles. "Sounds like a weird teacher."

"Yeah, I guess she's kind of weird." I tuck the hair behind her ear. "But I love her."

She stares at me for a moment, then she climbs on top of me so she's straddling my lap. "I think she loves you, too."

I laugh, grabbing her face as she leans in to kiss me. "Shouldn't you eat something first, so you don't pass out?"

She narrows her hazel eyes. "Are you rejecting me?"

"I would never. I just think you should eat something first. You look sort of pale."

Her jaw drops at this comment. "My skin is always pale."

I draw in a long breath, gazing longingly at the swell of her breasts. "I can't believe I'm about to say this, but I think there's something we need to talk about before we do that."

Her mouth closes and she suddenly looks confused. "What do we need to talk about?"

I let out a soft chuckle. "A lot of things, but mostly… the fact that I'm not sure how to deal with this new phase of our relationship. The part where I'm supposed to forgive your dad."

Her shoulders slump as her gaze falls to my chest. "Yeah, I guess we should talk about that."

I lift her chin again. "Rory, I don't want to hurt you."

"How would you hurt me?"

"I don't know. All I know is that I'm entering uncharted waters here." I take her face in my hands. "The person I love more than anything in this world happens to be related to the person I thought I hated more than anyone for the past six years. You have to understand how difficult it is for me to just… suddenly change the way I feel. He's your father, but… it's not that easy for me."

She winces as if she's in physical pain. "Are you saying… you can't be with me?"

"No," I respond firmly. "I'm not saying that at all."

"Then what *are* you saying?"

Rory

Houston sighs heavily as he lets go of my face. "I think… I need some time to get used to this."

I narrow my eyes at him. "What does that mean?"

"It means I think we should step back, give ourselves a chance to get to know each other better, all the gritty stuff and the boring stuff, all of it, before we jump into this again." He reaches up and grabs my face again. "I want to do it right this time. No moving in together from the first day. No drunken tirades and unresolved tension. Just you and me, without all the other bullshit. Getting to know each other… Forgiving each other."

The sharp sting of rejection throbs in every part of my body. "You don't want to live with me."

"I just think we need time to sort everything out before we jump in headfirst again."

My stomach burns with hunger and shame as I push his hands off my face. "You couldn't have told me this last night? Or did you have to fuck me five times before you could be sure you didn't want to live with me?"

He grabs my hands to stop me from sliding off his lap. "That's not fair, Rory. A lot has changed since we got here last night. Liam is gone. We both know what happened to Hallie. And your dad… You need your dad."

"This is about my dad?" My chest aches as his gaze falls. "Are you asking me to choose between you and my dad?"

His eyes snap up. "What? No! That's not what I'm asking at all."

"Then what is it?" I demand. "You said it yourself, a lot has changed since last night. I have no job, no home, no book. I've lost everything except you, and you think *now* is the best time to put some distance between us?"

"You haven't lost everything. You'll have a job when we get back to Portland. And I'm sure Kenny will have no problem sharing your apartment, or even my apartment, until he finds something else. And your book will be better the second time."

I groan with frustration. "You don't get it. I don't want to *think* about that book, much less rewrite it."

The muscle in his jaw twitches. "It's not just a book. It's our story."

"It *was* our story," I reply, my voice taking on a hard edge. "Now it's gone."

He turns his head and stares off into the distance as he considers this. I stare at his hands, where they rest on his abdomen, holding mine. His thumbs absentmindedly stroke the tops of my fingers. There's a raw scrape on the knuckle of his right hand and my stomach tenses as I realize it's probably from his scuffle with Liam last night.

If I had taken the time to listen to Houston when I was still in Portland, none of this would have happened. I know I didn't make Liam do what he did, but I'm not dumb enough to believe I'm blameless. I have to accept responsibility for my role in Liam's death. Only then can I begin to forgive myself. I couldn't have known what Liam was capable of, but now I know what Houston is capable of.

He spent weeks orchestrating a plan to try to make my dreams come true. Then he came running to me in my time of need. The least I can do is listen to him.

"I don't want anything else to come between us," he begins, turning back to me. "I don't know how we've survived this far, but I know I'm not going to risk throwing that away again." He squeezes both my hands. "I wasn't lying when I told you I would put that ring on your finger, but you need to let me do it the right way. Not the way I've done it in the past." He brings my left hand to his lips and plants a soft kiss on my knuckles. "All I'm asking for is a little time."

I let out a deep sigh. "So, are we supposed to just be friends or something?"

He chuckles and the sparkling hope in his eyes makes me smile. "Nothing would make me happier than calling you my friend."

"You're so full of shit."

He laughs louder. "I'll admit it would be nice to be friends with benefits."

"No," I say, shaking my head. "I'll do whatever you want, but no benefits."

His eyebrows shoot up. "But all I want is benefits."

I stare at him, trying not to smile at the devious look in his eyes. "After all the trouble you went through to get me back, I owe it to you to make sure we do this right."

His expression turns serious as he takes my face in his hands and plants a kiss on the tip of my nose. "You were worth every second of it."

I lean my forehead against his, inhaling each breath he exhales. His hands slide down to lightly caress my neck and a chill races through me. He fingers whisper over my shoulders as his breathing quickens and he parts his lips. I lean closer to him, my mouth almost on his, when he tightens his grip on my shoulders and gently pushes me back a few inches.

I'm too stunned to speak. He's really serious.

His eyes narrow a bit, as if he's unsure about what he just did. "This is going to be very hard."

My mouth drops open as I feel his erection growing beneath me. "No kidding."

He nods. "Maybe I should eat something—I mean, *we* should eat something."

Suddenly, a palpable sadness comes over me as I realize this may be the last time I'll be this close to Houston for a while.

"Can you hold me first? Just for a little while?"

He tilts his head to the side as his gaze skims over my face. "Come here."

He wraps his arms around my waist and pulls me close, crushing my body against his as I coil my arms around his shoulders and lay my cheek on his solid shoulder. We sit like this for a while, with me trying not to brush my lips over his neck and him trying not to make it obvious he's breathing in the scent of my hair. Our chests press together until our heartbeats are synced and our muscles begin to relax. With every breath I take, I feel his hold on me loosening and I know that, like every scene in every book I've ever read, this will end soon. But I've never dreaded an ending more than this one.

Reluctantly, I pull away from him and he reaches for my face. I grab his hand before he can touch my cheek. There's sadness in his eyes as I gently lower his hand.

"This isn't the end," he says, as if he can read my thoughts.

I nod. "I know. It's the unraveling."

His eyebrows scrunch together at this word. "The unraveling?"

"The unraveling comes just before the resolution. When we get to the resolution, that will be the end."

The left side of his mouth turns up in a half smile. "Well,

Professor Charles, I must say this is much more difficult than I imagined."

"What's more difficult?"

"Paying attention when you're fully clothed."

I smack his arm, then I slide off his lap. "Get used to it."

Part 5: Acceptance

"Then, she let it go."

Houston

It took two days and three meetings with Detective Dana Locke for us to get the go-ahead to leave California. Locke explained that any criminal or civil proceedings against the security guards or the hotel would probably see us called back to testify in the coming months. For now, we're free to go about our lives as if the worst is behind us. If two nights spent sleeping in separate beds in the same hotel room has taught me anything, the worst is far from over.

The lousiest part of those two nights wasn't trying to keep myself from having sex with Rory. Though that took considerable effort. The worst part was listening to her crying in the middle of the night and not knowing what to do. I broke the separate beds rule the second night, to comfort her. But as she laid her head on my bare chest, just the whisper of her breath on my skin awoke the beast. She tried to ignore the tent I'd constructed under the covers, but eventually she burst out laughing. I suppose there are worse ways to comfort someone.

By the time we land in Portland at a quarter past noon, Rory and Kenny have hashed out their new living arrangements over text message. Rory and I throw ourselves, and Skippy, into the back of a cab outside the airport. She gives the driver the cross-streets to her mother's apartment in the Pearl District. I know Rory's not exactly happy about giving up her apartment to Kenny and moving in with her mom, but I'm glad she'll be just a few blocks away from me now. Once this cooling-off period is over, it will be much easier to move her into my apartment if she's nearby.

I give the driver the cross-streets to Barley Legal headquarters and Rory cocks an eyebrow at me. "What?" I reply. "I've been gone for almost four days. My assistant needs me to sign some stuff."

"You don't mind your assistant seeing you like that?"

I look down at the same T-shirt and jeans I've been wearing for the past four days. I would have purchased an extra outfit or two in Palo Alto if I'd known how long Detective Locke would keep us there. I opted instead to have my clothes laundered at the hotel, which gave Rory endless opportunities to mock me while I walked around the suite in a bathrobe. I pretended to begrudge her taunting, but the truth is I was happy to be a source of levity.

"I sign Adaline's paychecks. I doubt she'd dare to judge me for wearing the same outfit I wore last week."

"Adaline? That's your assistant's name?" She continues staring out the window. I can't see her face, but the taut thread of jealousy in her voice in unmistakable. "It's a beautiful name," she concludes.

"For a beautiful girl," I reply coolly.

She whips her head around and narrows her eyes when she sees me smiling. "You're trying to bait me. It's not going to work."

"We'll see."

She leans forward to address the cab driver. "You can drop him off first, please."

I chuckle. "Anxious to be rid of me already?"

"No, I just want to pay for my portion of the ride after we drop you off." She sits back and smiles at me. "We're going dutch now, aren't we?"

It dawns on me as the driver pulls up in front of the large brick Barley Legal building that Rory has never been inside. When the cab pulls up next to the curb, Skippy stands up on the seat between us, wagging his tail as he expects this is his stop.

"Sorry, bud. You have to go home with that mean woman," I say as I take a few twenties out of my wallet and hand them to the driver. "Unless you two want to come inside and see where all the magic happens."

Rory wraps her arms around Skippy's chest to keep him from escaping as I reach for the door handle. "Do they allow mean women in there? Or would that destroy some of the magic?"

I shrug. "Come inside and we'll find out."

"I'd rather not live dangerously anymore, thank you," she says, pulling Skippy onto her lap.

I nod. "Another time." I stare at her hands clutched around Skippy's black fur for a moment. "Call me anytime you want to talk."

"I know," she replies automatically, refusing to meet my gaze.

"I'm serious," I say, reaching out to lift her chin. "I know your mom's going to drive you crazy. And there'll be times you just need a place to get away. I don't care what time of day or night, call me or come over. I'll stop by to give you a key soon."

She looks me straight in the eye, but I can't decipher the quizzical expression she's wearing. "I don't want the key, but I'm sure I'll be calling you. In fact, can I ask you for my first friendly favor?"

"Anything."

She presses her lips together as her eyes glisten with tears. "Don't forget me this time."

I lean forward, gently pressing my lips to her forehead, then I whisper in her ear, "Never."

I resist the urge to reach up, run my fingers through her hair, and kiss her. I settle for letting Skippy lick my cheek instead, then I hop out of the cab and into the rain, where I watch my Scar taken away from me.

Troy joins me on the sidewalk with his hoodie pulled tightly over his head. We both watch as the cab turns the corner and disappears. "I'm sure you're doing the right thing," he says, patting me on the back.

He's referring to Rory and me taking a break to get to know each other. I told him about it in one of our many conversations over the past few days when he was shitting bricks, thinking that Rory or I was going to be charged in connection with Liam's death. Luckily, the whole altercation was recorded on the hotel's surveillance cameras, and clearly showed that neither Rory nor I were in any way responsible for Liam going into cardiac arrest. I didn't even call my lawyer to come to California. Of course, when I told Troy about our plan to take a break, he thought it was the stupidest thing he'd ever heard.

I shake my head and let out a deep sigh as I head toward the entrance to the Barley Legal Pub. "I'm so fucking in love with her. This is going to be torture."

"No one's making you do this."

"I am," I reply, opening the door for Troy to enter. "She needs to know that I'm serious. And I need to know that she's serious."

Troy laughs, though I can barely hear him over the sound of the lunch-rush customers. "The girl's been serious about you since she was in diapers," he shouts, waving back at the bartender, Wilma, who's actually waving at me.

I nod and smile at her as we both head toward the kitchen. "Yeah, that's what I thought until I divorced my wife for her and she thanked me by moving six hundred miles away." I grit my teeth against this painful truth. "She needs time… to get to know the real me, not this heroic image of me she's built up in her head."

Troy cocks an eyebrow as we enter the bustling kitchen area. "I think that might be the most mature thing I've ever heard you say." He covers his mouth and gasps. "My little Houston is growing up."

"Shut the fuck up. I'm serious as hell," I reply, shaking my head. "This is going to be pure torture."

He shrugs as he snags a couple of beers out of the cooler. "Just keep reminding yourself how long she waited for you. You can wait a few more months for her."

Once I sign the checks for Adaline, I head back to the elevator to leave. Troy is standing there waiting for me.

"Oh, yeah. Thanks for picking up my car from the airport," I say, pressing the call button. "The last thing I needed was to get it towed for parking in overnight parking for three days."

"No sweat." As soon as we step out of the elevator onto the first floor, he heads for the employee lot in the back of the building. "You coming?"

"I'm just gonna check on a few things in the kitchen," I reply. "You go ahead."

His face scrunches up in confusion. "What are you talking about? I'm taking you to get fitted for your tux."

He opens the back door and we stand there for a moment, as if the pouring rain will suddenly stop just so we can walk to Troy's car. If there's one thing I've learned recently, it's that rain is a constant. Your time is better spent building a strong boat than wishing for the rain to stop.

"You may suck at relationships," Troy remarks, "but you're still my best man."

I shake my head as I step out into the parking lot. "I may suck at relationships, but at least I don't suck wedding-planner dick."

A homeless man rounds the corner of the building into the lot, probably hoping to take cover under the eaves of the shipping dock.

"Touché," Troy says as he continues toward his vintage Ford Torino. "I'm deep-throating this fucker ten times a day lately. He's got me dancing like a fucking single mom at a strip club."

His voice trails off as I make my way toward the homeless man, whose rain-soaked stench I can smell from ten feet away. He sees me walking toward him and turns around to head out of the lot. He probably assumes I'm going to remind him he's trespassing in a private lot.

"Hey, man," I call out.

He holds up his hand as if to say, *No need to say anything. I'm already leaving.*

"Hey, I'm not telling you to leave," I say, louder this time.

He stops and the pattering sound of the rain coming down on the trash bag he's using as a hood breaks my heart. I don't know who this guy is or how he came to be homeless, but that's exactly why I feel myself being drawn to him. There are billions of humans in this world with billions of secrets. Some of those secrets are toxic enough to destroy us. Send us spiraling into a bottomless pit until one day we're sleeping on a street corner or staring down the barrel of a gun.

He looks at me through the damp scrabble of hair matted around his gaunt features. "What do you want?"

His voice is raspy and hollow. He's naturally suspicious of me as I approach him, but something in his eyes tells me he knows I mean him no harm.

I come within a few feet of him when I stop. "I was hoping I could take you to get something to eat."

He narrows his eyes at me, almost angry with this suggestion. "Are you gonna try to convert me? 'Cause I don't need no religion."

I laugh at this. "Nah, man. I was just thinking you might want something to eat. Someone to talk to."

He's silent for a moment before he nods. "Okay."

I turn around and shout at Troy that we'll have to reschedule the fitting for the tux. Then I lead the silent homeless man around the corner toward the front of the building, where we enter the pub together. Once we're seated at a table in the second-floor dining area, he shrugs when asked what he wants to eat. I order him a soda and a few of the pub favorites, then I instruct our waitress to make herself scarce.

The man finally speaks up once he's had a few sips of Coke. He tells me his name is Justin Holmes. That he's been homeless since he got back from Afghanistan and his parents couldn't deal with his PTSD and his refusal to take medication. He swears he doesn't do drugs. He only drinks.

About an hour into lunch, he becomes very quiet again as he sets his filthy napkin on the table. "Why are you doing this?"

I smile as I lean forward, resting my elbows on the table. "I had a sister once. She had a lot of dreams. Lots of things she wanted to do, but she died before the world could see how amazing she was." I look him in the eye and he meets my gaze as he waits for me to finish. "You want to know why I'm doing this? Because everyone deserves to have their story heard."

Rory

I'm not surprised to find my mom waiting outside in the rain with her umbrella when the cab pulls up to her apartment building. I'm also not surprised to find that the wad of cash Houston handed the driver a few minutes ago was *way* more than enough to cover my cab ride. I *am* surprised by the driver's honesty and refusal to charge me another cent.

He sets my suitcase on the curb and nods his head as he hurries back into the dry sanctuary of his cab. My mom is dressed in all black as she rushes over with her black umbrella. For some reason, the image of a bat pops into my mind.

"I'm fine, Mom," I insist, swerving out from underneath her rayon wing.

"Suit yourself," she replies, rushing into the lobby of her building.

The cool slate floors and the crackling warmth coming from the fireplace on our right seem to contradict each other, but it does smell inviting. I haven't visited my mom's building since last summer, but if I recall correctly, the building manager had an air-freshener system installed in the ventilation ducts running through the lobby. Right now, they seem to be pumping out the scent of blackberry and leather-bound books. An odd combination, though quite appropriate for my mother.

She takes me past the doorway that leads to the mail room, and straight to the elevator. "How was your flight?" she asks, unable to keep herself from glancing down at the pool of rainwater collecting beneath me and my suitcase.

"It was fine. First time I get to fly first class and the flight wasn't even long enough for them to serve us warm cookies."

She flashes me a tight smile as we step inside the elevator. "You don't have to pretend everything is okay, Rory."

Skippy and I step into the corner of the elevator and stare at the panel as she presses the button for the fourth floor. My vision blurs and I blink furiously, successfully preventing the tears from falling. I've cried enough the past four days to last me for quite a while.

"I'm fine," I say, refusing to look at her.

"That's the third time you've said *fine* since you stepped out of that cab."

I turn my face away from her because I can't stop the flood of tears this time. She takes my suitcase as the elevator doors slide open and I let her pull it behind her until we reach apartment 405. Two and a half years ago, when my mom first moved into this apartment, I teased her about the unit number. I said, "Of course you live in 405, the number responsible for endless gridlock and misery." It was a terrible joke about the horrendous traffic on the 405 freeway. Now, it seems more like a self-fulfilling prophecy.

The moment the door closes behind me, Skippy gallops away somewhere behind me, probably to lie down on my mom's bed, his favorite place at Grandma's house. My mom sets her damp umbrella in the stand and takes me into her arms. The pain is everywhere. Every inch of my skin, my bones, my insides, everything aches. And I don't know what hurts more, losing my book and my home, that I played a part in Liam's death, the possibility that I never really knew my best friend, or that Houston wants to figure out his life without me.

"Everything's wrong." I squeeze the words out through the tears. "And I didn't see it coming."

She strokes my hair. "Oh, honey. If we could see these things coming, they'd never happen."

I gently push her away and head for the bathroom to get a tissue off the counter. She follows me in, watching me in the mirror as I wipe my face. She looks like she wants to tell me something, but she doesn't know if this is the right time.

"What is it?" I ask, tossing the tissue into the waste bin.

"Your father's coming. He wants to check on you."

I shrug, too upset to care. "That's fine."

"Fine?" She purses her lips. "Surely you're familiar with *other* adjectives?"

"I don't feel very familiar with anything or anyone right now, Mom."

She tucks a piece of hair behind my ear. "It may feel that way, but you have a lot of people who love you, Rory. Don't forget that." We stand in silence for a moment, before she chimes in with more news. "I invited your father over for dinner. Come with me to the store to get a few things."

"For dinner? What is this, some kind of intervention?"

She rolls her eyes. "You don't have to come with me, but feel free to shower. Your father won't be here for another four or five hours."

"Are you saying I stink?"

"It's the traveling. Airplanes have a certain… smell."

I sigh as I realize the next few weeks or months, however long I have to endure this living arrangement, are going to be more painful than I imagined. "Bye, Mom."

"I'll be back in a few minutes. Do you want anything from the market?"

"An apartment."

She shakes her head as she leaves the bathroom. I wait for the sound of the front door opening and closing before I head back into the living room to get my suitcase. That's when I notice the stack of freshly laundered blankets and pillows on the sofa. I have to remember not to invite Kenny over here. The only reason he agreed to keep my apartment in Goose Hollow is because I lied about my mom having an extra bedroom she wasn't using.

"This is the unraveling," I remind myself aloud.

My mom said she had cleared out a few drawers and some hanging space in her walk-in closet for me to put my clothes away. But the moment I throw the suitcase on my mom's bed and open it, the smell of Liam's cologne hits my olfactory nerve and I'm frozen. I stare at the colorful mashup of cotton and denim, unable to make sense of it.

Then I realize this suitcase is the rest of my life, everything thrown together haphazardly then shaken up until none of it makes the least bit of sense. And running through every inch of fabric, every frayed thread of memory is colored, scented, by Liam.

I shove the suitcase off the bed and it lands with a loud thump on the wood floor, startling Skippy, who was napping peacefully on my mom's pillow. He jumps off the bed and sniffs the toppled contents, barking at the pile of clothes a few times. He can smell it too.

By the time my mom returns from Whole Foods with two bags of groceries, every article of clothing I own is stuffed into her washing machine. Lights and whites mixed with darks, bras mixed with jeans. I don't care. I'm wrapped in the bathrobe my mother keeps hanging in her bathroom for guests, as if her apartment is a luxury hotel. It might as well be.

I'm aware my father has been paying my mother a generous sum in alimony for the past six years, but I've never cared to ask how much. There's no way my mother could live this well on a teacher's pension. And now that I'm reminded just how *well* she's been living, I wonder if she was so willing to take his money because of what she suspected he'd done, as some form of retribution.

My mom raises an eyebrow when she sees me in the robe. I try not to think of the irony of her mocking me when I was just mocking Houston for this very thing yesterday.

"Do you need help with dinner?" I ask, eager to do anything to keep my mind off everything.

She sets the bag of groceries on the kitchen counter and shakes her head. "No, I have it covered, but can you help me with something on my computer? It's over there on the coffee table. I can't seem to remember the password for iTunes."

"Did you try resetting it?"

"Of course I did, but it asked me some very strange verification questions. I think my account was hacked."

A spark of pain fires in my chest at the mention of being hacked, but I try not to let it show as I make my way to the sofa. I grab the laptop off the coffee table and set it in my lap. When I open it up, there's a picture of Skippy above the space to enter her user password. I roll my eyes at my mother's attachment to my dog.

"What's your password?" I shout at her as she turns on the faucet to wash some produce.

"Skippy nine zero," she calls back to me.

Skippy90.

My dog's name followed by the year I was born. Nice to see my mother takes Internet security so seriously.

I type in the password and expect her desktop to open up for me, but what I see instead takes me by surprise. My mom has Microsoft Word open to a document titled "The Story of Us - First Draft." I glance at the bottom of the document and see the word count: 143,767. I can tell right away that this isn't my book. This is *her* book.

"Did you fix it?"

Her voice startles me and I slam the laptop shut. Then I remember I was supposed to be helping her with something, so I open it up again. I type the password once more and the sight of the document gives me heart palpitations. I want to read it, but I also don't want to.

"Did you fix it?"

I look up and she's staring straight at me with a tomato in one hand and a very large chef's knife in the other. "N-no. Not yet."

"What's wrong with you? You look like you've seen—" Her gaze falls to the computer in my lap and her eyes widen. "Oh, my God. Close that! Close it now!"

I slam the laptop shut and she drops the tomato and knife on the counter before she hurries over to retrieve it. "I didn't read it," I assure her.

She doesn't say anything as she disappears into the bedroom and slams the door behind her. I find myself struggling. One moment I'm trying not to listen to the noises coming from her bedroom, then the next I'm listening for any hint of a drawer opening, trying to determine where she could be hiding the laptop. After all, she did read *my* book without my permission.

She exits the bedroom a minute later and heads straight for the kitchen, where she picks up the knife and tomato again. I don't know if I should approach her in this state, while she's wielding a sharp object, but I can't just say nothing.

I enter the kitchen slowly, watching as she peels an onion. "I didn't read it, Mom. I swear."

She shakes her head, but again she doesn't say a word.

"Mom, please say something. Anything."

She bites her lip as she cuts the onion in half and the resounding thwack of the knife hitting the cutting board sends a jolt of anxiety through me.

"Be careful, or you'll cut yourself."

"I will be just fine, Rory," she says, her voice taut with an unreadable emotion.

Is she angry? Embarrassed? Annoyed?

"Fine? Surely you're familiar with *other* adjectives?"

She rounds on me and the fiery anger in her eyes turns my smug grin to ashes. "I know I shouldn't be upset with you," she says, pointing the knife at me. "Especially since I read your manuscript without your permission. But I'm upset." She throws her hands in the air. "I'm upset. Okay?"

"Okay, Mom, give me the knife," I say, approaching her slowly.

She looks at me like I'm crazy, then she looks at the knife in her hand as if she's seeing it for the first time. She shakes her head as she drops it onto the cutting board and turns to face me.

She opens her mouth to say something, but nothing comes out. Her hands slide into the front pockets of her black apron, then they come out again as she tries to think of something to say. Finally, she grabs the counter for support.

"I've been working on that book for a very long time. And it's embarrassing that I haven't stopped. I should have deleted the damn file years ago."

"I know how you feel, Mom."

"No, you don't understand." She lets out a deep sigh and looks me in the eye. "I've been working on it since the day I met your father. I… Please don't tell him."

"He doesn't know?"

She scrunches up her face in disgust. "God no. The man is clueless. He wouldn't recognize a book about him unless it was leather-bound and published by the *Harvard Law Review.*"

I shake my head in disbelief. "You mean to tell me you were married to the man for, what, twenty years and he never asked what your book was about?"

"Oh, he asked plenty of times. I lied."

"Why?"

She stares at the floor for a moment before she looks up at me. "I don't know. And now that I think of it, that had to be some kind of sign. You told Houston right away, but I could never bring myself to tell your father. I guess I figured if I wasn't going to get it published, it didn't matter."

My face falls as I look around the kitchen and notice all the produce, the water boiling on the stove, the bottle of red wine aerating on the counter. "Mom, are you… still in love with him?"

She looks at me with utter horror in her eyes. "What? No! No, no, no, no, no. Absolutely not."

"But…" I wave my hand at all the trappings of a romantic dinner. "What's all this?"

Her shoulders slump. "It's for you. Your father wanted us to have dinner so he could talk to you about seeing a therapist. He wanted to take us to dinner, but I knew you wouldn't go for that. So I offered to cook."

"So this *is* an intervention?"

She shrugs and casts me a sheepish grin. "Please don't tell him about the book," she pleads.

"I won't," I mutter, taking a seat in a dining chair as the gravity of the situation begins to hit me.

"And do us both a favor and feign gratitude when he offers to pay for your therapy."

I open my mouth to protest, but my mother's severe expression stops me. "Fine."

"It will be good for you, Rory."

I look up at her and my smug smile returns. "I'll go to therapy if you show me your book."

Rory

Three days later

"What is the point of having a dishwasher if you still wash the dishes before placing them inside?"

My mom casts me a look of utter exasperation. "Rory, the role of clichéd young adult does not suit you well. Just rinse the glass and be done with it."

"Oh, so now I'm playing a role? Just another *character* in your book, am I?"

She lets out a harsh sigh as she reaches for the glass in my hand, but I yank my arm back.

"I can rinse the damn glass," I say, turning to the sink and flipping on the water to full blast.

A bit of water bounces off the glass as I rinse it, splashing both my mother and me in the face. I chuckle softly as she smacks the faucet handle down to turn the water off.

"Stop acting like a child."

I place the glass in the dishwasher then cross my arms over my chest. "Well, that's what I've been reduced to, isn't it? Your dependent child? No job. Living with my mom. No boyfriend. I just need a cat to complete this English-major cliché. Is there anything about self-fulfilling prophecies in your book?"

She shakes her head as she turns on her heel. She's not in the mood for the same argument we've been having for the past three days since I agreed to accept my father's financial assistance with seeking a therapist.

"I'm not allowing you to bait me into this argument again," she replies tersely as I follow her out of the kitchen. "I will show you the book *after* you've completed your therapy."

She enters the living room, where she grabs her iPad off the coffee table and proceeds to curl up on the sofa as if the argument is over.

"Are you kidding me?" My laughter sounds a bit hysterical. "I could be in therapy for *years* for all the shit I've been through."

"Watch your language, Rory."

"You didn't seem to mind my language when you were reading *my book*!"

She shoots me a look that could slice me in half. "I was editing your book. There's a difference."

"So I need to offer to edit your book in order for you to show it to me? Is that it?"

"Don't be ridiculous."

"Oh, because you couldn't possibly learn anything from me, could you?"

Her glare softens. "That's not what I meant."

The knock at the door saves me from further response. "Bye, Skippy!" I shout toward the bedroom as I snatch my purse off the stand next to the front door and exit the apartment without saying good-bye to my mother. This pettiness is not like me.

Houston and Kenny are standing in the carpeted hallway, their faces positively beaming with sunlight when juxtaposed against the gun-metal gray color on the walls. My shoulder bumps Houston's chest as I exit the apartment in a hurry. He looks down at me, his smile melting into a puzzled expression.

"You dyed your hair auburn?" The sexy easygoing smile he flashes me is infuriating.

"Yes. Can we go now?"

"What's the rush?" he asks with a chuckle.

I turn to Kenny, as if he's the one who asked the question. "My mom and I had a fight. We can't go in there right now."

Kenny's bright blue eyes dim as his shoulders slump. "But I wanted to see my Peppermint Patty."

I roll my eyes as I set off toward the elevator. "Please don't call her that. It's already weird enough that she read the sex scenes in my book. Now my best friend has an affectionate nickname for her?" I punch the elevator button then glance at Houston long enough to catch the skeptical look on his face. "She infiltrated my life and now she's refusing to afford me a shred of honesty in return."

Houston and Kenny are silent as we enter the elevator, and also as we descend to Parking Level One. The silence continues as we approach Houston's SUV in guest parking, nothing but the sound of my heels clicking against the pavement and echoing off the concrete walls. Houston deactivates his car alarm, then, out of habit or chivalry, he arrives at the passenger door before me, ready to open it for me.

"Don't do that," I say before he can reach the door handle.

He cocks an eyebrow. "I'm not allowed to open your door?"

"No. I'm perfectly capable of opening car doors on my own, believe it or not."

He rolls his eyes and sets off to the driver's side. I sigh as I reach for the handle, but Kenny beats me to it.

He giggles as he opens the door for me. "No rules that say I can't open your door, m'lady."

My mouth curves into a reluctant smile. "Thank you."

"Not so fast. My services aren't free. I require payment in the form of awkwardly long hugs." He holds out his arms to me. "Aurora, it's the first time I've seen you in three weeks."

I wrap my arms around his waist and press my cheek to his shoulder as he envelops me in a warm hug. "Three weeks is a long time?" I ask.

He gasps. "With everything that's happened, it's practically a lifetime."

I let him go, making sure not to look at him as I climb into the car. "I don't want to talk about the past three weeks."

I slam the door shut and pretend not to notice the icicles forming inside the car during our silent ride to Killer Burger. I know Kenny and Houston are not intentionally being cold. They're probably just trying not to upset me, but somehow the silence feels even worse than the cause of the silence.

"I'm sorry," I mutter as Houston turns left onto Stark Street. "I didn't mean to be short with either of you. I'm just frustrated."

Houston takes his eyes off the road to flash me an easy smile. "You're not the only one."

I shake my head as I turn in my seat to look at Kenny. "Can you forgive me?"

He tilts his head as he pretends to ponder my request. "I guess there's still room in my heart for the girl with the dirtiest mind I've ever known."

Houston laughs. "You don't know the half of it."

I gasp as I smack his arm. "Did my mom show you my book?"

He looks at me like I'm crazy as he rubs his arm. "Are you forgetting that I was there?"

Kenny bites his lip, trying not to smile when he says, "Fifty Shades of Houston."

I grab the water bottle in Houston's cup holder and throw it at Kenny, who dodges it quite deftly. "That's not funny."

"Not even a little bit?" Kenny says, and I shoot him a

piercing glare. "Okay, it's terrible that the book is gone, but you have to admit that it will be a lot more fun creating new sex scenes, right?"

Houston doesn't look at me as he turns right on Third, but I can see the confusion register on his face. He doesn't know I haven't told Kenny about our "friends with no benefits" arrangement. I guess a part of me has been hoping that Houston would change his mind and save me the trouble of having to explain. I guess I was wrong.

"Did I say something wrong?" Kenny asks tentatively.

"No," I reply with a sigh. "We're just… not together right now. But…" I look to Houston for help, but he's busy checking the cross-traffic on Alder. "We don't want to make a big deal about. It's just something we're trying."

"Speak for yourself," Houston finally responds. "I, for one, want to throw a party in honor of the bluest balls this side of the Willamette."

"It was *your* idea!" I shriek.

Kenny gasps. "Houston! After everything we did? How could you?"

Houston shakes his head as he turns into the lot on Second Avenue. "On second thought, I think Rory's right. Let's not make a big deal about this."

I lean my back against the inside of the passenger door and smile. "Fine, but there's one thing we need to get straight. Are we allowed to see other people?"

Houston slams on the brakes so hard my seat belt goes taut and cuts into my neck.

He narrows his eyes at me as his mouth hangs open in disbelief. "Did you really just ask me if you could see other people?"

"I was kidding," I reply, my heart racing as I try to sit back to release some of the tension on my seat belt.

He finishes pulling into the parking space. "Kenny, can you wait outside for us?"

"Yes, sir," Kenny mutters as he slides out of the SUV and shuts the door softly behind him.

Houston glares at me and I stare right back at him. "Don't bullshit me, Rory. Were you kidding?"

My gaze falls to his heaving chest and I swallow hard as I try to think of a good response. "I… No, but… I mean, obviously I don't want to see other people. I guess I was just trying to get a rise out of you."

He draws in a deep breath and lets it out slowly. "Rory, look at me." He waits until I look him in the eye before he continues. "We need to get this straight. I didn't suggest taking a break so I could fuck other girls. And I swear to God, I don't know what I'll do if I see you with someone else. Please don't put me in that position."

"I would never do that."

He nods as he slides the key out of the ignition. "Thank you. Now let's go have a fucking burger."

"A fucking burger?" I say, reaching for the door handle. "Is that the kind of burgers they serve in Fifty Shades of Houston?"

He shakes his head as he steps out of the car. "Be careful there, little lady, or I'll be showing you fifty shades of no mercy tonight."

I laugh as I slide out of the passenger seat and land on the asphalt. "I think you'll be the one begging for mercy tonight."

"Game on, baby."

"Game on."

Houston texts Troy as we walk through the parking lot and Troy instantly responds, telling us he's seated in the bar area. When we enter Killer Burger, it's packed, though I expected no less on a Friday night. The line queued up at the counter to order a burger is at least six deep.

"Maybe you should order for me, so I can go say hi to Troy," I suggest to Houston, but he shakes his head. "Am I not allowed to leave your side?"

He grins at this question. "You go right ahead, Miss Independent Woman."

"Thank you," I reply with an exaggerated rolling of the eyes.

"Oh, you two are too adorable," Kenny says, hooking his arm in mine. "I want a José Mendoza, well done."

Houston turns to me, awaiting my order. "And you?"

I bite my lip as I ponder what kind of burger I want, savoring the way his gaze occasionally falls to my mouth. "I'll also have a José Mendoza. And he should be..." I take a glance just below Houston's belt then allow my eyes to rake over his chest on the way back to his face. "*Very* well done."

From the corner of my eye, I can see Kenny shaking his head. "Girl, you are begging for a pegging," he mutters.

Houston laughs, his gaze still locked on mine. "Well done, indeed," he replies with a nod, then he sets off to get in line to place the order.

Kenny and I trail off arm in arm toward the bar area, which is just to our left through an entryway with a large neon bar sign hanging above it. The moment we step through the entryway, I jump about fifty feet in the air when someone shouts my name. I look to our right and Troy is seated on a stool at a table in the corner. Next to him sits a lovely girl who looks about my age. Her platinum-blond hair and horn-rimmed glasses scream hipster, but at least she's wearing a friendly smile.

I wave at him as Kenny and I make our way to the table. "Troy!" I say, slipping my arm out of Kenny's to give Troy a hug. "You look great."

He smiles. "Thanks. It must be all the gluten-free bacon I've been eating. Who's this?" he asks, referring to Kenny, and something in his face tells me he thinks I brought a date with me.

I suppose there's no harm in having a little fun with Houston's friends.

"Troy, this is my fiancé, Kenny," I reply, threading my arm through Kenny's arm again and resting my head on his shoulder. "Kenny, this is Troy."

Troy's eyebrows practically disappear into his hairline as Kenny reaches out his hand to shake.

"Nice to meet you, Troy," Kenny says, purposely making his voice deeper to play along with me.

Troy shakes Kenny's hand quickly, then turns to the blonde. "Honey, this is Rory and… Kenny. Rory and Kenny, this is my fiancée, Georgia."

"So nice to meet you, Georgia," I say, maintaining a firm grip on Kenny's arm as I stare up at him with googly eyes. "Isn't he dreamy?"

Kenny shrugs modestly. "Oh, how I love this woman." He looks down at me, narrowing his eyes in typical soap-opera fiery passion. "I just can't get enough of her."

Without warning, he wraps his arms around me and lowers me into a dip as he pretends to kiss me passionately. Our lips are about an inch apart, but Troy and Georgia can't see from their vantage point. I press my lips together firmly to stifle my laughter as Kenny stares into my eyes and moves his head around to make it look like he's kissing me.

"You can do better than that, Kenny."

Houston's voice startles us both and Kenny drops me like a sack of potatoes onto the sticky floor. I land pretty hard on my ass and Houston and I burst into laughter.

"Oh, my God. I'm so sorry, sweetie," Kenny says, offering his hand to help me up, but I'm laughing too hard to get a good grip.

Houston hands Kenny the tray of burgers then reaches down and scoops me up off the floor as if I weigh as much as a José Mendoza.

"Put me down," I say, trying not to look him in the eye or I may kiss him.

"Unhand my fiancée!" Kenny demands, though he's forgotten to drop his voice an octave and I'm pretty sure the jig is up.

Finally, I look up at Houston and he's smiling like a kid on Christmas. "Put me down." I repeat my demand, though with less force this time.

"Oh, you're going down all right," he says as he gently lowers my feet to the floor.

Once we're all seated and situated with our burgers, I kindly explain to Troy and Georgia that Kenny is actually my friend.

"And the only man allowed to touch me," I add, then I wink at Houston as I take a big bite of my burger.

"You're a fast learner," he remarks, then he takes an even bigger bite of his burger.

"Rory and I used to work together when she was a lowly grocery clerk," Kenny says. "Now she's a writer and she's too fabulous for me."

"Fabulously unemployed," I reply.

"Are you looking for a job?" Georgia chimes in. "Our salon is looking for a shampoo girl, if you're interested."

I smile at her unexpected offer. "Thanks, but I'm going to talk to my old boss next week. Just taking a few days off to get… settled."

"I already told you I can talk to Benji for you," Houston says, tearing a sheet off the roll of paper towels in the center of the table. He hands it to me and points at the corner of his mouth. "You've got a little something right there."

I snatch the paper towel out of his hand and wipe the burger sauce off my lips. "I'm fine. I don't need you to talk to anyone for me."

As the evening goes on, I learn that Georgia is a stylist at a hair salon in the Alphabet District. She and Troy met through a mutual friend, who also happened to be his ex-girlfriend. They dated for a little more than a year before he popped the question over Thanksgiving dinner last year.

"Congratulations," I say, shifting uncomfortably on my barstool as I try not to think of the Sierra Nevada box containing an engagement ring, which I ordered Kenny to give back to Houston a few weeks ago.

"Houston's gonna be the best man," Troy adds with pride.

I glance at Houston and he shrugs, though I can't discern why. Does he think it bothers me that he's going to be the best man in Troy's wedding?

Georgia reaches out and places her hand on my forearm. "I know we don't know each other well yet, but I've heard so much about you." She smiles, leaning forward as if she's going to tell me a juicy secret. "We think it'd be great if you were a bridesmaid. That way you and Houston could walk down the aisle together."

Time seems to slow down and I find myself unable to formulate a response. I blink a few times and turn to Houston, but the horror in his eyes tells me he knew nothing about this. I turn back to Georgia and her penciled eyebrows are raised in anticipation of my answer.

"I… I don't think that's a good idea."

Her smile fades instantly. "Oh, I'm sorry, that was probably too much too soon. I'm… I thought you two were together."

Her last sentence comes out more like an accusation. Troy gently places his hand on her forearm. "No, baby, they're not together… right now."

"Why not?" she says, her lip curled in mild disgust.

Troy sighs as he places his hand on her arm and leans in closer. "Baby, we'll talk about it later."

"Why?" she shrieks. "If she doesn't walk down the aisle with him, I'll have to ask my stupid cousin to do it. And you know I can't have her in my wedding. She'll ruin it!"

I couldn't be more uncomfortable if we were sitting here watching my parents have sex. I glance across the table at Houston and he's trying not to laugh. I shoot him a burning glare and he shakes his head.

"We should probably get going," Houston says, taking my hint as he steps off his barstool. "Don't you have the early shift tomorrow, Kenny?"

Kenny slides off his stool. "I do, but I'm taking the MAX home. I have to make a stop at a friend's place."

My jaw drops. "Kenny, do you have a friend I don't know about? Is he a *special* friend?"

"Not as special as you," he replies.

We say our good-byes to Troy and Georgia, though Georgia no longer seems in the mood for niceties. Then, I give Kenny an awkwardly long hug outside Killer Burger. As Houston and I walk to his car through a light drizzle of rain, I feel my awkwardness reaching new heights. I'm suddenly acutely aware of the way I walk and the sound of my heart beating in my ears and what my breath smells like. It feels as if we're on a first date, but we most certainly are not.

Houston throws caution to the wind and opens the passenger door for me. I thank him as I climb inside, my pulse racing as he shuts the door and our eyes lock through the window. I turn away quickly and take slow, deep breaths as he rounds the back of the car to the driver's side.

He climbs in and slides the key into the ignition, but he doesn't turn it. "Rory?"

"Yes."

He's silent for a long moment, then he shakes his head and turns the key. "Nothing."

He turns on the radio to fill the silence on the drive back to my mom's apartment. We're both lost in our thoughts until "I'm on Fire" by AWOLNATION comes on and I begin to imagine Houston's hands on me, his body sliding over mine, his thickness moving inside me.

"Oh, God. Can we turn this off?" I plead.

"Gladly," he says, but we both reach for the stereo at the same time.

The moment our hands touch, pinpricks of electricity detonate in my fingertips. A current of heat sizzles through me straight to my core. I draw my hand back, holding it protectively against my belly as if I've been physically burned.

Houston turns the music off just as he pulls onto my mom's street. I breathe a sigh of relief as I unlatch my seat belt and reach for the door handle, ready to exit as soon as the car stops moving.

"Rory?" he says, and my hand freezes over the cool chrome handle.

I swallow hard as I turn to him slowly and meet his gaze. "Yes."

His eyes travel down my face, lingering on my mouth, making no effort to disguise his wonderment as he stares at my chest, then he drags his gaze back up to my eyes. "You look beautiful tonight."

I let out the breath I've been holding and mutter my thanks as I hop out of the car and power walk into the apartment lobby. God help me. What have I gotten myself into?

Rory

Hi, Rory,

Sorry for contacting you via email. I know you asked Detective Locke to give me your phone number, but I just couldn't bring myself to call you. It's not because I blame you, I just haven't figured out how I feel about all this yet. It's very surreal and overwhelming.

Anyway, the reason I'm getting in touch is to tell you that Liam's funeral will be held the day after tomorrow, Monday, at Pioneer Cemetery in our hometown, Salem. I don't think you should come for the ceremony, but it will conclude around 4 p.m., if you feel the need to come later.

My brother wasn't perfect. I know that. And maybe none of this would have happened if I'd gone to the police when he told me what he did to Savannah's car. I also know Liam was lost.

Ever since we were little, he used to make up these stories. These elaborate lies that I easily fell for. It was kind of cute, even funny, when we were in grade school. And it came in handy when he needed to dig his way out of trouble in high school. But as the years went on, it got to the point that I began to wonder if any of us ever knew the real Liam. I guess we'll never know.

Despite this darker side of him, there was no one who could make me laugh harder than him. Liam was my only brother, and I loved him more than words can say. So, while I don't blame you for what happened, I also don't know if I can face you knowing that I kept quiet when he told me you two were moving to California. I'll admit I was hoping he'd changed. My parents will never say it, but you were the last good thing in his life, and for that I thank you.

I know you cared for Liam and I also know you lost someone very close to you a few years ago. The grief counselor I spoke to at the hospital told me something that I wanted to pass on to you. She said it's important to remember that grief is necessary and that the grieving process never ends. That sometimes, even after you've gone through all the stages of grief, and you've finally reached acceptance, something as heavy as another loss or as simple as a single memory can set you back to Stage One. Grief never ends, but with time we learn who and what we can turn to for strength, and it becomes easier to rise after each fall. Take care of yourself.

-Leah

My hands tremble as I close my laptop. My mom takes a seat across from me at the round dining table and slides a steaming mug of coffee toward me. I stare at the white mug with the words *World's Greatest Teacher* painted on the side.

"What's wrong?" she asks, her voice gentle and soothing.

I wipe tears from my face as I look up. "Liam's funeral is tomorrow. His sister sent me an email."

"Are you going?"

"I wasn't invited. She wanted to let me know where it was being held and what time it would end in case I wanted to drop by afterward."

Her face tightens with suppressed anger. "I see. Well, that was kind of her to let you know."

"It was. It was *very* kind," I reply forcefully. "She didn't have to do that."

"You're right. I just hate the idea of anyone blaming this on you. You're not responsible for what he did."

"She doesn't blame me… She blames herself."

The tautness in her features melts into regret. "Oh. Well, that's not good."

I let out a long sigh as I wipe the last remnants of moisture from my face. "No, it's not good. It's just natural."

I stand from the table, sliding my phone out of my pocket as I head for the bathroom. I dial the number, closing the bathroom door behind me as it rings in my ear. My heart races as I try to think of what I'm going to say when Houston picks up.

"Hey, why are you awake this early?" he says, and the sound of his voice instantly calms me.

"It's 9:30. It's not that early," I reply, my voice echoing off the walls of my mother's bathroom.

"It's early for someone who's been waking up at noon for the past week."

I consider sharing with him how, after our venture to Killer Burger, last night was the first night I fell asleep before two a.m. Then I question whether I want to reveal this vulnerability to him so early in our friendship experiment. Then I realize I have no choice. If this were Kenny, I would tell him why I woke up early, without hesitation. And I could have called Kenny right now, but I chose to call Houston instead. And there's good reason for that.

"You know I haven't been sleeping well," I reply, referring to the three nearly sleepless nights we spent in Palo Alto. "Well, last night was the first night I fell asleep early."

He's silent for a moment as he allows this to sink in. "That's good. I'm glad you're feeling a little better. Maybe I should take you out for burgers every night."

I chuckle. "Actually, I have a favor to ask you. A huge favor."

"Nothing's too huge for my Scar."

"Okay, that was half innuendo and half insult."

He laughs. "And half-true. What do you need?"

I draw in a deep breath and let it out slowly. "I need you to take me to Pioneer Cemetery on Monday at four p.m." The silence on the other end of the phone is amplified by the frantic pounding of my heart. "Houston, please say something."

"Why do you need to go there?"

"That's where they're burying him."

I almost ask him when the last time he went to Pioneer Cemetery was, but thankfully I stop myself before I make such a crass mistake. Still, the silence between us is making my mind scramble for something to fill the void.

"Houston?"

"I'm here. I'll take you."

"You will?" I reply, unable to disguise my astonishment.

"Yeah, I'll take you. Be ready at 3:15. Monday traffic on the 5 freeway is a bitch. We'll need at least forty-five minutes to get there."

I let out a sigh of relief. "Thank you so much."

"What are you up to today?" he asks, obviously eager to change the subject.

I hesitate as I consider lying about what I have planned for today. It's frightening how easy it is to lie to someone we love for the sake of sparing their feelings.

"I'm going to brunch with my dad."

"Do you still need me to take you to Kenny's to get your car back?" he replies, without missing a beat.

"No, I haven't gotten the parking permit from the building manager yet. She was supposed to give it to me yesterday, but I guess she didn't get around to it. I'll let you know as soon as I have it."

"Sure," he replies. "Enjoy your brunch. I'll see you Monday."

"Houston?"

"Yeah?"

I want to say *I love you so fucking much it hurts*, but I'm pretty sure that's against the rules, so I settle for "Thank you… for being a friend."

He sighs softly and the sound sends a chill through me. "There's nothing I wouldn't do for you… as a friend, of course. Please don't ask me to have sex with you. I don't want this to get awkward."

I roll my eyes, though I'm silently thanking him for diffusing the heaviness. "All right, *friend*, I'll see you Monday."

"See you then, sexy."

Houston

As soon as I see Rory exit the front of her mom's apartment building and set off on foot toward the streetcar, I get out of my car and walk toward the building. She climbs into the streetcar without a single glance in my direction. When I enter the lobby, the brunette standing behind the concierge desk flashes me a seductive smile.

"May I help you?" she asks, her voice low and sultry.

"No, thanks. Just going up to visit a friend in 405."

Her eyes follow me as I head for the elevator. "Let me know if you need anything."

I shake my head at her obvious attempt at flirting. Either she doesn't remember that I came here last night to pick up Rory or she doesn't care. Either way, I have to make sure to steer clear of that one.

My heart pounds with anxiety as the elevator climbs quickly to the fourth floor. By the time I knock on Patricia's door, my mouth has gone dry.

She pulls the door open and her eyes widen with genuine surprise. "Houston. You just missed Rory. She went to—"

"I know where she went. I'm not here for Rory."

She shakes her head. "I'm not doing any more editing."

"That's not what this is about. Can I come in?"

She lets out a heavy sigh as she opens the door. "She'll be back in about an hour."

"I'll make this quick."

Rory

I take the streetcar to Pioneer Square to meet my dad at the Urban Farmer restaurant, where apparently my father has a standing reservation every Friday at seven p.m. for dinner and every Saturday at eleven a.m. for brunch. I suppose I shouldn't be surprised. It's one of the trendiest fine-dining restaurants near the courthouse. It makes sense that he would utilize it to impress clients.

I make my way up to the eighth-floor atrium of The Nines hotel. As I enter the Urban Farmer, my first impression is that the restaurant is stunning. It's just a large open room with urban country furnishings, but the entire space is bathed in diffused natural light from the skylights in the ceiling seven floors above us.

"Hey, sweetheart."

I tear my gaze away from the ceiling and my dad is standing right in front of me. "Hey."

He smiles at my obvious wonderment. "Impressive architecture. I can introduce you to the owner if you're looking for a career change."

My jaw drops. "Really, Dad? We haven't even sat down yet

and you're already hinting that I need to get a job?"

He nods toward the hostess station. "Come on."

The hostess seats us at a table near the bloody Mary station, where guests are lined up to create their own custom cocktails. Just the thought of drinking alcohol at eleven a.m. makes me queasy. I don't know how I used to do it when Houston and I lived together six years ago.

"So what did you want to talk about?" I ask, as soon as the hostess is gone.

He chuckles. "Not wasting any time today, are you?"

"I'd rather not."

"Okay," he says, leaning forward to rest his elbows on the table. "Rory, I want you to work for me."

"What?" I reply with a chuckle, thinking I must have misheard him.

"Not the response I wanted, but just hear me out." His face is serious as he steeples his fingers and looks me in the eye. "I've been speaking with Ava this week and we're starting a foundation: Hallie's Hope. It will directly benefit organizations that are dedicated to helping victims of abuse get counseling as well as educating the families. You'd probably start out by helping us write funding requests and grant applications. But eventually… Ava and I think you should be the voice of Hallie's Hope."

Our waitress arrives with a basket of bread and a beaming smile. I try not to look too uncomfortable as I order a glass of ice water and my dad orders his usual Arnold Palmer. Some things never change.

Once the waitress is gone, I gather my jaw off the table and respond. "This is not what I expected."

"Well, I guess that's better than an immediate no," he replies. "I know this is sudden. And I don't expect you to say yes right now. Think about it. Mull it over for a week or two. We're meeting with my tax attorney February 17th, so we really need to get an answer by then, so we can loop you into the meeting or get someone else."

"Wow," I breathe. "So… this is moving forward with or without me?"

He nods and I nod in return. A solemn acknowledgment that this is our new reality. My father and Houston's mother are now working together.

After a somewhat awkward brunch, I return to the apartment in a bit of a daze, but this doesn't stop me from noticing that my mother is in her bedroom with the door closed at one in the afternoon.

"Mom, I'm home!" I shout so she can hear me through the door.

I listen to the sudden flurry of movement coming from inside the bedroom. Then I hear her turning the lock on the door before she comes out. She had the bedroom door *locked*? I don't even want to know what she was doing in there.

I head for the kitchen to pour myself a glass of water. "Hey, Mom."

"How was your brunch?" she asks, sounding a bit out of breath.

I glance at her, noting the slightly pink flush to her cheeks. "It was… shocking."

"Shocking?" she replies curiously. "How so?"

"It doesn't matter," I say, placing the pitcher of water back in the refrigerator. "Do you mind if I take my laptop into your bedroom? I'm going to try to Skype that therapist today."

"Of course!" she replies.

I watch her face for any sign of panic that I may discover what she's been up to while I was gone, but she looks genuinely enthusiastic about my Skyping this new therapist. I guess she feels her secrets are safe.

I take my laptop and my glass of water to the bedroom,

shutting the door behind me. Plopping myself down onto the bed, I set the laptop in front of me and open up the Skype application. I'm not surprised to find a contact request from Dr. Katherine Little. I accept the request and cross my fingers as I call her.

To my surprise, she answers the call almost immediately. Her video feed pops up and she looks like… me. Or what I'll probably look like in twenty years if I decide to dye my gray hair auburn. She's about my mother's age, with striking green eyes only slightly hidden behind her square-rimmed glasses.

"Rory, hi! It's so nice to finally meet you," she says, her voice clear and congenial.

"Hi, Dr. Little. I didn't know if you'd be available. I guess I was just… hoping you would be."

"Oh, please call me Katherine. And I'm almost always available. I take two to four patients a day, but there are days I don't have any. Like today. So I'm all yours."

I cringe inside as I remember today is Saturday. "I'm sorry to bother you on a weekend."

"No, don't apologize. I just finished taking the dog for a walk. I'm in for the day. I'm happy to speak with you." She adjusts her laptop screen or her camera a little, then she sits back in her chair. "So, your father told me you might have some things to talk about. I just want to start off by saying that you're not at all obligated to tell me anything. Of course, the purpose of talking to a professional about things that are bothering us is because we're able to offer an objective perspective. So the more you talk, the more you get out of this."

I nod, though I have absolutely no idea where I'm supposed to start. How do I explain to her the utter clusterfuck that is my life?

She smiles. "How about we start with a simple question? How are you feeling today?"

I take a deep breath. "Confused."

"Can you elaborate on that? Is there something that prompted your confusion?"

"Yeah, my dad. He just asked me to work for him. And part of me is happy that he and Ava—Ava is my best friend Hallie's mother. Hallie's dead. It's a long story. Anyway, I'm happy that Ava and my dad are working together on something so positive, but another part of me knows that this will not go over well with Houston."

"And who is Houston?"

"Ava's son, and my ex-boyfriend… kind of."

She scrunches her eyebrows together. I'm pretty sure she's the one confused now. "Okay, how about you start from the beginning? I have a feeling I've been dropped into the story somewhere toward the end."

I chuckle. "No kidding. Um… okay. It all started when I met Hallie, when we were eleven. Actually, I guess it started before that."

I give Katherine a forty-five-minute distillation of everything that's happened over the past fourteen years. Through it all, she nods and asks the occasional question, but mostly she just listens. And I find myself, for the first time in a long time, feeling like I'm entitled to my feelings. By the time I'm done, I already feel lighter.

Katherine purses her lips, then presses them together. She does this for a while as she considers everything I've just told her. Finally, she leans forward and asks me a very unexpected question.

"Can I ask why you feel the need to tell the story of you and Houston?"

At first, I'm a little offended by the question. As if she's implying the story doesn't need to be told. Then I draw in a deep breath, and it only takes a moment for me to realize she's not asking why people need to read the story. She's asking why *I need* to tell it.

I shake my head in dismay. "I don't know."

She nods, looking very pleased with my answer. "There you go. This is progress."

I let out an awkward chuckle. "How is that progress?"

"Because we just discovered something we need to explore further." She reaches for a notepad and a pen. "How about we do this again next week, same time? And in the meantime, I'd like to give you a little homework assignment. I'd like you to come up with at least one reason why you need to tell the story of Houston and Rory. And hopefully you'll also have a decision about whether or not you want to work with your father. If not, we can discuss that next week, too."

We end the call and I close my laptop feeling different. Like my problems are not roadblocks, they're just speed bumps. They're manageable, with a little extra perspective.

I let out a huge sigh of relief. My trepidation over talking to the therapist has been fully erased. Then, I look around my mom's room and I remember that she was in here earlier doing God knows what.

I shake my head as I stand up and head for the door. I am not going to snoop through my mom's things. Besides, I have enough to worry about without trying to figure out what she's up to. Like how I'm going to tell Houston that my dad wants me to work for him. Unless Ava has already broken the news to Houston for me.

Houston

The Monday traffic on the 5 freeway was worse than anticipated. We arrive at Pioneer Cemetery twenty minutes before it closes at five p.m. The rain is coming down lightly, and the sun has almost completely set. The dying sunlight fuses with the precipitation, casting a misty emerald luminescence across the cemetery. The mineral-rich scent of freshly dug soil is thick in the air. The only good part about arriving this late is that there's no sign of stragglers at Liam's grave site.

I park the car and reach for Rory's hand. "Wait. Do you want an umbrella?"

She shakes her head. "Please don't insult me."

I smile as I squeeze her hand. "Didn't take long for the rain to wash the California off you."

Though she clearly refused my offer of an umbrella, I still feel the need to wrap my arm around her as we walk toward the grave site. Something about being at a cemetery at sunset feels ominous. I want to keep her close in case the grave robbers and ghouls come out for a haunt.

The grave has already been sealed and covered with a fresh slab of sod, not that I'm surprised. A guy in one of my classes at

UO used to work at Pioneer Cemetery. Shortly after Hallie's funeral, I overheard him discussing how coffins are buried. He bragged about being able to put a coffin in the ground and cover it with dirt and sod in less than fifteen minutes. The crew who put Liam in the ground is long gone. All that's left is a muddy rectangle surrounding the fresh carpet of grass and a few flower petals strewn about.

Images of that night at the hotel flash in my mind and I grit my teeth against the memory of the fury in Liam's eyes. The man is dead and I'm still angry over his deluded sense of entitlement. Rory never belonged to Liam.

Rory slinks out from underneath my arm and takes a step toward the grave. I grab her wrist to stop her from stepping directly on it. Fresh soil can be unstable, especially in rainy conditions. The last thing I need is for her to get sucked into Liam's grave.

She glances at my hand curled around her wrist, then she looks up at me. "Do you mind? I just want to pick something up."

I let go of her and she kneels just outside the murky rectangle of sod. I can't see what she's reaching for until she pulls it out of the grass. A young dandelion weed. She stands and tucks the tiny golden flower in her pocket. The tension in my muscles eases as I realize why we're here. Because Rory never belonged to Liam, but that doesn't mean that a part of him won't always belong to her.

"Let's go see Hallie," she says, her voice cracking under the strain of her emotions.

With eight minutes left until closing, there's not much time to visit my sister's grave, but I don't mention this. This is the first time I've been here with Rory since Hallie's funeral. I guess there are worse people to get locked in a cemetery with.

I park the car along the curved road, the place that marks the upper-right bend in the heart-shaped path at Pioneer Cemetery. As we walk through the maze of headstones, I notice the scent of fresh soil is gone, replaced by the crisp scent of grass coated in cold rain. The temperature is dropping quickly, and I'm pretty certain Rory's jacket is almost soaked through, just like mine. I'm concerned about her not being able to feel the cold properly with her emotions running high.

The moment we get to Hallie's grave, Rory sits down cross-legged on the squishy grass. She pats the ground for me to sit next to her. I stare at the headstone for a moment, unsure if this is the time or place to make myself comfortable. I swallow the lump in my throat as I prepare to tell Rory I'll wait for her in the car, but when I look down at her she's covering her face with her hands.

I let out a sigh as I drop to my knees in front of her and reach for her face. "Hey, you don't have to hide your tears."

She lets her hands drop into her lap, but she doesn't look up at me. "It feels like something is ending."

"Yeah, I know what you mean."

She stares at the headstone for a moment before she reaches out and traces the year 2008. Letting out a soft sigh, she looks up at me with a question in her eyes. I hold my breath as I wait for her to speak.

"How often do you come here?" she asks.

Rory can see through me better than anyone.

"Three times since the divorce. Before that… never. Not since the funeral."

She nods. "Can you bring me with you next time?"

"Of course."

She sighs as she glances around the cemetery. "There's something special about this place. It's like a portal, to what or where I can't figure out."

"A portal to a higher dimension. Like we were living in 2D, and now we're in full 3D high-def."

She laughs. "If Hallie were here she'd make fun of you for saying that."

"She is here." The words come out of my mouth before I can stop them.

Rory looks me in the eye. "I guess she is. She's everywhere."

We sit in silence for a while, the rain disguising any evidence of tears. When the last wash of sunlight disappears over the horizon, and the darkness falls over us, I know we have to get going before we get locked in.

Rory is still cross-legged in front of me, but her eyes are closed. I reach for her hand slowly, afraid of startling her. The moment my skin touches hers, she gets up on her knees and throws her arms around my neck. I wrap my arms around her waist and hold her damp, trembling body tightly against mine.

She presses her lips to my ear and murmurs, "Thank you."

The sensation of her lips on my skin sends signals to body parts that should not be awakened at my sister's graveside. "Stand up, baby," I whisper as I release her.

She lets go of me and I help her up. The moment she's standing, she wraps her arms around my waist, burying her face in my chest. She's not ready to leave.

I stand with her a while longer, rubbing her back to keep her warm. When my fingers start to go numb with cold, she finally stops trembling. I tilt my head back and grab her face to look her in the eye.

"We have to go, Rory."

She nods in agreement, though I can sense her reluctance. And I can't figure out if it's because she doesn't want to leave Hallie or Liam or me.

Once we're in the car, I turn the heater on full tilt to blast the chill out of us. I round the bend in the heart-shaped road and head back toward the entrance on Hoyt Street. As soon as the cemetery gates are in sight, my heart drops. The chest-high gates are closed and chained.

"How are we gonna get out?" Rory asks, unable to hide the

hint of panic in her voice.

"Wait here," I say. "There has to be someone left at the funeral home. I'll just hop that fence and walk over there. They'll let us out."

She breathes a sigh of relief. "Oh, thank God. I thought we were trapped."

"I'm gonna lock the doors. Don't open the windows or doors for anyone."

"Okay."

The moment I walk away from the car and hop over the gate, the City View Funeral Home comes into view and I get a bad feeling. The windows are dark and there are no cars in the two parking spaces out front. I cross the street and forge ahead, hopeful that someone who can help us is in there. But after ten minutes of knocking and worrying about leaving Rory alone, I finally decide to give up.

As I cross the street toward the cemetery, the rain begins to come down harder. I race across the small driveway and my heart races when I see Rory standing just inside the gate.

I climb the fence quickly and wrap my arm around her shoulders to guide her back to the car. "What are you doing out here? I told you to stay in the car."

"I was worried about you," she says, her teeth chattering as I open the passenger door for her. "Is someone going to let us out?"

"No one was there."

Her eyes widen. "We're stuck in here?"

I shake my head as I try to come up with an answer better than the truth, then I remember I promised to never lie to Rory again. "There may be a groundskeeper who'll come by tonight and let us out. But if not, then yes. We're stuck here for the night."

Her mouth drops open in utter horror. "I'm sorry. It's all my fault."

"Bullshit. I could have carried you to the car and forced you to leave. It's not your fault. And, hey, look on the bright side," I reply, raising my voice to be heard over the sound of the rain battering the top of my car, and Rory looks at me as if I'm insane to even suggest there's a bright side. "Spending the night in a cemetery will probably be the ultimate test of our friendship."

She rolls her eyes as she climbs into the passenger seat. "You call that a bright side? I call that a nightmare."

I decide to pull my car back into the curve of the heart-shaped road, to hide us from view of the cars driving past the cemetery. After a couple of hours of basking in the warmth of the heater and fighting over what music to listen to, our clothes are finally beginning to dry. And a break in the storm arrives.

"We have to hurry up," I say, stepping out of the car.

"Hurry up, why?" she asks, her eyes wide with confusion. "What are you doing?"

I flatten the backseat of the SUV and open the moonroof. "Get back here."

I pull off my slightly damp jacket and roll it up to use as a pillow. Then I lie back and stretch my arm out so Rory can lay her head down. The sky is dark, with just a few twinkles of starlight breaking through the patchy cloud cover.

She lets out a soft chuckle. "This isn't how I imagined this day ending."

"What did you imagine?"

"I guess I thought we'd both leave feeling sad and maybe even angry."

I let out a soft sigh. "Guess we're growing up, huh?"

She gasps as she points her finger through the moonroof. "Oh, my God! Did you see that? It was a shooting star."

"Now you're seeing things?"

She smacks my chest. "I swear I just saw a shooting star."

I laugh as I grab her hand so she can't abuse me anymore.

"Okay, okay. I believe you. I guess you'd better make a wish."

"You don't believe me. You're just humoring me."

"You'd better make a wish before you lose your chance."

I try not to laugh as she closes her eyes. She's silent for a moment, then her mouth curves into a gorgeous smile as her eyelids flutter open.

"Done."

"What did you wish for? A groundskeeper?"

She gazes into my eyes, still smiling. "An answer."

A drop of water lands on my cheek and I quickly reach up to hit the button to close the moonroof before the rain gets in. Without the moonlight, the back of the car gets considerably darker. When I look down at Rory, whose head is still lying on my arm, her eyes are locked on mine.

I reach up and brush my thumb over her soft cheekbone. "What kind of answer?"

She shakes her head. "I can't say. At least, not now."

"Okay," I whisper, my gaze locked on her mouth as I trace my thumb over the ledge of her bottom lip. "I'll let it slide, for now."

Her breathing quickens as I slowly lean in closer. "Houston?" she breathes, her voice thin as a wisp.

"Yes?" I say, my reply brushing over her lips.

"Stop."

And with that one simple word, the spell is broken.

"Shit. I'm sorry," I say, lying back to stare at the boring ceiling of the car. "I guess I got a little carried away."

She chuckles. "You don't have to apologize. You're certainly not at fault. I was about to kiss you when I remembered our brilliant conversation from the hotel."

I reach down to discreetly adjust my crotch. "Brilliant is one word for it. Crazy would be another one."

"Nah, I'd still go with brilliant. You were right." She turns on her side so she's facing me. "There's a lot of stuff we need to sort out, a lot of questions we need answered before we can go down that road again."

"I know the answer to one very important question," I reply, turning on my side to face her. "The answer is yes. Yes, I want to play Strip Truth or Dare."

"Yes, because getting naked with me is definitely the way to play it safe."

"Who said we have to play it safe?" I smile as she shakes her head. "I'm serious, Rory. I can't leave the heater on in the car all night or I'll run out of gas. I'm going to have to turn it off soon. And once the temperature drops into the twenties outside, it's not going to be much warmer in here."

"What does that have to do with getting naked?"

I shake my head. "I'm disappointed in you, Rory. You're the one who laid next to me—naked—while reading me that book about the girl and boy who had to sleep naked in a sleeping bag to stay warm."

"Ah, shit!"

I laugh at her outburst. "Don't worry. The cemetery opens at eight. We'll only have to lie naked together for four or five hours, tops."

She narrows her eyes at me. "Oh, you're loving this, aren't you?"

"Not yet, but I'm sure I will be in about three or four hours when it's time to strip."

She lets out a heavy sigh. "Fine. I guess we may as well have some fun while we're at it. Truth or dare?"

"Dare."

"Of course," she mutters. "I dare you to… lick my eyeball."

"You're sick." I lean in close and she begins to giggle as I hold her eyelids open. "Stop laughing. One wrong move and… This tongue is strong enough to poke an eye out."

Her body shakes with the effort of holding in her laughter, and she blinks violently the moment I touch the tip of my tongue to her eyeball.

"Ew! That felt so weird!" she cries, rubbing her eye. "What did it taste like?"

"Didn't really taste like anything. Maybe a hint of salt."

"Ew. You tasted my salty eye boogers," she says, still rubbing her eye.

I shrug. "That's probably the only part of your body I hadn't tasted yet, so I'm cool with being able to say I've conquered every inch of you. And now you have to take off an article of clothing," I say, pulling her hand away from her face to stop her from killing her eyeball.

We both sit up and I help her out of her jacket, but she quickly drapes it over her legs for warmth as she sits cross-legged. I sit across from her, our knees touching as I grab the rolled-up jacket I was using as a pillow.

"Here. Put this on."

"Isn't that cheating?" she asks, taking the jacket from me.

"I won't tell if you don't," I reply with a wink. "My turn. Truth or dare?"

"Truth."

"Scaredy-cat."

She shoves my shoulder. "Just ask the question."

"Okay, is it true… that you want me to put my tongue on other parts of your body right now?"

She glares at me. "Yes, it's true. Now you have to remove an article of clothing."

I yank my T-shirt off without protest and she smiles as she stares at my chest. "Wanna touch?"

She shakes her head. "My turn. Truth or dare?"

It's about midnight when she's down to her bra and panties and I'm down to my boxer briefs. That's when I look at the fuel gauge and realize I'm going to have to turn the car and the heater off. I grab my phone off the folded pile of clothes next to me and set the alarm for five a.m. We need to make sure we're awake and dressed at least a few hours before the cemetery opens.

I reach into the front to pull the key out of the ignition, and when I turn back Rory has her hands behind her back, unclipping her bra. "What are you doing?" I blurt out.

"What do you mean? You're the one who reminded me about that stupid book. I'm getting naked."

I let out a nervous chuckle. "I didn't think you would get *completely* naked."

"Now you don't *want* me to get naked?"

"No, you're right. I remember… it didn't work when they tried to keep their underwear on."

The straps of her bra loosen and she watches me as she lets it slide off her shoulders and down her arms. My heart races at the sight of her full breasts, the nipples pink and perked up with the cold that's already seeping in. She hooks her thumbs in the waistband of her striped panties.

"Wait. I'll do that."

I kneel before her, leaning in close as I hook my thumbs into the waistband. Her chest is heaving with anticipation as I slowly push them down her thighs.

"Oh, God," she whispers as I slide my left hand behind her neck and my right hand between her legs. "Oh, God. Oh, God. Oh, God."

I hold her neck firmly to watch her face as I bury my finger inside her. "Truth or dare?" I murmur, gathering her wetness and bringing it forward to use it as I caress her clit.

She gasps. "Truth?"

"Is it true that you're dripping wet and all mine?"

Her stomach muscles contract as the orgasm builds. "Oh, God, yes."

I lean forward, kissing her slowly as I continue lightly massaging her clit, bringing her to the edge then stopping more than once.

"Is it true you want me to make you come with my mouth?"

"False," she breathes. "I want you to fuck me."

I chuckle as I continue stimulating her. When her body begins to curl inward and her legs are quaking, I slow down to finish her off gently. She leans her head back, exposing her neck to me as her body goes limp.

I slide my hand out from between her thighs. "God, you're beautiful when you come."

She lets out a sexy laugh as she pulls her head up and looks me in the eye. "This is so wrong."

I chuckle as I shrug out of my boxer briefs. "It's not nearly wrong enough." We both lie down on our sides, her back to my chest. I kiss her neck and shoulder as I reach forward and slide my hand between her legs again. She gasps, still tender from the last orgasm. I move my fingers lightly over the inside of her thigh until I reach the inside of her knee. Grabbing her leg, I pull it backward to drape it over my thigh as I enter her from behind.

She cries out in pain, but I know from experience it's the kind of pain she welcomes. I slide farther into her with each thrust, sinking my teeth into her shoulder to stifle my moans. Our bodies are slick with sweat and the heady fragrance of sex. The scent is an intoxicating musk, surrounding us in an invisible blanket of lust. I wrap my arms tightly around her middle, digging my fingers into her softness as I grind into her from behind.

"My turn," she says, her voice thready. "Truth or dare?"

"Truth," I say, slowing my thrusts so I can answer her question.

She wets her lips before she continues. "Is it true that… I'm the only girl you've ever loved?"

I slide out of her and turn her over onto her back. Then I

climb on top of her, looking into her eyes as I slide right back in.

"One hundred percent true," I reply.

She smiles as she threads her fingers through my hair. "Good."

Keeping my thrusts slow and deliberate, I make love to Rory as if this is our last night together and she's the only girl I've ever loved.

The Zucker's store on Belmont looks exactly the way it did before I was promoted to work in the wine bar at the Zucker's on Burnside last August, with one exception. They have their own wine bar now, which opened shortly after I left for California. As expected, Kenny is still the North Star of this store, shining brightly and reliably from his perch behind register three.

I wave at him as I walk past register one. "I'll be back," I say, continuing toward Jamie's office in the rear corner of the store.

He blows me a kiss and I pretend to catch it and tuck it safely in the back pocket of my jeans. The customers probably find us annoying, but I don't care. I pass through the produce section and knock on the oak slab door to Jamie's office.

"Come in," she shouts from inside. She must have seen me coming on the surveillance feed.

As I walk into Jamie's tiny office, the same office where I ran into Houston almost six months ago, I'm surprised at how normal this all feels. Even with everything that's changed since the day my life collided with Houston's, being here still feels like just another day on the job. I don't know if that's good or bad.

Jamie is leaning back in her chair with her Converse sneakers propped up on the desk, talking on her cell phone. "Did Grandpa tell you he wants us to get together for Easter? I won't even be here. I'll be in Bali. You have to talk to him, Benji. I am *not* canceling my honeymoon… All right, I have to go. Rory's here… You too. Talk to you later."

She lowers her feet to the floor and snatches a hair tie off the desk to pull her strawberry-blonde hair into a ponytail. "Hey, Rory. Sorry about that. You know Grandpa and his need to have everything his way."

"I think I remember a thing or two about Grandpa John. I'm sure he'll understand about the honeymoon," I reply, taking a seat in the chair across from Jamie.

Jesus. It feels like everyone's getting married these days. Meanwhile, I'm playing sex games in the back of a car at a cemetery. Thank God Houston agreed we should go back to being just friends and we must *never* speak about what happened three nights ago. To anyone. Ever.

Though I guess Pioneer Cemetery can thank us for putting on a show. If they ever *were* haunted, I'm pretty sure we scared away all the ghosts that night.

Jamie opens up the manila folder on her desk, my personnel file. "Well, I can't give you your old job at Burnside back. We're on our third replacement at the wine bar and it looks like this guy is going to stick around. But I can offer you your old job back over here. We can always use another cashier."

"Oh." I try to force a smile, but the idea of going back to being a cashier suddenly feels like a huge step back. "Okay. I'll have to think about that."

"No problem. I know it's kind of hard taking a step back. I wish I had something else to offer you."

"No, I understand. It's just that I have another job offer."

"Oh, really? From who? Freddie's?"

I laugh at her suggestion that I'm playing her against Fred

Meyer, another local grocery chain. "No, from my dad. He wants me to help him set up a charity."

Her eyes widen. "Wow. That sounds like a big responsibility, but I'm sure you're up to the challenge."

"Yeah, we'll see," I say, letting out a sigh as I stand from the chair. "It was great seeing you, Jamie. Do you mind if I take the week to decide on the position?"

She smiles as she stands. "Take your time. We'll still be here."

I wait in the wine bar, sipping an ice water, until Kenny's shift is over. Then we cross the street to the Laughing Planet Café to get smoothies. Kenny gets a Jungle Juice and I opt for a PB & J.

"Not watching your calories today, are you?" Kenny says as we take a seat on a couple of stools at the counter.

My mouth drops open in shock. "Can't a girl get her peanut butter fix without accusations of failed diets?"

"I'm sorry, honey. You're right. I'll come by your apartment later with a trough of peanut butter. Oink oink!"

I smack his arm. "Don't be mean. Are you telling me I've gained weight?"

He laughs as he leans out of my reach. "No! Of course not. I'm just teasing you. You look radiant as ever. Exactly the right amount of junk." He sits up straight and takes a sip of his tropical smoothie. "So how did it go with Jamie?"

"As expected. She offered me the cashier position."

He cocks an eyebrow. "You don't look very jazzed at the idea of working with me again. Should I be offended?"

I take a sip of my smoothie, my eyes practically crossing with delight when I suck a ribbon of peanut butter through the straw. "No, it has nothing to do with you. It's my dad."

Kenny sighs. "When is it *not* your dad?"

"He offered me a job."

His eyes widen. "At the law firm?"

"No. He wants me to help him set up a charitable foundation

for victims of sexual abuse… Hallie's Hope."

His jaw drops and I wait for him to respond, but he just stares at me in silence.

"Kenny, say something."

There's a wild spark in his eyes. "This is perfect."

"What?"

"You heard me. It's perfect. Now you and your dad and Houston can finally move forward in a positive direction."

I heave a deep sigh. "It's not that simple. My dad is working on this with Houston's mom, Ava."

"Even better!" Kenny squeals. "Rory, you have to do it. If you take the job at Zucker's, I swear to God I will never speak to you again."

"What? How could you even say that?"

"Because I love you. And I won't let you pretend that you can just go back to the way things were six months ago. Everything's changed. *You've* changed." He reaches up to grab my shoulders, then stops and winces sharply as he begins massaging his neck. "Ah, shit. I forgot about that."

"What's wrong with your neck?" I reply, my mind conjuring the worst scenario. "Do you have neck cancer?"

He looks at me like I'm crazy. "No, I do not have neck cancer. I have a crick in my neck. I think I slept on it wrong."

The way he refuses to look me in the eye when he says this tells me he knows exactly how he got a crick in his neck, and it has nothing to do with sleeping. "Kenny Rhodes, did you have sex last night?"

He takes a long pull on his straw, drawing out the moment, then he breaks into an uncontrollable grin. "Yes, ma'am."

I gasp. "With whom? And why have I not met him?"

"Because I don't know how serious it is yet."

I raise my eyebrows skeptically. "It must be pretty serious if he's killing your neck like that. Look at you. You can't stop smiling."

He covers his face in shame. "I know. I know. It's ridiculous."

"No, it's not. It's beautiful," I say with a small sniff.

He uncovers his face and turns to me slowly. "Rory, are you crying?"

I shrug as I wipe at my tears. "I'm just happy for you."

He's silent for a moment as he waits for me to compose myself, then he holds his arms out for a hug. "Come here, gorgeous." He squeezes me so tight, I instantly feel my emotions leveling off. "Take the job with your dad, Rory. Everything's going to work out with you and Houston. I promise."

I sniff loudly. "How do you know that?"

"Because if it doesn't, he'll have to answer to me."

I laugh as he lets me go and looks into my eyes. "Speaking from experience," I reply, thinking of our night spent in the cemetery, "I don't think there are many things that could scare Houston. But that… That might just do it."

Kenny rolls his eyes. "Oh, you'd better believe Houston doesn't want me bringing my wrath down on him. You may not know this about me, Aurora, but I am well versed in the art of Brazilian jujitsu. One of my mother's *many* boyfriends got me into it when I was fifteen."

"Fifteen? Didn't you come out when you were sixteen?"

He shrugs. "Yes, you caught me. I was schtooping my eighteen-year-old jujitsu instructor."

I gasp. "Kenny, did he abuse his position of authority?"

He smiles sheepishly. "In the best way possible."

Houston

I can tell by the bored look on Rory's face that the last place she wants to go right now is to the grand opening of the wine bar in the Zucker's Lake Oswego store. But sometimes *friends* have to go to boring grand openings to support their friends. At least, that's what I told her last night when I asked her to come with me. I just wish I could figure out why she's been in such a pissy mood lately.

I know she's frustrated with the whole dynamic of being just friends, especially since our little "setback" at the cemetery a couple of weeks ago. And I know I have no place trying to decipher Rory's moods. I have a terrible track record with not being able to figure out my own ex-wife's personality disorder.

However, having lived with Rory before, I know that when her mood changes, it usually has to do with an external problem, not an internal problem. And, though being just friends is frustrating as hell, it doesn't really justify her shitty attitude. Something else is wrong, and I'm going to figure it out. Even if that means taking her to a boring grand opening, surrounded by all her old coworkers, to force it out of her.

"What did Kenny say when you invited him?" I ask as I exit the 405 freeway.

She sighs as she continues to stare out the passenger window. "He said he was busy doing fun stuff with his new boyfriend."

"Have you met him yet?"

She turns to me with her eyebrow cocked. "His boyfriend? No," she replies bitterly. "He's good enough for Kenny to choose to hang out with him over me, but he's not good enough for me to meet."

"Yet," I reply with a grin that I hope hides what I'm thinking. "I'm sure he'll introduce you soon enough."

"Why are you grinning? Have you met Kenny's boyfriend?" Her second question comes out as a shrieking accusation.

"No, I haven't met him," I reply with a chuckle. "I'm just saying you need to be patient. Give Kenny time to figure out how he wants to introduce you two."

She shakes her head. "I don't need him to *plan* an introduction. I can meet his boyfriend in a damn Starbucks restroom, for all I care. I just don't like feeling like I'm being kept in the dark."

I bite the inside of my cheek to keep from laughing out loud. When I approached Patricia for her help a few weeks ago, I knew it would be difficult keeping another secret from Rory. Especially when the last two secrets I kept from her—Hallie's suicide note and my involvement with Patricia and Hannah—seemed to blow up in my face. Still, I'm confident that the secret I'm keeping from her this time will only have positive consequences. At least, I really hope that's the case.

Rory and I enter the Lake Oswego store and the aroma of brewed espresso and freshly corked wine is rich in the air. A long line of customers is queued up at the counter in the wine-slash-espresso bar on our right, while a dozen or so others are seated at the tables. A group of employees in their green Zucker's T-shirts are gathered just outside the wine bar with a few managers from other locations who are here to celebrate.

Rory looks a bit uncomfortable as we pass a display of Valentine's Day greeting cards and fresh floral arrangements tied with pink and red ribbons. "You didn't tell me Jamie was going to be here," she remarks.

"Of course she's here. So are Benji and Peter."

Rory knows Benji as the manager of the Burnside location where she worked. Peter is Jamie's brother, who manages the Burlingame location. Rory met him at the grand opening of the first wine bar on Burnside, where I had to stealthily avoid running into Rory. But I don't understand why Rory's shocked to see Jamie here.

Rory puts on a smile as we approach the group. "Hey, Benji," she says with phony enthusiasm.

Bella, Benji's wife and Rory's old boss, turns around at the sound of Rory's voice. Bella's holding their newborn son in her arms and Rory's facial expression and body language change immediately.

"Oh, my goodness!" she says when she spots the baby, but this time her enthusiasm is absolutely genuine. "Can I hold him?"

Bella's red lips curl into a proud smile. "Of course you can," she says, positioning her arms to perform the handoff. "Look at you, Rory. You look great. Have you lost weight?"

Rory laughs at this as she carefully takes the baby into her arms. "Not that I know of. I don't own a scale, but if my jeans could speak, I'm pretty sure they'd tell me I need to lay off the chocolate."

"Really?" Bella remarks. "There's something different about you. Maybe it's the sex glow?" She winks at me and I shake my head.

"It's definitely not that," I reply, trying not to sound too sexually frustrated.

Rory rolls her eyes as she gently taps the tip of her index finger on the baby's pouty bottom lip. "He's so beautiful. What's his name?"

"Theodore, but we call him Teddy," Benji replies. "Figured we'd keep the tradition of presidential names going."

Rory's eyes are locked on Teddy's. "Did you know your dad was named after Benji Franklin? I didn't," she says, speaking in a bright singsong voice.

Teddy's eyes are fixated on Rory's. He reaches up and grabs a chunk of her auburn hair and stares at it, utterly mesmerized. Then his round face breaks into a glowing smile.

"Oh, my God. He's smiling at me," Rory says, glancing at Bella.

Suddenly, my pulse races as I imagine Rory as a mother. I never realized how much I wanted to see that until now.

I slide my phone out of my pocket and take a step back to take a picture. Rory continues to speak to Teddy and his eyes dart around excitedly, seeking out the sound of her voice. I snap a couple of photos then I text the pictures to Rory, to show her how mesmerizingly beautiful she looks right now. But the spell is quickly broken when Jamie busts into the conversation.

"So how's the job with your dad going?" Jamie asks.

Rory hands the baby back to Bella, and the look on her face changes from pure delight to complete horror. "What?"

"What job?" I ask, addressing my question to Rory, but it's Jamie who answers.

"I thought you knew," Jamie says, but the expression on Rory's face makes it plainly obvious that Jamie has brought up something Rory didn't want me to know.

I can demand that Rory tell me what Jamie's talking about, or I can take a few deep breaths and try to make it through the rest of the grand opening without further embarrassment. Since I have as much riding on this grand opening as Jamie, Benji, and Peter, I opt for the second option. I'll pretend I'm not totally fucking floored that Rory has kept a secret from me until we leave.

Thankfully, after meeting with a few of the employees and customers, Rory and I are able to duck out of there an hour later. The moment we're both inside my car, the tension between us is thick enough to carve with a chainsaw. I make no attempt to start the car before I address the issue.

"You didn't tell me you're going to work for your dad," I say, my voice taking on a hard edge.

"That's because I haven't decided yet."

"Well, Jamie seems to think you've made your decision." I turn to her and she's staring at the dashboard. "What happened to writing your book?"

"Maybe I don't want to write the book anymore," she mutters.

I draw in a deep breath to calm myself. I don't know if I'm just pissed that she's going to work on the charity we've both successfully avoided discussing the past couple of weeks since our parents concocted this ridiculous idea, or if I'm more upset that she's giving up on telling her story. *Our* story.

"You spent years working on that book, and now you're just going to give up on it?"

"It's *my* book, Houston," she says, her chest trembling with each breath she takes. "*My* book. *My* life. *My* business."

"It became *my* business the moment you called me telling me you needed me."

She turns to me with rage lighting up her hazel eyes. "Oh, you were involved *way* before that, Houston. You were involved from the moment you gave my book to my *mother*!"

I chuckle at this accusation. "Now you're getting mad at me for something you were *thanking* me for last month?"

"Go ahead. Laugh. Do you know what it's like to lose almost three years of work? No, you don't," she says as the first tears roll down her cheeks. "Do you know what it's like to have the most private moments of your life revealed to your own mother? It fucking *sucks*. And now she won't even return the favor. You're *all* keeping stuff from me. You, Kenny, my mom, my dad. And I'm *so fucking sick of it!*"

I reach for her, but she smacks my hand away. "Rory, you had a major setback. It happens," I begin, and she rolls her eyes at me. "Do you think I got my business up and running on the first try? I've made a shit ton of mistakes along the way, and I keep making them, but most people don't let something like that stand in the way of achieving their dream."

"Maybe writing isn't my dream anymore."

I shake my head. "Don't do that, Rory. Don't hurt yourself to try to prove a point to me."

"Take me home," she says, sitting back in her seat and shifting her gaze to the dark clouds hanging over the Zucker's parking lot.

"So that's it? You don't want to talk about it? You're just going to give up and go work for your dad?"

She lets out a soft puff of laughter as she shakes her head. "Listen to yourself. Do you even hear what you're saying? You're actually angry that I want to work for a foundation set up to help people like Hallie? Do you know how insensitive you sound right now?"

I clench my jaw as I slide the key into the ignition and turn on the car. "Fine. Let's go."

"Oh, how convenient. Now that the tables have turned on you, you don't want to talk about it anymore. Just take me home."

The twenty-five-minute drive to Patricia's apartment is excruciatingly silent, with Rory too proud to admit that she's using her father's foundation as an excuse to give up on her dream and me refusing to admit that the foundation is a positive thing for both of our families, and the lives and families of people like Hallie. I'm not stupid or insensitive. I know my mom and James will do good things with Hallie's Hope. But I don't want any part of it. And I don't think it's unreasonable that I don't want Rory to give up on her dreams just to assuage our parents' guilt.

I understand why James and my mom need this foundation. They both knew about what happened to Hallie, and they both feel like they didn't do enough to help her when she was alive. But this isn't Rory's cross to bear.

Rory's story isn't Hallie's story. Hallie's story is over.

Rory

"Don't call me tonight," I say as Houston pulls up in front of my mom's building. "I'm too angry to talk to you right now."

"I won't."

His response is so cold and unexpected, I hop out of the car and slam the door shut before he can see my reaction. My chest aches as I walk quickly across the lobby, ignoring the friendly greeting from the guy working the concierge desk. I punch the elevator call button furiously, hoping the doors will slide open soon. Mercifully, the doors open for me before the first tears fall, and I tuck myself into the corner near the control panel as I wait impatiently for the elevator to close and take me up to the safety of the fourth floor.

Houston is wrong. Giving up on my book does not mean I'm giving up on my dream.

I haven't told him about my sessions with the therapist, because I think I need to keep that area of my life to myself. I need to work out the problems I discuss with my therapist on my own. My biggest issue is that I'm always reacting instead of acting. I spent five years of my life on cruise control, just waiting for the next speed bump or inevitable crash. Complacency was a way of life for me.

Not anymore.

I don't think Liam came into my life at the same moment as Houston out of sheer coincidence. I don't know if it was God, fate, the universe, or karma, but I think Liam came into my life to teach me a lesson about impermanence.

I never once considered that all the work I put into my book could be wiped out in an instant. Or that everything I thought I knew about Hallie could be called into question, more than once. I know now that nothing lasts forever. Not even the all-consuming love that once defined you as a person.

So maybe Houston and I are finally becoming who we were always meant to be. He always saw me as the storyteller. And I always saw him as the hero. But maybe the truth is that we're just two fucked-up people who have no business trying to fit the fucked-up pieces of our fucked-up lives together.

I guess it's fitting that this realization should come the day before Valentine's Day. It was six years ago today that I asked Houston if our story had to end, and he responded with, "I hope it never ends."

The truth is that every story ends at some point. It's just that some stories end happier than others.

February 17, 2015

The meeting with my dad's tax attorneys is just as boring as I imagined it would be. I spent the entire two hours taking notes on the various legal forms of a nonprofit organization, and the advantages that come with each form. Some of the legal and financial jargon goes over my head, but by the end of the meeting, I'm pretty certain they've settled on establishing Hallie's Hope as a public-benefit nonprofit corporation. I hide my unadulterated excitement when the meeting ends, keeping my business poker face on as my dad and I exit the conference room at his law office.

"When are you going to get an office for the foundation?" I ask as we head down the hall.

My dad glances over his shoulder to make sure the tax attorneys are gone before he responds. "I already have office space, very close to your mom's apartment in the Pearl District. I'll get you a key soon so you can set up your desk. If all goes well, we should have the foundation up and running in six months, which means you'll have plenty of time to help me with hiring and getting all the offices set up."

"Help you with hiring? I don't know anything about hiring people, especially not for a nonprofit."

He laughs as he reaches for the door handle. "I have complete faith in your ability to learn as you go. You need to give yourself a little more credit."

He opens the door and my heart leaps into my throat. Ava is sitting in one of the visitor chairs in my dad's office. The moment she sees me, her face lights up as if she's never been happier to see someone in her entire life.

"Oh, Rory," she says, covering her mouth as her eyes well up with tears.

"I'll leave you two to catch up," my dad mutters as he exits the office, closing the door softly behind him.

Ava stands from the chair and I'm frozen as she makes her way toward me. "You look so beautiful," she says, reaching up to touch my hair.

I don't know how to respond. I didn't realize how much I

needed to see Ava until now. And now I feel like a complete idiot. Does she know about my fight with Houston? Does she know we haven't spoken in four days? Is that why she's here? No, that's ridiculous. She's obviously here to talk to my dad. She doesn't know anything about how I've spent the past four days checking my phone every ten minutes for missed calls and texts from Houston.

I throw my arms around Ava's waist and grip her in a tight hug. "I'm sorry I haven't been down to see you."

She laughs as she wraps her arms around me. "Oh, honey, don't be silly. McMinnville isn't exactly around the corner from here. And you've been busy."

"No, I haven't been that busy. I'm sorry I never came back."

She rubs my back. "It's okay. We all dealt with it the best we could. The important thing is that you're here now. If Hallie were here, she'd want you to be a part of this."

I sniff loudly as I let go of her, cringing when I notice the wet spot on her jean jacket. "Sorry."

She glances at the spot and waves off my apology. "Not like I'm not used to a little rain."

I smile when she winks at me, then I let out a deep sigh. "Do you really think Hallie would be happy with what we're doing? I mean, she didn't even want us to know."

She smiles at my question. "She wanted you to know. She just didn't know how you'd react." She takes a beat before she continues. "She told your father because she desperately wanted others to know. And…" She presses her lips together and draws in a deep breath through her nose as she tries to get a grip on her emotions. "And I'm so glad she told him, because it helped me understand the dynamics of their relationship. And now we can help other victims find the courage to use their voice."

I nod as I finally understand what all this is about. Hallie's Hope is Hallie's story. And now that she's gone, I have to tell the story for her. And this will help others like her tell *their* stories.

When Dr. Little asked me why I wanted to tell the story of Houston and me, I couldn't come up with a valid reason. I told her I couldn't complete her homework assignment because I didn't have the answer to that question. Now I do.

I wanted to tell the story of Houston and me because it made me feel close to Hallie. But it wasn't our story I needed to tell. It was hers.

"Thank you," I say, and Ava looks a bit confused. "For coming here today and for doing this with my dad."

She waves off my gratitude. "Oh, please. I'm the one who's grateful for you two." She reaches out and grabs my hand. "Houston loves you more than anything. And even if he doesn't agree with everything we're doing here, you and your father are now a part of our family. He'll understand that soon enough."

I hug her one more time before I head back to my mom's apartment. Though I'm in a bit of a haze now, wondering if Ava *was* there to try to set things right between Houston and me. No, that's just my narcissism rearing its ugly head again. Not everything is about me and Houston. And our problems are not so easily fixed. It will take a lot more than a heartfelt speech from Ava to make things work between us.

When I enter the apartment, my mom is in the kitchen and the sound of the coffee machine sputtering its final drops into the carafe is like music to my ears. I follow the rich aroma into the kitchen and find her pressing start on the dishwasher.

"Can I have a cup?"

My mom jumps two feet in the air at the sound of my voice. "Jesus, Rory! You scared the life out of me." She glares at me when I laugh. "Very funny. Give the old woman a heart attack. Ha ha."

"You're not an old woman, Mom. You're fifty-one."

She rolls her eyes as she reaches into the cupboard for a

couple of mugs. "I may not be an old woman, but I am a wise woman. And I know a stubborn woman when I see one."

"What? What are you talking about?"

She pours one mug of hot coffee then replaces the carafe on the burner instead of pouring the second cup. "I'm talking about you and this stupid argument you had with Houston."

My eyes widen with shock. "Where is this coming from?"

She shrugs as if she doesn't know, but she continues as if she knows exactly what she's getting at. "I think you're taking your frustration with me out on Houston, and it's not right," she says, her gaze locked on the kitchen counter. "My decision to not show you my book has *nothing* to do with Houston's sincere attempt to help you get your book published."

This is clearly an ambush. Either Houston put her up to this or she thinks siding with Houston will get me so angry with her that I'll go running back to Houston. She's probably just tired of me moping around the apartment, cramping her single lifestyle.

"You mean Houston's attempt to *hide* the fact that he was helping me get my book published? The way *everyone* seems to hide *everything* from me these days?"

"I understand you need someone to take out your frustrations on, but Houston is not the one who wronged you. *No one* has wronged you, Rory. What we did with your book, we did out of love for you, and you *know* that. So stop behaving like a spoiled teenager and go apologize to Houston."

I narrow my eyes at her. "Are you *seriously* taking his side?"

She sighs heavily. "Rory, six months ago I would probably have been the last person you'd expect to take Houston's side in an argument."

I laugh at this. "Well, maybe you weren't so wrong about him. Maybe he *was* just a cocky frat boy after all."

"No. Things have changed. I've changed. You've changed. *Houston* has changed. And you can't keep treating him like the man who lied to you. You can't keep punishing him for keeping Hallie's letter from you." She sets her mug down on the counter and steps forward, taking my face in her hands. "He loves you, Rory. And I know, beyond a shadow of a doubt, that he only wants what's best for you."

I look into her eyes and my heart drops. I can't speak.

She lets go of my face and smiles as she realizes her words have struck a chord. "He's spent a lot of his valuable time and effort, time he could have spent trying to get over you after you repeatedly rejected his apologies. He spent that time doing everything he could to make your dreams come true. Now it's your turn to swallow your pride and show a little gratitude. You have to go to him this time."

Her words are so sharply true, they cut me down to nothing. How could I not see how selfish I've been? Yes, I have a right to grieve Hallie's and Liam's deaths, but I don't have a right to take my anger and frustration out on the one person who loves me despite the fact that I've repeatedly dumped all my baggage on him over the past few weeks. The one person who's been more of a friend to me than anyone since I lost Liam, though he's had every right to keep his distance.

It takes me ten minutes to walk the few blocks to Houston's apartment, and another five minutes for me to work up the nerve to use the key he forced me to take a few weeks ago. He usually gets home from work sometime around six or seven p.m. I can wait a couple of hours for him. That will give me time to think of what I'm going to say.

I enter Houston's apartment and I don't know why I'm surprised to see it's a mess. Houston used to help me clean our old apartment when we were at UO, but only after lots of cajoling and threatening to withhold sex on my part. And I guess it's a bit of a cliché that guys tend to let their bad habits take over in the midst of a breakup.

I could push aside the pile of clean laundry he tossed onto the sofa and wait for him. Or I could put away the laundry and throw away the three greasy boxes of pizza on the counter. And do the dishes in the sink. Oh, who am I kidding? I have to clean this mess.

I shake my head as I clean Houston's apartment, mildly disgusted with how much my mother's habits have clearly rubbed off on me these past few weeks. When I'm done, I smile and breathe a sigh of relief as I sit back on the sofa. He won't just accept my apology. He'll be begging me to come live with him after he sees this.

My smile quickly disappears at this thought. *Holy shit.* Have I been domesticated?

My heart races as panic sets in. Maybe I should just leave. I can call Houston later and apologize to him over the phone. Then I can start looking for an apartment of my own with the first paycheck my dad gives me next week.

I stand from the sofa and head for the kitchen to grab my purse off the table in the breakfast nook, but the sound of the door opening stops me cold. I watch in horror as the door handle turns and Houston walks in. For a long moment, he stares at the sofa, which is conspicuously free of all laundry. Then his gaze shifts to the coffee table, where there are no more empty bottles of Gatorade. Then he turns toward me and his eyes widen with shock.

"What's going on here?" he asks.

Just the sound of his voice, which I haven't heard in four excruciatingly long days, stirs emotions inside me. I can't leave without apologizing. I need him to know how sorry I am as much as he needs to know it.

"This is me apologizing to you," I reply. "I know why you wanted me to write the book, but I can't do it. Not because I don't love you, but because that book is *not* us."

He drops his keys in a bowl on the coffee table. "Not anymore, it's not. It was erased."

I take a few steps toward him. "Houston, since the day I ran into you in Jamie's office last August, I've learned an important lesson. A lesson that I only recently understood when someone gave me a very eye-opening homework assignment."

His eyebrows shoot up. "Homework assignment? What are you talking about?"

I shake my head. "It doesn't matter. What matters is what I learned from it."

He lets out a frustrated sigh. "What did you learn?"

I take a few more steps, until I'm so close I have to look up at him. "I learned that, whether it's the love between father and daughter or the love between a man and a woman, you can't erase love. Not with a delete button or six years or six hundred miles." I reach up, brushing the tips of my fingers over the sandpaper scruff on his jaw. "That book isn't us. *This* is us. Just you and me, getting through every day. That's our story."

His gaze is fixed on something behind me as the muscle in his jaw twitches. "I guess I began to equate fighting for the book with fighting for us." He sighs heavily as he shifts his gaze to my face. "But you're right. We're living the story right now." His hand comes up, landing on my cheek, rough and warm against my skin. "And there's no one else I'd rather live it with."

He takes my face in his hands and I hold my breath as I close my eyes and wait for his mouth to fall over mine. His lips taste citrusy, like orange Gatorade. His tongue parts my lips and slides into my mouth, sending a shiver of warmth cascading through me. Every tilt of his head and brush of his lips adds fuel to the fire building in my core, until I'm panting like an animal in heat. But we can't have sex until we've hashed out the dynamics of our arrangement.

Reluctantly, I place my hands flat on his solid chest and push him back. "We have to talk."

He looks down at me, his lips still parted and eyes hooded with lust. "There'll be time for that later."

I push him back again as he leans down to kiss me. "No, we have to talk now."

He lets out a groan that's packed with so much sexual frustration I almost laugh. "Fine. Let's talk."

I sit on the sofa and pat the cushion for him. "I think we should move in together."

"Great. So do I." He lunges toward me and I laugh as I push him away.

"I'm serious, Houston."

"So am I," he insists, his hand landing on my thigh. "I'll help you move your stuff in tomorrow, but tonight I have other plans for you."

I narrow my eyes at him as he slides his hand upward. He glares back at me for a moment before he rolls his eyes and lets out another groan as he removes his hand from my crotch and sits back.

"All right. Let's talk," he says. "I'll help you get moved in whenever you're ready."

"And you're not going to hold my new job against me?"

His head snaps in my direction. "Of course I won't do that. I'm not a total jerk. Do you promise you won't hold my job against me?"

I cock an eyebrow. "Why would I hold your job against you?"

"You know I love my job, Rory. And there are going to be times when I don't come home early, because we're testing out a new flavor or a new system. And there'll be times I come home a little drunk for the same reason. I love my job. And just like you don't want me to tell you how to do your job, I need the same thing from you."

I can't help but smile. "I love that you have a passion for

beer. I would never get mad at you for that."

He bites his lip as he looks down at me, his blue eyes dark with desire. "You know what else I have a passion for? Dinner. I'm *very* hungry."

I chuckle. "I get it. You want to perform oral sex on me. But can we please finish our conversation first?"

"What else do we need to discuss?"

I take a deep breath and let it out slowly. "Birth control."

His eyes widen. "Oh, yeah."

"I've been on the pill for a while, but, well, you know it's not one hundred percent effective." A sharp pain twists in my chest as I think about the abortion I had six years ago. "We need to agree on what would happen if… if I should become pregnant."

Houston turns his body toward me and takes my face in his hands. "Now it's my turn to apologize." His eyes shine with a steely resolve. "I'm sorry I asked you to get an abortion. Maybe we weren't ready back then, but I have no doubt that you would have been an unbelievable mother. And you would have whipped me into shape. I made a huge mistake. I know that now."

I blink furiously to clear my vision. "Thanks, but you don't have to apologize. Neither of us were ready."

"Maybe not. But if you were to get pregnant now, I'd hope for twins. Or triplets. Fuck, I'd have a *thousand* kids with you."

I laugh out loud. "No, no, no. No triplets. And you can take custody of your thousand kids and go live in a shoe for all I care."

He smiles as he leans in and stifles my laughter with a deep kiss. The kind of kiss that could make a girl forget her name. When he pulls away, I draw in a large breath of Houston-scented air, as I'm suddenly feeling a bit woozy.

He brushes his thumb over my bottom lip as he stares at my mouth. "Is it dinnertime yet?"

My chest heaves as he looks up and our eyes meet. "I hope so. I'm starving."

"We've lived together a week and you're already cheating on me."

Houston's eyes widen at my accusation, then he lets out a nervous chuckle. "What are you talking about?"

He closes the front door behind him and my gaze follows him as he hangs his coat in the closet and crosses the room toward me. He drops his keys in the bowl on top of the coffee table, where my feet are propped up, then he takes a seat next to me on the sofa. I turn my cheek to him when he leans in to kiss me on the lips.

"So you're not denying it?" I say, crossing my arms over my chest.

"Rory, how can I deny something that's so completely ridiculous?"

I turn to face him, fixing him with a savage glare. "I saw it!" I reply, pointing at the TV. "You binge-watched three episodes of *Breaking Bad* without me."

He hangs his head, but I can still see him trying not to smile. "You're right. I cheated. But it's not my fault, baby," he says, looking up at me. "They got me with those damn cliffhangers."

I shake my head and let out a heavy sigh. "Well, now you're

going to have to watch them all over again with me. That's your punishment."

He leans in and kisses my neck. "Do I have to pay attention, or can I practice my knitting while you watch?"

"Practice your knitting? Is that code for sticking your needle in my loop?"

He brushes his lips over the sensitive skin along the curve of my neck. "You catch on quickly."

My eyelids flutter as he lays a trail of kisses up my neck and buries his nose in my hair. His hot breath thunders in the shell of my ear, sending shivers through me.

"I'd better get an awesome sweater out of this," I say, my voice shaky with desire.

"I'll make you a whole fucking winter wardrobe," he replies, sliding his hand under the Barley Legal T-shirt I'm wearing. "And I'll throw in a pearl necklace free of charge."

I shake my head, unable to hide my grin. "So generous."

He yanks my top off roughly and I laugh as he twirls it over his head and tosses it onto the floor somewhere near the TV. His lips land on my neck and I swallow hard as he sucks on my flesh while undoing my bra. He slides the straps off slowly, then he unceremoniously chucks it onto the floor with my shirt.

His large hands grab my waist and he lifts me up so he can place me in the corner of the sofa. His eyes are wild with hunger as he tugs my panties off. My back is against a pillow while my head rests against the back of the couch.

Pulling off his T-shirt, he smiles as he kneels down on the floor in front of me and spreads my legs apart. "Have you been thinking about me today?" he says, sliding a finger between my wet folds.

"Yes," I reply, my chest heaving with anticipation.

One of his hands spreads my lips apart while his other finger lightly caresses my throbbing clit. "Did you touch yourself?"

My eyelids flutter as the pleasure builds. "No," I breathe. "I wanted to wait for you."

He softly squeezes my clit between his thumb and forefinger and I whimper. "Next time, I want you to touch yourself, but I want you to call me first so I can listen. Okay, baby?"

His voice is so commanding, yet reassuring. Just the sound of it is getting me close to coming.

I nod. "Okay."

He lowers his head between my legs and my eyes roll back as the orgasm builds. He kisses my clit firmly, then sucks on it the way he sometimes sucks on my tongue. Every nerve ending in my body is zinging with pleasure. A warm rush spreads through me. I grab the back of his head to hold us both steady as my legs begin to quake.

"Houston." I whisper his name the first time, then it comes out progressively louder the next six times, until I have to push him away because I can't take it anymore.

He pulls his head back and chuckles as I writhe with the aftereffects of the orgasm. "That was a good one," he says, sliding a finger inside me.

I flinch a little at how quickly he finds my G-spot, then I shake my head adamantly. "No, please. Give me a minute."

He smiles as he pulls his finger out and slips it into his mouth. "Mmm… That's like your secret sauce."

I laugh as I try to sit up, but he places his hand on my shoulder to push me back. He shakes his head as he grabs my hips and angles my body a little. He stands up and I marvel at the sexy cut of his muscles, the way they move as he takes his pants and boxer briefs off. I draw in a deep breath as he straddles me with one of his knees on the seat cushion and one foot on the floor.

He bends down and brushes his thumb over my bottom lip. "I was fantasizing about this mouth all day today."

He kisses me slowly and my breathing quickens as I taste

myself on him. His tongue plunges inside my mouth and I reach up to hold his face as I suck on it. Threading his fingers through my hair, he grabs a chunk of my hair and tugs my head back. Adrenaline courses through me, making me tremble as I watch him stand up while maintaining his hold on my hair.

"Open your mouth," he commands me.

I lick my lips then open my mouth wide as his erection advances toward my face. The corners of my mouth burn as his cock stretches my lips. He thrusts slowly at first, his eyes locked on mine, occasionally pulling out to ask if I'm comfortable. But I know when his grip on my hair tightens and he pushes in farther that he's going to come soon. My eyes begin to water as he hits the back of my throat and activates my gag reflex. He eases up a bit and I take the opportunity to curl my fist around his cock. Wrapping my lips tightly around my teeth, I pump my fist and bob my head in a sensual rhythm. He grips the back of the sofa to steady himself, and tears slide down my temples as he finishes in my mouth.

Twenty minutes later, Skippy is seated patiently at my feet as I stand in the kitchen wearing nothing but a Ducks T-shirt I found a few days ago, stuck between the wall and the back of the hamper. I dig through the utensil drawer for the microplane I brought with me when I moved in, then I use it to shave some Parmigiano-Reggiano cheese onto our postcoital dinner salads. Houston enters the kitchen freshly showered and fully clothed in a T-shirt, jeans, work boots, and jacket.

"Where are you going?" I ask, making no attempt to hide my disappointment.

He shrugs as if to imply that this isn't his choice. "Just got a text from Troy. Pilot vat sprang a leak. We've got hot mash all over the floor, and one of the guys slipped and burned his arm. I'll be back as soon as I can."

"But you haven't eaten," I protest.

He kisses me on the forehead and pats Skippy on the head. "I'll grab something in the restaurant. I'll be back soon."

I sigh as I take my salad to the living room, feeding the grilled chicken from Houston's salad to Skippy while catching up on *Breaking Bad.* Houston is gone no more than twenty minutes when I get a text message from him that makes me smile.

> **Houston:** Make sure you have Skippy close by to comfort you while you watch episode 13.

> **Me:** Thanks for the tip.

> **Houston:** There's more where that tip came from.

> **Me:** Very punny. See you soon. :)

When I wake in the morning, Houston is laid out facedown on the bed next to me. He came home at almost midnight last night and headed straight for the shower, claiming he was covered in sour mash. When he fell asleep, I resisted the temptation to smell the clothes he threw in the laundry basket.

Houston hasn't given me a reason not to trust him. And I will continue to believe him until I get a solid reason to suspect he's doing something other than working late, as he has been doing more frequently over the past two weeks since they started testing out a new summer ale in their pilot brewing system. I'm guessing that whatever happened with the vat yesterday will only set them back, and he'll probably have to work late again tonight.

Glancing at the clock on the nightstand, I realize Houston will be getting up for work in about twenty minutes. I don't have to start getting ready for work for another couple of hours, so I decide to make us some breakfast. He'll need a good meal to deal with the aftermath of whatever happened at the brewery yesterday.

Sliding out of bed, I stealthily leave the bedroom. I wash my face and brush my teeth quickly before I head to the kitchen to cook. The orange juice is freshly squeezed, the eggs have been whisked, and the bacon is sizzling in the cast-iron skillet by the time Houston stumbles into the kitchen.

His hair is sticking out in all directions and a large crease slashes across his left cheek. He squints at me through the light pouring in through the floor-to-ceiling windows. All I can think is that he looks absolutely exquisite, the way the morning light bounces off his golden-caramel hair and paints buttery streaks of light over his taut abs and broad shoulders. He's glowing. God, the man is hot, sizzling perfection. I can practically hear the fizzle of the fuse in my head, followed by the loud *pop!* of fireworks going off inside me.

"Look out!" he shouts, reaching for me as if he's about to save me from an incoming grenade.

He yanks me away from the stove, but not before the grease in the skillet pops, splashing a walnut-sized blob of hot grease onto the top side of my forearm.

"Shit!" I scream, with only one thought in my head: Get to the sink!

Houston beats me to it. He grabs me by the waist and sets me down on the counter next to the sink, then he turns on the faucet. I place my arm under the stream of cool water and sigh with instant relief. Then I let out a few curse words as the stinging returns.

"Are you okay?" he asks, his eyebrows knitted with genuine concern.

I sigh as I pull my arm out of the water and laugh. "Maybe you should turn off the flame on that skillet."

He reaches back and turns off the range, then he turns back to me, shaking his head in dismay as he examines the screaming pink mark on my arm. "What would you do if I wasn't here?" he says as he grabs a blue ice pack out of the freezer and holds it against my arm.

I flinch a little as the cold gives me a good shock. "Um… exactly what I just did? It's not like I'm going to die from a grease burn." I remove the pack from my arm and set it on the counter. "It's too cold."

I coil my arms around his neck and he smiles as he spreads my knees apart to get closer to me. He slips his hands under the Ducks T-shirt I'm wearing, his eyes widening as he slides his hands over my bare ass and realizes I'm not wearing panties.

"No panties and you're sitting on the counter? You're a dirty girl," he murmurs, his mouth hovering over mine as his hand slides between my thighs.

He kisses me slowly as his finger glides into me. I moan into his mouth and this only urges him on as he uses his other hand to grab my ass firmly and pull me closer to the edge of the counter. His finger pierces me deeper as the rough of his palm rubs hot friction into my clit. And just when I think I'm getting ready to climax, he removes his hand from between my legs and tilts his head back to watch my face.

"I think it's time for a little pre-breakfast appetizer."

I bite my lip with anticipation as he kneels before me and kisses the inside of my knee. His gaze drops as he becomes completely focused on the task at hand. His mouth plants a slow trail of kisses over my thigh, drawing out the anticipation until the sweet throbbing ache between my legs becomes almost painful.

I thread my fingers through his hair, clutching a handful as I gently encourage him to go for the prize. He chuckles at my impatience, but he quickly obliges my hints. His hot mouth covers my clit, kissing and lightly sucking until I can hardly breathe. The orgasm hits me like a freight train. But Houston doesn't allow me to give up there.

With my muscles still twitching, my limbs still warm and pliable, he stands up and slides into me. I wrap my legs around his hips and his fingers bite into my ass as he watches his cock thrusting in and out of me. He looks up at me for a moment, to see if I'm also watching.

"You see that?" he says, turning his attention back to the way his cock moves back and forth in a seamless rhythm. "I'm knitting you a baby sweater… Purl in front…" He slides out of me and rubs the tip of his cock over the crease of my ass. "Purl in the back?"

I laugh. "Purl in front, knit in the back. And… with that monster? You must be out of your mind."

He shrugs as he slides back into me. "We've got plenty of time to work our way up to that."

He plunges into me slowly and methodically, taking his time until the pleasure becomes too much for him. For the last few minutes, he fucks me hard and deep. His large hands have a firm grip on my ass as he pounds into me. I cry out each time he slams into my clit, and another orgasm ripples out from my core. He thrusts into me faster for a brief moment, before he begins to slow down, his cock twitching as he finds his release. His hand slides between us, rubbing my clit to finish me off while he's still inside me.

"Oh, God," I breathe, my body trembling as I pull him closer, resting my cheek on his solid, sweaty shoulder.

He buries his face in my neck as he wraps his arms around me and holds me tightly against him. His cock continues to twitch inside me as he breathes heavily into my hair. Then he opens his mouth and scrapes his teeth over my skin, his tongue tasting me as we both try to catch our breath.

"I have to get going," he says, though he makes no move to pull out of me.

"But you haven't had breakfast," I reply, slipping my fingers into his hair and smiling when I see goose bumps sprout on the back of his neck.

He finally pulls out, slowly, and tucks his monster back in its cage. "I'll eat at work. I gotta get back there before the repair guy shows up to fix the valve on the vat."

He lays a soft kiss on my cheekbone and another on the corner of my mouth before he heads to the bathroom to take a quick shower. I try not to think crazy things like the possibility that Houston's having an affair, or that… he hates my cooking! He always has to leave when it's time to eat.

He spends five minutes in the shower and another ten minutes getting dressed and doing his hair. He's out the door before I've even finished scrambling my eggs. Once the breakfast dishes are cleaned, I take a shower and get ready to finally see the new Hallie's Hope offices around the corner at ten a.m. Only, when I arrive at the address my dad gave me, no one's there and the key he gave me for the front door doesn't work.

I call his cell and he picks up right away. "Dad, the key to the office isn't working."

"What? That's impossible. I had the copy made from my own key. Are you sure you're using the key I gave you?"

"Yes. It's the only key I have other than my apartment key. I still haven't gotten my car back from Kenny."

"You haven't gotten your car back yet? Honey, you need to do that. If you're going to be working for me, you'll need a car to go to meetings and fund-raising events."

"I know, I know. I just haven't gotten around to it yet. I wasn't able to get the parking space at Mom's building, and now I'm waiting for them to assign me one here. It never ends."

He chuckles. "Well, hopefully you're all settled now and you won't need to worry about this stuff anymore for a while."

I sigh as I think about my insecurity over Houston's work habits, and how I promised him before I moved in that I wouldn't get upset if he had to work late. God, I'm such a typical girl. I almost hate myself.

"Honey, is everything okay with Houston?"

"Yeah, everything's fine. I'm just frustrated because now I have to go back to the apartment and be alone again. When can you get me another key?"

A male voice in the background asks my dad a question and he tells the person to wait a minute. "Sweetheart, I'm about to go into court. I'll have to call you back when it lets out and we can set up a time to meet and exchange keys. Okay?"

"Okay, Dad. Good luck."

"Thank you."

I walk back to the apartment wondering if I should be happy that I got out of work or annoyed that I'm going to have to find a way to meet my dad to exchange keys later. I don't know if it's okay to invite him here, even when Houston is gone. Houston has been very supportive when I've talked about my new job over the past week, but I can still sense some tension when the topic is broached. We're not out of the woods yet.

The rain begins as I turn onto our street, so I walk briskly past the yoga center toward the building entrance. When I enter our apartment, the place reeks of bacon. Despite the fact that it's raining and about fifty degrees outside, I open all the windows and begin burning a vanilla-scented candle. I reach into the coat closet to get my coat, when I notice something familiar sticking out of the pocket of the coat Houston was wearing when he left for work last night.

My heart races as I wonder how much of a violation of his privacy it would be for me to slip the Sierra Nevada tin box out of his coat pocket. I mean, he did once give me that box, even if I did give it back to him. It was *mine* at one point in time.

I stare at the corner of the tin box for a couple of minutes, but I finally give in to my baser instincts and slowly slide it out of the coat. The moment I slip it out of his pocket, I notice something is wrong. There's no sound or movement coming from inside the box.

I swallow hard as I carefully lift the lid and find the folded envelope containing Hallie's suicide note. I pull the envelope out and my heart drops. The ring is gone.

Why is the ring gone? There could be a million reasons. Maybe he's having it sized. No, that doesn't make sense. I haven't gained or lost weight. Have I? No, that's ridiculous. If I haven't noticed I've gained weight, then Houston definitely wouldn't notice. But then, why else would the ring be missing from this box?

Either he gave the ring to someone else (ridiculous) or he took it to a jeweler (plausible). But for what? Houston definitely doesn't need to sell the ring for money. And if he doesn't need the money, then the only explanation is that he doesn't think he needs the ring. Now that I've moved in with him, there's no reason to come home on time. No reason to share a meal with me. And now, no reason to marry me.

Rory

I make a quick stop to take care of some personal business before I walk the ten or so blocks to Killer Burger. When I spoke to Kenny yesterday, I insisted that I needed to meet him to get my car back, but that I also had some things I wanted to discuss with him about Houston. In return, Kenny insisted I meet him at Killer Burger, so we could get a bite to eat while we chat. And I'm not one to deny a man his craving for a José Mendoza. But the moment I enter Killer Burger and spot Kenny seated at a table near the window, I realize José has been replaced.

Kenny is sitting next to a gorgeous man who appears to be a few years older and a few inches taller than him. His friend has dark hair, cropped in a military buzz cut to show off his perfectly shaped head. And even from about ten feet away, I can tell he has the brightest blue eyes I've ever seen on a human. As soon as Kenny spots me, he leaps out of his chair and runs to me, and the guy next to him stands up a bit awkwardly.

Kenny throws his arms around me. "Aurora, my love. I've missed you."

I hug him briefly. "I've missed you too," I say as he locks arms with me and leads me toward the table. "Who's your friend?"

Kenny beams as his friend flashes me a stunning smile. "Rory, this is Pedro. Pedro, this is my best friend, Rory."

Pedro is dressed better than I am, and when I shake his hand I'm pretty sure his hand is softer than mine.

"Nice to meet you, Rory," Pedro says in a deep, smooth voice, which, if I'm not mistaken, is laced with a tinge of a Texas drawl. "I've heard a lot about you from Kenny."

The way he glances at Kenny and holds on to each syllable of his name tells me this is *him*, the guy who's been killing Kenny's neck. This is the boyfriend Kenny has been keeping hidden from me. And by the looks of it, they're in love.

"I *think* I've heard a lot about you, too," I reply, looking to Kenny to confirm this is him.

He rolls his eyes. "Yes, it's him."

Pedro laughs. "I hope it's all been good things."

I take a seat across from Pedro, watching his subtle yet favorable reaction when Kenny brushes against him on the way back to his seat. The sight of it makes me so happy I could cry.

Kenny sits down and stares at me for a moment. "Oh, no, sweetheart. No tears allowed."

I dab at the corners of my eyes. "I'm sorry. I know I'm being a total girly-girl. I guess I'm just a little… emotional today."

Kenny shakes his head. "Girl, you're emotional every day." He holds up his hand to stop me from voicing my gut reaction. "And you are *entitled* to be."

I roll my eyes. "Nice save. Did you two order?"

Kenny lays his hand on Pedro's bicep and I'm pretty sure he gives it a light squeeze. "Honey, can you order for us? We both want a José Mendoza well-done."

"Hey, you don't know if I want to change my order," I protest.

Kenny fixes me with a look of utter exasperation.

I smile as I turn to Pedro. "And an iced tea, please."

Both Kenny and I stare at Pedro's perfect ass as he walks away, but Kenny interrupts me with a gentle smack on the top of my hand. "He's mine. Don't get any of your crazy redhead ideas."

"Crazy redhead ideas? Are you comparing my life to an *I Love Lucy* episode?"

He smiles as he reaches across the table and takes my hand in his. "So what do you think of him?"

I glance over my shoulder at Pedro then turn back to Kenny. "He's gorgeous, and polite. And you look very happy, so I'm very happy for you."

He raises his arms in the air and smiles. "I am happy. Wheeeee…."

I laugh. "And he's obviously very into you."

Kenny beams at my words. "You think so? I mean, not that I question his sincerity, it's just, you know… It's hard to believe something so good can be so real."

His words make me think of Houston and the reason why I wanted to meet with Kenny today. I want to know what happened to the ring. And if Kenny doesn't know, maybe he can help me stop worrying that I've made a terrible mistake by moving in with Houston. Maybe he can help me realize that something so good *can* be so real.

I glance at Pedro again and he's at the front of the queue, which means he'll be back here any minute. Now I feel slightly annoyed that Kenny brought him. Not that I didn't want to meet Pedro, but I really wanted to talk to Kenny alone. How is he going to hug me and tell me everything is going to be all right with a table and a hot Pedro between us?

Then it dawns on me. Maybe I shouldn't be talking about this with Kenny. I should be discussing this with Houston. In our hearts, Kenny and I are still best friends, and we will always be there for each other. In reality, we both have new BFFs.

"Rory, you say you're happy for me, but you don't look happy."

I look up at Kenny. "I just had a very sad thought. I came here to talk to you about Houston. You see, I didn't come straight here from our apartment. I made a stop—"

Kenny stands up suddenly, and I look over my shoulder to see Pedro approaching. "I'll help you," Kenny says, making his way to Pedro and plucking the drinks off the tray he's carrying.

I sigh and force a smile as Kenny dishes out our burgers and fries, but I've suddenly lost my appetite. I shove down a few fries and a couple small bites of my burger, but Kenny quickly realizes something's wrong.

"Aurora, the last time we were here you inhaled that burger in about two seconds."

I stretch my mouth into an even bigger, phonier smile. "I'm just tired. I didn't get enough sleep. I can't digest food when I'm tired."

Kenny gets very serious as he tears a paper towel off the roll in the center of the table and wipes the corners of his mouth. "Rory, do you remember the last time we came here? You and I pretended to be engaged and I dropped you on your junk?"

I smile at the memory. "Yes, I remember that quite well." My eyes widen as I begin to suspect what he's getting at. "Are you and Pedro *engaged*?"

They both laugh hysterically at my suggestion and Kenny shakes his head. "No, honey. We're not engaged, and I'm actually talking about you right now. Pay attention."

My brow furrows. "What are you getting at?"

He reaches into his back pocket and pulls out a small ivory envelope. Written in precise calligraphy on the outside of the envelope are the words *Page No. 1*. He holds it out to me, but I find myself gripped with fear as I try to imagine what's inside that envelope. Is it page one of my book? Is it page one of a breakup letter from Houston? The last time someone handed me an envelope in such a dramatic fashion, it contained Hallie's suicide note, and the landscape of my world was irrevocably changed.

"What is it?" I whisper.

"Open it and you'll find out," Kenny replies, his smile never wavering.

I take the envelope from his hand and I'm immediately taken by the lush creaminess of the paper and the weight of it. I take a deep breath as I lift the flap and pull out an ivory slip of paper about the size of an index card. The edges are frayed, as if the paper is very old, but it's obviously been artificially aged. The words on the page are written in handsome storybook calligraphy.

Once upon a time, a beautiful princess named Aurora was born under the majestic brilliance of the northern lights. Her parents established their kingdom in the enchanted emerald hills of McMinnville, where it rained from sunrise to sunset. Aurora spent most of her days tucked away inside the warmth of the castle, reading and telling fantastic stories to all who would listen.

1

I read the note a few times, trying to make sure I'm reading what I think I'm reading. Finally, I look up at Kenny and the beaming smile on his face tells me I'm right.

"Is this what I think it is?"

"If you think it's the first page of a beautiful fairy tale, then you are partially correct. If you also think it's the first hint in a very carefully planned scavenger hunt, then you are even more correct. But that's all I can say."

I think about the things I came here to talk about with Kenny and I'm beginning to think that none of that stuff matters. I don't need answers to the questions I came here with. All I need to know is where I'm going, and apparently, that's to my old castle in the kingdom of McMinnville.

Kenny hands me my car keys, but looks at me like I'm crazy when I bolt up from my chair to leave. "Hold up, Princess Aurora. You're not leaving without me." He turns to Pedro and my stomach flutters as they exchange a tender kiss. "I'll see you tonight."

I shake my head as we walk out to the parking lot. "It should be illegal for two people that good looking to be together."

He chuckles as he grabs the keys out of my trembling hand. "You can't drive right now. You're a nervous wreck. And I'd very much like to reach the end of this scavenger hunt in one piece."

I smile as he opens the passenger door for me. "Where does it end?"

He shakes his head. "Nuh-uh. You're not getting it out of me."

I take a deep breath and stuff my hands between my thighs to try to calm the trembling. "How long have you known about this?" I ask as Kenny pulls my Toyota out of the lot.

"Can't tell you that either."

"What can you tell me?" I continue. I figure he'll slip up eventually if I badger him enough.

"Well, I can tell you that you are a nosy little twat who wants me to spoil the ending of a very special fairy tale."

I gasp. "Kenny, how could you speak to me like that?"

He smiles. "You can give me a clean, hard soap-opera slap when we get to our destination."

"So who else is in on this? It's a proposal, right?"

Kenny mimes pulling a zipper across his lips, turning a lock, and flicking away an imaginary key. "Not talking."

I roll my eyes and lean forward to turn on some music. It feels weird sitting in the passenger seat of my own car. It looks different from this angle. Like, I never realized how old-school-cool this car is until now. I have a cassette player. I should be cementing my geekdom by making mixtapes for me and all my friends.

I settle on an indie-rock station, then I sit back and close my eyes, letting the sound of the rain battering the windshield soothe me as I try to imagine what awaits me at my old house in McMinnville. Thinking about this fills me with buzzing anxiety, so I decide to open the notes app on my phone and create a playlist for my first mixtape, which I will give to Kenny. By the time I'm done arranging the order of my favorite lovemaking songs for Kenny to use with his new boyfriend, and trying to sneak some more information about this scavenger hunt out of Kenny in the process, our one-hour car ride is over.

The moment we pull up in front of the house I spent most of my life in, I'm overwhelmed with emotion. This house is so ingrained in my psyche, it's still the location where most of my dreams take place. Whenever I read a book, this is the house I imagine. It's as much a part of me as my hair color, and yet I've tried my hardest to put it out of my mind for the past six years, afraid that embracing my memories of it would open some mental floodgates, and my mind would become overrun with memories of the past. Now, as I gaze at the two-story house with the white siding and slightly droopy overhang shading the porch, I realize I'm ready to do away with those kinds of silly superstitions and embrace every part of me.

I turn to Kenny, smiling through my tears. "Hallie and I got into a lot of trouble here."

"I can only imagine."

I look at the house a minute longer, trying to see if I notice an ivory envelope tucked into a bush or lying on one of the steps, but I see nothing. And of course they wouldn't leave a paper envelope out in the yard while it's pouring rain.

"Where's the envelope?" I ask.

"You have to knock on the door."

I nod as I wipe away the tears so I don't frighten whoever answers. "I'll be right back," I say, sliding out of the car.

I race across the concrete walkway and up the steps to the door I've opened a million times. I can't just walk in anymore, so I press the doorbell and my heart stutters when I hear the clear chimes coming from within the house.

Ding-dong-ding.

I used to get so excited when I heard that sound, knowing it was usually Hallie coming over to rescue me from my boredom. The doorknob begins to turn and my heart races as I anticipate receiving the next page in the story, but when the door opens, it's not at all what I expected to find.

"Mom?"

For a moment I think that maybe she purchased the house back. Then she smiles as she pulls the door wide open, revealing a small elderly woman with a back as crooked as a fishhook.

"Honey, this is Beverly," my mom says. "She's the new owner of this house and she's very excited to meet you."

Beverly looks up at me, smiling brightly. "I'm sleeping in your old room," she says. "I don't like that big master bedroom."

I laugh as I reach my hand out to her. "It's very nice to meet you, Beverly. I'm Rory."

That's when I notice Beverly's hand is tucked behind her crooked back. She looks up at my mom and her smile widens as she brings her hand forward, brandishing an ivory envelope.

"Nice to finally meet you, Rory. This is for you," she says, looking very pleased with herself.

"Thank you so much, Beverly," my mom says, giving her a hug.

"Anytime, honey. You two are welcome here anytime." Beverly turns to me, then stares at the envelope. "Well, aren't you going to open it?"

I laugh as I lift the flap and pull out page two.

One day the skies darkened, and a storm descended upon the land, sweeping away many of the villagers, even Aurora's fairest and most lovely friend Princess Hallie. Aurora cried in her tower for many days and many nights, until finally she fell into a deep sleep from which no one could wake her. Then, handsome Prince Houston galloped into McMinnville, seeking to avenge his sister's death. But the prince did not find vengeance. He found his mother Queen Ava, who spoke of forgiving the heavens for unleashing the storm.

2

"Ava?" I barely speak the word in a whisper, but Beverly hears me clearly.

"She's just around the corner," she says proudly. "I think she skipped her daily walk today. Must have had something pretty important to do."

"Thank you, Beverly," I say, leaning down to give her a gentle hug. "Thank you so much."

She pats my back. "Go on now. You don't want to keep her waiting."

My mom gives Beverly a kiss on the cheek, then we head out into the storm. I signal to Kenny, who's still sitting in my car, that we're going around the corner on foot. He seems to hesitate for a moment, like he's wondering if he should take the car. He decides to walk with us to Ava's house.

We turn the corner onto 10th Street and arrive within seconds. It was always convenient having Hallie just around the corner and two houses down. It meant the corners of our backyards almost touched, which helped when we wanted to sneak out together without the nosy neighbors seeing us leave through our front doors.

When Ava opens the front door, her eyelids are a bit pink and puffy, though her cheeks are dry. She's been crying recently.

She takes me into her arms. "He's been through so much," she says, her voice cracking. "But I'm so happy to know you'll be there to get him through whatever else may come."

I swallow the lump in my throat. "I'll always be there, for him and for you. You know that, right?"

"Of course."

She holds on a bit longer before she releases me and hands me the envelope that rests on the table in her foyer. God, it's the same table she had when Hallie was still alive. But it's the framed picture of Hallie on the table that siphons the breath from my lungs.

Ava must look at this photo every day, but this is the first time I've seen this picture in more than six years. I take the envelope from Ava's hand, but my gaze is still fixed on Hallie. It's her senior class photo. I remember the day she took this photo, we were laughing like hyenas because Hallie had painted a big black mole on her nose before taking her picture. When Ava got the proofs, she asked the photographer to retouch the photo to take out the mole before he printed them. Hallie and her mom had a big fight over whether Hallie had the right to mess up her class pictures. In the end, Ava won.

Now I look at the retouched photo and I can't help but smile. We all remember people the way we want to remember them. I remember Hallie as the funniest, most selfless and stubborn sister I've ever had. And that's how I want everyone else to remember her.

"Hurry up. The suspense is killing me," Kenny urges me on.

I open the envelope and wipe the tears from my face as I read the third page.

After many years sleeping, Princess Aurora was woken with true love's kiss, and she and Prince Houston were happy for some time. But Aurora soon found the stories she told becoming darker and less colorful. With the help of King James, Aurora set out to explore the kingdom untethered by pen and parchment. One day, she came upon a home where young children orphaned by the great storm that took Hallie could seek shelter and hope.

3

"Hallie's Hope."

Ava smiles. "I think you know who's waiting for you there."

"My *dad*?" I reply with disbelief. "Is my *dad* in on this, too?"

"The surprises just keep getting bigger," my mom says with a smug grin.

I don't say it aloud, because I want to find out where this scavenger hunt ends, but I'm pretty certain my mother played a larger role in this than anyone else. Who could write a fairy tale based on my life with Houston other than the one other person who read my book? And suddenly, I find myself feeling guilty for all the ranting and raving I've done over the past few weeks. The tantrums I've thrown because my mom won't let me see her book.

"I guess we should get going," I say, tucking the envelope into my back pocket.

"I'll go get the car," Kenny volunteers enthusiastically.

We all pile into my Toyota and head to the Hallie's Hope office in the Pearl. Kenny and my mom spend the one-hour drive chatting about fall fashion, while Ava and I discuss work, carefully avoiding the topic of all the burning questions I have about what other surprises await me today.

Kenny is able to find a parking spot on the street not far from the entrance to our building. When we head up to the second floor, we find the door to suite 201 wide open. Upon entering, my jaw hits the floor when I see that the front office is completely set up with brand-new furnishings. Off to the right is a play area for children, and straight ahead is the door to the back office area. Just to the right of the door is a window looking onto the receptionist's desk, where my father stands wearing a proud expression.

We all head through the door to the back office.

Right away, my dad hands me a key. "Sorry I've been giving you the runaround with this key the past couple of days, but we weren't ready yet."

I laugh as I think of how frustrated I've been that my dad has been putting off getting me an office key ever since I called him to tell him mine wasn't working. "Thanks," I say, tucking the key into my pocket.

"This is your desk for now," he continues, indicating the receptionist's desk. "But your office is already set up and waiting for you down the hall once you hire someone to run the front desk."

I sigh as I turn to my dad. "Thank you, but I'm not here to get a tour of the office, am I?"

He smiles as he steps forward and takes both my hands in his. "Houston came to me about a week ago to tell me his plans, and to ask for my blessing."

"He came to *you*?" I reply, my voice cracking as I realize this really is a proposal. And not just any proposal. This is Houston setting aside all his pride and resentment… for me.

My dad nods solemnly. "Yes, he came to me, and I was just as surprised as you probably are right now. The truth is, I should have been the one to come to him. But you know how guilt works. It's a great deterrent to getting things done." He takes a moment to compose himself as his eyes begin to water. "Houston's a good man, sweetheart. And if I have to hand my little girl over to anyone, I'm happy it will be him. I have every confidence he'll take care of you the way you deserve to be taken care of, like a princess."

He takes me in his arms and we both comfort each other for a while, because even though this whole day has been planned as a new beginning, something else is also ending. The brief moment in time when my father rose to the challenge, giving me an opportunity to save me from myself, has ended. Now it's Houston's turn to rise to the challenge of ruling my unruly soul. God help him.

My dad finally lets me go and reaches into his back pocket. He hands me the envelope and I take a deep breath before I open it up and read the fourth page aloud.

When Aurora told the children stories of her long-lost friend Princess Hallie, they delighted in the colorful tales of humor, and found solace in the knowledge that the storm had spared them. They had been given a second chance. With a heart full of love, and many new stories that begged to be told, Aurora returned to the kingdom and found Prince Houston in the Reflection Garden.

4

"The Reflection Garden? At the museum?"

"He's probably waiting there right now," my dad replies.

My heart races as I remember the last time Houston and I went to the Reflection Garden. The *only* time Houston and I went there. It was the day Hallie died. The day of our first hug, our first kiss, and the first time we made love. Just the thought of going back there, to where it all began, fills me with throbbing dread. But I guess if Houston and I are going to make peace with our past, so we can have a future together, there's no better place to do that than the Reflection Garden.

My father insists on driving us to the Jordan Schnitzer Museum of Art in his BMW, claiming it has more space to fit three people in the backseat. And I make no attempt to object. But when we reach his car on the parking-garage level, Kenny is the one who begins to act up.

"Patty can sit on my lap," Kenny says with a wink.

My mom shakes her head, though I can see her blushing through her makeup.

"Over my dead body," my dad says, sliding into the driver's seat. "Patricia, you sit up front."

"Nonsense," my mom says, pursing her lips as she opens the back door. "Don't listen to him, Kenny."

I stand next to the passenger door, unsure if I should sit shotgun or give it to Ava.

"Rory, your mother sits in the front," my dad insists in the same authoritative tone that used to scare me into doing my chores. "Now get back there so you can keep Kenny in line."

I try not to laugh as Kenny watches my mom and me switch places. She slams the door after she takes the front seat and Kenny waits for me to get in, expecting me to sit in the middle.

"I can't sit in the middle. I'll get carsick," I protest.

His eyes widen. "Are you kidding me? You're going to make me sit on the hump?"

"I thought you liked sitting on the hump."

He gasps. "You dirty girl."

"Okay, kids. Enough fighting. Get in the car," my dad calls to us over his shoulder.

"Get in." I push Kenny toward the backseat and he smacks my hand away.

"Daddy, she's pushing me," Kenny whines.

"That's enough," my dad replies. "Be nice, Rory."

Kenny sticks his tongue out at me as he slides in next to Ava and I sit on his other side, forming an awkward Kenny sandwich. I shut the door and Kenny leans in to kiss my cheek.

"Love you, sis."

I roll my eyes as I pretend to wipe away the cooties on my cheek. "I guess I love you, too."

The thirty-minute drive to the university is excruciating. Between the thunderous pounding of my heart in my ears and Kenny's insistence that we need to sing "Wheels on the Bus," my anxiety skyrockets to a level I've never experienced. It's so bad that I beg my dad to drop me off near the loading dock behind the museum before I vomit in his car. Thankfully, the clouds have parted and the rain has ceased in this part of Oregon. I hope that's a sign.

Kenny, Ava, and my mom get out of the car with me while my dad sets off to look for parking. It takes a few minutes for my anxiety and my stomach to settle, which gives my dad enough time to park the car and meet us near the security entrance in the back to get a parking permit. With the permit secured, we head around toward the front of the building to the main entrance.

"Are you okay, Rory?" my mom asks.

I nod, but I don't say anything. I suddenly feel as if I'm walking toward a gallows, which is ridiculous. I've wanted to marry Houston since I was eleven years old. It's not the impending proposal that has me so anxious.

"Wait!" I shout, stopping at the base of the stairs that lead up to the museum entrance.

Everyone stops and looks at me, their eyes and mouths gaping with confusion.

"I have to go in there alone," I continue. "I'm sorry."

"Don't be sorry, dear," my mom assures me.

Ava looks a bit disappointed, but she puts on a smile. "We understand. This is a special moment for you two. We'll be out here waiting to celebrate when you're ready."

My dad kisses my forehead. "I love you, sweetheart."

I climb the damp steps toward the museum entrance slowly, my chest tightening as my mind flashes back to the last time I climbed these steps. When I enter the museum and reach the ticket counter inside, I try to hand the attendant my money, but the woman working the counter informs me my entrance fee has already been paid for. Then she smiles and hands me my ticket.

As I walk through the museum, memories of the day Hallie died come racing to the forefront of my mind. I recall the way Houston and I drifted through the halls of the museum like a couple of zombies, as if *we* were the ones who died that day. And if someone had told me back then that we were doomed to walk the earth with an insatiable hunger that could never be fulfilled, I would have believed them.

My memory serves me well, and I find the Reflection Garden on my first try. Beyond the concrete pillars and green foliage surrounding the reflection pool, Houston stands lost in thought, right next to the statues where we stood more than six years ago. I watch him for a moment, wondering what he's reflecting on. Is he thinking about the day Hallie died? Is he troubled with doubt that I may not show up today?

As if my questions have been sent to him in ripples across the reflection pool, Houston looks up at that moment and our eyes meet.

Houston

The Reflection Garden is an open-air courtyard in the center of the museum. A shallow rectangular pool runs down the center of the interior courtyard, with lush greenery running the length on each side. Behind the greenery, the garden is enclosed in a waist-high brick wall, atop which concrete pillars prop up a ceiling that covers the exterior courtyard, where visitors can take shelter from the storm.

But I know a secret no one else knows. The storm has passed.

I've been waiting patiently at the east end of the pool for more than an hour, a silent sentinel watching over the dribbling stone fountain, which is flanked by two statues of children playing archaic instruments. I guess it's called the Reflection Garden for a reason. The beautiful green foliage and sparkling blue pool, the calming sound of the trickling water, and the sweet fragrance of the blooming camellia shrubs all amount to an atmosphere that is ripe for reflecting.

I'd like to think there's a simple reason why people visit reflection pools. When you look into one on a clear day, you see your own mirror image. When there's a storm, and the rain is splashing the surface, or the wind whips the water up in rippling waves, it becomes impossible to see a clear image of anything. It's easy to feel as if you're lost in the storm.

But storms don't last.

If I had one wish in this world, it would be that I could have convinced Hallie of this.

As I stare at the water flowing out of the seashell-shaped fountain spout, I feel a strange humming in my chest, a ripple like those on the surface of the pool. I look up and turn my gaze to the west entrance. Rory is standing there wearing her army-green anorak and black skinny jeans that are ripped at the knees. Her auburn hair is pulled into a messy ponytail that droops a bit from the humidity, but I've never seen her look more beautiful.

I step away from the statue, toward the exterior courtyard, and she begins to jog toward me. When I reach the end of the corridor, I widen my stance a bit and hold my arms out as she leaps into my arms. I chuckle as the force almost knocks me over, but I manage to hold my balance as she coils her arms around my neck and her legs around my hips.

"You scared the shit out of me!" she scolds me, her voice thick with tears. "I thought you were cheating on me."

I laugh as I tighten my arms around her and bury my face in her neck. "You should know better than that."

"I know. I'm sorry." She pulls her head back, leaning her forehead against mine as I carry her toward the fountain. "You're the sneakiest person I've ever known, and I love you for it."

I smile and kiss the tip of her nose before I set her down next to the statue. "I think I won the right to say I love you more."

She shrugs as she wipes tears from her pink cheeks. "For now. I may have a few tricks up my sleeve."

I narrow my eyes at her, then I reach up and grab the Sierra Nevada box, which rests on top of the statue's pedestal, just under the lip of the seashell fountain. The moment she sees it, she shakes her head as more tears begin to fall.

"I was going to put page five of the story in here," I begin, "but then I realized that spelling out the happy ending in plain English would completely defeat the purpose of the fairy tale." I smile at the mild confusion on her gorgeous face. "You see, in real life, there are no happy endings, because real life, real *love*, has no ending. So all of this… This is our happy beginning."

Her mouth curves into a smile that could knock the earth off its axis. "Happy beginnings are my favorite."

Then, both her hands come up to cover her mouth as she watches me slowly lift the lid of the tin box just enough to loosen it, but I don't lift it off enough to reveal the contents. She waits for me to continue, but she soon realizes this is as far as I'm going.

She drops her hands to her sides and narrows her eyes at me. "You're going to make me say it?"

I shrug. "It can't hurt."

Her lips tremble as she tries to stifle her tears long enough to ask the question I want to hear. "What's in the box?"

I chuckle as I hold the lid in place. "I'll give you a hint: It's not Gwyneth Paltrow's severed head."

"Oh, thank God," she whispers, as if that were a real possibility.

I shake my head as I slowly lift the lid and place it back on top of the stone pedestal. Then, I pluck out the engagement ring and place the box next to the lid. Drawing in a deep breath, I take time to revel in this moment. Rory has no idea how I planned to do this, and now she has no idea what I'm going to say.

She looks back and forth from my face to the ring I hold between my index finger and thumb. I can see her making a concerted effort to keep breathing as her body trembles, and I'm pretty sure it's not the fifty-degree weather, which she's so accustomed to. I'd better do this quickly before she passes out.

I lean forward, holding the back of her neck as I plant a soft kiss on her forehead. "Breathe, baby."

She nods as she takes a few deep breaths. "I'm okay."

I smile as I look her in the eye. "You once told me that you can't erase love. Do you still believe that?"

"Of course."

"Good, because you and I have gone to hell and back together, but it has never changed my love for you. And I'd go through it all over again if it meant we still ended up right here, right now. 'Cause there's no one else I want by my side when the shit goes down. Just like there's no one else I'd rather have sex with in the middle of a dark cemetery."

She smacks my arm. "I'm so glad I came in here alone."

I chuckle as I reach forward and grab her left hand. Her momentary burst of anger quickly melts into tearful anxiety. I rub the top of her hand with my thumb to try to calm her.

"Rory, the world is a different place when I'm with you. It looks brighter. It feels easier. It *smells* better." I smile as she lets out a congested chuckle. "Every morning, when I wake up next to you, I feel like I've already conquered the day. And there's nothing I can't face, because somewhere deep down, etched into the shattered fragments of my dusty soul, is the knowledge that, if I don't fuck this up, I get to wake up next to you again tomorrow."

I get down on one knee and she presses her trembling lips together. "Rory… will you be my one and only best friend with benefits for the rest of our lives? Will you marry me?"

She nods for a few seconds, a look of mild panic in her eyes, as if she can't find her voice. For a moment, I worry that maybe she's having trouble breathing. Then she opens her mouth and lets out a sharp, stale breath.

"Yes!" she yells. She continues to nod her head and whisper *yes* as I stand up without sliding the ring on her finger.

Laying the ring flat in my palm, I bring my hand up so she

can see the words *You can't erase love* engraved on the inner surface.

"Oh, my God," she whispers.

I clench my jaw, but it's not enough to stop a tear from escaping the corner of my eye as I slide the ring on her left ring finger. "I love you, Scar."

"I love you more."

I smile at her continued attempts to one-up me, then I take her delicate face in my hands and kiss her. Her lips taste of salty tears and waxy lip balm and I've never tasted anything so perfect. She begins to pull away when she's overcome with giddy laughter.

"Oh, my goodness. I can't believe you did all this for a proposal," she remarks, clutching the front of my shirt as she looks up at me wide-eyed with glee. "You know I would have said yes if you proposed to me on the toilet."

"I'll remember that for my next marriage." I laugh at the mean glare she shoots me. "You can probably guess who helped me write that fairy tale."

She nods as she gets choked up again. "My mom. I owe her a massive fucking apology."

"She's more understanding than you think." I brush my thumb across the moisture on her cheek. "We wanted this to be the happiest happy beginning ever."

"Happy doesn't even begin to describe it," she says with a smile, but the way she's looking down at her hands tells me she's hiding something. "But I have a feeling my happiest happy beginning is yet to come."

I chuckle. "Of course, the wedding day."

She shakes her head. "Nope."

"I don't get it," I reply, cocking an eyebrow at the cunning gleam in her eyes.

Rory

I smile as I realize I also get to surprise Houston today. "It just so happens I have a note of my own for you."

I reach into my back pocket and retrieve a folded piece of pink paper. When the receptionist at the clinic handed me the pink slip of carbon-copied paper, I couldn't make sense of any of the tiny letters and all the medical jargon. I was able to comprehend the date printed at the top of the pink paper: October 5, 2015. And, oddly enough, I was able to make out the words scrawled on the small white prescription note stapled to the top of the pink lab results: CitraNatal 90 DHA.

I was so happy to see Kenny at Killer Burger with his new boyfriend this afternoon, and also happy that I finally had an answer for my recent mood swings, but I was sad that I didn't have Kenny all to myself to break the news to him. And even more anxious because I wasn't sure why Houston had been acting so strangely these past few days. Now I know the answer to both of our recent shifts in behavior.

My pulse echoes in my ears, tickles my fingertips as I watch Houston reading the text on the pink sheet of paper. His eyes sweep side to side as they scroll down the page, his face morphing from confusion to shock to the sexiest smile I've ever laid eyes on.

He looks up at me, his mouth still curved into an uncontrollable grin. "Are you fucking kidding me?"

I shake my head. "I'm pregnant."

His smile disappears as he tosses the paper onto the ground. His gaze wanders over my face as tears well up in his eyes. He reaches his hand out and gently places it on my abdomen, his chest heaving as tears slide down his cheeks.

"Houston, are you okay?" I ask, my voice wavering.

His gaze snaps up, locking on my eyes. "Fuck yes. I made a human."

I chuckle as I reach up to wipe the tears from his scruff, but he doesn't seem to notice as his gaze drops to my belly again, as if he's afraid the baby will disappear if he looks away. His hand slides up my abdomen, underneath my shirt. I draw in a sharp breath when the cool skin of his palm lands on my skin. His other hand reaches up, grabbing the back of my neck as he leans his forehead against mine. We both watch as his hand slides just beneath my waistband.

"There's a baby in there," he says, his voice full of wonderment.

"Yeah, we made a human," I reply, then I hold my breath as his hand travels upward, the tips of his fingertips whispering over my ribs.

His smile returns as he looks into my eyes. "And the story continues."

I smile. "It never ends."

His lips fall gently over mine in a kiss that's as intoxicating as a bottle of liquor. As his tongue brushes against mine, the sting of his stubble on my lips and his fist tightening around my hair fill me with blazing warmth, until I can hardly stand on my two feet. Sensing my unsteadiness, he wraps one solid arm around my waist, locking it there as he tilts his head back to gaze into my eyes once more, a victor relishing in the splendor of his spoils.

"I told you I would get that ring on your finger," he says proudly as he slowly releases his hold on my waist.

"I'll admit I had my doubts," I reply, holding my hand up to look at the sparkling diamond ring.

He shakes his head. "No, you didn't."

I look up at him. "What are you getting at?"

He smiles as he reaches up and brushes a piece of hair out of my face. "Somewhere deep down, you've known since you were eleven years old that we'd end up together. There's a reason your heart refused to let go."

I stare at the ring on my finger as I think of eleven-year-old me and fourteen-year-old me and twenty-four-year-old me, all of us madly in love with different versions of the same man.

"I guess you're right. I even loved you through your faux-hawk phase. That must mean we were destined to be together."

"Make fun all you want, but I'm being serious. Don't you see what's happening here?"

I narrow my eyes at him because I'm not sure if he knows that he said those exact words to me the first time we spent the night together. "What's happening?" I ask, fully aware that this is exactly how I responded that night.

"This is the way we rise," he replies with a smile.

"What do you mean?"

He takes both my hands in his. "When we were in California, you told me that we were in the midst of the unraveling. That's the lowest point in a story, right?"

I smile as I realize he's been googling story structure. "Right."

"That means that no matter what happened after that, even if we were to break up, we'd still have nowhere to go but up."

I chuckle nervously. "I have no idea what you're getting at."

"The point I'm trying to make is that, technically, anything that comes after the unraveling is better than nothing. The worst outcome is for the story to end right after everything unravels." He smiles at the bewilderment in my eyes. "What I'm trying to say is that even if I'd never gotten you back, I'd have been happy knowing that you were out there somewhere… rising."

Epilogue

"It is easier to build strong
children than to repair
broken men."
- Frederick Douglass

Rory

My fingers move furiously over the keyboard, each sentence materializing on the page fully formed and mostly coherent. The words flow out of me like water from a hose, unstoppable and refreshingly clear. When my editor told me we needed to move up the deadline a few weeks, so we could get galley proofs to a few more reviewers that signed on to the promotional tour, I didn't panic. I knew I'd have the first draft done by the new deadline.

Writing this book, a fictional novel loosely based on Hallie's life, has been almost a religious experience. Every day, I put Austin down for a nap and I sit at the desk in our bedroom to write. The words come with ease and my fingers move at lightning speed trying to keep up with my fluid thoughts. It's not as if I have a muse sitting next to me whispering the words in my ear. It's more like the muse is inside me. Like I'm possessed by something otherworldly. Something divine.

Of course, when I'm done and I sit back and read what I've written, that's when the doubt sets in. The fear that I'm not qualified to tell such a delicate story, at least not with the grace and wisdom the story deserves. Still, I sit down every day and write anyway. Every day, for a few hours, my muse locks away the crushing cynicism of my inner critic behind a door in a dark corner of my mind, hiding the key until the work has been done.

I wish writing my wedding vows were that easy.

I type the last sentence in the chapter and close the laptop as I reach for my phone on the desk in my bedroom. Turning on the phone, I find three voicemails, two from Kenny and one from my mom. I touch Kenny's number and wait for the call to go through. He picks up on the second ring.

"Rory, I know you're writing, but I'm having a bit of a crisis here," he says, and I can hear a man's voice in the background, arguing over the color of something.

"Kenny, I can't take another wedding crisis right now. The wedding is in *one week*. We don't have *time* for any more crises."

"That's what I told this woman. We told her, Rory. We said we wanted white silk tents and she's trying to give us ivory tents. Ivory tents! Who does she think is getting married? The *Golden Girls*?"

I put the phone on speaker and set it down on the desk, then I hang my head in my hands and let out a long sigh. "Kenny, just get the ivory tents. I can't take another disaster. I'm just… so over this whole thing."

"Nuh-uh. You are getting what you paid for if I have to spin you some white silk tents out of my ass."

I laugh. "I didn't know your ass was part silkworm."

"Honey, my ass is whatever you need it to be. Don't you worry about a thing. Sid and I've got this."

I smile as I end the call, the sound of Sid yelling at the silk-tents woman still echoing in my ears. Making Kenny my maid of honor and setting him up with Sid Burnham, my wedding planner, has been a roller coaster for me. At first, Sid and Kenny hated each other. I'm pretty sure that's because Sid has a not-so-secret crush on Kenny, but Kenny is completely committed to Pedro. After they got in a huge fight over the reception menu a few weeks ago, I finally sat them down and threatened that if they couldn't get along I was going to cancel the wedding and elope to Vegas. Since then, they have been the best of friends.

I check the time on my phone before I tuck it into my pocket: 1:22 p.m. Austin usually wakes up the moment Houston walks through the door for lunch. I glance at the baby monitor on the desk and see the steady movement made by Austin's slow breathing. Houston isn't home yet.

I switch off the baby monitor and head out of the bedroom then down the hall toward Austin's room. The door is wide open, exactly the way I left it when I put him down for his midday nap. I tread lightly across the wooden floor toward his crib. Peering through the dark-gray slats, I can't see him because of the crib bumper. Once I'm standing next to the crib, I find him lying on his back, his pink lips slightly parted, his long eyelashes twitching slightly at the rapid movement beneath his eyelids. My prince is still in a deep sleep.

I hate waking him up when he looks this peaceful, but I need to keep him on a schedule, lest we surrender to more sleepless nights. I reach down and lightly run my fingers through the soft patch of light-brown hair on the top of his head. His head twitches, then his eyelids begin to flutter. His tender bottom lip juts out like he's about to start wailing, so I scoop him up into my arms.

"It's okay, sweetheart. Mommy's here."

He blinks his eyes a few times and I gently wipe the moisture from his eyelashes. He leans back to try to get away from my hand and I chuckle.

"You want to call Daddy?" I ask him, and he instantly stops fussing when he hears the name of his favorite person in the world.

He opens his hand and presses his thumb to his forehead to make the sign for daddy. Then he says the only word he knows how to say: "Da-da."

I smile. "Yes, daddy. Let's go call Daddy."

I secure Austin in his high chair and set the phone down on the tray so we can call Houston. He picks up on the third ring, but I can tell by all the noise in the background that he's still at the brewery.

"Baby, I can't come home for lunch today, but I'll try to get home early tonight."

Austin's face lights up at the sound of Houston's voice and he reaches for the phone.

I move the phone just out of his reach. "Austin wanted to call you to say hi. He's listening."

"Aw… Hey, buddy, Daddy'll be home soon. I love you."

Austin smiles broadly, showing all six of his teeth as he smacks the tray, making the phone jump. "Da-da!"

Houston laughs and Austin reaches for the phone again.

I take the phone off speaker and press it against my ear. "Please don't be late tonight," I plead. "My mom's coming at six. I need you here to keep me from killing her."

"Oh, shit. I forgot she was coming tonight," he replies. "All right, I'll try my best, but you know I have that inspector coming by to do another inspection of the roof. It all depends on if he gets here on time and whether or not he passes us."

"Oh, he'd better pass us or we're gonna have to figure out a way to fit 110 people into our living room."

"I told you not to invite so many people," he grumbles. "Maybe if we had a bigger house we could actually fit 110 people in our living room."

"Are we gonna have this argument again?"

"No, we're not," he says, and I can hear the smile in his voice. "I'll be home as soon as I can. I love you."

"Love you too."

I sigh as I end the call and give the phone to Austin so he can play with it while I make us both some lunch. I got a nontoxic, water-resistant, and shockproof case for my phone when I realized it was Austin's favorite toy. He mostly just chews on it or throws it across the room, but once in a while he'll focus on the screen for a few seconds when I open up the baby apps. I guess I'll just enjoy these few years before he asks us for a phone of his own, before he becomes more interested in endless text conversations with his friends than phone calls to his daddy.

I grab a bag of fresh peas out of the refrigerator and sit down at the kitchen table next to Austin's high chair as I begin shucking them. The peas bounce as I drop them into a glass bowl, occasionally bouncing onto the table and rolling away to land on the floor. I'll clean those up later.

I look around the kitchen with the sleek black cabinets and creamy white marble counters and the modern baby-proofed living room. Instantly, I find my blood pressure rising as I think of Houston's comment: *Maybe if we had a bigger house we could actually fit 110 people in our living room.*

The age-old question city couples with children must grapple with: Do we stay in the city or move to the suburbs, where our children can presumably play outdoors without having to schedule a playdate?

Austin's first birthday is coming in less than three months and Houston and I are already struggling with this question. Houston wants to move the family to a multimillion-dollar lakefront estate in Lake Oswego. He imagines himself teaching Austin how to row and fish. I imagine the cringe on my friends' faces when I tell them I'm moving into a home with way more space than we need, in *Lake Oswego*. And soon our home will be full of *things*. Things we *need* to buy because there's so much space to fill, and God forbid we should have an unfurnished room. We're not college students anymore, you know?

And all our *things* will collect dust, unless someone—*me*—

spends all day dusting and sweeping and mopping. Then Houston will see how stressed out I am because all I have time for is Austin and the new house. I never have time to write or work at Hallie's Hope anymore. So he'll hire a housekeeper to do all the dusting and sweeping and mopping. And soon I'll become just like all the other wretched "real housewives" of Lake Oswego. Just the thought turns my stomach.

At the heart of the argument is another even more important question: Do I trust that Houston knows what's best for our family?

My gut reaction to that question would be a resounding *yes*. But if I sit and dwell on it just a moment, I begin to wonder if Houston understands how important this city has become to me. How important it is to *us*. I love that it takes Houston five minutes to drive to work and that he gets to come home for lunch almost every day. I don't want to imagine what it would be like if his commute were to take an hour or more during heavy traffic.

The argument is dead for now, since the house Houston was coveting for months was snatched up a few weeks ago in a cash deal by an investment company. Though, I'm sure Houston will set his sights on another lake house soon.

Once Austin and I have had our lunch, I pack up the baby bag and get the stroller ready to take him for a walk outside in the August sunshine. But when I get down to the lobby, a paramedic van is parked in front of our building, its lights flashing as a small crowd forms on the sidewalk.

Libby, the concierge, smiles at Austin as I approach her desk. "Hey, Austin. How are you today?"

I push the stroller closer. "What's going on out there?"

Libby shrugs. "I don't know. I think it's a homeless man who passed out. Maybe heatstroke?"

I sigh as I see that at least four or five of the people crowded on the sidewalk are homeless men. I'm not afraid of homeless people. I've never had any negative encounters with them in all the years I've lived in Portland. I did have an instance where a homeless woman tried to reach for Austin in his stroller when we were standing on the corner waiting for the light to change.

It could have been an innocent gesture. Maybe she wanted to feel his soft skin. Or maybe she wanted to wipe away a bit of drool or hand him a toy he'd dropped. I don't know, because my motherly instincts kicked in and I hurried off in the opposite direction.

I felt awful as I rounded the corner and quickly checked Austin to make sure he was okay. I don't want to be the kind of judgmental jerk who assumes that just because someone is homeless it means they're dangerous. Still, the sad truth is that a large percentage of homeless individuals suffer from mental illness. And some of them are a danger to themselves and others.

Staring out at the crowd of people on the sidewalk, I turn and flash Libby a tight smile as I head back to the elevator. "I guess we can go for a walk later once it's cooled down a bit," I say, and she smiles, knowing all too well that the heat has nothing to do with my decision to head back upstairs to the safety of our air-conditioned apartment.

A few hours later, I put Austin down for his six o'clock nap at 5:48 p.m. and Skippy plods over to lie on his dog pillow under the window, while I sit on the sofa with my laptop to take another crack at my wedding vows before my mom arrives at six. Thirty minutes later, my mom hasn't arrived yet, but Houston walks through the door with his skin flushed and dripping sweat.

I slam the lid of my laptop shut and place it on the coffee table. "What happened to you?"

He instantly peels his sweaty T-shirt off and uses it to wipe the perspiration from his face. "I was on the fucking roof for the last three hours trying to fix some aluminum flashing on one of the steam vents."

I leap off the sofa and head to the kitchen to get him a glass of cold water. "Why didn't you call a roofer?"

He follows me into the kitchen and the sharp smell of his sweat fills the room as he leans in to kiss my cheek and take the glass of water from my hand. "The roofer couldn't make it out until tomorrow, but I got the inspector to agree to come back first thing tomorrow morning. This roof permit is a fucking nightmare."

"We can have the wedding on the second floor," I say, trying not to sound too disappointed.

He guzzles the entire glass of water and chuckles as he places it in the sink. "Don't start that. I know you want to do it on the roof and I'm going to do everything I can to make it happen. We're not giving up yet."

I smile as I grab the shirt out of his hand and use it to dab the sweat on his chest. "You look like you could use a cold shower."

He smiles as he reaches up and roughly grabs my jaw, then he kisses me hard.

I trace my fingers down his six-pack abs and undo the button of his jeans as I slide down to my knees.

Houston

Rory knows there's no weapon more powerful in a woman's arsenal than a well-timed blow job. She wants the wedding to take place on the roof of Barley Legal. And she's willing to literally get down on her knees and beg me to make it happen. Not that I don't think it's a great idea. At night, the roof has a great view of Mount St. Helens, the downtown lights, and the river. And with the Barley Legal building taking up almost a full city block, the roof is by far the most spacious place in the building. No walls and not a whole lot of equipment to get in the way of the mingling.

Of course, when I spoke to our insurance company and the city of Portland, they both agreed I'd need a permit to make sure the roof was safe for 110-plus people. It can definitely support the weight, but we needed to get some adjustments made to the safety rails a few weeks ago, and now we have to fix some flashing around the steam vents. It doesn't matter that we're shutting down all the brewery equipment and there won't be a single molecule of steam coming out of those vents on the day of the wedding. The roof has to pass inspection or not only will there be no wedding, but they'll shut down the brewery until those flashings are up to code.

When she's done showing her appreciation for my hard day at work, Rory takes a few minutes cleaning herself up in the bathroom while I wake up my main man, Austin. I brush my thumb over his cheek, the same method I use to wake Rory in the morning, and he responds the same way, smiling as he reaches for my hand. Rory says Austin is my mini-me, but she doesn't realize all the small ways he's like her. Like the fact that they both like being woken up the same way, and they both have smiles that can bring me to my knees.

I scoop him up and he giggles as I nuzzle my nose in the crook of his neck. "Is that funny, little man?" I say, nuzzling him some more until he's squirming with laughter.

I carry him out to the kitchen and Rory is already setting up his bowl of mushy peas for dinner. I fly him around the kitchen like Superman a few times before he "lands" in his high chair. His chubby cheeks are rosy with glee as I strap him into the chair and lock the food tray in place. Rory hands me the bowl and I sit down to feed him a few spoonfuls before I let him try it on his own. Rory read an article in a baby magazine that said we need to start teaching him how to feed himself now. According to the article, the more he learns the way real food feels, the less likely he'll be to put strange objects in his mouth later.

I try not to laugh as he very predictably chucks the baby spoon onto the floor. Bending down to pick it up, I let him have a go at the peas with his chubby fingers. Then I head over to drop the spoon into the sink.

"What kind of smoothie is this?" I ask as Rory hands me a glass. "It looks like Austin's watery shit."

Rory rolls her eyes as she finishes pouring the rest of the brownish-green liquid out of the blender into another glass for herself. "It's the new hemp protein powder I just bought. It makes everything look like poop, but it tastes better than that chalky muscle-building stuff you were buying."

I take a long drink from the smoothie then smack my lips. "That's some damn good poop." I lick some smoothie off the corner of my lips and cock an eyebrow. "Wait… Did you put peanut butter in this?"

"Why? You don't like it?"

My eyes widen. "You're pregnant."

"What?" she says, her voice going up a couple octaves.

I glance at the high chair where Austin is making a mess out of his bowl of baby mushed peas. I turn back to Rory. "You stopped putting peanut butter in your smoothies after you had Austin. Now you're doing it again. You're pregnant."

"Oh, please. By that logic, I should have been pregnant the first time I got a full night's rest after Austin was born. There are a lot of things I stopped doing after I had him, and some of those things I started doing again, like sleeping and putting peanut butter in my smoothies. And some of those things I will never do again, like putting peanut butter on my hot dogs and—"

"Forcing me to have sex so you could go into labor?"

"I did *not* force you! And I was already four days past my due date. It was perfectly safe."

"It's okay, baby. I like it when you take advantage of the medicinal powers of my monster cock."

She shakes her head, trying not to smile as I set down my smoothie on the counter and come up behind her, laying my hands flat on her abdomen.

"Maybe we should let my monster have a peek and see if he can diagnose your peanut butter craving more accurately than I can."

I pull her back until her back is flush against me, then I brush my lips over the soft curve of her neck. I'm positive she can feel my erection growing against the top of her ass. She sets her glass down on the counter and turns her head to kiss me on the mouth as my hand slides under the waistband of her jeans. She grabs my hand and I sigh as she yanks it out.

"My mom will be here any minute," she says, reaching for her smoothie again. "And you have to stop doing that in front of Austin. Pretty soon he's going to understand what happens when Daddy's hand disappears down Mommy's pants."

"He already understands. Don't you, buddy?" I say, taking a seat in the chair next to Austin. "That's why I'm your favorite. You want to be just like Daddy when you grow up. Making the girls squirm." I glance at Rory and she shoots me a deadly look.

"Can you take a break from making the girls squirm long enough to get your son cleaned up before his grandma gets here?"

"I think I can handle that." I grab the bowl of mushed peas off the tray and unlock it. Then I unfasten his seat belt and pull his chubby body out of the high chair. "Let's go get you cleaned up for your grandmonster."

"I heard that," Rory shouts as I set off toward Austin's room.

"Did she say why she's late?" I shout back at her as I pull some clean pajamas out of his dresser and grab a clean diaper off the shelf, placing them both on the changing table.

"She didn't say. She's acting weird again," Rory shouts back at me as I take Austin into the bathroom.

I give Austin a quick bath, then I hand him off to Rory so I can take a shower myself. By the time I come out of the bathroom with my towel wrapped around my waist, Patricia is already in the living room with Rory. I can hear her cooing and fussing over Austin. I try to make it past the hallway entrance unnoticed, but Patricia glances at me as I walk by.

"Hi, Patricia!" I call out as I keep walking toward the bedroom. Once I'm dressed in some pajama pants and a T-shirt, I come outside to greet my mother-in-law properly with a kiss on the cheek. "How are you doing, Patricia?"

She shrugs. "Oh, you know. If it's not the menopause, then it's something else. When a woman gets to be my age, she's lucky if she can remember to put her panties on."

"Mom!" Rory whines. "We don't want to hear that kind of stuff."

I laugh as I offer to take Austin off her hands and she gladly hands him over. He's a hefty boy, even at nine months old. He's definitely going to grow up to be tall and strong like his dad.

"Oh, Rory," Patricia says, waving off Rory's embarrassment. "You'll see when you get to be my age. You'll begin to care less about what's appropriate."

Rory looks worried. Ever since her mom started experiencing menopausal symptoms earlier this year, she's turned into a different person. The prim and proper grammarian has become a hot, sweaty mess. She and Kenny have become even closer, which Rory doesn't like one bit. She says it limits her time with Kenny because her mom has become unbearable. On that point we agree. Menopause is no joke. If this is what I have to look forward to with Rory in twenty years, then I think I might have to start saving my pennies for a good divorce lawyer.

Well, maybe not a divorce lawyer, but a good therapist might come in handy.

"Is this yours?" I ask Patricia, pointing at the purple suitcase standing next to her.

"Yes. Do you need to borrow it for your trip?"

I smile as I grab the handle. "We're fine, thanks. We've got plenty of room in our suitcases."

"Because we haven't packed yet," Rory says, placing her hand on her mother's back to lead her into the kitchen.

"Houston, you can't let Rory slack off or she'll never pack her suitcase," Patricia calls to me over her shoulder. "I'll never forget the time she forgot to pack for sixth-grade summer camp. She ended up throwing a bunch of clothes straight from the dryer into a duffel bag just so she wouldn't miss the bus. She ended up taking two of her father's pairs of jeans and none of her own."

I laugh softly. I've heard this story at least twice before and I know how much it annoys Rory when her mom tells the story because she insists Patricia doesn't remember it accurately. But Rory doesn't try to correct her. She just leads her mother to the kitchen table and begins making a pot of tea.

I carry the suitcase into Austin's room, then I push the rollaway bed out of Austin's walk-in closet into the bedroom. I set him down in the crib while I set up the bed, then I take him back to the kitchen with me. Rory and Patricia are sitting with their cups of tea, Patricia wearing a smug grin as I enter.

"Did I interrupt something?" I say, reaching into the fridge for a bottle of breast milk.

I place it in the bottle-warmer machine and press the on button, then I reach into the drawer for one of the nipples.

"My mom is dating someone," Rory says, sounding almost bored.

"I'm not dating anyone. I'm too old to date," Patricia insists.

"Then what do you call it when old people have sex?" Rory replies, though she cringes a little in anticipation of her mother's reply.

"Oh, Rory, don't give me that look. You can't expect me to be alone forever. I've told you before, we all have needs."

Rory scrunches up her face as if she's in physical pain. "Please, not the *needs* discussion."

Patricia rolls her eyes. "Fine. I'm screwing someone."

"Ew. No, that's not the appropriate response, Mom."

Patricia pushes her cup of tea away and begins fanning her face. "You know where you can stick your appropriate response."

I try not to laugh as Rory hangs her head in shame. "You need some ice water, Patricia?"

"Yes, please. Thank you, Houston."

I grab her a glass of water, then I grab Austin's bottle out of the warmer and screw the nipple on. He reaches for the bottle as I sit down at the table with them. Cradling him in my arms, I lean down to kiss his forehead and draw in a long breath of his clean baby scent. His cheeks perk up, smiling even as he sucks on the bottle.

Rory watches us for a minute before a guilty look comes over her. "I want to take the laptop with me on the trip."

I stare at her, taking deep breaths to calm myself so I don't blow up. "We agreed you'd leave the laptop at home. It's our f— It's our honeymoon. You can't—" I'm about to say that she can't work on our honeymoon, but a small voice in my head questions who I am to say what she can and can't do on our honeymoon. It's *our* honeymoon, not just mine.

I glance at Patricia and she's absentmindedly tracing her finger in circles over the whorl in the top of the walnut dining table. I sigh as I realize Rory brought this up in front of her mom so I would be outnumbered.

"We'll talk about it later," I mutter, and she rolls her eyes.

When I look down at Austin, his eyelids are becoming heavy. Rory gets me a baby bottle filled with water and I switch it for the bottle of milk. He continues sucking, rinsing away the sugars in his mouth with the water, until a few minutes later he's fast asleep.

I think the most beautiful thing about babies is the way they look when they're asleep. Part of that beauty comes from the knowledge that they're not lying awake at night or tossing and turning with nightmares about weddings or honeymoons or in-laws. When you watch a baby sleeping, you know he's truly at peace. You know you're seeing someone at the most perfect time of their lives, before the smolder of the world has cured their heart into a breakable mold.

I know I should trust Rory to do the right thing. If she thinks she needs to bring the laptop with her on the honeymoon, she must have a good reason for it. Still, there has to be some compromise. For instance, if she can bring the laptop, I can buy a lake house.

Sounds fair to me.

Rory

It's 2:30 a.m. and my mom is standing in front of the open refrigerator, fanning herself with the door. I'm annoyed. Not only did she wake Austin up when she got out of bed to cool herself down, but now she's standing between me and the pitcher of water I need to pour myself a glass.

I clear my throat softly. "You okay, Mom?"

She whips her head around. "Oh, I'm sorry. Did I wake you?"

"No, it was Austin, but I settled him down."

I don't mention that it was her who woke him. No need to rub it in. Still, it's hard to feel like my mom is here to help when her presence is already disturbing the delicate balance of Austin's routine. He just started sleeping through the night five weeks ago and it's been pure bliss. The first night it happened, I woke up at six a.m. feeling confused and out of sorts. It took me a few minutes to realize this was because I'd just had my first full night's rest in almost eight months.

"Did I wake him?" she asks, still fanning herself with the fridge door.

"I don't think so. Are you feeling okay?"

She sighs. "I'm burning up. If it's not hot flashes, it's night sweats. It's a waking nightmare."

"Is there anything I can do? I have a small desk fan in the bedroom. I can put that in Austin's room and point it at you. It's not very powerful, but it should give you a little comfort."

"That would be wonderful. Thank you." She looks around as if she's just realized where she's standing. "Oh, dear. Am I in your way?"

I smile. "Just getting some water."

She grabs the jug of filtered water and hands it to me, then closes the fridge. I hit the night-light button on the microwave and reach for a glass in the cupboard. She watches me as I pour myself a glass of water, and I get a strong feeling there's something she wants to say.

"Would you like some?" I ask, holding the glass out to her.

She smiles as she takes it. "Thank you."

I pour myself some more and put away the pitcher, then I lean back against the counter and sip my water as I wait for her to speak her mind.

She sets down her glass. "How are your vows coming?"

I sigh, glancing toward the living room to make sure Houston hasn't gotten up. "Not well. I don't know what's wrong with me. I seem to be having some sort of wedding-vow block."

"Maybe you're still harboring some latent fear from losing your book? You had some beautiful ponderings on love and commitment in there. Is it possible you feel like they're gone forever?"

I shrug. "I don't know what it is. Every time I sit down to write them, I draw a blank. Then I find something else to distract me: Austin, my book, Houston, Hallie's Hope, the wedding, whatever. My list of distractions is long."

She smiles. "Well, that's what I'm here for, to distract you from your distractions so you can focus on the wedding. You'll find the right words. I'm sure of it."

I nod then guzzle down the rest of my water. "Good night, Mom."

"Good night, sweetheart."

My head jerks to the side and I open my eyes to find Houston brushing his thumb over my cheek. I smile as I grab his hand and wrap it around me as I snuggle up to him.

"Good morning," I murmur, planting a soft kiss on his scruffy jaw.

"You and your mom had a slumber party last night?" he asks, sounding amused.

For a moment, I panic that he overheard our conversation about me having trouble with my vows.

"She was having night sweats," I reply. "She must have woken Austin when she got out of bed. I thought I'd turned off the baby monitor fast enough for it not to wake you. Sorry."

"Is your mom okay?" he asks, absentmindedly brushing his thumb over my bottom lip.

"I think so. I mean, she's as well as she can be, but something's still off. I just can't put my finger on it."

Houston slides out from underneath me, propping himself up on his elbow as his other arm disappears under the covers. "You can't put your finger on it?" He smiles as his hand slips inside my panties. "Can *I* put my finger on it?"

His finger slides between the throbbing folds of my flesh. I close my eyes and tilt my head back as he lightly massages my clit. He gently rolls me onto my side, his hand never losing contact as he brings his body flush against my back. His other arm slides under my head and turns my jaw toward him to kiss me, swallowing each of my moans.

It's a technique we both adopted after Austin was born, so we wouldn't wake him with our sex noises. Instead, we feed each other our cries of passion through an unrelenting kiss, which has only served to make sex even more interesting. Of course, there are certain positions where kissing just isn't possible. In those cases, we've had to be creative, or maybe *kinky* would be a better word. I'm not a fan of ball gags, but there's something about having a scarf tied around my mouth and hands that gets me hotter than I thought possible.

He removes his hand from between my thighs and guides his erection inside me, then he spreads my knees apart as he works his way in. I drape my leg over his and reach up to firmly grasp the back of his neck so our mouths don't lose contact. The muffled sounds of my whimpers are punctuated by the smack of skin on skin. I worry briefly that Austin will wake up soon and, in turn, wake my mother, who will hear us having sex.

Just as this thought crosses my mind, Houston slams into me, hitting my cervix and calling forth a sharp moan from deep inside my throat. He chuckles, continuing to kiss me as his finger finds my clit again. Every time he slams into me, his finger presses firmly on my sensitive nub, sending a shock of pleasure through me. The pleasure builds quickly and I soon find myself digging my nails into the back of his neck to keep from screaming.

"Oh, fuck," he whispers against my mouth. He slows his thrusts as he releases himself inside me. "Holy fuck," he says as my muscles contract around him. "Good fucking morning to you, too."

I chuckle. "We'd better get up before Austin does."

He thrusts into me one more time as he hugs my body tightly against his. "Your mom's here to help. If he wakes up, she'll take care of him."

I laugh as he slides his hand between my legs again. "I'd stay in bed with you all day… if my mom weren't here. But she is. We have to get up."

He groans as he slides out of me then smacks my ass before rolling out of bed. "By the way, you *are* pregnant. Your cervix has that soft pregnant feeling. You should go to the doctor."

My jaw drops as I sit up in bed. "Are you kidding me? I can't be pregnant. I only got pregnant with Austin because I forgot to take my pill a couple of times. I haven't forgotten to take my pill in months."

He shrugs as he grabs some clean boxers out of a drawer. "I'm just giving you my dick's very scientific diagnosis."

"*Pft!* Your dick needs to go back to medical school."

Once we're all showered and dressed, Houston obliges my request to sit down and have breakfast with me, Austin, and my mom. Houston insists my mother should sit down while he helps me set the table and fix the baby's morning porridge. I've been slowly introducing almond milk into Austin's diet, mixing a little in with the breast milk. The goal is to stop pumping soon. I told myself I wouldn't go beyond six months' breastfeeding, but then I read some articles that suggested children who are breastfed longer have higher IQs. I'm willing to do just about anything if it's good for my mini-Houston.

Well, almost anything.

I set down a plate of bacon, a basket of toast, and a French press of dark-roast coffee in the center of the table as Houston sets down three plates of scrambled eggs. I sit next to Austin to help him eat his porridge. My mom pours us all a mug of coffee and I thank her when she passes me the carton of cream.

"Are you going to pick up the dress today?" she asks, stirring some sugar into her coffee.

"Yeah, Kenny and I are leaving in a couple of hours. Our

flight to Seattle leaves at 1:15. We should be back by seven."

"That should be fun," she says, raising the mug to her lips.

I flash her a tight smile. "If you consider rushing from the airport to the designer's studio then back to the airport fun, then I guess so."

She sets down her mug and reaches out to tickle Austin's neck. "Well, at least Austin and Grandma will finally get some quality time together. Right, angel?"

Austin squirms a bit, his face scrunching up as if he's about to start giggling, then he lets out a loud belch followed by a small pocket of vomit.

"Oh, no," I say, grabbing my napkin and using it wipe his mouth.

He spits some regurgitated porridge into the napkin as I wipe, then his face screws up like he's about to cry.

"Oh, no, sweetheart. It's okay."

By the time I unlock the tray on his high chair, Houston is already there to undo the straps and pull him out. Austin lets out a pitiful whimper and sniffs a couple of times before Houston calms him.

"Did he throw up because I was tickling him?" my mom asks.

"No, it's not your fault," I insist, though I'm pretty sure it is, since Austin has never vomited this particular brand of porridge since I started giving it to him a few weeks ago.

Houston disappears into the bedroom, probably to change Austin's shirt. I try to eat a few bites of scrambled eggs, but I find myself becoming anxious over the prospect of leaving my baby alone with my mom for so many hours. I know it's ridiculous to feel anxious about that. She took care of me on her own while my dad was away at work. It's not like a hot flash is going to make her forget how to hold a baby. However, forgetfulness is another symptom of menopause. I don't know what I'd do if I came home to find she'd forgotten to lay him on his back instead of his stomach, or she forgot to feed him. I know. It's ridiculous. I'm being a helicopter mom, but I can't help it. He's just so precious to me.

"Maybe I should send Kenny to Seattle by himself," I mutter, holding the coffee mug in front of my mouth as if this will soften the blow.

She cocks a silver eyebrow at me. "You don't trust me."

"It's not that I don't trust you. It's just that I don't even know why I have to go. Kenny would be perfectly happy to pick up the dress without me."

She huffs at this excuse. "Really, Rory. I'm going through menopause, I don't have brain damage. I can still spot a lie like that a mile away."

"It's your first day here, Mom. I should be here to ease you into this."

"*Ease* me into it? Please, by all means, *ease* me into this new role. Lord knows I've never taken care of a baby before."

"It's not the same as it was when I was a baby. You can't just tickle him all day or stick a bottle in his mouth to make him shut up."

She glares at me. "Do you hear yourself?" She pauses to register her shock. "At least when I got married, I had no problem writing my vows!"

Houston walks in, looking very confused. "You haven't written your vows?"

I stand up to take Austin from him. "I'm still working on them. They'll be done soon."

"She hasn't written a single word," my mom says, crossing her arms as she sits back in her chair.

I bounce Austin on my hip as I wait for Houston to say something. He just stares at the dining table, truly at a loss for words.

"Houston, that's why my mom is here. I've only had time to

take care of Austin and write the book. Now that she's here, I have all the time in the world to write my vows. They'll be done in no time."

He squints at me as if he's trying to figure me out. "I've had mine written for months. When I asked you about your vows last week, you said they were almost done. You lied to me?"

"I was ashamed," I reply, laying my hand on his chest. "I just want to get them right."

He heaves a deep sigh as he grabs my hand. "I have to go. I have to meet the inspector in a few minutes. I'll see you later." He kisses my cheekbone and Austin's forehead. "See you later, buddy." He waves at my mom. "Bye, Patricia."

As the front door closes behind him, I turn on my heel to face my mom, flashing a scathing glare in her direction. Then I set about making another half bowl of porridge for Austin while carrying him in one arm. By the time I have him seated in his high chair with his new breakfast, my breakfast is cold. I stare at the plate of rubbery eggs and cardboard toast and sigh.

"If you're going to be here for the next seven days, you cannot stir up trouble between Houston and me." I look her in the eye and she purses her lips. "I will not hesitate to call Ava to replace you if you can't stay out of my marriage."

Her shoulders slump in defeat. "I'm sorry. I shouldn't have said anything to Houston about the vows."

I nod as I grab my plate and Houston's to take them to the sink. As I'm shoving the leftovers into the trash bin, my phone vibrates in my pocket. I pull it out and breathe a sigh of relief when I see Kenny's name.

"Hey, are you almost ready?" I ask, balancing the phone between my ear and my shoulder as I rinse the dishes.

"Rory, have you gotten RSVPs from Houston's uncle Ned or Benji and Bella?"

I slip the plates into the dishwasher and shut the door as I try to think whether I've heard from either of them. "No, actually, I haven't. Have you?"

"No, and it's weird because they were on our probably-definitely list. I'm going to try to get in touch with them and see if maybe the invite got lost in the mail or it just slipped their mind to RSVP."

"Sounds good to me. Do you have RSVPs from everyone else?"

"No, there are a few we had on the maybe list who haven't RSVPed. I'll try to get in touch with them if I find there was some kind of widespread mail issue or something."

"Okey-doke. I'll see you in two hours."

"See you soon, my blushing bride."

Kenny and I arrive at the bridal studio in downtown Seattle just after 2:30 p.m. The moment we enter the store, I get the same bubbly feeling in my stomach I got the first time I came here. The studio is a three-bedroom bungalow converted into a bridal studio, but made to look like a 1920s Parisian loft. The creamy wallpaper and vintage furnishings in various shades of sage green and soft pink make you feel as if you've drifted into another world, a dream world where feminine beauty and afternoon champagne cocktails rule.

Misty Green—yes, that's her real name—spots us as she's hanging a dress on a rack in the next room. "Rory! It's so good to see you," she says. "Come inside."

We enter the parlor where she was hanging the dress, then she leads us through to the fitting room. And there it is, the only dress hanging on a silver rack next to a large silver-framed mirror that's leaned up against the wall. The dress is covered in clear plastic, but I can still see that it's as breathtakingly beautiful on a hanger as it was when I first saw it on the runway last year.

The designer named this dress the Secret Garden, and it couldn't be a more perfect name for this classic vintage design. A full-length flowing silk organza skirt skims the floor while a floral lace overlay covers the bodice and climbs over the chest like ivy up to the tops of the shoulders, forming a deep V-neck pattern. Under the lacy V-neck overlay is a delicate sheer organza scooped across the neckline and over the shoulders in soft flutter-cap sleeves.

My hands are trembling a little as Kenny and I head into the dressing room to try it on. Even the rustling of the plastic makes me giddy with excitement. But when I step into the dress and Kenny tries to zip up the lower back, the zipper encounters some resistance on the last couple of inches.

"Holy jugs, Batman. You can see your cleavage through the sheer neckline," Kenny says, looking down at my chest as he continues to try to force the zipper up. "Did your boobs get bigger?"

The neckline comes together a few inches below the nape with a single pearl button. The entire center of the back of the dress is open, with the delicate lace extending from the front bodice to encircle the lower back.

I adjust my boobs a little inside my bra, trying to separate them a bit, then I suck in my belly. "Try the zipper again."

He yanks the zipper and this time it goes all the way up. "Honey, you may need to lose five pounds this week."

"I can't lose five pounds in a week!" I snap at him and his eyes widen. "Sorry, it's just that Houston thinks I'm pregnant, but I really don't want to be pregnant during the wedding and the honeymoon."

"Is everything okay in there?" Misty calls to us from the other side of the dressing-room door.

"Just fine!" I shout back, then I turn to Kenny and whisper, "Undo the zipper."

"But you haven't even looked in the mirror."

"I don't care. It looks fine. Just take it off me. I can't breathe."

He quickly unzips me and I sigh with relief as I slide out of the dress. "You're gonna need to get a good backless corset or do a liquid cleanse this week."

My hands are still trembling as I pull on my jeans. "I have to go to the doctor first. I can't do a corset or a cleanse if I'm pregnant."

Once the wedding dress and the two bridesmaid dresses are packed up in boxes, the boxes are wrapped in two layers of plastic wrap and a layer of thick brown shipping paper, so we can check them as luggage on the return flight. Kenny and I take our seats on the plane and Kenny takes advantage of his first-class seat by ordering a gin and tonic before takeoff. Though I'd love an ice-cold beer, I order a plain club soda instead.

"I can't wait to get home," I mutter, reaching up to open the air vent a bit more.

Kenny's phone chimes and he lifts it off the console between us to check the text message. "Oh, my God."

"What?"

The worried look on his face makes my heart race. "It's Benji. He said he didn't RSVP because his invitation said the wedding was on a Wednesday and he and Bella can't make it."

"A Wednesday?" I reply loud enough to get the attention of the passengers across the aisle. "That doesn't make sense. It clearly says the wedding is on a Saturday. Did he read the invitation wrong?"

Kenny shakes his head and holds up his phone to show me the photo Benji sent him. It's a picture of the invitation Benji received, and underneath my and Houston's names are the words Wednesday, August 10, 2016. It's supposed to read Saturday, August 13, 2016.

Kenny and I look at each other and speak one single word at the same time: "Tessa."

Rory

There is no way in hell Houston can find out I allowed Tessa to design and produce our handmade wedding invitations. He had only two requests for our wedding. The first was that we get married in Portland. The second was that we couldn't use Tessa for the invitations. And I agreed with him one hundred percent on both points. At least, I agreed with him before I saw her work.

When Sid and I began working together, I was adamant that I wanted most, if not all, of the vendors we used to be small, local artisans. He showed me an album of various wedding invitations, and I narrowed my choices down to four different styles. Three of those four were by Contessa Designs.

I thought it was just a coincidence. Maybe the designer just liked the word *contessa* and wanted to use it in her business name, like the Barefoot Contessa. When I called the designer on the phone, she introduced herself as Contessa and she was very friendly. She didn't stutter or pause when I introduced myself as Rory. I was certain she was not the same Tessa who had attacked me at Wallace Park.

Of course, I was wrong. There she was when I entered Contessa Designs near Lloyd Center. My fiancé's ex-wife, sitting behind a gorgeous vintage writing desk, her blonde blunt-cut hair glistening under the warm lighting. Her eyes were fixated on the sleek screen of her Mac computer, her bracelets jingling as her slender hand pushed the mouse around, probably working on a new design.

I almost turned around and walked out. She hadn't seen me yet. I still had time to leave. Then I thought of those three wedding invitations and I knew I wasn't going to find a better designer in Portland.

When she sat me down to look at style albums and discuss concepts for my invitations, she was bursting with excitement and ideas for designs so beautiful they made me salivate. I found myself thinking, *Wow… She's not as awful as I thought she was.* Not once during our whole meeting did she try to crack me over the head with a thermos.

We even chatted a bit about how she's doing. She told me she opened Contessa Designs a few months after her hospitalization, and she's now happily involved with a man she met at, of all places, a friend's wedding. She seemed happy and stable. Not once did I think she would send out invitations with the wrong date.

"What are you going to tell Houston?" Kenny asks as we slide into the backseat of a cab outside Portland International Airport.

"Nothing," I reply without a missing a beat.

Kenny raises his eyebrows. "Lucy, you got some 'splaining to do. You can't just ignore this problem."

I sigh heavily. "I am not going to tell Houston. No way. Not in a million years. I'm… I'm going to have to talk to Tessa."

"And you think she's just going to admit to sabotaging your wedding?"

"Well, what am I supposed to do? Try to get hold of 150

people to ask them to confirm that they RSVPed for the correct date?" I groan with frustration. "Ugh. I'm so stupid for trusting her."

Kenny smacks the top of my thigh. "You are *not* stupid. You just wanted the best invitations for your wedding, so you gave Tessa the benefit of the doubt. That doesn't make you stupid. It makes you kindhearted… and a bit of a risk taker."

I shake my head. "It doesn't matter. I don't have phone numbers for all 150 people on the list. Some of them are in Houston's contacts and he'll notice if I get home and start puttering around on his computer." I turn to Kenny, a desperate plea in my eyes. "We have to go to Tessa's shop and ask her how many invitations she messed up. You have to come with me."

Kenny cocks an eyebrow. "Um… You're the one who just said you were stupid for trusting her. Now you want to go ask her to confess to screwing up your invitations? And you really expect her to tell the truth?"

"You never know. She sent the invitations out eight weeks ago. Maybe she was just having a bad day, or maybe she didn't get enough sleep and it was an honest mistake."

He lets out a deep sigh as he slumps down into the backseat. "Fine, but if Houston finds out about this, it was *your* idea to keep this a secret, not mine. Got it?"

I nod. "Got it. Thank you, Kenny," I say, linking my arm in his and laying my head on his shoulder. "You're the best maid of honor a girl could ask for."

Houston

"Baby, can you make me one of those poop smoothies you made yesterday?" I ask Rory when I enter the kitchen to find her balancing Austin on her hip while pouring almond milk into a sippy cup.

She shakes her head as I take the baby from her. "I'll make you a poop smoothie if you make Austin his dinner. There's some shredded chicken and mashed sweet potatoes in the fridge."

"I can do that," Patricia offers, hurrying past me to beat me to the refrigerator. "You go sit down and spend some time with the baby. I'll get his dinner ready."

I take a seat in a dining chair and Skippy plops down at my feet as I sit Austin on the table in front of me. "You and I are getting treated like kings today." Austin wobbles a little as if he's going to fall sideways, but I catch him. "Are you drunk, buddy? Has your mom been spiking your boob juice?"

"Make fun all you want. You're not the one who has to stick your nipples in a machine all day Friday."

"Rory, watch your language in front of the baby," Patricia

scolds her.

"What?" Rory laughs. "*Nipples* isn't a dirty word. Nipples are a part of the human body, and they also happen to be part of a bottle. Just like pussies are cats and cocks are roosters. These are not bad words, Mom."

Patricia huffs as she sticks the bowl of baby food in the microwave. "For heaven's sake, you have an English degree. You should know better than that. Language is meaningless without context, and context is what makes those words inappropriate."

I turn back to Austin so I don't have to witness another battle of the English majors. "Baby, did you find out what happened with my uncle Ned's invitation?"

"Houston, don't let him sit on the table," Rory replies, completely ignoring my question. "I don't want him to grow up thinking it's okay to sit on the kitchen table."

I sigh as I pull him into my lap and grab his toy zebra off the high chair to keep him busy. "What happened with the invitation?"

"Kenny and I are still looking into it. In fact, can I look at the contacts on your laptop? I don't know if I have the right phone number for your uncle. And there are a few other numbers I need, just to verify this invitation debacle isn't a bigger issue than we think it is."

"Of course, you don't have to ask. You know I have nothing to hide from you."

She flashes me an uncomfortable smile, but she doesn't reply. Something tells me she's hiding something from me.

Patricia sets a bowl of warm chicken and mashed potatoes on the table. Skippy sits up straight, his wet black nose sniffing the air. I glance at Rory to make sure she's not watching me, then I hand him a small piece of Austin's chicken.

"Is something wrong?" I ask Rory, to cover up the sound of Skippy licking his chops.

She heads over to join us at the table. "Are you talking to me?" she replies, placing the sippy cup of almond milk and my poop smoothie next to Austin's dinner bowl.

She takes a seat in the chair next to me and leans forward to scratch Skippy behind the ears, but his attention is still laser-focused on Austin's bowl.

I blow gently on a spoon of mashed potatoes before I slide it into Austin's mouth. "You just look a little worried," I reply. "Did something go wrong with the dresses?"

"No. Well, not really. Kenny had a little trouble zipping me up."

I cock an eyebrow at her. "Kenny goes in the dressing room with you?"

She rolls her eyes. "Oh, please. Does that even warrant a response?"

"Have you gained weight or is it just my seed growing nice and plump inside you?"

She shrugs. "I don't know. I have an appointment with the doctor tomorrow morning." She stares at the zebra plush toy on the table for a moment, lost in thought. "What if we postpone the honeymoon?"

"What?" I reply with a chuckle as I spoon some chicken into Austin's mouth. "Why would we do that?"

"It's just that there's so much up in the air right now. I may be pregnant, which means I won't be able to drink or do anything remotely fun in Maui, like parasailing or horseback riding. It seems like a waste of a honeymoon to do it while pregnant."

I look at Patricia to see her reaction and, as expected, her arms are crossed over her chest and her eyebrow is cocked with harsh skepticism. In other circumstances, I would consider Rory's concerns legitimate. But with all the turmoil between Rory and Patricia these past two days, I'm almost certain this has more to do with Rory trying to find a way out of leaving Austin for a week than feeling like she won't be able to have fun in Maui. Rory's trying to heighten the tension between her and her mother so that Patricia can throw in the towel, leaving us no choice but to cancel the honeymoon.

I smile at Rory and she smiles back, probably thinking I'm going to agree with her. "Baby, I don't need to go parasailing or horseback riding to have fun with you. That shit is for tourists. You can still hike up a volcano while pregnant and you can still hike up my volcano." I wink at Rory and her face drops, but this gets a laugh out of Patricia. "See, Patricia, I know how to use context."

"Yes, you do, young man. And I completely agree with you, as usual."

"As usual?" Rory chortles. "Fine. If you two want to team up against me, that's fine." She shoots up from her chair. "I'm going to take a shower and go to bed. You can put Austin down tonight."

"I can do that," Patricia offers.

Rory turns to me. "Don't forget that you agreed to stay home tomorrow. I know you have something big going on at the brewery, but it's Saturday. It's my last full day to write and run errands. You have to be available in case my mom or I need you."

I smile as Austin spits out the last bite of mashed potatoes and reaches for the zebra. "I'll be at your beck and call, m'lady." I glance at Patricia as she clears her throat. "Pardon me, *m'ladies*."

When I wake at 6:22 a.m., Rory is already showered and blow-dried and sitting at the kitchen table with her makeup case and a cup of coffee.

"Where's Austin?" I ask, grabbing a mug out of the cupboard to pour myself a cup.

"I peeked in on them a few minutes ago. They're both still asleep," she replies, making that weird monkey face she makes when she's putting on mascara.

"Where are you off to so early?"

She uses her hands to fan her eyelashes as she responds. "Kenny and I are going to meet the cake designer. She wants us to try a couple of new filling recipes she came up with. She works from 12 a.m. to 8 a.m., so we have to head out early."

I sit across from her, setting my coffee on the table. "I don't get a say in the filling?"

"Your groom's cake isn't changing. This is for the actual wedding cake."

I don't bother mentioning that the groom's cake is only being served at the rehearsal dinner, so technically I should still have a say in what she puts in the wedding cake. But I've learned to choose my battles wisely when it comes to the wedding.

I tilt my head as I think I hear Austin. Rory is already on her feet, but I hold my hand up to stop her. "I'll get him, baby. You finish getting ready."

She watches me as I get up from the table and head for the bedroom. I can feel her eyes on my back as I walk away. That woman is going to drive Austin crazy when he's a teenager if she doesn't loosen up before then.

When I enter the bedroom, Patricia is out of bed and reaching for Austin.

"I can take him," I say, sidling up to the crib.

She pats my arm and smiles. "Good morning, Houston."

I smile as she leaves the room, but when I turn back to Austin something's wrong. His face is flushed bright pink and he's crying softly, almost silently, as he rubs his eyes. I scoop him up and he rubs his face all over my T-shirt.

"What's wrong, buddy?" I say, reaching up to feel his forehead. *Shit.* He's burning up.

Rory startles me when she enters the room. "I have to go now. I'll see you later," she says, puckering up for me to give her a kiss.

I kiss her lips and she quickly turns her attention to Austin, who's still rubbing his eyes.

"What's wrong with him?" she asks, reaching up to lay her hand on his forehead. "He has a fever."

"I'll give him some Tylenol. You go ahead. You have a clinic appointment, don't you?"

"That can wait. Why does he keep rubbing his eyes?"

She reaches up and we each take hold of one of Austin's chubby hands to pull them away from his face. He begins to cry louder as Rory tries to examine his eyes.

"They're both pink and his eyelashes are stuck together. Do you think he has pink eye?"

I shrug. "How could he get pink eye? He was here all day with your mom yesterday and she's fine."

"Unless she took him somewhere. Mom!" she calls out as she leaves the bedroom.

Oh, man. Here comes another argument, I think as I follow Rory into the kitchen, where Patricia is stirring sugar into her coffee.

"Did you go anywhere with Austin yesterday?" Rory asks, assuming her mother-hen pose.

Skippy plods into the kitchen and heads straight for his bowl of water. Patricia watches him as she seems to be trying to remember what she did yesterday.

"We went to Hallie's Hope. I needed to talk to your father about… about the fund-raiser in Vancouver next month. And I let Austin play in the playroom for a little while."

"Unsupervised?"

Patricia glares at her. "Of course not. Your father and I were in there with him."

"Were there any other kids in there?"

Patricia nods. "There were a couple of other children, but they looked healthy. I wouldn't have let him play in there if they were sniveling and feverish."

Rory sighs and turns to me. "I'll take him with me when I go to the clinic. Maybe the doctor can spare a moment to check him out. I'll be back in an hour."

As soon as Rory's gone, I give Austin some baby Tylenol and let him chase it down with a bottle of whole breast milk, no water or almond milk added. Less than two hours after he woke up, he falls asleep on my chest while I'm lying in bed watching a recorded episode of *SportsCenter*. He doesn't even stir when Patricia knocks on my bedroom door.

"Come in," I call out, and his wispy eyebrow twitches.

Patricia pushes the door in slowly, glancing at the TV as I mute the sound. "I can come back later if you're busy."

"I'm not busy. What do you need?"

She sighs as she wrings her hands. "I wonder if maybe we should ask your mother to come and take over. I… I don't want to cause any more trouble."

I look down at the fuzzy brown hair on Austin's head as I try to think of an appropriate response. The truth is that I think my mom's easygoing temperament is better suited for the role of babysitter, but my mom is too busy with the foundation to watch Austin for more than a week. She made it very clear that she was only available to take care of Austin during the honeymoon as a "last resort." I don't begrudge my mother her priorities. Hallie's Hope has given her a purpose, and we're not all cut out to be caregivers.

"Patricia, don't let Rory's frustration get you down," I begin. "She's under a lot of stress right now with the wedding and the honeymoon and leaving Austin for the first time for a whole week… And not to mention the possibility of being pregnant. The last thing she, and any of us, need right now is for Austin to get sick. But no one believes this is your fault. And if he's sick, they'll give him some antibiotics and it should be cleared up before we leave next week. Simple as that."

She nods, though she doesn't look convinced by my words of encouragement. "Thank you, Houston." She gazes at Austin for a moment. "I don't tell you often enough, but my daughter is lucky to have you."

As soon as she leaves, I get on the phone and call Troy.

He picks up on the first ring. "Where the fuck are you?"

"Good morning to you, too."

"Jesus, we had an angry crowd of brunch customers this morning."

I laugh as I imagine the scene. Saturday and Sunday brunch and dinner are by far the busiest times for the Barley Legal restaurant. Those are the only times we have to open up the second-floor dining area. Except that the second floor is closed today, and all week, until after the wedding next weekend. We have a delivery of white silk tents coming in today from a vendor Kenny found at the last minute. The warehouse isn't clean enough to store the tents, so we have to use the second-floor dining area, which means there's probably an hour or longer wait to be seated for brunch today.

"I'm home with the baby," I say, smoothing down Austin's hair and kissing the top of his head. "He's sick. How's that other thing going?"

"Lookin' good. I think we'll be done on time."

"Good. Thanks for putting in the extra hours on this."

"No sweat, bro. You coming in later? I think it would really help morale around here. These guys are working their asses off."

I pause as I think about my promise to Rory to stay home in case she needs me, then I think about how hard the guys have been working to put out this latest order. I'm sure Rory won't have a problem with my dropping by the brewery for an hour or two once she gets back from the doctor's office.

"I'll be there."

Rory

I didn't lie to Houston about having to meet the cake designer at the bakery this morning. I just didn't tell him that I'm *also* going to visit Tessa afterward.

After Kenny and I settle on the cake designer's latest concoction—hazelnut macchiato Chantilly cream—we decide to walk the thirteen blocks from Irvington to Contessa Designs, since Tessa won't arrive to open up the shop for another forty minutes or so. We stroll casually arm in arm as if we don't have a care in the world, when the reality is that in two days, my world has gone from a slow simmer of day-to-day wedding errands to a violent rolling boil of wedding disasters. But it feels nice to be out here on a pleasant August morning, meandering through the streets of Portland as if we're just taking a leisurely stroll. Maybe on our way to the farmers' market or to a lazy brunch.

I sigh as we turn the corner at 9th Avenue. "Houston suspects something. I'm going to have to tell him about Tessa."

Kenny shakes his head, but I can't see his eyes behind those new prescription sunglasses he's been wearing all summer. "I'd say I told you so, but that's not my style. What I will say is that you have nothing to worry about. You and Houston are as solid as my buns of steel."

"That's comforting," I mutter.

He smiles, reaching for my hand. "I know, feel them. They're beautiful. I've been working with that new trainer. I'm deadlifting 325 now."

I smile, then I realize I'm not going to be able to deadlift anything at the gym until I find out if I'm pregnant. "Yeah, well, I deadlift a twenty-four-pound baby almost all day long, so I'm sure by the end of the day I've deadlifted more than you."

"You know, Rory, if you need someone else to look in on Austin and Grandma Patty while you're gone, I'm more than happy to do it. You know the old saying, 'Keep Austin weird.' I believe that's Uncle Kenny's job."

I squeeze his arm. "I'd love that."

We arrive at Contessa Designs eight minutes before nine a.m. and Tessa still hasn't arrived. My doctor's appointment is at 10:30 a.m. I hope Tessa doesn't decide to come in late today because it's a Saturday. I need this issue with the invitations solved and behind me.

"I got an email from my editor. She says I'm not going to hear from her until Houston and I are back from Maui."

"Awesome!" Kenny says, holding up his hand for a high five.

I lightly smack my hand against his. "Yeah, great. Now I have no excuse to bring my laptop on the honeymoon and I'm not going to be able to get any work done. I'll be swamped when I get back."

Kenny purses his lips. "Rory, it's a honeymoon, not a business trip. Treat it as such."

At ten minutes past nine, I start to feel physically ill. Kenny is standing with his hands cupped against the glass storefront, trying to peek inside the shop.

"Ooh… She has one of those cube-y artificial intelligence things in there. She probably uses it for evil. 'Cubic, remind me that tomorrow I have to murder my parents,'" he says with a giggle.

"I'm going to have to go home and tell Houston."

"Tell Houston what?"

Kenny and I spin around and stare wide-eyed as Tessa approaches the front door. "Good morning," we say in unison.

She smiles. "A good morning for murdering my parents," she says, blowing on her fingernails before she sticks the key in the lock.

"I didn't mean that the way it sounded. I was just…" Kenny steps behind me, putting his hands on my shoulders as he leans in and whispers in my ear, "Mommy, help me."

I shrug him off. "Tessa, we need to talk about the invitations."

She smiles as she pushes the door open and holds it for us. "Sure. Was there a problem with the invites?"

I stuff my hands in the pockets of my jeans to keep myself from punching her in her smug face as I walk into the shop. "Yes, there was a problem."

"Have a seat," she replies, waving us toward two ivory armchairs in a sitting area to the right.

I watch as she places her purse on top of her vintage desk then takes a seat across from us in a plush wine-colored armchair. "At least two of the guests received invitations with the wrong date. Do you know how that could have happened?"

She looks back and forth between Kenny and me for a moment, then she sighs as her shoulders slump. "I'm sorry."

"You're… you're sorry? Are you saying you did it on purpose?"

She stares at the small mirrored coffee table between us as she speaks. "When you called me asking me to make your invitations,

I didn't know if you were doing it to rub it in my face or, like you said, you just really loved my work." She swallows hard. "I kept telling myself to be a professional. Don't say anything stupid. Don't *do* anything stupid… But then Eric and I got in a fight and I… I had a few drinks. I'm not supposed to drink, but it was just standing there on my desk… That *stupid* bottle of champagne given to me by a client who knows nothing about my… about my…"

"Stop."

Tessa looks up at me in confusion, as if she just realized who she was speaking to.

"You don't have to explain," I continue, taking a deep breath. "I can't believe I'm going to say this, but I'm sorry."

She looks even more confused now. "For what?"

"For asking you to do the invitations. I should never have come here. And not because you kind of screwed me, but because you're right. You had no way of knowing whether I was here to rub the wedding in your face. I wasn't, by the way. I just… love your work. You… have a gift." I glance at Kenny and he's dabbing his finger at the corner of his eye. "Kenny, are you crying?"

"Just look away," he whispers.

I chuckle as I reach out and grab his hand to give it a squeeze. "Oh, Kenny, I love you." I hear a loud sniff and when I look at Tessa, she's wiping away tears.

"Oh, my God. I'm so sorry. I'm just really emotional lately," she says.

I shake my head as I realize I'm the one who's possibly pregnant and these two are the ones crying. "Tessa, I'm sorry, but I have to ask. Was it just those two invitations, or were there more?"

She shakes her head vigorously. "It was just the two. I did it to his uncle Ned because he always hated me. And the other couple, you were talking to one of them on the phone while you were here. I think it was the woman. And you sounded like good friends, so…"

I feel a twinge of anger at this confession, but I try not to let it show. "Thank you for your honesty."

She smiles. "I really am sorry. I was just in a bad place, but everything's better now. In fact, I'm getting married too." She holds out her hand to show me a beautiful diamond ring on her left hand. "Eric and I worked everything out and we're getting married in Massachusetts in the fall. Eric's family is from Massachusetts."

I try not to smile too broadly as I say a silent prayer that Eric and Tessa will move to the East Coast to be near his family. "That's fabulous. Congratulations!"

"Thank you," she says, then she gasps. "You and Houston should come! Oh, hold on, let me get you an invite."

She leaps to her feet and races through a door into a back office area. As soon as the door closes behind her, I turn to Kenny. His eyes are wide with shock.

"Oh, my God. What do I do?" I ask, my heart racing. "I can't accept an invitation to her wedding."

Kenny shakes his head. "This is your fault for being so damn nice to her. Now she wants to be your friend. If she murders her parents, just imagine what she does to her friends." He stands up quickly. "We should just leave. Hurry before she comes back."

"We can't just leave," I say, batting his hands away as he tries to pull me out of the chair.

"Rory, you're like that character in the scary movie who wants to investigate. Don't just sit there. Run! Run your booty off before Tess-zilla catches you!"

"Tess-zilla?"

Kenny freezes at the sound of Tessa's voice. I slowly tilt my head to the side to see past Kenny, and sure enough, Tessa is standing right there next to her desk.

"Kenny has an overactive imagination," I say. "And he used to act in the theater."

Kenny looks at me like I'm crazy and I shoot him a deadly glare meant to communicate the need to play along. "Oh, yes!" he squeals as he turns around to face Tessa. "I wanted to be an actress when I was in high school. I auditioned for the part of Juliet because yummy Hayden Blackley was playing Romeo, but stupid Mrs. Garrett and her stupid perpetuation of gender roles in the theater. As if the whole school didn't know she hadn't shaved her pits in twenty years."

Tessa stares at him, slack-jawed and dumbfounded.

I take the opportunity to stand up and approach the desk. "Sorry about that. We should probably get going. Thanks for talking to me… and telling me the truth."

She flashes me a tight smile. "Sure." She holds out a creamy lavender envelope. "Here's your invitation. I realize this is kind of weird. And I wouldn't expect you guys to come. I mean, not in a million years, right?" We both chuckle, though I make a concerted effort not to laugh harder than her. "But my therapist says I'm ready to start making amends. So if you do decide to come, we'd be… delighted to see you there."

I've never seen someone look more uncomfortable in my life. I sigh as I realize I can't reject her invitation. I have to at least accept the invitation, then I can go home and mail her the RSVP saying that we can't make it. But if I take this invitation, then that means….

"Do you want to come to our wedding?" The words are out of my mouth before I can stop them. "I mean, you already have all the information."

Did I really just say that? I made it sound as if I'm only inviting her because she already knows where and when it's going to take place.

She smiles. "Thanks. I'll talk to Eric about it and see if we can drop by."

I nod as I smile back. "Great." I continue nodding my head for far too long. "Great. We'll just get out of your hair."

"Oh, don't forget your invite," she replies as I begin to turn around.

I smile as I reach for the lavender envelope. "Of course." I swallow hard as I clutch the invitation to my chest. "See you around."

Houston

Luckily, Austin is awake by the time Rory returns from the bakery. Rory is obviously in a rush and worried that she's going to miss her 10:30 a.m. appointment, so I offer to drive her to the clinic myself. This will win me some points for later when I tell her I have to go into work.

Our family practitioner, Dr. Winslow, is more than happy to squeeze in a checkup for Austin while Rory is whisked away by an assistant to another room to have her blood drawn. Austin is asleep and drooling on my shoulder as Winslow informs me that our suspicions were correct. Austin indeed has contracted conjunctivitis, but we won't know if it's bacterial or viral for another week. If it's bacterial, the eye ointment he gives us should clear it up before the wedding. If it's viral, it may or may not clear up on its own before then.

Winslow hands me the prescription for the ointment as Rory reenters the exam room. "You want to try to get it on the inside of his lower eyelid. One of you will probably have to restrain him while the other applies the ointment."

Rory takes the prescription from my hand and glances at Winslow's chicken scratch. "What is this for?"

Winslow smiles. "It's pink eye, as you both suspected, so it's quite contagious. Make sure you wash your hands well before and after you apply the ointment." He closes Austin's medical file as he heads for the door. "It's probably best if you three just wait in here. The lab should have your test results in just a few minutes."

As soon as the door falls closed, Rory looks up at me with desperation in her eyes. "He has pink eye? Did he say how long it would take to clear up?"

"He said he should be fine in time for the wedding."

She covers her face with her hands, and shakes her head. "I have to tell you something."

I get a bad feeling in the pit of my belly when she says this. "What do you have to tell me?"

She uncovers her face and looks up at me. "I used Tessa for our wedding invitations."

"You *what*?"

Austin is startled by the intensity of my voice. He raises his head from my shoulder, jutting out his bottom lip as he begins to whimper.

"I'll take him," Rory says, reaching for Austin.

I turn away so she can't reach him. "Why would you use her?" I ask calmly as I try to rock Austin back to sleep.

Rory's gaze is still fixed on the baby as she tries to think of a response. "It just happened. I saw some of her invitations, but I didn't know they were hers."

"How could you not know they were hers?"

"Because the name of the company was… Contessa Designs."

I cock an eyebrow as I glare at her. "Are you kidding me?"

"I realize how stupid it sounds… *now*. But when I called her eight weeks ago, she didn't seem to recognize me. I was sure it wasn't her. Now I realize I was just in denial."

"In denial?" I reply with a chuckle. "Un-*fucking*-believable… So this is what the whole invitation debacle is about? Your little secret backfired on you?"

Austin is still fussing and Rory is giving me that look, the look that says, *How long are you going to pretend you can shut him up faster than my boob?*

I roll my eyes as I step aside so she can sit down on the chair with the worn blue fabric and wooden arms. Then I hand her the baby. As soon as she lifts her shirt, Austin is feeling around for his flesh bottle. She unsnaps the front of her bra and he latches on like a champ.

When I look up at Rory, she's smiling as she whispers something to him that I can't hear. Then she kisses his temple and I can't help but smile. I shake my head as I realize there's no fucking way I can stay mad at this woman.

"So what's happening with the invitations?" I ask, all the harshness in my voice wiped clean.

She looks up at me, an apology in her eyes. "We worked everything out, but…."

"But what?"

She brushes her fingers through Austin's hair for a few seconds before she answers. "I invited her to the wedding."

I immediately start laughing, and it takes me a few seconds to stop. "You are something else."

"I had to. She invited me to *her* wedding—in *Massachusetts*."

I shake my head. "This is just what I need. My ex-wife and my fiancée getting chummy."

"She's the one who invited me *first*."

"But, Daddy, she hit me first."

"She *did* hit me first."

"Which is exactly why you're not supposed to hire her or invite her to the wedding," I reply. "What's next? Is she gonna share a bed with us in Maui?"

She slides her finger into the corner of Austin's mouth to stop the suckling now that he's back to sleep. "I'm sorry. I messed up. But I really don't think we have to worry about her coming to the wedding. She looked just as horrified by my invitation as I was by hers."

I step forward to take him from her while she fixes her bra and shirt. He barely stirs as I fold him into my arms. I kiss the top of his head and think about what it would be like to have another one of these in eight or nine months. My chest is flooded with warmth at the thought of Austin running around the yard of our lake house with his little brother or sister.

Rory's still sitting in the chair, leaning forward with her elbows on her knees and her hands clasped in front of her mouth, as if she's praying. I open my mouth to speak, but the exam room door swings inward, interrupting me.

Dr. Winslow's face looks bright and cheerful as he announces, "You're pregnant!"

Rory stands from the chair, her eyes widening as she stares at the doctor. "But I'm on the pill. I don't understand how this happened."

Winslow's face becomes a bit more sober when he realizes this is not the news Rory wanted. "Oh, well, these things happen. Especially if you have a history of it happening before, as in your case."

"So I'm just going to keep getting pregnant?"

I press my lips together to hold back my laughter. Winslow looks at me and seems to relax as he turns back to Rory.

After some additional reassurance that Rory has many other birth-control options at her disposal, we leave Winslow's office and I drop Rory and Austin off at the apartment before I go to pick up his prescription. By the time I get home thirty minutes later, they're both asleep in our bed while Grandma Patricia is busy making something in the kitchen.

Perfect.

I set the prescription down on the kitchen counter. "When Rory wakes up, can you give her this and let her know I'll be back by three?"

The first and second calls from Rory come while I'm helping the guys load cases of beer onto a pallet. The sounds of the warehouse drown out the ringtone and it isn't until I stop moving for a moment, while watching Seth and Jorge wrap the pallet in plastic, that I feel the vibration of the third call come through.

I step out of the warehouse onto the loading dock to answer the call. "Hey, baby. What's going on?"

"You promised you were staying home today," she replies, sounding annoyed.

I jump off the dock onto the asphalt parking lot to put some more distance between me and the guys. "I know, but we have a big shipment going out and you were asleep, so I thought I'd come in to lend a hand. I'll be home in less than an hour."

"I need to give Austin his medicine and I need you to hold him down while I do it."

"Ask your mom to help you. That's what she's there for."

"She's not here!"

"What? Why? Where did she go?"

Rory sighs. "I don't know. She said she was going to the store, but she's been gone over an hour. I called her before I called you, but she didn't answer. She just texted me telling me she would be home soon. She's probably having sex with her secret boyfriend."

I laugh as I realize Patricia's trying to get some before she's stuck with the baby for a week. "I'll be home in ten minutes."

Patricia gets back to the apartment shortly after I get there. Her cheeks are flushed and she's wearing a lazy freshly fucked smile. Rory sits next to me on the sofa, her gaze following her mother across the living room. Patricia heads straight for the baby's bedroom without saying a word.

"Ten bucks says she's getting a change of clothes to take a shower and wash away the sex smell," Rory says, holding out her hand for me to shake.

"That's a losing bet if I ever heard one," I reply, dumping out the bag of Knock-Knock Blocks onto a blanket on the floor so Austin can play while he has some energy from his nap.

"What are we going to do if Tessa shows up at the wedding?" Rory asks while typing something on her phone, as if it's a casual question that doesn't require her full attention.

She's trying to downplay the seriousness so I don't get upset. I'm fully aware that she broke the news to me about Tessa while we were at the doctor's office because she knew it was a safe place. She thinks I don't know when she's hiding something from me or when she's trying to manipulate my emotions, but Rory's so bad at being deceptive. Her emotions give her away. It's one of the things I love most about her.

Of course, the downside is that Rory is easily manipulated. She doesn't realize there's a good chance Tessa emotionally manipulated her into getting a wedding invite. It's possible Tessa did it without consciously knowing what she was doing, so I can't really be mad at either of them. But I'll be damned if I'm going to have Tessa anywhere near us on our wedding day.

"We have two choices," I begin, handing Austin a black and white block. "You can call Tessa and tell her you don't think it's a good idea for her to come to the wedding or I can call her. Your choice."

She looks up from her phone, her eyes locking on mine. “I’ll call her.”

Rory

Somehow, in less than six days, I manage to call Tessa and break up with her, make two last-minute trips to the florist, safely lose two pounds of bloat so I can zip up my wedding dress with ease, get Austin cleared of all pink-eye symptoms, pump a week's worth of breast milk, and not have an emotional breakdown when Kenny gives the most hilarious and beautiful toast at tonight's rehearsal dinner.

The wedding rehearsal on the roof and the small private dinner on the second floor went off without a hitch. Sid got some partitions to block the view of the area where the tents were being stored. Then he pushed a few tables together and created beautiful rustic place settings and centerpieces. Since the only people invited to the rehearsal dinner were the wedding party and close friends and family, Sid made eighteen unique place cards, which were actually personalized thank-you cards from me and Houston.

By the time Houston and I have said good-bye to everyone, the only ones left in the restaurant are me, Houston, my mom and dad, and a few of the kitchen staff who are staying late to clean everything up.

My dad kisses me on the cheek and pats Houston's arm. "You two have done a great job. I'm not looking forward to giving my little girl away tomorrow, but I have no doubt you two will make it worth the while."

"It's not too late to take her back," Houston says, placing his hands on my shoulders. "My refund policy is pretty lax."

I shrugs his hands off. "Thanks, Dad. We've worked really hard to make this perfect for everyone."

My mom smiles. "You've done a beautiful job. You should be very proud."

She glances at my dad and he glances back at her. There's an awkward silence, then they both open their mouths to speak at the same time. My mom chuckles as my dad offers to let her go first.

"Oh, no, you go ahead," she insists.

He smiles at her, but not a cordial smile. There is something else in his smile. Something I've seen before. My heart races as he gazes at the floor for a moment, lost in thought, before he looks up at me, still smiling.

"Rory, your mother and I are… We're engaged."

I look back and forth between them, waiting for the punch line. "This is a joke, right?" I reply with a chuckle.

His smile disappears and my mother's eyebrow shoots up. "Sweetheart, we wanted to tell you before the honeymoon because we know you've been suspicious, and we don't want you to feel like you have to worry about what your mom is doing while you're gone."

My heart is punching my chest so hard, I feel as if it might explode. I stare at a spot on the wall just to the left of my dad's face because I'm afraid to look at him.

"You're… You're the *secret boyfriend*?"

My dad laughs and my mom scoffs at this characterization of their relationship.

"Rory, please, your father and I aren't *secret* boyfriend and girlfriend. We're grandparents, we're not teenagers."

I turn to my dad and he's looking at the floor trying to hide a sneaky grin, because he knows damn well they've been behaving like teenagers.

He puts on a straight face and looks up at me. "She's right. We're partners. And we're adults, so we have every right to conduct our relationship as we see fit."

"Partners…?" I reply, my voice trailing off. "So that means… you're getting remarried?"

They turn to each other and my dad nods. She smiles like a schoolgirl who just got an A on her spelling test. Then she holds out her left hand to show me a diamond ring that looks almost twice as big as the three-carat diamond ring Houston bought me more than seven years ago.

My jaw drops. "Holy shit, Dad."

My mom purses her lips. "Rory, language."

My dad shakes his head. "Oh, how I've missed this."

Houston chuckles. "You'll get tired of it pretty soon."

I grab my mom's hand and bring it closer to my face to get a better look at it. "You guys are serious."

"Don't get any ideas," Houston says, squeezing my shoulders. "I didn't get you a new, bigger ring because your old ring is special."

I wave off his explanation. "I don't need a bigger ring. I'm just admiring it."

My mom tugs her hand gently. "Can I have my hand back?"

I chuckle as I let go. "Well, this is weird."

"Why is it weird?" my dad replies, a warm smile spreading across his face as my mom links her arm in his. "Your mother and I have loved each other since we were teenagers. But even the smartest people sometimes forget to put love first. I'm sure you both understand that as well as we do."

I'm suddenly overcome by a gust of emotion as I think of the years Houston and I denied our feelings for each other.

I throw my arms around my dad. "Congratulations," I blubber.

"Thank you, sweetheart," he murmurs into my hair as he holds me tightly.

Once I've smeared most of my makeup on his blazer, I let go of him and turn to my mom. "Mommy."

She laughs softly as she wipes away a tear.

I hold my arms out to her. "I'm so happy for you."

My mom and I hold each other for a long while, and I spend much of that time wondering how this happened. I want to ask, but I'll save my questions for later. Right now, I just want to revel in the joy of having my family together. And, I definitely don't say this aloud, but I'm relieved to know my dad will be around while Houston and I are on our honeymoon. In case my mother's menopause demon needs to be exorcised.

Houston and I arrive at our apartment a few minutes before eleven p.m. to relieve our neighbor Janice of her babysitting duties. Houston pays her while I check in on Austin. He's deep asleep in his crib, his perfect little mouth hanging slightly open. Though his pink-eye symptoms have been gone for a couple of days now, I lay my hand on his forehead just to be sure, and I'm pleased to find he feels as perfect as he looks.

When I come out of the room, my mom is waiting for me in the hallway. Her back is to me as she watches Houston and my dad talking to each other in the living room.

I tap her on the shoulder and she jumps. "What are they talking about?" I whisper as she turns to me.

She smiles as she takes me by the arm and pulls me into the bathroom. "You're not supposed to know." She reaches for my hair. "Let me help you with those bobby pins."

She begins taking the bobby pins out of my updo. I keep my mouth shut as she removes each pin while humming a song I don't recognize at first. After a few more notes, I smile when I realize she's humming the theme song to Austin's favorite cartoon.

I'll let them keep their little secret for now, but as soon as Houston and I are in bed, I know just how to get it out of him.

Houston

Rory and I lie in bed together for the last time as an unmarried couple. Both of us stare at the ceiling in silence. I don't know what she's thinking, but I'm thinking about the conversation I just had with her dad, and I'm worried about how Rory is going to take the news when I break it to her.

"How does it feel to know this is our last night living in sin?" I say, my voice amplified by the darkness.

She chuckles as she turns over and lays her hand on my chest as she looks up at me. "I'm so happy I'm finally going to be an honest woman."

"An honest woman? Does that mean you're finally going to be one hundred percent honest with me?"

She gasps. "I'm always honest with you."

I laugh louder than I probably should, considering it's almost midnight.

"Okay, so I may have forgotten to tell you about Tessa," she concedes.

I clear my throat. "Honest woman."

"Okay, okay. I deceived you. And I'll always be honest with you from now on. But the same goes for you," she says, trailing her fingers down my abs until she reaches the waistband of my boxer briefs. "You have to tell me everything. No more secrets."

I grab her face and tilt her head up to kiss her tenderly. Her hand slides into my boxers, slowly inching downward until her fingers are wrapped around the base of my cock. I thrust my tongue into her mouth and she whimpers as her hand glides up and down the length of my erection.

She pulls her head back and looks me in the eye as she lowers herself off the bed so she's standing at my bedside. "Sit up," she whispers.

I smile as I realize I'm getting a BJ the night before my wedding. This almost feels like cheating.

She sinks to her knees then slowly pushes my boxers down and tosses them away. Spreading my knees, I suck in a sharp breath when she grabs the head of my cock and slides her fist down the shaft.

"No more secrets," she repeats just before she licks the tip.

"Fuck," I hiss as she takes my cock deep into her mouth.

She's not wasting any time. Her head bobs back and forth like a well-oiled piston. I lean my head back and close my eyes, biting my lip to keep from alerting Patricia in the next room.

Her right hand twists as she moves it up and down in time with her mouth. I reach down and move her hair away from her face, then I watch as she takes me in and pulls me out. I twist my fingers in her hair and slide my hand to the back of her head, holding her steady as I get closer to climax. As soon as I do this, she pushes off.

Licking her lips, she looks up at me. "What were you talking about with my dad?"

"What? I don't know. I'm… fuck."

She leans forward and traces her tongue around the tip of my cock. "What were you talking about?"

"Shit," I whisper as I realize this was a trap, and I fell for it.

She lightly runs the tips of her fingers up and down the length of my erection as her other hand massages my sac. "No more secrets."

I chuckle as I shake my head. "You literally have me by the balls. This is not fucking fair."

"You're the one who said you wanted one hundred percent honesty," she replies, then she takes me into her mouth, pushing me farther inside until I hit the back of her throat.

She pulls away again as she feels me getting close.

"This is cruelty to animals," I say.

She laughs. "Are you calling yourself an animal?"

"You're damn fucking right," I reply, taking her by surprise as I reach down, pick her up, and toss her onto the bed next to me.

She laughs as I position myself between her legs and lean down to kiss her neck. Sliding into her, I let out a groan of relief that makes her laugh even more.

"You think it's funny that you almost gave me the bluest balls of the century," I say, lifting her leg as I thrust into her.

She smiles as she looks up at me. "I almost had you."

I shake my head as I place her ankle on my shoulder and push her leg back until I'm close enough to kiss her. She whimpers into my mouth and I groan into hers as I plow into her, releasing my load in the free-loading zone. God, I love it when she's pregnant. After this one shoots out in nine months, I'm going to convince her to do this a few more times.

Rory

When we arrive at Barley Legal in the afternoon, the restaurant has been closed down for the day and the rolling gate entrance to the back parking lot is locked. A security guard stands just outside the gate, letting in only wedding guests and members of the wedding party. Houston's parking space is open for him as he pulls in, and his aunt Melissa is just stepping out of the car in the next space.

As he pulls the key out of the ignition, I'm hit with the sudden realization that this is really happening. I'm getting married. And not to some guy I settled for. I'm getting married to the boy I used to write stories about. The guy whose name filled the pages of my journal for more than a decade. The man who commissioned my mother to write a fairy tale about us. I'm literally marrying my Prince Charming and I still haven't written my wedding vows.

I can feel Houston watching me as I stare at the dashboard. I flinch when he grabs my hand, then I chuckle as he gives it a gentle squeeze.

"You getting cold feet?" he asks, though the confident smile on his face tells me he knows damn well I'm not having second thoughts.

"Just thinking," I reply.

"What are you thinking about?"

I smile as I take his hand in both of mine. "I wrote a story when I was twelve. It was about you and me."

He chuckles. "Is it in that box of stories in your storage unit?"

I shake my head. "It got lost during one of the many times I changed dorms after we broke up."

His smile disappears. "I'm sorry."

"It's not your fault. I should have taken better care of it." I smile as I rub my thumb over the palm of his hand. "I guess that's a lesson I had to learn twice."

He closes his hand around mine. "Are you okay, Rory?"

I look up at him and nod. "In that story, you and I got married and had three kids. One of them was named Hallie after her aunt."

His smile returns. "Knowing Hallie, she probably forced you to name our fictional child after her."

My gaze falls back to our hands. "She never read the story. She never read *any* of the stuff I wrote about you. I was too afraid to show anyone that stuff. It was like… my deepest shame. I was in love with a boy who would never love me back. Somehow, I thought that made me defective, and I didn't want anyone to know." I look up again and sigh. "I think I finally understand why she didn't tell us… If I was ashamed of being in love, I can't even begin to fathom how she felt."

He stares at the steering wheel for a moment before he replies. "Everyone deserves to have their story heard." He looks up at me, his gaze filled with intensity. "You're the only one I trust to tell Hallie's."

I let go of his hand, chuckling as I wipe away a tear. "Too bad

I'm pregnant. I could really use a few drinks to get through this wedding."

He smiles as he glances over his shoulder at the Barley Legal building. "I think Wilma might have a few virgin drinks you can enjoy in your condition."

I grab my purse and lean over the console to kiss him. "Let's go get married."

The entire first floor of the restaurant has been decorated for the wedding. Small, lush floral arrangements dot the center of each dining table, surrounded by twinkling garlands of twig lights. More strings of twig lights hang from the ceiling and along the edge of the staircase leading up to the second floor, where Houston and I are headed.

The white silk tents have been moved out of the second-floor dining area, taken to the roof to be set up. The second floor has been partitioned into four separate dressing areas with silkscreen dividers that seem to glow from within.

Houston brings my hand to his lips and plants a soft kiss on my knuckles. "Next time you see me, I'll be standing underneath that star you wished on."

It takes me a moment to realize he's talking about the time we got locked in the cemetery and I made a wish on a shooting star. "Next time I see you, you'll know if I got my answer."

He smiles as he bows his head then disappears into the dressing area on the right. I head into the dressing area on the left and find Kenny dressed in a slim nude Gucci three-piece suit and a soft wine-colored tie to match my floral crown and the lilac arch. He's setting up my makeup on the dressing table as my mom sits on a settee in the corner with Austin on her lap. Skippy lies beneath the dressing table as if he's waiting just for me.

"Where are the bridesmaids?"

Kenny looks up at the sound of my voice. He opens his mouth to reply when I hear two voices coming from the dressing area next to us.

"We're in here!"

Within seconds, Jenna and Misha come rushing into my dressing area. Though no one could ever take Kenny's place, Jenna and I became friends last year when she started working for Hallie's Hope as a bookkeeper. She's a year older than I am, and she has a three-year-old son who isn't quite keen on playdates with Austin yet.

Misha came to Hallie's Hope in December, trembling and bloody after being brutally raped by her boyfriend. She was eighteen and I'd never seen anyone so frightened. We worked with the authorities to get her boyfriend arrested, then we worked with her family to make them understand she hadn't brought this upon herself. She helps out with general office work at Hallie's Hope occasionally, and she's starting community college later this month.

They're both in the nude dresses we picked out for them, each dress its own unique design.

"Oh, my goodness. You guys look gorgeous," I say, fanning my face as I realize I'm going to cry again. "I hope I'll look as good as you."

Misha waves away my compliment. "Girl, you're going to look a billion times better than us. Where's your dress?"

I look around, but I don't see it anywhere. "Kenny, where's the dress?"

"Sid's picking it up from the shop where we took it to get steamed. He should be back by now. I'll call him."

I look around at the others as Kenny leaves to make the call. "So… where's Georgia?"

Troy's wife was supposed to be here by now to do my hair and makeup. Where the hell is everybody?

"I'll call her," Jenna offers. "My phone is in the other dressing room. I'll be right back."

I sit down on the plush velvet stool in front of the dressing table and watch in the mirror as Misha comes up behind me. "Your makeup looks great. Maybe you should do mine."

"She'll probably do your hair first," she says, grabbing the paddle brush off the table. "I'll brush it out so it's ready when she gets here."

I smile and hold up a finger to stop her. "Hold on." Glancing over my shoulder, I call to my mom. "Can you bring Austin to me? He likes playing with my makeup."

My mom sets him down on my lap and he breaks into a huge grin when he sees all the makeup on the table. He laughs as he smacks the mirrored surface of the vanity and reaches for a tube of lip gloss. I have a change of clothes for him and plenty of baby wipes to clean him up, so I let him have at it. By the time Kenny returns, the three of us ladies are in stitches watching Austin paint bright pink lip gloss all over my cheeks.

"Oh, no. You're already trying to turn him gay," Kenny remarks.

I laugh as I dodge the lip-gloss wand just before it almost goes into my nostril. "He's destined to be fabulous. Right, Austin?" He smiles at me and giggles when I rub my nose against his. "You love your momma, don't you? You're a momma's boy." He giggles again. "Can you say *momma*? Mom-ma."

He stares at my mouth as I repeat the word a couple more times. He smacks his lips together a few times before it finally comes, crystal clear and as angelic as I imagined it would sound. "Momma."

"Oh, my goodness. Did you hear that?" I say, glancing at Kenny.

"I certainly did."

He says it again and I laugh as I squeeze him in my arms.

"Your daddy's gonna be so jealous. He's not so special anymore."

Sid and Georgia arrive one right after the other and I spend a few minutes cleaning myself and Austin up before I hand him over to Grandma again. Ninety minutes later, it's the moment of truth. Time to see if my dress still fits.

Kenny holds the dress as I step into it and he carefully pulls it up, being careful not to smear the makeup on my chest. He grabs my hips and gently spins me around so he can zip me up. I consider sucking in my gut, but I won't be able to hold that position all night, so I just hold my breath and wait. The zipper slides up cleanly and I sigh with relief.

Kenny claps his hands. "Yay! It's okay if your baby is born a little on the Kate Moss side, because at least you look fabulous."

I roll my eyes as Georgia continues fretting over every piece of hair and every inch of makeup, spraying hairspray and dusting me with finishing powder every few seconds.

"Okay, that's enough," I say, pushing her hands away as she attempts to adjust another flower in my crown.

She steps back to look at me. "Oh, my God. I'm so nervous."

Sid rolls his eyes at her. "Honey, go get your husband before he drinks himself into oblivion."

Kenny holds the bottom of my dress as I step sideways to get a look at myself in the full-length mirror. He covers his mouth and shakes his head. "You're an angel," he whispers.

"Stop it. You're gonna make me cry."

Sid sighs as Kenny turns away to hide his face. "You heard the woman. Stop it."

"Oh, you leave me alone. I'm not your slave boy anymore," Kenny replies, though he's already making his way out of the dressing area. "I'll see you at the altar, gorgeous," he says, winking at me.

"We should start making our way up there now. You're on in ten," Sid says, adjusting the lapels of his slim gray suit and checking his dark hair in the mirror. "Let's go."

We turn away from the mirror to leave, only to find my dad standing at the entrance of the dressing area.

Sid flashes me a tight smile. "I'll be right outside." He points at the invisible watch on his wrist. "Ten minutes."

My dad steps into the dressing area, taking a look around as if he too is having trouble with this new reality we find ourselves in today. He stops a couple of feet away from me and looks me up and down with a proud smile on his face.

He nods solemnly. "Yeah, this is just as difficult as I imagined it would be."

I shrug. "It could be worse. I could be marrying a tree," I say, referencing a case he refused to take on a few years ago where a woman wanted to sue the state of Oregon for the right to marry a tree she had fallen in love with.

He smiles, but I can sense a sadness behind it. "I wanted to come here and talk to you before the ceremony to give you a chance to take everything in. I'm sure once the ceremony is over, you'll want to celebrate and not have to worry about any of this stuff."

"Dad, you're kind of scaring me. Are you dying or something?"

He chuckles. "No, sweetie, it's nothing like that. I just wanted to thank you."

"Thank me for what?"

He takes a moment to think before he responds. "For forgiving me and letting me give you away." He smiles as he reaches up and lays his hand on my cheek. "It's one of those things you dream of doing as a father, from the moment your little girl is born. And there was a long time where I didn't think I deserved to have this honor. Today, I feel like one lucky bastard."

I smile as I try to swallow the painful lump in my throat. "I'm the lucky one, Dad." I shake my head as I realize there's no use trying to stop the tears. "If it weren't for you, I wouldn't be writing something that makes me feel good. I wouldn't be doing something that makes me feel like I matter. Thank you… for bringing our family back together."

He takes me into his arms. "I'm going to try my hardest never to let you down again." He holds me gently for a while, then kisses my forehead as he pulls away. "I've got to go take my position, but there's one more thing I need to do." He reaches into his pocket and pulls out a key ring with three keys dangling. "I didn't want to wrap these in a box and have you open them in front of everyone at the reception. I didn't think it would be fair to everyone else."

"What are they?"

He smiles as he places the keys in my hand. "They're the keys to the house my investment company bought four weeks ago in Lake Oswego."

"*Your* investment company?"

He slides his hands into his pockets and shrugs. "Houston's a good man. He's an excellent father and I have no doubt he'll make a great husband. I know this because he already knows something important about being a family man, and that's the importance of sacrifice." He smiles that knowing smile again, as if he has a secret. "Someone once told me that you can't hide behind self-pity as an excuse for being a bad parent." He holds his hand up to stop me from interrupting him. "Wait. I'm not calling you a bad parent. I'm saying that you can't pity yourself for having to move to a beautiful suburb. You have to do what's best for Austin, no excuses. Are we clear, young lady?"

I sigh as I realize my dad is right. "This is what you and Houston were discussing last night?"

He nods. "There are times when you have to make tough decisions for the sake of your children's future." He reaches up and pinches my chin. "Even when they're twenty-six years old."

I roll my eyes. "Thanks, Dad."

"You're welcome, sweetheart."

The moment he's gone, Sid is back and he looks annoyed that my conversation with my father has us running late. "It's okay. It's okay," he insists as he waits for me to freshen my makeup. "They can hold the music a few more minutes."

He looks a bit nervous as he helps me into the elevator. The elevator doors open onto the roof and I'm surprised to find my mother is standing there with Austin in her arms.

She gasps when she sees me and it startles Austin. "Oh, I'm sorry. I was going to get his bottle." She claps her hand over her mouth. "Look at you."

Sid shakes his head. "Nuh-uh. You have to go sit down, Grandma."

She rolls her eyes. "If he starts crying in the middle of the ceremony, it's your fault," she says as she stalks off through the lilac arch, past the rows of guests to her seat in the front.

Sid touches a button on his headset and speaks into the microphone. "Roll tape." He looks over my hair and dress one more time and nods with approval before he speaks into the microphone again. "Cue music."

The speakers, which have been pumping out "Air (on the G string)" by Johann Sebastian Bach, go silent as I make my way toward the arch, where the wedding party waits for their cue. And then it comes. The band, which has been waiting patiently on a stage about forty feet behind the last row of guests, begins to play "Best Day of My Life" by American Authors.

As rehearsed, Jenna and Misha begin skipping down the aisle arm in arm, singing along to the music as the guests cheer and clap. Then Kenny and Troy link arms and walk down the aisle together, waving and blowing kisses to the crowd. Then I have to hold back my tears as the dog trainer gives Skippy a treat and points at Kenny and Troy. Skippy gallops after them, stopping right in front of Houston at the altar. He licks Houston's face as

Houston unclips the ring box from his collar.

My dad grins as he sticks out his elbow, and my heart races as I slip my arm through his. Every step we take down that aisle feels less and less real, until I'm almost there and I feel as if I'm floating. Houston's wearing a boyish grin when I get to the altar, and the moment I see it I'm filled with relief. I still don't know what the hell I'm going to say when I get up there, but I know now that it doesn't matter.

I turn to my dad and his eyes are watery as he leans in to kiss my forehead.

"I love you, sweetheart. Go be happy."

The tears start and Houston chuckles as he reaches down to help me up the two steps onto the podium. "I want to say my vows first," I whisper to the minister so as not to get picked up by the microphone hanging above us.

He looks a little taken aback by the change in plans, but he takes it in stride. I try to pay attention to what the minister is saying as he talks about love and commitment, but my mind keeps drifting to what *I* want to say. Finally, the sound of someone clearing their throat gets my attention. It's the minister. He nods at me and I realize this is it.

I draw in a deep breath as I look into Houston's blue eyes and my hands begin to tremble. "This will probably surprise everyone except for Houston, but I haven't written any vows for today." There's a small rumble of laughter and at least one gasp from the guests. "But," I continue, directing my attention back to Houston, "in my defense, I've probably written my vows for this wedding about a thousand times since I first laid eyes on you."

I try not to laugh when there's a collective *awww* from the crowd.

"As I tried to write my vows, I couldn't pinpoint one single thing about you or one single moment that made me realize I was in love with you. Then I tried comparing what we have to some of the greatest love stories: Jane and Rochester, Elizabeth and Mr. Darcy, Ana and Christian…" Houston lets out a hearty chuckle along with the guests. "I could write a thousand sonnets and essays and chapters and none would come close to capturing the warmth I feel when I catch you sneaking food to Skippy, or how safe I feel when I'm lying in your arms, or how joyful I feel when I see you playing with Austin."

He smiles as I take a moment to compose myself. "Take your time, baby."

I smile as I wipe the tears off my chin before they can drip onto my dress. "I guess what I'm trying to say is that there are no words to describe what it's like to fall in love with someone the moment you see them. And to have that love returned with as much honesty and passion as the way you've loved me back, there are no words to describe it other than… You're not just the love of my life, you're the best friend I've ever had." I take a deep breath as I look into his eyes. "No friendship, no love."

Houston

It takes everything in me not to kiss her right then and there. Part of me thinks, *Hell. We're already breaking the rules by letting her say her vows first.* But then I think about how this is Rory's day as much as it's mine. I want to make sure that when the minister says, "You may now kiss the bride," it's as epic as she's always imagined it would be.

I clear my throat as I suddenly feel everyone's eyes on me. "Well, not to brag or anything, but I've been writing my vows for a long time, too. And mine have been done for over two months."

She shakes her head as she laughs along with the guests.

"But I must admit, it's kind of daunting having to come second to that. Of course, that's one of the things I love the most about you, your ability to string words together and make them into something more beautiful than even you can comprehend." I squeeze her hands lightly as she smiles bashfully. "It's a gift, and one that makes me proud, not just to be with you, but also to know you."

I let out a deep sigh as I prepare to say the vows I've been memorizing in my office for months. "Rory, when I imagine my future stretched out before me, where I'll go, what I'll do, where I'll live, it's all hazy except for your face. There's nothing I know for certain other than how much I love you and need you. For the rest of my life, I want to share every important and utterly insignificant moment with you.

"I want to inhale the scent of your skin after a rainstorm. I want to watch from the doorway as you put our children down to sleep. I want to see the sunlight glimmer on your hair as you're watering the garden. I want to hear you laugh too loud after you've had one too many beers. I want to see you cry tears of joy when your first book is published."

I reach up, brushing my thumb across her cheek to wipe away a tear. "You're probably wondering who helped me write these wedding vows."

She lets out a congested chuckle as she nods.

I smile as I gaze into her eyes. "You did." I pause, relishing the look of confusion on her gorgeous face. "You've changed me, Rory, in more ways than I can count. You've made me a better man… A man who knows how to quiet a screaming baby. A man who worries about his dog while he's away at work. A man who listens not just to the words you say, but to the way you say them. A man who knows how to write wedding vows."

She bites her lip as she tries not to laugh.

I lean forward and plant a soft kiss on her forehead then whisper, "This is how the story ends, with a promise of forever. I love you, Scar."

I take her face gently in my hands and look at the minister for the cue.

He clears his throat. "You may now kiss the bride."

I plant a tender, lingering kiss on her lips. She laughs as she turns her head away to stop my embarrassing display of affection.

Then she leans in and whispers in my ear, "That was the answer I wished for: How does it end?"

I grin as a surge of joy-fueled adrenaline floods my body, and she yelps as I scoop her up into my arms and shout, "I killed Mufasa!"

Troy jumps off the podium and falls to his knees as he wails at the sky, "Nooooooooo!"

Skippy tackles Troy, smothering him with kisses as Rory gently pummels my chest and demands I put her down.

My mom stands up from her seat in the front row and points at me. "Put her down, Hugh."

I laugh as I gently set her down on the podium, so as not to mess up her dress. "You ready to watch the rest of us get drunk, Mrs. Cavanaugh?"

Rory rolls her eyes, but she can't wipe the stupid grin off her face. "Only if I get to pour the beer into the beer bong, Mr. Cavanaugh."

"Deal!" I say, and we fist-bump before I grab her hand and we set off down the aisle.

The guests all reach into the drawstring bags they received upon arrival, pulling out handfuls of barley to toss at us as we walk past them. We make it to the lilac arch without getting any barley in our eyes, and as soon as we walk through the arch, the band starts playing "Evergreen" by Broods.

We all retreat down to the first floor for the reception. Once everyone is seated for dinner, and champagne has been served, Troy arrives at the long table reserved for the wedding party with a six-pack of cold beer. He sets two down in front of me and hands one each to Kenny, Jenna, Misha, and himself.

I smile as I hold up my two beers so Rory can see the labels. "Houston, we have liftoff," I say, reading the new label on our Barley Legal Double IPA. Then I read the label on our summer ale. "Into the Northern Lights."

She smiles and shakes her head as she watches the waiters going around with trays of cold beer on offer to the guests. "Do they even know this is a sexual innuendo?" she says as her mom accepts one of the beers and takes a long swig.

"They'll figure it out," I say, reaching over to stroke Austin's face as he lies peacefully asleep in Rory's arms.

Troy and Kenny both give highly embarrassing toasts in the middle of dinner service, then we all manage to stuff down at least one slice of the most expensive and delicious cake ever. By the time we head back upstairs for more dancing and drinks, the rows of guest seating have been replaced by a dozen tables that take up half the area on the roof. The other half is covered in a wooden dance floor and stage for the band.

The sun has almost completely gone down, painting dramatic swaths of billowy pink clouds across the western horizon. In the east, the stars are twinkling as they get ready to make a dazzling entrance. And here in the middle, on a rooftop in Portland, I feel high enough to touch the sky.

At 10:30 p.m., Rory and I begin saying good-bye to all the guests as our car will be arriving at eleven to take us to the airport for the trip to Maui. We find Kenny and Pedro on the dance floor, slow-dancing to "Come Find Me" by Emile Haynie.

Kenny gasps when he sees us and realizes we're there to say good-bye. "Oh, no. You're leaving me," he says, giving Rory a one-armed hug and a kiss on the cheek because she's still refusing to let go of Austin.

I give her arm a playful squeeze. "My girl has biceps that don't quit."

She rolls her eyes as she turns to Kenny. "We'll be back in eight days. Don't forget that you and Pedro are coming with us to see *Wicked* at the Keller Auditorium when we get back."

"Psh!" He waves off her reminder and Rory's eyes widen when she sees a ring on his finger. "Honey, I wouldn't miss that if

I was on life support."

"Or getting married?" Rory replies.

Kenny's jaw drops as he clutches his hand to his chest. "You saw it?"

"Uh, how could I miss it? Are you getting *married*?"

Pedro smiles as he stuffs his hands into his pockets and shrugs. Kenny bites his lip as he tries to contain his excitement.

"Oh, my God. I want to scream, but I don't want to wake Austin," Rory says, and instead of screaming she hands Austin to me so she can give Kenny a proper hug.

Once Kenny and Rory have congratulated each other, Rory demands I give Austin back as we set off to say good-bye to the others. We find my mom, Jenna, and Misha chatting it up at a table not far from the altar. My mom instantly breaks down into tears when she realizes we're leaving.

"I'm so proud of you two," she says, giving me a monster bear hug. "I always knew you two would get back together, but what you two have done here tonight has surpassed my wildest dreams. I know Hallie is out there somewhere, cheering you two on every step of the way."

Rory and my mom wipe away each other's tears. "Wherever she is, she's just as proud of you as we are."

My mom sniffs loudly. "I'll drop by to give Patricia a break as often as I can while you two are gone. Now go on and have a beautiful honeymoon."

We find Patricia and James chatting near the elevator and they walk us down to the second floor to get our luggage. The back parking lot is crowded with tired guests trying to sort out their designated drivers and get the hell out of here. We head to the front entrance of Barley Legal, where the car will pick us up soon. Skippy sits obediently at our feet as Rory begins to sob when she realizes it's time to say good-bye to Austin.

Patricia reaches for the baby. "Rory, he's going to be fine.

Give him here."

A car drives by with my cousin Hunter hanging out the back passenger window holding a bottle of Barley Legal up in the air. "Houston, we have liftoff!" he shouts, then he guzzles the rest of the beer.

"Put that shit away!" I shout back, and all we hear is the roar of laughter inside the car fading as they drive off. I shake my head as I turn to Rory. "They'd better not be driving drunk. I thought Kenny and Sid coordinated the designated drivers."

"They did, but participation was voluntary."

Patricia reaches for Austin again as Troy stumbles out onto the sidewalk with a plate of cake.

"Damn. This is the best fucking cake I've ever had," he slurs through a mouthful as Skippy sits down at his feet, watching for any crumbs that may fall. "You scored mega points with this cake, Rory."

Rory closes her eyes as she rests her cheek on Austin's forehead. "I don't know if I can leave him."

Troy looks down and sees Skippy waiting patiently for a treat. He breaks off a piece of cake with his fingers and raises his hand as if he's going to toss the piece of cake into the street. Luckily, he glances at me first and sees the disbelief on my face.

"Are you fucking kidding me?" I say, taking the plate of cake away from him. "Go find Georgia so she can take you home."

He looks at the piece of cake in his hand and giggles. "Oops. Sorry, Skip." He stuffs the cake in his mouth. "Congratulations, bro," he says, holding his frosting-covered hand out to me.

I shake my head as I take his hand and give him a man hug. "Thanks, man. Now go sleep it off."

He flashes us all a drunken half smile as he heads back inside. When I turn around, I find Skippy has stolen the whole slice of cake off the plate in my hand, and he's now trying to skulk away unnoticed.

“Skippy, come back here,” I call out sternly as he prepares to step off the curb.

He glances back at me, his doggy eyebrows scrunched together in a classic guilty expression. But the moment I take a step toward him, he sets off bounding into the street. Rory lets out a bloodcurdling scream as another car full of cheery wedding guests plows toward him.

I race into the street and swing my arm underneath Skippy’s body, trying to keep my momentum going as the car comes straight at us, but in a state of panic he struggles to get away from me and slides through my arms. There’s no way I’ll be able to pick him up and get to safety fast enough now. As I bend over to scoop him up again, all I see is the grille of the car coming at my face. All I hear is the screech of rubber on asphalt. And in that split second before impact, all I can think is that Rory finally got her answer. This is how the story ends.

Rory

My heart stops as my dad rushes into the street. A green Subaru is parked at the curb in front of me, blocking my view of Houston and Skippy. My entire body goes weak and my mom notices just as my arms begin to slacken. She takes Austin from my arms and my heart pounds as I take a few steps to the left. And that's when I see them.

The driver of the car—Houston's warehouse manager, Seth—and my dad are standing over Houston and Skippy. The front of the car is about four feet away from where they're splayed out. Houston is lying on his back on the asphalt grinning as Skippy licks his face. I pull the skirt of my dress up as I step down into the street.

Houston takes Skippy in his arms, chuckling as he hugs him tight. "You almost killed me, you bastard. Over a piece of cake."

I smile at Seth as I approach and he flashes me an apologetic grin. "You both almost killed me," I say, standing over Houston.

Houston stands up as my dad takes Skippy by the collar and leads him back onto the sidewalk. "I'm sorry, baby, but Skippy and I are a team. You knew that when you married me."

I shake my head as we step out of the way so Seth can pass. "Well, you nearly gave me a heart attack. I love Skippy, but if you ever risk your life like that again, I will personally murder you."

"Does that mean we won't be climbing any active volcanoes in Maui?"

A black Mercedes arrives at eleven p.m. sharp to take us to the airport. The driver stuffs our luggage into the trunk as Houston and I say our final good-byes.

I don't want to wake Austin, who's sleeping like an angel in my mother's arms. I also don't want to leave without squeezing his squishy body just one more time.

I compromise by stroking his feather-soft hair as I whisper in his ear, "I love you, my sweet boy. Be good for Grandma and Grandpa."

My stomach aches as I walk away from him toward the car. I want so badly to take him with us, but that's just me being crazy. This isn't a family vacation. This is a honeymoon.

Houston holds the back door open for me, and I get close enough to smell the leather interior before I freeze as I remember what Kenny said to me the other day.

"Wait." I step around Houston and knock on the driver's window. "Can you pop the trunk?"

The driver, a young guy who looks like he's been eating too much lomi-lomi at the luau, looks a bit confused at first. Then he hits the button to release the lid on the trunk.

Houston follows me to the back of the car. "What are you doing?" he asks, as I try to flip my suitcase over to get to the zipper. "Here. Let me do it."

He turns the bag over and unzips it for me, then takes a step back so I can dig through the layers of neatly folded clothing. My fingers bump against something hard. I slide the laptop out and walk it over to my dad.

"Take this with you to the office, please."

My dad nods. "Sure thing, sweetheart."

When I walk back to the car, Houston has already zipped up the suitcase and slammed the trunk shut. He holds the back door open for me, shaking his head as he watches me slide into the backseat. He rounds the back of the car and takes a seat next to me.

The car drives off toward the 5 freeway entrance as I sit in silence, waiting for Houston to say something about the fact that I tried to sneak the laptop onto our honeymoon. My fingers tap the leather console between us as I stare out at the lights of downtown Portland. We're crossing over the Broadway Bridge toward I-84 when I finally decide I can't take it anymore. I open my mouth to speak, but Houston speaks first.

He's looking out his window at the shimmering surface of the Willamette River when he says, "I'm not mad. I'm just thinking."

"About what?" I ask anxiously.

He turns to me, and the soft smile he's wearing puts me at ease. "When Hallie died, I think we can both agree that the worst part was that we didn't see it coming."

I nod in agreement. "Which is why it hurt so much when you kept the letter from me."

He sighs. "If Seth hadn't stopped his car in time, and you had lost me tonight, that probably would have been the worst part. Knowing that the whole night, while we were celebrating, you were blissfully unaware that it was our last night together. You'd have spent the next few months or years mourning all the things we never got to do. All the things you never got to say."

My anxiety ratchets up a notch again. "What are you getting at?"

He smiles as he grabs my hand. "Maybe not knowing when someone you love is going to be taken away from you isn't the worst part. Maybe it's the best part, because it allows you to enjoy your last holiday with your sister or your last night with your husband."

I smile as I realize he's right. "And maybe the key to acceptance is knowing that you did all you could do, and said all you could say."

He nods as he squeezes my hand and gazes into my eyes. "Promise me that if I die before you, you'll remember that."

I let out a soft chuckle as I shake my head. "Not a chance."

He laughs as he leans over and kisses my temple. "Then, for your sake, I hope you go first."

I gasp as I push him away. "You're so mean."

He laughs as he sits back in his seat. "I'm not that mean. I knew you were hiding that laptop in your suitcase and I never said a word."

I narrow my eyes at him, unsure if he's telling the truth. "You didn't know."

"Yes, I did," he replies with a smug grin. "And your editor emailed me a note of congratulations a few days ago, so I also know that your editor told you she wouldn't be contacting you while we're on our honeymoon. Which means you were bringing that laptop for no good reason."

My jaw drops, but I can't think of a single coherent response.

He laughs. "Caught red-handed, but you'll learn," he says, shaking his head. "You can't get back the time you should have spent climbing your husband's volcano in Hawaii instead of staring at a computer screen."

"Oh, so now every time you want me to do something, you're going to ask what I'd do if it were my last day with you?"

"What *would* you do if it were your last day with me?"

The question sounds sort of flippant and casual, but I have a feeling he wants a serious answer. I'm silent for a while as I try to think of one, but it only takes a few seconds for the answer to come to me.

"I'd find a way to go with you."

He smiles as he reaches up and brushes his thumb over my cheekbone. "And that's why not knowing the ending is the best part."

The end.

Acknowledgments

I've always thought that good fiction is a means of conveying the truth. When I began writing this series in December 2014, I set out to write a love story that conveyed the truth about storytelling, and how it's such a powerful force to help us heal. I'm not sure if I even came close, but here are the people who helped make this dream a reality.

As always, I have to thank my beta readers: Paula Jackman, Cathy Archer, Sarah Arndt, Kristin Shaw, Carrie Raasch, Erin Fisher, Heather Carver, and Beverly Cindy. This series has an unconventional storyline, told through an unconventional format, with unconventional characters, and these girls never missed a beat. They even agreed to read a book on story structure! Not many betas who will power through a "boring" nonfiction book so they can become better beta readers. But I have no doubt these ladies are the cream of the crop. It's a privilege to have worked with them on this series.

Thank you to Tamara Paulin and Deanna Roy for being there with positive words and the occasional reality check when needed. So glad I finally got to meet you in Austin, Deanna.

Sarah Hansen, Cover Sorceress. Somehow, she always knows exactly what I want in a book cover without my even telling her. Thank you for always fitting me into your schedule, especially when I decided to change *The Way We Break* cover about one week before the cover reveal date. Whenever a new writer asks me for advice on how to be a successful author, I always tell them one of the most important ingredients in a successful book is a great cover. And then I refer them to you. Only the smart ones take my advice. Thank goodness or you'd never have time for me.

Big thanks to my editor, Jessica Anderegg of Red Adept Edits. Thank you for seeing what I couldn't see and for calling me out on the things I'd prefer to ignore. I've worked with many editors and I'm so glad I've found one who not only knows what to look for but who also knows how to communicate a solution. Also, it takes a special kind of editor to admit when the manuscript just didn't need a lot of editing.

Huge thanks to my copyeditor, Marianne Tatom. I can't believe how many typos this woman can find. I always turn in my manuscripts with confidence, thinking there won't be more than 20 or 30 corrections. Then I get them back with over 200 corrections and my ego is quickly deflated. This woman is amazing, and the absolute best copyeditor to have when two of your characters are English majors.

Thank you to all the bloggers who shared the cover reveal and those who participated in the blog tours and release activities. And a big thank you to Holly Malgieri of Holly's Red Hot Reviews for handling *The Way We Break* launch. And to all the bloggers and readers who took the time to read the book and post their reviews during release week. You are such a huge part of what makes this indie book community thrive. Keep supporting the indie authors you love and we'll keep writing the uncensored versions of the romance books you love to read.

To the readers who have messaged me and shared your excitement for the release of each book in this series, thank you for taking time out of your day to think of me and reach out to me. Your enthusiasm kept me going on days when the writing became more difficult than usual.

To Arielle, for helping me develop the idea for this series and for making it possible for me to write a book in three months while moving out of state. Though you've turned me into an empty-nester at thirty-seven years old, I stand in wonderment of your independence and optimistic anticipation of the journey ahead.

To my father. Thank you for teaching me that we all deserve to be forgiven.

Also by Cassia Leo

CONTEMPORARY ROMANCE

Forever Ours (Shattered Hearts #1)
Relentless (Shattered Hearts #2)
Pieces of You (Shattered Hearts #3)
Bring Me Home (Shattered Hearts #4)
Abandon (Shattered Hearts #5)
Chasing Abby (Shattered Hearts #6)
Black Box (stand-alone novel)

EROTIC ROMANCE

KNOX Series
LUKE Series
CHASE Series
UNMASKED Series
Edible: The Sex Tape (A Short Story)

PARANORMAL ROMANCE

Parallel Spirits (Carrier Spirits #1)